In addition to the bestselling Recluce saga, **L.E. Modesitt, Jr.** is the author of the acclaimed Spellsong cycle, and many science fiction novels. He lives in New Mexico.

Find out more about L.E. Modesitt, Jr. and other Orbit authors by registering for the free monthly newsletter at www.orbitbooks.co.uk

Praise for L.E. Modesitt, Jr.

'Resplendent . . . fantasy with an inventive and expertly handled scenario, life-sized characters and flawless plotting'

Kirkus Reviews

'An intriguing fantasy in a fascinating world'

Robert Jordan

'Fascinating! A big, exciting novel of the battle between good and evil and the path between'

Gordon R. Dickson

'Modesitt has created an exceptionally vivid secondary world, so concretely visualized as to give the impression that Modesitt must himself have dwelt there'

L. Sprague de Camp

L·E Modesitt JR

MAGI'I OF CYADOR

www.orbitbooks.co.uk

An *Orbit* Book

First published in the United States by Tor Books 2000
First published in Great Britain by Orbit 2001
Reprinted 2002

Copyright © 2000 by L. E. Modesitt, Jr.

The moral right of the author has been asserted.

A CIP catalogue record for this book
is available from the British Library.

ISBN 1 84149 027 X

Printed and bound in Great Britain
by Clays Ltd, St Ives plc

Orbit
An imprint of
Time Warner Books UK
Brettenham House
Lancaster Place
London WC2E 7EN

Robert Edward Janes
In memoriam, for the dreams he had.

NORTHERN

CANDAR

Gulf of Candar

Gulf of Murr

RECLUCE

EASTERN OCEAN

The WORLD

E.Mitchell 1995

OCEAN

Gulf of Austra

AUSTRA

Brysta

Valmurl

NORDLA

WESTERN OCEAN

Swartheld

Luba
Cigoerne

Afrit

Atla

South River

MEROWEY

HAMOR

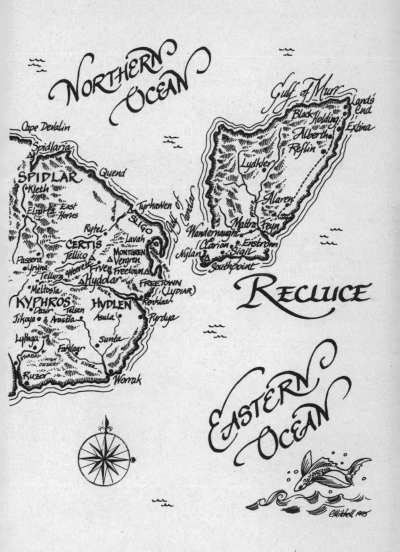

Characters

Kien	Magus, Senior Lector, "Fourth Magus"
Lorn	Son of the Magus Kien
Vernt	Younger son of Kien
Jerial	Eldest child and daughter of Kien
Myryan	Youngest child and daughter of Kien
Nyryah	Consort of Kien
Toziel'elth'alt'mer	Emperor of Cyador
Ryenyel	Consort-Empress of Cyador

MAGI'I

Chyenfel	First Magus and High Lector
Kharl	Second Magus and Senior Lector
Liataphi	Third Magus and Senior Lector
Abram	Senior Lector
Ciesrt	Student/Magus
Jysnet	Lector
Hyrist	Senior Lector
Rustyl	Student/Magus
Tyrsal	Student/Magus

LANCERS

Rynst	Majer-Commander, Mirror Lancers
Luss	Captain-Commander, Mirror Lancers
Allyrn	Student/Lancer Undercaptain
Brevyl	Sub-Majer [commanding at Isahl]
Dettaur	Student/Lancer Officer
Eghyr	Captain
Helkar	Captain
Jostyn	Captain
Juist	Undercaptain
Kyl	Undercaptain

Maran	Majer [Patrol Commander, Geliendra]
Meylyd	Commander [Geliendra]
Thiataphi	Commander [Syadtar]

OTHERS

Bluoyal	Merchanter Advisor to the Emperor
Dustyn	Factor in spirits [Jakaafra]
Eileyt	Enumerator
Fuyol	Head, Yuryan Clan
Ryalth	Woman merchanter
Shevelt	Merchanter heir [Yuryan Clan]
Veljan	Merchanter [Yuryan Clan]

Lorn'elth,
Cyad

I

THE MAN WEARS white trousers and a white tunic, belted with white leather and secured with a glistening white metallic buckle. His boots are white, including the thick leather soles, and his hands are encased in white gloves. The only items of color upon his body are the pair of gold starbursts—one on each of the short square collars of his tunic.

A dark-haired boy wearing shimmering gray trousers and a short-sleeved shirt of the same shimmering fabric holds the man's left hand. Both walk along a corridor. The floors, walls, and ceiling are all of white granite, except for one window of a glass-like substance so dark it appears nearly black. The black window is on the man's right, exactly halfway between the two metal doors, each also of shimmering white metal.

When the pair reaches the window, the man halts, bends, and lifts the boy, holding him so that their heads are almost even with each other. The man inclines his head toward the dark expanse of glass. "There. There is the First Tower."

The dark-haired youth, his amber eyes shielded by the ancient dark glass, stares at the glittering trapezoid of light beyond the wall. The dark transparency filters out all that lies beyond the wall except for the blistering light that is the Tower.

"One day," says the man, "one day, Lorn'elth . . . you and your brother will be Magi'i of the Rational Stars. One day, you will direct the workings of Towers of Light to harness the power of chaos and to continue to bring peace and prosperity to Cyad and to all of Cyador."

Abruptly, the boy shivers, then stiffens, though his eyes do not leave the chaos light of the Tower.

"To be of the Magi'i—it is a long and difficult struggle." The man smiles at his son, and even his sun-golden eyes smile. "But as you grow older, you will see that it is worth the effort, for nothing compares to the glory that is Cyad, and the peace and the grace of her people."

The magus slowly lowers Lorn'elth to the polished white stone floor and takes his son's hand once more. They continue along the corridor to the second door, where the father raises his hand. A flicker of golden energy flashes from a point just beyond his gloves to the door. Then he slides the door into its recess—to his left. The two enter the second corridor, and the magus closes the door behind them.

Another window awaits them midway down the second white stone corridor.

At this window, the man again lifts his son, speaking softly as he does. "You will be the ones who will transfer the pure chaos energy from the towers to the fireships, to the firewagons, and to the firelances of Cyador. You will ensure that the fair city remains so, and that her people bless the Emperor and the Magi'i of the Rational Stars."

Serious-eyed, the boy watches through the darkened glass—not so dark as that in the first corridor—as the six-wheeled firewagon rolls silently into the shimmering enclosure that flanks the chamber holding the mighty tower. Figures scurry and remove the square cells from the rear of the vehicle, replacing them with other cells that almost glitter. Then the firewagon rolls out, and another rolls in and halts.

"This is the heart of Cyad, and Cyador, and it can be yours, Lorn'elth." The father lowers his son once more. "It will be yours."

The two return as they came, their heavy boots whispering but slightly on the hard stone of the corridor.

II

RISING ABOVE THE bay and the Great Western Ocean to the south are puffy white clouds, clouds not dark enough to forecast rain at any time soon, nor high enough to block the sun that casts its mid-day autumn light upon the playing field that had been carved from the hillside generations earlier. There on the field, with a gentle sea-breeze cooling them, a score of students alternate jerky bursts of speed with sudden stops, their polished wooden mallets glistening as they jockey for position on the reddish surface. All wear white trousers and undertunics, but the undertunics bear green collars and green borders upon the sleeves.

"Lorn!" calls one student as the polished wooden oval skitters from his mallet toward another youth.

"Thanks!" With his dark-brown hair and wiry frame, Lorn is neither the largest nor the smallest on the playing field, but he streaks past a defender, his mallet almost lazily precise as it strikes the oval that is weighted unevenly. Lorn slips one way, and the oval flashes the other way, yet both Lorn and the oval meet at full speed beyond the defender as Lorn sprints inward and toward the trapezoidal frame in the middle of the circular field of play. His eyes take in the last defender and the smaller redheaded player dashing toward the goal. Lorn smiles and flicks his wrist, calling, "Tyrsal, it's yours!"

Lorn's mallet strikes the oval, and it skitters over the packed clay toward Tyrsal.

The small and redheaded Tyrsal darts around the taller and more muscular young defender and swings his mallet. The oval spins, but lifts off the clay and accelerates toward the trapezoidal goal. When it strikes to one side of the goal frame, it veers sideways and skids into the net of the opening.

"Goal!" The redhead jumps up in glee. "I got by you, Dett!"

"That's the last time, Tyrsal!" The tall and heavily muscled blond student drops his mallet and tackles the redhead, whose polished wooden mallet skids across the smooth red clay as both students lurch toward the ground.

Despite Tyrsal's struggles, Dett handily dumps the smaller youth onto the clay and raises an arm as if to strike Tyrsal.

"Bruggage! Bruggage!" Four other youths jump on top of the two who struggle.

The dark-haired Lorn is the second to slam into the pile,

but the first to put his shoulder and then his elbow into the midsection of the larger Dett.

". . . oooffff . . ."

Dett struggles to take his hands away from the squirming Tyrsal, to fend off the hidden attack on himself.

A low voice whispers in the muscular boy's ear, "Don't do it again, Dett. Ever."

"Says who?" The bully gets his knees under him and one hand on the clay and starts to elbow his way clear, unsure of who has spoken to him.

Snap . . . snap!

The other students fall away from the larger figure, who bellows, then staggers upright holding an injured hand, coddling two fingers that have already begun to swell. "Barbarians! Sheep-loving swill-drinkers!" Dett turns toward the students who had piled on. "Cowards! You just wait . . . You'll see."

"Dett . . . hurt his hand."

". . . couldn't happen to a better fellow . . ."

". . . bullied enough . . . deserved it . . ."

". . . careful . . . get you . . ."

Even before he rises, neither the first nor the last, Lorn slips the polished pair of wooden rods back inside his belt. After he stands, he limps slightly as he walks toward the mallet he abandoned, bending gracefully and scooping it up left-handed.

Tyrsal, the last to scramble up, quickly extinguishes a grin and avoids looking at the injured Dett.

"That's it! Over here!" orders the schoolyard proctor, a tallish man with a pointed goatee and wavy black hair that stands away from his head. "All of you. You know the rules! Bruggages are forbidden!"

The score of students slouch toward the proctor and the columns of the low white stone building behind him. None move to brush away the smears of reddish clay upon their student garments, nor lift their eyes to the shimmering white of the Palace that stands farther to the south and which dominates the gradual slope rising from the harbor, nor even to the white structures that lie uphill of the school, the dwellings of the senior Magi'i and Mirror Lancer commanders.

"Line up! All of you."

Lorn somehow materializes in the second rank, nearly in the middle, the expression on his face one of mild concern.

"What happened? How did Dettaur'alt's hand get injured?" demands the proctor. His eyes travel the youths, picking out a stocky student. "Allyrn'alt? You always know."

"Ser . . . Dett fell on Tyrsal, and everyone tripped in the bruggage. When we got untangled, Dett was holding his hand. I guess he fell on it." Allyrn'alt's face is carefully blank.

"Tyrsal'elth?"

"I made the goal, and I jumped around. I must have bumped into Dett, ser. We all got tangled in the bruggage. Maybe Dett's hand got kicked by someone's boot." The small redhead looks apologetically at the proctor.

"Ciesrt'elth?"

"No, ser. I wasn't even in the bruggage, ser."

". . . never is . . ." murmurs someone.

"Quiet!" The proctor turns to another. "Shalk'mer?"

"Ser . . . I got tangled up, but I didn't see anything." The square-faced merchant's son looks directly at the proctor.

"Lorn'elth? You wouldn't know . . . of course, you wouldn't." The proctor shakes his head. "You never see anything."

"I'm sorry, ser." Lorn looks contritely at the proctor.

"All of you, except Dettaur'alt, get back to your studies." The proctor sighs and motions for the muscular injured student to follow him toward the healer's room.

Before he turns to follow the proctor, Dett's eyes rake over the other students, but each in turn meets his eyes openly, without flinching.

III

CYADOR IS A paradox, one wrapped in an enigma, and offered as a riddle to the world it dominates by its sheer force of being. No land, no ruler, can contest the might of Cyador, yet its people look no different from other folk, except by their raiment and their deportment.

The Towers of Chaos descended from the Rational Stars, yet they serve those upon the land and water, those who can but observe the distant chaos of those stars, yet who can bring such chaos upon their foes.

For does the White Empire not have the fireships of war that can destroy all other vessels? Yet the trade vessels that dock at Cyad and Fyrad and Summerdock are carried there by sails, and not by the power of chaos.

Do not the firewagons roll endlessly across the finest of granite roads that link all of the Empire together, carrying passengers and cargoes smoothly and speedily? Yet even within mighty Cyad, are not the white streets of the great city filled, not with firewagons, but carts and carriages pulled by horses, by men on horseback and women on foot?

Does not the Emperor, Protector of the Steps to Paradise, Ruler of the Towers of Chaos, command the firelances before which quail the barbarians of the north and east? Yet those firelances are borne by lancers who ride the same horses as do the barbarians, and those lancers also bear blades, even if such blades are of white cupridium, against which the poor iron of Candar cannot stand.

Do not the towers of chaos send forth light so bright that it must be shielded by solid stone? Yet the Palace of Eternal Light is lit by the diffuse chaos of the sun and the lesser chaos of oil lamps.

Is not the Emperor himself a figure of might and majesty? Yet all in power fear that an emperor may again arise who is truly mighty, like the one who is seldom mentioned by the high in Cyad.

Maintaining this paradox, this enigma that is Cyad, that is the task of the Magi'i, and the duty of every magus who has ever lived and ever will live, now and forevermore. . . .

> *Paradox of Empire*
> Bern'elth, Magus First
> Cyad, 157 A.F.

IV

IN THE BLESSING and warmth of chaos, in the prosperity which it engenders, and for the preservation of all the best of our heritage, whether of elthage, altage, or merage, let us give thanks for what we receive." The silver-haired man at the north end of the table lifts his head and smiles.

The family is seated around the dining table on the covered upper balcony, from where they can look downhill and south directly at the harbor—and to the west and slightly uphill at the Palace of Eternal Light. Although the sun has set, the sky remains the purple that precedes night, and the white stone piers of the harbor glitter above the darkness of the Great Western Ocean. The Palace gleams a shimmering white—both from the white sunstone from which it was constructed all too many years before and from the innumerable lamps which bathe its endless corridors and vaulting halls in continuous light.

The dining table around which the family sits is lit but dimly by two lamps set in gleaming cupridium brackets, each affixed to a pillar, the two closest to each end of the table. None of those seated appear to be affected by the dimness. The mahogany-haired Nyryah, who sits at the end of the table opposite the silver-haired Kien'elth, lifts a silver tray that holds both dark bread and sun-nut bread and tenders it to the sandy-haired young man on her left. "Go ahead, Vernt."

"Ah . . . thank you."

"And don't take all the sun-nut bread," suggests Myryan from where she sits across from the still-lanky Vernt. "We like it, too."

"There's plenty there, children," suggests Nyryah, "and there's another loaf in the kitchen."

Vernt grins and takes one slice of each bread, then passes the tray to Lorn, who takes only a single slice of dark bread before passing the tray to his father. Kien'elth, like his younger son, takes one slice of each, and hands the tray to Jerial, dark-haired, and the eldest child. She, like Lorn, takes but a slice of dark bread, and smiles across at Lorn as she hands the tray to Myryan, also black-haired, and the youngest of the four siblings. Myryan takes a single slice of sun-nut bread and returns the tray to her mother.

The fowl casserole that had been set before Kien'elth makes a circuit of the table, but all helpings are so similar in size that they would have to have been weighed for an outsider to determine which is the largest—or the smallest. After the casserole comes the dish of buttered and nutted beans.

When Myryan sets down the serving spoon for the beans, all six begin to eat, silently for a moment, until each has had at least one mouthful of something.

"You were a little late, dear," suggests Nyryah.

"We had to chaos-charge a second complement of fire-wagons," replies Kien'elth. "The two new companies of Mirror Lancers are being sent along the Great Eastern Highway tomorrow. The barbarians of the northeast have tried to attack the cuprite mines. While they were thrown back across the Hills of Endless Grass, the Emperor has determined that the lancers of the northeast shall be more greatly reinforced to carry the message to the barbarians that they may be reminded of the futility of such attacks."

Myryan smiles.

"You find that amusing?" asks Vernt.

"The name's amusing," she admits. "Nothing's endless, not even the Rational Stars. So how can grass be endless?"

"The barbarians are endless," says Vernt. "Every year there are more of them."

"More doesn't mean endless."

"And they're just as stupid every year. Tens of scores of them try to cross the border, and most of them die." Vernt looks at his father. "There must have been more than usual if you had to do more chaos-charging."

"I was told that the lancers have it well in hand," answers his sire.

"And they will push the barbarians back across the not-so-endless Grass Hills," Myryan says, "no matter what the barbarians call the grass."

"I do believe we've heard this before," suggests Kien'elth politely. "We decided the name was a barbarian affectation." He clears his throat, then takes another mouthful of the fowl casserole, nodding as he tastes it.

"We just ought to take over all of Candar—the western half, anyway," says Vernt. "That way, we wouldn't have to worry about the smelly barbarians."

"The chaos-towers can't be moved," Lorn points out. "That's why Emperor—"

"Lorn," interjects Kien'elth quickly. "Not at dinner."

"Yes, ser."

"We don't need to move the towers," continues Vernt, seemingly oblivious to his father's warning to Lorn. "The barbarians' iron blades are so soft that a cupridium blade cuts through any of their weapons." The younger son snorts. "We don't need firewagons and highways to conquer them."

"No—but would you want to live in a mud-brick hut or a tent?" Kien'elth laughs. "You wouldn't get cooking like this, or cities like Cyad or Fyrad or Summerdock."

"We've heard this discussion before, too," interjects Jerial. "Cyador already has more land than we'll ever need, and so do the barbarians. They don't attack from need, but from perversity. They want to take what we've built, because they're too lazy and too stupid to make things for themselves."

"They do not have chaos-towers, nor could they fabricate them if they wanted to," says her father gently.

"They don't have to live like swine," counters Vernt. "You can smell them from kays away."

"They weren't born with your advantages," Kien'elth points out.

"We've sent teachers out to the north and east." Vernt's voice rises. "And those that weren't killed had to kill the barbarians to escape with their lives. . . ."

"Maybe they don't want to learn," suggests Jerial, with a hint of a laugh in her voice. "They don't like books as much as you do."

Lorn quietly finishes his casserole, and, while the others are looking at Vernt and Jerial, and while his mother has slipped away from the table to bring the dessert platter, he slips a slice of sun-nut bread from the tray and onto his platter. He eats it in precise motions before finally speaking. "They still think we took their land."

"We didn't take anything, did we?" asks Myryan. "I thought most of Cyador was the Accursed Forest before the founders came, and it killed either the barbarians or us whenever it could. They didn't live here. They couldn't have lived here." She shakes her head. "It doesn't make sense. We're not using land that they ever could have farmed or herded on. I agree with Jerial. They're just lazy."

"They are what they are," replies Kien'elth, "and we aren't going to change that. We can only deal with our own lives." He clears his throat. "Lorn . . . have you ever met Aleyar? She's Lector Liataphi's next-to-youngest daughter?"

"He's met them all." Vernt chortles.

Lorn manages not to flush. "She is blonde, I believe, and quite well spoken."

"I told you so," Vernt hisses.

"Father . . ." Jerial begins.

Kien'elth turns to his eldest daughter. "Liataphi has no sons. I am not asking Lorn to consort with her. I am asking if he would at least talk to the young lady. There's no harm in seeing if he likes an eligible young woman."

". . . and it would be kind," Myryan says with a sad smile.

"Because her older sister Syreal ran off with that merchanter, and that means that unless she consorts with a Magi'i she'll lose her standing in the Magi'i?" asks Jerial.

"It's true, isn't it?" counters Myryan. "We're lucky. We have brothers who are carrying on as Magi'i. Aleyar isn't, and she's sweet."

"You know her?" asks Nyryah.

"I like her," replies Myryan. "She's too gentle to be consorted to a lancer or a merchanter." She looks at Lorn. "And she is pretty."

Lorn shifts his weight in his chair almost imperceptibly, then smiles. "I'll make a point of talking to her."

"That's all I ask," Kien'elth says, as he turns and smiles at Myryan. "Lector Kharl'elth said that the only young lady his son ever talked about was you."

"Ciesrt?" Myryan's expression reverts to one of polite interest.

Lorn glances from her to their father, who in turn watches the wavy-haired Myryan closely.

"Ciesrt'elth," corrects Kien'elth. "You know him, Lorn."

"He's in my student group," concedes Lorn.

"He works hard," adds Vernt. "Lector Hyrist'elth says he wishes all the students worked as hard."

Across from Lorn, Myryan's face tightens ever so slightly.

"He's pretty serious," Lorn adds.

"These are serious times," Kien'elth begins, clearing his throat in the way that Lorn knows a long pontification is about to begin.

"It sounds like a good time for sweets." Nyryah sets the wide white-glazed platter in the center of the table, then reseats herself. "Baked pearapple creamed tarts." She smiles at her consort. "You can talk about serious times after dessert, dear."

Kien'elth laughs. "Undermined at my own table."

"A good dessert doesn't wait," counters Nyryah, "and if

you do, you won't have any tarts with this bunch drooling over them."

Myryan and Vernt laugh. Lorn and Jerial nod minutely at each other, but the corners of Lorn's mouth turn up ever so slightly as he glances at the warm smile his mother has bestowed upon their father.

"Outstanding!" Kien'elth beams as he takes the first tart. "The barbarians and the serious folk have nothing like this."

"They might." Vernt frowns, as if in thought, then adds, "But they probably don't."

"You can't even argue just on one side, Vernt," says Jerial after a mouthful of her tart. "Maybe you should become a counselor. That's what they do—they argue both sides of everything."

"What about something like being the Hand of the Emperor?" asks Myryan guilelessly.

"Myryan," cautions Nyryah. "One doesn't talk about the Hand."

"Especially since no one knows who he is," adds Jerial dryly. "That's not wise."

Kien'elth, his mouth filled with the creamy tart, shakes his head and finally swallows. "Argumentative counselors get sent as envoys to the barbarian lands. Besides, no Magi'i should stoop to being a counselor. Mostly, they mediate between merchanters."

Amused smiles fill the faces around the table, smiles followed by silence as they enjoy the tarts.

"There are a few tarts left," offers Nyryah when all have finished, glancing toward Lorn, "and since you didn't have as much of the sun-nut bread . . ." She looks at Vernt, on whose face a frown appears and quickly vanishes, "and since you look positively starved, Vernt . . ."

Myryan raises her eyebrows.

". . . and you're still growing, youngest daughter," Nyryah smiles at Myryan and concludes, "there are enough extra tarts for each of you."

"The last thing I need is another tart," observes Jerial,

glancing down at her slender waist. "I should not have had the one."

"You could eat three every night, and it would scarce show," counters her mother, "but I know how you feel."

Kien'elth glances at his consort. Nyryah raises her eyebrows, and he closes his mouth quietly.

Lorn eats a second tart, deftly, with motions that are neither hasty nor dawdling, yet leave no crumbs upon his fingers or his mouth. "Excellent. You must tell Elthya." He smiles at his mother. "If I don't first."

"You'll not only tell her, Lorn, you'll charm her out of a third," says Jerial.

"A fourth," suggests Myryan. "I'd wager a silver he had one this afternoon when they were cooling." Her warm smile turns toward Lorn.

He shrugs. "It might be."

His sisters laugh. Even Vernt, seated beside Myryan, smiles. So does Nyryah, although the mahogany-haired woman's smile is more knowingly ironic.

As the family rises and as Elthya and the shorter serving girl step forward out of the shadows to clear the table, Kien'elth beckons to Lorn. "I'd like to talk with you for a few moments, Lorn."

"Yes, ser." Lorn, slightly taller and slightly broader across the chest than his father or his younger brother, follows Kien'elth along the outside upper arched portico until they reach the open door of the study.

The study is lit by the pair of oil lamps at each end of the pale oak table-desk. Their silvered mantels—and their separation—cast an even glow across the room so that the shadows are faint against the warmth of the blond wood panels that comprise the walls and the amber leather of the volumes set in the bookcase that is built into the wall beside the desk. The scents of frysya and baked pearapples linger in the room, reminding Lorn of the glazed tarts that had followed dinner.

Kien'elth turns and stands between his desk, empty except for the lamps, and the stand that holds the shimmering white cupridium pen that is yet another mark of his position as a magus. The polished white oak case that holds his chaos glass rests on the small octagonal table to the right of the desk proper.

Lorn's eyes pass over the glass, though he has often felt its power when his father has employed it to observe him from afar.

After a moment of silence, the magus turns to his dark-haired son. "I spoke with Lector Hyrist'elth."

Lorn nods, waits for his father to continue.

"He is not displeased with your studies, Lorn, but he is not pleased, either. He and I both feel that while you learn all that comes before you, and more, you learn because it is easier for you to learn than to oppose us." Kien'elth smiles. "I have seen you on the korfal field. There, you are unfettered, almost joyous. I would wish you to show such joy in learning and in studies."

"I learn everything that I can, ser," Lorn replies carefully, knowing he must choose his words with care, for his father can sense any hint of untruth—as can anyone within the family—and Lorn does not wish to have his father use his chaos glass to follow him continually, though he can sense when Kien'elth—or any of the Magi'i—seek him with a glass. Most of his actions are innocent enough, but there is little sense in provoking his father into deeper inquiries. "It is true that, presently, learning for me is not so joyous, but I will persevere until, I hope, it is such."

"All Cyador rests on the Magi'i," says the older man. "Without the chaos towers, the firewagons would not run, and neither lancers nor foot nor crops could be carried to where they must go. The barges could not run the Great Canal. Without the chaos chisels, the stone for the roads would have to be quarried by hand, and it would take years to pave but a kay of road. The Great Eastern Highway alone . . . Without chaos glasses, we could not see the storms or the larger barbarian forces, . . ."

Lorn listens politely as his father continues.

". . . and that is why it is a great honor and a worthy duty to become a magus, and a goal for which you should strive."

"I understand that, father."

"Lorn . . . you nod politely, and you apply yourself diligently enough, and you have mastered the art of chaos transfer, indeed more than mastered it, and you have even learned the basics of healing from Jerial, though that be more of a serving art than a magely one, and you have, I know, the skill to truthread, and that is something but a handful ever fully master."

"Is that not what I am required to do, ser?"

"You are capable of more, far more. You have the talent to become one of the great mages. But that requires more than talent." Kien'elth looks squarely at his oldest son. "I would hope that you would see such." He shrugs. "I have told Lector Hyrist'elth that, if you do not show great love of your studies, I will seek an officership for you with the Mirror Lancers. You possess the skills to direct the lances of an entire company already, and perhaps the time on the frontiers would rekindle your love of chaos."

Lorn continues to meet his sire's searching study. "I will do my best for the year ahead, ser, but I can promise only diligence and hard work."

"That I know you will provide, Lorn." Kien'elth shakes his head slowly. "But each one of the Magi'i must possess the very fire of chaos within himself or the chaos with which he works will consume him as surely as a firelance will consume whatever its fire strikes. If you cannot find such passion, no matter how great your skill, you would be better as an officer of the Mirror Lancers than as the highest of the Magi'i." His lined face and silver hair do not hide the sadness within him as he beholds his eldest son.

"I understand, father. I will do what I can do."

Kien'elth nods. "I know."

Lorn cannot disguise the frown as he closes the polished wooden door behind him and steps from the study into the open pillared corridor that rings the upper levels of the house. As he had sensed, Jerial waits in the shadows. Lorn turns to his older sister.

"How is Father?" asks Jerial. "He was quiet at dinner, and

you're frowning. It must have been a serious discussion."

"It was. We discussed how, without the Magi'i, the Great Eastern Highway—and the Great North Highway—would still be under construction," Lorn finishes with a smile, "since even the North Highway's length is four hundred and ninety three kays. We also talked about how I should build a new chaos tower when I finish my studies."

"Lorn . . . someday you're going to have to be serious."

"I am serious." The dark-haired young man smiles at his older sister. "I'm always serious." The smile fades. "Too serious in my studies for father. He wishes that I approach them as a lover."

"Well . . ." Jerial grins, "you've already had enough experience there, brother dear. Surely . . . surely . . ."

Lorn laughs. "Ah . . . if I could."

Jerial smiles, then slips away.

After a moment, Lorn shrugs and takes the outside steps down into the rear garden, past the fruit trees and the grape arbor. He pauses by the rear gate, in the shielded darkness, and concentrates on his adaptation of chaos transfer.

Hssst! A small firebolt arcs from his fingers onto the white stone, splashing like liquid flame, rearing up a good two spans into the gloom.

Lorn quickly steps on the twig that has caught fire and stamps out the small fire with his heavy white boots. "Careful . . ." He glances around, but there are no sounds beyond the murmurs that drift from the servants' quarters beyond the garden. He should have used even less chaos.

After a last look at the house, he leaves by the rear gate, and walks down the paved and spotless alley to the lower street, above which tower the three levels of the family dwelling.

Lorn strides along the Road of Perpetual Light, eastward, away from the taverns frequented by the higher-ranking lancers and the cider-houses that cater to the students. The cylar trees overhanging the white-paved street whisper in the night breeze, and the autumn perfume of the purple arymids fills the cool air.

Lorn senses red-dark chaos . . . or trouble, and wonders what it might be. His eyes note little distinction between twilight and night as he strides purposefully eastward, almost welcoming the reddish-whiteness that he nears—after the talk with his father.

A couple walks toward him, nearly in the white and sparkling center of the wide walkway flanking the road, and Lorn can see from shimmering blue attire that both are from the merchanters. The man is slender, and his attention is upon the red-haired woman he escorts. Chaos lurks behind them, in the hulking figure that follows, apparently unseen in the shadowed darkness of the trees.

Lorn eases onto the same side of the road as the skulker who moves toward the couple, but the student magus is too late as the heavy and tall man leaps and strikes the male merchanter, with a blunt club or some such. The man collapses in a heap, and the woman turns to flee, but the attacker grabs her arm.

"Halthor! Let go of me!" she screams. "Help! The Patrol!"

The man called Halthor drops the club to muffle her screams with his oversized hand.

Lorn steps out of the shadows, then ducks and picks up the truncheon as Halthor releases the woman. Lorn moves as if he had seen the large fist coming and steps under the giant's arms, bringing the short wooden truncheon into the vee of the man's ribs. Something cracks. The giant gasps, standing there immobile.

Lorn's eyes glitter gold for but an instant as he speaks. "I believe that all would be best if you jumped off the southernmost pier in the harbor and inhaled as much water as you can."

The taller man shivers, then turns, breathing laboriously, and begins to walk westward along the Road of Perpetual Light, ignoring the fallen trader, the woman merchanter, and Lorn.

Despite the sudden knife-like headache that has shivered through his skull, Lorn lowers the truncheon and turns toward the woman in shimmering blue, his voice filled with concern. "Are you all right?"

"Ah . . . I think so. Yes." She does not quite shiver, as she bends toward the fallen man.

Through slightly blurred vision, Lorn sees that she is a redhead, and lightly freckled, with creamy skin, and a full figure under the shimmering blue tunic.

"What did you do?" she asks. "He . . . just turned away and left."

"Just offered an opinion. . . ." Lorn's laugh sounds easy. "He won't be bothering anyone soon." The warm and friendly smile appears as he also steps toward the fallen junior trader. "We need to attend to your friend."

The male trader squints, rolls to his knees, glances up at the redhead, then at Lorn. "What did you do to Halthor? He'd like as kill you, student magus or not." He slowly rises to his feet, but he shivers and staggers.

Lorn extends a hand. "As I told your lady friend, I offered my opinion to the fellow, that he take himself elsewhere."

"He's never heeded anyone's advice before." The trader groans as he straightens up. "Cracked in my skull."

"This . . . young man," says the woman, "offered it rather persuasively. Halthor was almost doubled over. He has a cracked rib or two, perhaps."

The male trader lowers his head and holds it in both hands. "My head's splitting."

"I'm sure it only feels that way," says the woman.

Lorn's fingers brush the man's skull.

"That's better," admits the wounded trader.

Somehow the slight healing Lorn can offer the trader also lessens his own headache, if marginally.

"Are you a healer, young ser?" asks the woman.

"Me?" Lorn shakes his head ingenuously. "I've picked up some from my older sister, who is, but I'm afraid I'm poor in comparison to her." He looks eastward, along the white stones of the road, past two couples who are strolling in a leisurely fashion down the cross-street toward the pavilions that wait on the beach front park. "I think you do need to lie down before long. Are your . . . quarters far from here?"

"No. Just two streets up." The trader takes a step and pales, then takes another.

"Are you sure you're all right, Alyet?" asks the woman.

"For two streets . . . yes."

Lorn takes the man's arm once more. "Just lean on me."

"And me." The woman takes his other arm, and the three walk slowly eastward until they reach an archway on the uphill side of the way.

"There . . ." mumbles Alyet. "There."

The woman and Lorn guide the trader up three steps and toward a darkened doorway to the left. She fumbles a shining brass key from Alyet's belt wallet and unlocks the door.

Once inside, they cross a small sitting room that holds but a small table with two chairs, and a low settee under the high window. A sleeping chamber barely big enough for the bed and a chest lies through a narrow archway.

They help Alyet lower himself onto the bed that is draped with a dark blue coverlet.

"Are you sure he'll be all right?" asks the woman.

"He has some bad bruises, and a lump on his skull, but nothing's broken, I think," Lorn ventures, "and his head will ache for days."

"Ryalth . . . be careful . . . sorry . . . don't think I can see you home," Alyet apologizes.

"I'll make sure she's safe," Lorn promises. "Don't you worry."

Ryalth raises her well-formed but narrow eyebrows. She does not protest as they leave Alyet's quarters.

Once they are back on the Road of Eternal Light, standing beneath the arch of curved white stone—merely alabaster, and not sunstone—Lorn turns to Ryalth, "We should decide what we should do tonight."

Her eyebrows arch. "I do not know you, ser, and you appear to be a student."

"I am indeed a student, but that's all the more reason for you not to worry. Besides, you scarcely need to end the evening on such an upsetting note." Lorn takes the young woman's hand and smiles winningly.

V

COOL WINTER SUNLIGHT angles through the high windows and strikes the age- and chaos-whitened granite walls well above the heads of the five figures in the discussion room, illuminating the space with an indirectly intense light. Four student Magi'i sit on straight-backed chairs facing the Lector who stands before them in shimmering white tunic, trousers, belt, and boots.

Lorn wonders, not for the first time, whether the Lector's smallclothes shimmer as well, even though he knows his father's do not—but somehow, a Lector who monitors his studies is more forbidding.

Ciesrt'elth shifts his weight in his chair, and it creaks. Lector Abram'elth ignores the sound and looks across the group of four with eyes that glow golden, as do the eyes of many of the senior Magi'i. "The time has come for you to once again observe a chaos tower, this time in light of the knowledge that you have acquired and with all your senses, and not just your eyes. You will be escorted in pairs. Ciesrt'elth and Rustyl'elth will be first. Tyrsal'elth and Lorn'elth will be the second group. You two in the second group will wait here."

After the other three leave and the golden oak door closes, Tyrsal glances at Lorn. "Why would it look different now? The tower, I mean?"

"We've seen one before, and we've seen the drawings. It probably looks the same, just like the drawings, except it would have to glow with chaos. It is a chaos tower. That's probably what the Lector wants to know—whether we can sense the chaos." Lorn smiles and laughs gently.

"Maybe it doesn't look like that at all with chaos senses. Maybe we just thought we saw a tower before."

"What would be the point of deceiving us about that? It would just be a waste of time."

"They say that none of the halls in the Palace of Eternal Light are actually the way people draw them," Tyrsal counters. "And that they change them all the time."

"That's different. Anyone can request an audience with the Emperor or his Voice or his Advisors. They don't know who might be coming in, and I suppose the Emperor cannot trust anyone. Except the Hand, and that's because no one knows who he is. The senior and more talented Magi'i could use a chaos glass to scree the Palace. That's why they have lancers and firelances behind the screens throughout the Palace. Here . . . the only ones who see the towers are the Magi'i, and the older students."

"Have you . . . a chaos glass?" Tyrsal stumbles over his words.

"Hardly. If my father didn't discipline me for that, the Lectors certainly would, and I'm not sure father wouldn't be worse."

"Ah . . ." Tyrsal swallows, then quickly asks, "What about the workings of the fireships and the firewagons? They're all sealed, and anyone besides a magus who opens them gets chaos-fried."

"Exactly," suggests Lorn.

"I suppose you're right," Tyrsal concedes.

"Maybe I'm not, but we'll find out soon enough."

"Do you know if we're going to see the same tower or another tower for the Magi'i?"

"The same, I'd imagine."

"They all have to be close, don't they?"

Lorn shrugs. "They could be anywhere in the Quarter. They do have to be surrounded by the heavy granite and sunstone, but everything in the Quarter of the Magi'i is built that way."

"That's true." Tyrsal lapses into silence.

In time, the door to the discussion room opens, and Lector Abram'elth follows the other two students back inside. He does not close the wooden door to the corridor.

"Not a word," the Lector says to Ciesrt and Rustyl, "not until we depart the room." He beckons to Lorn and Tyrsal.

The remaining two students rise, and Ciesrt and Rustyl re-seat themselves in the cool mid-day winter light that the very stones of the building have amplified in some indefinable fashion.

Without speaking, the Lector leads Lorn and Tyrsal out of the discussion room and along the corridor toward the private study rooms of the Magi'i of the school, then through a gleaming cupridium door, and along a narrower corridor which ends in another cupridium door that has neither latches nor handles nor knobs.

Knowing what must come next, Lorn watches the Lector with his senses as the man lifts his hand. The flash of golden energy follows, and Lorn withholds a nod of understanding as Abram'elth eases the heavy door into its recess. The three enter the second corridor where the floors, walls, and ceiling are all of white granite Lorn remembers.

Abram'elth stops and turns to the two students. "Up ahead you see the black shield. When you look through the black shield, you will see the Magi'i tower—the one that powers chaos cells used in the school and in the Palace of Eternal Light." The Lector pauses, then adds. "Study the tower, not only with your eyes, but with your senses, and see the variants of chaos that exist. Do *not* even think about transferring chaos. If you do, both the tower and I will consume you with unfocused chaos."

"Yes, ser." Lorn's and Tyrsal's responses are nearly simultaneous.

"Tyrsal'elth, you may go first."

"Yes, ser." The redhead takes his place before the darkened square that is neither glass nor metal nor any substance yet made in centuries within Cyador, a single pane so dark it appears black. He stands there for a very long time before he steps away.

Abram'elth's eyes and senses shift from Tyrsal to Lorn. "Lorn'elth." The Lector's voice rumbles in the granite-walled corridor.

Lorn walks to the window shield, where, through the dark aperture, he studies the shimmering tower enclosed within the insulated granite walls of the chaos-power station. He recalls a similar such vision, clearly unauthorized, from many years before, long before he had first seen a tower as a student magus.

Knowing that, he concentrates, but his eyes reveal to him little beyond the glaring silhouette of the tower. His chaos senses focus on the reddish-white chaos surrounding the bluish-white barrier that blocks the core from touching even the air that surrounds it. He feels, though he could not explain why, that the tower, this particular one, teeters on the edge of . . . nothingness . . . as if poised to fall into the world, or out of it. Yet the reddish chaos and the bluish chaos do not touch, although each pulses in response to the other.

After a time, Lorn steps away, his face expressionless.

After he does, the Lector studies Lorn, then Tyrsal, before he speaks. "What did you sense?"

"The pulse of chaos," Lorn says mildly. "It is constant, yet ever-changing."

"It is constant within chaotic bounds," the Lector affirms. "It produces the same amount of chaos energy at all times." He turns to Tyrsal.

"The chaos that surrounds the core," offers Tyrsal.

"There is a barrier there," confirms Lorn.

Abram'elth nods slowly. "Precisely, and that barrier must remain for the tower to continue operating."

"What happens if it doesn't, ser?" inquires Tyrsal.

"Then the tower will cease to be." The Lector frowns. "Your lessons should have taught you that."

"Yes, ser." Tyrsal looks down.

Lorn realizes he must speak or forfeit the opportunity. Offering a guileless smile, he says slowly, "But there is chaos— or something like it—on the other side of the barrier. Wouldn't that escape or something?"

The Lector's frown deepens as his eyes flick to the dark-haired student magus. "How do you know that?"

"You told us that there were several kinds of chaos, and asked us to try to use our chaos senses to determine them,"

Lorn replies easily. "The chaos behind the barrier feels different, as you said it would."

"I did say that," muses the Lector, almost to himself, then he straightens. "No one knows for certain what will happen if the barrier fails, and no tower has yet failed since the first years of the founding of Cyad nearly two hundred years ago. And one of the tasks of the Magi'i, as you will discover, is to ensure that no tower does fail."

Tyrsal and Lorn do not exchange glances, but they might well have, for Lorn knows that the Lector misleads with his last statement—not exactly a lie, but a statement verging on it, and Lorn knows Tyrsal understands that as well. Lorn also knows that Abram'elth does not know that Lorn and Tyrsal can sense such, for most students cannot sense such shading of the truth.

"Remember, the towers are the heart of Cyad and Cyador."

"Yes, ser."

The Lector believes his last statement, and that belief troubles Lorn more than the statement that had preceded it.

The two follow the Lector back along the corridor to the door where, again, Abram'elth raises his hand and focuses chaos before sliding the door open.

Once the three have traveled the white granite corridors and are back in the discussion room, where Ciesrt and Rustyl are waiting, the Lector surveys the four students.

"Tomorrow, you will begin your advanced chaos-transfer training in the firewagon hall. Consider what you have seen. You may speak of it only to other Magi'i or to students as advanced as you, and to no others. We will know if you speak otherwise. You may depart for the day."

VI

THE EMPEROR TOZIEL'ELTH'ALT'MER looks through the tinted glass windows of the Palace. His eyes focus on the harbor of Cyad, and the piers that house the White Fleet—although there are but two of the white-hulled fireships tied there presently. To the east of the fireships are tied a handful of coasting schooners, a brig that flies the jack of Brysta, and two other deep-sea vessels without jacks or ensigns flying.

North of the piers and closer to the Palace, the sunstone-paved streets glisten. The shops to the west sport green and white awnings, and under those immaculate canvases are the cafes and bakeries for which Cyad is known. Those who walk the streets are well-clad, whether in the shimmercloth affected by the Magi'i, the higher merchanters, or lancer officers—and their households—or in the hard-combed and tightly-woven cotton of the common people.

"Yet the least of the common folk is clad like a noble among the barbarians, and lives in greater comfort and cleanliness," murmurs the Emperor. "And that is as it should be." He turns and walks past the Great Hall, past the three-story-high gilded doors that can open so silently and swiftly that an observer who blinked might well miss their operation. Behind him follow two figures uniformed in silver-trimmed green, each with hand firelances—used but by the Palace Guard and those Mirror Lancers who guard the outside of the Palace of Light.

The Emperor Toziel—for he thinks of himself without the multiple identifiers attached to his name—steps through a silently-opening and cupridium-clad door that brings him to his own entrance to the small receiving hall. After a moment, composing himself, he steps through the archway and seats himself on the sculpted malachite and silver chair on the dais. He looks out over a marble-floored room merely large enough for two or three of the Cyadoran firewagons that speed endlessly along the Great North Highway.

Those waiting cross the shimmering and spotless white tiles, bow below the dais, and offer their felicitations.

"Your Mightiness . . ."

"Mightiness . . ."

Toziel gestures toward his Majer-Commander of Lancers, standing on the left of those who await his scrutiny. "If you would, Rynst'alt . . ."

"There were nearly ten score barbarians in the raid on Pemedra, and nearly that many in the raid on Inividra. We have not seen such raids, not on the base outposts, in many years. The Mirror Lancers killed about half those in the first raid, perhaps a third of those in the second. The barbarians vanished, as expected, into the Grass Hills. They appear as endless as the blades of grass in those hills." The gray-haired officer in cream and green bows slightly as he finishes speaking, as if apologizing. "We have sent additional charged firelances to the north, and replacement lancers as well."

"Thank you, Rynst'alt." The tired-faced and silver-robed figure shifts his weight in the sculpted malachite and silver chair and turns his head toward the golden-eyed magus with the crossed cupridium lightning bolts on the breast of his tunic.

"The replenishment tower continues to provide chaos flow for the lances and the firewagons, sire. We were required to charge nearly double the number of wagons this fall as compared to the numbers in any recent year in the past generation."

Toziel nods. "High Lector Chyenfel'elth, can we move any of the towers that prison the Accursed Forest?"

"No, sire." Chyenfel'elth bows. "Attempting to move them would be far too great a risk."

"What about replenishing chaos for the lances from those towers? They could be moved down to Fyrad on the Great Canal."

"That we can do for now. For how many years we do not know. You should be aware, sire, that two of the ward towers have already failed. It will take all the chaos of those remaining to build the permanent barrier you have approved, sire."

"You do not know yet even if you can accomplish this," Toziel points out.

"We must try, sire. The towers will not remain forever."

"And, if I rescind my approval?"

"You do as you see fit, sire. The Magi'i obey."

"How long will it take to build the barrier?"

"It is not precisely a barrier," Chyenfel says cautiously.

"It will bar the Accursed Forest, will it not?"

"Yes, sire. We cannot say how long the process will take. We estimate a full two seasons, if aught goes well."

"And that will provide protection for the realm of chaos for generations to come? And keep the Forest from reclaiming Cyador?"

"As we discussed . . ." Chyenfel says smoothly.

"On a lesser scale, I know."

"Yes, sire."

"I will consider this, and I will talk to the Hand." Toziel turns to the next figure, clad in shimmering blue. "How stand the warehouses, Bluoyal'mcr?"

Bluoyal bows stiffly. "All have been inspected and their contents enumerated . . . this autumn season is a little different from any other autumn season . . ."

"Have you been able to purchase the additional cuprite?"

"Yes, sire, although in the quantities required, the . . . acquisition necessitated spending nearly a thousand golds beyond what we had estimated. You may recall, sire, that we had discussed that possibility."

"We had." The tired eyes of the Emperor watch each of those who act as though they serve him and Cyador.

VII

A COOL MIST shrouds Cyad, a mist that holds the tang of salt air, the fragrance of the late-blooming aramyds, and the faintest odor of the bitterness that reminds Lorn of chaos, an acridness far stronger within the Quarter of the Magi'i, but omnipresent throughout the great white city. Occasional drops of rain slither through the silvery mist, and the white stones of the buildings and roads of Cyad are gray with moisture.

Lorn slips along the covered portico on the upper level of the dwelling and then down the outside steps to the garden,

staying close to the inside wall. In his left hand is a loosely
rolled bundle that appears to be a towel. Once in the garden,
he takes the path by the wall toward the postern gate, for
that is directly under his mother's window, and unless she
leans out the window, she could not see him pass below.

There is a bench outside the rear gate, where Elthya and
the other servants often gather to talk, but no one will be
there while dinner is being prepared. After he eases the gate
closed, in the afternoon dimness, he quickly pulls off his
green-trimmed student whites and dons the shimmering blue
merchanter tunic and trousers, then switches his white boots
for the dark blue boots, before adding a blue belt. He rerolls
his own clothes and places them and his boots into the pitch-
coated basket that he had left earlier and replaces the basket
back under the feathered conifer beyond the gate.

He walks swiftly down the alley and across the Road of
Perpetual Light, still taking the alley downhill past two other
roads until he turns westward on the Road of Benevolent
Commerce. The heavy heels of the merchanter boots barely
whisper on the stone pavement. His stride is that of the other
junior merchanters who scurry to the beckoning of others.

As he passes the Empty Quarter—a coffee house, almost
a cafe, that caters to the most junior of merchanter appren-
tices—and outland sea-traders—he nods to the two appren-
tices sitting in the near-vacant establishment, giving them a
perfunctory smile of acknowledgement.

"Who's that . . . ?"

"Some junior enumerator . . . friend of Alyet's and
Ryalth's . . . saved Alyet from Halthor one night when he
guzzled too much. . . ."

". . . can't figure Halthor drowning . . ."

". . . anyone'll drown . . . drinks and walks the piers . . ."

". . . looks young for an enumerator . . ."

". . . Ryalth says he's good . . ."

". . . at what?"

Lorn represses a grin as he hurries westward along the
Way of Benevolent Commerce until it intersects with the
First Harbor Way. The corner is identified by the green-

lettered placards inscribed in the angular Anglorian script on the walls of the warehouse that stands on the southwest corner. Only in the trading district of Cyad do such placards exist. Elsewhere, one must know where he goes.

On the northwest corner, a woman in shimmering blue waits for Lorn under the awning by the Honest Stone—the unofficial merchanter coffee house for the warehouse district of Cyad.

Lorn waves and smiles as he nears.

"I was afraid you weren't coming." Ryalth snorts angrily. "After all you said."

"I'm sorry." Lorn offers an easy and fully apologetic smile. "I got here as quickly as I could."

"We'd better go. Aljak said at the eighth bell." Ryalth heads toward the harbor, walking on the right side of the white-paved First Harbor Way, as much by custom as to avoid the near-silent cart on the left drawn up the gentle incline by a white pony.

Lorn inclines his head to the bearded carter who walks beside the pony, leading him, then says quietly, "We have some time."

Ryalth glances behind them, as though she fears they are being followed.

"Don't worry," Lorn assures her. "All we're doing is buying cotton."

"With our own coins—not clan coins—and there's no one to back us if it's not good."

"That's why I'm here, remember?" Lorn says.

"You can slip back into that mighty house if this doesn't work."

"It's worked before. Why would today be any different?"

"Because it's Hamorian cotton. Or that's what Aljak has let it be known. You can't trust him, not even so much as Jiulko."

"He was the one who had the oils—Jiulko?" Lorn touches Ryalth's arm, gently, offering reassurance.

"I don't know why you talked me into this," Ryalth murmurs.

"So that you can start your own merchanter house. Merchanter women can refuse to consort, or consort by choice if they have a business worth more than five hundred golds. Remember?"

"Don't remind me."

"My sisters would like that kind of choice," Lorn says softly.

"Why would they need it? They're protected women."

Lorn smiles faintly, deciding against arguing. "If we take this Aljak's cotton . . . If we take it, did you arrange for a cart?"

"Sormet has the next warehouse . . . he'll let us use his hand cart and charge me a silver for storage until I can sell it, if it's less than a season." Ryalth grins. "The oils . . . he got a silver for an eightday. So he'll be happy."

"If the cotton's good."

"Some of it will be good," predicts Ryalth.

The two swing to the left and around a two-horse wagon that lumbers uphill. The wagon bed is covered, as required in Cyad, but the covering does not totally block the acrid odor of dyes carried in the small demicasks.

"Green dye," Lorn murmurs.

"You'd think you'd been born a merchanter, sometimes, and then . . . other times." Ryalth shakes her head.

"That's why we work together."

Ryalth laughs. "No . . . we work together because you want to sleep with me, and it's the only way you think I'll keep seeing you."

Lorn smiles, slightly more than faintly. "Well . . . you're still seeing me, and you have a lot more golds."

"Alyet says you'll leave me once you become a full Magus."

"More likely that you'll leave me," he counters, laughing again. "I'm too young for you. You've told me that more than once."

Ryalth turns again, this time along the Road of the Second Quay, which is the second street back from the stone piers where the trading vessels tie up.

Although the road is spotless, for it could not be otherwise in Cyad, an air of disuse permeates the road that appears narrower than it is, running as it does between the high and largely windowless warehouses of gray stone. The acrid scent of ancient, chaos-carved stone drifts up and around Lorn, a scent that he has discovered few others discern.

"His place is on the next corner, away from the harbor."

"Are any of these used any more?" Lorn gestures to the warehouse to his right.

"Most of them are empty. Aljak probably doesn't pay a gold an eight-day to rent the space. It belongs to the Jekseng clan, but they only have two ocean traders and a coaster left." She adds wryly, "I wish I had *just* two ocean traders and a coaster left."

"Is that it?" Lorn nods toward the half-opened timbered door framed by weathered granite that had faded into a whitened and dingy gray shade more attractive from the hillside above than from where he viewed it.

"Yes." Ryalth squares her shoulders, her hand brushing her belt wallet as she steps toward the open door.

Lorn follows Ryalth through the opening created by a heavy wooden sliding door being rolled back perhaps five cubits. He enters the warehouse a step behind her, his posture conveying that he is indeed her lackey—or hired enumerator. His chaos senses flick across the racked items, stopping for a moment on the barrels of seed oil stacked in a cube to the left of the doorway. He does not nod, but his eyes sparkle, as he takes in the other items—a pallet of dark timbers; five tall amphorae, one slightly cracked, with darkness seeping from the crack; a stack of what appear to be bales of wool; another set of nine curved canisters, half again as large as the amphorae. . . .

"Ah . . . the lady merchant from the House of the Lesser Traders." Aljak steps out of the gloom at the rear of the cavernous structure toward the comparatively small groupings of goods just beyond the open warehouse door.

Lorn focuses on the heavy-set but massively broad trader

with the oiled curly black hair and the bush-like beard.
Heavy bronze bands girdle overlarge wrists.

"Trader Aljak." Ryalth inclines her head. "Sormet said you
might have some cotton . . . some *good* Hamorian cotton."

"That I do. That I do, lady merchant. Aljak has what
others lack." The big trader offers a rolling belly laugh that
echoes falsely through the big warehouse, then turns and
walks a good fifteen cubits before pointing at five bolts of
off-white cloth, each hung on a rack above the stone floor
of the warehouse. "Here ye be. Five full-length bolts of Hamorian first rate cotton, thread count guaranteed tighter than
sixscore to the span, ready to bleach and dye. Twenty-five
for the lot or seven and a half for each bolt, and I pick the
bolts."

Ryalth nods, then moves forward.

Aljak steps back, his eyes flickering toward the darker section of the warehouse to the east.

Lorn sees the other two men, nearly as big as the trader,
with blades, iron blades, in the scabbards at their belts. His
eyes flick back to the barrels of seed oil, then to Ryalth. As
Ryalth examines each bolt of cotton, Lorn studies each with
his chaos senses.

After looking at the last bolt, Ryalth straightens and steps
toward Lorn.

He steps forward and murmurs, "The first two, the ones
closest to the door, are garment class cotton, close to it. The
other three are leavings or burlap or something wrapped in
the good cotton."

"He's asking five golds a bolt, if we take all of them."

"What's a bale of garment class run?"

"Bales are for raw cotton. Bolts are finished. I could sell
it at ten a bolt to Guvell." She frowns. "Maybe fifteen if it's
really good."

The two burly men, each topping Lorn by a head, appear
just behind the trader.

"What say you, merchanter?"

"Offer him eight for the first two bolts," Lorn suggests,
noting the short timber leaning against an empty rack. He

does not let his eyes even register its presence as he bends toward Ryalth. "Tell him we'd love to buy his cotton, but that it's far more than we need."

"We'll take the first two bolts for eight golds total," Ryalth offers firmly.

"Eight golds for that which will bring twenty, or perchance thirty. Ah . . . my friends . . . Well . . . perhaps you don't wish to buy my cotton after all. Sooner or later, you will. You merchanters won't have the golds to keep buying shimmer-cloth from the Hamorians, not with the barbarians pushing at your borders." Aljak and the two guards ease forward. Each guard bears a heavy club, besides the blades in the scabbards. Aljak has a coil of velvet rope in his left hand, and the teeth that his smile reveals are crooked and yellow.

Lorn hides a frown, his attention on Ryalth—and the two thugs.

"And lady merchanter . . . perhaps you would like to spend some time with a real man, not a girlish enumerator." Aljak laughs harshly. "To seal a bargain, shall we say."

"When I tell you, dash toward the oil barrels . . . all right?" Lorn murmurs to Ryalth.

"You won't pay me twenty-five? How about twenty-five just to leave here?" Aljak laughs again, and the two guards step away from him, as if to flank Lorn and Ryalth.

"Now!" Lorn says.

As Ryalth bolts for the oil barrels, the student magus concentrates—hoping he can pull chaos from enough places—then flings the firebolt into Aljak.

Hsssttt!

"Aeeeeiii! Dung-devil . . ." Aljak's words are cut off.

The two guards freeze as they see the pillar of fire. Lorn uses the interval to cast two more firebolts. *Hssst! Hssst!*

The other two figures writhe, screaming, momentarily, before they topple into charred heaps.

Lorn scans the rest of the warehouse, but the space is empty, as he expected. Aljak had not wanted witnesses. So far the student magus cannot sense the unseen presence of someone scanning the warehouse with a chaos glass. That is good, since he has used chaos in ways reserved but to upper-level mages. He wipes his damp forehead, ignoring the sudden headache. "Ryalth, I need some help."

Ryalth's eyes are wide as she steps away from the oil barrels. "What . . . what . . . did you do?"

"A small firelance, like the emperor's guards have," Lorn lies. "I'm not supposed to have one, and it would be best if you didn't mention it." He steps toward the small table behind the last stack of goods, nodding as he sees the small chest on the table. His fingers and his chaos senses deftly work a thin stick, and the lock clicks. He opens the chest and nods.

"Who . . . who would I tell?" asks Ryalth, looking over her shoulder toward the door as she hurries toward the young magus.

Lorn picks up a two-cubit length of greenish cloth from the samples on the table. Then, after pocketing perhaps fifty golds, he wraps the small strongbox in the cloth and hands it to Ryalth. "Here. It's yours."

"What?" Ryalth steps away, not taking the wrapped chest. "Aljak's family will be looking for anyone with more golds . . . they'll know it's stolen."

"Maybe not." He glances at the three charred figures. "Take it, please."

"What?" She reluctantly accepts the cloth-wrapped and heavy oblong.

"Come on." He tugs her toward the warehouse door, then gestures. "Stand right inside the door. Be ready to run. Tell me if anyone's watching."

Ryalth raises her fine reddish eyebrows.

"Please." Lorn follows her, but halts a dozen paces beyond the rack oil barrels, his eyes on the redhead in blue.

When she reaches the timbered door, she glances out, and then back at Lorn. "There's no one near. Some people at the cross-street up the way, though. They're coming this way."

"They're not near now?"

"No."

Backing toward the door where Ryalth waits, Lorn concentrates on summoning chaos right into the middle of one of the center barrels of oil, ignoring the headache that builds even more.

Whhhooossshhh! The wall of flame is so sudden and massive that he stumbles out the door, dragging Ryalth with him.

Turning toward the figures less than a hundred cubits north, who have already turned toward the warehouse, and gesturing toward the blaze, Lorn yells. "Fire! Fire in the warehouse!"

"Fire! Fire!" Ryalth's voice adds to the clamor.

The heads of three others at the corner turn.

From a narrow doorway across the road, a tall man runs toward them. "It's the clan warehouse! You! What caused it?"

"Oils, I think. We were talking about cotton, and all of a sudden there were flames everywhere." Lorn glances at Ryalth. "Excuse me, ser. I think she's a bit faint."

"Who are you?" demands the trader, studying the two young people in blue. "What clan?"

"I'm an enumerator." Another *whoosh* of flame flares from the warehouse, and the merchanter looks at the flames, then back at the two. Ryalth leans, almost dramatically, on Lorn's shoulder. The trader dashes past them toward the flaming section of the warehouse, gesturing toward the three men who have piled out the opposing warehouse as well. "We've got to get the water on the next building. Don't let another one go."

Lorn takes Ryalth's arm. "Let's get out of here. Don't drop that."

They hurry back along the road until they reach the Second Harbor Way and turn uphill.

Ryalth glances back toward the increasing pillar of smoke. "Did you have to do that? That could burn a whole block."

"It won't. The roof's slate, and there's nothing to burn but the oils. Maybe whatever was in the amphorae." Lorn pulls Ryalth to the side of the Way as a fire brigade wagon careens past. "Aljak was ready to kill both of us. That's why no one else was there—except he would have spent longer with you." He offers a crooked smile as they walk swiftly uphill and then eastward along the Lower Hill Road away from the warehouses. "Not that I fault his taste."

"You're frightening sometimes, Lorn."

"Me? I'm just a student." He grins disarmingly.

"That's hard to believe at times." Without stopping, Ryalth looks down at the wrapped cloth. "This is heavy."

"You've got your five hundred golds, more or less."

"I can't take all that."

"You have to. I took what I dared. If I had more, my family would find out in days, if not sooner."

At the corner of the Second Harbor Way and the Road of Benevolent Commerce, the unofficial border to the merchanter quarter, they stop under a tall feathering conifer, shielded from above by the spreading dark green branches and by the afternoon mist. Lorn is breathing heavily, but the worst of his headache has faded. He stands there silently for a moment, thinking. Abruptly, he turns to Ryalth. "Do you have any scent? A vial of what you use?"

The redhead frowns. "Why?"

"Just dab some on me."

She fumbles in her belt wallet, her arm still around the cloth-covered strongbox. "You know that the City Watch wouldn't be pleased with this."

"They don't care about scent," Lorn jokes.

"They care about people setting fires," she whispers as she dabs some of the scent oil on his wrist.

"Better fires than outland traders assaulting Cyadoran merchanters," he counters, adding, "More of the scent."

"More? What's on you will cover any scent of smoke." Her eyebrows lift. "You *want* your family to know you've been with someone?"

"It's better than having them ask what I've really been doing," he points out. "Remember, when you live in a Magi'i family, questions are dangerous."

"People say that . . . is it true?"

"Only a handful of Magi'i can truthread, but the Lectors can, and my father is a Lector." Lorn gestures. "Dab more on my skin, my neck," he suggests, "as much as you can spare."

"You already reek." She wrinkles her nose.

"Fine. Then, they'll all be ready to condemn me."

"And me," Ryalth points out.

"They don't know you, and they'd have to know your name to ask a decent question."

She shakes her head, then glances along the road. "I think I'm glad I'm not from the Magi'i."

Lorn straightens the blue tunic. "You said I could always retreat to my mighty house."

"It sounds as bad as an inbred clan house."

"It's not that bad. My sisters are nice. So are my parents."

"I'm sure they are." Ryalth pauses, then adds, "I'll save your share of the coins."

He shakes his head. "They're yours. I took some, but you took most of the risks," he exaggerates.

She frowns, but says nothing.

"I'll need some favors before everything's done. Call the coins advance payment." He smiles broadly.

"I can't afford favors that expensive."

"I won't ask for anything that big." He leans forward and touches the line of her cheek. "Use them to get yourself free." Then he squeezes her hand and steps from under the conifer, hurrying uphill.

After a moment, Ryalth swallows and begins to walk eastward.

There is no one near the postern gate as Lorn quickly changes into his student whites, leaving the blues and the blue boots in the basket tucked behind the small tree. He readjusts the square of cloth in his belt wallet to ensure the coins are muffled, and then walks briskly through the garden and up the steps.

"You're late, Lorn." His father stands at the top of the steps. "Your mother is worried. It would be kinder if you let us know when you're going out."

"Yes, ser. I'm sorry. I know. I lost track of time. I didn't expect to be so late." Lorn's statements are all true, and he makes sure he doesn't look anywhere close to the billowing smoke that rises to the southwest of them.

His father's nose wrinkles, and he shakes his head. "That's a merchanter scent, isn't it?"

Lorn tries to look bewildered.

"Don't dignify it with a falsehood, Lorn."

"Yes, ser. I mean it is. A merchanter fragrance."

"Do you know what you're doing? What if . . . ?" His father doesn't finish the question.

"I've been careful about that. There won't be any child," Lorn says absolutely truthfully.

"Lorn . . ." His father shakes his head again. "I trust you have not attempted a chaos compulsion with the girl."

"No, ser. I wouldn't do such with her."

"Chaos compulsions are odious, and over time, they weaken those who use them, and make them susceptible to the compulsions of others." Kien's voice is stern.

"I have not with her, and I will keep your advice, ser."

"Good. Would that you will be so amenable to showing greater interest in your studies. If not, perhaps a time in the lancers will settle you down . . . though this is not the best time."

Lorn knows he cannot manifest any greater interest in his studies, although he has come to enjoy learning for its own sake, feeling the sense and the power involved in transferring chaos from the tower outlets to the firelances, and in seeing just how much chaos he can press into each weapon. He also is less than enthused about the thought that he could be posted to the frontiers and use a lance or blade in earnest, even if his skills with the blade are among the best among the students, including those like Dettaur who had been born with a blade in his hand. Using a blade in earnest would definitely increase the odds of an earlier demise than Lorn would wish.

"Vernt was right, then . . . about the barbarians?" he asks his father.

"There have been more attacks than in any time in memory—or in the records," his father admits. "And they have even used archers in the far northwest." A faint smile appears on Kien'elth's thin lips. "All the attacks have been repulsed, and most of the barbarians killed."

"But they keep attacking?"

"Yes . . . Enough . . . we can talk about it at dinner. After you wash off some of that scent. I'll tell your mother that you're here."

"Yes, ser." As he hurries toward the wash chamber, Lorn can sense his father's unease, as though there is far more left unsaid. Yet, Lorn does not wish to push, not when he has apparently misdirected Kien'elth's inquiries about his actions of the afternoon.

VIII

THE CORE OF a fully functioning tower maintains an isochronic/isotemporal barrier of approximately nine hundred nanoseconds. This temporal "dislocation" effectively provides the points of energy polarity which generate the raw power fed to the converter system . . .

The dislocation also provides a barrier against the operating impingement of the physical energy transfer/generation/entropy laws of the spatio-temporal coordinates of the systems hereafter described . . .

This impingement effect is illustrated by more than ten local years of observation. No tower in which the isochronic/isotemporal barrier has failed [failure being defined as a barrier separation of less than 150 nanoseconds, with an error margin of three percent] has ever functioned again in the spatio-temporal coordinates in which this world is currently situated. . . .

Tower cores have been run continuously without shutdown for the operating life of a Mirror Ship. The longest known continuous operation documented prior to the space-time shift translocating the colonizing/planoforming expedition . . . was eighty-seven elapsed standard Anglo-Rationalist years.

Given that a standard storage cell [model CD-3A] discharges power at the same amplitude as before the transspatio-temporal shift, but for more than quadruple the previous duration, and that power amplitude requirements/discharges from various powered end-use equipment [i.e., electrocell carriers, motor/dynamos, laselectroburst rifles, antipersonnel electrolasers] varies by user, locale, and even spatio-temporal planetary locales, accurate determination of tower core life is unlikely.

Consequently, despite considerable depletion of technical personnel and transport equipment, in the interests of pragmatism and maintaining a viable colonial structure with the infrastructure necessary to adapt to the local parameters and paradigms, as described in Section IV, the remaining tower cores have been located in physical circumstances that would appear as most conducive to their continued and uninterrupted operation . . .

Maintenance can be accomplished on the secondary systems [see Section V], as well as the energy transfer and conversion systems, since these are located outside the core, and the power transfers are accomplished by field manipulations and impingements. Such maintenance should be held to an absolute minimum, however, since macular cellular degeneration has already been observed among personnel with high exposure within the operating confines of the basic system, in contravention of previously established principles and tolerances . . .

Overview
Maintenance Manual [Revised]
Cyad, 15 A.F.

IX

LORN GRINS AS he peers into Myryan's chambers. "How's the studious healer?"

His younger sister looks up from the old and cushioned maroon armchair she had claimed years earlier from the second-floor sitting room when their parents had considered sending it down to the first-floor servants' quarters. She has a black leatherbound book in her lap, and her green-trousered legs are slung over one arm of the chair. She pushes a shock of black and wavy curls back off her high forehead. "Lorn . . ." She grins back. "You're full of horse dung. Jerial's the studious healer, and we all know it."

"You're the natural one, though." He slips through the door and closes it gently behind him, dropping easily into the straight-backed chair that has been turned out from the writing desk. He ignores the half-written note on the leather desk pad.

"What were you doing yesterday?"

Lorn shrugs, half-embarrassedly. "Everyone knows. I was with a girl."

"She wears a nice scent, even if it is a merchanter fragrance. Who is she?" Myryan offers a knowing smile.

"A merchanter," he responds.

"She's more than that," Myryan says. "Are you—"

"Don't ask . . . please?" Lorn offers a truly embarrassed smile, hoping his expression displays enough chagrin.

"I won't . . . since you asked." Her amber eyes smile with her mouth. "But only since you asked. Jerial would have asked anyway. Is that why you're here?"

Lorn ignores the question and asks Myryan, "You're worried about Ciesrt, aren't you? That father will consort you two?"

"How observant." She shakes her head. "I'm not mad at

you, Lorn. Father doesn't see it, and consorting is one thing where what mother thinks doesn't matter."

"Consorting is political." Lorn shrugs again. "We know that. It doesn't matter whether you like someone."

"It's unfair." Myryan almost pouts, but reins in the expression. "You can have a merchanter girl, and all anyone cares about is to make sure there's no child, and you're back in time for dinner, and there are a few laughs about wearing too much scent. Can you imagine what would happen if I arranged a tryst with a handsome merchanter—or an outland trader?"

"You wouldn't like the outland traders. They do smell, most of them."

"Is that why . . . ?" Myryan arches her eyebrows.

Lorn laughs, easily and openly. "I don't think so."

"You saved her from a fate worse than death?"

"Once or twice," Lorn admits.

"How can you say that and be telling the truth?" Myryan shakes her head, trying not to laugh. "You're impossible."

"What about Ciesrt?" Lorn asks again.

"He's dull as a pillar, and he's not even sweet. People think he's nice because he's quiet. He's quiet because he's only half alive. He only talks about being a magus."

Lorn nods.

"Father doesn't want to see." She shakes her head and looks down.

"I won't promise . . . but maybe I can do something. Talk to father, or Vernt."

"They won't listen. Ciesrt's going to be a full magus, and no one could be a more wonderful consort than that." Her voice, normally full and warm, carries a bitter edge that Lorn hears seldom and likes not at all.

"Talk to me about healing," Lorn suggests.

"Jerial knows more."

"I'm not interested in knowing. I'm interested in seeing and feeling," Lorn replies. "Scroll or book learning aren't enough." His mouth quirks into a self-deprecating smile.

"It'll be hard for you," Myryan says.

"If you say so."

"I mean it. You've been handling chaos."

Lorn raises his eyebrows.

"Don't look at me like I'm daft. There's a white shimmer around you. Father practically glows all the time. So does Vernt. You're not so bad."

Lorn nodded. "And there's a blackish haze around you and Jerial, but it's stronger around you."

"You can see it?"

"More like feel it," he admits.

"Good. Vernt can't, you know. He thinks healing is all imaginary because he's order-blind. Father can't sense it, either, but he knows it works."

"Father is a pragmatist." After a pause, Lorn adds, "About most things, anyway."

"And there are two kinds of chaos," Myryan continues, "the deep white-gold kind—like surrounds the Quarter of the Magi'i—and the ugly reddish white kind, and that's what you feel when a wound goes bad or someone looks like they're going to die. Healing's not what people think it is," Myryan states flatly. "A good healer can combine order—that's the black—with wound chaos, so that someone can heal, and we can bind things together for a time—"

"But their bodies have to heal by themselves," Lorn finishes.

Myryan waits.

"How do you bind or wrap the order to someone?" he finally inquires.

Myryan laughs. "I asked Kyrysmal the same thing. People have chaos and order within them. You have to work with that."

"Show me."

"Are you sure? They say that the Magi'i shouldn't work with both." Myryan looks intently at her older brother.

"I'm not going to be a magus," Lorn replies. "Before year-end, I'll be a lancer, and healing will help."

"You're going to give up on magery?" Myryan's eyes flick toward the closed door, as if to make sure that Lorn's words do not leave the room. "What will father say?"

"He already knows, but he's hoping that it won't come to that."

"But why? Father says you do well at your studies and that no one learns things better than you do."

"I don't like being confined between walls of granite. That much chaos . . . presses in on me." Lorn shrugs helplessly. "I can't hide that. Lector Hyrist would have thrown me out a long time ago if father weren't a Lector and if my studies weren't so good. The Magi'i want people who eat, think, breathe, and sleep chaos transfers and manipulation. Like Vernt . . . or father."

"All right." Myryan sighs as she swings her legs around and stands. "Give me your hand. If you had a slash there that wasn't healing it would be red and maybe puffy . . . really, you wouldn't need healing. You could—"

"Cut it open and drain it, and wash it with clear winter brandy or something." Lorn smiles. "I know." He stands and extends his hand. As she steps closer, he can smell the clean scent of frysya. "But if I were going to lose it . . . ?"

"I'd reach out and gather free order . . . like this."

Lorn's senses follow hers as the unseen but still real darkness forms above his left hand. He tries to replicate her order-gathering. After a moment, a smaller, more diffuse, block of darkness appears beside hers.

"Oh . . . you should have been a healer."

"Men aren't healers—not in Cyador," he points out.

"Like women aren't Magi'i," she replies.

Near-identical ironic smiles appear on each sibling's face. "How do you bind it or move it?"

"You take the affinity within your body. . . ."

Lorn's eyes and senses are fully intent, his amber eyes both searching and hard as he concentrates on his sister's demonstration of order healing.

X

Two FIGURES STAND on the westernmost balcony of the Palace of Light, enjoying the comfortable breeze that heralds the beginning of the cool but moderate winter in Cyad. Below them, the green and white awnings on the small plaza to the west and north of the harbor piers ripple with a gust of wind coming off the Great Western Ocean, enough of a gust that the rippling is visible nearly a kay away on the Palace balcony.

"Someone used chaos to create the fire in the warehouse district," First Magus Chyenfel says to the Majer-Commander of Lancers.

"Was there any damage beyond the one warehouse?" inquires Rynst.

"No. The damage was confined to the western end. It had been rented to an outland trader by the Jekseng clan."

"Outsiders, again. Everywhere, from the barbarians to the traders, we have difficulties with outsiders." After a pause, Rynst ventures quietly, "Some had mentioned seed-oil burning."

"It was—but you cannot get that heavy oil to burn with a striker—or even a fallen candle or lamp." Chyenfel smiles ironically, his sungold eyes flashing.

"Cammabark?"

"There wasn't any sign of an explosion, and there were bodies and bones there. The dead men didn't try to run."

"The fire was to cover their murder, then. Anyone important?"

The High Lector and First Magus shakes his head. "No. The bodies seem to be those of the man renting the warehouse—a most unsavory Hamorian thought to be a smuggler—and his two bodyguards."

"How unfortunate. How very unfortunate." Rynst lifts his

eyebrows. "Then we cannot suspect the Hand of the Emperor?"

"No . . . not in a dispute between traders, not unless it is far more than it seems to be. But then, you know that." Chyenfel smiles lazily. "You would like to know who the Hand is, would you not?"

"Many would."

"True," muses Chyenfel. His face hardens. "Perhaps, just perhaps, the most unfortunate demise of this Aljak may put an end to a string of recent disappearances among the merchanters."

"You do think it was retribution?" Rynst turns so that the afternoon sun falls full on his back, bright if cold in the green-blue sky, and so that he can watch both the First Magus more closely and the harbor.

"It probably was, but we don't know who killed Aljak." Chyenfel offers a theatrical shrug. "Unhappily, the man comes from a prominent Hamorian trading family. They have threatened a ten percent increase in the cost of Hamorian goods . . . or so Bluoyal tells me."

"They cannot make that stick, not when the Austrans will bring the same goods for a five percent increase. Then, the Hamorians, should they want the trade, would have to go back to the old prices."

"That is true, and even Bluoyal would agree. Yet . . . there is one thing."

"Oh?" offers the Majer-Commander warily.

"There was a trace of chaos beneath all the charred goods and ashes."

"You have assured me that all your Magi'i would not do such."

Chyenfel nods. "I have already spoken with every magus. All are innocent. None are hiding anything."

"Does that mean a wild chaos wielder? Or that one of your Magi'i can evade the truthreading?"

"Even those few skilled at truthreading cannot evade another's reading. Since no Magi'i are involved, it means the chaos was directed in another fashion. There was no spray.

That I could tell even after the fire, and wild types do not have that kind of control."

"So . . . a former Magi'i?"

"Those who have such talents are weeded out early—they are dead or in the lancers on the frontier." Chyenfel fingers his smooth chin. "And we follow those who hold chaos with the glasses until they can no longer do so or until they die. None have been detected in Cyad in seasons, if not years."

"You have the impossible, then, and that is less than satisfactory, especially in these times."

"It could have been a small firelance—as your guards for the Emperor carry," suggests Chyenfel almost idly.

"I would bc most pleased to accompany you as you question each of them." Rynst smiles tightly.

"I thought you would be." Chyenfel returns the smile.

XI

TWO FIGURES IN blue sit on a carved wooden bench that overlooks the harbor of Cyad. Below the low hill, a half-dozen ships are tied at the white piers. Cargo carts roll along the granite wharves, carts filled with the wool brought from Analeria, cotton from Hamor across the Eastern Ocean, tin ingots from Austra, and other goods from wherever the tall-masted ships sail. A single white-hulled fireship is moored at the lancer pier.

The redheaded woman shivers in the cool breeze. "Lorn?" Ryalth pauses. "Aren't you cold?"

"Me? No."

"I am." She eases next to him, so that their sides touch. "You're warm, like a banked fire, or the sun."

"I'd rather not talk about fires."

"I have a gift for you." Ryalth's voice is soft.

"You don't have to give me anything," Lorn insists, as he turns. "The coins and the strongbox are for you. I told you that. Don't spend them on me."

"It's not that kind of gift. It's something I've had for a long time."

Lorn raises his eyebrows. "You don't have to do anything like that for me. You know that."

"I know I don't *have* to. This is because I want to." Her smile is warm, even as she shivers again.

Lorn grins, and puts an arm around her. "You *are* cold."

"That helps. You're warm." She pauses, tilting her head and looking at him directly. "Do you ever wonder where the Firstborn came from? What they were like?"

Lorn frowns and shrugs. "They came and used the chaos-towers to create Cyad and Cyador. They imprisoned the Ac-cursed Forest and opened the lands of the east for us. They built the firewagons and—"

"That's history," Ryalth interrupts him gently. "We know a lot about *what* they did. But all the books and scrolls talk about is that they came from the Rational Stars and what they built once they came here. Don't you wonder about them? What kind of people were they?"

"They were people like us." Lorn laughs gently, turns and touches her cheek with his right hand, then bends forward and brushes her cheek with his lips.

Ryalth gently disengages him. "Were they?"

His brow wrinkles. "First you talk about a gift, and now . . ."

"It's all the same thing." She extends a shimmering ob-long. "It's here."

"What is it?"

"It's an old, old book. My mother's mother had it. No one knew she did. Father said no one could make anything like that then, or, I suppose, today. He told me to keep it. Never to sell it, no matter what I was offered."

Lorn looks into her deep blue eyes. "Don't give it to me, then. It's yours."

"Then you'll have to keep it for me," she says.

"I couldn't do anything like that . . ."

"Open it to where the leather marker is. I want you to read me the words there." Ryalth forces the thin volume into his hands.

Lorn takes the book, its cover as unmarked and as smooth as if it had been created in his fingers at that very moment. He turns it sideways, seeing the light flare across the silvered green binding fabric as the winter sun's rays strike it.

"Open it," Ryalth insists.

He slides open the book, his fingers almost slipping on the pages that are more like shimmercloth than paper or parchment, a surface so smooth it makes shimmercloth rough by comparison. The letters are clear, but somehow slightly more tilted and angular than Lorn is used to reading.

"That one." The redhead points.

Lorn's eyes go to the title. He reads it . . . and continues.

SHOULD I RECALL THE RATIONAL STARS

There I had a tower for the skies,
where the rooms were clear,
and the music filled the walls.
The light clothed the halls,
and the days were long.
The nights were song.

Should I recall the Rational Stars?
Or hold my ruin on this hill
where new-raised walls are still,
Perfect granite set jagged on the dawn,
with striped awnings spread across the lawn.
Then, gold was known as gold,
and long slow stories could be told.
White flowers filled the darkest room,
flowers that never lost their bloom.

Should I recall the Rational Stars?
And should I raise anew

old chaos-towers in the darkest wood,
leaving nothing where the forest stood,
turning the dark of day to sunlit pride,
to see frail windows throw the rainbow wide,
with passages and courts in bloom
and white flowers in the darkest room?

Should I recall the Rational Stars?
I had a tower once, across heavens from here,
with alabaster edges and silver domes.
Raised above the fields and homes,
it flagged my fires, flew my fear.

Oh . . . take these new lake isles and green green seas;
take these sylvan ponds and soaring trees;
take these desert dunes and sunswept sands,
and pour them through your empty hands.

Lorn swallows, despite his resolve not to show any expression.

"It's sad, isn't it?"

He shakes his head. "I don't know."

"You do know," she insists.

"Why . . . why did you bring this?"

"Because it's yours now. Because I want you to keep it and read every poem in it."

"It's yours," he insists once more.

"You have to keep it and read from it. At least every few days. Promise me."

"I promise." Lorn nods slowly. "You don't sound like a merchanter lady now."

"Do you think that we're all just one thing? That I can only be a hard trader lady? That you can only be a logical magus?"

"You have to concentrate to be good."

"You . . . we . . . have some time for other things." She grins. "Other things besides making love, too."

He looks down at the book, mock-mournfully. "Are you making me choose?"

"Silly man! We have time for both."

Lorn looks at the green-silvered cover, so fresh, and so spotless, and so ancient, and he wonders.

XII

WEARING THE MERCHANTER shimmercloth blues and blue boots, Lorn walks hurriedly along the Road of Benevolent Commerce. His destination is the building that serves the Clanless Traders, the structure in which Ryalth has opened a very small office, mainly, he suspects, to legitimize her status as a woman free trader. He hurries because he has seen his father walking up the steps to Lector Chyenfel's study in the Quarter of the Magi'i. That had happened in mid-afternoon, as Lorn had passed along the lower Tower corridor—and Lorn had known at that moment that he was now headed for lancer training.

There might have been another reason for Chyenfel to summon Lorn's father, but Lorn strongly doubts it, and that means he has little enough time before he is sent off for lancer training. Far too little time for what needs to be done, because he has no doubts that once the Lectors know he has been notified, he will be well watched until he is out of Cyad, and probably far longer than that. He hopes the summons comes because of his studies, and not because of anything else—such as the chaos compulsion he used on Halthor . . . but no one has said anything, and Ryalth has only mentioned the trader's death as an accident.

The absolute certainty in his father's voice was more than enough to discourage Lorn, for about magely matters, he knows his father is always correct. He pushes away those thoughts as he casually studies the street he travels.

No one he knows—or who knows him—looks out from the Empty Quarter as he passes the coffee house, but the awning that shields the vacant outside tables is furled, and any patrons are well inside and out of the wind.

The air holds an icy chill, despite the bright winter sunlight, and the salt air bites at his exposed face and neck and hands.

He stops and waits on the edge of Third Harbor Way West as a white-lacquered enclosed carriage, drawn by a matched pair of white mares, whispers past him. A gust of wind brings a hint of warmth, and the smell of fresh-baked bread, followed by the tiniest hint of erhenflower scent, possibly from the woman seated in the shielded carriage.

Two lancer rankers stand on the far corner, their eyes following the carriage, and Lorn cannot help but smile at their all too obvious interest. Then, will he end up standing on a corner in some out-of-the-way town like Syadtar? Or one of the towns bordering the Accursed Forest—like Geliendra or Jakaafra?

Lorn shakes his head, then crosses the Way and takes the white stone sidewalk on the far side down the gentle slope of the Third Harbor Way to the lower plaza—the merchanters' plaza. Even in the late afternoon chill, a handful of the green and white striped awnings remain up over a few carts. Lorn makes his way around the carts toward the squat white structure in the northwest corner of the plaza, his boots nearly silent on the hard white paving stones.

Once he has stepped through the squared open archway of the Clanless Traders' building and is out of the wind, Lorn can feel his face begin to thaw. Despite the near-abandoned look of the plaza from outside, within the building is filled with figures in blue, as well as some in red, or green, or white. None seem to mark the passage of the enumerator Lorn emulates, at least not beyond an occasional frown, as he takes the wide central stairs at the back of the covered central hall flanked by balconies that rises all three stories.

Ryalth's trading place is little more than a cubby with two doors swung wide at the back of the third level, so far into the northeast corner that only the balcony railings can be seen from her doors. The redhead sits behind a true desk with drawers, an antique of battered and time-darkened white oak, writing in what appears to be a ledger.

As Lorn steps through the open doors, he clears his throat, and with a hint of a smile, asks, "Lady Trader?"

"Yes?" Ryalth looks up and her mouth opens, then closes.

Lorn steps forward until his trousers brush the edge of the desk. "I wished to see you, honored trader." His smile is both tentative and guileless.

"You shouldn't be here—not at this time of day. Enumerators' times are either first thing in the morning or close to the close," Ryalth murmurs, then adds more loudly, "I would that you had come at a more appropriate time, young ser."

"I won't be able to do that," Lorn whispers. "I'll be leaving Cyad tomorrow or the next day, from what I've overheard, and there's nothing I can do about it, and I couldn't have come to see you once they told me." He cocks his head inquisitively, and says in a normal voice. "I apologize, honored trader, but I was nearby, and thought I would not be presuming too much. I do apologize."

"You're leaving—Like that?" she murmurs. "Why?"

"Because I'm not a dedicated enough believer for the senior Magi'i, and I'm either leaving, or I'll be found dead in a chaos transfer accident." His voice is low. "I care for you . . . and I wanted to let you know. If I wait until it's official, then I couldn't tell you."

Ryalth shakes her head ruefully.

He slips a purse into her hand. "Business. I'll be back, one way or another, and I couldn't take these. I wouldn't have them without you. Use them as you can." He offers a warm smile.

"A purse? Like that, and you expect me to wait for you? As if I were bought and paid for like . . . cotton?"

"No." Lorn meets her eyes. "I care for you, well beyond our shared interests." He swallows and shrugs. "I can't ask you much . . . not with what's happening. But if you'd wait . . . at least a bit."

"I'd have to. Then . . . we'll see." Ryalth laughs softly, not quite bitterly. "But you have to take the book and read it . . . all of it."

"You're sure? I could be gone for years."

"Then . . . it's even more important. Read it." Her words are half choked, half hissed.

"I will."

"Promise?"

"Promise." He reaches out and squeezes her hand, then lets his hand fall away as he hears footsteps in the open arched corridor.

"I appreciate your interest, but there won't be anything where I can use you for at least another eightday," Ryalth says firmly, although her eyes are bright.

"I see. I will check with you then."

"During enumerators' times, if you would," Ryalth adds.

Lorn can see the brightness in her eyes, and feels the same in his own. He swallows. "Yes . . . Lady Trader."

Then he turns, letting his shoulders droop, a gesture not totally of pretense, and walks dejectedly down the corridor toward the plaza overlooking the white harbor.

As he leaves the plaza, he can feel the chill of his father's chaos glass surveying him, but he has already done what must be done, and he doubts that Kien'elth will pry further.

He hopes for that, at least.

XIII

EVEN THE EMPERORS of the Land of Eternal Light embody the elements of paradox that infuse and suffuse Cyador. . . .

Most paradoxical is the treatment of the memory of the Emperor Alyiakal. Despite his many successes in establishing the current borders of modern Cyador, and his formalization of the balanced power structure that has come to govern Cyador, he has become the "One Never to be Mentioned" among the Magi'i and Mirror Lancers of Cyad. The

Magi'i wish to forget him because he was a stronger magus than the First Magus and turned his back on what he saw as the ever-narrowing traditions and inbreeding of the Magi'i, then became a Mirror Lancer officer who used his magely abilities to lead the northern Mirror Lancers in the devastation of Cerlyn and the establishment of the northeastern cuprite mines. By doing so, he assured peace with the northern barbarians for more than a generation, and a continued supply of cuprite ore for the continued formulation of cupridium. When he used those same lancers to become Emperor, he insisted that the chaos energies be diverted from mere experimentation to power chaos-cells for stonecutting and thus the building of the Great Highways of Cyador, the completion of the Palace of Eternal Light and the strengthening and lengthening of the Great Canal. . . . Yet for all this, for which he and his memory should be revered, the paradox is that he remains the magus of whom the Magi'i will never speak.

The Mirror Lancers avoid his name because it reminds them all too clearly of their deficiencies in arms and other skills and because his success continues to imply that merely being a Mirror Lancer is less than sufficient to be a successful or great holder of the Malachite Throne. . . . The simple fact that no Lancer commander has since matched his feats makes the comparison even more odious . . . and, again, the paradox is maintained: the greatest Mirror Lancer officer in the history of Cyador is the least known as such.

Even the merchanters dislike the image of Alyiakal, for they have none of the talents that he embodied, and, therefore, they cannot aspire to place one of their own, truly their own, upon the Malachite Throne, yet it was largely the result of his policies as Emperor through which they came to prosper. . . .

Paradox of Empire
Bern'elth, Magus First
Cyad, 157 A.F.

XIV

LORN WALKS SLOWLY along the covered upper portico of the dwelling, trying to ignore both his faint headache and the patter and splatting the sudden winter rain, such a change from the frost of the day before or even from the dryness of the afternoon. His head seems to pulse with the hissing of the rain and the dripping of the larger droplets that have rolled off the tile roof and fall onto the edge of the walks and the walls.

He finally stops outside the open door to his father's study, waiting for a moment, as if to see whether his sire will notice. When there is no response or invitation, Lorn steps into the study. "You summoned me, ser?"

In the storm-dim gloom, lightened by the oil lamps at each end of the pale oak desk-table, Kien'elth looks up from the scroll he peruses. "Sit down, Lorn." The silver-haired magus sets the scroll aside. The crossed lightning bolts on his tunic radiate a faint golden light of their own.

Although the silver-manteled lamps cast an even glow across the room, suffusing with a warm light the blond wooden wall panels and the dark amber leather of the volumes set in the bookcase built into the wall beside the desk, the room is chill. Lorn lowers himself into the hard seat of the single armless and straight-backed wooden chair. He faces his father and waits.

"I have been talking to Lector Hyrist'elth *and* Lector Chyenfel'elth. . . ." Kien'elth's fine eyebrows lift as if asking for Lorn's response.

"Yes, ser."

"They have noted that while your knowledge and scholarship remain outstanding, you do not manifest the love of the Magi'i and our works that are necessary for true success as a magus." Kien'elth studies his son. "We have discussed this before, Lorn, and I had hoped you would change your approach to your studies and to the senior Lectors."

"Ser. . . . I have learned a great deal, and even the Lectors have indicated that my studies have been superior." Lorn lets a puzzled expression cross his face. "Have I not been diligent and enthusiastic in my studies?"

"Mere excellence in studies is not enough for a magus, Lorn. Enthusiasm for studies alone is not sufficient, either. One must always carry the awareness that the Magi'i are what distinguishes Cyador from the barbarians or the Hamorians—and what distinguished the Rational Stars from the black angels. Without the understanding of chaos as the font of life and the core of prosperity, a flame lance is little more than a brighter, sharper barbarian blade. A firewagon is little more than a more powerful eight-horse team."

"I have always understood and accepted that, Father," Lorn says truthfully.

"Yes . . . you have. But you have not understood that there is a greater good beyond personal accomplishments." The older man offers a rueful smile. "Nor do you understand with your heart that golds are mere counters in a child's game, or that all Cyador rests on how the Magi'i balance chaos and the black order."

Lorn represses a frown. While his studies and his practical work as an advanced student magus have touched upon the balancing of chaos with the cold and deadly nature of order, this is the first time his father has directly mentioned such balancing—or even suggested that he has observed Lorn's clandestine merchanting ventures.

"I have prevailed upon my friendship with Captain-Commander Luss'alt to have you accepted as a probationary officer trainee. Luss'alt is in charge of the Mirror Lancer operations throughout all Cyador, under Majer-Commander Rynst'alt. You also know, I am certain, that lancer training is well away from Cyad." Kien'elth pauses.

Lorn considers both the words and the pause. Knowing that his father is a closer acquaintance of Rynst'alt than would be normal from their relative positions within the Quarter of the Magi'i, Lorn also understands that there is much he does not understand, except that his father thinks it is important that Lorn know a favor has been called in, and that Rynst'alt has not been involved. "Yes, ser."

"High Lector Chyenfel'elth and Lector Hyrist'elth are most impressed with your talent, but not your attitude." The older man gestures as if to wave off any objection Lorn may raise. "Yes, you are most respectful. Yes, you learn everything before you, and more. Yes, you have greater mastery of chaos forces than any other student magus and probably a mastery greater than most of the fourth level adepts, and even some third level Magi'i. And you have greater potential than that, even if you receive no more training. However . . ." Kien'elth draws out the word. "Now is not the best of times for a talented magus to manifest less than perfect adulation."

"So Vernt is safe, then?" inquires Lorn, understanding his own danger, if not precisely all the possible forms that danger could lead to were he to remain a student and become a full magus. If he were allowed that far. Then he realizes what else his father has said and nods.

"He is safe. He does not have either excessive talent or excessive skepticism, and he will learn more, because he is patient, if not so precociously brilliant as his elder brother."

"Is this because the towers are failing?"

Kien'elth raises his eyebrows. "I should have guessed that you would puzzle that out." He pauses, steepling his fingers together. "It would not be wise for me, or for you, to discuss this farther. So let us talk of other matters. You may recall that the barbarian attacks are increasing, and increased attacks require greater chaos transfers for firewagons and firelances. A greater number of firelances must be charged and transported north and west. Likewise, more lancers must be raised and trained, and more cupridium blades must be forged." Kien'elth smiles, but his golden eyes remain concerned, and their expression does not match that upon his mouth.

Lorn understands. His father—all the Magi'i—live and work where the truth, or falsehood, of every word they utter can be sensed and used in one fashion or another—at least by the most talented of the Magi'i. That understanding breeds caution even in settings that others might consider safe from scrutiny.

"The need for more lancers means a need for more junior officers, and that affords you an opportunity." This time, his father's smile is more complete. "Although Luss'alt and I do not, shall we say, see exactly eye to eye, he needs more capable junior officers, and he has heard of your skills with a blade. He has not heard of where you have been . . . such as this afternoon. I would not repeat such a visitation as that before you leave Cyad, no matter what her charms may be."

"Yes, ser. Thank you. Very much. I will do my best."

"I'm sure you will. And in the Mirror Lancers, success is measured more by ability than by attitude." Kien'elth laughs. "Not totally . . . but more."

"I understand." Lorn also understands the warning. The Mirror Lancers are no different from the Magi'i, except that most Lancer officers cannot truthread, and therefore must judge more by actions than by hidden intent revealed by truthreading.

"You will leave for Kynstaar tomorrow. There will be a firewagon departing from the school. You will doubtless face some difficulties, there, but . . . you have surmounted such before, and I have every confidence that you will again."

"Yes, ser." Lorn nods.

Kien'elth stands slowly. "I wish . . ." He shrugs apologetically.

Lorn also stands. "I know, ser. It's not your doing."

"I can still wish, my son."

Lorn lowers his head for a moment.

After he leaves the study, Lorn walks slowly along the covered portico of the upper level of the house, pausing to look southward through the rain that is beginning to taper off toward the gray stormy waters of the harbor, waters more often than not usually an intense blue, with the intensity of the water's color underscored by the white sunstone piers. Today, the piers are gray, like the sky and the water.

Then he descends one level and slips toward the rear of

the dwelling. There, he pauses before the closed door of his older sister's chambers.

"You can come in, Lorn," Jerial calls.

He opens the heavy oak door, slowly, and closes it behind him.

As usual, Jerial wears a form-fitting tunic—this one of a silky black that shows her petite but well-endowed figure. She stands beside a polished white oak table desk that is almost empty, and her eyes are intent as she studies Lorn. Beyond the narrow archway, Lorn sees the bed chamber, with the dark blue coverlet set neatly on the narrow bed, and the tables as neat as the sitting room where they stand.

"Dice?" Lorn looks at the six white cubes on his sister's table. "I suppose there's the uniform of a beardless junior lancer in your wardrobe?"

"No." Jerial smiles back. "That of a young merchanter, a spoiled youth who has more coins than sense. Someone who loses most of the time, but loses little, and wins seldom, but well. Not, shall we say, a scholarly enumerator."

Lorn looks from the dice to the wardrobe and then back to the dice.

"Why not?" asks Jerial. "I can be a healer, or a brood mare. Neither will gain me golds nor independence."

"You have the golds invested in the Exchange?" Lorn raises his eyebrows.

"No. The Bank of the Clanless Traders. There's no interest, but far fewer questions."

"Something like Jeron'mer?"

"You might say so," Jerial replies, "but I'd appreciate your not asking."

"In case you're forced into being a brood mare? So I can't reveal anything to father?"

Jerial nods, then smiles wryly. "I like Cyad, Lorn, but not enough to consort with someone I detest. So far, I've managed to steer father away from people like Ciesrt. . . ."

"I see." His sister's words remind Lorn—again—that he has yet to do anything about the impending consorting of Myryan to Ciesrt. His eyes light on Jerial's face, taking in the determined and set chin, the hard and piercing blue eyes. "What's Ciesrt's weakness?"

Jerial shrugs. "He has no strengths."

Lorn nods. "And no principles, except self-interest."

"You, my brother, do well enough to conceal such." Jerial's eyebrows both arch.

"Maybe I'm like him, then."

"No one would ever say that, even Dettaur, and he detests you. He thinks you're the one who broke his fingers years ago."

"That could be a problem in time to come. I'm leaving for Kynstaar in the morning," Lorn says quietly.

"Is that why you're here?"

"I thought you'd like to know." He grins insouciantly, as if he were on the korfal field or in a coffee house.

"At least you can be an officer, and Dettaur won't be that senior to you."

"If I don't get thrown from a mount or 'accidentally' incinerated by a firelance, you mean?" Lorn's laugh is half humorous, half deprecating. "I have some chance of surviving there."

"You have no illusions, brother dear?" Jerial's laugh is somehow both ironic and supportive. "That will doubtless help."

"I wanted to talk about healing," he says.

Jerial nods. "You would."

"I've seen you and Myryan do it. There's a black mist that enfolds you—is that why you like black?"

"Black has its uses, one of which is illusion."

"Ciesrt wouldn't like black," Lorn notes. "About the healing?"

"I think of it almost as an order of sorts. It's the opposite of the surging power of chaos, and there really are two kinds of chaos, the unclean kind in a wound and the kind in the towers and the power cells of the firewagons—"

"You've never been near a tower," Lorn says.

"I don't have to be. Father has been clear that the chaos that powers the firewagons is the same as the chaos that comes from the towers. You've all talked about how the Magi'i transfer that chaos into the firewagons, and I've certainly been close enough to firewagons to sense the difference."

"And you've looked with all your senses. Most healers don't."

"Except healers raised in this house," counters Jerial.

"That's true enough." He glances from Jerial to the dice, and then back to her fine-featured face, a visage that, for all its beauty, might have been carved from sunstone or granite.

"What do you want to do with what I show you?" Jerial asks.

Lorn offers a lazy smile, hoping he will not have to respond verbally.

"Brother dear . . . you're sweet when you want to be, but you *use* everyone and everything." Her hard smile softens. "Sometimes."

"I've tried not to hurt either of you."

"You've learned to use people, including us, without hurting them, but it's still use, Lorn. Remember when you gave both Myryan and me those chaos-cut emeralds set in cupridium."

"Yes," Lorn admits warily.

"You never told mother and father, did you?"

"No."

"But they knew all the same." Jerial smiles as if the answer were obvious.

"I suppose so."

"How would either of us wear something that costly without mother or father asking?" She laughs. "That way, you created the impression of modesty and caring." A shrug follows. "I know you care, but you also wanted them to know you cared, and you impressed them all the more by doing it quietly." A crooked smile follows. "And . . . they couldn't ask you how you managed to come up with all those golds."

Lorn flushes.

"How did you? Gambling . . . or theft?"

Lorn steels himself, then shrugs reluctantly. "Neither.

Trade. You know that. That's why you talked about enu-merators."

"You aren't allowed to handle coins, and the Lectors—oh . . . who is it? What woman, I should ask. It would have to be a merchanter woman." Abruptly, she laughs. "The scent! Of course." Jerial shakes her head. "So much scent that we all thought . . ."

"I don't believe you've met her," Lorn says quietly. "I've known her for over a year. Over two," he corrects himself.

"Do you . . . I won't ask that."

"Thank you."

"You must want to know about healing badly . . . or you wouldn't have given away so much. You can't use it on yourself, you know? Except to keep flux-chaos out, if you have the strength."

"I know."

"Very astute." Jerial nods. "I'll show you some more." She smiles. "Myryan told me what she showed you."

"A man has no secrets. . . ." he protests.

"From his sisters?" She laughs warmly. "Not too many, but you hold more than most men."

Lorn sincerely hopes so. Most sincerely.

XV

LORN STANDS BESIDE the immaculate white oak desk-table in his own chambers, glancing out through the glass window at the cold mist that has replaced the earlier rain. He will be leaving in the morning for Kynstaar, and his promise to Myr-yan remains unfulfilled. He purses his lips as he looks toward the rain he does not see.

The problem with Ciesrt is not the student magus himself, who is about to become a fourth level adept, but his sire, Kharl'elth, the Second Magus and Senior Lector. Consorting Myryan to Ciesrt is advantageous to both families. The talent for handling chaos runs strongly in Kien'elth's children, even in Vernt, if slightly less powerfully, and any children that Myryan might bear will have a far better chance of holding the talent than those of anyone else that Ciesrt might take as consort. The alliance will also benefit Vernt, and both parents—even Lorn. The one person it will not benefit is the sensitive Myryan.

Lorn frowns. With the little time he has remaining, so far as he can determine, he has limited choices. To remove Ciesrt's father or to persuade his own father to act otherwise. Can he justify murdering a man because his sister Myryan is unhappy with her proposed consort? Yet Lorn has promised to do something.

He has to do something.

For a few moments more, he watches the misting rain. Then he turns quickly and walks out of his chamber, leaving the door open. He makes his way up the stone steps to the uppermost level of the house, pausing briefly in the open air of the covered portico to look through the late twilight toward the harbor, mostly obscured in mist and rain, with the evening beacons not yet lit for late-arriving ships.

Finally he approaches the study door, closed—and knocks. The brief chill that is in the mind and that betokens screeing crosses him.

"You can come in, Lorn."

Lorn steps into the warmth of the study and closes the white oak door behind him. His father looks up from behind the wide desk, but does not stand. The two look at each other for a time.

Lorn waits, the bare hint of a smile on his lips, an expression that is one of his most somber.

"It's too late for last chances, you know," Kien'elth says mildly. "I warned you for almost two years about your lack of enthusiasm."

"I know. You did what you could. That wasn't why I wanted to talk to you. It's nothing about me."

Kien'elth raises his fine white eyebrows, then fingers his chin. "Lorn, pardon me if I appear somewhat . . . skeptical . . . but many of your exploits have not exactly borne the stamp of altruism. I felt your mercantile ventures were, shall we say, useful for your education and understanding of how Cyad operates, and you did maintain yourself with a certain dignity and were not involved in anything too sordid." The older man clears his throat. "What did you have in mind?"

"I'm worried about Myryan, ser." Lorn wasn't sure how else he could put it. "She's more sensitive than most people realize. That's why she's a good healer, of course."

"You don't think she should be a healer?"

"She should be a healer. I'm not sure she should be a consort," Lorn says slowly, deciding against elaborating immediately.

"Lorn . . ." Kien'elth draws out his son's name, as he always has when he disagrees with Lorn—or anyone else.

Lorn steels himself to wait, knowing that his father always draws things out to make an adversary more uncomfortable and to force revelation or haste.

Kien'elth looks directly at his son, as if to press for more explanation. Lorn resists the impulse and continues to wait.

A wry smile crosses Kien'elth's face, and he finally speaks. "Your mother was a most sensitive healer, but she has managed to be both consort and healer."

"Yes, ser." Lorn nods. "But much of her ability to be both has rested upon you, ser."

Kien'elth laughs. "You'd use my own vanity against me, Lorn. Or anything else, I suppose."

"Vanity or not, ser, it's true."

"I can tell you believe that—mostly." Kien'elth leans back slightly in his chair and steeples his fingers, not looking quite directly at his son.

Lorn waits, noting absently that the pattering of the rain on the roof has returned. Or perhaps the pattering is sleet, since the sound is harder than that of rain droplets. He cannot tell, because both windows are shuttered.

"Tell me, Lorn . . . are you opposed to Myryan's becoming a consort of Ciesrt—or of anyone?"

Lorn offers a frown. "I think that Myryan is not ready to be consorted to anyone. I also think that being consorted to someone like Ciesrt would harm her. I don't think she could continue her best as a healer, and . . ." He shrugs in trying to convey without saying exactly those words that being a consort might have extremely detrimental consequences for his younger sister.

"No one is ready for being consorted. I wasn't; your mother wasn't; you won't be; and Myryan's no exception." Kien'elth's words carry a sense of finality, as if the argument is over.

"Myryan's different." Lorn's tone is stronger than he intended.

"You believe that. You really do." Kien'elth shakes his head, and his sun-gold eyes somehow darken. "All you young people think that you're different, that we were never young, not the way you are, that we never felt what you feel, that we can't possibly understand what you're going through." Kien'elth snorts. "I'd wager that every generation has felt that way about its parents."

"I'm not suggesting that, ser. Not at all. I'm suggesting that, out of the four of us, Myryan *is* different. Jerial will handle anything that comes to her, and so will Vernt. I hope that I can. At the very least, Myryan needs more time to learn who she is. And she needs a consort who is as considerate as you have been to mother." Lorn fears he has said too much, but what he has already said has made little impression.

The pattering on the roof rises to a violent drumming, then abruptly dies away, and a gust of cold air sweeps into the room through the closed shutters, indicating that perhaps one of the windows is not completely tight.

"You would judge such?"

"No, ser. I would offer my thoughts and my understandings to you. I offer them in part because I will not be here after tomorrow, and I do fear for and care for my sister. Were I not leaving, I would not speak."

"Such caring does you credit, Lorn, but do you not think that I also care for the well-being of my daughter? Do you not think that I see her sensitivity? That I wish to see her

protected in times that are likely to be turbulent and changing? That I can only offer her that protection through a consort who is strong and well-placed?"

Lorn almost responds, then checks his tongue, and nods.
"I have never questioned your concerns for us. Or your efforts to help us as you can. Any decision about consorting
Myryan will be yours, and I know you love her dearly. So
do I. I would only see the best for her, ser, and I have offered
my concerns to you, knowing you will do as you must."

Kien'elth shakes his head slowly. "Still . . . you surprise
me, Lorn. There are times when I wonder if you were ever
a child."

Again, Lorn waits for his father to continue.

"You remind me more of Toziel'elth'alt'mer than anyone
in our family, with layers upon layers hidden behind your
eyes." Kien'elth straightens. "I hope so, because you will
need all that devious honesty, and more, in the years ahead.
Now . . . I will think upon what you have said. That is all I
will promise."

Lorn bows his head. "Thank you, ser."

"If that is all . . . ?" Kien'elth rises.

"That's all, ser. Thank you for hearing me."

"I'd be a poor father if I didn't listen, Lorn." Kien'elth
clears his throat again before he adds. "I'll think about your
words, but we don't always have the choices others think we
do. Try to remember that."

"Yes, ser." Lorn bows again before he leaves the study.

Outside, he looks out through the darkness, seeing the
fragments of white on the neighboring roofs, white tatters
that are all that remain of the brief hail that has pelted Cyad.
Night has replaced twilight, and the harbor is marked only
by the pier beacons, while the Palace of Light beams through
the mist that enshrouds Cyad.

Lorn walks down the steps and then enters his own room.

Myryan sits at the straight chair turned away from his
desk.

"Myryan . . ."

"You were talking to father about me, weren't you?" She stands quickly to face him. "Weren't you?"

"Yes."

A faint smile crosses her face, and she half-consciously pushes back strands of curly black hair. "You upset him. I could feel it. He upset you, didn't he?"

"Some. I don't think he understands, and . . . that bothers me."

Abruptly, she lurches forward and hugs him—tightly. "Thank you . . . don't know if . . . but . . . thank you."

As he holds Myryan, Lorn's eyes burn, for he fears that his effort may have been too little.

XVI

IN THE CHILLY midday light, Lorn stands by the sunstone bench beside the main entrance to the Quarter of the Magi'i. Beside the bench is a single canvas bag, containing smallclothes, toiletries, and a few small personal items, including, buried deeply, Ryalth's ancient book, the book he has promised to read and has not—yet.

Behind him, the squared arches of the entrance glitter in the sun. The light reflecting off the chaos-altered sunstone shifts moment to moment even though the sky is clear and cloudless, all traces of the rain and hail of the day before gone, except for hints of dampness on the stones where the sun has not struck.

As he waits, Lorn turns and studies the square arch that leads into the center building, a structure seemingly of smooth stone and tinted windows. The arch itself bears no decorations, no carved figures, no embellishments. Then there are few embellishments and only scattered statuary throughout Cyad. The City of Light is its own art, Lorn reflects as he notes that the only breaks in the seamless stone are the words across the center of the arch itself.

"Chaos is the heart of life; the Magi'i serve life and

chaos." He murmurs the words to himself. Is that why he will never be a magus, because he cannot bend himself to serve? Or serve blindly? He frowns, but the frown vanishes as he turns toward the sound of heavy footsteps.

Ciesrt, nearly as lanky as Lorn's brother Vernt, but more broad-shouldered and far heavier on his feet, lumbers awkwardly toward Lorn.

"Greetings," Lorn offers.

"So . . . you're going to be a lancer?" Ciesrt half-smiles, but the smile conceals nervousness.

"I'm being sent for lancer training. If I become a lancer officer depends on how I do." Lorn follows the words with a rueful smile.

Ciesrt nods, thoughtfully. "I suppose it doesn't matter how good we are, but only how well our efforts are seen by those above us."

Lorn conceals another frown. He hadn't expected something like that from Ciesrt. "Someone has to decide."

"You always wanted to be the one, Lorn," Ciesrt adds quietly. "You're pretty good at concealing it, but . . . not good enough for the Magi'i. Maybe you'll do better with the lancers." Ciesrt's muddy-green eyes fix on Lorn. "Sometimes, it's better to go with the chaos flow on more than the surface."

Lorn nods, waiting.

"Good luck." Ciesrt offers a half-smile, then turns.

"Thank you." Lorn watches the lanky student magus for a moment, wondering if he had indeed made a mistake in not trying to deal with Ciesrt's father. Yet . . . all he had to go on were his feelings, and he didn't think murder should be based on feelings alone. Should it?

He turns at the sound of another set of lighter steps on the white stone pavement.

The red-haired Tyrsal stops short of the bench. "I'm sorry, Lorn. I don't understand. You were the best student."

"It's probably better this way."

"Is there anything I can do?" Tyrsal grins. "I mean, here in Cyad. If you're careful, you can take care of yourself

better than I could. I still remember how you handled Dett."
The redhead frowns. "He's probably a lancer officer now.
You'd better be careful."

"I will." Lorn pauses. "You could stop by the house a few
times and talk to my sisters. You've met them, haven't you?"

"Just Myryan."

"Jerial's my older sister. They're both healers, but Myryan's got several years before she's finished."

"Like Kylernya, except she's just started."

"She's that old?" Lorn remembers Tyrsal's sister as barely
waist-high, watching a korfal game.

Tyrsal nods. "It will be a while before she gets into real
healing." He pauses. "I'd be welcome at your house?"

"You're a student magus in good standing." Lorn laughs
gently. "If you're worried about it, tell Vernt that I asked
you to."

"We'll see. I will call on them." Tyrsal pauses. "Are you
sure that's all I can do?"

"For right now." Lorn shrugs. "I really don't know what
to expect . . . but if I need anything else, I'll let you know."
If I can.

"I'll be here," Tyrsal promises, before he turns away.

The lancer firewagon is late in getting to the Quarter of
the Magi'i, and Lorn has been waiting on or standing beside
the hard sunstone bench for most of the afternoon before the
vibration of six chaos-driven wheels shivers through the
pavement, and the shimmering white vehicle slows to a stop
opposite the squared stone arch. Shadows from the uphill
buildings that hold the chaos towers of the Magi'i cast two
bars of darkness across the gleaming white lacquer of the
firewagon. The curved glass of the driver's station reflects
the shadowed sunstone behind Lorn enough so that Lorn cannot see the driver of the vehicle that looms at least another
six cubits above the smooth pavement.

As Lorn stands quickly, he can sense the flickers of chaos
from the storage cells that are hidden behind the shining
white cupridium panels at the rear of the firewagon. As
quickly as the former student mage has stood, a lancer officer

in a cream and green uniform is already out of the forward compartment. The two single silver bars, one on each side of his short stiff green collar, glow. The officer's eyes take in Lorn and the canvas bag beside the bench. "You Lorn?"

"Yes, ser," Lorn answers.

"Hop in. Rear compartment. Only three of you today. Be close to midnight before we reach Kynstaar."

As the officer watches, Lorn opens the side door to the rear compartment, a door of white-lacquered cupridium, light, but stronger than iron.

"Put your stuff under the seat."

"Yes, ser." Lorn glances at the two other young men. One is clearly older and far burlier than Lorn, with a swarthy complexion and a short-trimmed black beard—one of the first beards Lorn has seen on a young man. The second is slighter and far more wiry than Lorn, with hair that is somewhere between sandy-blond and light brown. "I'm Lorn."

"Akytol'alt," rumbles the larger man.

"Kyl'mer," follows the slighter figure.

"Well . . . I was Lorn'elth," Lorn corrects himself as he places his bag under the curved white oak bench seat and seats himself beside Kyl and facing Akytol and the other seat, "but that will change."

"One way or the other," snorts Akytol.

Even before Lorn closes the door, the vehicle begins to glide away from the Quarter of the Magi'i with the thin and distinctive whine that marks all firewagons. Despite the hardness of the lightly padded seats, their curvature makes sitting tolerable, and the suspension is strong enough that the ride is almost without bumps.

Through the right window, just before the firewagon turns north, Lorn takes what may be his last look for a long time at the Palace of Light, its windows bright with the light from the innumerable lamps within its sunstone walls. Despite the gleaming whiteness and the lights, for a moment, or so it seems to Lorn, the Palace seems empty.

"Ever lifted a blade?" asks Akytol.

"I've had some training," Lorn admits.

"Some? Well . . . better than most." Akytol shakes his head, then leans back and closes his eyes.

Lorn turns to Kyl. "If one might ask . . . ?"

"How did a merchanter's son get sent off to lancer training?" Kyl shakes his head. "Another time . . . if you would."

"That's fine by me." Lorn nods. He suspects neither of them is interested in revealing much, especially not with Akytol present.

Kyl turns his head to watch the buildings on the west side of North Avenue pass by.

In turn, Lorn watches those on the east side—and the few carts and carriages, and the scattered handfuls of people, a few in shimmercloth, but most in the green cottons of workers and crafters. Before long, Cyad lies behind them and the firewagon has turned eastward onto the Eastern Highway. The sun has dropped below the horizon, and the clear green-blue sky has begun to purple.

Lorn sees as well as senses the glow of chaos that surrounds the firewagon as it rolls through the twilight toward Kynstaar, the only sound the low rumble of the six cupridium-coated iron wheels on the whitened granite of the Great Eastern Highway. To an outsider the vehicle would indeed resemble a horseless and fire-swathed wagon or carriage.

Across from him, Akytol sits back, his eyes closed, a faint snore punctuating his sleep. Kyl glances nervously from Lorn to Akytol, and then for long periods out the tinted window. There is no sound from the front compartment and the unnamed lancer officer.

Finally, Lorn closes his own eyes. He can do nothing until he reaches Kynstaar.

Lorn'alt, Isahl Undercaptain, Mirror Lancers

XVII

LORN'ALT STANDS RIGIDLY in formal lancer whites, white-scabbarded sabre at his side, white garrison cap set squarely in place over his short brown hair. He is the fourth man in the front line of five new Mirror Lancer officers, listening to the graying but trim lancer commander standing on the podium before the score of new undercaptains ranked in the open sunstone arena—an arena nearly empty except for the officers who had trained them, who had whittled down three score possible candidates to the score who remained nearly a year later. A score had left voluntarily, and a score had died or been too severely injured to continue.

". . . you are the first line of defense against the barbarians of the north. At times, you will be all that stands between Cyador and the black order of death. . . ."

Standing one rank back and three junior officers to his left is Kyl'alt, and somewhere farther to the rear, surprisingly, is Akytol'alt, towering over most of the other new undercaptains. Lorn concentrates on the commander's words, as though they were new, as though he had not already heard similar banalities all his life.

". . . never has our world had a land that offered so much to so many for so long . . . never has our world had a light that has shone so brightly as that raised by Cyador . . . and you are here to ensure that light will shine forever, and that peace and prosperity will reign endlessly. You are a Mirror Lancer officer. Never forget that! Never forget that you are here because generations of Lancer officers have stood between the dark tide of the order of death and the light and prosperity of chaos. That was their duty, and they did it well. May you carry out your duty as well."

After a moment of silence, the commander adds, "You will step forward as your name is called." He pauses, then announces, "Undercaptain Bruk'alt."

When the commander calls Lorn's name, the former student magus steps forward as had the others. The commander hands the two silver bars to Lorn.

"Thank you, ser."

"Don't thank me, Undercaptain. You earned them, and you will continue to earn them every day you are on duty in the service of Cyador—and even when you are not."

"Yes, ser."

"Lorn'alt . . ." the commander offers in an even lower voice.

"Yes, ser?"

"Perchance I am wrong, but you could easily have been first in the training company." The flint-gray eyes never leave Lorn's.

"Ser . . . I wanted to do well, but I also was more concerned about learning everything I could. I made mistakes that way, ser."

The faintest of smiles crinkles the commander's lined face. "I hope that's the truth, Undercaptain Lorn. The Lancers have no place for officers who let someone else be first to blunt the charge, and then rise to take credit. Do you understand that?"

"Yes, ser."

The commander nods brusquely, and Lorn turns and steps back to his place in the formation.

"Undercaptain Jykan'alt . . ."

XVIII

LORN STANDS IN the narrow hallway, sabre at his side, white garrison cap tucked in his belt, waiting for his interview with the majer who will inform Lorn just what duty he will undertake for the Mirror Lancers in the service of Cyador. Although it is early winter, nearly a year after he had left the Quarter of the Magi'i, the air flowing through the outside arch to his left is warm and moist, more like spring in Cyad, carrying with it a hint of arymid. But then, Kynstaar is actually south and east of Cyad, where the southern currents of the Great Western Ocean first touch Candar before swinging westward and north.

Lorn shifts his weight, trying to hear the conversation beyond the door, but even his magus-honed skills can only enable him to catch phrases.

". . . being posted to Hristak . . . Great Canal south to Fyrad . . . Majer Derin'alt . . . two scrolls . . . and seal ring . . . understand?"

"Yes, ser!" Rydenber's words are far louder and clearer than the majer's.

After Rydenber steps out through the open white oak door, Lorn waits a moment before entering Majer Styphi's office. Light floods into the small space from an open window to Lorn's right and the majer's left. The office contains little besides the desk, an oil lamp set head-high in a bronze bracket on the stone wall, and two chairs.

Majer Styphi sits on one chair, behind the small desk that he dominates. At his right hand is a neat stack of scrolls. His cream and green tunic is slightly wrinkled, and darkness fills the hollows under his eyes, but his green eyes are hard and fix on Lorn. "Undercaptain Lorn'alt?"

"Yes, ser."

"You're being posted to Isahl. First, you will take the lancer firewagon tomorrow morning. It will take you and a number of others to the transfer station on the Great North Highway. There you will wait and take the regular firewagon to Syadtar. That's where you will pick up the replacement lancers and Nytral—he's a seasoned squad leader. Then you'll take the lancers and the replacement mounts on the trade road northwest to Isahl. Sub-majer Brevyl is the area commander. You'll report to him." The majer hands a scroll to Lorn. "This scroll confirms that." He hands a cupridium seal ring to Lorn. "There's your seal ring. Don't lose it. Nytral will ask to see it, just like every other good squad leader you'll command when you're coming in alone." A second smaller scroll follows. "Here are his posting orders. There are two copies there for you—one goes to Commander Thia-taphi's clerk in Syadtar, the other to Nytral. You understand?"

"Yes, ser." Lorn slips the seal ring onto the third finger of his right hand. The ring fits well enough that it will not slip off.

"You'll draw a mount in Syadtar. Choose it carefully."

"Yes, ser."

"Get your kit together. Then spend some time with your fellows. Most of you won't see each other for some time."

Lorn bows once more before he turns and leaves.

Kyl is waiting outside in the group of undercaptains who have yet to see Majer Styphi. He glances inquiringly at Lorn. "Where are you headed?"

Lorn grins. "Where every good lancer goes. To fight the barbarians of the Grass Hills. In a town called Isahl."

"It's better than the guard detail in Geliendra where you have to patrol the borders of the Accursed Forest," volunteers Kyl.

"Right," murmurs someone. "Dark-angel-right . . ."

"You won't get Forest duty, Kyl," Lorn says. "You know trade. They'll probably assign you to one of the coast patrols to deal with smugglers or something like that."

"I'll know in a bit." The sandy-haired undercaptain inclines his head toward the building door and Majer Styphi. "I wouldn't mind that." Kyl smiles. "I wouldn't mind anything, actually."

Lorn is not so sure that he would be equally happy with all duties, but since he has no choice over his duty assignment, he sees no point in comparing the potential satisfaction of duty assignments he would be unlikely to get. "I'll talk to you later, and you can tell me where you're headed."

"I will," promises Kyl.

As Lorn turns, he overhears the comments.

". . . good as he is . . . not many make it back from the Hills of Endless Grass. . . ."

". . . anyone who does makes full captain and majer quick though. . . ."

". . . maybe . . . but he was magus-born . . . some don't like that. . . ."

Lorn takes in the low words most would not have believed he has heard, then nods to several others as he passes, walking back to the small cubicle that contains his uniforms, his weapons, and his handful of personal items.

The firewagon to the north will not depart until the following morning, assuming it is on schedule, and that will leave him time to write scrolls to his parents, to Myryan . . . and to Ryalth . . . before he follows the majer's advice and talks a last time with the other new undercaptains.

And, as he promised, he will read from Ryalth's book, though he does not know if he understands the Firstborn any better for all the words he has read in the green-silver covered volume.

XIX

AS THE LOW orange light of dawn fills the front compartment of the firewagon, Lorn yawns and rubs his eyes. Although he had garnered a short night's sleep on a hard cot at the highway transfer station located in Ilypsya—a town beside the Great North Highway that Lorn had never heard of— after more than two days of near-continuous travel from Ilypsya, except for short comfort stops, Lorn is tired. The flickering chaos that envelops the vehicle bothers none of the other passengers, it seems, but Lorn finds himself still studying it. Even though he is no longer a student magus, in a strange fashion the flickering almost seems to nag at him, more so than when he had studied chaos.

The six wheels rumble more loudly than those of the lancer firewagon that had brought him to Ilypsya, but that might well have been because the regular coach carries a good fifty-score stone of goods in the hold between the small front compartment and the larger rear compartment, where a good half-score passengers are squeezed together.

A slight snoring comes from the merchanter in blue shimmercloth slumped in the bench facing Lorn. The trader is a young man no more than a handful of years older than Lorn, if that, but who sports a short brush mustache in a clear effort to appear older. Beside the young merchanter is an older man in deep brown—a wealthy miller returning to Syadtar, Lorn has gathered, and on the far left sleeps another mid-aged man also in brown who has spoken but little since Lorn joined the others at Ilypsya. The last man in the front compartment, to Lorn's left, also sleeping, wears the crimson-trimmed brown of a regional guard, but the silver stars in his collar signify that he is a district commander. As Lorn's eyes light on him, his head turns, and he emits a grunt.

Ignoring the ripe odor of male bodies confined in too warm a space for too long, Lorn stifles another yawn and shifts his weight on the curved and lightly padded white oak of the seat he has to share only with the district guard commander, at least until the next stop, unless that stop is Syadtar. Each firewagon, Lorn knows, can make but one run to Syadtar and back before the chaos in the cells in the back of the vehicle must be replenished, and the vehicle makes but two round trips every eightday. Were he not a lancer officer, Lorn's passage-fare would have been at least a gold—and in the crowded rear compartment.

Abruptly, the merchanter sits up and glances out the window. "Getting close to Syadtar, I see."

Lorn follows the other's eyes, but the hills to the north look no different to him from the ones he had seen the night before—or not enough different to indicate anything. But he is used to the forests and irregular hills north of Cyad itself—not the scattered farms and the grasslands of the east that are north of the Accursed Forest and the Great Canal that links the fertile lands between the rivers with Fyrad. "Because the farms are closer together?"

The merchanter shakes his head. "The hills. They're longer here—like they've been stretched out. They get shorter and steeper as you go west. Much more rugged, they are."

Lorn nods.

"You'll see. Are you going to Isahl or Pemedra?"

"Are those the only two choices?" Lorn counters.

"For a new undercaptain, they are. You're probably pretty good with a blade and a firelance, I'd wager. No?"

"Better than many," Lorn admits.

"That's why you're there. Glad you are. Wouldn't travel this route weren't for the lancers. Barbarians be through Syadtar like grease through a goose." The merchanter laughs. "Grease through a goose. Faster than coin spent by a pleasure girl."

The miller sits up. "Begging your pardon, trader, but it be early, and Syadtar is not here yet. Some of us lack the endurance we once had."

"My apologies," offers the young merchanter. "My apologies, ser."

The miller grunts and closes his eyes.

"You'll see," murmurs the trader to Lorn, leaning back with a wry look at the miller before closing his own eyes.

Lorn closes his eyes for a time, but he can no longer sleep to the rumbling of the wheels, and his eyes stray back to the window.

The first sign that the firewagon is approaching Syadtar is the appearance of scattered farmhouses—similar in their green tile roofs, green ceramic privacy screens before the front doors, and the green shutters open but ready to be closed against night or weather. Yet each is subtly different, with a lighter or darker shade of cream or off-white plaster on its walls and with different types of bushes and trees planted to create privacy areas behind the dwellings where the girls and the women may appear without being revealed to passers-by.

Then comes something Lorn has not seen before in Cyador—a white sunstone city wall—one nearly ten cubits high. There are no guards, but the firewagon passes through the open heavy oak gates and well-kept ramparts and twin guard towers.

Past the gates are the wide white-granite streets of the

small city, with the scattered green and white awnings, although those are furled in the early light of day, except for one, which signifies a coffee house. Lorn frowns momentarily.

"You're right," says the merchanter, stretching. "Won't be many coffee houses afore long, not with the blight."

"Blight?" Lorn asks involuntarily.

"Order blight—blacks spots on the underside of the leaves, then, poof! No more coffee plants."

"Magi'i will find something to stop it, or the healers," rumbles the district guard commander, slowly straightening on his part of the bench he shares with Lorn.

The firewagon is slowing, and Lorn's eyes go back to the buildings they pass. Syadtar is a miniature of Cyad, at least in that the buildings are all of white sunstone, but smaller than those of the great City of Eternal Light—and there are far fewer of more than one level. The light is more intense, even early, perhaps because there are no trees within Syadtar. Lorn sees none, at least.

"Maybe they will, honored ser, but shipments of the beans have dropped to nothing from the fields north of Fyrad, and those from Geliendra are half what they were last year."

"Don't be underestimating the Magi'i, trader," suggests the district guard commander. "Most of those that have are ashes."

"Ah . . . yes, your honor." The merchanter's mustache bobs as he swallows.

"Bah . . . not that much honor in being a district guard. The lancers have the honor." The older man's eyes twinkle as he winks at Lorn.

Lorn hides a smile, but says, "Without the guard, the lancers would be spread far thinner."

The merchanter looks from one armsman to the other, bewildered, then looks to the window. "We are here, sers."

"Good." The commander winks once more at Lorn.

The firewagon slows under a large covered sunstone portico.

After a moment, one of the green-uniformed drivers opens

the door of the front compartment. "Syadtar, officers, kind sers."

Lorn glances to the District Commander.

"Go ahead, Undercaptain. Let a stiff commander take his time. You have much farther to go than do I."

"Thank you, ser." With that, Lorn reaches under the curved and lightly padded bench seat and pulls out his kit, then steps out into the sunlight, for it is far too early for the tile roof above to shade passengers or the firewagon itself. After slipping the white garrison cap from his belt and donning it, he glances at the firewagon driver, or one of the two, standing beside the open glass cupola. "Do you know which way to the Lancer headquarters?"

"Go one block east, to the Avenue of the Square, then head toward the hills. It's about a kay north."

"Thank you."

Carrying his kit in his left hand, Lorn begins to walk eastward, feeling a hint of dampness on his forehead where the front of the garrison cap rests.

"Poor bastard . . ."

Lorn holds in a wince at the pity in the driver's voice. He thinks he knows what he is facing, but more than a few people seem to think his assignment is a death sentence.

Two youths in faded blue undertunics and trousers careen down the street, then, seeing Lorn, abruptly dash down a side alley. An older man in a brown tunic so faded it is closer to tan leans on a walking stick and shuffles down the other side of the white-paved street, his eyes fixed on the paving stones. The creaking of a cart echoes from somewhere up the alley Lorn passed, but he sees neither cart nor whatever pulls it.

One block east, as the driver had said, is a small square. In the center is a statue, the figure purportedly of Keif'elth'alt, the first Emperor of Light. Lorn doubts that the original emperor had possessed such heroic proportions. On the south side of the square is an inn, its side porch shaded by a green and white awning. The scent of roasted fowl drifts toward Lorn, and he stops, then shakes his head, before turning northward. He does take the shaded eastern side of the street.

He passes a coppersmith's shop, then a cooper's, but both doors are closed. The door to the chandlery a block later is open. Lorn pauses, then steps inside. After his eyes adjust to the dimness, he moves toward the side counter, trying to keep both his kit and his scabbarded sabre from banging into the table that holds various leather goods. He pauses to study the travel foods on the counter, looking over the differing shapes, all covered in wax.

"Those not be what you'd be wanting, ser, I'd wager," offers a cheerful voice. A woman stands behind another counter, to Lorn's left. She points at a tray before her. "Fresh honey-rolls . . . well . . . not that fresh . . . baked late yesterday."

Lorn takes in her smiling face, and the short-cut but tight-curled black hair and the clear but dark skin. "They look better than the travel fare."

"For eating now, they are." With her words, surprisingly, comes the hint of erhenflower scent, a fragrance Lorn would have thought too dear for most in Syadtar.

"How much?"

"A copper each for the small ones. Three coppers for two of the large."

Three coppers find their way from Lorn's belt wallet to the woman. "Thank you." He takes two of the larger honey rolls. Before he is fully aware of it, he is licking the crumbs of the second off his fingers.

She extends a wooden cup of water. "You'll need this."

"Thank you." Lorn forces himself to drink the water more slowly than he had gulped down the honey rolls. "Thank you very much."

"You're most welcome. If you would wait a moment . . ." She slips away from the counter, only to reappear with a bucket and a small towel. "You could use this, ser."

"Ah . . . I wouldn't wish to impose."

"My brother was a lancer." Her smile is strained.

"I'm sorry."

"That's all right."

Lorn takes the towel and bucket, and washes his face and hands. He has to admit that he feels less grimy, and probably looks a bit more like an officer. "Thank you, lady." He hands back the bucket and the towel.

"You know, I've seen a score of young officers walk by here in the last year or so, and not a one has stopped. Why did you . . . if I might ask?" She drops her eyes.

"I was hungry." Lorn grins. "I don't think well when I'm hungry, and . . . I stopped." He pauses. "I don't mean I stopped because I wasn't thinking . . ."

The woman grins back. "You sound like Cailynt."

Lorn shrugs helplessly.

"I'm glad you stopped," she says, "but you'd best be on your way." After the briefest of pauses, she adds, "Cailynt would have made a good officer."

"He probably would have," Lorn agrees.

"Calenena? We got a customer? You be ringing me . . . you hear!"

Lorn puts another pair of coppers on the counter, and says in a low voice, "Take care." Then he grins warmly, and turns toward the door.

"I took care of it," Calenena answers.

Lorn steps back into the bright sunlight, blinking as his eyes readjust.

Another block northward, he passes a potter's shop. The smell of wood burning tells him that a kiln is being fired. His brows knit. Places like potters' and coppersmiths' shops aren't allowed in the main section of Cyad, and some trades, like rendering and tanning, are not allowed anywhere in the city. Yet he sees the potter and has smelled the tannery. Is everything within the wall? Are the barbarians that much of a threat? Or had they been at one time?

He keeps walking, realizing as he does that there are few trees in Syadtar—no cylars or arymids, no straight or feathering conifers, just a few scattered scrub cedars here and there.

The Mirror Lancer enclave is clear enough. The street ends

at another white granite wall and an archway with the two
lancer guards, each under a projecting roof to shield them
from the sun. Lorn shows the seal ring, and steps past them.
Once inside the archway and past the open gates that are
swung back inside the compound, Lorn glances around, then
heads for the largest building.

After walking the hundred cubits from the gates, he slips
through the open front archway into the coolness of a stone-
walled corridor.

"Ser?" A lancer ranker looks up from behind a table a
mere ten cubits inside the corridor. His left sleeve holds two
green slashes a span or so above the cuff—showing he is a
senior squad leader.

"Yes, squad leader?"

"If you're reporting for duty, ser, you need to go to the
next building."

"I'm going to Isahl, but I'm supposed to pick up a squad
leader, replacement lancers, and mounts."

"They'll help you there, ser. This is Commander Thiataphi's headquarters, ser. The support centers for the outposts
are in the next building."

"Thank you."

Lorn turns and makes his way to the next building, con-
siderably smaller, with a plain weathered white oak door,
standing ajar. He peers inside, at the two lancers who sit at
opposite sides of a large table on which are stacked scrolls
of various sizes and sorts.

". . . need three more for the replacement company . . ."

". . . good thing you got the mounts . . ."

Lorn steps inside, and, at the slight whisper of his boots,
the older and bearded squad leader stands, followed by the
younger.

"Ser? Can we help you?" The senior squad leader pauses,
studying the weary junior officer. "Would you be the new
undercaptain for Isahl?"

"That I am," Lorn admits. "Undercaptain Lorn'alt." He
shows the seal ring. "I'm supposed to find a squad leader

named Nytral. I have his orders." Lorn extracts the somewhat battered smaller scroll from his tunic.

"I'm Byrten, ser. Senior lancer clerk for the outposts." As the man shifts his weight, Lorn can sense the stiffness and the pain in his motions.

"It's good to meet you, Byrten." Lorn shrugs. "I'm supposed to report here, but I wasn't given much in the way of details."

Byrten hides a smile. "Chorin . . . go find Nytral. Tell him his undercaptain's here."

"Ser? By your leave?"

Lorn nods and steps aside to let Chorin by him.

"De the day after tomorrow afore all the supplies and replacement lancers be ready, ser. Till then, you'll have a room in the officers' building—that's second back, and I'll show you after you're set with Nytral. Or he can show you."

"How many replacement lancers are there?"

"Two score," replies Byrten.

"And how often do they need replacements?"

"When Sub-Majer Brevyl needs them—sometimes once, sometimes twice a season." Byrten's smile is thin.

Two score lancers six times a year? From one outpost on the edge of the Grass Hills? Lorn nods thoughtfully, deciding not to ask how many undercaptains are needed as replacements.

"How long a ride is it to Isahl?"

"Three days, more or less."

"And what sort of supplies will we be taking?"

"You'll be escorting five wagons—four horse team on each." Byrten glances toward the door, where the rail-thin Chorin reappears, followed by a ranker with a single green slash on his sleeve. Both halt just inside the door. Nytral is short and stocky, and his right cheek bears a faded purple starburst scar. His thick black hair is cut short, and his thick black eyebrows are bushy. The deep brown of his eyes conveys a flatness, as if Nytral has seen too much for his eyes to reveal. The flat eyes look at Lorn, eyes that are wary, waiting.

Lorn extends the set of smaller scrolls. "Undercaptain Lorn'alt. These are your orders."

"Yes, ser." Nytral takes the scrolls, then looks at Lorn'alt.

The two other lancer rankers watch, eyes flicking from Nytral to Lorn.

"You can unroll them," Lorn says. "They're yours, but one copy has to go to Commander Thiataphi's clerk."

"Ah . . ." suggests Byrten.

"You take it first?" asks Lorn.

"Works better that way, ser," suggests Nytral. "Byrten draws us supplies, and he can't draw for more than we got on roster."

Lorn nods, wondering how much more he needs to learn, and whether he can—in time. "If there's nothing else Byrten needs to tell me . . . ?" He looks at the senior clerk.

"No, ser. Just check every morning. Tomorrow we should have the replacement roster done, and the supply list."

"I'd like Nytral to look at those with me," Lorn says.

"Yes, ser."

The undercaptain looks at his squad leader. "Let's go on outside, Nytral."

"Yes, ser." Nytral's voice is deferential, but level.

After leaving the support building, Lorn crosses the small courtyard until he stands in the shadowed corner on the southeast side. Then he turns to Nytral. "I understand you'll be able to let me know what I should know and don't on the way to Isahl." Lorn offers a smile, one simultaneously open and yet professional.

Nytral does not return the smile. "Could be, ser."

Lorn laughs, gently. "I know chaos, firelances, and blades. I don't know lancers and barbarians, and you do, or you wouldn't be a squad leader assigned to a green officer. I also don't know what supplies we should have, and what we might get shorted. You do."

Nytral's lips crinkle slightly. "There be that, ser."

"More than that, I'm sure." Lorn laughs self-deprecatingly. "Do you know where I draw a mount? And how we can find out about just what our replacement lancers are like?"

"Wouldn't be much good to you, if'n I didn't, ser."

"Let's start with finding my room so I can drop off this kit, and then look for the kind of mount that will be best for Isahl." Lorn smiles. "Lead on."

Nytral gestures toward the three-story, narrow, barrack-like building in the northeast corner of the compound. "There." He walks out of the shade across the white paving stones of the courtyard. "Front entrance there is to the officer's rooms. You can take whatever one you want on the top level. Stables are out back, beyond the wall. . . ."

Lorn matches steps with the squad leader, listening, and yet studying the compound, trying to memorize where everything is.

XX

AFTER HAVING SELECTED a mount, and getting a tour of the rest of the Mirror Lancer compound from Nytral, Lorn finds himself yawning more and more as they walk back from the armory, a heavy-walled and squat building located inside another set of walls in the northwest corner of the compound. Lorn's boots are scuffing the stone as well.

"Ser . . . begging your pardon, but best you get some sleep afore you eat with the senior officers tonight." Nytral glances at Lorn.

"Because they'll be sizing up the new undercaptain? You're probably right, and there's not too much more I can do until tomorrow anyway." Lorn yawns again. "I'll see you in the morning, and we can go over the supplies and everything."

"Yes, ser."

Lorn turns and walks back to the quarters building, and up two long flights of steps. His room is stark—one narrow pallet bed, a small table by the bed with an oil lamp, a single armless wooden chair, and a set of wooden pegs on the wall for hanging uniforms. The single window bears ancient glass, and the shutters are inside the casement.

After slipping the latch bar in place behind him, Lorn levers off his boots and strips to his small clothes. By then he is struggling to keep his eyes open.

Despite his fatigue, Lorn wakes in mid-afternoon, in a chill. As he was sleeping, someone had been screeing him, and it had not been his father. But why? To see that he was indeed where he had been sent?

He rolls upright and rubs his eyes. Since he is awake, he rises and then uses the cold shower in the semi-communal bathing chamber in the middle of the uppermost floor. After drying and dressing in a clean set of lancer whites, he heads back to the outpost support building where some discreet inquiries of Chorin locate the officer's laundry service, set, obviously, in the rear of the ground floor level of the quarters building.

Lorn returns to his room and carries his soiled whites down to the small room where a gray-haired and bare-footed woman in gray stands over a wash tub, swirling the wash with a wooden paddle. A second thigh-high tub stands to her right. The odors of warmish water and soap fill the bare-walled space.

Lorn waits, but the woman does not turn in his direction. Finally, he clears his throat.

She looks up, then steps toward him. "Ser . . . ser . . . those I cannot wash until tomorrow."

"That's fine."

"A copper for each uniform, you know."

Lorn nods. "There is just one."

She bobs her head and takes the uniform. "Tomorrow night."

"Thank you." Even before he finishes his words, the washerwoman has set his whites on a table by the tub and is back at work with the wooden paddle. He steps outside, into a gentle, but unseasonably warm breeze for winter in Syadtar—that is what he feels. He checks the white garrison cap, although the breeze is scarcely strong enough to worry about.

There is time before dinner. So he walks around the compound, studying more carefully what Nytral had shown him earlier. Under grayish-green tiled roofs, the buildings are of clean-lined granite and sunstone, the granite for the main walls, and the sunstone for the minimal trim and arches. Both types of stone have been bleached out by time and the residual impact of the chaos-chisel cutting used to shape the stone blocks. With the late afternoon sun glinting on the windows of Thiataphi's headquarters, Lorn can see that some of the window panes are clearer than others, by the reflection of both light and the chaos within the sunlight. The window casements are all of stained and weathered white oak, but barely visible, since all the shutters in the compound are inside the windows.

The outpost building, although old, has been added to the compound later.

Lorn smiles as Chorin hurries out the door and scurries toward Thiataphi's headquarters.

". . . two, three . . ."

At the sound of cadence-calling, Lorn turns to watch a line of men in white marching along the west wall of the compound, just outside the shade.

". . . have to march before you ride . . . two, three . . . keep the chaos on your side . . . two, three . . ." calls a burly squad leader, breaking the cadence to add, "You're not tough, and the barbarians will eat you like honeycakes . . . pick it up in the rear!"

Hoofs clatter on the stones, and a Mirror Lancer in white, wearing the red sash of a messenger, rides up to the hitching post outside Thiataphi's headquarters, dismounts, hurriedly ties his mount, and rushes inside carrying a white leather dispatch pouch.

As Chorin eases out through the stone archway, the Lancer clerk's head turns as if he is trying to hear what the messenger might be saying or what he brought.

Lorn smiles, watching.

When Chorin sees Lorn, he begins to walk quickly back

to the outpost building, without looking back at the junior officer.

At the sound of the fifth bell of afternoon, Lorn turns back toward the quarters building. By the time he reaches the dining area, a small hall with a table long enough for a score and a half, and folds his garrison cap and tucks it in his belt, there are already a number of officers gathering within the sunstone finished room. The fireplace behind the head of the table is dark, and the walls are bare, except for a series of miniature mirror shields on the north wall, each with a design color-etched into the polished cupridium. The cupridium catches the indirect early evening light coming through the windows on the south wall, enough so that light plays across the shields.

From the rank insignia he can see, he is the only under-captain, with six captains, two overcaptains, one sub-majer, and one majer standing at places around the table, and with the gray-haired Commander Thiataphi himself at the head of the table.

As the other officers seat themselves, Lorn watches, then moves so that he is at the very foot of the table on the left side.

Each place has a brown platter and a heavy glass wine goblet—glass, not crystal nor metal. The servers are lancers, but each wears a green overtunic. On the serving platter first presented to the commander are slices of beef, covered with a brown sauce. The second platter is heaped with yellow noodles, and four large baskets of dark bread are set at intervals along the table. Then comes a deeper dish filled with something green.

Lorn waits and takes as much as he dares of the beef, noodles, bread, and ackar, a bitter leafy vegetable he had seen far too much of as a boy. The server fills his goblet with a maroon wine.

Commander Thiataphi lifts his goblet, and the other officers begin to eat. Lorn follows their example, listening to their conversation as he does.

"White mounts handle the sun better . . . chaos-colored, you know, and the white reflects better. . . ."

". . . darker coats shield them better . . ."

". . . so why do the chestnuts breathe harder and lather earlier?"

". . . got you there, Helkar . . ."

". . . doesn't matter now . . . not in winter . . ."

Lorn takes a bite of the overcooked beef, following it with a mouthful of equally overcooked noodles. The wine, while a plain red, is far better than either the beef or the noodles, but Lorn eats everything on the chipped brown platter before him, then waits for the senior officers to finish and take any second helpings.

". . . scouts say the Jeranyi are gathering the eastern tribes, the ones north of the cupric mines."

"Some of them have started carrying polished iron shields—work almost as well as a mirror shield against the fire lances . . . with those iron-headed arrows . . ."

"Their bows aren't that good, not from the saddle."

"Yet . . ."

"Ought to go in and take the iron mines . . ."

"You want to get ferric poisoning . . . be my guest, Helkar. Besides, none of the barbarians work metal that well."

"You don't get it from the ore . . . only after it's smelted and turned into weapons . . . Rather take out the mines than risk getting ferric poisoning and order death."

Lorn keeps a polite smile on his face when he isn't eating, taking in the attitudes of the lancers, partly amazed at some of the misconceptions that seem common, even among officers.

The serving dishes, after being refilled by the lancer servers, make their way down to Lorn, who takes additional slices of beef and a pile of the gravied noodles. He has eaten two mouthfuls of his seconds, then stops to break off a chunk of the moist brown bread.

"Undercaptain? Lorn'alt, is it not?" calls Commander Thiataphi.

Lorn swallows quickly. "Yes, ser."

"You're from Cyad, are you not?"

"Yes, ser."

"How do you find the north?" asks the commander.

"Warmer than I would have thought in winter, ser." Lorn offers a polite smile.

"That's why the barbarians want our lands. One reason, anyway. On the other side of the Grass Hills, there's snow. Or there was last eightday, according to the report from Sub-Majer Brevyl. Don't forget to draw a winter jacket, and winter boots."

"No, ser. I won't." Lorn hasn't thought about either, and hopes his face does not show his ignorance.

"You from a lancer family?"

"No, ser." Lorn decides against volunteering his background.

"That's right," Thiataphi says with a guffaw. "You're one of the magus-born who's good with a blade." He shakes his head. "Do some of the Magi'i good to get out on the borderlands, see what the barbarians are doing."

Not knowing how to respond to that, Lorn nods politely.

"You'll see. Sub-Majer Brevyl will ensure you do. Just like he did with all the others here. Except me, and I made sure he saw just what they were." The darkness in the commander's words is scarcely concealed.

Lorn manages to finish the second helping on his chipped platter just before the servers clear the platters, and replace them with smaller plates, each bearing a rolled and fried paelunka that has been dipped in condensed sweetsap. He continues to listen as the conversation drifts away from him.

". . . all that snow to the north . . . grass'll be green early, and that means more raids."

"If it ever melts . . ."

". . . doesn't melt early, stay green longer, and the raids'll start later and last longer, either way, we need to draw more trainees."

". . . could be right about that . . . need more undercaptains, too . . ."

Lorn finishes his paelunka and sips the wine, very slowly, listening.

Abruptly, Thiataphi rises, and so do the other officers. Even though caught unaware, Lorn rises with them.

One of the captains draws up to Lorn as they leave the officer's dining hall.

"I'm Helkar, the one they're always telling that I'm wrong."

"Lorn."

"I noticed you didn't say much about ferric poisoning, but you have to know something about it, don't you, if you were a magus."

"I know something about it," Lorn admits.

"Was I right about it? That it's got to be used in a weapon?"

"Mostly." Lorn pauses. "And you have to have been using firelances, and directing them for a long time. Otherwise, you'll probably only get a burn in addition to a slash or a cut."

"Why do the Magi'i warn us so much? Burns, those I can handle."

"The Magi'i handle more chaos than firelances, much more."

"Ah . . ." Helkar frowns. "You'll have to worry more about iron then?"

"I shouldn't."

"Good." Helkar laughs. "You'll have enough to worry about with Brevyl anyway."

"Is he that hard?"

"Is cupridium tough? Does a firelance burn?" The captain shakes his head. "He's fair, but best you do as he orders, or you'll find yourself leading a half-score of troublemakers who don't know one end of a lance from the other against four score raiders." Helkar laughs. "And if you make it through that, he'll decide you're the one to train and lash all the troublemakers in the whole outfit into formation."

Lorn nods, stifling a yawn. He is still tired from three days' travel in firewagons and wonders if one good night's sleep will be enough to recover. "Is this your duty assignment now?"

"Me? Working for Commander Thiataphi? Not likely. I'm here like you, picking up replacement lancers, except I'm headed back to Pemedra tomorrow. A few less barbarians there, and a lot more snow. You can see the Westhorns from there, and that wind comes off them in winter, and it'll cut right through you."

"How many lancers are you taking back?"

"Four score, with two squad leaders." Helkar shrugs. "Takes near-on four days, and there's always a chance of a raiding party, but it's less early in the winter. The barbarians get bored or run out of food before spring, and they'll start raiding while there's still snow everywhere." Another laugh follows. "Trailing them through snow and mud, we all enjoy that."

Lorn nods.

"You look order-dead." Helkar half-thumps Lorn's shoulders and turns. "Good luck with Sub-Majer Brevyl."

"Thank you." Lorn walks slowly up the two flights of stone steps, concentrating so that his white boots do not scuff and so that he does not trip. A night's sleep will be good. Very good.

XXI

LORN BENDS FORWARD in the saddle and pats the shoulder of the big white mare, then straightens and looks ahead along the road that curves its way between yet another set of hills. The grass that covers the hills is brown, but it does seem endless, with each hill that the detachment rides over giving way to yet another, and then another. After the first morning, for two days all Lorn and the lancers have seen are grass hills. Part of that sense of endlessness is because they are not crossing the hills directly, but angling northwest from Syadtar.

Every so often there are small copses of bushes or low trees bearing their gray winter leaves, generally along streams so small as to be almost invisible from more than a hundred cubits away. The wind is cold, but not bitter, and blows out of the northwest, almost into Lorn's face, carrying a clear odor of wet grass and the hint of mold.

At the top of the hill on the north side of the road are two lancers Nytral has sent out as scouts. One remains reined up, watching the column of riders, while the second vanishes beyond the hill crest, shadowing and following the road from the heights as it winds generally northwest.

Lorn glances over his shoulder at the forty-odd new lancers riding behind them. Most appear painfully young, even to Lorn, and some struggle managing the firelances in the holders, even though the lances are little more than three cubits long. Lorn scarcely notices his any more.

"You ride pretty well, ser. You come from a lancer family?" asks Nytral.

Lorn turn in the saddle and looks at his squad leader. "I had to learn it on my own, Nytral. Spent a lot of extra time in officer training working with mounts. Seemed a good idea."

Nytral frowns.

"I came from a Magi'i family. I didn't take to being kept in a granite tower playing with chaos. The Magi'i didn't want me dabbling in trade. So it was strongly suggested that I become a lancer."

"Ah . . . being a magus family, ser . . . ?"

"When the head of the Magi'i, who sits at the right hand of the Emperor, suggests that a young man become a lancer officer, it's generally a good idea to agree. Besides, it got me out of the towers," Lorn points out.

Nytral glances at Lorn. "That be making more sense, ser."

"Because Isahl is one of the places that the barbarians always raid, and we lose a lot of lancers and officers here?"

"They tell you that, ser?"

"No." Lorn laughs cheerfully. "They sent me here."

Nytral shivers and looks away.

Lorn shrugs. Best that Nytral knows Lorn's background early on, and understands that Lorn doesn't intend for it to bother him, or adversely affect him. He turns and studies the riders behind him again. Then he turns his mount and rides back along the column, looking at each lancer as he passes.

Only a handful meet his amber eyes.

Near the end of the column, where the wagons rumble along, he turns the mare again, and lets her keep pace so that he rides beside the lead teamster.

"How are the wagons going?" he calls.

"Be fine, ser," answers the gray-bearded lancer with the crossed green sheaves on his sleeves, his right hand on the leather leads for the four-horse team. "A mite heavier than I'd like, but the roads stay dry, for another day, and all be well."

Lorn nods, raises his hand, and urges the mare back toward the front of the column, riding almost on the shoulder of the road and letting her move just slightly faster than the lancers, so that he can study each as he rides past, without seeming to do so.

When he reaches the front of the column, the road has begun to curve between yet another set of hills, and Lorn can see that it slopes gently upward at an angle along a ridge that extends a kay or more both east and west.

"Have to climb this one, ser."

Lorn nods as he eases the mare closer to the squad leader's mount.

"Sent out another pair of scouts," Nytral says quietly. "Been a few attacks here, 'cause you can't see the road."

Lorn follows Nytral's gesture. A pair of scouts has reined up at the ridge crest, where they pause before one turns his mount and rides down the road at a quick trot.

"Trouble . . ." mumbles Nytral. "Knew it!"

The scout has barely reined up before the words of his report tumble out. "Barbarians, ser. On the rise a kay northeast of the top there."

Lorn glances past the scout at the half-kay of road that remains before the first of the column reaches the crest. "How fast are they moving?"

"They're not riding, ser. They're waiting."

"A kay away and they'd have to ride down and then up?" asks Nytral.

"Yes, ser."

"We'd be better to get to the top," suggests the squad leader.

"Order it," Lorn says.

"Quick trot! Quick trot!"

Lorn keeps the mare abreast of Nytral, letting the squad leader set the pace as the column hurries toward the ridge top, raising heavy dust that the teamsters and the trailing riders will have to breathe. After reining in the mare at the crest of the hill, beside Nytral and the two scouts, Lorn looks out, squinting against the sun that barely warms the mid-afternoon.

"Barbarians . . ." Nytral says. "Don't look like raiders, but you can't ever tell, crazy as they are."

The score of mounted figures on the opposite hilltop are less than a kay away. The riders are bearded, with large blades in shoulder harnesses. Several have shields fastened somehow to their saddle in front of their left knees, and some have shields strapped over the bags behind their saddles.

"They won't attack . . . not now," Lorn observes.

Nytral raised his eyebrows. "With them . . . you never know."

"Do they use those shields?"

"Yes, ser." Nytral looks toward the barbarians. "They could have those out in a moment."

"Let's just wait and see if they do."

Nytral turns his mount. "Form up—eight abreast. Lances ready! Four abreast. Lances ready!"

Lorn watches the barbarians as Nytral chevies the raw lancers into formation. Abruptly, the barbarians turn their mounts and begin to ride back northward along the ridge line.

"They won't do that in the spring," Nytral prophesies as

he turns his mount and eased up beside Lorn. "And they'll have more."

Lorn has few doubts about that.

"We should wait, ser. Make sure they're well along."

"Good idea. That will let the wagons catch up, too."

"Wagons . . . wish the firewagons and the paved roads came out this far," murmurs the squad leader. "We'd get more supplies faster."

Lorn laughs. "No, we wouldn't. They'd just move us farther north, then."

"Probably right about that." Nytral shakes his head, his eyes still on the riders headed northward.

After a moment, Lorn says, "Oh . . . Nytral. There's a lancer back there, about the third back on the left. Tall fellow, but he's swaying in the saddle. Might be sick . . . or something worse."

Nytral looks at Lorn. "That be Beryt. Used to be a squad leader. He likes the malt too much, ser."

"But he fights well out where there isn't any ale or brew?"

Nytral smiles. "Yes, ser. One of the best."

Lorn nods, then readjusts the white garrison cap, still watching the barbarians as they dwindle from sight.

XXII

THE ROAD CLIMBS over a low rise between two hills, running westward. From the saddle of the white mare, Lorn can see a long and shallow valley ahead, one with more than a handful of Cyadoran-style brick dwellings dotting the eastern end of the valley, all with thin plumes of smoke rising through the cold air toward the cloudless green-blue sky overhead. The only trees are the infrequent and scraggly scrub cedars.

"There you are, ser," said Nytral. "Isahl's at the far west end. Be a bit afore we can see the outpost."

"We haven't seen that many farms until now," Lorn says, hoping Nytral will offer more information or opinion.

"Ha! Wouldn't see any here, except that they're all welcome in the walls if the raiders did come. They won't though. Not while Sub-Majer Brevyl's here."

"How many lancers are assigned here?"

"Don't tell me that, ser, not in figures, but we got five companies, and that's ten squads. When we're all lined up in formation—happens once in a while—I counted near-on tenscore, and that didn't take in the cooks and such."

"That should allow plenty of patrols."

"Not that many. Figure you need a company for a recon patrol; and a company to deal with a small raider band, and near-on everyone if all the barbarians in a tribe join a raid."

"Does that happen often?" Lorn leans forward and pats the mare on the neck.

"A full-tribe raid? Nah . . . not more than once every few years, if that. Once three summers afore last, but it was dry in the north. Figure they were hungry . . . or something."

"The raids, have they been happening for years? Or just in recent times?"

"Long time. Once heard Commander Thiataphi say he'd been an undercaptain out here. You tell me how many years that is, ser." Nytral laughs.

"More than a few." About fifty cubits back from the road, on both sides, Lorn notes the even irrigation ditches, brick-lined, and the miniature dams and sluice gates designed to channel the water to the fields, though the ditches are empty under the winter sun. "The barbarians try to tear the irrigation systems?"

"No. Mostly, they're after women and weapons, and horses—and whatever lancers they can kill while they're at it." Nytral lapses into silence.

Lorn looks northward as they pass a homestead, one with a house that could have been dropped into the outskirts of Cyad or Syadtar, with its green ceramic privacy screen before the front door, privacy hedges in the rear of the dwelling, and green shutters. The two outbuildings are of brick, but larger than those Lorn has seen elsewhere in Cyador. The one barn is nearly a hundred cubits long and twenty high—at the top of its tiled roof.

Even after riding two kays into the valley, Lorn has to squint against the glare of the late afternoon sun for a time before he can make out the general outline of the outpost, far larger in the ground it covers than the compound in Syadtar or the officers' training base in Kynstaar.

After another kay or so, Nytral offers, "There, ser, you can see it better."

The outpost has been built around a hillock at the west end of the long and shallow valley. The outer sunstone walls are a good eight cubits high and enclose corrals, barns, and an inner wall that holds an armory, and several long barracks—all built of stone and roofed in tile. On the lower part of the hillside, Lorn can see both a raised water cistern and what appears to be a spring with protective walls running from the spring to the armory.

"Have the barbarians ever breached the walls?" asks the undercaptain.

"Stories are that they killed most of the first garrison, generations back. Emperor said it wouldn't happen again . . . so they built Isahl to stop any attack. Patterned after Assyadt, except the west Jeranyi haven't caused as much trouble in a few years. Anyway . . . no attacks . . . leastwise, haven't happened since."

Lorn nods.

A kay from the outpost, they turn northward onto a short road leading to the gates in the approximate center of the southernmost east-west wall. There are four guards stationed at the closed gates at the end of the road. Two stand outside the closed gates and two above them on the low parapets. All four watch as Lorn and the replacement lancers approach.

Nytral glances at Lorn.

Lorn rides toward the gate alone, offers the seal ring for inspection to the square-faced and older guard who steps forward. "Undercaptain Lorn'alt . . . reporting to Sub-Majer Brevyl with supplies and replacement lancers."

"Good to see you, ser." The sentry steps back, and the gates swing open.

Once inside the extensive outer walls, which could only stop a small raiding party or discourage a larger band of barbarians, Lorn can see more clearly the second inner wall that surrounds the main compound, set at the base of the low hill perhaps a third of a kay northward.

The inner gates, while guarded by a halfscore of lancers, are open. One steps forward.

"Ser?"

"Yes?" answers Lorn politely.

"Being as you're new, the sub-majer'd be seeing you afore you go to quarters." The young orderly's voice is firm, if high.

"Where do I go?" asks Lorn politely.

"The corner tower in the right . . . where there's a guard at the door. There's a hitching post there."

"Thank you." Lorn nods his head, then urges the mare forward.

A lancer with the double slashes of a senior squad leader on his sleeves appears from the barracks building closest to the gate, his eyes lighting on Nytral. "Nytral's back! Even brought some wagons."

Lorn glances at Nytral. "You can settle things while I report to the sub-majer?"

"Yes, ser. They'll be fine."

"Thank you."

"My job, ser."

Lorn guides the mare to the right, toward the tower that indeed has a single guard standing by the square-arched doorway. There, he dismounts and ties the mare to the unused hitching post, then steps forward toward the lancer.

"Through the door, ser. Kielt will see to you, ser."

"Thank you." Lorn steps out of the mild but chilly wind and into the narrow corridor. A dozen cubits down the corridor yet another lancer sits at a small table beside a closed door.

Lorn steps forward and offers the seal ring to the lancer.

"Undercaptain Lorn'alt reporting for duty." The formality of the words sounds almost pompous to Lorn, but he waits.

"One moment, ser." The bearded older lancer slips through the door and closes it.

He returns almost immediately. "Sub-Majer Brevyl will see you now, ser." The lancer holds the ancient but spotless white oak door for Lorn to enter the sub-majer's study.

"Thank you, Kielt." Lorn ignores the slight flicker of the lancer's eyes and steps through the door.

The study is not large for an officer who commands an outpost as large as Isahl, for the room is less than fifteen cubits by ten, and contains but a table-desk, a single scroll case, the wooden armchair from which Brevyl rises, and four armless straight-backed wooden chairs that face the desk. There are two other chairs in the corners. High windows on the wall behind the desk offer the sole source of outside light, although two wall sconces contain unlit oil lamps.

Sub-Majer Brevyl is a short and slender man, half a head shorter than Lorn, with a thin white brush mustache. His short-cut white hair is thick, and his green eyes dominate fine features and an even nose.

"Ser, Undercaptain Lorn'alt." Lorn offers the order scroll to the sub-majer.

Brevyl lays the scroll on the corner of the desk, unopened. "Please sit down, Undercaptain. It is a long ride from Syad-tar." He pauses, then asks, as Lorn seats himself, "Did you see any barbarians along the road?"

"One group, ser. They were about a kay away, and they turned north when they saw us."

"Too bad they didn't get closer." A wry smile crosses the sub-majer's face as he picks up the scroll, unrolls it, and sits down to read through it. After a moment, he looks at Lorn, all traces of a smile vanishing from his face. "Do you know why you're here, Undercaptain Lorn'alt?"

"Because there's nowhere else I can be," Lorn says evenly. "Except perhaps Pemedra or the Accursed Forest."

"Or Inivridra in the spring or fall," adds the sub-majer. "And you'll see all four before you make majer. Without returning to Cyad except on leave between assignments." He pauses. "Doesn't seem exactly fair, does it?"

Lorn waits, attentively.

"I'd like an answer, Undercaptain."

"What's considered 'fair' has to defer to what is necessary for the well-being of Cyad, ser."

A frown replaces the bluff humoring look on the sub-majer's face. "I didn't ask for a student answer, Undercaptain."

"Absolute loyalty is required of both lancers and the Magi'i, ser. Any lancer seeking to become a magus or any student magus seeking to become a lancer comes from outside and has to demonstrate both ability and absolute loyalty."

"You're testing my patience."

Lorn represses a sigh. "Ser, it's not fair. It can't be fair, and you know that, and I know that. Ser . . . what do you want from me?"

Brevyl smiles, crookedly. "Just that. The reasons don't matter. The politics don't matter. Your background and obvious education don't matter. All that matters is that you know that you'll get the nastiest assignments you can handle. They won't be more than you can handle because that wastes lancers and endangers other officers. Are you up to that, Undercaptain?"

"I don't know, ser. I think I am, but what I do is what counts."

"You're honest, Undercaptain Lorn. Let's hope you're as good as you think you are. You'll ride patrols for the first four eightdays with Zandrey. You'll be the second-in-command, and that means you do exactly what he says—unless the barbarians get him. You'd better make sure they don't, because you don't know dung about the way they operate."

"Yes, ser."

"You listen and you ask questions, quietly and when there aren't any rankers around. You carry out Zandrey's orders and learn all you can. It won't be as much as you should know, but it might be enough if you work hard and learn fast. Do you understand?"

"Yes, ser."

"No . . ." Brevyl shakes his head. "All undercaptains just think they understand. On your way out, tell Kielt to set you up on the officers' level of the barracks, and then go find Zandrey. He's not on patrol today. He'll be here somewhere."

"Yes, ser."

"Formality is fine, Undercaptain. Ability and luck count more."

Lorn waits, deciding against another polite response.

"At least you listen." Brevyl snorts. "Go get yourself settled. Zandrey's next patrol is the day after tomorrow."

"Yes, ser. By your leave, ser."

Brevyl gives a dismissive nod, and Lorn stands, offers a slight bow, and turns. He closes the door behind him.

Outside, Kielt waits, standing beside his table.

"The sub-majer said that I was to ask you about being set up on the officers' level of the barracks."

"Very good, ser." Kielt rings the handbell on the table, turning as another lancer appears. "If you would take over, Rueggr?"

Rueggr nods once.

Lorn follows Kielt out of the brick-walled tower. Now that the sun has dropped behind the hills, the wind sweeping out of the north is chill, and he is glad of the winter jacket.

XXIII

THE OFFICERS' STUDY at Isahl contains several flat tables that can serve as desks, as well as a good half score of battered armless oak chairs. The polished stone floors are largely covered with worn green wool rugs that take the chill from the stone and muffle the sound of boots. The south windows are high, but large, and on a long table against the smooth stones of the north wall are eight large strongboxes, each with a cupridium lock. Each has a bronze plate on it with the name of a company. Lorn's company is Fifth Company, and the bronze key to his lock is fastened inside his green web officer's belt.

He sits on the opposite side of a table from Captain Zandrey. Zandrey is black-haired, brown-eyed and stocky. Like most lancer officers, he is clean-shaven, but in the afternoon light, his dark beard is beginning to show. "Sub-Majer Brevyl has decided that Nytral will be your company squad leader. Each squad is a score, and there's a squad leader for each."

Lorn nods, wondering if it had taken a promotion for Nytral to agree to serve under Lorn. He almost shook his head. Nytral could have been ordered to serve. Was the promotion to encourage Nytral?

"You look skeptical, Lorn."

"No, ser. I just wondered about Nytral's promotion." Lorn tries to make his voice as guileless as possible.

"He was overdue, actually." Zandrey snort. "Rumor has it that he asked to serve under you, and Brevyl was so surprised that the man volunteered for anything that he promoted him on the spot."

"He seems to know a lot," Lorn ventures.

"He does, more than most of the senior squad leaders, but he says what he believes, and some officers and other squad leaders are less than pleased with his attitude."

"Right now, that's fine with me." Lorn nods. "What about the patrol tomorrow? What exactly do we do?"

"Patrol." The captain laughs. "We'll ride northward, looking for barbarians or signs that they've been around. We might see some, and we might not, but they'll know we've been looking. The one thing that is certain is that when we don't patrol, there are more raids."

"Nytral said that the barbarians were mostly after women, weapons, and mounts."

"He's mostly right, but they'll sometimes take children, and sometimes silvers and golds, if a homesteader has any."

Lorn frowns.

"You wonder why anyone lives out here? Simple. They don't have any choice. Thieves, swindlers, and people who've failed the Empire—if they haven't killed anyone, they can choose to homestead beyond the great highways for a score of years. Some like it and stay. Others leave, but sometimes they work a deal with someone in Syadtar—turn it over to a younger son or a troublemaker who's headed for worse. Anyway, we're here to protect them as well as the towns and cities farther south. Strange, when you think about it . . . protecting folks who've forfeited the Emperor's justice." Zandrey shrugs. "Can't question too much here, or you'll end up questioning your own mind."

"Is there anything about the barbarian tactics?"

"Tactics? Most wouldn't know a tactic if it walked up with a cupridium blade and cut them out of the saddle."

"That would seem to make them unpredictable."

"I wouldn't say that," replies the captain. "They're direct—like a big iron hammer. And there is one thing you can count on with the barbarians. They don't believe in doing anything that's not honorable." Zandrey's words were dry. "In two years here, I've never seen an ambush. They don't attack at night, or in the rain or snow. They ride at you, but they don't cluster, and they don't try to pick off officers. They also don't back off attacking officers. Any Cyadoran is like any other, and they hate us all."

Lorn wonders why. From what he knows of history, the hatred makes no sense, and that means he doesn't know enough of history or that the barbarians are irrational. Somehow, he thinks that the history is more suspect than the barbarians' rationality.

Zandrey stands and stretches. "Go over your squad rosters until you know the names. Last thing you need to be doing on patrol is trying to remember names. It's hard enough to match names to faces at first."

Lorn stands and replies. "Yes, ser."

"And you'll need to check the firelances in the morning, each one as it's issued."

Lorn nods.

"See you at dinner."

Lorn waits until Zandrey turns before letting an ironic smile cross his face. Are all the outcasts on the northern border? He shakes his head before turning to head toward the stable to check on both his mare and his company's mounts.

XXIV

UNDER THICK GRAY clouds, the mist seems to billow out of the north and across the brown grass of the endless hills. Although it is near mid-day, the clouds and mist give the impression of twilight. The mist droplets congeal on the back of Lorn's neck and then roll in tiny rivulets down his back under the white oiled leather of his winter jacket.

Lorn shifts from one leg to the other, putting his weight on one stirrup, then the other. He half-stands in the stirrups, just trying to stretch his legs.

They are less than twenty kays north of Isahl, and in another world. The patrol travels a narrow clay path on the north side of a valley that holds little besides a small brackish lake they had passed earlier, and a handful of scattered earth brick dwellings and barns. The dwellings are scarcely that, without privacy screens or glass in the windows. Rough cut and oiled shutters, often pieced together from old boards, are swung closed against the damp and chill. The thin lines of smoke from the chimneys are lost in the gray of the clouds and mist.

The only living creatures visible besides the lancers and their mounts are the sheep of a single small herd—grayish lumps against the brown grass—beyond the last barn on the south side of the road.

So far, the only tracks in the road are those of the patrol and of a single cart that has left span-deep ruts in the clay-like mud that has almost frozen.

Lorn glances a half-kay or so ahead, where Zandrey leads the Third Company, then back along his company's two squads. For the moment, Nytral rides with Shofirg—the Second squad's leader. Beside Lorn is another older lancer, Dubrez, whose bearded face holds a dourness that has been unchanged since the patrol began the day before.

The road slowly curves northward at the west end of the valley, rising to pass between two slightly lower hills, where there are a handful of scrub cedars, a few bushes and mostly taller grass.

"This place have a name?" Lorn finally asks Dubrez.

"This valley? Not that I know, ser. Most don't, not properlike. This one's the valley with the sour lake. Next is the one with the burned-out house. That sort of thing . . ." Dubrez lapses into silence.

Lorn shifts the reins from his right hand to his left, flexing his fingers, trying to warm them inside thick white gloves that keep out the worst of the chill—but not all of it.

Cold and fat droplets of rain splat against lancers and their mounts, just enough to cover both with a thin sheet of water, before the cold rain ceases, and is in turn replaced by the finer droplets of the seemingly endless mist.

"How often are we likely to run across barbarians?" Lorn asks the squad leader quietly.

"Don't, ser. Not in winter." Durbrez to the hills to their right. "Up there, probably a few now. Or could be. We don't patrol, and in an eightday, there'll be raiders in most of these valleys. Wintertime . . . they don't want to fight, and it be too cold for them to stay out too long and guess where we'll be. We patrol . . . they watch some. We don't patrol—they raid. Dung-eaters . . . every last one of 'em." The squad leader grunts and is silent.

Lorn studies the column ahead, and the faint puffs of white coming from the lancers' mounts, wondering if any raids take place during the winter, or if the patrols are just to keep the lancers in shape.

"Be some raids," Dubrez adds, as if he has thought about his earlier words. "Some raiders desperate . . . maybe two or three every winter . . . not like the spring and summer and fall, though."

Three or four raids—and those are considered as insignificant? Lorn looks northward at the darkening clouds.

XXV

AS HE HALF-LISTENS to Nytral, on yet another patrol, Lorn studies the road and the west end of the valley they are about to leave. The road curves northward, again rising into the lowest point between two hills. Directly to Lorn's right, there is a sheep path or trail that angles eastward through two switchbacks and over the hill, probably into the next valley in what seems an endless series of hills and interlocked valleys. The cold wind is scarcely more than a breeze, but it still chills Lorn's ears, despite the winter garrison cap with the ear-flaps.

". . . just can't ever tell, ser . . . might be a raid now . . . might not be one for eightdays," declares Nytral, as he rides beside Lorn in the chill, gray, and sunless afternoon. With the last of his words, the senior squad leader offers a shrug.

Lorn nods faintly at the phrases he has heard more than a few times over the past three eightdays, then glances northward at the sound of hoofs thudding on the frozen clay of the road. A lancer gallops southeast from the Third Company toward Lorn and Nytral, steam puffing from his mount's nostrils.

"Never can tell, ser, but that'd be looking like a raid the scouts found."

Not about to second-guess his senior squad leader, Lorn just keeps riding until the lancer reins up.

"Ser . . . there's raiders over the hill, spoiling a herder's place. Captain Zandrey's orders be for your company to ride the path there, along the ridge, and then start down toward the herder's place. Says you be making noise so as to spook 'em out along the road, and that's where he'll be."

"Tell Captain Zandrey that we'll be following his orders."

"Yes, ser." The lancer offers a head bow, then turns his mount.

Lorn glances at Nytral, who smiles crookedly.

"Fifth Company! We're taking that sheep trail—two abreast!" Lorn orders.

"Yes, ser!" answers Dubrez, the squad leader riding directly behind Lorn.

"I'll ride back and tell Shofirg, ser," offers Nytral.

Lorn nods as he guides his mount northward across the brown grass toward the trail that begins perhaps a half-kay northward of the road. The frozen brown grass crackles under the mare's hoofs, and a few murmurs drift to Lorn on the light cold wind.

". . . they get the road . . . we climb goat paths . . ."

". . . leastwise . . . undercaptain's up front . . ."

". . . supposed to be there . . ."

The trail is steeper and narrower than it had appeared from the road, so that the lancers ride single file. The sound of hoofs scrabbling on the frozen clay mixes with the mumbles of lancers, pitched low enough that Lorn can no longer distinguish anything but the general tone of dissatisfaction. He glances back, but the Third Company has vanished into the pass between the two hills.

The wind is stronger nearer the crest of the hill, and when Lorn finally reaches the top and is about to look down on the next valley, the chill gusts almost take his breath away. Below them the sheep path meanders downhill through a series of switchbacks to a small valley, an oval no more than two kays across at the widest point and less than four kays along its east-west length. A single clump of buildings set beside a long pond are the only sign of settlement—except for the dozen or so horsemen reined up outside the largest building, while other figures scurry around a long and narrow sod barn.

Lorn urges the mare into a slightly faster walk, the best he dares on the steep and hard ground of the path. His eyes flick from the path to the holding, and then to the line of lancers that follows him down the slope.

Nytral and Lorn have reached the second switchback on the way down the northern side of the hill when screams reach them—carried on the light wind. Lorn looks westward toward where the road enters the valley, but the undercaptain cannot see Zandrey's company, and he wonders where the Third Company might be, since taking the road surely had to have been quicker than crossing a frozen field and then climbing and descending the hill.

One of the raiders gestures, as if to note Lorn's company of lancers, but none of the raiders seem to stop their depredations—and another scream wavers through the chill air.

"Bastards, they are. Every last one of 'em," mumbles Nytral.

"They know we can't reach them quickly." Lorn still looks for Zandrey, but cannot see the Third Company anywhere. Is there a bridge down . . . or another group of raiders? Or is Zandrey going to let Lorn make the first attack?

As the last of the Fifth Company descends the path, finally lining up in formation, and begins its advance, the barbarians suddenly mount and begin to ride westward—away from Lorn.

"They're running!" comes a yell from behind Lorn.

"For now," counters Nytral. "Hold formation!"

"Hold formation!" Lorn orders as well.

As the Fifth Company reaches a flatter area of brown grass perhaps five hundred cubits south of the midpoint of the long pond, a series of flashes appears to the west—flashes of fire-lances.

Lorn conceals a frown. Has Zandrey been waiting beyond the low rise all along—letting the holders be killed and tortured—until Lorn charged the raiders into ambush?

"Third Company's got 'em!"

"Hold formation!" Nytral orders again.

As his Mirror Lancers near the holding itself, Lorn studies the ground, noting the closeness of the earthen dike that holds back the waters of the shallow pond, and the narrow space between the northern end of the pond, and the steeper hills that define the northern side of the valley.

The firelances of the Third Company flash again, and amid the flashes come the screams—of mounts—not of men.

Close to half a score of the raiders wheel their mounts and turn away from Zandrey's firelances, heading toward the northeast, as if to circle the frozen and narrow pond that extends almost a half-kay to the north, even though it was created by an earthen dike no more than four cubits high.

Lorn glances at the raiders' course, and then at the pond, and the orders seem obvious, so obvious that his words seem ponderous and slow. "Dubrez! Take your squad around that pond! On the far side!"

"Yes, ser!" Dubrez offers Lorn the first smile the under-captain has seen from the dour veteran.

"We'll take this side in case they turn," Lorn tells Nytral.

"Best send a half-score along the edge of the pond on this side," suggests Nytral.

"It's that shallow?"

"Yes, ser."

"Do it!"

"Shofirg!" bellows Nytral. "Take a half-score on this side of the pond, up toward the north end."

"Yes, ser!"

"We'll take the rest down this side."

Lorn, Nytral, and the remaining half-score of Shofirg's squad quick-trot southward along the southern and western edge of the long pond. They near the holding buildings and ride toward the melee that now seems to involve all of Zandrey's company and all the raiders except the handful that had already fled.

Suddenly, two more riders in leathers turn their mounts from the melee and begin to gallop toward the pond, heading eastward and almost directly in front of Lorn and the half squad that rides behind him. As the pair sees the small squad, they veer more toward Lorn's right, trying to ride between the lancers and the frozen pond.

Lorn turns the mare nearly due north and urges her into a

gallop, half aware that Nytral and the other ten riders have fallen back momentarily.

As they race eastward, the two raiders lean forward in their saddles, yet manage to draw long blades that glisten like order death, even while spurring their mounts toward the low embankment that forms the south side of the pond. Lorn leans forward, giving the mare her head.

Both raiders rein up, and seeing the single lancer officer, turn and charge Lorn.

With a cold smile, Lorn reins up the mare. By the time she has halted, the raiders are less than a hundred cubits from him, and closing rapidly. He pulls his own firelance from the holder and levels it at the left rider of the pair.

Hssst! The reddish-white chaos-bolt bisects the barbarian chest-high.

Hssst! The second bolt takes the right shoulder and the head of the second raider.

The two raider mounts slow to a walk, as if hampered by the limp figures slumping in their saddles.

". . . order dung!"

". . . never seen an officer do that . . ."

Lorn hears the comments, but keeps the lance leveled for a few moments longer before flicking the fire stud to the safety position and replacing the weapon in its holder. The acrid and metallic scent of chaos fills his nostrils for a moment, then is carried off by a gust of cold wind. He turns the mare slowly as Nytral and the rest of the squad rein up. "Have someone get those mounts."

"Ah . . . yes, ser." The senior squad leader gestures. "Get the mounts!"

"Yes, ser!"

Nytral's face is stiff, not quite pale, as he looks at his undercaptain. "Ser . . . that must 'a been a good hundred cubits."

"More like seventy." Lorn knows his smile is lopsided, knows that he should have waited until the riders were closer. "Might have been a bit lucky."

". . . once . . . luck . . . not twice . . ."

Nytral's eyes go to the lancer whose voice had carried, and the eight lancers all close their mouths. The remaining two are farther east, leading back two riderless mounts.

Lorn looks to the northeast, where the flashes of firelances have died away. He gestures toward Nytral. "Let's make sure everything's right with Dubrez and Shofirg."

"Follow the undercaptain!" Nytral orders.

Lorn lets the mare walk evenly back eastward along the southern side of the pond.

Dubrez and his squad are formed up at the northeast end of the iced-over pond. Shofirg and the half squad he had taken have already joined with Dubrez's squad, and Shofirg offers a head bow to Lorn as the undercaptain nears. Lorn returns the gesture. After searching the dead raiders, several lancers mount hurriedly, without looking in Lorn's direction.

One lancer's saddle is empty—or rather two lancers are strapping a lancer's body across it. Two other lancers are tying seven mounts into a tieline of sorts. Three other mounts are loping northward, the steam of their breath lost against the frosted brown of the hills.

"Stopped 'em all, ser. Fought like black angels, but did 'em no good." Dubrez gestures. "Got some mounts, too. Leastwise, good for cart horses or the knackers."

"I imagine the sub-majer will decide that," Lorn says. "You did a good job."

"What we're here to do, ser." Dubrez pauses. "Any come your way, ser?"

"Just two," Lorn answers. "We stopped them. You and your men did the hard work." He gestures toward the southwest. "Let's head back to the homestead there and join up with the Third Company."

"Yes, ser."

"Four abreast!" orders Nytral.

"Column by fours!" echo Shofirg and Dubrez.

"Captured mounts to the rear," adds Nytral.

For a time, the only sounds are those of the mounts' heavy breathing and their hoofs on the frozen ground.

"Are the raiders always like that in the winter?" asks Lorn.

"Pretty much, ser," answers Nytral. "They'll run if they can, and fight if they can't. In the spring and summer, they fight. Don't ever seem to run then."

Lorn nods, his eyes searching the area to the west, but the slight rise beyond the holding blocks any view of the Fifth Company, and there are no flashes that would indicate the use of firelances.

As they ride westward, past the dike and the end of the stock pond—if that is what it is—Lorn studies the buildings of the holding. The door of the house hangs crookedly on one iron strap hinge, and a single figure in gray lies beside the door. Lorn cannot tell whether the corpse is a man or a woman. Another dark-haired figure lies on a bale of hay beside the barn door. That figure is of a girl, one not yet a woman, all clothes ripped off her. Lorn swallows as he sees the slash across her throat. He swallows again.

As they reach the west side of the holding, beyond the barn, Lorn can see over the rise where the Third Company has formed up. Zandrey's lancers are walking their mounts toward the holding and Lorn's company.

As the captain sees Lorn and his company, Zandrey gestures for the Fifth Company to halt.

"Halt them," Lorn tiredly tells Nytral.

"Company halt!" orders Nytral.

"Squad halt," echo Shofirg and Dubrez.

Zandrey rides up toward Lorn, and Lorn continues toward the captain. Both officers rein up with less than a score of cubits between their mounts.

Lorn's eyes are flat, cold, as he waits for the senior officer to speak.

"Good job!" booms Zandrey. "Not a one got away. Most of the time, we can't do that with one company, and some escape."

Lorn nods.

"You did just the right thing in charging them toward us," Zandrey continues. "Too bad about the peasant holders, but if we'd have charged before you got down the hill, most of the raiders would have escaped."

The wind whines, and the chill drops around Lorn. He glances up to see that, sometime during the fighting, the sun has dropped behind the hills to the west, and the cold of winter in the Grass Hills had returned.

"We'll overnight here," Zandrey says. "Barn's big enough for the men, and the dwelling for us and the squad leaders."

Lorn nods, unwilling to speak for the moment, his thoughts on the dark-haired, dead herder girl not that much younger than his own sister Myryan . . . and the charge that Zandrey had never considered making.

XXVI

IN THE DIMNESS of his cold quarters, under the flame of a single lamp, Lorn sits on the edge of the narrow bed, holding a green-silvered book, marvelling at the clarity of the angled characters that date back to the founders. The cover remains pristine, unmarked, its silver shifting from one faint shade of green to another as he turns it in his hands. With all he has had to learn, and the tiredness that comes from that and seemingly endless riding, he has read little. He looks at the back cover, but it too is untouched by time.

Yet the slim volume is missing two pages, and Lorn suspects that one would have been a title page and the other would have born the name of the writer, for there are no inscriptions anywhere within it that say when the book was written or for what purpose or by whom. There are no numbers, no strange cursives or codes. There are just the poems, and no one in Cyad writes poems, not publicly, not that Lorn knows. And no one has in generations, at least not poems shared beyond a family or a lover, and not that there is any restriction on writing them. It is just not done.

His lips curl. Just as it is not written that a student mage who is not properly reverential shall not become a full mage.

He fingers the pages of the book again. He can scarcely

see where the cuts had been made to remove the pages, and the material of each page seems stronger than shimmercloth. No knife he knows would cut such tough material so cleanly. But the pages have been removed.

He opens the volume, almost at random. He has promised to read it, every page. He knows Ryalth must have had a reason, a reason well beyond sentiment, for though she has feelings, those emotions will not betray her.

He reads the words on the page before him once. Somehow, unspoken, they are not satisfactory. He murmurs them softly as he reads them again.

> Although the old lands are in my heart,
> in towers that anchored life with certain art,
> in eyes that will not again see bold
> the hills of Angloria or surf at Winterhold,
> I greet the coming evening, and the night,
> proud purple from the strange and setting sun
> and the towered ragged course that I have run,
> towers yet that hold the chaos of life,
> and struggle with order's unending strife,
> for endless may they hold our light
> against the long and coming night.
>
> Worlds change, I'm told,
> mirror silver to heavy gold,
> and the new becomes the old,
> with the way the story's told.

Lorn shakes his head. The words, or most of them, are familiar, but hint at a meaning beyond the obvious. Yet Ryalth had asked a question when she had given him the book. What were the Firstborn like?

Will the volume in his hands tell Lorn that?

The lancer undercaptain slowly closes the ancient yet ageless volume. He will read more. In time. He has years at Isahl. Years.

XXVII

DESPITE THE CLEAR green-blue sky, and a bright sun nearly at its noon zenith, the winter wind whistles out of the northeast, chilling Lorn's cheeks and ears, driving through the light earflaps on his white winter garrison cap. A faint dusting of snow lies scattered on bare patches of ground beyond the shoulder of the road and on the brown grass that stretches toward the lonely single hut and barn to the south of the road that is less than a narrow cart track.

The hoofs of the lancers' mounts clunk faintly on the frozen clay of the road that stretches northeast past the single stead toward a gap between two hills. Beyond those hills, according to Nytral and the maps, lies another valley, one where three families raise black-wooled sheep and some few field crops.

Using his chaos senses, Lorn practices listening to the comments of the lancers in the first company behind him.

". . . winter patrols . . ."

". . . lot of riding . . . last eightday . . . first raiders all winter . . ."

". . . probably the last, too . . ."

". . . like that last winter . . . two bunches all winter . . . turned and rode away."

". . . let the undercaptain hear that . . . or the sub-majer . . . be riding every patrol till you hit the Steps."

". . . lancers don't hit the Steps to Paradise . . . get buried under 'em . . . Drext . . . even the officers."

"Specially the officers." A low laugh follows.

Nytral, riding beside Lorn for the moment, turns in the saddle, and the murmurs die away. The only sounds are the low whistle of the wind, the *whuffing* of mounts, and the dull clumping of hoofs on the frozen road.

Lorn smiles at Nytral. "Officers are the ones who send them out on winter patrols."

"You hear more than most officers, ser. That'd not be always good."

"So long as I know what they think, and so long as I listen to you and my own judgment, knowing what they think is better than not knowing."

Nytral frowns momentarily.

One of the lancers earlier sent forward as a scout reappears on the road leading to the gap in the hills, but he rides southeast toward the Fifth Company with the measured pace that indicates he has found nothing disturbing ahead. Since the patrol is but Lorn's second alone, the undercaptain is perfectly willing not to be riding into trouble with barbarian raiders.

"Looks good, ser," observes Nytral.

"That's fine."

The scout turns his mount to ride beside Lorn, and Nytral guides his mount to the scout's right.

"What did you find?" Lorn asks.

"Road's clear to the holding in the next valley, sers," the lancer reports. "No hoofprints on the road or the grass. Herders are out some, one or two, anyways."

"Good," grunts Nytral. "What about fires . . . cookfires?"

"Fires from most of the chimneys, maybe all. Could smell something cooking."

Both Lorn and Nytral nod, nearly simultaneously.

Once the column, rising two abreast on the frozen road, reaches the low crest that overlooks the next valley, Lorn again studies the valley, trying to fix the details in his mind, hoping that he can, and knowing that the more he can retain, the better the chances for his success and survival over the years ahead. On a slight rise in the middle of the valley are dwellings clustered together and surrounded by an earthen dike tall enough to seem high from where the company rides nearly three kays away. The whitish smoke from the chimneys is blown into a low line that stretches from the northeast to the southwest.

"Cold as a trader's heart at tariff time it be, ser," offers Dubrez, riding behind Lorn and to his left.

"Or a lancer's blade in winter?" asks Lorn.

"Colder 'n a *good* lancer's blade, ser."

Nytral laughs once.

Lorn merely nods.

Below the crest, the road turns more directly eastward, and they travel another kay before they begin to near the earthworks in the center of the elongated oval valley. The earthworks are not insubstantial for a small holding, rising a good six cubits above the level ground, and close to nine above the base of the shallow ditch on the outer side of the earthen wall.

"It wouldn't be easy for the barbarians to get over that," Lorn observes.

"Easy enough to climb, but the old man here was an archer for the Mirror Foot years back. Taught his kin."

"So the barbarians could climb over, but they'd have to leave mounts behind, and a handful of men and women with bows could pick off most of them?"

"Don't know as most, ser, but raiding parties are not often more than two or three score, five maybe sometimes, and they'd lose maybe a score, and get little enough . . . some sheep, a woman or two, maybe a young girl, and some flour and maize, and fewer mounts than they'd lose in a raid."

A single herder stands by the open gate on the west end of the earthworks, apparently the sole means of entry to the holding. The herder beckons toward the gate, and Lorn and Nytral guide their mounts toward the man in the sheepskin jacket and leather trousers.

"Might as well bring your patrol inside the dike, sers," calls the herder.

"Thank you," Lorn responds. As he rides through the open, but narrow, timbered gate, Lorn notes the huge pile of rocks on the top of the earthworks, and the chutes that would funnel those rocks behind the gate. He shakes his head at the amount of effort behind the herders' defenses.

The single visible herd of sheep is clustered in a corral beside a long and low, sod-walled barn, and the corral is well inside the earthen dike that protects the holding. The man who has beckoned them also wears a bulky hat with heavy earflaps that Lorn momentarily envies. The local lumbers toward them as Lorn and Nytral—and the Fifth Company—rein up and wait.

"Greetings there, sers!" calls the herder. "Leastwise, you picked a sunny day to visit Ram's End."

"Greetings," Lorn returns.

"Hear tell that there were raiders west 'a here . . ." The white-bearded herder looks at Lorn but briefly, then drops his eyes.

"There were," Lorn admits. "They killed everyone in a holding. We caught and killed them all."

"All?"

"Every last one, and the undercaptain killed two himself," snaps Nytral.

The herder shivers, a gesture visible despite his heavy coat and hat. "Come spring, their kin'll ride for blood."

"They ride for blood anyway," Nytral points out, a harsh laugh following his words. "This springtime, there'll be fewer riding."

"Fewer raiders are always better for us—specially for the herds."

"They pick off animals?"

"Last time they came into the dike, they lost near-on a score. We lost not a soul." The herder shrugs. "Be five years back or so. Figure they'll be forgetting afore too long."

"Their memories aren't that long," Nytral agrees.

Lorn glances at the lancers of his company, sensing their cold and impatience, then looks directly at the herder, waiting.

As he receives the long searching glance of the undercaptain, the white-bearded herder clears his throat, once, twice, before finally speaking. "Sers . . . we be a poor folk not to offer . . . but . . . we be not wealthy, either. But bread and some mutton stew we could spare for you and your men."

Lorn glances at Nytral, catching the minute nod. "We would welcome that, but only what you can spare." He pauses, then adds, "and perhaps the use of your barn to let them warm themselves before we ride on."

"Might as have to take turns, sers . . . with two score mounts. . . ." The herder offers a crooked grin. "But seeing as we're glad to have a patrol now and again. . . ."

"And you'd like us to come back a lot more in the spring?" Lorn grins.

The herder grins back. "Can't say as any of us'd mind such."

"We'll accept your hospitality, herder—but only for a bit." Lorn nods to Nytral.

"First squad . . . you'll eat and warm first! Shofirg, have 'em follow the herder! Second squad . . ."

Lorn remains in the saddle, waiting to eat and warm himself with Dubrez's squad. His eyes look to the frozen hills that barely seem to rise above the earthworks of Ram's End, the Grass Hills that shelter all too many barbarians, he fears.

XXVIII

LORN SITS AT the corner desk in the officers' study, the one in the northwest corner—where the chill and the wind seep in around the high window overhead and plummet down to make it the coldest spot in the room. Even the low fire, fed by both dried dung and the peat dug by the lancers on disciplinary duty, fails to lift all the chill out of the study.

The undercaptain reads over the words of his last report, ignoring the drafty chill at his back and upon his neck, wanting to ensure that Overcaptain Chyorst and Sub-Majer Brevyl will have little to criticize—or at least as little as Lorn can manage.

. . . The valleys to the west of Ram's End showed no sign of raiders, and the people there had not reported seeing any barbarians in the past four eightdays . . .

. . . Two mounts were lamed from being ridden

and slipping on the icy surface of the road beyond
Eryutn . . .

Lorn looks down at the words again and frowns, then
glances at the notes he had jotted down at the end of each
day of patroling. There should be more to report, but he can
think of nothing, nothing to convey the chill and the empty
kays that had followed one after another as the Fifth Company has ridden patrol after patrol for the past four eightdays.
One raid more than five eightdays before, and empty roads
and empty hills ever since.

As the chill of a screeing glass sweeps over him, Lorn
freezes momentarily, then looks at the report he holds once
more, studying it until the unseen inner chill passes. That
chill is clearly not felt by any but him, and certainly not by
the three captains clustered around the next desk, sharing
several bottles of wine that one has brought back from his
midwinter furlough—a luxury Lorn will not see until after
his first complete year at Isahl.

Lorn half-hears their words as he looks up from the last
words of the report that will go to Sub-Majer Brevyl in the
morning.

". . . that double patrol put a stop to their raids . . ."

". . . can't do double patrols all the time . . . too many areas
don't get covered, and they'll know it. . . ." The squat and
swarthy captain who replies to Zandrey's observation is Jostyn, an officer Lorn knows only from the officers' dining
hall.

"Barbarians know too much," suggests Eghyr, a blond and
rail-thin captain who always has a smile on his lips, but seldom in his eyes.

"They just watch, and when we go one way, they go the
other." Zandrey takes a small sip from the goblet, still nearly
half full for all that the three have been drinking ever since
dinner.

"Lorn!" calls Jostyn, lifting a hand and beckoning to the
undercaptain. "You can't write reports all night. Have a glass
with us. . . ."

"We'd like you to share some of this Alafraan," adds Zan-drey more temperately. "We don't get it that often, and it'll spoil by the time I get back from patrol."

"You could leave it for us," counters Jostyn. "Warm us up with the coldest part of the winter yet to come."

"Not the coldest," corrects Eghyr. "The longest, but not the coldest."

Lorn sets the report face down on his desk and pulls his chair over to the corner of the desk where the three are seated.

"Lorn will enjoy his first glass more than you'll enjoy your fifth," says Zandrey with a laugh, pouring a goblet he has produced from somewhere half-full and handing it to the undercaptain.

"Thank you." Lorn takes the goblet with a smile, lifts it in salute to the three and takes a very small swallow. The amber wine tastes warmer than it is, with a hint of both pearapples and trilia . . . and something else that he cannot identify. "It's good."

"Far better than what we usually get," comments Eghyr, "thanks to Zandrey."

"My uncle's a vintner in Escadr."

"If this is his wine, he is very good." Lorn has never heard of Escadr, and he had thought he knew nearly every town in Cyador.

"He is good, even if no one's heard of Escadr. It's a tiny little town south and east of Biehl—not all that far from the rugged part of the Grass Hills way to the northwest," explains Zandrey. "And I tell everyone that because no one's ever heard of it."

"He said the same thing when he offered the first bottle," interjects Eghyr.

Lorn nods and takes a second, smaller sip. The Alafraan is indeed excellent, far too good for a Lancer outpost at the base of the Grass Hills.

"City lancers never appreciate a bottle of Alafraan," mumbles Jostyn, cradling his goblet. "Don't know what it is to ride a Patrol through the Grass Hills—or watch the white walls of the Accursed Forest for some giant stun lizard or cat big enough to cross the wards and take cattle or sheep."

"You haven't patrolled the Accursed Forest." Eghyr laughs gently, but coldly.

"Sasym did. Saw both."

"He probably did, but he wasn't much good with a lance, and that's . . ." Zandrey breaks off his comment with a shrug.

"You stay here for even a year, and you'll never be a city lancer again," says Jostyn, nodding toward Lorn. "All of 'em in Cyad . . . just city lancers."

"Not all," observes Eghyr. "Captain-Commander Luss'alt and Majer-Commander Rynst'alt served in every Grass Hills and Accursed Forest post."

Lorn does not ask how Eghyr knows, but resolves to be most careful around the blond captain.

"Maybe that's why they're where they are," suggests Zandrey.

Eghyr casts a quick glance at the stocky Zandrey.

Zandrey's brown eyes reveal nothing as he lifts his goblet for another sip of the Alafraan, a swallow that seems far larger than it is.

"That's the big secret, you know," adds Jostyn, his words even more slurred. "Most lancer officers are city lancers . . . never spent any real time on the borders, never seen a barbarian across the shimmer of a blade. . . ."

Lorn nods, but his eyes and attention are on Eghyr and Zandrey.

XXIX

THE EMPRESS RYENYEL affixes the silver clips to her thick and dark red hair, hair too coarse by the standards of Cyad had any one seen it closely or dared to comment upon it. She studies her freckled visage in the shimmering cupridium mirror set in its silver stand upon the glistening marble vanity before straightening. The half-length mirror reveals a figure somewhat too full to be called imperially slim.

She turns and walks from her robing chamber into the salon where the Emperor waits, standing before the long white divan in his silver audience robes.

His eyes flicker appreciatively from her to the divan.

She laughs. "I doubt we have the moments for that, my dear, but I thank you for an expression dearer than words."

The slightest flush suffuses his face, then fades. "Would that there were more such moments, Ryenyel."

"I would wish such, also." She pauses. "You appear most impressive, dear one. As always. What audience awaits you this afternoon?"

The light wind that brings the early and warm spring air into the Palace of Light whispers through the half-open window, bringing the renewed fragrances of trilia and aramyd, and the Emperor Toziel glances past his consort toward the tinted panes of that eastern window, the one overlooking the Quarter of the Magi'i. His eyes focus on the chaos- and age-whitened granite buildings, and he shakes his head ever so slightly. "I must—we must—again review the conditions of trade with Hamor and Austra, and the pirate-traders of Hydlen and Lydiar. I have asked Chyenfel for greater particulars about his . . . project . . . but particulars seem to turn to smoke when I inquire." Toziel laughs ruefully.

"I take it that Rynst and Chyenfel still maneuver over the firelance that never was, and attempt to discover who might be the current Hand," the Empress murmurs as she steps forward and kisses her consort softly on his left cheek.

"Or if the incident was caused by a renegade magus unreported by the Magi'i." Toziel chuckles. "Come . . . I need you to listen to the latest innuendos and veiled threats."

"After these years of my accompanying you, one would think he would know my modest role or who the Hand might be. . . ." the Empress begins.

"He doubtless must, but it is best not to mention the name, my dear. Chyenfel can use a chaos glass to see where he is not, and he reads lips, and others may as well."

"I doubt he is *that* accurate, love. He does not ever talk

about the chaos glasses and their accuracy, and he would do so if he dared." A quirky smile appears on Ryenyel's lips.

"It is to his benefit, and ours, not to say aloud what his glass may show." Toziel steps toward the door that leads to the private corridor that will take them to the audience chamber, holding it for her.

"So gallant . . . yet." Her smile is warm and affectionate.

"I am merely the Emperor. Chyenfel and Rynst are the gallant ones, striving to save Cyador from enemies without and within."

"And Chyenfel will present his facts most carefully. . . ." A smile crosses Ryenyel's generous mouth. "Then Rynst will ask a few gentle but revealing questions, and Bluoyal will look at each densely, as if their words make no sense."

Toziel smiles at his consort. "That is why you accompany me, and why the Hand must remain in the shadows, for I need you both."

Their feet barely seem to brush the polished white stones of the corridor as they glide toward the audience chamber, preceded by a pair of Palace Guards and followed by a second pair. All four guards carry small firelances and, since they are not Mirror Lancers, wear green uniforms edged in silver trim.

The door opens as the Emperor and his consort approach the Lesser Audience Hall, then closes behind them. Toziel gracefully takes the sculpted malachite and silver chair on the dais, while Ryenyel seats herself in a silvered chair a pace back and to his right. The marble floor of the audience hall glistens in the light that pours down from the high oval windows.

The three advisors wait—the gray-haired Rynst, Majer-Commander of the Mirror Lancers; the almost-delicate, but steel-willed and sun-eyed Chyenfel, High Lector and First Magus; and the heavy-eyed and ponderous Bluoyal, First Merchanter.

Toziel nods, then speaks. "Have each of you finished your investigations surrounding last fall's murder of the outland trader?" The Emperor looks at Chyenfel.

"An investigation cannot be termed complete without a resolution," offers the High Lector. "The weapon and its wielder have not been located. The loss to the Treasury from having to purchase goods from the Austrans has amounted to more than a thousand golds in less than a full season."

"That would be a significant loss over time, it is true, were it to continue," muses the Emperor, his fingers brushing his chin.

"Most significant," agrees Chyenfel.

"What words might you add, Majer-Commander?" Toziel tilts his head toward the head of the Mirror Lancers.

"Every chaos weapon in the armory has been accounted for—and so has every *Lancer* who has ever carried one in Cyad, Your Mightiness." Rynst smiles. "Unlike every Magus."

Ignoring the faint emphasis on the word "Lancer," the Emperor of Light straightens in the malachite and silver chair.

"Ah . . ." Bluoyal clears his throat gently.

"Yes, Merchanter Advisor Bluoyal?" The Emperor's baritone is clear, mildly inquisitive.

"Ah . . ." Bluoyal extends a scroll. "I have taken the liberty of making my own inquiries, and I trust that you will find them helpful in considering the most sagacious advice of the First Magus and the Majer-Commander of Mirror Lancers."

Neither Rynst nor Chyenfel looks at the older merchanter.

Toziel lets the guard at his left hand take the scroll, which passes quietly to the Empress, then lets his eyes fix on each of his principal advisors in turn before speaking. "It would seem that further investigations are unlikely to result in farther progress." Toziel smiles broadly. "Should any new *facts* appear, I will hear them gladly, but it would appear that after all these seasons, the murder of the outland trader should be laid at the hands of unknown assailants, perhaps smugglers or other outland traders jealous of this Aljak's initial success in Cyad."

"Sire . . . that casts much disrepute upon the merchanters and the harbor guards," suggests Bluoyal.

"Then let none say anything, and should anything appear,

why then, we will know who sharpens his blade." Toziel lifts both hands theatrically. "Enough." He looks at the First Magus. "High Lector Chyenfel . . . how goes the effort with the Accursed Forest?"

"As we have informed you, we have created a replica of the sleep barrier—a small forest far to the north where the method has been tried and met with great success."

"Except you do not know how long those wards will hold." Toziel frowns, then erases the expression as if it had not been.

"That is true. But we have near-on a half-score of years of observation, and the barrier yet holds. We dare not wait until the other chaos towers begin to fail, not when so much is at stake, Your Mightiness."

"That may be." Toziel offers a nod that does not convey agreement.

Chyenfel does not speak, but replies with a head bow.

"What of the shipyards, Rynst?" Toziel's eyes turn to the sabre-slender Majer-Commander.

"We cannot replace the fireships, your Mightiness, but we are about to build a sailing vessel, based on the material from the archives, which is speedier than all others upon the Great Western Ocean, and we feel that we can build similar vessels if you find the need pressing, sire. The use of cammabark as a cannon propellant appears promising. . . ."

"You had mentioned these matters before. Is there anything new? Or any unforeseen problem?"

"Ah . . . such vessels are not inexpensive. . . ."

"They will cost more than you had told me, and armed versions will not protect our trading vessels as well as the fireships do. Thus, we will need more ships, and the tariffs on the merchanter clans will be greater, and the profits lower . . . and few are pleased with the prospects. Is that what you meant, Rynst?" asks the Emperor.

"Yes, Your Mightiness."

Toziel glances at the heavy-set Bluoyal. "Are my surmises about trade correct?"

"Ah . . . I would judge so, Your Mightiness."

"More lancers will be needed as ship marines," suggests Rynst.

"Requiring more golds," adds Chyenfel.

"Perhaps each of you could provide estimates in an eight-day . . . or two," suggests the Emperor Toziel. "I would prefer that you not discuss those estimates with each other."

"Yes, ser." Chyenfel agrees quickly.

"As you command," adds Rynst.

"As you require," concludes Bluoyal.

Toziel stands, and the three advisors bow. Then the Emperor and his consort depart, Ryenyel remaining a half-pace behind Toziel until they have left the audience chamber and until the door has closed behind them. They return silently to the Empress's salon.

There, the two sit side by side on the white divan. Toziel's hand caresses his consort's neck, and then her shoulders.

She turns. "Chyenfel believes what he tells you, my dear."

"That is worrisome. I would rather that he did not."

"You would have him lie?" she asks.

"No. I know he deceives, but when he does not lie, I cannot tell where he deceives."

"That is true, and they will all start rumors, except Rynst, and his truths will be taken as rumors."

He laughs sardonically. "Of course. But it will be interesting to see exactly what kind of rumors each creates."

Ryenyel offers a tired shrug, then massages her forehead with her right hand.

"I am sorry. Audiences such as that are hard for you," he offers.

"They are hard on you, too." She leans her head against his shoulder. "Each knows something, and should each know what the others do . . ."

"Hush . . ."

"That is why there is an Emperor, and yet each would replace you, and each would fail, and why yet we search."

"You are kind, I fear."

She shakes her head, even as it rests against his shoulder. "I am not kind, for I help you to do what no other can do, and we both suffer."

He turns so that his arms enfold her . . . gently.

XXX

LORN STANDS IN his stirrups, trying to stretch his legs while the mare travels a section of road that is damp but appears firm. The early spring or late winter wind carries alternating gusts of chill and warmth past the undercaptain, but everything is brown—the grass, the road itself, the hills to the south and north. The puddles in the road are muddy brown.

The mare's forelegs are coated with brown from the mud of the road, and even the lower parts of Lorn's once–cream–colored trousers are splattered with the mud that remains cold and greasy despite the clear and bright mid-morning sun.

"One time when riding the fields be faster . . ." The words drift forward from one of the lancers in Shofirg's company, carrying on a light gust of wind to Nytral and Lorn.

Nytral shakes his head. "The fields be like the great swamps below the Accursed Forest. You take a mount there, and he'd be in over his fetlocks, then hock deep afore you know it. The barbarians know it, and we'll not be seeing them for another eightday."

"So we're the mud patrol? To see when the ground firms up and when they're likely to begin their attacks?" Lorn's eyebrows arch as he asks the question.

"Aye. That be why the Fifth Company rides now."

"To save the others for the first attacks . . . that makes a sense of sorts." After all, Brevyl had told Lorn that he'd be handed nasty jobs, but not more than he could handle, and a mud patrol certainly fits the description of nasty and within his capabilities.

At Lorn's open and humorous laugh, Nytral looks quiz-zically at his superior.

"It's about what Sub-Majer Brevyl promised," Lorn says. "He does keep his word. You have to admit that."

"Be times we all wish he'd not, ser."

"Probably."

Lorn's eyes drop to a single sprig of green in a muddy patch a half-dozen cubits off the shoulder on the north side of the road. There is but the faintest hint of red within the center of the tight-curled wild-flower.

"Blood-drop," he murmurs to himself, looking to the northern hills that conceal the barbarians beyond.

XXXI

IN THE LATE afternoon, before dinner, Lorn sits at the corner table in the officers' study, his fingers carefully clasping the bronze pen whose nib will bend too easily should he exert too much pressure. He dips the pen into the inkstand and continues the scroll to Ryalth, ignoring the chill in the room where the heat from the always-inadequate but long dead fire has much earlier died away.

> . . . have not received a scroll from you lately, but I hope that is from either oversight or the lack of interest in my stilted writing, and that you are well and pros-pering in your trade. If you have any spare coins, a few might go to copper futures on the exchange . . . only a few, though.

He half-smiles, half-frowns, his eyes going to the folio of maps set by his left elbow. He should be studying those maps, for he knows his understanding of the terrain he pa-trols is still not instinctive—and it should be, for the time will come when he will not have the luxury of looking at a map.

He purses his lips and continues with the scroll.

. . . most presumptuous of a lancer to offer mercantile advice to a merchanter, but you know I have never
lacked presumption.

. . . our patrol schedule is being increased now that
spring is about to arrive in the Grass Hills . . . and I may
be the one with little ability to write or to have my
missives sent southward to you. . . . You would be
pleased to know that I have heeded your advice about
reading, and have taken care with that with which you
entrusted me.

After affixing the closing and his signature, Lorn folds the
letter flat, then glances around the still-empty study. With no
one near, he holds the stick of green seal wax over the paper
edges and focuses the slightest flare of chaos he has drawn
from around him on the tip of the wax. Almost as the droplet
of green wax strikes the paper, Lorn presses his seal ring to
it.

"Much easier . . ." murmurs to himself.

He still must write Myryan, a task he always postpones
because he is still unsure whether his words to his father
about Ciesrt will have made any lasting impact. Since he has
received but a single scroll from his younger sister, and that
far too many eightdays ago, he worries.

Finally, he takes a smaller section of paper, then gently
cleans the bronze nib of his pen. He looks at the blank paper,
then pauses.

Chyorst—the sole overcaptain at Isahl—walks into the officers' study, surveying the entire room before his eyes come
to rest upon Lorn. The overcaptain turns towards the junior
officer, deliberatively.

Lorn slips the pen and paper under the folio of maps and
stands as the overcaptain walks toward him.

"Maps?" Chyorst's eyebrows lift.

"Yes, ser. I try to match them with what I've patrolled
and study where I may be assigned."

Chyorst nods. "Can't hurt. Might help so long as you remember that maps are only an incomplete representation of

what's out there." The overcaptain looks around the study once more before asking, "Have you seen Jostyn, undercaptain?"

"No, ser. Not since last night."

"Thank you." Without another word, the overcaptain steps away from Lorn, and then leaves the officers' study.

Lorn waits for a time before he returns to his letters.

XXXII

AFTER ENTERING THE square tower that holds the sub-majer's study, removing his winter jacket and brushing the dampness from the oiled white leather, Lorn hangs it on one of the pegs on the wall rack set forward of Kielt's table.

"Go ahead, ser," says the senior squad leader. "He's waiting."

"Thank you, Kielt." With a nod to the lancer ranker, Lorn opens the white oak door and steps into the oblong room on the first floor of the square tower. As usual, Sub-Majer Brevyl looks up from the table desk with the hard green eyes that are half-bemused, half-impatient. The sub-majer's thick white hair has been trimmed shorter than normal, shorter even than that of a new lancer recruit. He motions for Lorn to take one of the armless chairs facing him.

Although the late afternoon is cloudy, with the indirect light from the high windows weak, only one of the lamps in the pair of wall sconces is lit, and the single lamp does little to dispel the gloom. Sleet patters on the glass of the windows, briefly.

Lorn eases himself into the proffered chair, then waits for his whip-thin commanding officer to speak.

"Undercaptain," says the sub-majer dryly, "your next patrols will be the most dangerous for some time."

"Ser?" Lorn eases forward in the chair, knowing that reaction is exactly the opposite of what Brevyl intends.

"It's simple. You've survived a raid or two. You're beginning to know the land and your men and squad leaders, and it's almost spring. You think you know something." The white-haired officer barely pauses. "Don't you?"

"More than when I came, but I have more to learn, ser." Lorn can sense that an answer of some sort is required.

"So much more that you might as well say you still know nothing. If you think the winter patrols were nasty, you don't know what a tough patrol is. If you thought freezing to and from Ram's End was disagreeable . . ." Brevyl shakes his head. "In another eightday, the barbarians will begin their spring raids. Everyone has been telling you how tough that will be, but I'd wager that no one has told you why. Do you know why?"

"No, ser."

"Because a raider's life isn't worth dung until he's killed three lancers—or more. He can't take a woman from his own clan—they do know about inbreeding—and he can't take a woman from another clan without those kills. So he has to kill lancers to get laid, because their women are property, and playing around with a proven warrior's daughter could cost him his personal jewels or his life. And if he takes a Cyadoran woman, she's fair game to be stolen or raped by any blooded warrior. Same thing if he takes a woman from one of those dirty hamlets or villages they call towns."

Lorn nods slowly.

"Their women aren't any great prizes, and the few good ones go to the proven warriors or the young ones crazy enough to take on a Mirror Lancer company . . . or smart enough to get away with it." Bervyl shakes his head. "All you are is an obstacle in the way of some young barbarian buck's crotch-ambitions, a game counter to add to the stack so he can stop having damp dreams and start in on the real thing."

"You make it sound like they don't think life is worth much, ser." Lorn says quietly.

"Until a barbarian gets to be a full-blooded warrior, it isn't," Brevyl replies dryly. "I tell this to every young undercaptain who comes through. They all hear me out, and then more than half of them die in their first spring or summer." A snort follows a brief pause. "I don't care about the stupid ones dying. Better that way than letting them grow up and getting entire outposts all killed off. But stupid officers can kill good lancers, and good lancers are getting hard to come by these days."

"Yes, ser."

Brevyl draws a deep breath.

The mannerism is deliberate. Lorn can't imagine Brevyl being that dramatic naturally. The undercaptain waits for the next verbal riposte.

"One other thing . . . Undercaptain."

Despite his resolve, Lorn stiffens ever so slightly within himself.

"No lancer officer with magus blood leaves Isahl until I say he does, just like none leave the Geliendra outpost until Maran says he does. No lancer with magus blood gets to be a majer until we both let him go on, not that there have ever been many of you." Brevyl smiles. "Tomorrow, you're headed east. The attacks are later there, and the raider bands smaller. Plan on being out an eightday, and being attacked twice. At least. So be careful how you use your firelances."

Lorn nods respectfully.

Brevyl stands to dismiss the undercaptain. "Just *try* to remember half what I told you, and you'll live longer and save more of your lancers. And they're the ones who will keep you alive." Brevyl inclines his head toward the study door.

"Thank you, ser."

"Don't thank me, Undercaptain. Just remember."

Lorn leaves the study, nodding to Kielt as he closes the door behind him. He takes his jacket and dons it before walking from the square tower out to the courtyard and into the sleet that has returned to pelt roofs, stones, and lancers alike.

XXXIII

IN THE COLD sun of late morning, the brown grass stretches unmarked for at least three kays in every direction from the narrow road on which Lorn and Nytral ride eastward. Nearly two kays ahead of them are two scouts, large black dots on the brown line of the road that slowly climbs the long swell that is not steep enough to be a ridge or hill. Behind Nytral and Lorn ride the two squads of the Fifth Company.

"Still another ten kays to Pregyn," Nytral says.

The senior squad leader's words are barely audible above the impacts of hoofs on the road and the rising whistling of the wind that sweeps southward across the fields that only hold last year's browned and flattened grass. With the wind comes the odor of vegetation that has molded, frozen, and thawed—an acrid scent, sour but slightly sweet.

"The maps show that the road's flat. Is it?" asks Lorn. He has never been northeast of this unnamed valley, let alone to Pregyn, a hamlet a good forty kays to the north of Isahl and the northernmost and most isolated of the communities south of the Grass Hills to claim allegiance to Cyad and the Emperor.

"Most ways. The climb out of Four-Holders—next valley—is steeper than the way in, but it's flat after that, boglike until you get to the real hills that border the Westhorns."

At the crest of the hill, Lorn slows his mount and studies the long and sinuous valley that holds four families—a clan structure almost, Lorn suspects, from the layout of the holdings with their multiple dwellings and community stock barns. Each holding has an earthen berm around its buildings and stock pens—earthen because trees are far too scarce and more valuable for shade or fruit or windbreaks than for timber.

In the depression on the northern side of the valley, a kay from where the Fifth Company descends the hill, there are

long parallel trenches. Lorn nods—peatworks. The two
scouts have now almost ridden to a point on the road abreast
of the peat diggings, although the road is more than a kay
south of the boggy depression, and little more than a thin
lane winds over the rolling grasslands from the main road to
the bog.

Slightly flattened by the wind, trails of smoke rise from
the chimneys of all four holdings. A good sign, reflects the
undercaptain.

"Not real friendly-like here," cautions Nytral about the
time when they reach the beginning of the valley floor and
the road turns more to the northeast, angling across the long
and curving valley.

"Any reason?"

"Say we don't come here enough, let 'em take the barbarian attacks by themselves."

Lorn nods, but does not comment.

As the Fifth Company nears the first earthen berm, the
wind gusts around Lorn, mixing warmer damp air with
cooler swirls. Lorn's nose wrinkles, then relaxes, as he sniffs
the smoke—burning peat—an odor far better than that of the
dung burned in many holds.

There is a gate in the first earthen dike. Less than two
hundred cubits from the right side of the road, it stands half-
open, with a bearded figure in a sheepskin jacket waiting.

"Shofirg!" orders Nytral. "Send up four lancers."

Lorn and Nytral follow the four lancers up the rutted road
toward the gate, where all six rein up twenty cubits back
from the holder.

"We'd be welcoming you, and your company of lancers,
ser," offers the holder. "Don't have much, ser, but you'd be
welcome to the water and to stand down and rest."

Nytral eases his mount past the holder and partway
through the gate. After a moment of studying the area, he
turns in the saddle and nods curtly to Lorn.

"We thank you," Lorn tells the bearded man, who inclines
his head briefly to the undercaptain.

"Two abreast!" Nytral orders. "Straight to the troughs. In formation, by squads."

Lorn guides the white mare through the gate and to the north side where he and Nytral watch as the lancers ride past them.

The ground inside the four-cubit-high embankment is earth churned by sheep and cattle, dark frozen mud that will turn into oozing slop within eightdays, if not sooner. The odor of manure permeates the air, mixing with the sweet-smoky odor of burning peat. The doors to the sod-walled stock barn beyond the water trough are closed and barred, although Lorn can hear the lowing of cattle.

"Water by half-squads! You be starting, Dubrcz!" Nytral orders, his words ringing across the holding.

After the first squad has watered and remounted, Lorn waters his mare before Shofirg's squad while Nytral watches. The young officer then watches as Nytral rides his mount to the trough.

The holder now steps nearer to where Lorn sits astride the mare.

"Have you seen any trace of the barbarians lately?" Lorn asks the local.

"Little early for raiders," says the redbearded figure. "Bogs on the north side still show ice. . . ."

Lorn takes in the man's words, not understanding the exact importance of when the ice might melt as a predictor, but understanding fully the herder's feeling about its accuracy. "Have they ever attacked before the ice melts?"

"One time I recall, ser . . . be the year afore the last."

Nytral remounts and guides his mount back beside Lorn's.

"Would that we'd be able to offer more, ser. . . ." The holder's voice is almost pleading.

Lorn understands the plea, but were he to pay, even a few coppers, for every watering or every meal offered to his company, his purse would be empty well before the end of each patrol. Worse, the holders would come to expect it, and Lorn knows where that would lead. "I would that you could, too, holder. I would that I could offer you some poor recompense." He smiles. "Perhaps we will be able to remove some barbarians."

"You do that . . . and you be doing more than most in these days." The herder inclines his head, slightly.

The last of Shofirg's men remounts, and the younger of the two squad leaders turns his mount toward Lorn and Nytral. "All the mounts have been watered, sers."

Lorn leans forward in the saddle, toward the herder. "Thank you." Then he nods to Nytral.

"Ride out, by squads, two abreast." While Nytral does not yell or shout, his voice carries throughout the holding—and well beyond the earthen dike, Lorn suspects.

Although it nears mid-day when the Fifth Company is clear of the holding wall and fully on the road northeast, the light wind is but fractionally warmer, still a mixture of warmer and cooler air. The road itself remains frozen except for a few muddy spots where small bumps face directly south and trickles of water ooze from the raised and thawing ground.

Neither Nytral nor Lorn speaks until the company is well beyond the first of the four holdings in the valley.

"They don't think we've done much," Lorn observes.

"The Lancers never do as much as anyone wants, ser. Specially out here. Might be different if the Emperor . . . if His Mightiness'd ever been a real lancer. Or if we had more lancers. Never enough lancers, never have been, I been thinking. . . ."

"No." Lorn frowns. Nytral's speculations are not good for the sub-officer's future, not with anyone besides Lorn.

"Best not be thinking what can't be."

"That's probably a good idea," Lorn agrees. "There are only so many firewagons and so many lancers, and there's not much we can do about it."

For a time, they ride without speaking.

Herders from the other three holdings do not appear as the Fifth Company nears, and passes, their earth dikes. Nor are their gates opened.

By mid-afternoon, the Fifth Company nears the eastern

end of the winding valley, a valley empty of all herders and herds—except those within the earthen dikes that they have since passed. The scouts have ridden out of sight over the top of the hill, and the column of riders, two abreast, starts up the gentle incline.

Lorn glances up at the sound of hoofs. Two scouts spur their mounts down the road from the crest of the low pass that leads out of the Four-Holders Valley and toward the next valley, that of the Burned-Out-Stead.

"Frig!" mutters Nytral under his breath. "Frigging raiders . . ."

"Halt!" Lorn raises his arm, then gestures downward. Behind him, the riders of the company rein up.

Lorn and Nytral wait for the scouts, both scanning the road behind the scouts, as well as the brown grass and the few scattered bushes with their handfuls of gray winter leaves. Nothing moves except the lancer scouts.

"Raiders, sers! They're riding up the far side, almost half-way to the crest." The words burst forth from the younger scout before he has even fully reined in.

"A good four score. Could be more," adds the older scout.

Lorn turns in the saddle. Behind them, less than a hundred cubits back, is a low depression, and west of that a slight swell.

Nytral's eyes follow Lorn's. "Best we can do, ser."

"We'd better do it, then."

"Column back to the rise, Shofirg!" Nytral orders.

"Squad two back to the rise, Dubrez!" Lorn's voice, seemingly less penetrating than Nytral's, carries to the second squad.

Dubrez nods and replies. "Second squad to the rise!"

Lorn turns the mare, and the others follow his lead, until the Fifth Company has reformed on the highest ground nearby, in a single long line, slightly convex, that for all its apparent length will still be flanked on both ends by four-score barbarian raiders.

"We'll let them come to us," Lorn decides.

"Not reined up, ser?" Nytral's voice holds a slight edge.

"No . . . but we won't charge until they're hitting the dip in the ground there."

"Won't slow 'em much."

"Will anything?" Lorn raises his eyebrows, then pushes back the once white garrison cap.

Nytral laughs, not quite hollowly.

In the colder afternoon wind, each moment seems longer than the one that preceded it, and the hillside and road that lead out of the valley remain empty.

"They were riding up, sers," insists the younger scout, although neither Nytral nor Lorn has even looked toward the lancer. "They were."

"They'll be here," Nytral says. "This time of year they don't turn back."

Lorn surveys the line of lancers once more, then checks his own firelance. He can feel the chaos stored within it— red and golden white. His eyes flick from the Fifth Company to the hill above and then back to the lancers.

One moment, the hill is empty. The next finds mounted figures riding down toward the Mirror Lancers.

"Lances ready!" Nytral orders.

Forty lancers pull their three-cubit-long white firelances from holders and level them, waiting for the raiders to close, for Lorn's command to charge, and for the inevitable order to discharge chaos.

Lorn looks at the sweep of riders—five score, if not more, arrayed in a loose formation no more than three deep. Unlike the mounts of the barbarian bands he has encountered earlier, these horses bear no saddlebags or gear stowed behind the saddle—not that he can see. The riders carry long blades, blades bared to the sun, each weapon a half blade longer than Lorn's own sabre. Even across the half-kay that separates the two groups, the raiders' bared iron blades shimmer with the ugliness of death-ordered iron.

The undercaptain forces himself to wait, to measure the closing distance. He moistens his lips, watching, as the riders loom larger, bearded men bearing long blades, surrounded by another sort of chaos—the chaos of blood-lust?

As the raiders near the uphill depression, charging toward the Fifth Company, yells and unintelligible battle cries suddenly burst forth and spill across the brown grass of the gentle slope that has slowed them not at all.

"Now!" snaps Lorn.

"Forward! Forward and discharge at will!" orders Nytral. "Discharge at will!"

The Mirror Lancers of the Fifth Company move forward, ponderously, slowly at first, but when the two forces are less than a hundred cubits from each other, the Lancers are moving almost as fast as the barbarians.

". . . Slay the white demons!"

". . . Death to the demons!"

Other calls fill the air, but all are from the barbarians.

Abruptly, the barbarian line changes—gaps appearing here and there. But the gaps are not so much gaps as the result of groups of three barbarians charging toward a single lancer.

Hssstt! Hssst! . . . With less than fifty cubits between the leading barbarians and the lancers, golden-white chaos bolts flare from the firelances.

Lorn holds back on using his lance, though he rides forward toward the raiders, and finds himself leading the fray.

Five riders are swinging toward him as he finally lifts his lance, and triggers it. *Hssst! Hsstt! Hsstt!* . . . Not all the bursts strike barbarians, and he ducks and throws himself sideways and under one of the swinging iron bars that promises death if it strikes him full.

Then, gasping, he finds the mare has brought him through and beyond the barbarian line—practically alone. A good forty cubits to his right, Nytral has emerged, and the squad leader charges back toward the mix of men tangled with each other.

Lorn wheels the mare and rides back—more deliberately, his eyes flicking across the field. Less than twenty cubits before him, a barbarian lifts, not a long and unwieldy hand-and-half blade, but something like a sabre somewhat more curved than that of a lancer. The barbarian ducks as he nears the melee, and starts to slash across the unprotected left side of a lancer.

Hssstt! Lorn flicks a short bolt of chaos from the lance into the barbarian's back, then urges the mare toward the next group of fighters, men hacking at each other, silvery cupridium blades against the order-death-infused, edged iron bars of the attackers. Absently, Lorn wishes he could use a sabre as well in his left hand as in his right.

Hsstt! The chaos transfixes another bearded barbarian.

Two more barbarian riders turn their mounts, then, inexplicably, ride toward a group skirmish to Lorn's left. Lorn follows them, picking off the laggard with his lance. He wonders how long the chaos charge will last, careful as he has been. He can sense that a goodly fraction remains yet.

A single wavering yell echoes across the afternoon, and a good three score riders ride across the hillside, not back the way they had come but toward the hills on the northern edge of Four-Holders Valley. Beside and around the road, the Fifth Company finds itself without attackers, except those that have fallen.

Lorn takes a long deep breath, feeling sweat cooling on his forehead and the back of his neck. He counts quickly. There are six Mirror Lancers lying on the brown grass, and he can see blood on the winter jackets of half a dozen more. He hopes some of that blood is not that of the lancers. Close to a half-score barbarian mounts are without riders, and more than a score of dead or dying raiders lie sprawled or crumpled in the trampled brown grass.

The light, cold wind cannot carry away the odors of blood and death, not all of them, nor the odor of damp dead grass churned up by more than a hundred horses.

Lorn walks his mount back to where the barbarian with the odd-looking sabre has fallen. He dismounts and reclaims the blade and the scabbard, fastening them behind his saddle. Then he remounts and rides back to where Nytral is reforming the company. No one has noticed his efforts.

"Squad leaders. Report," Nytral orders as Shofirg and Dubrez ease their mounts to a halt opposite Lorn.

Shofirg's winter jacket is slashed open across his left shoulder, and blood smears the oiled white leather. "Lost four lancers, five wounded. Eight lances with chaos charges left," replies Shofirg.

"Two lancers gone, three wounded. Eleven lances . . . most are low, though," adds Dubrez.

"Use the barbarian mounts for the blades and any shields they left. You know what to do with our dead."

"Sers . . ." both squad leaders incline their heads, then turn their mounts, heading back to their squads.

"Have they done that before?" Lorn asks after a moment. "Sending three men after a single lancer?"

Nytral frowns. "Hadn't seen that."

"They did," Lorn assures the senior squad leader. "That's why there were gaps in their attack to begin with. They figured out that a lancer has to concentrate on a single attacker at a time."

"Didn't look that different," replies Nytral. "Could be they've been doing it for a while." He pauses, then adds. "Lot more raiders in that party than most. Lot more."

"How many are there usually when they attack?"

"Most times, maybe a few more than a company."

"They had more than twice what we did," Lorn observes, then adds, "We're headed back. We've got only about two-thirds of a company, and not many chaos charges."

"They'll be back . . . afore sunset tomorrow," predicts Nytral. "Even if we head back. They'll follow."

"With more horsemen?" asks Lorn.

"No . . . They can't go back to the clan without wounds or trophies. The raiders rode off . . . they didn't get much."

"Will they try an ambush, you think?"

Nytral pulls at his chin. "Not so as you'd say that. Low light . . . some place where we'd not suspect . . . nor see . . . but no sneaking round . . . usually don't pick off scouts . . . can't count on that, though."

"We'll have to be careful, then." Lorn has been getting the feeling that there is little predictable about the barbarians except their desire to kill lancers—and their success in doing so despite the effect of the firelances. The antique sabre, still solid, and Brystan, he thinks, raises another set of questions, ones he will not voice, about how better blades, if older ones, are reaching the barbarians, and why no senior officers have mentioned the change.

Lorn'Alt, Isahl, Captain, Mirror Lancers

XXXIV

IN THE HOT air of late summer, his third summer in Isahl, Lorn shifts his weight in the saddle. Then he blots the sweat off his forehead with the back of his hand to keep it from running into his eyes. His hand comes away damp and slightly reddish from the road dust, and he is careful to wipe it on the square of cloth tied to his saddle. Even so, his cream uniform is streaked with pink from the dust, as are those of all the lancers in the Fifth Company.

To the west of the road that hugs the east side of the valley, the grasslands stretch almost four kays or more before another set of hills. The tips of the blades of grass, some of which would reach shoulder high on his mare, have already begun to brown.

Ahead to the north lies the Ram's End Valley, and beyond that one of the valleys with an abandoned and burned-out holding, one that had never been re-inhabited, Lorn suspects, because there are no streams in the small valley and but one meager spring. He wonders, not for the first time, why the Grass Hills are drier now than in distant years past when the first holders were sent forth from Syadtar.

He cocks his head slightly to better catch the murmurs drifting forward from lancers in the first squad.

". . . better Captain 'n most . . ."

". . . no great shakes . . . all we do is ride and get attacked . . . ride and get attacked. . . ."

". . . you want to chase barbarians all over the Grass Hills?"

Lorn represses a frown, then beckons to his senior squad leader.

The square-bearded and craggy-faced Dubrez eases his mount toward Lorn. He has been senior squad leader for over a year, ever since Nytral lost a leg to a barbarian blade and hobbled back to his home in Summerdock.

"I'm thinking we need a pair of scouts to look two or three valleys ahead—way ahead." Lorn turns in the saddle, as if to face Dubrez, and raises his voice so that it will carry back to the complaining lancers. "They might be able to find some barbarians so we don't have to ride quite so far."

"Yes, ser, Captain," Dubrez replies, a slight twinkle in his eye.

Lorn unsheathes his cupridium sabre, lifts it, and then studies the razorlike edge that can drive through the best of the barbarian blades. "I'm still thinking. I heard some of the men saying it might be a good idea."

The murmurs from the riders behind die away.

"Of course, we wouldn't be close enough to support them, not unless they were very careful and could get a start on the raiders." Lorn shrugs. "Wouldn't want them to get their throats slit so some barbarian can claim a woman."

"No, ser." Dubrez nods.

Both turn in their saddles and ride silently for perhaps half a kay before Dubrez speaks. "There's more complaining now."

Lorn nods. "There will be more."

"Not good, ser."

"We both know that."

The company remains still—or the murmurs low enough that Lorn cannot discern them even through his chaos senses—even after the lancers ride over the low pass and along the gentle ridge.

As the Fifth Company descends into the Ram's End valley, Lorn turns his attention to the holding, far closer to the south end of the valley and the route back to Isahl than the majority of holdings in the lower part of the Grass Hills. Most holders set their steads somewhere close to the center of the valley. Not so Ram's End.

Something bothers Lorn, and he keeps studying the holding as they near it. "What do you think, Dubrez?"

"Quiet . . . no one out, and it's near mid-day."

Lorn nods and keeps riding, watching.

Then, they reach the stream and the wide and shallow ford,

Lorn sees hoofprints—more than a mere handful, and as he looks toward the sod walls of the holding, he can sense that all is less than well. The gate is off its straps—that he can see from nearly a half-kay away—and, though it is almost mid-day, the line of smoke from the cookhouse chimney is but a thin gray line, as if from a dying cook fire.

The single small herd of black-faced sheep to the southwest of the gate are unattended—something that Lorn has never seen in three years—except in the aftermath of a barbarian attack. Lorn sees two silent shapes sprawled in the grass—a herder . . . and a long-haired sharp-muzzled black herding dog. Dark splotches stain the green and brown of the grass.

"Lances ready!" he snaps.

Dubrez turns in his saddle and echoes the command, an echo amplified by the individual squad leaders.

"Spread formation! Forward!" Lorn adds.

The Fifth Company reforms into a line abreast and rides toward the open hanging gate of the hold. The lancers cover but another hundred cubits before two sharp whistles pierce the noon air, and the sound of hoofs rises from within the sod walls of the hold. Then riders pour through the sundered gate, the first forming a rough wedge before the gate as if to allow those who follow to escape.

"Charge! Discharge at will!" Lorn orders. He spurs his mount, as do the Mirror Lancers behind him, trying to cut off the barbarians, or keep them trapped, against the sod wall.

A half-score of rough-clad riders gallop clear of the left flank of the Fifth Company, riding westward hard. The remaining twoscore raiders squeeze their mounts into a tight wedge that gallops toward the Fifth Company.

Hsst! Hssst! Two short bolts burst from Lorn's lance. One strikes a barbarian, and then Lorn is using both firelance and sabre to parry one heavy iron blade, and then another, before the mare carries him past the edge of the barbarian wedge, and he turns his mount.

"First squad! Shofirg! Turn about!" Lorn's orders rise above the flashing and hissing of the firelances. He follows his own orders and wheels the mare, charging toward the western flank of the barbarian wedge, guiding the mare past a grim-faced lancer, and then slashing his sabre left-handed across the neck of an unprepared barbarian who barely started to turn before the chaos-reinforced blade separates his head and torso.

Lorn swings away, more westerly, as perhaps a half score of the barbarians break through the Lancer's line, but the first squad, following Lorn's command, has already re-formed.

Hssst! Hssst! After a last few flashes of chaos, the fire-lances are discharged and silent, and cupridium blades ring against dark iron.

Lorn slows the mare, eyes studying the swirl of bearded barbarians with dark blades, and cream-clad lancers with bright sabres, ready to lend his blade, as necessary. A wide-eyed barbarian breaks clear of the fray, and turns his mount westward, as if to escape.

Lorn raises the firelance, calmly. *Hssst!*

The barbarian slumps in the saddle, then slides downward, one boot still caught in a stirrup, his weight and length dragging the mount to a halt.

A second raider pulls clear of the fray, and Lorn again aims his lance, letting a short burst of personally-raised chaos burn through the man's back.

Lorn waits, but no other raiders try to escape, and, as the last barbarian pitches out of his saddle, the clangor fades.

"To the hold!" snaps Lorn, moving the mare northward and through still-milling lancers. "The hold. Now!"

"The hold!" echoes Dubrez, and then Shofirg.

As Lorn rides in through the sagging gate, a bearded giant darts from the open door of the house, then lunges sideways and grabs a small figure—a dark-haired waif who, surprisingly, recalls Myryan to Lorn.

Lorn turns his mount and pulls the firelance from its holder, again—calling on the force beyond pure chaos, for he knows there is little of the stored chaos left in the weapon. He lets the mare walk slowly toward the barbarian.

There is blood on the trousers of the bearded man who holds the struggling girl before him, as a shield against what Lorn may do. "You lift that lance any more, demon, and I'll kill her!"

A line of whiteness streaks from the silvridium tip of the lance, a line so thin it is almost invisible.

The barbarian convulses as his face blisters into charcoal, then vanishes. The knife wavers, then falls from dead fingers, leaving a slash across the small girl's face, and the headless barbarian corpse pitches sideways.

The girl, suddenly released, staggers toward the still figure half-leaning, half-sprawled against the earth brick wall of the house.

". . . captain did it again . . ."

". . . hush . . ."

Lorn's eyes flick across the area of the holding inside the sod walls. One dark-haired, slightly heavy-set, young woman—the one the girl clings to, sobbing—had been flung against the ceramic screen that shields the front door of the farm house. Her neck is at an angle that shows it has been broken. The second girl, scarcely ten, continues to sob loudly, clutching the dead woman, perhaps an older sister.

Except for the lancers of the Fifth Company, nothing moves.

Is there sobbing from within the house?

"Dubrez . . . have someone watch the little girl . . . and check on anyone else here. No liberties with her! Or anyone else. None!" Lorn's voice cuts like the sabre at his side, and he gestures at the four nearest lancers. "You four! Follow me!"

He turns his mount westward, riding back out through the gate and turning westward to follow the barbarians who have ridden away from the road, and toward the nearest hill.

Two hundred cubits or so beyond the sod wall, he glances at the lancers who follow. The leading rider, the youngest, is white-faced.

Lorn smiles and returns his attention to the faint track of chaos that he follows through the high and browning grass.

More sweat drips from under the brow of the lightweight and white summer garrison cap, sweat that he blots away as they continue riding westward.

The lancers cover a kay through the browning late summer grass, then two kays. Lorn can sense that, as they reach the slightest of inclines leading toward a thin stream marked by young willows, the barbarians are not that far away, and he lets the mare slow her walk.

The half score of barbarians have watered their mounts and watch from their saddles as Lorn and the four Lancers ride toward them.

"Blades ready," Lorn says quietly. He knows the firelances of the four are without chaos charges. His fingers touch his lance, but do not grasp it, as he continues to ride forward.

"You will die, white demon," announces the broad-shouldered giant in the center of the ten barbarians. The man is doubtless two heads taller than Lorn, and four stones heavier, without a finger's worth of fat anywhere.

"Why do you kill the holders? They don't attack you." Lorn's voice is level, as he continues to let the mare walk slowly toward the barbarians.

"These lands were our lands in the time of our grandsires' grandsires. They will be ours again." The language is the guttural barbarian tongue only loosely related to Cyadoran or the Anglorian from which it came.

"Why did you kill the girl?" asks the captain.

"Women serve men. She would not serve us. Besides, she was white-spawn." The man laughs, mockingly.

Lorn lazily raises the light lance, seemingly without pointing it, then concentrates, as he sweeps it sideways. The thin line of chaos bisects the six barbarians in the center of the group—and their mounts—one after the other. The giant is still clutching for his immense blade as his upper torso crashes into the tall grass.

". . . dung-frig . . ." hisses a lancer behind Lorn.

The pairs untouched—two men at each end—look almost blankly as mounts scream and riders fall. Without pausing, Lorn turns the lance to the two at the south side.

Hsst! Hsst! With two almost-delicate bolts of chaos, two more barbarians fall.

After sheathing the firelance, almost automatically, Lorn turns his head to the remaining two raiders. "Go!" He forces the words out, fighting against dizziness, and a headache that threatens to cleave his skull in twain. "Tell your clan what happens to those who kill girls and women."

The two raiders glance at the slender Mirror Lancer captain and the four lancers who flank him.

"Tell them!" Lorn forces a cold laugh. "Brave warriors, tell them."

"Never!" The younger warrior raises his blade, order-death edged iron, and charges toward Lorn.

Despite the dizziness, Lorn draws his own shimmering cupridium blade, then spurs the mare, leaning forward, focusing into the blade that chaos he can draw from the air and land around him, and from the dead and dying.

Reddish white light flickers from the cupridium, seemingly lengthening the blade, until it is almost a lance.

The young barbarian's eyes widen. He tries to lever the bar-like greatsword toward Lorn more quickly, but he is too late, and the light fades from his eyes as the chaos lance flicks past the death-ordered iron. He spews from his saddle.

The older barbarian warrior has turned his mount and gallops northward.

Lorn clutches his saddle with his knees, barely hanging onto his sabre. His head rings as though it were a bell struck with an iron mallet, and knives of white pain lance through his eyes.

Slowly, ever so slowly, he eases the cupridium sabre back into its scabbard. Then his fingers close around the water bottle. Each movement is slow, deliberate, as he lifts the bottle to his lips and drinks.

Only then does he turn the mare back toward the wide-eyed and silent lancers who have ridden with him.

"Darkness, ser! Never seen a light lance do that," blurts the youngest.

Lorn offers a lazy smile over the anger boiling inside him,

a smile forced despite the dizziness and agony that he must
fight to stay mounted. "Do what?"

". . . ah . . . what you did, ser."

The shrug is an effort, but Lorn makes it seem effortless.
"I killed some barbarians. That's what we're here for. Gather
the good mounts and follow me." Ignoring the moans from
one bearded figure lying on flattened grass, a man who will
die shortly, Lorn turns his mount back eastward, back toward
the raided holding.

After a time, he can hear the mounts of his lancers as they
hurry to catch up with him. He does not look back until the
youngest lancer draws nearly abreast.

"Only got two mounts. One other lame—you killed the
others, ser."

"Two will be fine, Yubner." Lorn's voice is professional,
neither warm nor cold.

"Yes, ser."

Yubner drops back, and the murmurs begin, voices low
enough not to be heard, except by a lancer officer trained in
chaos use.

". . . ever see that . . ."

". . . more 'n once, Yubbie . . . more 'n once, and you'd
not be saying a thing outside the squad. Understand?"

". . . just . . . killed 'em . . . doesn't matter which hand
holds sabre. . . ."

". . . they'd do that to you, boy . . . done it to a lot of lancers . . . see those girls? Why you think we're out here?"

"But . . ."

". . . not a word . . . See how many a' us come back . . .
look at the other companies . . . Captain Jostyn . . . 'member
that?"

The murmurs die away as Lorn and the four near the gate
to the holding.

From his saddle, Dubrez studies Lorn as the five ride
slowly through the broken holding gate. The last two lancers
following Lorn each lead a barbarian mount. The senior
squad leader rides toward the captain, then reins up as Lorn
does.

Dubrez nods slowly, then announces, "Lost seven lancers, ser. Took down near-on two score, maybe more."

"There were ten who tried to get away. We killed nine," Lorn says flatly.

"Your lancers didn't have any chaos charges left in their lances," Dubrez murmurs quietly. "None of us did. They aren't charging the lances as much as they used to."

"That's why one got away," Lórn lies. "I didn't want to risk our men, and we did get all but him."

"Nine out of ten . . . can't outwager that." Dubrez laughs, once, harshly.

"Who survived among the holders?" Lorn asks.

"Two older women, two boys, one woman, and the girl. That's all, ser."

"They'll have to ride back with us, at least to some other holding, if not to Isahl."

Dubrez glances at the dead raider by the house, the one whose head Lorn had burned off. "We must have killed close to three score . . . and they'll be back in an eightday or a season—who knows—and we'll have to fight with less chaos in our lances."

"Maybe . . ." Lorn offers. "Can you get a few of those barbarian mounts for the holders? They can't stay here, and we might as well head back. Not much more that we can do here."

"True, ser." Dubrez's smile is grim. "Should be able to find six good mounts." He turns his mount. "Stynnet! You and Forlgyt get six gentle mounts. Holders'll ride out with us. We're headed back to Isahl, captain says."

"Yes, ser."

Dubrez nods to Lorn, then rides toward the stock barn, to let the animals out so that they will not starve until they can be claimed—or slaughtered by another barbarian band.

". . . three score, and he killed a score of 'em hisself . . ."

Lorn can only remember killing slightly more than a half score, but there is little point in protesting such. He has long since lost count of the barbarians he has killed. He slowly studies the holding, as if to note the details for the report he will have to write when he returns.

The girl Lorn saved freezes as his eyes sweep across her. Then she begins to tremble.

The Lancer captain maintains a cool smile and lets his eyes travel past the girl and back toward Dubrez. "Let me know when we're ready."

"Yes, ser."

Lorn unfastens his water bottle and takes a deep and long swallow, still ignoring the headache, the intermittent double vision, and the unseen hammer blows to his skull.

XXXV

TWO MEN STAND on the shaded east balcony of the third level of the Palace of Light, the balcony that is closest to the smaller audience hall preferred by the Emperor Toziel. The shade and the bare hint of a cool ocean breeze are not enough to keep a sheen of perspiration from their foreheads on one of the hottest of summer afternoons in many eightdays. The breeze dies away, and the air is so still that the harbor to the south and even the Great Western Ocean are shades of flat shimmering blue that offers no hints of whitecaps. The stillness and the heat keep any hint of the trilia blooms in the gardens below from rising to perfume the upper levels of the Palace.

One of the double doors that offers access to the balcony is slightly ajar, enough so that the two men can hear if the calling bell is being rung. In the corridor just inside the Palace, but a good ten cubits from the octagonal panes of the ten-paned doors, stand a pair of Mirror Lancers, each armed with both a rapier and a short firelance.

"You have not shown great enthusiasm for the plan of the First Magus to subdue the Accursed Forest," offers Luss'alt, the Mirror Lancer Captain-Commander, second in Lancer authority only to Rynst'alt.

"I have not, nor should you," replies Kharl'elth, the Second Magus, a red-haired figure in white shimmercloth. His green eyes bear but a hint of gold. "The First Magus plans for a future that may never be. He would turn the chaos towers that surround the Accursed Forest into the mists of time . . . and then trust that the three chaos towers of the Quarter will sustain us."

"They have for many generations," points out Luss evenly. "Rynst has said that the plan will imprison the Accursed Forest. Then there would be more Mirror Lancers to fight the barbarians."

"With fewer charges for their firelances, and fewer firewagons to carry supplies." Kharl shakes his head. "The Accursed Forest is the same as it has been always. Some of the great beasts escape. They kill a few peasants and some livestock. To stop a few such deaths over the generations ahead, Chyenfel would sacrifice years of chaos-charges for firelances and firewagons." The Second Magus studies Luss, then asks, "Have the barbarian attacks become fewer over the years?"

Luss returns the question with a crooked smile. "You well know that each year brings more attacks."

"The Mirror Engineers already send chaos-cells powered by the Forest towers to the Mirror Lancer outposts of the north. How will your lancers fare without such? Or if the firewagons can travel less frequently?"

"I have asked such of Rynst, and he but replies that eastern Cyador will fall, should the Accursed Forest slip its wards."

"None know that," Kharl points out. "Even in the first days of Cyad, the Accursed Forest did not even reach Kynstaar. Better to lose some lands, if need be, than to lose all of Cyador to the barbarians of the north, for they indeed would destroy all we and our forbearers have wrought."

"The Majer-Commander believes that the Mirror Lancers can hold the borders . . . even with few firelances." Luss shrugs. "We always have."

"Perhaps they can. Perhaps they can." Kharl smiles. "They

might require a few more officers . . . accomplished in other fashions."

Luss's face becomes impassive.

"Then it has been many generations . . . since one such rose through the ranks," offers the Second Magus.

"That is not even an acceptable jest," Luss replies coolly.

"There are rumors about the Majer-Commander. . . ."

"He is not, as well you know," Luss replies.

"Then . . . why does he encourage such as Captain Eghyr, or that offspring of a merchanter—Dymytri—or Senior Lector Kien'elth's son. . . ?"

"They are most useful in combat or in dealing with the problems of the Accursed Forest. Eghyr is most successful in killing barbarians, and young Lorn is also quite capable. . . ."

"I did not know. . . . You have not mentioned him in over a year," observes the Second Magus and Senior Lector. "I presume, then, he is still alive?"

"As you *should* know, Lorn'alt became a captain last year. He's in his third year at Isahl. That is one of the main Jeranyi attack points. Commander Thiataphi had orders to use him on the barbarian pursuit details."

"The mortality is . . . what . . . fifty percent?" asks Kharl'elth, carelessly wiping perspiration from his narrow forehead and angular and clean-shaven face with a white cloth.

"He is a young man of enormous skill and intelligence. The Majer-Commander is most impressed with the reports of his actions." Luss smiles. "He is rather good at killing barbarians, as well, and there are many to kill."

"You have named three brilliant lancers with possible elthage talents, and, if they survive, all could come back to Cyad. I was not aware that the Mirror Lancers encouraged such." Kharl'elth shakes his head ruefully. "The Majer-Commander might like that, but it would not be good for Cyador. Not now."

"Do not worry. There have been many such over the generations. If they survive their patrols against the barbarians, they will get patrol post commands on the edge of the Accursed Forest." Luss smiles. "And if they still show traces of elthage talents, and the ability that might earn a promotion, then, well . . . our friend Maran knows how to deal with a brilliant Lancer magus."

"I had thought so, but we of the Magi'i do have some concerns." Kharl offers a wry smile. "You always have matters so very well in hand, dear Luss."

The Captain-Commander frowns, then asks, "Why did Captain Lorn's father not become more than a senior lector?"

"Kien'elth is a most respected senior lector, and one of the most devoted of the Magi'i. He is a magus among Magi'i. As such, it is unlikely that he will live long enough to advise Captain Lorn, should the young captain avoid the fate you and Maran have planned. Most unfortunate, I dare say." Kharl's warm smile does not reach to his green eyes.

"None escape Maran," declares Luss. He blots his forehead. "Few days are as warm as today. Perhaps we should attend our superiors."

"*Few* escape Maran," corrects Kharl. "Thiataphi did, but he understands. Is it not true that he has requested that he receive a stipend before being considered for a position with the Majer-Commander in Cyad?"

Luss nods.

"How feels Rynst about the policy of . . . discouraging . . . lancer-magi'i?" inquires Kharl.

"Not strongly enough to oppose it. Not when all the senior Mirror Lancer officers support it," replies Luss. "What of the First Magus?"

"He is most opposed to any who might handle chaos outside the Quarter and the discipline of the Magi'i, and on that we are in full agreement. Full agreement." Kharl smiles. "Perhaps we should stand ready to attend the results of the audience."

Luss nods, once more, evenly.

XXXVI

AFTER A DINNER of heavy mutton, soft potatoes probably left from the harvest of almost a year earlier, and bread harder than some barbarian blades, Lorn has repaired to the officers' study, where, under the sunlight of a summer evening pouring through the high windows, he rereads his patrol report, then nods, and sets it aside to submit to Overcaptain Zandrey in the morning.

Then he lifts the first of the personal scrolls that had been awaiting him on his return from patrol—the one from Myryan. While he has hurried through it once, he needs to reread it. His eyes fix on the graceful letters.

> Dearest Lorn,
>
> It seems so long since I saw you, and it is, more than three years. . . .
>
> . . . have almost finished my training as a healer, and now I go to the lancers' infirmary every fourth day, and to the Healers' Indwelling every other day. . . . Healing is hard, but rewarding in its own way. Jerial said that a long time ago, but we get different rewards. An eightday ago, I received a healer's pin, but I don't know where it came from. I can't wear it yet, not until after the ceremony next sixday. It's beautiful, green lacquer over gold. A messenger brought it from Syang the goldsmith, but no one could say who had sent it, except that the purchase was arranged through a small merchanter house. It is all very strange, and I wish you could be here for the ceremony, but you won't even get this until I am truly a healer. . . .

Lorn pauses. His warm and waifish little sister—a healer. And the golden pin . . . he has his ideas about that, too, but they are but ideas without confirmation—yet.

Vernt is finally seeing someone. He won't tell anyone, except father, and I think father is the one who arranged it all.

. . . would have liked to have sent you a baked pearapple creamed tart, but they don't travel. I remember how you sneaked them from the kitchen, and once you brought me one. They tasted better that way. . . .

After he finishes Myryan's scroll, Lorn runs his hand through his short brown hair. What can he say? Finally, he picks up the bronze-nibbed pen and dips it, then slowly begins to write.

Your scroll was waiting when I came off patrol. I was glad to hear that you are finally a healer . . . like to tell you that I had something to do with the healer pin. I can't. I would have liked to, but I've never even seen a healer's pin. . . . Summer here is hot. It is hotter than Cyad, but drier . . . also would have liked that pearapple tart . . . miss things like that, but, mostly, I miss the family, and the way we talked, even with Father's long lectures. . . .

When he finishes his reply to Myryan, he picks up the second scroll—the one he had received just before the last patrol, the one from his father that he had not had time to answer before riding out to Ram's End, and the barbarian raid.

Lorn slowly unrolls it and rereads carefully, as if he had not seen it before.

. . . While I did heed your advice about Myryan's need to mature more, in the end, I have decided that her being consorted to Ciesrt is far better than any of the alternatives, and they will be joined by the time this reaches you. I do know of your concerns, and they are good ones, and I do not

write this to mollify you. All I ask is that you return to Cyad and see her before you judge too
harshly. . . . Vernt is well-respected and appreciated by the older Magi'i . . . am comforted to know
that you are now a captain. According to Luss'alt,
the first two years are the most dangerous, although
he says that any lancer's life is dangerous. . . .

The scroll continues, with pleasantries, and then concludes:

. . . I can see the patterns of the Rational Stars,
and some change and some do not, and some always shine brighter, no matter where in the heavens they swing.

Lorn purses his lips. His father has seldom talked of the
Rational Stars, and never written of them, for the Rational
Stars are the emperor's heritage, and not that of magus or
lancer. Then, there is the timing. Myryan's scroll had been
written later, yet it does not mention or even hint at Ciesrt.
Lorn had decided not to mention what she had not. Jerial
has not written at all. But that leaves the question of how
should he respond to his father? He takes another sheet and
once more dips the pen.

Father,
I am sorry that it has taken a while to write back,
but I have been on patrol and have just returned. . . .
. . . I appreciate your waiting to formalize a consortship between Myryan and Ciesrt'elth, and I will
follow your suggestions in that regard . . .

"Especially since there's nothing else I can do," Lorn murmurs under his breath, glancing around. "Not from here."
The young and pale blond undercaptain—Cyllt—enters
the study and takes the desk-table farthest from Lorn to seat

himself and peruse a single scroll. Beside the scroll Cyllt sets a nearly full bottle of the darker Byrdyn—not nearly so good as the amber Alafraan.

Lorn nods politely before dipping the pen in the inkwell and continuing his response.

> I have not mentioned consorting in my messages
> to Myryan, since she has not brought that up. . . .
> Patrolling takes special skills, and I have been
> lucky enough to serve with those who have been
> able to impart them to me. . . .
> I have been told that after three full years, I will
> have a half-season's home leave, whether I am to
> remain at Isahl or be posted elsewhere. What may
> be my next duty will be decided in the early fall,
> I would gather. . . .

He finally closes.

> . . . and I look forward to seeing you this winter.

Lorn has saved the scroll from Ryalth for last, for those are as infrequent as they are welcome, and he wishes to re-read it before replying. He notes again that the passage marks indicate it was sent from Fyrad, as are all her scrolls, and hence their infrequency, and after his earliest scrolls to her, has since dispatched his missives to the trading house address in Fyrad as well—a far wiser course, he suspects.

> My dear lancer captain,
> Your scrolls remain an unending surprise. This
> poor merchanter can scarce reply to your elegant
> words. I will not try. I will but say that the con-
> stancy which you never professed exceeds all that
> I have heard professed elsewhere.
> The Ryalor Trading House—

Lorn still winces at the name she had chosen, despite the

fact that he knows he provided most of the coins to give her the start.

> —continues to flourish, and we now have shares in three coasters and two long-haul ocean traders. Some of those shares are great enough so that before long, we could well own one or more. The long contracts in copper have prospered so much that I have resold one at enough of a profit that we could lose all on the other and still come out with coins.

He laughs to himself. She writes as though he knows truly what she has done.

> The word has been spread that my consort works the distant lands, and we know that is certainly true in some ways, if but for my unacknowledged merchanter partner . . . although I have accomplished some frivolities on his behalf.

Lorn's forehead wrinkles at the mention of frivolities, for all Ryalth's words carry messages between the lines, and that is probably wise. All he can do is wonder and shake his head. He is in Isahl, and Ryalth is in Cyad, and furloughs have allowed him only so far as Syadtar. He is a lancer officer, and she is a merchanter. He smiles. While a magus could not consort with a merchanter . . . it would be but a mere scandal if a lancer officer did.

At Lorn's self-mocking and ironic laugh, Cyllt glances toward Lorn, then quickly down at his scroll for a moment, before the undercaptain refills his heavy goblet with the Byrdyn.

> Ryalor House is consulted now and again by several Hamorian and Austran traders. It is almost as if it were one of the smaller clan houses. We are not that large, yet who ever would have imag-

ined that oil and cotton would have led so far?

I have engaged an enumerator. He is nothing to compare to the first. He is most polite, but he keeps calling me sire. He says it is habit. There are but two other houses and no clans headed by merchanter women. . . .

"Here comes the overcaptain," Cyllt murmurs.

Lorn slips Ryalth's scroll under those from his father and Myryan but does not move the report or the blank paper on which he will reply to Ryalth.

The brown-haired and stocky Zandrey glances at the heavy goblet beside Cyllt. "Wine can become too much of a friend here in Isahl."

"Yes, ser."

Lorn keeps his nod to himself, recalling Jostyn, who'd taken to carrying bottles in his saddlebags—first Alafraan and then the cheapest fermented fruit dregs—until the barbarians had caught him off-guard. For a time, Sub-Majer Brevyl had banned all wine in the study and at Isahl, to punish the officers for not letting Brevyl know that Jostyn was a danger.

"You knew," Brevyl had said to the remaining officers when he'd gathered them together. "You knew, and no one told me. Good lancers were killed, and that shouldn't have happened."

Besides the wine leaving Isahl—if but for a season—so had Overcaptain Chyorst, as a mere captain. And they'd later heard he'd died patroling the Accursed Forest, although his body had never been found.

"Ask Lorn there about what wine did to other officers," Zandrey says. "Or not, as you choose." His smile is mirthless, and he turns and walks toward Lorn.

Unlike Cyllt, Lorn stands, if easily. "Ser."

"Sit down, Lorn." Zandrey pulls out a chair.

Lorn re-seats himself.

"Nice patrol . . . Kielt talked to Dubrez," the overcaptain

says conversationally, although in a low voice. "Over three-score barbarians . . . that's a lot for Ram's End. I checked the old reports. There hasn't been a raiding party that large there in more than a score of years. Assyadt out west, yes, but not this far east and north."

Lorn lifts the report. "Would you like this? I just finished it."

The overcaptain shakes his head. "Drop it in my box in the morning. Did you notice anything different?"

"They formed a wedge to charge us. It wouldn't have worked as well if we had full lance charges."

"I got a scroll from Eghyr. He said they were doing that at Abyfel." Zandrey's lips form a crooked smile.

"He's the overcaptain for the west sector there, isn't he?"

"He is. He'll probably make sub-majer in another two years."

"He's very sharp," Lorn says.

"Not so sharp as you. You could be an overcaptain for one of Jeranyi sectors, Lorn," observes Zandrey. "Another two years and you'd be ready." A short laugh follows. "Two years after that, it might happen."

"That's what the younger sons of the Magi'i do, isn't it? Most of them? Before they die, I mean?" Lorn's words are gentle, almost flat.

"Those who aren't talented enough to become Magi'i or stupid enough to get killed by the barbarians," ripostes Zandrey. "Or who don't get too fresh with their overcaptains." The hint of laughter beneath his last words undercuts their seriousness.

"I don't think I'll be an overcaptain for a barbarian sector." Lorn's voice is languid, an ease of tone unmatched by the coldness in his amber eyes.

"You're meant for something." Zandrey shrugs as he stands. "Nothing ever seems to get to you." Then he grins. "Just remember the rest of us poor struggling lancer officers when it happens."

"If you'll do the same for me, ser." Lorn stands and returns the grin.

Cyllt's eyes harden as he glances from Zandrey to Lorn and then back at the departing overcaptain.

Lorn reseats himself to finish the scroll to Ryalth, which will be sent to a trader in Fyrad, from there to make its way to her through some indirect route of which he is totally unaware. His lips curl in a slight smile. That is to protect her, except that she was the one to arrange it, to protect him. As in this, as in everything in Cyador, little is as it seems, even under an emperor of the Rational Stars.

At the other table, Cyllt takes a long swallow of the Byrdyn.

XXXVII

THE HOT WIND blows out of the northwest, away from the raiders and directly into Lorn's eyes. He squints slightly as he looks along the low rise, easing his white mare along the side of the Fifth Company until he is barely forward of all the lancers, if on the flank.

The barbarians have formed into two wedges, almost a half a kay away. As Lorn watches, a series of yells echo through the afternoon air, and the two wedges begin to move, then to hurl themselves across the late summer grass at the Fifth and Second Companies. Dust rises over the brown-tipped grass that is but knee-high on a mount.

"Cyllt! First squad on the right wedge!" Lorn orders. "Dubrez, have Shofirg's squad support the Second Company."

"Yes, ser!" Dubrez answers.

"Yes, ser." The undercaptain's response lags Dubrez's.

Lorn slips his lance from the holder, keeping it low, and aiming it with his chaos-senses, at the knees of the horse that leads the left wedge of the raider attack.

Hssttt! The single line of chaos flame is brief, going unseen and unheard beneath the thunder of the sixscore barbarians who charge the Mirror Lancers. The horse goes down, and so close are those that follow that another four horses are tangled in the mass, slowing the entire left wedge. As the barbarians near, Lorn can make out clearly that most now bear polished iron shields, small round ovals that they raise to deflect the chaos bolts from firelances that no longer hold the power of years previous.

"Lances ready!" Dubrez orders. "Lances ready."

Lorn uses his lance covertly once more, for he draws chaos from where he can find it, not from the inadequate chaos charges within the lance haft. A second well-chosen mount topples, and more physical chaos snarls the left wedge of the charging barbarians.

"Now! Dubrez! Forward and discharge at will! Short bursts!"

"Forward! Short bursts!" orders the senior squad leader. "Short bursts!"

Hhsst! Hhsst! The short bolts of golden-white chaos drop many of those barbarians at the front of the wedges, but the mass of horses and riders strikes the advancing Mirror Lancer line, which slows and bends.

A barbarian, unbalanced by the weight of both shield and hand-and-a-half blade, slashes too wildly. Lorn's cupridium sabre flashes like a short stroke of lightning, and he is past the dying barbarian, driving the chaos-reinforced blade through another's shoulder.

Lorn senses another rider to his left, and twists his body out of the way of the unwieldy big blade, using a backswing to sever the attacker's neck from the back. He recovers in time to turn the mare and take down another raider from behind, then spurs his mount out of the center of the melee, using the sabre to weave a shimmering line of defense.

Once clear, he wheels the mare, then waits for a moment, before engaging a raider about to blindside a lancer tied up with one of the barbarian giants. Although the barbarian senses Lorn's approach, he is too late—and takes a deep slash across the shoulder. His big blade spins downward, and he tries to smash the iron shield across Lorn's sabre hand— his left—but that too is slow and late. The sabre slashes across the struggling barbarian's neck, and Lorn pulls clear of the swirl of barbarians and lancers, a swirl that suddenly separates into two forces once more.

Almost as quickly as it has begun, the skirmish is over, and Lorn watches as perhaps three score raiders ride northward. Several sway in their saddles.

Around Lorn rises the chaos of death and the stench of blood. He glances at his own sabre, smeared with blood. Dark splotches also decorate his left forearm, and dapple his trousers. He wipes the sabre clean with the cloth attached to his saddle, then sheaths it.

"Find the wounded first!" snaps Dubrez. "Dispatch any of the barbarians. They'd do worse to you." His words are directed at three of the newer lancers, for whom this has been the first or second barbarian attack.

Their sabres out, the three men walk slowly from fallen figure to fallen figure.

"One of ours, here."

Two other lancers appear with dressings, and the three continue onward through the bodies. Once a sabre flashes, but none of the three speak.

Ignoring the headache that comes with drawing chaos from the grasslands, Lorn lets the mare carry him slowly to a section of the trampled grass free of fallen mounts, or dead or dying lancers and barbarians. He takes a slow, deep breath, his eyes on the northwest part of the grassy ridge. The raiders are well out of sight beyond the first range of hills to the north.

Lorn turns his mount.

Dielbyn, the senior squad leader of the Second Company, rides slowly toward Lorn.

Lorn waits.

"The undercaptain . . . ser . . ."

"He fell," Lorn acknowledges. "Bravely." All officers die bravely.

"Yes, ser." Dielbyn's eyes do not look away from his captain's.

After a moment, Lorn nods, then asks, "How many in the Second Company can fight?"

"The second squad took most of the charge . . . six left there, ser. Ten from the first squad. Four of 'em won't be much good in a fight."

Lorn considers. The Second Company had been a half-score under strength before they had started the patrol. "Can the wounded ride?"

"Yes, ser. Slowlike. Except for Cymion. Won't last much longer, though."

Dubrez sits on his mount thirty cubits away, waiting.

"Get them ready to move out," Lorn says.

"Yes, ser."

After Dielbyn returns to reform the Second Company, Dubrez rides closer to Lorn before reining up. "Lost four, ser. All in Shofirg's squad. Three with wounds in Gylar's squad."

"Thank you." Lorn considers. After starting the patrol with thirty five lancers, the Fifth Company still numbers nearly a score and a half, but the Second has less than a score of lancers. Majer Brevyl will not be pleased with two companies returning, but two raider bands as large as the one the Fifth and Second Companies had vanquished would be unlikely, and if Lorn presses on, few if any of the wounded will survive. Lorn also knows that neither company will be soon reinforced, nor are fully recharged firelances likely to arrive to replace those discharged in fighting the barbarians.

Lorn's smile is fixed as he prepares to order the return to Isahl. Behind the smile, he wonders. How long can he continue to hold back barbarians with fewer men and firelances less fully charged? At times, he is already feeling that he can draw no more chaos for his own use without risking his own life.

XXXVIII

LORN REMAINS STANDING before the desk-table in the square tower, the late afternoon light from the high windows cascading around him, illuminating the dust motes that hang in the air, some of which seem to glitter with minuscule points of chaos. His eyes watch the newly promoted Majer.

". . . you destroyed three score, but lost more than a score yourself. Then you turned back without completing the patrol." Brevyl's voice is flat. So are his green eyes.

"Yes, ser."

"You could have pressed on," the Majer observes. "Others have. That is what lancers do, if you don't recall, Captain."

"Yes, ser, I could have." Lorn keeps his voice even, emotionless. "We would have lost all the wounded, and we wouldn't have seen any raiders. If you wish, ser, we'll return to patrol tomorrow."

"If any of your wounded survive, Captain." Brevyl pauses. "I liked you better when you were a polite and subservient undercaptain." The Majer snorts. "You're supposed to kill barbarians, Captain, not offer me reasons why you aren't."

"Yes, ser."

"You'll return the day after tomorrow. I'll transfer a half score from Zerl's company to yours. Not the Second. Combine both squads under Dielbyn and use them as a third squad. You can have a score of charged lances. That's all."

"Yes, ser." Lorn bows. "We'll be ready, ser."

"And Captain . . ."

"Yes, ser?"

"The Majer-Commander likes lancer officers who follow orders and die. He has little use for lancer officers who impose their own priorities."

"Yes, ser." Lorn meets Brevyl's eyes.

After a moment, Brevyl is the one to look away. "You may go, Captain."

Lorn bows again. He also inclines his head slightly to Kielt, the senior squad leader and the Majer's doorkeeper, on his way out of the tower.

He crosses the courtyard and turns northward toward the barracks.

Dubrez stands by the side of the barracks building as Lorn approaches. "Ser?"

Lorn smiles. "Tell the men they have tonight and tomorrow off. I'll talk to Dielbyn. The Majer is restructuring the

Second as a third squad of the Fifth. That will probably be until we get another officer and some reinforcements."

"That could be spring, ser," ventures the senior squad leader.

"It could be. It could be in a pair of eightdays, too." Lorn pauses. "Don't tell the men about the Second yet."

"No, ser. Best to let Dielbyn tell 'em." Dubrez's smile is ironic. "Won't hurt to have another squad, a full one."

"No. It won't." Lorn glances toward the stables, where he can see several lancers still grooming mounts, then back to Dubrez. "I'm going to the infirmary. Then I'll find Dielbyn."

"Yes, ser."

Lorn's boots barely whisper on the hard stones of the courtyard as he walks along the north side of the barracks. He steps through the untended and time-darkened white oak door. The infirmary consists of a long bay at the north end of the barracks, with a dozen pallet bunks on each side. In more than two years, Lorn has never seen more than a half score lancers in the infirmary, and he has used his healing talents secretly and sparingly, for the energy required is great, and he does not wish that talent known. What he plans is a somewhat greater risk, but if all the wounded die, he risks even greater displeasure from the Majer.

There are three lancers laid out in the infirmary bunks, lying in the alternate bunks on the south side. Lorn's eyes flick to the first man, almost sprawled on his back, his undertunic half ripped away from his chest. With each intermittent breath, the lancer gurgles, then shudders. His eyes are wide open, seeing nothing. The captain can sense the whitish red of chaos that envelops the man, chaos so raw and pervasive that Lorn knows the man will die within the day.

Slowly, Lorn walks past the dying man and an empty pallet to the third bed, where a stocky blond lancer is propped up with horsehair pillows, covered with a faded gray cotton cloth.

"Ser?" asks the lancer, who wears a wood and leather brace around his lower left leg.

"I wanted to see how you're doing, Eltak." Lorn offers a smile.

"Be all right, ser."

"I'm sure you will be." Lorn nods and leans forward, his fingers touching the brace. "It's not causing a sore, is it?"

"No, ser."

Lorn has to struggle to summon the smallest bit of dark order, so opposed to the flow of chaos, to squeeze away the clump of red chaos that lingers where the broken bones meet. He keeps smiling as he straightens. While the bone is set, and healing, and Eltak will recover, he will limp. "You'll be riding again in a season."

"Thought so, ser."

Lorn nods and moves past another empty pallet to the third lancer, where he stops. An angular young man with wiry black hair lies propped up with pillows, a dressing across his right shoulder. Lorn has to search his memory for the man's name, although the lancer is in Shofirg's squad. After a moment, Lorn asks, "How are you feeling, Stynnet?"

"Felt better, ser, and I'd feel even better iffn they'd let me go."

Lorn can sense the points of red chaos beneath the stitches and the dressing. While they are small, without a healer, they will grow until Stynnet will be dying like the older lancer in the first bed.

"You're not as well as you feel, lancer," Lorn says gently. "Close your eyes. Keep them closed until I tell you to open them."

"Ser?" Stynnet's forehead crinkles. His mouth opens as if to protest.

"If you want . . ." Lorn stops and fixes his eyes on Stynnet. "Lancer . . . don't argue. Just do it."

Stynnet swallows. "Yes, ser." He closes his eyes.

Lorn lets the tips of the fingers of his left hand rest lightly on Stynnet's skin just above the top edge of the dressing. Trying to call up what little he has learned from Myryan and Jerial, Lorn tries to let the black mist of order—the order-death of chaos, but a necessary one here—around the points of wound chaos he can sense, one point after another, until they vanish. They may return, but Stynnet's own chaos-order balance can cope by then—Lorn hopes. He straightens and takes a slow breath, not showing the momentary dizziness that swirls around and through him.

Stynnet's eyes are still closed.

"You can open your eyes, lancer."

"Ser . . . felt funny . . . what did you do?"

"Just offered some good thoughts. . . ." Lorn feels as though his smile is lopsided. "We want you back riding."

"Ser . . . ?"

"Yes?" Lorn waits, a more easy smile upon his lips.

"Nothing, ser." Stynnet does not conceal a slight frown.

"You'll be fine, Stynnet." Lorn nods and turns. He still has to break the news to Dielbyn about the lancers of the Second Company being attached to the Fifth. Then, he will ensure that the promised lances are indeed charged and ready—perhaps slightly more charged than Brevyl anticipates. How much of that he can do he is far from certain, and it will entail another splitting headache—in more ways than one.

Once more . . . he must balance what he can do with what he would choose to do. And without overtly revealing any more than he must to survive.

XXXIX

THE HARVEST SUN is barely peering above the eastern wall of the outpost at Isahl when Lorn slips silently through the time-stained white oak door and into the north barracks for another one of his unannounced inspections before a patrol.

He can hear voices from the bunks past the columns on his right which separate the marshalling area from the bunking spaces of the company's two squads. A slender brown-haired lancer walks past the columns barefooted, on his way to the jakes, Lorn suspects.

The lancer's head jerks up. "Ser?"

"Quiet, Yubner," Lorn murmurs, putting his index finger to his lips.

Yubner swallows.

Lorn smiles and motions for him to continue.

With a look back over his shoulder, Yubner hurries away, his bare feet slapping on the cool stone tiles of the barracks floor.

Lorn eases toward the square granite columns, listening as he does, recognizing the rough-edged voice.

". . . don't know what he did . . . don't care . . . they didn't think I was going to walk out of there. Gwinnt died. Eltak and I didn't. . . ."

"Maybe he's a black one. . . ." The words choked off, as if they had been stopped by Stynnet's angular hand around the other lancer's neck.

Lorn has to strain to make out the words hissed by Stynnet. "You say one word . . . and you'll end up with a lance in your back . . . I was dead . . . didn't know it . . . don't care if he's the head of the Black Angels . . . first one in line and stands behind his men . . . angel-damned few officers do . . . you hear me?"

"Ulp . . . hear you . . ."

Lorn steps back toward the barracks door, where he turns and waits for Yubner to return, or for another lancer.

Yubner returns before another lancer appears, walking far more cautiously, eyes surveying the open marshalling space between the two ends of the barracks. The south end is empty, since the Fourth Company had left on patrol the day before. Yubner glances apprehensively at his captain, but does not speak.

Lorn steps toward Yubner. "You can announce me, Yubner. Make it loud."

"Yes, ser." Yubner squares his shoulders. "Captain in the barracks! Captain in the barracks."

Boots scuffle. Several wooden foot chests shut, and the murmurs of various conversations die away as Lorn steps past the pillars. His voice is not loud, but carries. "Let's take a look at the gear you'll be using today."

Lancers stand beside their foot chests, waiting.

The barracks are standard. Each lancer has a pallet bunk, the head to the brick wall, the foot to the center, with the wooden uniform chest flush against the foot of the bed. On the wall beside each bunk are three pegs—one for the winter jacket, one for the uniform of the day, and one for the lancer's garrison cap. Each bunk set opposite another and is separated from those that flank it by six cubits. A single narrow window also separates each bunk from the next. The aisle between the foot chests is six cubits. The first squad bunks on the east wall, the second on the west wall.

At the third bunk on his left, Lorn pauses, sensing as much as seeing a spot on the hilt of a sabre. "Westy . . . show me the blade, if you would?"

"Yes, ser." The lancer swallows, but complies and lays the bare sabre out for Lorn to check.

Lorn studies the cupridium blade. "You're not getting it clean under the guard."

"Yes, ser."

The captain nods and continues down the aisle. At times, he barely glances at a lancer's pallet or gear. At other times, he stops.

"Would you open the foot chest, Sherzak?"

"Ah . . . yes, ser." The muscular lancer flushes, but lifts the top, to reveal uniform tunics neatly folded.

"And the tunics, too, if you would."

Under the trousers beneath the tunics are three bottles of Alafraan. Sherzak looks impassively at his captain.

"I could break them and have you clean up the mess," Lorn says mildly. "Or I could make you scout alone on patrol today." Lorn pauses, but not long enough for the lancer to speak. "But anything like that would hurt the Company and waste good wine. Take those to Kielt—right now—and tell him that I said they're to go in the strong room, along with other personal valuables, until you have furlough. It is valuable." Lorn's smile is wintry. "There won't be a next time, Sherzak. Is that clear?"

"Yes, ser."

Lorn nods and continues down the center of the barracks, then halts opposite a foot chest. "If you would open the chest, Skyr?"

"Yes, ser."

A muffled snicker comes from somewhere at the lancer's resigned tone, but Skyr lifts the lid.

"At the bottom . . . in the rear."

Skyr removes all the tunics and trousers and smallclothes. A slightly more curved sabre, another antique Brystan sabre, lies there in a worn dark brown scabbard.

Lorn lifts his eyebrows.

"Wanted a trophy, ser. I'm sorry, ser."

Lorn smiles, not unpleasantly. "Just turn it in to Kielt. After patrol. Less questions that way." He still wonders how the barbarians had obtained Brystan sabres, especially ones relatively new, like his, although the style of Lorn's is antique, as is that of the one picked up by Skyr.

"Yes, ser!"

Lorn stops one more time, at the next-to-last bunk on the right side, where he addresses a stocky red-haired lancer.

"Teikyl, have those boots resoled after this patrol, and tell the bootmaker to use the thicker leather this time. Tell him that I said that."

"Yes, ser."

Lorn nods and checks the last two bunks. When he is finished, he turns and walks slowly back up the center space between the bunks, his eyes meeting those of each lancer once more as he passes. He stops and turns just short of the pillars that form the barrier separating Fifth Company's space from the marshalling area. "You and your gear look good. Carry on."

Then he continues past the pillars and turns toward the door to the courtyard.

". . . never know when he'll show up . . ."

". . . just *knows* . . ."

Lorn pauses, as if to check the pointing on the bricks beside the doorway, letting his chaos senses try to pick up what Stynnet is saying to Yubner.

". . . he hear . . . ?"

". . . don't know . . . got that smile . . . told me to announce him. . . ."

Lorn steps through the doorway and into the faintly orange light of dawn.

Fifth Company has another patrol to ride, one that Lorn hopes will be uneventful, even as he prepares for it to be otherwise.

XL

LORN STEPS INTO the study in the square tower and glances toward the outpost commander. The darkness under the Majer's eyes is obvious for the first time Lorn can recall. Brevyl's face is almost gaunt, and his short bushy hair is thinner. The faintest hint of raspiness edges his voice as he gestures. "Take a seat, Captain." He lifts a scroll slightly, then sets it on the table-desk.

Lorn nods and settles into the armless wooden chair, his own eyes remaining on the white-haired majer.

"You're being ordered to the main outpost at Geliendra, Captain Lorn. You will command a company whose duty is to guard the ward-wall and to protect the Mirror Engineers. After home leave in Cyad." Brevyl snorts, lifting the order scroll from the desk again, before dropping it on the polished wood. His eyes flick to the doorway, as if to ensure that the white oak door is securely closed. "Stupid orders. Waste of training."

There is little Lorn can say. He says nothing, waiting for the majer's next words.

"I didn't like you, Captain, when you came here as a green undercaptain. Well . . . you're as good a captain as I've got, better than most I'll ever get, and I still don't like you." The majer leans forward. "That doesn't matter. I respect you. You work hard. Lancers all want to serve under you, and they follow your orders to the word. You kill more barbarians and lose fewer men than any officer I have. I have to respect all that. I don't have to like you."

Lorn nods slightly.

"You know that most of the senior officers in Cyad don't like Magi'i-trained lancer officers. Neither do the Magi'i. And they like the good ones even less. In a word, they're afraid of you. They have been afraid of men like you for the past four generations, ever since Alyiakal made himself emperor. They don't want it to happen again." Brevyl snorts. "It couldn't happen now, but they don't see that. If it did, it wouldn't last because the chaos towers won't last that much longer. What earthly good would a magus-born Emperor be without the chaos powers of the towers?"

The majer studies Lorn, then continues. "You didn't blink an eye at what I said. You knew all that before you came here. You said it didn't matter that they were twisting a splintered staff up your rectum. I've heard that before from others. All words." Brevyl leans back. "You believed those words, and you went out to learn how to kill barbarians and lead your men . . . and save them."

"Yes, ser. I tried."

Brevyl brushes away Lorn's words with his left hand. "So . . . now they'll send you to Geliendra, and if you're not careful, one night a stun lizard or a big cat will appear, and you'll disappear. No one will see the creature of the Accursed Forest, but you'll be gone." Brevyl's smile is harsh. "I don't like you, but sending you to Geliendra is a waste of a good captain when I don't get many. They'd rather see half of Cyador fall to the barbarians than risk another emperor like Alyiakal. They forget he was the best emperor in a century. All they recall is that he was a magus-born lancer." The majer laughs once more. "He was an emperor who didn't bow and scrape to the Magi'i . . . or ask the price of everything from his oh-so-dear-and-valued merchanter advisors."

Lorn has not heard more than offhand references by his father to the origins of the mighty Alyiakal, references that had prompted covert research in his sire's books. He waits, sensing that Brevyl has indeed told the truth in all of what he has said. Lorn hopes the majer may add more.

"That's all, Captain." Brevyl stands and extends the scroll. "You can leave tomorrow, or the day after, at your choice. You're off patrols, right now."

Lorn stands quickly, gracefully, and takes the scroll. He bows his head. "Yes, ser. Thank you for everything, ser."

"And, Captain?"

"Ser?"

"I never said anything except to give you your orders and wish you well with Majer Maran. He's very good at what he does."

"Yes, ser." Lorn bows again. "Yes, ser."

Brevyl watches, unblinking, as Lorn turns, then opens the aged white oak door that predates the emperor Alyiakal.

In the narrow corridor outside the majer's study, with the order scroll in his hand, Lorn nods at Kielt.

"Be wishing you a good trip and success, ser," offers the senior squad leader.

"Thank you, Kielt." Lorn walks slowly out of the square tower and into the gray fall afternoon. A light mist seeps down from the low-hanging clouds, leaving a glistening sheen of water on the stones of the outpost courtyard.

"Maran." Lorn murmurs the name to fix it in his mind. Brevyl had dropped the name advisedly, most advisedly. The question wasn't why so much as what he expected of Lorn— and Brevyl definitely expected something. Then, Brevyl had always been like that, never acknowledging the slightest possibility that Lorn might have some magely abilities. The Mirror Lancers were happy to benefit from those abilities, but would never acknowledge them in any positive way. That Lorn understands all too well.

After standing for several moments in the misty courtyard, Lorn begins to walk toward the officers' barracks.

XLI

LORN FOLDS THE heavy winter tunic and lays it on the bed next to the other uniforms he has folded before he will pack them in his kit bags.

As he lifts an undertunic, he catches a flash of greenish light and picks up the silver-covered volume. He flips through the pages he has not read recently. Had the ancient writer written aught about duty changes from a bad outpost to a worse one? His lips quirk as another question surfaces. Why is there no poetry written in Cyad? Lorn frowns. He cannot remember ever seeing a written poem before Ryalth— yet he had known what the verse had been. He stops at the one verse that catches his eye and reads softly, aloud, if barely.

> Do not ask me which carillon has rung
> or if the Forest's silent god has sung.
> Best you watch white granite towers,
> raised in pride, doze in the dusky sun
> until the altered green-bloody rivers run
> down to the coming night where chaos cowers.

Wondering how and why chaos could cower, Lorn still winces at the images, and riffles through the unmarked pages until he comes to a short verse standing by itself—about smiles. Perhaps . . .

He reads.

> Smiles are so fragile,
> like images on the pond of being,
> reflections only made possible
> by the black depths beneath.

What had been written is not exactly a poem, he reflects. Still . . . do not smiles hide depths no one wishes to see?

Poetry will not help with the Accursed Forest, nor speed him to Cyad and Ryalth. He closes the book, and slips it into the bag between his smallclothes.

XLII

IN THE ORANGE light of dawn at Syadtar, Lorn stands beside one of the fluted white columns supporting the sunstone portico that shelters travelers waiting for the firewagons which link the farflung cities of Cyador. The chaos-powered vehicles roll along the polished stone highways from warm and western Summerdock to the southern delta city of Fyrad, from Cyad to Syadtar, as they have for more than two centuries.

With the threat of the chaos-towers failing, Lorn had at first wondered why the use of firewagons was not curtailed— except that such would make no difference until a tower actually failed. He smiles, thinking about how Lector Abram'elth had let that slip.

In the cold morning breeze, Lorn stretches as he waits for the firewagon that will carry him back along the Great Northern Highway until it joins with the Great Eastern Highway, where he will transfer to another firewagon to carry him back home to Cyad. The two green canvas bags at his feet carry uniforms and little else, save the antique Brystan sabre, wrapped in his undertunics, and Ryalth's silver-covered book, in his smallclothes.

At the second set of columns, a good thirty cubits to Lorn's left, stand a half score of passengers who will be travelling in the rear compartment. Among the brown and gray tunics are the maroon cloak of a mastercrafter and a yellow cloak trimmed in purple. The woman wearing the yellow cloak is gray-haired and carries a leather instrument case, possibly a sitarlyn. Lorn is not sure of that, having been raised in the household of a magus where the order vibrations would skew the use of a chaos glass or even shatter it.

Boots scuff on the clean white stones of the platform. Lorn turns to his right and watches a heavy-set merchanter, followed by a porter and a hand cart. On the hand cart are three roughly cubical canvas-wrapped objects, each about two cubits on a side.

"Here." The merchanter points down beside the column adjacent to the one flanking Lorn.

The porter silently tilts the two-wheeled handcart into an upright position, then carefully checks the three containers to ensure they rest securely on the cart's carrying ledge.

The clean-shaven and gray-haired merchanter in blue nods brusquely and looks toward Lorn, taking in Lorn's cream and green uniform and the double bars on the lancer officer's collar. "Furlough, Captain?"

"Duty change," Lorn answers pleasantly.

The merchanter laughs pleasantly. "You're one of the good ones, then."

"Good enough."

"The poor ones never make captain before they hit the Steps. The fair ones stay here until they get unlucky or old." The merchanter nods. "Seen them come and go, one way or another."

"Are you with a clan house?" Lorn asks, noting the fine cut of the man's blue shimmercloth tunic and the polished cupridium boss on the silver belt buckle.

"Stitheth. One of the oldest in Syadtar."

"What kinds of goods . . ." Lorn lets his voice trail off, as if he were uncertain as to whether he should even inquire.

"Durables—clays, timbers from Jakaafra, leathers, well, hides really . . . all kinds—from the finest in gaitered stun lizards to bull leathers for the most durable boots. Dyes and polishes, lacquers . . ."

"All very necessary goods." Lorn nods. The merchanter has been careful in his house description—using the word the "oldest" rather than "finest," although Lorn has few doubts that the Stitheth clan is among the wealthier houses, since Syadtar is far from the sources of all the goods traded by the house, and most would have to come by horse-drawn wagons rather than by firewagon because their bulk would make firewagon transport unprofitable. "Doubtless all most profitable in Syadtar."

"We have been fortunate," acknowledges the merchanter.

At the low rumbling of heavy wheels on stone, Lorn glances to the west, where the morning sun glints on the white-lacquer-like finish of the approaching firewagon as it nears the embarking portico.

Behind the curved glass canopy at the front of the vehicle, the two drivers—one white-haired, the other gray-haired—wear the green tunic of a transporter. All drivers are former senior squad leaders in the Mirror Lancers, something Lorn had learned at Isahl.

Eight passengers emerge from the firewagon, only one from the forward compartment, a magus of indeterminate age who nods briefly to Lorn and continues past the lancer officer carrying but a small duffel of white shimmercloth. The seven passengers from the rear compartment all wear brown or gray, except for a woman in the yellow of an entertainer.

All the passengers vanish into the streets of Syadtar.

As Lorn and the merchanter beside him wait, the two drivers and two porters slowly unload crates and baskets, while a young enumerator watches.

Then another pair of drivers appears—one bald and the other with salt and pepper hair. The driver with the black and gray hair begins to walk around the firewagon, checking each of the six wheels, the fastenings, and the array of chaos cells behind the rear compartment.

"First compartment. Travelers westward! Travelers westward!" announces the bald driver. "First compartment."

Lorn bends and lifts the two duffels, careful not to let sabre and scabbard strike the one in his right hand. As he walks toward the open front compartment door, the wind carries voices from the second platform to him.

". . . don't see why *they* get to travel first free . . ."

"Because half of them don't live long enough to get pensioned off, Vorkin. They can't take consorts with them, if they can find one, and they never are home. That's why. You want to live like that?"

"Still . . . wasn't *that* bad for your uncle."

"You weren't there."

"Saw enough, I did. . . ."

"Hush!"

A faint smile crosses Lorn's lips and vanishes.

Behind Lorn, the merchanter directs the porter toward the cargo bay of the firewagon, the space separating the smaller front compartment from the larger rear one.

Lorn has to bend forward to slide the duffels under the thinly padded curved bench seat, and he pushes them to the far side. Then he has to unclip his scabbarded sabre from his belt. After setting it against the outside wall of the compartment, he takes the rear window seat on the left side, so that he can see ahead.

Through the cupridium-braced white oak behind his head, he feels the rest of the goods and crates being loaded, and then the *clunk* of the cargo doors being closed.

The merchanter peers into the compartment, smiling as if in relief. "A bit of space here, captain. Until Coermat for certain, anyway." He takes the rear-facing seat on the right side, as if to be seated as far from the Lancer officer as possible, then stretches out his thick legs. "Might not be so bad this time." His words end with a yawn.

"It's better not to be cramped," Lorn agrees pleasantly.

"Closing up, sers." The bald driver peers into the compartment, before withdrawing and closing the door.

"You'll pardon me, captain. I had to do the accounts before I left, and there wasn't much lamp oil left." The merchanter nods politely, leans his head back, and closes his eyes.

The firewagon rolls forward slowly and smoothly picks up speed. Lorn watches the white sunstone buildings of Syadtar pass and vanish behind him.

He will not return to Syadtar. That he knows.

XLIII

THE FIREWAGON RUMBLES through the twilight toward Chulbyn, the town that exists only to serve as the station for transferring passengers and urgent freight from the firewagons plying the Great Northern Highway to those using the Great Eastern Highway. Even though the chaos cells that power the rear wheel motors are behind the second compartment, Lorn can sense the waning of the cells' power. This trip will be the vehicle's last, until those cells are replaced with the recharged cells periodically carried from Cyad to the replenishment waystations.

Across from him snores a thin senior enumerator, while the Stitheth merchanter sleeps quietly in the far corner of the firewagon's forward compartment.

The firewagon lurches ever so slightly, as if the wheels had struck something, and then crushed it, before the faintly rumbling sounds of normal travel resume. For a moment, the enumerator's snores cease. But only for a moment, Lorn reflects.

The firewagons on the Great Northern Highway are smaller than those on the Great Eastern Highway, for all that the travel distance from Cyad to Chulbyn is less than a third the distance to Syadtar. Has it always been that way? Leaning back in the seat that become harder and harder, Lorn fingers a chin getting all too stubbly.

Will Cyad seem any different? Lorn smiles. Different it will seem, but in what ways he does not know. He hopes he will be able to recognize those differences and that he can spend some time with Ryalth.

A frown replaces the smile. Has Myryan been able to deal with being Ciesrt's consort? He takes a long and slow breath. Should he have taken matters in hand there? Will he ever know? Does he want to know?

Outside the forward compartment of the firewagon, as

chaos powers the vehicle along the gleaming white pavement of the Great Northern Highway, the twilight deepens into night. Inside, the enumerator snores; the merchanter sleeps, and Lorn ponders the days ahead.

Lorn'alt, Cyad

XLIV

THE FIREWAGON PASSES between the two sets of angled whitened granite pillars that symbolically mark the northern boundary of Cyad, the City of Eternal Light and Prosperous Chaos, and at that moment those pillars are half in the late afternoon sun, half in shadow.

Lorn sits in the middle of the rear-facing seat in the first compartment. To his left is the silent Lancer majer who had boarded the firewagon in Chulbyn and who has spoken to no one. To his right is a black-haired and sharp-nosed merchanter, almost as silent as the majer. Across from Lorn sits a painfully thin young woman in the pale green of an apprentice healer, with her father by the door to her right. Her father—even more spare than his daughter—wears the unadorned white of a magus, without the lightning bolt pin of an upper level adept. The magus alternates between studying the younger men in the compartment, although his observations of Lorn are less intense, as if he has already decided Lorn is scarcely worthy of attention.

Lorn leans back, waiting until the firewagon completes its traverse of the city and arrives at the main firewagon station to the west of the Palace of Light. His thoughts are upon Ryalth and Myryan . . . and upon Jerial and his parents. None have seen him as a Mirror Lancer officer.

He does not look up as the chaos vehicle takes the upper Way of Far Commerce and passes the three-story sunstone residences of the merchanter clan principals, small palaces on the fourth highest hill within Cyad. Nor do his eyes lift as the firewagon, moving smoothly over the polished granite blocks that floor all thoroughfares in Cyad, glides by the exchange halls that dwarf all but the Palace of Light and the structures that comprise the Quarter of the Magi.

"You're from Cyad, then, Captain?" asks the majer, addressing Lorn for the first time on the entire journey of more than two hundred kays from Chulbyn.

"Yes, ser."

The majer nods. "I thought so. You've seen it before, many times."

In the seat facing Lorn, the magus lifts his eyebrows, and he tilts his head, as if viewing Lorn for the first time.

"Yes, ser." Lorn nods politely to the majer, but the other officer relapses into silence.

A time later, when the firewagon slows to a stop, Lorn eases himself erect. After the driver opens the door to the front compartment, Lorn nods to the magus. "Good day, ser."

"And to you, Captain." The thin man turns his head and murmurs, "Carefully, Kilenya." He slides out the open door, then turns to offer his hand to his daughter. The young healer apprentice looks neither at Lorn nor at her father as she takes a small green bag from under the seat and slips from the compartment.

The lancer majer eases his sabre from beside him, takes a single kit bag, and leaves as silently as he had entered so long before, offering a brusque nod to Lorn. In turn, the sharp-faced merchanter inclines his head to Lorn.

"Go ahead," Lorn says with a smile. "I've a great deal under the seat."

"For your courtesy." The merchanter nods once more, and slips from the firewagon.

Lorn reclaims his sabre and clips it in place before sliding out the two bags that hold his kit. Once on the platform under the granite pillars of the portico, he takes a slow breath of sea-perfumed air, air far damper than he has felt in three long years. He steps closer to the nearest pillar and sets down his gear, waiting for the others to leave the pillared portico, watching as the provincial mage and his daughter take the first waiting carriage, and the majer the second. The merchanter talks with a white-haired enumerator, both standing by a wagon waiting on the far side of the platform, presumably for some goods that will be unloaded from the center compartment of the firewagon.

Lorn picks up his gear and crosses the narrow way to the carriage-hire lane, where he addresses the first driver of the pair of carriages remaining. "The Road of Perpetual Light, at the crossing of the Tenth Way."

"Yes, ser."

Lorn opens the carriage door and sets the two duffels that contain his kit on the floor, then adds, "Straight down to the Third Harbor Way, and then out." He grins. "It's faster that way."

"Yes, ser. As you wish, ser." The driver bobs his head nervously with each word he utters.

Lorn slides into the uncovered carriage and closes the half-door, settling back into the upholstered seat and taking another long breath of the moist air of Cyad. For a moment, he glances up at the thin white clouds that seem to hang motionless.

As the two horses pull the carriage southward, Lorn studies the harbor, the white granite piers that hold near-on a dozen vessels, more than two thirds long-haulers with stern ensigns of either Hamor or Nordla. He sees but a single white-hulled fireship and two ships with the blue of Cyadoran houses, and he wonders if one might be a ship in which Ryalor House holds an interest. He laughs softly, telling himself he has no claim on Ryalor House or its assets. None whatsoever.

Except . . . he shakes his head.

The chill of a chaos-glass screeing him comes over him, as it has intermittently since he went to Isahl, although this imaging is warmer. His father? The feel is similar. He shakes his head. He must work that out—and somehow reconcile his father to Ryalth.

But can he even work matters out with Ryalth? Without her suffering for his transgression of having been a student magus? Will she even consider it? And what of Myryan? Is there anything he can do to remedy her consorting with Ciesrt? Or did he have but one chance where he has already failed?

His eyes do not truly see the City of Light as the carriage

conveys him toward the harbor and then eastward beneath and past the Palace of Light, for he wrestles with all the questions seething behind the composed expression upon his visage.

"Ser? This corner?" asks the coachman for hire. "Is this where you wished to be?"

Lorn straightens, glances toward the northwest corner, toward the four-story dwelling where he was raised. The house is larger than he recalls, a dwelling that would be a merchanter palace in Syadtar. "Yes."

"Three coppers, ser. It was half the city."

Lorn offers four, and opens the carriage half-door, easily lifting the two duffels, and instinctively managing to keep the sabre from striking anything as he alights. By the time he has carried his kit to the front and formal gate of the house, Jerial is standing on the lower steps, well before the green ceramic privacy screen that protects the main entrance overlooking the Road of Perpetual Light.

His composure shatters into a broad smile.

As his boots touch the steps beyond the gate, Jerial shakes her head. "I felt you were coming. Then I wasn't sure. You look so . . . removed, so Lancer-like—I almost didn't recognize you." Then she smiles, and for a moment, the formal facade of healer fades. "I was hoping it wouldn't be long after your last scroll."

Lorn drops his kit and hugs her, amazed once more at how small she truly is, for she has always seemed so much larger.

For but an instant, she clings to him before deftly slipping out of his embrace. "You're stronger."

Lorn understands. "I hope so. I tried to follow what you said." He pauses. "Where's Myryan?"

"She is consorted . . . father wrote you, I know. . . ."

He shakes his head. "I knew. I . . . Myryan . . ." He shrugs. "What you don't see is sometimes hard to picture."

"She and Ciesrt have a dwelling. You can see her in the morning. She spends the afternoons at the infirmary."

Lorn holds back the frown. He understands that message as well.

"Father used the chaos-glass, but he and mother are still waiting upstairs."

"Decorum," Lorn says dryly.

"Always," responds Jerial, her tone as dry as Lorn's has been.

Lorn picks up the duffels once more, and the two walk up the lower steps and then around the decorative tiled bricks of the privacy screen and into the lower entry. Side by side they ascend the marble steps of the formal staircase. Only the servants' quarters are on the lower level—where breezes are rare.

Lorn's mother—her once-mahogany hair now almost entirely white—stands at the back of the second-level entrance hall. Beside her is Lorn's father, in shimmercloth white, the bolts of chaos glowing on the breast of his tunic.

"It's so good to see you." Nyryah's smile is shy, if warm. She does not move toward her son.

"It's good to be here." Lorn sets down his kit, steps forward, and hugs her firmly. Her embrace is firm, but without the strength he has recalled.

When Lorn steps back, Kien'elth inclines his head to his son the Mirror Lancer captain. "Welcome home."

"Thank you."

"It's good to see you, Lorn. You have grown . . . in more ways than one." Kien'elth's smile is both welcoming and strained.

"I've tried." Lorn's smile is practiced and easy. "The Mirror Lancers make you work and think."

"Work, certainly. You have a few more muscles," offers Nyryah.

"I'm as scrawny as ever," Lorn protests.

"No, you're not," Jerial counters. "Mother would know."

Lorn shrugs helplessly.

"I would like a few words with Lorn." Kien'elth smiles, first at his son, and then at his elder daughter, and then his consort. "But a few words, and you may have him back."

"I will check the dinner," Nyryah says. "We may be able to find some tarts, or a pearapple pie."

"Mother . . ." Jerial smiles despite the slight exasperation in her voice.

"Lancer captain or not, I doubt that Lorn has lost his taste for sweets . . . of all kinds," Nyryah says firmly. "He does take after his father."

Lorn can't help but grin at his mother.

Even Kien shakes his head ruefully, if barely.

Lorn carries his bags up the second flight of stairs, leaving them in the third level foyer. He unclips the sabre and lays it across the green bags, then follows Kien'elth up the inner steps and to the study on the uppermost level. With an inner sigh, Lorn notes the slight shuffle in his father's walk and the thinning of his white hair.

The senior magus closes the study door before making his way to the chair behind the polished white oak table-desk. He sits carefully and not-quite-heavily.

Lorn takes the chair closest to the desk, careful not to let his boots scuff the polished wood of the legs. He waits as his father studies him in the comparative dimness of the paneled study. The sun-gold eyes have lost none of the intensity Lorn recalls.

"I said you had grown in more ways than one. I think you understand to what I refer," Kien states.

"Yes, ser."

"It is a dangerous course. Few complete it."

Lorn shrugs, understanding all too well why his father will not mention Lorn's growing power and control of chaos. "I've followed what Myryan and Jerial have advised as well, for my health, of course."

"They would know, but best you not mention that again, even to me."

"Yes, ser." Lorn forces himself to recall that he is back in the City of Light, where every statement may be truthread, and every movement caught in a screeing glass like the one which rests, covered, on his father's desk. He frowns, as his eyes study the light amber of the wood which frames the glass.

Kien follows his eyes. "Yes, it's only a year or so old.

The old one vanished when I traveled to Fyrad last year."

"That's odd," Lorn says.

"Most odd," reflects his father. "I packed it when I left Fyrad, but when I unpacked here, it was gone."

Lorn nods slowly. He is indeed back in Cyad.

"With no sense of it in a year, I doubt its fate will ever be known." Kien leans forward in the chair and studies his son. "You may recall Alyiakal?"

"The lancer emperor?"

"The lancer-magus emperor. Any Mirror Lancer who has such talents may well turn Cyador over to the barbarians."

Lorn waits.

"I'm aging, Lorn, and I am too fond of pontificating. Yet I would ask that you bear with me and not ask any questions." At those words, Kien'elth turns in his chair so that he does not look at the lancer captain and cannot even see Lorn. "All who are of the Magi'i are bound to serve chaos, and thus limited by chaos. Those who are lancers are restricted because Cyador can but support limited companies of the Mirror Lancers with firelances. A senior lancer officer who could muster chaos would not be so bound or restricted, and both the senior commanders of the Mirror Lancers and the most senior Lectors are bound to find and assure such never become senior officers. None speak of this; none who are not first level adepts or lectors know of such."

Lorn remains silent in the pause that follows his father's words. Technically, Kien'elth has not addressed his son, yet he has risked much even to speak as he has.

Kien turns back to face Lorn. "Some from Cyador romanticize the freedom of the barbarians." His white eyebrows lift. "Would you be one of those?"

"No. Once I asked myself about that freedom." Lorn laughs harshly. "That was before I got to know them."

Kien nods. "A man free of all restraints is a slave to chance and order. The barbarians are slaves to chance, even while they proclaim their freedom."

"They're dangerous, and there seem to be more of them every year," Lorn points out.

"I suspect it has seemed that way for many generations," Kien says. "Cyador endures, and the barbarians dash themselves in vain against the lancers."

Lorn nods, but he recalls Jostyn and Cyllt—and others who had shattered beneath such vain dashing.

"You'll be here for a season?"

"Five eightdays."

"Good. We'll get to see you." Kien smiles. "So will a number of young women, I suspect."

Lorn shrugs, looking appropriately sheepish.

The older man rises. "I will not keep you from your sister and your mother. Otherwise we both will hear of it."

With a smile, Lorn stands.

"We will see you at dinner?"

"Of course. Where else could I get pearapple cream tarts?" Lorn's smile expands into a broad grin.

Kien shakes his head as Lorn turns.

Outside the study, Lorn glances through the portico columns that ring the open sides of the upper level, his eyes checking the southwest and the harbor, though he cannot see the building that houses the Clanless Traders . . . and Ryalor House. After a moment, he walks slowly down to the second level, toward his own quarters, if they can truly be said to be such after his three-year absence.

In the foyer, he looks for his bags, but someone has moved them, and then continues toward the rear, slipping through the open door. His bags have been set beside the wardrobe beyond the archway to the sleeping alcove. The sabre lies across the desk. The chamber has not changed, except in the feel of disuse and the lack of small items. There are no spare coppers in the small tray in the corner of the desk, nor any paper in the open-topped white oak box beside the empty inkwell.

He glances at the bags, then offers a crooked smile to the emptiness of the room before turning and walking back toward Jerial's door.

"It's open. You can come in, Lorn."

Jerial sits behind the desk. She replaces the cupridium-tipped pen in the holder and stoppers the inkwell, her slender fingers quick and deft. The piercing blue eyes turn on her brother, and both narrow and finely defined black eyebrows arch into a question.

"A warning about not repeating the mistakes of my past," Lorn answers.

"Were they really mistakes?"

"In father's eyes, I suspect."

"There was more, but I won't press."

"Thank you." Lorn slides into the armless chair at the corner of the table desk that could have been a match to the one in his quarters. "How are matters with you?"

"For a healer without a consort . . . as can be expected." Jerial shrugs. "I'm good enough, and I can always be counted upon to be there. For that, all I receive is enormous condescension, but the pressure to be consorted isn't as bad." She displays a crooked smile. "I'm older now than most of the junior adepts who need consorts, and those who are left don't wish a sharp-tongued healer."

"Especially one with brothers such as yours?" Lorn's tone is idle.

"Vernt is most accepted."

"I would have thought so."

"And a lancer who fights the barbarians is respected."

"In short, I'm expected to die young and respectably, and Vernt will carry on." Lorn's tone is totally without bitterness, as though he states a fact so obvious that there is not a doubt of its veracity.

"No. You are expected to act heroically and effectively." The eyebrows arch a second time. "Isn't that what lancer captains do?"

"I'm only half what's expected, then." Lorn shrugs. "I'm not terribly heroic."

"I imagine you are very effective."

"The majer said something along those lines," Lorn admits.

"Good." Jerial pauses. "I presume you will offer some observations on the barbarians and the Grass Hills at dinner."

"Yes. And how the lancers serve Cyador and the Magi'i."

"That cream might be too heavy."

Lorn keeps the smile from his lips, but not his eyes, though he could have done that as well.

Jerial laughs softly. "I forget how well you deliver the outrageous."

"It's not outrageous. The Mirror Lancers and the firelances provided by the Magi'i are all that keep the barbarians of the north from turning Cyador into a wasteland." Looking perfectly earnest, Lorn squares his shoulders.

"Well . . . Vernt *might* believe you. If you began with the firelances."

Lorn's eyes catch Jerial's.

"He wants to be like Father, Lorn." Her healer's voice carries a trace of sadness. "He does not know Father."

"I'll be very careful . . . and very cheerful."

"That would be best. Mother is still most observant."

Lorn nods. "What about Myryan?"

"She is handling Ciesrt as well as possible. Your words to father gave her some more time."

"You're afraid it wasn't enough?" Lorn studies Jerial without seeming to do so, almost leaning back in the armless chair.

"She doesn't talk to me. Not really."

"I'll see her tomorrow," he promises.

"That would be good. Mother insisted, quietly, that you not face Ciesrt as soon as you arrived."

"She is not happy with the consorting."

"Neither she nor father saw any other choices. Myryan could not follow my path." Jerial's smile is tight.

"I feared that."

"You did what you could."

"I need some time to unpack." Lorn stands and stretches. "And to wash up before dinner. It was a long ride from Syadtar."

"And think?"

"That, too." He turns toward the door.

"Lorn?"

"Yes."

"When you need them . . . there are blues for a senior enumerator in your wardrobe, under the winter waterproof. I thought your friend needed, shall we say, advancement."

"Thank you." Lorn nods to Jerial, then steps out into the open corridor, walking slowly back to a chamber that is his, and is not.

There he opens the first green bag and begins to place his uniforms in the wardrobe, alongside the enumerator blues. A faint smile curls his lips.

After the clothes are unpacked, and he has slipped the silver volume into hiding with the smallclothes, he takes out the Brystan sabre he has carried across Cyador, resharpened and worked into shape, sensing the faint order-death sense of the worked and polished iron beneath the scabbard. He has taken one liberty with the blade, a significant one, for now the tip of the blade is edged on both sides, if only for a span on the heavy-backed side. His senses tell him that much of a true point will not weaken it, and for what he has in mind, he may need to thrust with it.

He can hold the iron without burning his hands, but there is no reason to, not when Vernt or his father might sense it. He smiles. He is, after all, entitled to a souvenir of his efforts against the barbarians, although he has kept its presence hidden from all the lancers at Isahl, and will from his family. Even should his father scree the iron, Kien'elth will say nothing directly.

Once he has folded the green bags and put them in the back of the wardrobe, he pulls off his boots, and then the uniform he has worn for too many days. There is a robe on one of the wardrobe pegs, which he slips on, before heading out the door toward the bathing chamber.

Once he is washed thoroughly and shaved, he returns to his room and lies across the bed. What can he do about Myryan . . . and Ryalth?

He does not ponder either long, for sleep claims him.

* * *

A gentle rapping on the door frame brings him awake, and he bolts upright.

"Dinner is almost ready," Jerial says from the other side of the closed oak door. "I thought you'd like to know."

Lorn has to clear his throat before he can reply. "Thank you. I dozed off."

"I thought you might."

There is silence, and Lorn can sense that she has slipped away to let him ready himself.

After hurriedly dressing, Lorn leaves his chambers and walks down the steps to the smaller, and warmer, inner dining area on the second level, his boots silent on the marble of the steps.

Even so, one of the servants nods to him as he nears. He does not recognize the brunette with the round face and the braided brown hair. "I'm sorry. I'm Lorn. I don't believe we've met."

"Sylirya, ser. I came here a season after you left." Sylirya keeps her eyes properly downcast.

"How have you found it?"

"Your family is most kind, ser. A better home I could not have found." She moistens her lips. "I must help cook, ser. . . ."

Lorn smiles cheerfully. "Do what you must."

He waits until she turns, then waits again as he hears his father's heavy steps on the stairs.

The magus whose hair has turned from shimmering silver to a flatter white over almost four years nods to his son. "You're still the first to the table." He looks around, then at Lorn. "Is Jerial here? You were talking to someone."

"The new servant—Sylirya."

"She's scarcely new, Lorn. It's been nearly three years for her, and for Kysia, and more than a year for Quyal—she's the new cook."

"What happened to Elthya?"

"Her mother fell ill, and when she went back to her town—I've forgotten the name—a widower she'd known when they were children asked her to be his consort." Kien spread his hands. "So we had to get a new cook. Quyal's as good as Elthya, but her cooking's different, more . . . western, I'd say. More spice."

The two men walk through the foyer and along the corridor to the dining area, where they stand by the door, waiting for the others.

"Too spicy?" asks Lorn.

"I did ask for a little less seasoning," his father admits.

They turn as Jerial approaches.

"Lorn was here, first, I'd wager," Jerial observes.

"Before me," their father confirms.

"Vernt should be here before long," Jerial says. "I heard him come in, but he'll wait for mother."

As she speaks, Lorn hears steps, and Vernt and his mother appear. Like his father, Vernt wears the white shimmercloth of an adept of the Magi'i, but without the lightning emblem. He has also added a short-trimmed beard, sandy-colored like his hair.

"The lancer has returned," the younger mage says. "Welcome back."

"Thank you." Lorn inclines his head. "It's good to see everyone."

"Can we eat?" Kien rolls his eyes.

"Of course, dear," responds Nyryah. "Why don't you just go in and sit down?"

Lorn follows his father. While Kien sits at the end of the table with his back to the window, Lorn takes the place to his father's right. Jerial sits beside Lorn, and Nyryah seats herself at the end opposite her consort. Vernt takes the place across from Jerial and Lorn.

Sylirya eases a large crock before Kien, setting a ladle beside it. Another woman brings in two trays of bread—sunnut and a dark rye.

"Thank you, Quyal." Nyryah nods at the second server.

"What—" begins Kien.

"Dinner is a beef stew. Quyal didn't know Lorn was coming," interjects Nyryah quickly.

"None of us knew when he was coming," adds Jerial.

Lorn shrugs.

"Just serve yourself, dear," suggests Lorn's mother to Kien.

"I will. I will." The older magus shakes his head.

Vernt offers the tray of nut bread to his mother, then takes two slices and sets them on his plate, before passing the tray across to Jerial.

"You look good." Vernt smiles happily at Lorn, then at the tray Jerial holds. "I still remember how you sneaked extras on the sun-nut bread. You'd pass it up to begin with, and then take three slices later."

Lorn grins easily. "Why not? You always tried to grab two right at first, and you always got caught. Now you can do it, and no one says anything."

"After all these years," Kien grumbles good-naturedly, "you two are still at it."

Jerial laughs. "They're brothers. Did you expect that to change?"

"I'm getting older. I could hope." Kien slides the crock toward Lorn, who serves Jerial and then himself, before passing it.

Vernt serves Nyryah and then himself, while Lorn pours a maroon wine for everyone.

"Careful with that Fhynyco," Kien tells Lorn. "It's better than Byrdyn."

"As good as Alafraan?"

"Alafraan? Now he's heard of wines we don't know." Kien shakes his head. "Boy goes off, and now he's a lancer who knows wines."

Both Jerial and Lorn laugh.

"I wouldn't," Lorn says, "except that one of the officers came from a vintner's family in Escadr."

"At least he admits it," adds Nyryah. "Now . . . start eating before it all gets cold."

Lorn needs little urging, and stew or not, the first mouthful tells him it is the best meal he has eaten since he left three years earlier.

"What is Isahl really like?" Jerial asks after Lorn has eaten several mouthfuls and half of the slice of nut bread he had slipped onto his plate.

Lorn swallows. "It's hotter in the summer, colder in the winter, and windier all the time. Outside of the outpost, there are no more than a score of families in the valley, and fewer than that in the adjoining valleys. The only trees are scrub cedars, and bushes . . ." Lorn's description is as accurate as he can make it. ". . . and everything has walls. Even the herders have sod walls around their holds."

"I wouldn't want to be there." Vernt offers a twisted smile. "It's too bad he can't tell that to some of the student mages."

"They wouldn't believe me." Lorn shrugs. "I wouldn't have believed me."

A slight chill passes over the room, and Lorn and his father exchange glances. Lorn takes another bite of stew, noting the minute nods between his mother and Jerial. Someone is using a chaos glass. To see if Lorn is indeed with family? Or to check up on Vernt or his father?

"What will you do while you're here?" asks Nyryah quickly.

"See you, visit friends, enjoy good food, and rest. All the things you can't do out in the Hills of Endless Grass."

"And then . . . ?" Vernt inquires.

"I'm off to my next post. In Geliendra. I've been told I'll have a company." Lorn shrugs. "In the Mirror Lancers, you find out when you get there." He takes a small swallow of the Fhynyco, stronger and smoother than Byrdyn, then helps himself to more of the stew.

"And after that?" Vernt persists. "Or do you know?"

"I could but guess." Lorn takes another bite of the stew before continuing. "If I make overcaptain, or sub-majer, I could be the second-in-command somewhere, or head a port installation . . . or . . ." He lets the words trail off.

"Seasons enough to worry about that," says Kien. "Best we enjoy the season at hand." He smiles at Lorn, and then at Nyryah.

"And you," she replies to the look of her consort, "are like your sons, wanting to know what sweets follow?"

"There is little wrong with that," counters the older magus.

Nyryah inclines her head to Sylirya, who slips away from the table, to return with a shallow bowl that she sets before Kien. Then the serving girl slips smaller porcelain bowls, fringed in gold, before each family member before retreating to the archway where she waits.

"You will have to do with dried pearapples and sweet brown sauce," Nyryah tells Lorn.

"I can manage that." Lorn chuckles. "I never saw pearapples in Isahl, or Syadtar, either."

"What is Syadtar like?" Jerial asks. "Is it dirty with narrow streets, like a barbarian town?"

Lorn shakes his head. "It's like any other town I've seen in Cyador. Granite and sunstone buildings, clean tile roofs, wide paved streets, houses like the smaller ones here in Cyad." He shrugs. "Except for the size of the buildings and how few there are compared to Cyad, the towns I've seen all are pretty much alike. That's until you get to the grasslands and the herders' holdings out in the Grass Hills."

"I don't think I'd like that," ventures Jerial.

Lorn senses he is being watched, but as he watches, never looking overtly, he can see no one. Nor is the feeling like that of being watched in a glass, as he has felt with his father, and, occasionally, at other times—as had happened earlier at dinner. Being watched, in his parents' home? Being watched by other Magi'i, in a glass, that he can understand. But who else would care?

He reaches for the pearapples, a smile still upon his lips.

XLV

A RAW WINTER wind whips off the Great Western Ocean and across the city of Cyad, bringing a chill that belies the bright mid-morning sun set in the cloudless green-blue sky. Wearing but his winter white uniform, trimmed in green, and white leather gloves, and without the sabre, Lorn walks quickly eastward on the walkway of the Road of Perpetual Light, stepping past the First Score Way. The carry-bag in his left hand is gray—something that could be carried by a lancer, a tradesman, or a merchanter. In it is the set of blue shimmercloth enumerator garments.

The dwelling where Jerial has directed Lorn is still farther to the east, almost out of the city. Lorn hurries, because he wishes to arrive at mid-morning—when Ciesrt will be at his tasks in the Quarter of the Magi'i.

When he reaches the Twenty-Third Way, Lorn pauses, readjusting the white dress officer's cap, as he mentally reviews the description provided by Jerial and compares it to the dwellings to his right. The two-story dwelling is of green glazed brick, with a blue tile roof, set in a slight hollow between two larger dwellings, blocked partly from the cooling ocean breezes. The privacy screen is of blue and green tiles, with a time-faded inset golden lily in its center.

He steps up to the ledge on the left side of the privacy screen and pulls on the green silken cord to ring the bell.

After a long moment, he hears steps, and the viewing shutter is unslit.

"Lorn!" Myryan rushes out the door and around the screen. She hugs her brother tightly and buries her head against his chest. "You're here! You came!"

He has to drop the carry-bag to return the embrace.

After the initial exclamation and hug, almost as suddenly, Myryan steps back and looks down. "I suppose consorted healers aren't supposed to do that." Her smile is partly sheepish, partly something Lorn cannot identify. "But you were out fighting the barbarians, and you came back safely, and you are my brother."

Lorn is conscious of just how thin and frail she appears, tall as she is, even in the loose-fitting healer greens. He can sense no chaos about her, no sickness . . . yet there is something. Around her is the faint scent of trilia and erhenflower, a combination much gentler than erhenflower alone, and not as overpoweringly sweet as trilia alone.

"You must come in." She bends as if to pick up his bag.

"I've got it." Lorn is quicker and has it in hand before she half-starts the movement.

"Same old Lorn. Do you let anyone do anything for you?"

"Sometimes."

"Ha! Tell me when." She doesn't wait for an answer, but walks around the ceramic privacy screen and through the still open front door.

Lorn follows with his carry-bag.

Beyond the front door is a small tile-floored foyer scarcely four cubits square with arches leading in three directions. Myryan leads Lorn to the left, into a chamber perhaps ten cubits long and six wide. The walls have been freshly plastered and painted in a green-tinted, off-white color, and the floor tiles recently regrouted.

Three narrow and shuttered windows grace the outside front wall, their lower sills two cubits above the polished but worn green ceramic tile floor. A narrow set of shelves stands between the left end of the windows and the corner, bare except for a single sculpted sunstone statuette of a magus looking up at a single step. In the other window corner is a waist-high circular table holding an oil lamp that had once been in Myryan's chambers. Facing the window is a settee upholstered in faded blue. To its left stands another table, of darker wood, holding a blue glass lamp. To its right, between the settee and the window table, is a straight-backed oak chair. The last piece of furniture in the room is a low padded stool set before the middle window.

Myryan steps to the windows, and one after the other, opens the shutters to let in the light. She turns and gestures around the small room. "This will have to do. We only have the one sitting room, and no portico." She stands by the padded stool and faces the settee.

Lorn sets down the bag and takes the straight-backed white oak chair that, from its patina, is probably older than either of them.

Myryan settles onto the stool. "When did you get back?"

"Last night." He smiles crookedly. "Jerial suggested that my arriving late in the evening at your door might not have been well-received. So I came this morning." He does not mention that their parents had offered no guidance, except indirectly through Jerial.

"Jerial never cared that much for Ciesrt." Myryan smiles wanly.

"She didn't offer any judgments."

"Does she need to?" Myryan's tone of voice is wry, much like their mother's can be.

"Jerial does things her own way," Lorn answers.

"She always has. I don't see that changing."

"How are you doing?"

"I'm still working as a healer." Her amber eyes sparkle for a moment. "And trying to turn this place into something respectable. All the walls were dark blue."

"With large gold lilies painted on them?"

"Small faded yellow lilies. Everywhere." Myryan laughs. "It was the best we could do. Ciesrt didn't want us to live with our parents, and I didn't want to live with his. So . . ."

"Junior second level adepts don't make that much."

"You're kind, Lorn. Third level. He says he'll make lower second this summer when the Lectors review all the thirds."

Lorn considers the dwelling—modest by the standards of where they grew up, but far from modest even compared to Ryalth's quarters . . . assuming Ryalth has not found larger accommodations suited to the success of Ryalor House.

Myryan follows his eyes. "We had help. Kharl'elth and father . . . and someone else."

"Someone else?" Lorn does frown.

Myryan shrugs, almost helplessly. "I thought it might have been you. Like the healer pin. There was a deposit made in an account at the Exchange in my name . . . as much as father and Kharl promised. I told Ciesrt that it came from mother's family. He just nodded."

Lorn could see Ciesrt nodding, accepting what he could not understand, and passing through life without considering anything beyond the Quarter of the Magi'i. "You have no idea?"

Myryan shakes her head. "I kept the golds for almost a

season, but there was never any hint of anything from anyone. Finally . . . well . . . I found the house. Tyrsal helped me, posed as a relative. We've only been here a season."

"You're happier here."

Myryan smiles. "Much happier. I've done some work outside, but I can't wait to start on the garden. The soil's good, and I can grow some of the better herbs, I think. And Jerial commissioned a bed and armoire for us. I don't know how she did . . ."

Lorn raises his eyebrows.

"Well . . . she didn't have to . . ."

"She made you promise not to tell, right?"

Myryan nods. "You won't, will you?"

"Chaos-light, no. What does Ciesrt think about all this?"

"He's pleased we have our own dwelling. None of the other thirds do."

"I'm glad you do."

"What about you?" she asks.

"I have a little less than five eightdays before I have to leave and report to Geliendra. You'll have time to fill me in." He smiles. "On everything. Almost everything," he quickly adds.

"Geliendra?" She frowns. "Be careful. The Magi'i are doing something there. I overheard Kharl . . . but he stopped when he saw Ciesrt and me."

"He is *the* Kharl'elth, and still the Second Magus?"

"Very powerful, and he makes sure the family knows it." Myryan's mouth crinkles into an ironic smile. "He spends all his time in the Palace. That's the way Ciesrt talks about it."

"Did you hear any more about Geliendra?"

"I didn't hear much. I wouldn't have heard that, but I'm not that comfortable when we go there, and . . ." She offers an embarrassed smile this time.

"You used your chaos-order senses?"

She nods, then adds, "All I heard was something about the importance of the trial period, and the interest of the Emperor. It was at a gathering, and he was talking to another

of the Magi'i. It wasn't Chyenfel, but we were never intro-
duced—I wasn't. Kharl took Ciesrt and introduced him."
Myryan's face hardens slightly. "Since I wasn't introduced,
I didn't ask who he was. I wish I had."

"It doesn't matter." Lorn means it. The information's value
is in the content and the speaker, not the listener.

Myryan brushes back a strand of curly black hair and
shifts her weight on the padded stool. "Sometimes, when I'm
there, I feel more like a settee or a table than a person."

"At Ciesrt's parents' dwelling?"

"They want us to have children, and she's always asking
me when she can expect a grandchild." Myryan's lips twist.
"I tell her that it's in the hands of chaos. It is, but not the
way she thinks."

"Jerial?"

Myryan nods. "She knows a lot. Sometimes that's helpful,
and she didn't even ask why."

"Does Ciesrt suspect?"

Myryan laughs gently. "He's order-blind, like Vernt.
Maybe that's why they get along so well."

"I didn't know they had become friends," Lorn says easily.

"Friends? I don't know. When they talk, they understand
each other, but they don't go out of their way." The healer
lifts her shoulders, then drops them. "That's with anyone—
both of them are like that."

"Vernt asked a question or two at dinner last night," Lorn
says.

"He probably had to force himself to do that."

"Ciesrt . . . does he talk much? To you, I mean?"

"He tells me everything he can about his day, and about
how many firewagon cells he charged, and why the cells on
the bigger firewagons are different, and how important what
he and the others do is for Cyad." She laughs softly. "I listen.
He means well, and, in his own way, he does want me to be
happy."

"I'm glad for that." Lorn turns in the chair.

"That chair is hard. You could sit on the settee."

He grins and stands, stretching. "I'm still a little stiff from the travel. Not used to sitting in a firewagon for days."

"You . . . the man who could outwait anyone?"

"Only if I have a reason," he points out. "Otherwise, I have trouble sitting still."

"That I find hard to believe, my dear brother."

Lorn rolls his eyes.

"I won't ask about other . . . matters." Myryan stands. "The kitchen isn't much, but I need to eat something, and so do you." She uncoils herself from the stool, standing as tall as Lorn, and motions for him to follow.

The kitchen has also been replastered and smells fresh and clean, despite the age of the dwelling. Somehow, the spare setting suits Myryan, Lorn reflects, watching her extract a wedge of cheese from the watercooler.

Deftly, his sister slices the hard cheese into finger-sized wedges, yet Lorn can sense her reluctance with the knife, and her relief when she wipes it clean and replaces it in the wooden holder quickly.

"The knife bothers you."

"Most healers have trouble with knives, even cupridium ones, but they're not as bad as the iron ones."

"The iron—"

"It's not the iron. I can hold iron, any kind of iron, and it doesn't bother me."

Lorn frowns. "I'd think . . . this can't be new."

Myryan laughs. "New? It's been a problem since the first-born. The Magi'i don't mention it because we're just healers, not wielders of chaos."

Lorn holds in the wince he feels.

"Take some of the cheese. You're pale. I'm a healer, and I can sense it." Myryan breaks off a chunk of the slightly stale bread and thrusts that at him as well.

"I didn't come to take food."

"I know. You came, and I'm glad." Myryan chews the bread and cheese before speaking. "Is this all right? I like bread and cheese. Ciesrt doesn't. He wants a hot breakfast and dinner. So I have the cheese at mid-day."

"Bread and cheese like this are fine," Lorn reassures her.

"They're not at all like what lancers get, even lancer officers. I didn't say much about food last night, but I think anything in Cyad would taste wonderful. This is better cheese." He raises his eyebrows. "What kind?"

"It's from the east, someplace called Worrak, I think."

"And the eastern barbarians actually make good cheese?"

"They're not all like those in the north," Myryan counters.

"No matter what father says?" Lorn smiles.

"Oh . . ." She pauses. "Father is beginning to look old. Didn't you see it? Sometimes, I wonder."

"His hair is white, not silver. But it will happen to us all," Lorn says.

"But it's so sudden. Last year, it *was* silver."

Lorn frowns.

"There's nothing I can do. Mother's doing what she can. I hope she doesn't try too hard."

"Too hard?"

"She's a healer, not just a mother. If she puts too much into helping father, then . . ." Myryan looks at Lorn.

"It could hurt her."

"It could. It will." Myryan wraps the cheese and replaces it in the cooler, then puts the bread in the keeper. She looks at the sandglass on the pedestal. "I don't want to go . . . but I'd better . . . they expect me."

"I'll keep stopping by."

"I hope so. You are my brother." Her smile warms him, but it fades too quickly as she continues, "I won't ask about other things, Lorn. I hope you work them out, but I shouldn't know. We have dinner at least once a week with Ciesrt's parents."

He nods, understanding too well. "Thank you. I hope so, too."

"I'm going to have to leave for the infirmary. Is there anything I can do before I go?"

Lorn wants to laugh. Anything *she* can do? He is the one who should have acted.

"Lorn . . ." Myryan's amber eyes catch Lorn's. "You did what you could. It's better this way. I can accept Ciesrt."

Accept. Lorn does not like the word.

"Would you mind if I just sat for a while in the garden?" he finally asks. "I need some quiet. I'll leave from there."

"You could stay here."

"I think I'd like the garden." Lorn does not wish to risk being seen in a glass within her walls without her present, for several reasons.

"If that's what you'd like." She smiles once more. "You've always needed some time apart from others. I'm glad that hasn't changed."

"I don't always want that distance, Myryan." He steps forward and hugs her. "I just can't change things. Not now."

She returns the hug, then steps back, and he wonders if he has changed so much that she must hang onto a few old mannerisms to assure herself that he remains the Lorn she knew.

After reclaiming the carry-bag and waving from the garden gate as Myryan walks out to the Road of Perpetual Light, Lorn steps back into the garden, finding the arbor.

Myryan may guess what he is doing, but she does not *know,* and one arbor is much like another in a screeing glass.

Some time after he senses that she is far enough eastward of the house that she cannot sense anything he may do, he steps into the corner of the arbor where the gray winter leaves of the grape are thick and will shield him from any eyes that may peer from the adjoining dwellings that rise above the blocks of the gray stone walls that enclose the rear garden of Myryan's dwelling.

Once he has changed into the blues and boots that he had carried in the bag, he stretches, then readjusts the tunic. The blues feel strange on him . . . as if he had outgrown them. He checks the fit, and the tailoring is perfect. With a snort, he smiles.

He emerges from the arbor as a senior enumerator, carry-bag in hand, and walks through the outside garden gate, carefully latching it behind him, and then heads along the Road of Perpetual Light, westward back toward the center of Cyad.

At the Fifteenth Way, long before he can be seen from his

parents' dwelling, he turns and walks southward to the Road of Benevolent Commerce. Bag still in hand, he follows it toward and then into the Merchanter section.

With the sun higher in the clear blue-green sky, the wind has softened and warmed, and more folk fill the walkways that flank the road. A wagon drawn by a single horse passes. Lorn notes the legend painted in yellow upon the green wagon sideboard: Tarfak House, Spices.

Perhaps Ryalor House should investigate spices. He smiles lopsidedly and continues walking, his steps quick and precise. As he passes the Empty Quarter coffee house, he can see that it appears more empty than three years earlier, and that the awning that once sheltered outside tables has been removed. So have the tables. Is there that little coffee left that it is too expensive for junior merchanters?

At the Third Harbor Way, he steps behind an empty wagon drawn by a pair of mules and crosses to the white stone walkway on the far side, where he turns harborward and walks down the gentle incline to the lower merchanters' plaza. Three carts remain under their traditional green and white striped awnings as Lorn strides around them to the northwest corner of the plaza, his destination the squat-looking white building of the Clanless Traders, where Ryalth has continued to maintain the small office of Ryalor House.

Once inside the squared open archway and off the relatively uncrowded plaza, Lorn finds himself at the edge of a swirl of figures in blue, as well as a few in red, white, or green. Seemingly without much notice, Lorn eases through and around the small groups of traders and hagglers and hangers-on and makes his way to the stairs at the rear of the high-arched hall. He glances up at the three stories of balconies and hopes that Ryalth has not moved her trading office too far.

She has not moved it at all—it remains the same two-doored area at the back of the third level, well into the northeast corner. Sitting at the small corner desk, she studies a ledger, her head down, and as he slips toward her Lorn can see that she has cut her hair far shorter than he recalls.

"Do you have a need of a senior enumerator, Lady Merchanter?" Lorn smiles, but he finds his heart is beating faster than it should.

"I have . . ." Ryalth looks up, and her mouth drops open. "You came," she whispers. "You really did."

Lorn can sense that no one is that near or listening. "I arrived last night . . . my parents expected me to spend some time there . . . so I came as soon as I could." He forces himself to cut off the explanation of why he did not want them suspicious of his immediate departure. "As soon as I could."

Ryalth quietly closes the ledger. "You still are trying to protect me, aren't you?"

"You seem to be able to take care of yourself." He smiles. "And you've protected me in so many ways. I never would have thought about scrolls going through Fyrad, or been able to set that up."

"That was easy." She pauses. "It was not difficult."

"Your enumerator?"

"Eileyt is still at the harbor, checking the accounts of the latest venture with the Jekseng clan. Dyes from Brysta—their green is better than anything on this side of the Eastern Ocean."

"Does Ryalor House have ventures with everyone?" Lorn shakes his head.

"It's better that way. Each thinks we're too small to stand alone, and that way I can spread the risks." Ryalth stands.

Lorn wishes to hold her, but his hand merely brushes hers. They both stiffen.

"I think I'd better close up," she smiles wryly. "I'm not going to finish reviewing these." She lifts the ledger, then slips it into the leather case she has pulled from beneath the desk.

Lorn watches as Ryalth extracts a wallet from the desk, then slips a lock bar in place and padlocks the bar. "It won't stop a Clan thief, but to break it will make enough noise that everyone will know, and they frown on that." She lays the thin and long leather wallet—almost a narrow pouch—on the desk top and fingers the golds inside into a position to allow her to fold it in half. She slips the folded wallet into the slots in the back of the heavy and overlarge blue leather belt she wears.

After Ryalth closes and locks the doors, the two walk briskly down the steps and out through the covered hall. A few heads turn at Ryalth's red hair, see the enumerator's garb, and turn back.

"Another enumerator . . . has three . . ."

". . . trades everything . . . but not a lot . . . doesn't lose much . . ."

"You should be so good, Tymyk."

"Everyone knows you," Lorn observes.

"I've made it a point," she says. "I've helped those I could, and cheated no one."

"The good and fair lady trader."

"Not always good."

The bleakness in her voice surprises Lorn, and he says nothing as they cross the open plaza outside the hall.

"You were right, when we first dealt with cotton and oil." She turns her head, and the deep blue eyes fix his amber ones. "I learned that again, the hard way. I find I have to remember that, but I don't like it."

Lorn nods, though her words send a cold knife down his spine.

They walk silently eastward along the Road of Benevolent Commerce, past a row of arymids with furled gray winter leaves, their trunks pale gray in the afternoon light.

"How long will you be here?" she asks quietly.

"Almost five eightdays. I get six, but that has to include travel from Isahl and then to Geliendra. That's my next post."

"And you sought me out within a day? Are there not scores of healers and women from high lancer families vying for your attention?"

"I wasn't interested." Lorn cannot quite keep his tone disinterested. "I would have sought you last night, but my family was watching. Someone has also been following me with a screeing glass, not always my father. I didn't come from the house, directly. I stopped to see Myryan and then changed in her garden arbor after she left for the infirmary."

"I would have liked to have seen that." Ryalth's lips quirk.

"I'm sure you would." Lorn laughs gently.

They pass the Fourth Harbor Way—the east one, although the ways are not distinguished on the placards by whether they are east or west of the harbor center.

"How is Myryan?" Ryalth asks after a time.

"I don't know. She seems healthy, but she's . . . more resigned than happy. The only time she seemed joyful was when she talked of the house and of her garden."

"Isn't that good?"

"I'm glad she has the house," Lorn says. "I can't imagine her living with Ciesrt's parents. He's the second highest of the Magi'i. Kharl, Ciesrt's father, I mean."

"That must be quite an honor for Myryan to be his consort." Ryalth's voice is even, hiding emotions.

"She didn't want it, and I tried to talk father out of it before I left. He waited to consort her, but he didn't change his mind." Lorn takes a deep breath. "I think Myryan would have been better without the honor."

"You'd do almost anything for those you love."

"Almost," Lorn temporizes, again wondering if he should have killed Kharl before the Lector knew Lorn was a threat.

"More than that, I think." Ryalth's voice is calm, slightly distant. "Your father knows that." After a barely imperceptible pause, she adds, "Don't you think?"

"Father? I think he doesn't know quite what to think. I'm not the Magi'i son he wanted, and I'm not exactly the lancer officer he suggested I could be."

"You survived and made captain," she points out.

"I'm . . . effective," Lorn says. "Not glorious." His eyes flick to the next Way, where a tinker's cart is tied before a smaller house, and where the maroon garbed tradesman pedals a foot-grinder and sharpens knives, deftly handling one, then another.

She nods, her lips quirking momentarily. "Maybe that's why you're a good trader."

"I'm not a trader. You're far better than I could ever be."

"You can see what will change," she corrects him. "I know what to do when you tell me what will happen."

"We make a good team." He smiles, happy to be walking beside her, as they pass the tinker's cart.

"You've never said that before."

"I haven't? I've thought it enough."

"There's much you think and don't share, Lorn."

He cannot but catch the edge of wistfulness behind the facade of the experienced merchanter, a wistfulness he doubts most would perceive. "I'm sorry." And he is, yet he knows that every word in many places they both frequent may carry to the wrong ears.

Ryalth points to the structure on the lower side of the Road of Benevolent Commerce, although she points upward. "I took chambers on the third level. The end stairs."

Lorn follows her through the archway in the wall and then through the simple shared formal garden—little more than trimmed dwarf cedar, two short flower beds turned under for the winter, and time-polished stone benches placed in areas shaded by the handful of feathering conifers.

"These came vacant. They only cost three golds a season more, and the balcony is more private," Ryalth explains, starting up the outside stone steps. "It seemed worth it. They're larger, and the breeze is better in the summer."

"And colder in the winter?"

"I haven't noticed." She smiles as she stops in front of the last door off the covered walkway on the third level.

"Better view up here," Lorn says.

"It is."

The key clicks in the lock, and she opens the door, waiting for Lorn to enter. He waits for her to enter. Both smile, albeit nervously.

He finally shakes his head and steps inside, past the narrow interior privacy screen. Then he turns, taking in her face and the deep blue eyes that he has recalled on so many nights.

Ryalth closes the door. She steps past the screen, and

Lorn's arms go around her, but not so quickly as hers encircle him.

The key clanks on the floor. Neither reaches for it as their lips meet.

XLVI

IN HIS UNDERTUNIC, Lorn sits in the small eating area by the door to the balcony, glancing over the empty plates that had earlier held a thrown-together omelet and almost fresh dark bread to take in Ryalth, her creamy freckled skin and the deep blue eyes that make even merchanter blue seem shallow by comparison, even above the bulky white cotton robe she had donned before she had made the omelet.

Lorn smiles, and Ryalth smiles back.

He sips the water from the goblet, pondering the early morning drizzle beyond the small window, wondering if it is the typical winter morning drizzle or whether it will lift as the sun rises higher into the sky.

The lady merchanter looks at the goblet Lorn holds. "I don't buy coffee any more."

"That's all right. It's too bitter for me."

"I liked it, but you can't get it for less than ten golds a tenth-stone."

"That much?" Lorn's mouth makes an "o" as he sets the goblet down.

"The blight. All the coffee bushes are dying, those that hadn't already. They're saying that the chaos strength of the Firstborn has faded, and that since they brought the coffee bushes, none will survive."

"I never heard that. It could be true," he muses, considering what he knows about the impending failure of the chaos towers.

"It is true. They're dying."

"No. I meant the reason." He finds a smile still upon his lips as he looks at her once more.

"I need to get ready. I still have a trading house to run."
Ryalth's face clouds abruptly.

"You're worried." Lorn pauses, then says, "And it's not about trading today."

Ryalth shivers. "I still don't know why you're here."

"Because I met you one night when I was a student, and nothing was quite the same after that."

She laughs, a forced sound. "You just wanted me in bed."

"At first," he admits. Then he grins. "And you just wanted to know what loving someone from the Magi'i was like."

"Someone sweet," she corrects.

He shakes his head. "I'm not sweet."

"You are inside, and to those you love."

"You know why I'm here," he points out.

"You never tell me, though. That's something I hate about the Magi'i. You—maybe not you—but most Magi'i use words as weapons, and none of you like to say anything beyond pleasantries because you're afraid someone will weigh the truth of your words and use it against you."

"They do," Lorn counters. "All that bothers you, but that's not what's worrying you."

"I'm fine."

Lorn conceals a frown. He stands and walks over to her, drawing her to her feet and nuzzling her ear.

Ryalth remains stiff, unyielding.

"I'd feel better explaining this way," he whispers. "You don't know how closely the Magi'i watch and how they use the chaos-glasses."

She nips his ear, slightly harder than necessary. "That's for not telling me earlier. I knew, but I wanted you to tell me."

"I'm sorry," he murmurs. "Will you tell me what else is bothering you?"

"I said . . ."

"It's not true."

"I would love a man who still remains Magi'i."

"He loves you." Lorn keeps his voice low, and his left

hand massages the tight muscles beside her right shoulder blade. "Tell me."

"Shevelt has been pressing me . . . he says I really don't have a consort," Ryalth says quietly, letting her arms encircle him, but loosely.

"Who is he? A spoiled trader?" Lorn's left hand continues to massage her tight shoulder muscles.

"The heir to the Yuryan Clan . . . shimmercloth, Hamorian cotton, spices . . ."

"Does he want a consort?"

Her smothered laugh is bitter.

"Come to Geliendra for my first furlough," he says. "A year after I get there."

Her eyebrows lift and she leans back to look at him. "Why?"

Lorn swallows, then bends to let his lips touch her left ear. "So we can be consorted there."

"You mean it." She shakes her head, pushing him away slightly before whispering back. "Why there?"

"Because it's not here."

She laughs at the dryness in his tone. "And?"

"If I'm followed here, anyone would think you're my mistress—" Lorn stops, not really sure how to voice what he thinks.

"I'm not?" Her eyebrows arch.

"You're far more than that." He hurries his next murmured words. "That anyone would think you are my mistress protects you."

She nods. "I think I understand. I don't like it."

"I'm trying. . . ."

"I know." She tightens her embrace for a moment. "I know."

Lorn holds her close, as she does him.

Ryalth will have to leave shortly, all too soon.

And Lorn will still have to handle Shevelt . . . before he leaves for Geliendra.

XLVII

LORN STUDIES THE city from the fourth-level portico of his parents' dwelling, watching the morning winter sun create shimmers that dance across the harbor and the Great Western Ocean farther to the south. Yet to Lorn's eyes, the white city does not seem so vibrant as usual. Is it because of the winter-gray leaves . . . or the absence of the green and white awnings, furled for the winter . . . or because he sees it differently?

The air is still, cool but warming as the sun climbs.

Sensing someone approaching, he turns to see the round-faced servant—Sylirya—carrying a small basket. She inclines her head to him.

"Good day, Sylirya."

"Good day, ser."

Lorn peers at the basket.

"Brushes and caustic, ser. To clean the tiles on the rear portico."

"That's a hard job. Mother used to give it to us when we were children." Lorn half-smiles at the memory, then adds, "Well . . . I won't keep you."

He steps back to let Sylirya pass and get to her duties, then turns and begins to walk back toward the stairs down to his chamber. The door to his father's study is open, and Kien stands there, a polished white oak walking stick in his hand.

"Oh . . . I thought you would have been in the Quarter," Lorn says.

"I was about to leave." The older man gives a self-deprecating smile. "At my age, I have some small leeway. Vernt left much earlier."

"Are you all right?" Lorn studies his father, but can sense nothing overtly wrong—except that the core of order-chaos that sustains each individual does not seem so strong as he has recalled.

"I'm fine except that I'm not as young I once was."

Lorn senses the shading of the truth, but lets the words pass.

"You're still seeing that merchanter woman, aren't you." Kien'elth's words are not a question.

"You know the answer to that, father. Why do you ask?"

"I worry. All parents do, even when their children are grown."

"She has been most helpful and supportive." Lorn's lips twist. "As a lancer, I'm not exactly sought after by those families with whose daughters I grew up."

"There are many honorable lancer families," Kien points out. "More than a few women have talked to your mother."

Lorn shrugs. "I think it best that any such talk wait for a successful completion of my next duty assignment."

"Perhaps . . . a successful consorting might prove useful."

Lorn's stomach twists, but he offers a smile. "That might well be, but that would present merely another set of dangers in years to come."

"Your . . . friend . . . has done well, Lorn, but she's not from an established house, and all she has gathered could be scattered in an instant. There is no house to back her."

"That is true."

Kien's eyes narrow before he speaks. "You will break off the relation. After you return to duty, of course."

"I can only do as I sense best, father."

Kien'elth winces visibly. His arms move, as if to raise the walking stick, but instead he but taps it on the floor tiles. After a moment, he says, "Vernt is seeing a lovely young woman."

"I wish him well." Lorn smiles. "He deserves a lovely young woman."

"You are treading a dangerous path, Lorn."

The lancer captain offers a lazy smile. "How dangerous is doing my duty as a lancer? Or seeing a woman who is a talented merchanter?"

Kien clears his throat, once, twice. Then he shakes his head. "Your mother and I have tried to follow the path of prosperous chaos, following the Light, and setting an example."

Lorn holds a sigh. How can he explain without giving away what he dares not put in words? "I appreciate that, and all you have done for me, and all that you have done that you do not think I know or understand. You gave me an extra year at the Academy for Magi'i, one others would not have gotten. You allowed me to grow in ways that were necessary and that you doubted. You respected my opinion about Myryan." He pauses. "Please do not think that I do not understand, nor that I do not appreciate all that."

Kien looks at Lorn for a long time before speaking, as if he, too, must consider his words most carefully. "I can sense your appreciation, and for that I also am grateful. Yet, as a senior Lector who has been privileged in my life to see and to hear much, and to serve Cyador to the best of my poor abilities, I cannot but worry about your not being able to use your talents where they will be most accepted and appreciated in the years ahead."

Lorn nods. "I, too, would like that, and in my own way, I will be striving for such. Perhaps I should be even more judicious in my conduct over the seasons to come." He smiles. "But I would hope, with the strain of the duties that face me, none would gainsay my poor efforts to take some comfort while on my home leave."

A wry smile crosses Kien's face. "I will suggest to any who inquire that after three years fighting barbarians, you do indeed merit some comfort. You are young for a lancer captain, and many will appreciate your words when that is pointed out. On your next leave, then, we will look forward to seeing a consort in keeping with your achievements and honor."

Lorn returns the smile. "That would be most acceptable, father, most acceptable."

Kien frowns, then shakes his head. Finally, he laughs.

"Your lack of reservation is so honest that it takes me by surprise."

Lorn spreads his hands helplessly. "I do listen."

"When you wish." Another headshake follows. "I must go, but I am relieved that we have talked."

"So am I."

Lorn walks down the steps with his father. Then standing on the steps outside the privacy screen, he watches as the older magus walks briskly westward toward the Quarter. A faint smile plays across Lorn's lips as he thinks about the consort who he knows is appropriate to his needs and accomplishments.

XLVIII

IN THE WARM air of the sparring room, Lorn lowers the exercise sabre, blots his forehead, and glances at the red-headed Tyrsal.

Tyrsal's exercise tunic is dark with sweat. He lowers his own blunted exercise sabre and shakes his head. "You're barely sweating, and I'm dying. I haven't sparred this hard in years. Not since you left. You could have killed me three or four times."

"Once maybe." Lorn grins.

"And . . . you were doing it left-handed. Don't think I don't remember which side you used before."

Lorn shrugs. "I've been working on it for a time." He grins. "For three years. Against the barbarians you have to be able to use whatever hand's free."

"Knowing you, you did more than that. You work on everything. That's why I never understood . . ." Tyrsal frowns and lets his words die away.

The two walk toward the open door, through which a cooling breeze blows, but stop perhaps ten cubits from it.

"I don't want to get too chilled." Tyrsal looks at Lorn.

"There's really no one to spar with any more. Even Vernt . . ."

"I know." Lorn laughs. "All he thinks about is chaos transfers and the way of the Magi'i . . . and finding the right consort."

"You haven't found one," Tyrsal points out, again blotting his forehead.

"Lancer captains aren't supposed to consort. Not until after their second tour of duty, anyway, and preferably not until they're overcaptains or even sub-majers. Now you . . ." Lorn raises his eyebrows. "What excuse do you have?"

"Me? I'm not a second-level adept with a generous stipend, and I don't come from a prosperous old-time Magi'i family. Remember, my father was the first Magus ever in my lineage, and he was the grandson of a clanless trader." Tyrsal rolls his eyes.

"There are Magi'i daughters who would have you. You're talented, and good-looking, and cheerful." Lorn pauses, and adds, "And loyal." He grins before going on. "And don't give me those words about poverty. You may have come from merchanters, but they were most successful ones. There are many young women who would like a young magus who would inherit what you will."

"You have someone in mind?"

Lorn shrugs, then pulls a scrap of gray cloth from his belt to wipe the sabre before replacing it in the battered exercise room sheathe. "Not particularly. I remember my father parading names past me." He frowns. "There was one . . . Aleyar, Liataphi's daughter. Blonde, very pretty. Well-spoken, and 'it certainly wouldn't hurt, Lorn, that she is the daughter of the Third Magus.' "

Tyrsal laughs at Lorn's imitation of Kien'elth's pedantic tone. Then the red-haired mage shakes his head. "There were two, you know. Syreal is blonde and sweet. She was older. Dett's age, at least. And she wouldn't consort with anyone, Lorn. Not anyone her family liked. . . . There was something there, rumors about a merchanter . . . but I didn't know what. If their father had sons, no one would care."

"What of the other daughters? Doesn't he have a bunch?"

"Salsyha—she's the oldest . . . she consorted with a Lancer commander. His first consort died of the flux when he was the port commander in Biehl years ago. Gives him some status, but she's got a tongue like a sabre, or so I've heard tell. The second daughter . . . she was to be consorted to a second-level adept—but she died suddenly. No one ever said why, but there were rumors that his rivals . . ."

"Too much influence from Liataphi?"

Tyrsal grins wryly. "You see why I'm not terribly interested in pressing a suit upon an unwilling lady?"

"What about the younger two?"

"Aleyar's sweet like Syreal, but she's younger than she looks, if you know what I mean. The other's too young, nine, I think." Tyrsal adds dryly, "Besides, being the consort of Liataphi's daughter might do little for my desires to live a long and uneventful life."

Lorn laughs.

"I have been looking, not urgently, you understand, for a quiet girl from a modest Magi'i family without ambitions."

"I wish you had been more interested in Myryan."

"I was. She wasn't interested in me."

"I'm sorry. I had hoped."

"I know, Lorn. She's not really interested in anyone. I could have, I suppose, and she would have been sweet to me, because she is. . . ."

"But you didn't want a consort merely to be nice to you?" The lancer captain nods. "I understand that."

"You know that. I don't know as my mother does."

"Is she pressing you?"

"She's never said a word." Tyrsal lifts his eyebrows and rolls his eyes.

"That's worse." After a pause, Lorn asks, "Are you working on that project for the chaos towers?"

"Which one?" Tyrsal snorts. "There's one for the Accursed Forest, some sort of new way to constrain its black order, and one to try to strengthen the barriers on the fireships, and a couple of others that no one even talks about."

"I presume you are continuing to ensure that the firelances are charged and that the firewagons cross Cyador in speed and comfort?"

"Absolutely! What else are unknown third-level adepts good for?" Tyrsal frowns. "I'd better get back. Exercise over a mid-day meal is approved, but excessive exercise . . ."

"Especially with a lancer?" Lorn grins.

"Who else would give me a decent workout?" The redhead walks toward the racks where the practice weapons are kept and replaces the sabre.

Lorn does the same, then turns to his friend. "Tomorrow, then?"

"Of course."

"And you're still coming to the house for dinner on five-day?"

"I wouldn't miss it."

After Tyrsal leaves, Lorn walks slowly back along the Road of Perpetual Light toward his parents' dwelling, a pleasant smile fixed upon his face, as he considers what he must yet accomplish.

XLIX

FROM WHERE HE sits on the edge of the settee, Lorn takes in the main room of Ryalth's quarters—the low ebony table before him, the straight-backed black oak armchair where Ryalth sits, and beyond that the green ceramic brick privacy screen that protects the door from the inside. Behind him and to his right is the alcove that contains the circular eating table and two armless chairs, and the door to the small balcony. To his left is the narrow archway to the bedchamber, and beyond that, the small bathing chamber. Lorn finds it hard to believe that two eightdays have already flown by.

His eyes light on the painting—the portrait of Ryalth as a young girl—wearing a high-necked blue tunic, and a thin golden chain. He has admired it every time he has come into her quarters, but never said a word. "Your parents had that done?"

"Just before they died," she affirms. "I was supposed to take the ship, too, but I got so sick that mother insisted I stay with my aunt Elyset. She was really my great-aunt, but I always called her 'aunt.' She died just before I met you." Ryalth gestured around the room. "Most of this came from her house—the things Wynokk didn't want. I did get to keep my bed, but everything else went to pay father's debts. He lost everything when the ship went down."

"You don't like to spend coins on yourself."

"Father did, and on us." Her smile is mirthless. "There was nothing left."

Lorn nods, then asks gently, "Why did you give Myryan the pin and the coins for the house?"

"I should have known you'd see that." She barely shrugs. "You love her, and you couldn't do anything. I didn't want you to be upset when you returned."

"And Kysia . . . you pay her to watch what happens in the house?"

Ryalth shakes her head. "How did you find that out? She's never laid eyes on you."

"Because someone has been watching me, and it wasn't the cook or Sylirya. I never have seen Kysia, except from behind or at a distance, and that means someone who knows about the Magi'i and doesn't want to be discovered. Besides, there was no other way you could have known what you needed to know to help Myryan." He lifts his hands helplessly. "No one else would have cared."

"You helped me . . . when no one cared, and you kept helping me. There wasn't much I could do to repay everything. I helped Myryan." The redhead looks down at the ancient blue wool carpet that displays a border of what appear to be interlocked ropes, surrounding a trading ship under full sail.

"Your father's ship?" Lorn points to the blue-hulled vessel portrayed in the carpet and partly obscured by the low table before him.

"No one wanted a carpet showing a sunken trader. I got to keep that, too."

"And that's why you invest in cargoes carried on many ships?"

She nods. "The profits are lower, but the houses will take our golds because it lowers their risks. I choose carefully. So far, we have lost but one cargo."

"You're a careful woman."

"Except with you."

Lorn is not sure exactly how to respond. "I suppose I am a risk."

"Not nearly so much as I'd thought, and you have made us more than a few coins."

He raises his eyebrows.

"You were right about the cuprite," Ryalth says. "What made you suggest that?"

"I couldn't say." Lorn smiles crookedly. "It felt right."

"Do you have any more 'feelings' like that?"

"Cider," he suggests. "Or something like it. Or wine."

"Because coffee is getting scarce?"

"More because there won't be any at all in a few years, I feel." He shrugs. "People will drink something else, but I don't know what."

"I'll have to think about that."

Another thought strikes him. "Iron . . . not immediately, but in another few years."

"Scarcely anyone uses it here."

"Other lands will, though."

Ryalth frowns. "I do know some traders who use the Hamorian Exchanges."

"I can't think of anything else. Not now." He stretches, glancing out to where the sun hangs over the dwellings higher on the hill to the west.

"You still haven't asked me to meet your parents." Ryalth offers a half-humorous pout.

Lorn understands it is but half-humorous.

"You'd frighten them—badly."

That draws a deeper frown from her.

"I mean it. They'd see how much I care. They couldn't avoid it. They'd also see how capable you are. Neither one could hide knowing that—not from other Magi'i."

"You're aiming to become the Majer-Commander, aren't you? Or trying?"

"It's been done before," Lorn replies lightly.

"Except you want me as well. Or do you want me because I can help you?"

"I've wanted you from the beginning. I never thought about using you to become a Majer-Commander . . . or anything else." He frowns. "I did want you to help me make some coins at first. I have to admit that, but that bothered me."

"So you gave me the chest out of guilt?"

"Guilt . . . and love."

"I don't think anyone knows you." Ryalth shakes her head. "Every time I see you, and every scroll you send . . . there's always something new, like a gem polished into so many facets that the sparkle doesn't ever let you see the stone."

"Do you want to see the stone?"

The redhead nods slowly.

Lorn stands and steps around the low table and takes her in his arms, kissing her, and then lifting her, carrying her to the bedchamber, where he lays her on the deep blue quilt. He lies beside her, holding her, and begins to whisper in her ear, half-nuzzling her as he does.

She listens, then stiffens, her eyes wide, as he adds two more sentences.

After a moment, Ryalth kisses him gently on the cheek, leaning back away from him slightly, before she murmurs in his ear. "Alyiakal must have been one of your ancestors."

"Not that I know."

"How could you?" She laughs and rolls away from him. "You said you had to have dinner with Myryan and Ciesrt. It's getting late, and I wasn't invited. I'm hungry, and you have to go." She offers a mischievous smile. "Should I dab you with a little scent?"

"I don't want to leave you." He cocks his head to the side,

taking in the deep blue eyes. "Actually the scent is a good idea. Ciesrt will tell his sire."

"Devious—"

Lorn gives a quick headshake as he senses the chill of a screeing glass. He draws her to him, as if passionately.

Her arms go around him, if not in passion, at least in comfort, and they hold each other for a time—until he can sense the chill fading. Slowly, he kisses her cheek, then leans back. "Thank you for understanding."

"I could almost feel . . . someone watching. . . ."

"They were . . . through a glass."

Ryalth shivers. "Do all Magi'i live like that? With the knowledge that nothing is private? Nothing secret?"

"Most can't sense it except faintly. Even my father has to be concentrating."

"You can sense that? And they wouldn't let you stay as a magus?"

"Being of the Magi'i isn't just ability," Lorn states flatly. "It also has to be the most important aspect of your life. Father's pointed that out several times, indirectly, since I've returned to Cyad."

In a fluid movement, she rolls away from him and off the bed and to her feet, slipping to the low vanity under the high north window. She opens the chest on the vanity and draws out a vial. "After that, you definitely need some scent." Her lips quirk in a smile Lorn knows is forced.

"I don't like leaving you." Lorn slips to his feet and walks up behind her, easing his arms around her waist.

"I know."

He can feel her sigh.

After a moment, she adds, "I know you're opposing your family, and I know you asked me to . . . come to Geliendra. . . ."

"But you want everything to be in the open."

"Yes."

He laughs, softly, almost bitterly. "All the senior Magi'i know about you and me. Were that were open enough." The bed chamber is silent, and he adds, more softly, "I will put our consortship in the open. Haven't I kept my word?"

"You have. You have more than kept it." Ryalth turns out of his arms to face him, but still holds his left hand. "We would not be here, had you not."

Lorn traces her jaw line with his fingers.

"I am not angry with you." Her eyes harden. "I cannot say the same for your parents. Or the Magi'i." Her fingers rise to touch his cheek, and she bends forward and whispers, "But I will come to Geliendra at the end of your first year."

"I will be there, with everything arranged."

"Good." A smile, bright and simultaneously wistful, appears. "You'd better get ready to go." She half-turns and reclaims the vial. "And you will wear some scent. Not so much as last time. I want them to understand I also have some small amount of taste." She dabs a fingertip of the fragrance on each of Lorn's cheeks, then holds his face in her hands, and kisses him gently.

He returns the kiss, equally gently.

Slowly, they separate.

Lorn reclaims his tunic from one of the wall pegs, then dons and fastens it.

"You are a handsome man."

He shakes his head.

"You are."

"I'm glad you think so. Very glad."

They walk to the door of her quarters, where he turns and kisses her cheek again.

"Be good to dear Ciesrt," she says as she opens the door.

"Only for Myryan's sake." Lorn offers a rueful smile and steps back.

Ryalth closes the door, and he turns and walks slowly down the steps and out to the Road of Benevolent Commerce.

He eases into a brisk walk up the Thirteenth Harbor Way East, and then turns eastward on the Road of Perpetual Light. At the click of hoofs behind him, he glances over his left shoulder to see a gig approaching. In it are a woman in healer green and a magus in white, looking perhaps ten years older than Lorn. Neither looks at him as the gig passes.

He walks almost another block before an open carriage passes in the other direction. This time, the two passengers nod. The man wears a lancer uniform with the simple starburst of a commander; the woman wears a formal green tunic of shimmercloth, and a necklace of emeralds set in silver that sparkles well beyond the carriage. Lorn nods back with a smile.

The sun is beginning to drop behind the trees on behind the dwellings set uphill of the Road by the time Lorn turns up the walk to Myryan's dwelling. A light and cool breeze sweeps up from the harbor, promising a cold evening. He smiles at the faded golden lily on the exterior privacy screen before he rings the bell.

The viewing slit opens, and then the door. "Come in, Lorn," Myryan says warmly, but she does not step from behind the exterior privacy screen.

He steps around the screen and into the house, where Ciesrt stands beside Myryan, a long-fingered hand on her left shoulder. His long fingers seem strangely delicate compared to Ciesrt's tall form and broad shoulders.

Myryan's nose wrinkles, just slightly, as Lorn nears them, and, suddenly, she winks.

Laughing inside, Lorn keeps a polite smile on his lips and inclines his head. "It's good to see you, Ciesrt." His voice is warm and friendly.

"You, too, Lorn." Ciesrt's nose twitches, and he rubs it inadvertently with his right hand. "It's been a while." He gestures to the left archway from the foyer.

"Thank you." Lorn follows the motion into the front sitting room.

There, Myryan and Ciesrt take the settee, leaving the sole armchair for Lorn. He settles himself and turns toward the couple. "I like the dwelling. You've done much with it, Myryan."

"She has, indeed," Ciesrt responds, proudly, putting his arm around her slender shoulders and squeezing slightly. "She is a wonderful consort."

"She's always been a wonderful sister," Lorn replies, "and an excellent healer, from what I have heard."

"She cooks well also, but before long, we will have a cook so that she can spend more time with her garden, and, some time soon, we hope, with the children."

"From what I heard," Lorn answers, looking at Myryan, "you've already done much with the garden."

"The soil by the wall is just right for brinn, and I started some astra plants in the fall. They feel strong. . . ." The healer's eyes brighten as she begins to detail her plans. ". . . it's cool enough for winterseed, but I'll need more lime for that. . . . Ciesrt said he'd crush it for me. . . ."

Lorn listens, enjoying the enthusiasm and the warmth in his younger sister's voice, and the sparkle in her eyes as she speaks of gardens to come.

Abruptly, Myryan stops and bolts upright. "Oh . . . I have to finish dinner . . . a few things, and I've been meandering on about gardening."

"I liked hearing about it," Lorn says.

"She loves that we have our own garden," adds Ciesrt.

"Just keep talking." Myryan stands, patting Ciesrt on the shoulder. "I can hear from the next room," she adds as she pauses by the archway, before disappearing.

Both men smile.

"She has so many talents to be a good consort," Ciesrt muses. "My parents were so pleased. Father, especially, likes that she understands so much, and that he can talk to her like he would me or any other of the Magi'i."

"Myryan's always been quick," Lorn admits. "She's very sensitive. She understands things without people having to yell at her or tell her twice." He hopes Ciesrt will understand exactly what he says.

"That's what I like about her," answers the young mage. "She knows what I need, without my having to explain everything."

Lorn nods. "She likes things calm and peaceful."

"It's so restful when I come home from the Quarter at

night." Ciesrt smiles. "So much better than I'd ever thought being consorted could be."

"Lancers aren't expected to become consorted until they've been captains for at least several years," Lorn says conversationally. "What are you doing now . . . I mean the kind of work?"

"Third level adepts do mostly support work . . . transfer chaos, clean up after projects, that sort of thing. I do some of the chaos cell transfer, and whatever else I'm called to do."

"It's an exciting time for a magus, Vernt tells me, with everything going on." Lorn leans forward, conveying an interest in what Ciesrt may offer.

"It is. All the projects . . ." Ciesrt shrugs.

"I understand. I'm going to be headed to the Accursed Forest. They say that what you're doing may be of some benefit to us poor lancer types there."

"Father is enthusiastic about it," Ciesrt responds. "I can't say anything, you understand, but they're working on a new kind of barrier." He shrugs. "I don't know much about how it works, but . . . it should help the Mirror Lancers greatly."

"If it does, we could move more lancers to the north," Lorn points out.

"If it does, you may not need lancers at the ward-walls, I hear."

Lorn nods. "There's much else that could occupy the lancers."

"How have you found being a lancer?" asks Ciesrt, after a moment of silence.

"I seem to have a talent for it," replies Lorn. "Or a talent for surviving while being one, anyway."

Lorn looks up to see Myryan standing in the archway, waiting, listening.

Ciesrt leans forward on the settee, his eyes on Lorn, apparently unaware of Myryan's return.

"You still do not talk of duty and commitment," points out Ciesrt.

Lorn fingers his cleanshaven chin before replying, understanding Ciesrt's allusion, and understanding, too, that he has been discussed by Ciesrt and his father, the Second Magus. "We all have a duty to uphold Cyador and the Path of Light," he begins slowly. "That is my commitment as well. You have found that way that best suits you, Ciesrt. I have found a way at which I am good. I am still working to see how to make it best suit me." Lorn offers an open smile. "It is harder when you are not born into the way for which your talents fit you."

"I can see that," Ciesrt says, a hint of patronage in his tone.

"What about you? How have you found being an adept?" counters Lorn gently.

"My father is, and his father was before him," Ciesrt says, "and his before him. So far as any know, we have all been mages and healers back to the days of the Firstborn of chaos. Father has a glass in his study . . . one so old . . ."

The familiar chill of a screeing glass passes across the room. Myryan and Lorn exchange glances, but neither speaks, letting Ciesrt, apparently oblivious to the chaos-glass scan, continue to address Lorn.

". . . goes back beyond the time of Alyiakal, but it's too fragile to use anymore. With all that tradition, why wouldn't I want to be a magus?" Ciesrt smiles. "I've found it rewarding. I like being able to help provide power for the firewagons, and the firelances you lancers use to halt the barbarians. It makes me feel worthy to direct chaos into the making of cupridium." The lips of the magus curl slightly. "I'd feel wrong saying these words to most lancers, but you were a student magus, and you are of the Magi'i, and you are Myryan's brother."

"I understand," Lorn says. "Most lancers wouldn't, not in the way you mean."

"That's it," Ciesrt says. "Most wouldn't."

Myryan clears her throat.

"Yes?" Ciesrt looks up, a look of annoyance passing swiftly across his face and vanishing as he realizes his consort has been in the sitting room.

"If you do not wish to eat cold emburhka . . ." Myryan ventures gently.

Lorn stands. "I am hungry . . . and it's been a long time since I've had emburhka."

Ciesrt also rises. "I'd forgotten . . . of course, you wouldn't. Not in the Hills of Endless Grass."

"I used mother's recipe—the way Elthya used to fix it."

Lorn can't help but smile at her half-mischievous, half-imploring tone. "I'm sure it's wonderful."

"It is. She's a wonderful consort," Ciesrt says proudly.

Lorn ensures that the smile remains on his face as he follows Myryan to the dining area. He will speak of small matters, and little else, for the remainder of the evening.

L

IN THE EARLY morning, even before he has eaten, Lorn pauses outside Jerial's door. Is she dressing . . . or already gone?

"Come on in," calls Jerial. "I've got a moment before I head off to the Healer's Center."

Lorn pushes the door open. Jerial is sitting on the straight-backed chair, pulling on her second black boot.

"You leave early," he says. "I wanted to talk to you."

Jerial looks up, then stands, and lifts the heavy green wool cloak off the back of the chair. "I leave early so I can get off early. The senior healers are happy to have someone there early. That way, the consorted healers, like mother and Myryan, can come in later."

Lorn nods.

"What favor do you need this time?" Jerial's smile is amused.

"Because I'm up early?" Lorn laughs.

"Because you're home and because you have that look on your face."

"I didn't realize I was that transparent."

"You're not. When I can't tell what you want is when you want something."

"Sisters . . ." He shakes his head.

"Lorn . . . I have to go soon."

"I'd like to find out anything you might know about a merchanter called Shevelt. With your other . . . activities, I thought . . ."

"I might know?" She wraps the cloak around her. "I do. He throws cold dice and doesn't understand why he loses. He bullies anyone he can, and he'll bed anything that has red hair. Why, no one knows. He's the senior heir to the Yuryan Clan . . . if his sire decides not to send him across the Great Western Ocean on an uncaulked scow."

"You've won more than a few coins from him."

Jerial shrugs. "He can't count when he gambles." She frowns. "That's not right. How often he wins is more important than how much he wins. He gambles against Jeron'mer because he usually wins—say eight or nine times out of ten. I win only once or twice, but it's ten times what he loses, and I pick the times when it's safe to win."

Jeron'mer—that is the merchanter name under which she gambles as a beardless and dissolute young trader. "What does he look like?"

"Big . . . broad shoulders. He's not much older than you, but he's already got a belly and jowls. He's strong. He picked up one of Fragon's guards and tossed the fellow through a door. He has a square brown beard, and he's going bald. He always wears scent, something like musk and roses." Jerial frowns. "Not too many people would miss him, but you ought to be careful. The Dyljani Clan hates him."

"That's a start."

"Here." Jerial rummages in the single drawer to her desk, then passes a short dagger to him.

"What's this?"

"A Dyljan ceremonial dagger."

Lorn takes a deep breath.

"She helped Myryan, and she's helped you, just by being there. I thought you'd find out. She could probably hire someone to handle him, but it would be neater if you did. It would also leave the impression that she has ways to remove people that can't be traced. You can handle matters so that even the Hand would not know."

Lorn wonders at the reference to the Hand of the Emperor and notes that Jerial is careful not to mention Ryalth by name, even in her own chambers. He takes the dagger. "Wouldn't someone suspect?"

"A lancer in a merchanter brawl? Or over commerce?" Jerial raises her eyebrows. "Even father doesn't understand it all. . . ."

"Where would I find Shevelt? After trading hours?"

"The Silver Chalice . . . most nights." Jerial steps toward the door to signify that she is leaving.

Lorn opens the door and steps back into the corridor.

Jerial steps closer and murmurs, "Oh . . . you might as well change into the blues in your own chambers, and take the back stairs. Just for outsiders, you understand," she observes. "Mother and father both know. So do I. Sylirya and Quyal could care less, and Kysia gets her wages supplemented by Ryalor House."

Lorn raises his eyebrows. "Nothing like living in a dwelling of the Magi'i . . . who else knows?"

"Besides half the senior Magi'i? They all think you're just bedding her to spite father, and unless something else comes up, why would they care? Kharl won't tell the lancer types, not unless it will gain him Chyenfel's position, and what would wearing blues to bed a merchanter really mean except that you're hot-blooded. You certainly aren't the first."

Lorn holds in the wince and the denial.

Her last low words chill him. ". . . don't let anyone know more . . ." She smiles brightly and says loudly. "Have a good day, and make sure you keep enjoying your leave."

"I'll try." He returns her smile with an ironic grin.

She nods and is gone.

Lorn scrambles down to the kitchen, where, standing in the corner, he gobbles down some cheese and bread, and a handful of dried pearapples. Then, he scurries upstairs and, following Jerial's suggestion, changes into the blues. He still does not head to the rear stairs until he knows no one is nearby.

His steps are quick as he walks westward along the Road of Perpetual Light, and then down Second Harbor Way east. Although the early morning is chill, the lack of wind and the bright winter sun make it feel warmer than it truly is.

As he nears Harbor Way, Lorn slips behind a group of three traders, keeping far enough away to seem respectful, but listening as he follows them.

". . . cuprite's still too dear . . ."

". . . be dear for years . . . risk in iron, though . . ."

". . . need an outland partner there . . ."

". . . dry winter in Hydlen they say."

". . . spring looks dry, and grain'll be getting scarce."

Lorn's eyes flicker from the three before him to the others in blue nearing the Plaza—mostly men, the majority bearded and arriving at the Plaza in groups of two or three.

"Enumerator! You're late!" Ryalth's voice snaps at him like a whip.

Lorn winces, and turns, bowing to Ryalth from where she emerges from the morning shadows cast by the pillared entrance to the Plaza. "I am most sorry, Lady Merchanter. Most sorry."

"Sorry does not matter. Once more, and you'll be working in Jera . . . or bilge crew on a Hamorian scow."

At the scorn in her voice and the snickers from the merchanters before and behind him, Lorn flushes. "Yes, Lady." He bows again.

Ryalth ignores him, turning and striding toward the harbor.

Lorn scrambles after her, another set of snickers in his wake.

". . . voice'll peel lead from a fireship's hull . . ."

"See why you don't cross her. . . ."

Obviously, Ryalth has a certain reputation.

For a time, he walks a half-pace behind her, to her right. She turns down the First Harbor Way East, and he follows, finally drawing up beside her once they are well out of sight of those who might have witnessed her scolding of him.

"You *were* late," she murmurs, not slacking her pace, as she turns onto the walkway beside the east seawall of the harbor.

"I was. I supposed I deserved that." He grins. "Did you enjoy it?"

"Actually, I did." A faint smile crosses her face. "I don't get to order the upper classes around much." The smile vanishes. "Eileyt is up in the office. This will have to be quick."

"Why did you want me to come with you?"

"You have a good sense about people, and there's something about L'Igek that bothers me." She frowns.

"Your senses are as good as mine."

"Better in some ways, but not in this case."

The two turn and take the outermost of the white stone piers toward the oiled wooden hull of the three-masted and square-rigged ship tied at the seaward end. As they near the vessel, Lorn makes out the name carved into the stern—*Redwind Courser*. The inset letters are painted a brilliant light green that stands out against the wood. A Brystan jack hangs limply from the stern staff.

Two armed guards, with iron-studded leather vests worn over gray shirts, stand at the foot of the gangway. Each wears a heavy leather belt from which hang both a truncheon and a slightly curved scimitar. Their heavy boots are iron-toed.

Ryalth stops a good three cubits from the pair. "Merchanter Ryalth and her enumerator, of Ryalor House," she announces.

"Let them aboard," calls a voice from the main deck.

Lorn glances past the guards to the pale-faced and full-bearded man in a green tunic and a short golden vest, then follows Ryalth up the gangway onto the polished wooden deck of the *Redwind Courser*.

"Lady Merchanter." The thin trader, a head taller than either Lorn or Ryalth, bows moderately. "We are most glad to see you."

"And we, you." Ryalth's voice is cool, assured, as she returns the bow.

Lorn follows her lead and bows as well, but his senses are already scanning the vessel, trying to discover what it is that had previously concerned Ryalth.

"Master L'Igek!" calls another younger man in green, also wearing a short gold vest, but a simpler one.

The Brystan bows to Ryalth. "If you will excuse me for a moment . . ."

"Not at all. Would you mind if I showed the enumerator around—just the open decks? His experience has been more in the grasslands than here."

"Be our guest." L'Igek smiles politely before turning.

"This way," Ryalth says coolly, her voice harder than when she had spoken to L'Igek. Lorn follows as she climbs the ladder-steps to the higher rear deck. They pass a raised platform that holds the ship's wheel and a rack designed, presumably, to hold navigation gear when at sea.

Lorn can understand Ryalth's feelings about the ship. While the people hold the normal ranges of order and chaos within their bodies, the ship itself is less than whole. He lets his senses range down the rudder that dominates the stern, but the wood is solid.

They parallel the taffrail and then head forward, descending the ladder on the seaward side of the *Courser*. Lorn stiffens, then murmurs to Ryalth, "Bracing . . . the keel itself is cracking . . . a weakness in the wood . . . something like that."

Ryalth nods politely, and murmurs. "Say no more. Not now." She adds more loudly. "That's the main hold cover there. Don't ask stupid questions."

Lorn bows his head and answers obsequiously, "Yes, Lady Merchanter. As you wish."

Ryalth's eyes harden. "Remember that."

L'Igek, turning from the junior officer or mate, smothers a smile as he nears them. "I have the agreements in my cabin." He gestures, then leads Ryalth through the open passageway on the main deck into the rear deckhouse.

Lorn follows.

"This enumerator is more . . . muscular than the last," says the Brystan in a low voice to Ryalth.

"They have differing talents," Ryalth replies off-handedly.

L'Igek laughs. "I like you, Lady Ryalth. Like a dagger, you reach the point quickly." He stops in the narrow passageway, steps past the doorway, and allows both Ryalth and Lorn to enter.

The master's cabin is cramped, with a narrow bunk flush against the rear bulkhead. Forward of the bunk is a circular table, bolted to the deck, with four low-backed chairs around it. Several scrolls and a pile of what appear to be bills of lading are stacked on one side, a closed ledger beside them.

The Brystan seats himself by the papers and waits for Ryalth to sit.

"You have a tenth of the oilseeds, and a twentieth part of the dried fruit. Do you wish a tenth of the gingerwood?"

"I would greatly like that," Ryalth admits, "but the House accounts will not cover that at present."

L'Igek nods as if he had expected the response.

"And how much do you wish to take of the return spice cargo?" asks the Brystan. "You had mentioned an interest there."

"As little as you will grant me the favor of," Ryalth says almost pleadingly. "We are but a small house, as well you know, and . . . you did hear of what befell the *Western Hare?*"

The pale-skinned Brystan nods. "I was not aware. . . ."

"Enough," Ryalth replies. "More than enough. We have shares in others, but I cannot promise what has not ported." She shrugs apologetically. "You will set out before we see those coins, yet I would not lose your favor."

"Fifty golds . . . I cannot accept less, not for the best in Hamorian peppercorns and cumin."

Ryalth winces. "For you, for your friendship, it will be fifty." She pauses. "But the usual arrangement."

"Of course. That will not change."

Ryalth extracts a wallet from somewhere and carefully counts out twenty-five golds, then eases them onto the polished wood of the table before L'Igek. In turn, the Brystan counts them. Only after that does he lift the pen and write out the exchange bill.

Once he has finished it, he extends the parchment to her. She reads slowly and carefully. Then she nods. L'Igek slides the inkstand across to her, and extends a quill pen. She signs, her cursive clear and precise: Ryalth for Ryalor House.

Then L'Igek signs and returns the parchment to her. "Always a pleasure doing business with Ryalor House, Lady Merchanter." L'Igek pauses, then grins. "Will we ever see a true man in your House?"

Ryalth returns the grin with a smile. "I am most certain you will. Perhaps sooner than you think."

"You have said such before." L'Igek rises.

"And I will again," replies Ryalth as she stands.

Lorn follows their lead, and trails them out onto the main deck.

"We sail with the evening wind," L'Igek announces.

"I wish you fair and following winds," the woman merchanter responds, "and an early and profitable return to Cyad."

At the head of the gangway, the Brystan bows again. "The combine will be pleased to know of your continuing support."

"I appreciate their forbearance." Ryalth nods once more.

Lorn waits until they are a hundred cubits from the ship and past the sweating figures unloading the coastal schooner that is tied up inshore of the *Courser.* "Why did you wait so long?" His tone is curious.

"When they want to insure, you get a better deal if you're late. They don't like holding the entire risk of a cargo. If I can't get a share, I'll find another master who has something I think I can factor for a profit. They keep my coins whether the cargo makes a profit or not. On this end, I have more control, but you can't buy shares in just incoming cargoes. Not and remain a merchanter for long."

Lorn nods, although he is far from sure he fully understands. As he considers her words, the two walk slowly northward on the walkway flanking the seawall, back toward the Trading Plaza for the Clanless Houses.

"If the *Courser* gets caught in any sort of storm, or rough seas, you'll lose fifty golds, plus your share of the outbound cargo," Lorn says finally when he is certain that they are well away from prying ears.

"That is true. If . . ." She draws out the conditional word, before adding, "Some vessels have made two or more passages with damaged keels, some even more. Some owners have knowingly sent out vessels with cracked keels."

"Why?" Lorn frowns. "Gambling on not having to replace a ship that's not worth it?"

"They didn't have the hundreds of golds necessary to repair the ship—or to replace it. It's cheaper to get a new captain and crew and offer him a fifty gold bonus to bring it back safely. Or sell it to another trader who isn't so concerned." She shrugs. "For all I know, L'Igek may know of the *Courser*'s problems. That may be why his buy-ins are cheaper."

Lorn pulls on his chin. Each moment with Ryalth teaches him that there is so much he does not know about trade. "You didn't think about telling him."

"No. I would have had to explain how I knew, and then none would ever trade with us again. They detest the Magi'i. That's also why I took the return cargo. It could come in, and if it does, or especially if L'Igek discovers the problem and survives, none of them would take another agreement from me." Her voice softens as she continues. "You know, there weren't such things as merchanters in the time of the Firstborn. The first merchanters—most of them—came from Spidlar—that's in northern Candar, east of the Westhorns."

"I know."

"But they were the only ones the Hamorians and Austrans would trade with, and in time, there were merchanters from Cyad as well."

"But that's why the Lancers and Magi'i frown on the Merchanters?"

"They also like to flaunt their superiority." She smiles.

"You don't think Bluoyal is every bit as sharp as the Majer-Commander of the Mirror Lancers?"

"He's the Emperor's advisor on trade?" Lorn laughs. "From what I've seen, he's probably sharper."

"The Magi'i and the Lancers don't think so. Your parents feel I'm below you."

"I don't."

"You aren't your parents."

At the shoreward end of the pier, Ryalth stops, well back from the carters who roll pushwagons of supplies toward the vessels moored along the piers. "I have to go back to the Plaza. I'm expecting a response from Nylyth House to a bid on shares of peppercorns from Atla. They're Hamorians."

"Do you—we—trade all over the world?"

"Only where we can make golds," she replies. "Only where we can make golds." She gestures eastward. "You'd best spend some time with your family. You've only another three eightdays left."

"Tonight?"

"Of course." For the first time during the morning, her smile is warm, radiant.

He shakes his head ruefully, smiling broadly as well. "That's what I look forward to."

Her eyes dance. "As you should."

He watches as she walks briskly back toward the Traders' Plaza. After a time, he turns and begins to walk northward toward the Road of Perpetual Light.

LI

LONG DAY?" LORN asks from the third floor landing of the formal staircase as Jerial walks slowly up one marble step after another.

"You're still here?" Jerial smiles up at Lorn as she nears the landing. "I thought you'd be elsewhere."

"I will be . . . later. What about you?"

"I'm too tired."

Lorn studies her face, clearly fatigued and drawn. Even the order-chaos levels in her body were depressed. "What happened?"

"You didn't hear?"

Lorn shakes his head. "I met Tyrsal, and then we sparred."

"There was a chaos explosion on the *Ocean Flame.* . . ." Jerial slowly shakes her head. "It wasn't that big, but it started a fire. There were many burned. I would have been home far earlier."

"Could you save any?"

"We'll see. I did what I could. They sent Myryan over to help, but we finally were dismissed."

"Because to do more would have injured you?"

Jerial nods. "I'll need a good supper and some rest."

The calling bell rings from the lower front door.

From where they sit in chairs in the third level sitting room, Lorn and Jerial frown.

"Feels like a lancer," she says.

"I'll get it." Lorn stands quickly. "You can sense that far away?"

"You could, if you worked at it." Jerial rises and straightens the green tunic, answering his unspoken question. "Sensing takes little energy. It's trying to re-balance the order and chaos that costs you."

"Just stay here." Lorn goes down the stairs quickly, reaching the privacy screen before Sylirya. "I'll see who it is." He steps around the inside screen, opens the door, and glances through the outer screen's viewing slit.

The figure in the dress uniform of a lancer is Dettaur'alt, taller, broader, and harder-faced, but still with the air of a schoolyard bully.

Lorn steps from beside the screen. "Dettaur, I didn't expect you."

The linked silver triple bars of a sub-majer glitter on the collar of Dettaur's cream and green uniform, and he inclines his head. "I was hoping to have a word with your sister Jerial, the distinguished healer, and to thank her."

Lorn gestures. "She's upstairs. Please come in." His eyes flicker toward the harbor where thin trails of smoke still drift skyward before melding into the gray of the high clouds.

"Thank you." Dettaur'alt bows again, before stepping into the house.

The two lancers head up the steps, Lorn trailing Dettaur ever so slightly.

When Dettaur steps into the third floor sitting room, he immediately bows to Jerial, who stands beside one of the upholstered armchairs. "Honored healer, I wished to convey my thanks for your efforts this afternoon. Several of the marine lancers may well survive solely because of your efforts, and one of them is the brother of my cousin's consort."

"Thank you." She motions for the visiting lancer to sit, and does so herself.

Dettaur takes the straight-backed white oak armchair across from her. Lorn sits on the other wooden armchair, to Dettaur's right.

"I heard that you aided many," Dettaur continues.

"That is what healers are for, ser. To heal. I am pleased that those efforts were of benefit to you and your family."

"Of much benefit," Dettaur insists, "and not just to my kin."

A faint smile plays across Lorn's lips, then vanishes as the more senior lancer turns in the chair.

"I did not realize you were on home leave, Lorn," Dettaur says smoothly in a deep and cultivated baritone from the back of his throat.

Lorn responds to the lie with a smile. "Even captains assigned to Isahl are privileged to get home leave every few years." He pauses, before asking, "Are you assigned here? Or are you on leave as well?"

Dettaur frowns at Lorn's familiar tone, and his eyes flick to the captain's bars on the junior officer's collar. "I've been fortunate enough to be promoted, and that requires a change of duty. The benefit of some leave goes with that." A false smile appears. "And you?"

"Merely a change of duty. The promotion came a few years back."

"We have not seen you in some time," Jerial offers an apparently sincere smile. "There must have been a reason why you came today."

"Actually, I came for two reasons, first, because of your efforts in the Lancer infirmary, and also because of your brother. I saw his . . . efforts in the exercise building, and his presence recalled your charms."

"I must admit my sparring was an effort," Lorn says easily. "I will be spending much of the few days remaining of my leave resharpening skills. I noted your proficiency, much improved from when we last sparred."

"I do regret that we will not have a chance to test ourselves against each other . . . this time." Dettaur smiles.

"There may be other times," Lorn smiles.

"Will we see you again soon?" asks Jerial politely.

"Alas, lady healer," says Dettaur, "had I not come today, reminded of your presence as I was by your brother, I could not have called at all. I leave the day after tomorrow in the morning for Assyadt as the second-in-command there." Dettaur's smile is directed at Lorn as much as at Jerial.

"I wish you well," Lorn says. "Assyadt takes many attacks from the Jeranyi."

"Fewer, once I am there," promises Dettaur.

"I am sure you will make your presence felt," Jerial says agreeably. "You have in so many ways."

"For a long time," Lorn adds.

Dettaur flushes. "For a captain, Lorn, you are . . ."

"Insubordinate?" Lorn shakes his head. "You have always sought what you wanted, and achieved it. That has gone on for years. It's hardly insubordinate to note what has occurred." Lorn's mouth forms the slightest smile. "Unwise, perhaps, but hardly insubordinate, Majer Dettaur."

"Unwise. I like that." Dettaur inclines his head to Jerial, then rises. "At your pleasure, healer, I will call again, although it will be a season or more."

"I'm sure I will be here for some time, Majer." Jerial's

smile is that of the professional warmth of a healer with a difficult patient. She inclines her head. "Until then."

"I look forward to that day, honored healer." Dettaur's smile contains a hint of triumph, but his voice remains perfectly polished as he bows, more deeply than necessary, to Jerial.

Lorn accompanies his former schoolmate down to the front door, then steps outside with the more senior lancer.

There Dettaur inclines his head, if barely. "Your sister is polite, attractive, and talented. It would be a shame for her never to consort."

"That is her choice."

"Perhaps I will change her mind."

"Perhaps you will."

"Or yours, Captain Lorn. Geliendra is far more challenging than mere barbarians."

"I appreciate the advice, Sub-Majer Dettaur." Lorn bows his head respectfully.

Dettaur's eyes glitter, but he returns the bow. "Convey my continuing regards to your sister."

"I will indeed."

Dettaur turns stiffly.

Lorn waits until the sub-majer has descended the steps to the Road of Perpetual Light before he re-enters the house. Then he hurries back upstairs.

"Dettaur asked me to convey his continuing regards."

"You know what he's suggesting, don't you?" Jerial notes from the armchair where she has remained as Lorn returns to the sitting room.

Lorn nods. The implication is clear—that Jerial will remain of the Magi'i only so long as Kien'elth remains alive, since Lorn is the eldest male, and he is of the lancers. Unless, of course, he dies before his father does, which would make Vernt the heir.

"He insulted your skills, and yet you were rather mild."

"I was using the sabre with my left hand, and he did not notice." Lorn laughs. "I trust he will remain as unobservant in the future."

"Your left hand? Why?"

"I may need it some day. In the lancers, not always do barbarians, or others, attack from where one can best defend himself."

"How long have you been using both hands?"

"Two years perhaps." Lorn pauses as their mother appears in the third floor foyer.

"That was young Dettaur, was it not?"

"It was," Jerial replies.

Nyryah glances from Jerial to Lorn. "I am surprised he would call. . . ."

"I'm not," Jerial says.

"You are a healer. He might hope, but you're certainly above him. He is a lancer, after all," suggests their mother.

"So am I," Lorn points out.

"By necessity, not by limitation of intellect or ability." Nyryah shakes her head. "I suppose I shouldn't say such, but these days there's scarcely much point in being too circumspect."

Lorn holds in a frown, and focuses what senses he can upon his mother. Yet he can sense neither the chaos of illness nor the darkness of death-order—or even a hint of either, although there is . . . something about his mother . . . something he cannot describe or even identify.

". . . never liked that young man, even when he was in school with you, Lorn. He wasn't on your level."

"He's two years older, and was a level ahead," Lorn replies.

"There was quite some talk when he broke his fingers in a korfal game. Among the healers, I mean." A faint twinkle flickers in Nyryah's eyes. "No one at the school ever figured it out, but then they didn't realize, as healers do, that the chaos of each person is as individual as eyes or the whorls on fingers. Sometimes, it lingers when men fight. A mage can change his chaos pattern, but most wouldn't think of that." She smiles wryly at her children. "Silly of me, I suppose, to remember something from years back."

Again, Lorn can only nod, accepting what cannot be acknowledged, not in Cyad, not when anywhere can fall within the ambit of a chaos glass.

Below them, two flights down, the front door opens, and Kien'elth steps into the foyer. He walks up the stairs with forced and deliberate energy. His breathing is labored. The three wait for him to join them.

Like Jerial, he moves slowly, his face pale and drawn, and he is breathing heavily when he reaches the third level. "Where have you been today?" Kien's eyes fix upon his elder son.

"I visited Tyrsal at the Quarter; we went to the little cafe off the Quarter for something to eat. Then I went over to the exercise building in the Lancers' Quarter and spent the afternoon sparring."

Kien nods. "I had not thought otherwise, but best I determine first."

"The chaos explosion?"

"You knew?"

"Not until Jerial told me." Lorn frowns. "It couldn't have been that large. I didn't sense anything."

"It wasn't large. A single cell failed in one of the fire cannons. But they were taking on oil for the lamps and other equipment, and a fragment of hot metal shredded one of the barrels." Kien gestures vaguely toward the harbor. "You should have seen the smoke."

"I might have, except that—" Lorn flushes "—I was worried about my sparring and thinking that I needed more practice."

Jerial raises her eyebrows, but does not comment on the nature of his practice, instead saying, "Dettaur just left, and he happened to notice Lorn at the exercise building. After that, of course, he found out about how I had saved a distant relative of his."

"Dettaur'alt is an honored protégé of Captain-Commander Luss'alt, Jerial, and much to be respected."

"I was very respectful, father, and even suggested that he would be welcome in the future, when he returns on furlough."

"Wise of you." Kien takes a deep breath, then sits down heavily in the chair where Dettaur had been sitting.

"Are you all right, dear?" Nyryah bustles over to her consort, touching his forehead lightly, frowning. A relieved smile crosses her face.

Jerial and Lorn exchange glances, as Lorn senses the slightest transfer of something between his parents. An almost imperceptible headshake from the younger healer to her brother is caution enough for Lorn to leave well enough alone.

"I'm better," Kien insists. "I just needed to sit down. We had to send replacement cells to the *Ocean Flame*, and there weren't enough younger mages there at the moment."

"So you pitched in as though you were twenty years younger?" Nyryah raises her eyebrows.

"What else could I do? If all the cells discharged . . . they could have thrown off the ship's tower . . . and we'd have lost another fireship." Kien half-throws his hands into the air. "What was I supposed to do?"

"Just as you did, dear," suggests Nyryah. "Except you shouldn't have charged up the stairs like a bull when you got home."

"Women . . ." mutters Kien.

Lorn and Jerial both laugh. Nyryah smiles indulgently.

LII

WEARING THE BLUES of an enumerator under a grayed waterproof, Lorn walks along the narrow way a good half-kay to the west and south of the harbor seawall. A mist verging on rain sweeps across the white city of Cyad, turning it gray. As with all storms, this one bestows a slight and nagging headache upon Lorn. In the long package also wrapped in gray cloth and then within oil-protected leather is a sabre, but not a Mirror Lancer's sabre.

Lorn's eyes finally make out the shimmering oval above

the cupritor's shop, an oval that shines through the misting rain. Once he is under the overhanging eaves that form a narrow porch, he wipes his boots on the horsehair mat, and then opens the door, stepping inside and closing it behind him. Inside, there is a foyer of sorts, with a half-door blocking entrance to the rear of the shop, where Lorn can see the chaos cells and the dipping vats, and even the special forges. A hammer rings through the building.

The very air bites at Lorn's nostrils, with a bitter taste that sears his palate as well. His eyes water, but he opens the waterproof enough to show his blues, before he steps up to the half door, on which has been fixed a polished plank the width of the door itself to form a narrow counter. How long he waits, he cannot tell precisely, but it is not an insignificant wait before a burly man, barely beyond youth, leaves his position by one of the dipping tanks and comes to the half-door.

Lorn bows his head slightly to the journeyman who steps forward to the door-counter.

"Yes, senior enumerator?" The journeyman waits for Lorn's response.

In turn, Lorn extends the stolen plaque of Dyljani House. Ryalth had not asked why he needed it, but it had taken her sources nearly two eightdays to obtain it, longer than he would have liked, but early enough, he hopes. "We have a . . . special need . . . for an outland trader."

The journeyman takes in the plaque, then raises his eyebrows as Lorn unwraps the scabbarded sabre, curved but slightly more than a lancer blade—clearly not a weapon of Cyad. He does not remark on the sharpened tip. "Yes?"

"The senior trademaster was told that you could coat this sword with a thin layer of the best cupridium, so that it would be acceptable for a master trader of Brysta to wear within Cyad, but enough so that it will fulfill its purpose." Lorn lets his voice edge slightly beyond concern, but not quite toward pleading.

The journeyman frowns. "That . . . that is something that master Wanyi will decide."

"As he should. We can but request," Lorn says in the polite voice of an enumerator.

Lorn waits as the journeyman dons a pair of heavy leather gloves before the younger man lifts the dark ordered-iron blade and carries it into the rear of the shop, and the white-haired man who finally looks up from the chaos-glistening forge. The journeyman also has taken the plaque, which he displays to the shop master even before he presents the sabre.

After a time, the younger cuprite-worker turns and heads back to Lorn—without the blade. When he reaches the half-door, he returns the plaque to Lorn. "For Dyljani House, he will do it, but only for five golds. And a good faith fee of five more."

"For the senior trademaster, it is worth such." Lorn has expected such, although the amount will leave him with but a few golds in his wallet. Both the plaque and the fee—a year's wages for a Lancer captain—are required to discourage almost all uses of cupridium except for the Mirror Lancers and the most wealthy. "He said I should provide half now, and half when the weapon is ready."

"That is acceptable."

Lorn lays the golds on the counter and receives a token in return.

"On threeday, it will be ready."

"Thank you." Lorn inclines his head. "I will so tell the senior trademaster, and I will return then." He turns and re-fastens the waterproof before stepping out of the shop.

Outside, the mist has turned to a freezing rain, driven off the Great Western Ocean so hard that it stings where it strikes Lorn's unprotected skin. Yet, after the air and the chaos mist in the cupridium-forming shop, the ice rain is more than welcome as Lorn walks carefully eastward. The rain should limit anyone screeing his actions, although there is nothing strictly forbidden about plating an ordered-iron sabre. Expensive and frowned upon, yes . . . but Lorn will need the weapon for more than one reason.

Lorn shakes his head and continues back toward the harbor, and eventually toward Myryan's dwelling. He stops by his parents' dwelling only long enough to change from the blues to a working lancer uniform before continuing on to see Myryan. By the time he has reached the Fourteenth Harbor Way East, the ice rain has become sleet that bounces off his waterproof and his face. His lancer cap is soaked, as is his hair, and cold water drips down his neck.

Myryan has been watching, for she opens the door quickly and beckons him to enter. "You're soaked, Lorn. How early were you out? Ciesrt left but a while ago. You didn't have to come, you know?" Absently, she smooths back her thick and wavy black hair.

Lorn eases the waterproof off, trying to limit the dripping to one point on the polished tiles of the entry foyer. "I didn't? How many days are left before I must return to duty?"

"Less than three-quarters of a score," she admits. "If I've counted correctly."

He grins. "So I had to come."

Her nose wrinkles. "There's something."

"I've been in the freezing rain and the sleet. . . ."

Her frown fades. "Probably nothing. Come into the kitchen. I actually made hot bread this morning—with cheese in it." She turns.

"That would be good." Lorn feels his mouth water as he follows Myryan.

LIII

THE SILVER CHALICE is a two-story structure hidden in the shadows of the second auxiliary warehouse of the Spuryl Clan, and stands a hundred cubits off Second Harbor Way West on an unnamed narrow way set between the Road of Perpetual Light and the Road of Benevolent Commerce. Behind the two archways that form a small portico are the age-varnished double doors to the Silver Chalice.

Lorn slides inside the right-hand double door, trying not to move too stiffly with the sabre inside his trousers and boot top. He wishes that he had the Brystan sabre, but it will not be ready for another two days, and if he is careful, no one will notice the difference. The Dyljani dagger remains behind the heavy blue leather of his belt.

The tile foyer offers three arches, and behind the center arch are most of those in the Silver Chalice—traders and full merchanters in blue, all men. To the left is a near empty small room with but a single bearded merchanter of indeterminate age with a woman also in blue, perhaps his consort or a cousin.

The muscular guard with the truncheon in hand nods to the right, immediately dismissing Lorn. Lorn takes in the near-empty side section where three young enumerators share one table, and a gray-haired enumerator and a woman in yellow sit in the corner. Then he moves slowly toward a table for two just beyond the arch, set so that the light from dim oil lamps will leave his face in shadow, yet from where he can watch both the traders in the larger center room, and those who enter.

The serving girl—in gray, not yellow, and not even so old as Myryan—looks down at him. "Same as last night?"

Lorn nods, and she turns toward the back. No one even close to Shevelt's description is in the tavern, nor has anyone been on the half-score occasions over the past two eightdays when he has frequented the Chalice. His other investigations and observations have been more fruitful, for which he is grateful.

A woman in entertainer's yellow staggers away from a merchant, pulling her ripped gown up across her chest, then throws the contents of a mug in the man's face. The man lurches to his feet, only to sit down as the bravo with the truncheon—nearly five cubits of silent muscle—appears before him.

Loud laughter rolls out of the center room as the merchanter sits down abruptly.

". . . got you, Fysl, she did . . . and Wosyl'll have a silver for her gown, too, and more if you're not watching your purse."

The serving girl in gray appears from the back, angling toward Lorn, who leans back slightly, watching as she sets the mug on the table with a slight *thump*. He eases three coppers into her hand. With a smile she steps away.

Lorn lifts the mug, but barely tastes the cheap red swill that passes for table wine. His eyes flick across the foyer as another merchanter steps inside, but the man is slender, and bent, and turns to the left, where he joins the couple waiting there.

"Fellow . . . seen you around . . . you the other enumerator for the red bitch?" calls the brown-haired and round-faced enumerator from the table of three.

"Ryalor, you mean?"

"Ryalor—you really think there's anyone but her?" The round-faced man laughs. "Her and two enumerators—that's all anyone sees."

"What about all the traders, Bercatl?" asks the man to the inquirer's left. "Lots of 'em, and they don't trade 'less there's coins."

Lorn shrugs and waits for a moment, until the men at the other table are silent. "Met her partner once. He's quiet. She listens to him. Don't know much about him."

The round-faced enumerator asks, "You serious?"

Lorn nods. "Told me not to say much, but I figure it doesn't matter if folks know he's real. He travels a lot."

The other two nod at their companion. "See. Told you, Bercatl. That's why they get contracts. She's safe here, and he's greasing the wheels in the outports. That's what they do in Tuylyn House, too, but they got teams that do the outports."

". . . can't . . ."

". . . Eileyt bets the House is bigger than anyone knows . . ."

". . . cause he works for 'em . . ."

"And who else'd know?"

Lorn looks past the three, politely, and the words die away. His eyes center on the archway, and the full merchants beyond.

Following an uneasy and lingering silence, the enumerators resume their conversation.

". . . Hamorians wouldn't trade fair without the fireships . . ."

". . . pretty fair . . . coins talk, too."

After a time, Lorn stands, leaves a copper by the goblet, and nods to the enumerators as he starts to leave the Silver Chalice. A few whispered words follow him.

". . . more than an enumerator. Walks like a bravo. . . ."

"Looking for someone, he is. . . ."

". . . wouldn't want to be the one he finds."

"Wouldn't want to be him if he finds what he's looking for, either. . . ."

"For a little house . . . got some scary folk there . . ."

Lorn hopes they continue to think so as he slips out.

He stops by his parents' dwelling, the lower garden only, to cache the sabre and the golden dagger, before hurrying back along the Road of Perpetual Light and thence downhill toward Ryalth's. The western sky is still partly greenish purple when he reaches Ryalth's quarters and rings the small trade bell.

Ryalth doesn't bother with the privacy screen, but opens the door and takes his hand. "You're later tonight."

Lorn offers an embarrassed smile. "Father hasn't been the same since the *Ocean Flame* explosion. I stayed and talked to him for a bit. He protested that I wasn't spending much time with the family." All of what he says is true, but he is aware of how close to his fingers he sharpens his blade, particularly given that Ryalth is far more sensitive than most merchanters.

She closes the door, and they walk toward the table. "I fixed some emburhka. It's warm, still."

"Thank you. It will be good." He smiles as he seats himself. "I wish I could have come earlier. I really do."

"I can tell that." She returns the smile. "Sometimes, I can sense how you feel." She pauses, and the smile fades. "Sometimes, it's as if you put up a screen to keep me from knowing anything." She fills the goblet before him with an amber vintage. "Try this."

"Habit . . . when you grow up in the Quarter of the Magi'i . . . you try not to reveal much. There's too much that people know or can find out anyway." He takes the goblet, sniffs, and breaks into a grin. "Alafraan! How did you get this?" The smile breaks. "You didn't pay a fortune for it, did you?"

She shakes her head, and her eyes dance. "Enjoy it. There's not as much market for it here as you might think."

Lorn takes a small sip, enjoying the mixture of fragrances, and the clean taste that calls up both spring and autumn.

Ryalth follows his example. "I wouldn't have known about it, except for you. I think we can also make some coins from it."

"Oh? How?"

"It's too delicate for the Magi'i . . ."

Lorn frowns.

". . . and too dear for the lancers, and too refined for most of the merchanters."

"It sounds like there's no one who can afford it who wants it," Lorn says. "I'm not sure I understand."

"Too much chaos surrounds the senior mages, and they're the ones who have the golds, and chaos off-puts the bouquet. That was what Esydet told me."

"So . . . what idea do you have in mind?"

"Send it by coaster to Lydiar. The Lydians will pay; we'll probably get three good cargos, two if we're unlucky before one of the big houses discovers the profit."

"So . . . after two, go to them and ask if they want shares, large shares, for their investment."

"I haven't wanted to let them know much about us. . . ."

"There's already talk," Lorn temporizes. "Let them think you're a facade for someone else."

"That's dangerous . . . especially with Shevelt pressuring me."

"I know." Lorn sighs. "I know. Maybe we can think of something else in the next few days. Either way, you can make some more golds from the Alafraan before . . . whatever. . . ." He laughs. "Is that life? Making of it what you can before . . . whatever?" His thoughts drift back to Jerial, Myryan, and his parents.

"You look so sad." Ryalth ladles the emburhka onto his platter, then sets the small basket of bread between them.

"I was thinking about my parents."

"You can't make everyone happy, Lorn. You can't live for them."

He sighs again, and feels every emotion in the sound. "I know. I won't. You know that. But . . . I'm not too sure how long father will live. Mother's keeping the chaos of age at bay. She is a healer, but . . ."

"They'll die at close to the same time?"

"I really don't know. So long as your body stays in balance, you can give a lot of balanced order-chaos force."

"But does she want to?" asks Ryalth, her voice softening.

"I don't know that, either." He snorts. "There's so much I don't know."

"That's true of everyone."

Lorn nods, then smiles at the warmth in her eyes, lifting the goblet to her.

She lifts hers as well.

LIV

THE MAGUS IN the shimmering white, with the silvered cupridium pin worn by only the three highest Senior Lectors on his collar, stands beside the Captain-Commander of the Mirror Lancers in an alcove twenty cubits from the three-story-high doors to the Great Hall—the main audience chamber of the Palace of Light. The polished white floor tiles reflect their images with but the slightest waver, portraying Luss'alt and Kharl'elth almost as clearly as might a glass.

Even Kharl's red hair and Luss's bushy black eyebrows hold their tints in their reflected images. The walls of the Palace shield them from the cold breeze that blows out of the north, creating small whitecaps on the harbor to the south, and far larger ones on the Great Western Ocean beyond.

"I suppose," Kharl says easily, "that you and the Majer-Commander have discussed increasing the number of companies of the Mirror Foot?"

"Why would the Mirror Lancers consider such?" Luss'alt frowns. "What is the need beyond duties as ship marines and guards?"

"No need, I suppose," Kharl replies. "Although . . ." He shakes his head, then smiles apologetically.

"When you beg me to ask a question, devious Second Magus, you have something to say of the nature you would have me guess. Guess I will not."

"I am sorry." Kharl smiles apologetically. "Some habits die with difficulty." He shrugs. "One dare not speak too directly in the Quarter of the Magi'i."

"You never speak that directly, honored Second Magus." Luss's bluff voice carries a hint of amusement. "But, if you would, a slight effort in that direction would be appreciated."

"Ah, yes, a slight effort." Kharl purses his lips dramatically, and his green eyes carry a sparkle of amusement, conveying an impression of youth.

Luss nods to encourage him.

"Was there not a fire upon the *Ocean Flame* an eightday past?"

"There was." Luss waits, as if to indicate that he has no intention of guessing.

"And it was caused, as you may have overheard, by the weakening of the barriers of one of the chaos cells that power the fire cannon."

"So it is said."

"You know that salt water weakens metals, and the basic order of the oceans wars against chaos reinforcement. Then . . . suppose . . . just suppose . . . that more cells are found to be weakened . . . or that the chaos towers in each ship suffer a similar degradation. . . ."

"Hmmm," muses Luss. "*If* that be the future, then we

would have to build our warships as do the Hamorians. As Rynst has already planned."

"Cannon of the old style *might* be possible," continues Kharl, "but without the threat of the fire cannon, other warships might well attempt to board ours . . . if you understand what that might entail."

"Devious mage . . ."

"You are the officer responsible for the Mirror Foot. They are trained near Cyad, as I recall. They *could* be stationed in the empty barracks by the eastern seawall. If times should become . . . unsettled . . . well . . . I trust you understand."

Luss's lips curl. "I will think upon your . . . suppositions."

"Of course, my friend. Of course." Kharl spreads his hands. "That is all I wished from you."

"Whatever it be, that is never all that you wish." Luss snorts loudly. "Never."

Kharl shrugs gracefully, as lithely as if he were still but a youth.

LV

IN THE BLUES of a senior enumerator, Lorn sits at the side table in the Silver Chalice, nursing a goblet of bitter red table wine and watching through the archway the bulging figure who has to be Shevelt—watching and listening.

The enumerators' section of the Silver Chalice is all but empty, except for a pair in the corner, a very junior blond enumerator far younger than Lorn with a dark-haired girl who giggles annoyingly and all too often.

". . . Isyt . . . don't say things like that. . . ."

". . . you are pretty . . . I wouldn't say so otherwise. . . ."

". . . you tell all the girls that . . ."

". . . none of them are like you."

Lorn glances toward the center section of the building, through the archway, to where Shevelt stands.

"Last one! Have to go and be nice to my dear brother!" bellows the big merchanter. "Last one!"

Lorn shakes his head, and rises, leaving three coppers on the table for the serving girl. He can only hope that Shevelt will not be all that long in leaving the Silver Chalice.

Without looking behind him, Lorn—a lancer attired as an enumerator—nods politely as he passes the bravo in the entry foyer. The bravo does not even return the gesture, but looks past Lorn toward the louder merchanters in the central room.

"It's always a last one, Shevelt? Is it really?"

"You'd be hurrying if your brother's consort had red hair. . . ."

A gust of laughter fills the room.

Lorn steps into the darkness outside the Silver Chalice, turning eastward, when a cold chill settles over him. He almost halts, so strong is the sense of being observed in a chaos-glass. But, instead of halting immediately, or stopping by the straggly tree barely twice his height, which he had picked out earlier for its concealing shadows, he continues walking, back in the direction of Ryalth's quarters.

"Chaos-light," he murmurs under his breath.

After finally managing to be at the Silver Chalice when Shevelt is, and when the man plans to leave and not drink all night, Lorn must pass up the opportunity—all because some magus is curious. And why? Lorn has done nothing—yet—besides his duty as a lancer, and besides showing an interest in an attractive merchanter lady.

He offers a wry smile to the night and keeps walking.

While his lady trader will be pleased to see him earlier than it has been, finding Shevelt has taken more time than Lorn would like. Yet he cannot undertake what he plans with an unknown magus watching him through a chaos-glass. If Jerial is right, all the senior Magi'i know he travels in merchanter blues . . . but that is all they should know.

He nears Second Harbor Way West, trying not to limp or to disclose the sabre tucked into his boot-top.

At least . . . at least Ryalth will be pleased to see him. Lorn just hopes the next time he finds Shevelt that the same magus does not choose that time to observe him.

The chill does not lift until Lorn is well past Fourth Harbor Way East.

LVI

THREE NIGHTS AFTER his first observation of Shevelt, once more in the blues of a senior enumerator, Lorn sits at the same side table in the Silver Chalice. He takes a sip from the goblet, half-filled with a vinegary red wine, and watches the burly Shevelt. He has little time left in Cyad, and can but hope the unknown magus does not decide to scree him this night.

At the table to his right are a pair of gray-haired enumerators, talking in phrases that rise and fall, sometimes audible over the louder merchanters in the main room, and sometimes not.

". . . no winter rain in Hydlen . . . snow's light . . ."

"Aye . . . both Easthorns and Westhorns . . ."

". . . know the lancers asked Ekyon for another five-score ranker sabres . . ."

". . . loved that, he did . . ."

The bravo in the entry foyer ignores the noise in the central room, though his fingers occasionally tighten around the golden oak truncheon.

Lorn takes another minute sip of the wine, shaking his head at the serving girl as she approaches. With her, from the back room, comes the odor of overcooked grease. At the young woman's frown, Lorn extracts a copper and lays it on the table, offering a brief smile to her.

She nods, and turns to the two enumerators.

"One more? And why not?" asks the older enumerator.

Lorn smiles, absently, as the server slips out of the smaller enumerators' section without looking back him.

". . . and he had to pay Wosyl? He should have paid her!"

Shevelt's laugh is loud, bluff, and annoying to Lorn, but he takes another sip of the bitter red wine—only a sip.

"You don't come here often enough, Shevelt! Don't be leaving so soon. . . ."

"I should come here to be insulted?" The big trader's over-hearty laugh booms forth once more, riding over the enumerators' conversation yet again.

". . . give as good as you get . . ."

"Can't stay too late . . . have some plans. . . ." Shevelt announces.

"Who is she? Another redhead?"

"No . . . Shevelt's going to journey to a strange land. She's blonde—all the way down." A bass laugh fills the room.

The laughter dies away as Shevelt lurches erect and lumbers toward an adjoining table. "If I didn't happen to be leaving, Vorgan . . . you would be. On the way to the Steps, mayhap by the long voyage. . . ."

Lorn leaves a pair of coppers on the table, nods to the gray-clad serving girl who returns with two mugs, and points to the three coppers on the wood.

The gesture earns him a fleeting smile.

". . . just joshing, Shevelt . . ."

"Off to your redhead, Shevelt . . . whichever one she is."

"When I finish my mug . . ."

Without looking back, Lorn departs the Silver Chalice, walking quickly, as if he will be late somewhere. He continues his pace all the way to Second Harbor Way West, where he slides into the late twilight shadows, and eases back perhaps fifty cubits and melds into the deeper shade that shrouds a straggly feathering conifer. He eases the left trouser leg out over the sabre in his boot—still the Lancer sabre, which means he will need a few other touches. Then he stands and waits beside the straggly tree barely twice his height, and but a score of cubits away from the arches that shield the double doors of the Silver Chalice.

The odor of overcooked grease melds with the salt air and other odors from the harbor. Only a trace of purple hangs above the low hills to the north and west, and the early night

air is warmer than it has been in more than an eightday, with
a trace of dampness that recalls fall not winter. Lorn remains
silent as another man in blue walks slowly from the west
end of the way and enters the Silver Chalice.

The right hand double-door opens, and then closes.

Lorn waits, but Shevelt does not emerge.

The sound of voices from the way behind Lorn drifts past
him, subsiding as the pair continues toward the harbor.

At last, the door opens and the tall and bulky figure in
blue that is Shevelt steps out into the night, stretching
slightly, before turning toward Lorn. Lorn waits until the
trader is within a handful of cubits before he moves.

"Trader, ser . . ." Lorn cringes, almost cowers as he scut-
tles toward Shevelt. "Trader, ser . . . a word. A word, please."

Shevelt turns, his face twisting.

Lorn backs away, but only slightly. "Ser . . . a good enumerator. I am. Good for all manner of goods and trades. . . ."

"Good? Begging in the streets? You disgust me, fellow."

"I'm better than any you have. . . ." Lorn whines, stepping
back another pace. "I can show you. . . ."

The bulky merchanter takes two surprisingly quick steps
and grabs the far smaller enumerator by the shoulder. "Who
do you think you are? I want an enumerator . . . I hire you.
You come beg at the hiring door." He starts to shake the
smaller man in blue, but the younger man slips from his
fingers and bends as if struck.

"Trash . . ." mumbles Shevelt. "Worthless scum . . . off
with you."

"Like you."

The coldness of Lorn's words, so at odds with the cringing
personality displayed a moment before, freezes the huge man
for the instant it takes for Lorn to whip the chaos-reinforced
sabre across and toward Shevelt's neck.

The merchanter gapes, but cannot even blink or form
words as the glitter of cupridium and the sparkle of chaos
cut through him. Both head and torso fall, a pair of dull
thumps on the white stones echoing faintly into the evening,
blood pooling around the momentarily twitching torso.

Lorn quickly takes out the golden scabbard and extracts the dagger, driving it into the dead man's back, rather than turn the body. He dusts the dagger's scabbard with chaos and leaves it by the head, then walks quickly along the shadowed edge of the warehouse, pausing in the deeper shadows to clean the sabre and replace it. The cleaning rag vanishes in a puff of chaos fire, and Lorn walks out onto Second Harbor Way.

Lorn has walked a good two hundred cubits when he nods politely as he passes two Mirror Lancer captains. He continues downhill for another three blocks before turning eastward onto the Road of Benevolent Commerce.

The stars are out full, and all hint of twilight has vanished from the western sky by the time he has reached Ryalth's quarters.

She has heard or sensed his approach and opens the door as he nears. She frowns briefly as she opens the door. "I'd hoped you would be earlier."

Lorn smiles wryly. "My parents wanted to talk, and then I was delayed by an obnoxious merchanter who didn't like enumerators on the same walkway. Extracting myself quietly took some time."

"You always do things quietly." After closing the door, she walks to the table.

"When I can." He offers a laugh that is not quite forced as he follows her. "I can recall a few times when it didn't work that way, and the results weren't quiet."

She smiles, an expression that combines humor, recollection, and wistfulness. "I recall one of those times. Some day you'll have to tell me about the others."

Lorn shrugs, almost sheepishly. "I broke a boy's fingers when we were in school, in a bruggage. . . ."

"A what?"

"A pile-up in a game—korfal. He suspected, but couldn't prove it." Lorn laughs. "A few days ago, he came to call on Jerial. He's a Lancer sub-majer. He deftly pointed out that she couldn't consider herself above him now, or at least not for any longer than my father lives."

Ryalth shakes her head. "In some way or another, the past comes back."

"Let's hope the good things do as well." Lorn pauses. "That does mean that he doesn't want me dead too soon."

"Oh . . . because your younger brother's a magus?"

"Exactly."

"Have you eaten?"

"Not since . . . this morning, I think. I had some dried pearapples early this afternoon, but not very many." He grins. "Kysia still has avoided meeting me." The grin fades. "It's probably better that way."

"Why don't you sit down? I waited, and I'm hungry."

Lorn holds back a wince at the sharpness of her tone. "I'm sorry." He glances at the covered dish in the middle of the small circular table.

"It's armenak—Austran creamed beef strips and noodles."

Lorn takes the ladle and serves Ryalth, then himself, offering her the bread first, as well. The armenak is strongly seasoned, but with a trilia-like tang, rather than with a chilled or pepper-like spiciness, and Lorn finds he has finished all he has served himself, when half of Ryalth's portion remains on her blue crockery platter.

"I was hungry."

"You usually are." She puts down the goblet from which she has hardly drunk and looks across the table at him. "You have to leave soon, don't you?"

"Before the end of the eightday. I can't risk being late in reporting for duty. Not as a Lancer captain with magus blood." His lips twist. "And not with senior officers waiting for mistakes."

Ryalth tilts her head quizzically.

Lorn nods ruefully. "I know. I know. But you're not a mistake. That's why I need a season or so to set things up."

Ryalth waits.

"I keep my word, lady trader, and that's one promise I want to keep. More than you know." He looks into her eyes and repeats the words. "More than you know."

"I'm glad."

They both smile.

LVII

CYAD IS SWATHED in gray, the sun sending but a dim light across the city. The fog outside the master cupritor's shop carries not only the scents of salt and the clamminess of the fog itself, but the acrid odors of acids and chaos-forming. The sounds of hammers and forges echo more loudly as Lorn, wearing the grayed waterproof, climbs the step to the narrow porch, where he wipes his boots.

After opening the door and stepping inside, Lorn closes it firmly behind him, walks forward, and waits at the countered half-door. When the young journeyman finally acknowledges him and approaches, Lorn shows the token he had received earlier and the Dyljani plaque. "I have come for the Brystan sword."

The journeyman inclines his head but slightly. "The modified *sabre* is ready, and the master would have it out of his place, masterful though the work is."

Lorn places the token and the five golds on the narrow counter—and two silvers.

The younger man takes the token, but leaves the coins on the polished wood and steps to the side and a rack that Lorn cannot fully see, returning with the sabre and the scabbard. He eases the weapon out of the scabbard for Lorn to see.

Lorn glances at it, in the manner of an enumerator unaware of and unconcerned with the intricacies of blades. "It looks as it should."

"The master also rebalanced the blade and adjusted the scabbard for the additional thickness and the point. That meant some additional rivets."

Lorn smiles, keeping the resignation from his lips, and adds another gold to the pile.

"We thank the house of Dyljani," responds the journeyman.

"The house of Dyljani thanks you and master Wanyi."

Lorn bows, then wraps the weapon in the gray cotton and the oilcloth before leaving the shop.

As he walks eastward through the heavy fog toward the harbor, swathed in his gray waterproof, Lorn hopes that his investment of more than a year's pay will provide what he needs.

LVIII

LORN STANDS IN the afternoon shadows on the upper level portico of his parents' dwelling, the wind from the Great Western Ocean in his face as he looks out across the harbor, taking in the scaffolds erected around the *Ocean Flame*, and the other fireship tied along the same pier farther seaward. From what he can tell, the two square-rigged ocean vessels on the adjacent pier are both Brystan, while the three schooners on the coastal pier are from Lydiar, Hydlen, and Gallos, if the colors of the ensigns flying from their sterns are any indication. Another vessel, with wind-billowed sails, cuts diagonally out of the southwest toward the harbor.

The wind has shifted and strengthened enough to clear out the heavy fog of the morning. Whitecaps fill the water that is as much gray as blue under the dark clouds that swirl in from the west, and the wind hints at colder weather approaching. Lorn can sense someone behind him, but he does not turn for a while.

When he does, his mother is still waiting, wearing a heavy green woollen cloak.

"I don't go to the healing center except on twoday and fourday. A small benefit of age and experience," she says. "I had hoped we could have some moments together before you left."

"Would you like to go down to the sitting room?" he asks as his eyes shift to her cloak. "It would be warmer."

"No. I like the wind. That is . . . if I'm properly attired." Her fine white eyebrows arch, under short-cut hair that has none of the mahogany Lorn recalls remaining. "The cloak is most warm." She walks toward the southwest corner of the portico.

Lorn follows and arranges two chairs so that they sit in a sheltered corner of the area where the family has often dined in warmer weather, the wind rustling and murmuring around them.

Nyryah arranges her cloak and fixes her eyes on her older son.

Lorn waits, knowing his mother will say what she desires as she wishes.

"I never have cared for young Dettaur," Nyryah finally says, "even when you were but waist-high and friends with him. He was bigger, and he hit you, sometimes when he thought no one was looking, but you never cried. His mother was my best friend when we were young. She was of the Magi'i, but her father was only a third level adept, and he died very young. She foolishly accepted Pyeal, but we all can do foolish things when we're upset."

"You never mentioned any of that."

"There was no reason to, not when you were young. We were more idealistic, then, I fear." She smiles, as if recalling a memory that gives her pleasure. "It is difficult to remain young and idealistic in Cyad. It is near-impossible to reach my age and retain all one's ideals." She frowns. "Perhaps it is better said that it is impossible to live up to those ideals."

"You and father have certainly tried," Lorn says gently.

"It may be. . . ." She stops and shakes her head. After a moment, she readjusts the cloak. "I feel old and foolish spouting grand ideas. . . ."

"What?" Lorn asks gently.

Nyryah purses her lips.

Lorn waits.

"Your father would disagree. Seldom do we disagree, you know? Still . . ." She pauses once more before continuing. "Cyad rests on the power of the chaos towers. All lands rest on some form of power. The towers are few compared to the size of Cyador. . . ." Her words trail off into the wind, yet again.

"There are a half-score fireships, each powered by a tower, and the half-score or so around the Accursed Forest, and those here in Cyad," Lorn says. "Few for a land that stretches more than fifteen hundred kays east to west."

"A quarter score in Cyad," Nyryah confirms. "At the beginning. You know, Lorn, that is a very narrow base of power. A handful of men control that power. Such creates the possibility for corruption, and that is why the Magi'i remove those from their ranks who will not put the service of chaos above self. That is why none know the Hand, and all meet him in darkness, except the Emperor. It has always been a struggle." Another quirky smile appears on her lips. "Your father reminds me of that constantly."

"He's reminded me," Lorn replies. "More than infrequently."

"There is one other thing, my son," she says slowly. "It is something so obvious that I doubt you have considered it."

Again, Lorn waits.

"You and Vernt, and even Myryan and Jerial, tend to look down on the lancer families, perhaps because there are three times as many lancer officers as Magi'i." Nyryah smiles sadly. "The number of lancer officers who are majers and commanders is less than the total number of Magi'i, and neither are numerous compared to all the folk of Cyad. You were raised among both, but how many lancer or Magi'i families are there here?"

"Two hundred Magi'i families?" Lorn hazards.

"Closer to three hundred, and the same number scattered throughout all the rest of Cyad, with most in Fyrad and Summerdock. Now . . . how many folk are there in Cyad?"

Lorn shrugs. "The Emperor's census is not made public. I would guess there are more than a thousand score."

"More than twice that." She coughs once. "Remember, a lancer officer is almost as exalted to the folk of Cyador as is a magus, even though it may not seem so among those with whom you were raised. Power is held by very few, and it has always been so, and, given the nature of the world, I fear it will always be so." She shakes her head. "What if the basis of power were in something accessible to all people? Would that make governing easier and less of a temptation for the corrupt? I don't know. I used to think so." She smiles. "I wander. I cannot ponder that forever. You may, perchance."

"Me? I don't think I'm the idealist you and father are."

"You?" A headshake follows the rueful single word question. "You have protected your idealism in a terrible way, my son. You believe those in Cyad are somehow better because the city itself is more magnificent."

Lorn does not know how best to answer such a statement.

"People will be who they are, you know. Some you can ignore. Some you can persuade, and some you can manipulate. That is where most, even in Cyad, scratch the line in sunstone."

Lorn nods.

"If you would do more . . ." Nyryah coughs, several times.

Lorn starts to rise, and she gestures for him to sit.

"Nothing of flux-chaos there," she finally says. "You can sense that for yourself."

He senses no flux-chaos within her, but the levels of order and chaos are far lower than he recalls. "You need more rest," he says.

"I do my best, dear. Holding on to your rest can sometimes be harder than we think." An enigmatic smile plays on her lips for a moment, then fades. "As I was saying, you have difficulty scratching lines. Some will attempt to do it for you. Others will act as you have."

"Yes?"

"You will soon reach that time when only one path lies before you. We all do. Your father did. I fear that holds for Jerial already. Straying from that course brings earlier death than holding to it." Her eyes harden. "Do you understand?"

Lorn nods slowly.

"I thought you might. Now . . . you have few enough evenings left here, and they are better spent with your friend than with us."

"You don't approve?"

Nyryah smiles. "You worry far too much about our approval. You must live the life you create, and you especially, unlike your brother, know far better who will aid in your creations. Your father can guide Vernt as a magus, as he could have you, but there is no one in this world of ours who knows the path you have chosen." She shifts her weight in the chair. "I am feeling the wind, and you need to do what you must."

Lorn stands and extends his hand for her to rise, feeling both the strength and the delicacy in her grip.

"She must be lovely, or Jerial would have made her displeasure known."

"She is . . . but beyond mere beauty."

"That is what I meant. You never did stop at appearances, Lorn." Nyryah walks steadily along the edge of the portico.

The clouds to the southwest have begun to lower, and the wind is damper, bringing spits of moisture that herald a fuller rain to come—and the storm headache for Lorn that is so common he can almost ignore it.

After escorting his mother down to her chambers, Lorn returns to his own rooms, where, for a time, he reflects . . . except before long, his thoughts are circling back upon themselves. Finally, he takes out the small silver book and selects a page, reading almost under his breath.

RIPENING

Like a dusk without a cloud,
a leaf without a tree,
a shell without a sea . . .
the greening of the pear
slips by.
Sly tree,
you know how . . . where . . .
So could we

> with reason,
> to follow,
> leaf by leaf by green,
> each second of the season,
> to hold the sun-hazed days,
> and wait for pears and praise
> . . . and wait for pears and praise.

Lorn frowns. Pears are rare in Cyad, and, once more, there is more to the words than their angular characters.

He smiles. He has no choice but to see what fruit will ripen in the years and seasons that lie before him. In the meantime, he sits on the edge of his bed and reads through the marked and ancient pages.

When late afternoon approaches, he re-dons the enumerator blues, and the waterproof and takes the rear stairs down to the rear garden gate.

"Who will aid in your creations . . ." he murmurs as he walks eastward along the northern walkway flanking the Road of Perpetual Light. In the continuing rain, the wind ruffles his hair and flaps the gray waterproof that covers the enumerator blues. ". . . no one who knows the path you have chosen. . . ." While those words could have meant that no one knows his goals, which he hopes to be true, the less obvious meaning is what his mother intended.

He hopes Ryalth has returned from the Plaza, and is relieved when she opens the door. Her eyes are both deep and opaque as she looks at him. She does not speak, but motions for him to enter. Lorn does so, stepping around the interior privacy screen and keeping a pleasant smile upon his face.

Ryalth closes the door gently, firmly, then faces him, her back to the green ceramic screen. "They found Shevelt's body last night—with a Dyljani dagger through his back. Everyone in the trading quarter was talking about it." She studies Lorn.

"I heard that he'd angered the Dyljani. . . ." Lorn says carefully.

"The plaque?"

"It is safe. Do you want it back?"

"No." Almost eye-to-eye, she looks levelly at Lorn. "You know that Tasjan denies the bad blood. Publicly, anyway. I suppose he has to. He's the Dyljani Clan Head. Shevelt's father Fuyol threatened to dismember all of Tasjan's heirs." Ryalth shakes her head. "Fuyol is as hot-tempered as his son was. Before he finished his screaming, at least four other house heads went to see him. They all suggested that such threats were unwise, and the rumor is that some of them suggested to Fuyol privately that a score of merchanters were quietly rejoicing at Shevelt's death. They also suggested that he name Veljan as his heir. Veljan's much more level-headed." The redhead looks at Lorn. "He's more dangerous, but that is because his consort is very bright. She is the middle daughter of Liataphi."

"The Third Magus?" Lorn's eyebrows lift.

"Liataphi has four daughters, and no sons. One daughter died years ago. Syreal was far too young when she threatened to run off if she couldn't consort with Veljan. There was a compromise. . . ." Ryalth breaks off and looks hard at him. "You knew this, didn't you?"

"I knew that Liataphi has no sons and that he has been trying to find younger Magi'i as consorts for his daughters. I'd heard Syreal consorted with a merchanter, but I didn't recall who that was, and I didn't know that there was a large settlement for her." He pauses. "It was large?"

Ryalth nods. "More than many."

"So the Magi'i would not be displeased with Veljan."

"One of Veljan's and Syreal's sons has the chaos talent and is being taught at the academy," Ryalth notes. "There are rumors that he will be accepted as a student mage."

"So long as Liataphi and Fuyol hold their power."

"They will." Ryalth steps forward and hugs Lorn. "You won't be here that long, and you haven't even hugged me."

"No . . . I haven't." His arms slip around her.

"You didn't have to do it," she whispers in his ear. "You didn't."

"I did," he murmurs back. "You would have had to handle

it, and you could, but this way . . . you can use those skills for something else, when I'm not around."

"I worry. . . ."

"I do also." Lorn steps back and offers a crooked smile.

So does she. "We don't have much time left, but you'll get something hot tonight."

They both find themselves flushing.

LIX

LORN LIFTS THE two green bags that contain his clean uniforms, laundered by the ever-unseen Kysia, and the ancient Brystan sabre that holds a shimmering cupridium finish and an edge that is every bit as sharp as the lancer sabre in the scabbard clipped to his green web belt. He has tested the Brystan weapon, and it feels better than his own sabre—except both are his.

He takes a last look around the chambers, checking to see that he has not forgotten anything, and then turns. With a wry headshake, he steps into the gray light outside his door and starts toward the formal stairs. He does not get far, because his parents appear from their chamber at the end of the corridor. Both wear heavy white woolen robes—lined with the finest Hamorian cotton, he knows.

"I know you don't like good-byes," his mother offers, "but it *will* be more than a year before you get back to Cyad." She steps forward to hug him.

"Two, at least," Lorn admits, lowering the kit bags and returning the embrace. He can feel the wetness on her cheeks, and he swallows. "I will be back."

"We know, dear." Nyryah gives him one more embrace before stepping back.

Kien'elth grasps Lorn's forearm with both hands. "It was good to see you, and to see how much you've changed in four years." He smiles. "I didn't think it would turn out this way, but you've done well, and I think you're happier doing what you do."

Even Vernt appears, standing behind his parents, although he is fully clad in the shimmercloth of a third-level adept. "Take care, Lorn."

"I will do that, but you be careful as well." Lorn steps forward and claps Vernt's forearm, adding in a lower voice, "The Quarter is just as unforgiving as the Accursed Forest." He can sense the frown that their father does not express, but he does not explain his words to either his brother or his father, who already understands what he has said, nor his reasons for voicing what they know without his advice.

Finally, he steps back, glancing around.

"You saw Myryan last night . . . didn't you?" asks Nyryah.

"I did."

"Jerial asked if she could be the one to see you off downstairs," Nyryah adds.

"We could all do that," insists Kien. "She shouldn't . . ."

"She asked it as a favor, and she never asks, dear." Nyryah looks blandly at her consort. "We should let her have that small favor."

"If Lorn doesn't think ill of us." Kien half-chuckles.

"That's fine. It doesn't matter where," Lorn replies, even as he wonders why Jerial has made such a request.

After another hug from his mother and handclasps from Vernt and his father, Lorn finally walks down the marble stairs, to find that Jerial, as the others have said, waits alone by the front door. Her face is composed, almost drawn, and her eyes flicker to the empty stairs behind Lorn.

"I didn't want to leave without . . . but . . . I didn't want to intrude. . . ." He sets down the green bags once more.

"I know you have to go." Jerial hugs him—a long and warm embrace, warmer than any Lorn can recall since childhood. Then she steps back and lifts something wrapped in cream shimmercloth—matching the fabric of the dress uniform he wears. She slips it into his hands. The object is roughly two and a half spans square and hard. Lorn can feel the polished wood beneath the cloth.

"It was father's," Jerial murmurs. "He thought he misplaced it several years ago. I knew you would need it sooner or later. It would be better if you didn't use it until you return to duty—away from Cyad. Vernt has no use for it; he has his own, and he'll never master it the way you will . . . the way you should . . . if you'd like to return to Cyad someday." Her smile is somehow both professional and warm—and disturbing. "If they hadn't let me see you off alone . . . you'd still have it."

Lorn bows ever so slightly, understanding. "Thank you. I can't tell you how much."

"Everyone has told you to be careful." Her eyes are bright, but the unshed tears do not streak her cheeks. "I will, too, but . . . believe in yourself, Lorn."

Still holding the screeing glass, he hugs her once more before stepping back, then quickly slipping the glass into the left hand bag, the one without the Brystan sabre.

"And I arranged a carriage for you. The driver is waiting. You don't need to start a journey to the Accursed Forest by carting those across Cyad on foot." She raises her dark eyebrows. "That's a lesson, younger brother. Save yourself for what you alone can do."

"Yes, elder sister."

They both smile.

Lorn lifts the bags and steps around the privacy screens, then walks down the steps to the waiting carriage.

"Firewagon portico, ser?" asks the driver.

"The one near the harbor," Lorn confirms as he slides the kit bags into the carriage.

"Yes, ser."

As the carriage begins to roll westward toward the harbor and the hint of filmy fog that irregularly shrouds the piers, Lorn turns and watches the house, but his mental images are of Myryan, who had cried the afternoon before when he had stopped to say that goodbye . . . and of a red-haired trader and the tears she—and he—had shed the night before.

His lips tighten, and his eyes harden.

Lorn'alt, Jakaafra

LX

AT THE *CREAAKING* from the front wheels, the round-faced
second level adept Magus who sits across from Lorn shakes
his head. "They need better maintenance." His eyes show an
occasional flash of the goldenness that may in future years
give him the sun-eyed appearance of more senior Magi'i.
Fine lines already radiate from the corners of those eyes, for
all that he is but a handful of years older than Lorn.

Lorn nods to the magus. Every few kays, a *creaaaaking*
has filled the front compartment of the firewagon that rolls
along the Great Eastern Highway toward Jakaafra. The sound
seems to come from the front wheels and lasts but a few
moments before fading away.

"Firewagons should be silent," the magus continues.
"Don't you think so, Captain?"

"They should be as well-maintained as possible," Lorn responds.

With a definitive nod, the magus looks to the undercaptain
on Lorn's right. "Don't you agree, Undercaptain?"

"Yes, ser," replies the dark-haired undercaptain. A faint
sheen of perspiration covers his forehead, but he makes no
move to blot it away.

Sitting on the left side of the compartment, facing forward,
Lorn watches the magus seated directly across from him, but
the man in white shimmercloth closes his eyes. After a time,
so does the black-haired undercaptain.

Seemingly the only one even half-awake in the late afternoon, Lorn rubs his chin, his fingers feeling the stubble and
the griminess of the long trip in the firewagon, and they are
not scheduled to reach Geliendra until late afternoon. He
shifts his weight on the too-lightly padded and contoured
bench seat, then once again glances out through the window,
a window whose ancient glass creates the slightest of distor-
tions, rendering the fields and dwellings that they pass less

substantial, as if they were not quite as they should be.

Once the firewagon had traversed those few kays of the Eastern Highway that bordered the northeast corner of the southern grasslands—roughly halfway between Cyad and Geliendra—the land beside the highway has become far more lush than that through which Lorn had passed on his way to Syadtar—or even that of the fertile areas around the lancer training base at Kynstaar. While he has expected to see the furled gray leaves of winter, there is green everywhere, much more than he would have expected. Yet Fyrad and the southeastern lands of Cyador are warmer, far warmer, than cool Cyad, at least in winter.

Wrapped in his own silence, Lorn watches, as outside the firewagon passes the towns, and then the well-tended holdings. Yet, for all the prosperity of those glazed brick dwellings with their intricate exterior green ceramic privacy screens, their immaculate brick outbuildings, their woodlots with their borders as neat as if they had been measured by an enumerator . . . Lorn feels vaguely uneasy. Is it because those houses are more truly Cyador than the massive sunstone and granite structures of Cyad itself? Or that such regularity is somehow at odds with the chaos that supports it? Or something deeper?

He frowns, letting his order-chaos senses reach beyond the firewagon, beyond the comforting warmth of the chaos cells at the back of the vehicle.

From what he senses, the regularity of the holdings that the firewagon carries him past is what it seems. Yet . . . something does not feel right. Or is it that he does not feel in accord with those regular holdings and what they represent? He can almost sense the chaos glass in his bag, as if it burned to be released. Yet he knows that the glass holds no chaos itself, and serves merely as a focus.

Lorn takes a long slow breath, and closes his eyes, hoping that he can sleep for some of the remaining ride to Geliendra.

LXI

As THE CARRIAGE driver reins up the two horses, Lorn glances at the twin pillared sunstone gates spaced wide enough for three carriages abreast, then at the white oak gates themselves, oiled and polished, but clearly ancient from their deep golden color. Two Mirror Lancer guards stand before each of the ten-cubit-high pillars that hold the gates, and the gates themselves are swung back into the compound, a sure indicator that they had not been built to withstand a true siege.

"We stop at the gate, sers," announces the driver of the open-topped carriage. "Be four for the two of you."

"Thank you." Lorn hands over five coppers, then opens the half-door, careful to swing his sabre clear, and then stepping down to and walking across the granite paving stones to the open luggage rack on the back where he pulls out his two green bags. He looks down, not quite sure why. While the paving stones are smooth and clean, as are all paving stones in Cyador, these bear traceries of fine hairline cracks.

"Ser . . . I could pay my own—" begins the undercaptain, reaching for his single bag.

"You could, Nythras, but consider it a favor that you'll repay when you're a captain," replies Lorn with a smile.

"Thank you, ser."

Neither of the guards looks directly at the two officers as they walk through the gates. Inside, Lorn pauses, glancing northward at the proliferation of one- and two-storied white granite structures inside the square of walls that stretch a good kay or more on a side. The compound at Geliendra is twice the size of the one at Syadtar . . . if not more.

The undercaptain glances sideways at Lorn.

Lorn offers a wry smile. "This is a new station for me, too, Nythras."

Although it is almost exactly midwinter, the air is warm,

as warm as late spring in Isahl, and damp, as damp as the sea air coming off the harbor in Cyad. Lorn takes a slow breath, trying to identify the muted fragrances and odors, a melange of scents that partakes of frysia, the decomposition of stable straw, and other floral scents new to him.

Lorn studies the layout for but a moment, then walks directly toward the large whitened granite building before them. While he can see officers and Lancer rankers entering and leaving the buildings farther to the north, there are none entering or leaving the nearest. He ducks inside the archway of the first building, glancing toward the junior squad leader who sits at a narrow table in the foyer at the end of a short corridor, much as Kielt had done at Isahl.

The squad leader looks up. "Captain, ser?"

"Captain Lorn. I'm reporting in. Is this the Commander's headquarters?"

"Ah . . . yes, ser."

"Where should I report?"

"The third building back, ser, the second archway."

"Thank you." Lorn smiles and steps back outside. In the damp and warm air of Geliendra, especially in his winter-weight uniform and under the direct sun, he is beginning to sweat. "Third building," he tells the undercaptain.

"You didn't think it was that one, did you?"

"No. But it's faster to ask than try them all." Lorn grins. "You only look uninformed once that way."

Lorn leads the way to and then into the front archway into the third building back, a low one-story granite-walled structure that, for all its cleanliness and spare lines, still radiates age. A heavy-set squad leader, one of the most rotund lancers Lorn has ever beheld, bulges over the wide table that holds a dozen wooden boxes, each filled with stacks of paper. He looks up as the two officers appear.

"This is where we report?" Lorn asks.

"Yes, ser." The squad leader's voice is a mellow tenor.

"Captain Lorn, reporting, squad leader." Lorn offers an easy smile along with the words.

"Undercaptain Nythras," the black-haired junior officer adds.

Lorn shows his seal ring, then proffers his orders. Nythras follows the captain's example.

"Squad Leader Kulurt, sers." The heavy-set lancer nods politely and scans the two scrolls before speaking again. "Captain Lorn . . ." The squad leader nods as he speaks, and his jowls quiver. "Commander Meylyd has been expecting you, and asked me to let him know as soon as you arrived. If you would wait for a moment . . ."

Lorn nods.

Kulurt heaves himself out of the white oak chair, nods again to the two officers, lumbers down the corridor directly behind his table.

Nythras glances at Lorn. "They know who you are."

Lorn doubts that is for the best. "They know who you are also. You'll see."

Kulurt returns almost immediately, breathing slightly heavily. "Undercaptain Nythras, the Commander will see you after he finishes with Captain Lorn," Kulurt explains to the more junior officer before gesturing to the corridor. "The Commander's study is the first door on the left, Captain Lorn."

"Thank you." Lorn leaves his gear against the wall and slips around the squad leader. The study door is open, and he steps inside. The study is roughly fifteen cubits square and contains little beside the desk and the chair behind it, a single chest-high bookcase to the right of the desk, and five armless chairs set out in a semicircle facing the desk. On the wall facing the door, two large windows, their panes and shutters open, admit both light and a pleasant breeze. All the furniture is of white oak, burnished by time into a deep gold. On the desk are three boxes filled with papers, an inkwell, and a pen holder. Fastened on the wall behind the commander's desk is a green-bordered wall hanging. Inside the border are four stylized golden towers set in a diamond pattern. Four narrow lightning bolts connect the towers, and within the lightning-bolt-enclosed diamond is the black outline of a single leafless tree—a tree with four gnarled branches twisting up and out from the trunk. The tips of the branches curve back from the lightning bolts.

Commander Meylyd is standing behind the polished golden surface of his table desk as Lorn enters and bows.

"Captain Lorn, ser."

The tall and slender commander offers a warm smile, with both his eyes and mouth. "Captain Lorn . . . it's good that you're here."

"I'm glad to be here, ser."

"After spending all that time on a firewagon, I'm sure you are." Meylyd responds, gesturing to the chairs before his desk and reseating himself. "I take it that your trip from Cyad was unremarkable."

"Just long." Lorn takes the chair on the left end, the one closest to the window.

"That's the way the patrols are here—most of the time." Meylyd nods, leaning back in the wooden armchair. He tightens his lips for a moment. "What do you know about what we do . . . or about the Accursed Forest?"

"Well, ser, I know that the Accursed Forest is a remnant of the wild order that once spread across all of Candar before the Firstborn. They pushed it back and confined it behind warded walls. One hears reports that at times it breaks free of those wards and must be pushed back within the boundaries." Lorn shrugs. "I understand that the Lancers patrol the walls and support the Magi'i and Mirror Engineers in bringing the wild order of the Forest back within the wards."

"That is in fact the basis of what we do here. You understand better than many, as might be expected from an officer raised in the City of Light." Meylyd purses his lips once more, leaning forward in his chair. "You'll be in charge of the Second Company in Jakaafra, Captain Lorn. There are two companies there on the north side. You and your company will patrol the northeast wall to make sure that the Forest remains within the wards. First Company patrols the towns outside the northwest wall." The commander stands. "It's good to meet you." He nods toward the door. "Majer

Maran will brief you on the specifics. He's in direct command of all the surveillance patrols. He's expecting you. The next door down."

"Yes, ser." Lorn stands quickly.

"I hear you are most capable, and this is a time when that experience will be valuable. If there is anything you need or think I should know, please let Majer Maran or me know." The commander smiles warmly a last time.

Lorn bows, then departs.

Majer Maran has clearly heard Lorn's departure, because he, too, is standing, as the captain enters his study, a chamber less than eight cubits square, and even more sparse than Commander Meylyd's study.

"Majer." Lorn bows, then straightens, studying the officer. Majer Brevyl had warned Lorn about Maran, but without specifics.

Maran stands slightly over four cubits, a good head taller than Lorn, with short, light-brown hair, mild brown eyes, and a thin brush mustache. His broad shoulders and muscular chest taper to a narrow waist and comparatively slender legs. "Greetings, Captain Lorn, and welcome to Geliendra." Maran bestows a warm and friendly smile upon the junior officer. "Please sit down."

"Thank you." Lorn takes the leftmost of the two chairs before Maran's table desk.

"There are many tales about duty here," Maran begins, sitting back in the chair behind the table desk. He sits up and rings the bell on the corner of the table. "Oh . . . I almost forgot."

Lorn wonders what Maran almost forgot, but leaves a faint smile upon his lips, although his concentration, and his chaos-order senses, are upon the door, which opens.

"Ser." A junior squad leader, thin-faced, appears with a tray, which he sets upon the corner of the desk.

"Thank you, Quenst." Maran's warm voice conveys appreciation.

A carafe and two mugs rest on the tray, as well as a dozen clean slices of white cheese, and as many wedges of thick cracker bread. A freshly sliced apple is laid out behind the cheese.

"Go ahead," Maran urges. "If you're like most of us, you don't eat much on a firewagon trip."

"That's true." Lorn lets his chaos senses flick across the carafe, and then the food, but can detect no flux that might indicate poison or other unsavory substances. So he samples a slice of cheese, an apple slice, and a wedge of the hard cracker bread, eating it carefully.

Maran pours two mugs of juice. "Redberry."

"Thank you." Lorn grasps the nearest mug and takes a small swallow.

"Patroling the Accursed Forest is not that dissimilar to patroling the Hills of Endless Grass," Maran says, "and yet it is also totally different." He smiles apologetically at Lorn.

"I understand dealing with barbarians," Lorn offers, "but exactly how does one patrol the Accursed Forest?"

Maran's warm smile turns ironic. "The Forest and the barbarians are much alike. They would invade Cyador and rob us of the fruits of chaos and prosperity. The Forest is a creation of wild order that would consume all of Cyador and return it to a forest where each creature would be ordered to destroy every man, woman, and child, because the wild order does not recognize us as a part of its patterns." Maran coughs, takes a sip from his mug, and continues. "The First-born pushed the wild order back into the smallest area possible, and confined it with barrier wards. There are a dozen chaos towers which provide chaos energy to the wards. Each tower provides enough chaos energy to power the wards for sixty-six kays, so that each ward receives power from two towers. There are eight wards evenly spaced over each kay of wall, and all are linked by cupridium cables encased in vitrified ceramic."

Lorn nods, wondering just how the Forest could escape such a chaos barrier.

"You ask, if you are like most lancer officers, how the Forest can escape such a prison." Maran pauses for another sip of redberry. "There are several ways. First, some of the trees can expel their seeds beyond the wall. Once such a seedling takes root, it grows quickly. That is why the area for a half kay back from the walls is continually tilled and sowed with salt to ensure that nothing will grow there. Second, the Forest has grown trees so large that when a branch breaks it falls across the wall. Full grown trees also fall, even when they appear to have no rot or illness. Trees or branches breach the barrier, and animals use such as a bridge to escape. We have found chaos cats over eight cubits in length, ten if you include their tails, which weighed more than fifty stone. You will see, on the wall in the officers' dining room here tonight, the remnants of the skin of a giant stun lizard killed here twenty years ago. It is twenty cubits in length. It took a special firecannon to kill it. Third, occasionally a tree will send a root under the foundations of the wall. The foundations go down more than fifty cubits." A crooked smile appears on Maran's face. "The Accursed Forest is a dangerous adversary."

Lorn waits.

"Seedlings can be destroyed by firelances, but if you destroy such, you send a lancer as a messenger immediately to the nearest Mirror Engineer detachment, with the *exact* location of the seedling. You can determine that because each ward on the wall is numbered. The first ward to the east of the north point is north ward one east; the second is north ward two east. . . . You understand? Roots are more dangerous, if infrequent, and all you can do is quarter off the area and destroy any animals that climb through them. Yes . . . they can be hollow. Fallen limbs require the most effort, because you will have to destroy all animals that try to use the limb as a bridge. The wards will eventually destroy the limb, but that could take anywhere from a day to an eight-day. . . ."

Lorn finds himself nodding.

Maran extends a thin book. "This is the patrol manual. You need to study it immediately." He shrugs offhandedly. "It is straightforward. Patrol the ward-wall. Contain the wild creatures of the Accursed Forest when it is breached. Protect your lancers and use them wisely. Oh . . . there is one structural difference here. We have one less squad leader per company. That means your senior squad leader also leads a squad." The warm smile returns. "I expect you will find time to study it. From here it is roughly a solid four-day ride to the post at Jakaafra."

Lorn takes the manual. The time to ride to Jakaafra is certainly understandable, since Geliendra is on the southernmost point of the diamond walls that surround the Forest, and Jakaafra above the northernmost.

"Your senior squad leader will be Olisenn. . . . You are expected to patrol thirty-three kays each day, and rest on the fourth. There are way stations every thirty-three kays, and, of course, an outpost at each corner of the ward-walls." Maran coughs lightly. "Tomorrow, when you're rested, first thing, we'll take a ride to the wall. There's really no other way to explain it, not really." Maran shrugs. "Some things have to be seen before any explanation makes sense. Then, the day after, you'll be in charge of taking the replacement lancers for both Westend and Jakaafra. You'll ride the wall, as, if you will, a quicker example of a patrol."

The majer rises. "In the meantime, we'll get you a room for a visiting officer. I'll give you a quick tour, and then you can get cleaned up and familiarize yourself with Geliendra. Please feel free to look throughout the compound and to ask anyone any questions."

Lorn rises. "You've been most helpful."

"Nonsense. The more you know, the better you'll do." Maran smiles his warm and friendly smile and gestures toward the study door.

LXII

THE LATE AFTERNOON air is far warmer than in many recent days when Bluoyal'mer steps onto the balcony where Luss'alt waits. After a glance at the Captain-Commander, the merchanter looks back over his shoulder, then steps away from the doorway into the Palace of Light.

The second-in-command of the Mirror Lancers does not speak as the Merchanter Advisor to the Emperor approaches, but waits for Bluoyal's words.

"The heir to the Yuryan Clan was murdered, and I wished to speak to you of it." Bluoyal bows slightly.

"That has been reported, and it is most unfortunate, but Fuyol of Yuryan has many heirs, I understand." Luss frowns, as if he is uncertain why Bluoyal has requested the meeting.

"Before I consulted with the High Lector or the Second Magus . . . I wished to advise you."

"Of what, Bluoyal'mer?" Captain-Commander Luss does not conceal his puzzlement. "The City Guards report to the Majer-Commander, but unfortunates within the city do die at times under the blade despite the efforts of the City Guards. Why would such a killing be of interest to the Magi'i . . . or me?"

"Ah . . . you do not know." Bluoyal nods happily. "That is best."

Luss waits.

"The heir was killed with a lancer sabre. A single cut of a lancer sabre."

"I wish that I could say that no lancer would do such to a trader known for his arrogance. Or that such has never happened." Luss offers a shrug and a smile. "Yet those who have their golds speak for them sometimes find themselves without voice."

"As happened with Shevelt," Bluoyal points out. "You know aught of this?"

"No. I wish that I could say that it had not happened. Or that all lancers were so effective. But it did occur. However . . . this trader was killed on foot and in the dark, as I recall. Those are not the conditions for which lancers are trained. Also, I recall something about a dagger. . . ." Luss raises his eyebrows.

"There was a dagger. It did not kill him. A healer was summoned. There were traces of focused chaos around the wound, and the killing wound was made by cupridium. Nothing else cuts the way a lancer sabre does."

Luss frowns thoughtfully. "That sounds far more like a renegade magus who has stolen a blade than any lancer officer I have known. Far more. And a lancer from the ranks, in the trade quarter? That would be impossible in Cyad. He would have been noticed immediately."

"We also looked into this. Someone stole a Dyljani trade plaque and used it as authorization to have a Brystan sabre plated and refinished with cupridium. . . ." Bluoyal lets the words drift off.

"You see . . . it could not have been a lancer. Lancers are constrained from keeping such weapons, and certainly someone would have noted an outland blade being reformulated with cupridium. Any lancer who attempted such would immediately have been noted."

"As I said . . . the man was noticed."

"Oh? Perhaps you had best explain how this might implicate a lancer." Luss waits.

"The Brystan sabre was replated—under false pretenses."

"You said such." Luss's voice betrays a trace of exasperation.

Bluoyal smiles crookedly. "There is one . . . difficulty. . . ."

"Oh?"

"The Brystan sabre was not delivered until the day after this Shevelt was murdered."

"Why are you telling me this?" questions Luss. "You claim the man was killed with chaos added to a cupridium blade that did not exist until the day after the murder. No lancer was ever seen, and the weapon was not handled by a lancer. Or is that what you wished to know?"

Bluoyal shrugs. "It is helpful. An enumerator ordered the blade to be plated, and reclaimed it. Yet no one knows who that enumerator was. Except that he was of average size and wore the garb of a senior enumerator and had ten golds and a Dyljani trade plaque."

"Ten golds? Someone could have hired a halfscore bravos for that."

"You see?"

Luss frowns.

"You do see. There are two threads. First, whoever killed this Shevelt did not wish it traced to him. Or her. Shevelt was a danger to someone. Or he knew something. That by itself is meaningless. It could have been over a woman. Or a slight. Anything. But . . . then we have someone who has taken the risk of stealing a trade plaque and spending ten golds to make a Brystan sabre cut like a lancer weapon. Yet no one has been killed in such a way in the eightday following. And the blade was not even finished when the killing took place."

Luss shakes his head.

"One other matter . . ."

Luss stares hard at the Emperor's Merchanter Advisor.

"The journeyman who dealt with the enumerator swears the man knew nothing of blades. I trust you understand what that portends."

"I fear I do. There is more here, and more than one man involved."

"Then you would not take it amiss if I discussed this with Lector Kharl?"

"Perhaps we both should," Luss suggests.

"A most excellent and worthy idea, Captain-Commander." Bluoyal blots his face with a green shimmering cloth. "Most excellent."

LXIII

IN THE EARLY morning light, Lorn rides easily beside Maran as the two lancer officers near the wall warding the Accursed Forest. Lorn's mount is a white gelding of moderate size, while Maran rides a fractious white stallion three hands taller at the shoulder than the gelding.

"You're lucky it's clear," Maran observes. "We often have an early morning fog in the winter, especially around the wall. It can make it difficult if the forest tries to use a fallen trunk as a bridge to escape because no one sees anything until the giant cats are loose and killing cattle or peasants or until a stun lizard has killed an entire wagon team."

Lorn nods, listening to the words and remembering them, neither accepting nor rejecting what the majer says.

Even from a kay away, the Accursed Forest towers into the sky, a mass of greenery that appears more like a dark, low-lying cloud than vegetation. The crown of the forest canopy rises at least two hundred cubits skyward, and the ward-wall itself appears as little more than a thin shimmering white line at the base of the trees it confines.

The grass through which the narrow road leads dies away, and the white paving stones continue toward the wall through a grayish white dirt that oozes the red chaos of salt-killed soil. The light breeze intermittently swirls powder-like soil and salt across the road. Lorn can also sense residual chaos—from firelances, or magus-bolts, or perhaps from the specal firecannon Maran had mentioned the afternoon before.

"It's amazing the first time you see it," Maran observes. "It's hard to believe that anyone could have built something this massive and so long. Remember, the part that's underground is ten times as deep as what you see."

As they approach the wall more closely, Lorn glances upward at the dark-trunked trees that appear evenly spaced just inside the wall. Each trunk appears to be set no less than thirty cubits from the next and no more than forty. At the height from which Lorn can see their bases across the top of the wall, he judges each trunk to be between ten and fifteen cubits in diameter.

Maran reins up the white stallion a good fifty cubits back from the wall, and Lorn follows the majer's lead.

Then Lorn studies the wall—a barrier not terribly high, perhaps five cubits high, low enough that he can look beyond it while mounted. Each white granite wall stone is an oblong two cubits long, one cubit high, and approximately one thick, from what Lorn can tell. The wall's thickness is three courses. He looks to the southeast, but there the wall seems to end less than a kay away, a spot marked by the fifty-cubit-high granite structure that stands a quarter kay back from the wall—the southernmost chaos tower. The tower is windowless and squat.

He glances back to his left, where the wall seems to stretch endlessly to the northwest, a line of white dwindling and then vanishing into the gray-green of the horizon. "It looks as though any one of those trees could fall and crush the wall."

"If it were a normal wall, they might. The bark and the outer layer splinter and shatter, but their heartwood absorbs all the chaos for a long time, and that allows all sorts of animals to use the trunk as a bridge." Maran snorts. "Then, to remove it from the wall proper takes special engineer equipment, and the engineers have their hands full. Sometimes, there are seeds that sprout as well."

"Even in the salted soil?"

"Even there, and at times the seeds and fragments get thrown or carried beyond the barrier strip."

Lorn glances from the wall back along the road. At most, one of the tallest trees would cover less than a quarter of the distance to where the grass begins. "How often does that happen?"

"An actual full trunk falling—perhaps ten a season in a bad season, five in a good season. Two years ago, there were close to three score in the autumn. That was the most ever."

Lorn frowns. Between twenty and forty tree trunks falling

across the wall every year? In a bad year, that might approach one an eightday.

"A giant cat or a stun lizard—they're about as dangerous as a company of barbarians."

"How many lancers do we lose every year?" asks the captain.

"Some years, perhaps a handful. Two years ago, we lost almost tenscore." Maran shrugs. "That was high." The majer turns his mount right, along the white paving stones of the twenty-cubit-wide road that parallels the wall, back along the wall toward the chaos tower.

Lorn follows, his eyes and senses still studying the wall.

Every two hundred and fifty cubits is a glittering cube of crystal, from which chaos radiates above the whitened granite. A stronger, but less obvious, line of chaos runs from ward to ward through the cupridium cables within the white ceramic casings set under the capstones of the wall, cables that link each cube with the next.

The entire wall glitters with chaos and power, yet it seems almost insignificant against the unseen wall of dark order that the Accursed Forest represents. Lorn does not quite shudder, but he wonders how Maran can accept the Forest so casually. His chaos-order senses range over Maran as they have over the wall, and he has to force himself not to stiffen in the white leather saddle. Smoldering beneath the pleasant exterior and the uniform of a lancer is a magus—or a lancer with the power of a second-level adept.

Lorn lets a faint smile cross his lips. His eyes lift and study the road and what lies ahead—the white granite structure that is one of the dozen chaos towers to power and reinforce the very structure of the ward-wall. A low chaos-reinforced white granite wall—built exactly like the ward-wall—runs from the chaos tower building to the ward-wall proper. Although it rises nearly fifty cubits above the dead and salted-soil area in which it is located, it too is dwarfed by the bulk and power of the Accursed Forest to its north.

Just what sort of chaos-power had the ancients used to

confine the Accursed Forest? And how had Cyador been able to maintain those wards for so long?

Knowing that he has more immediate problems than the source of the wards' power, Lorn glances from the wall to Maran, then back to the ward-wall.

LXIV

THE SUN HAS not cleared the crown of the Accursed Forest, effectively the eastern horizon, as Lorn's replacement lancers mount up around the second waystation on the southwestern ward-wall. The waystation is simple enough, a single low structure with stables and barracks for three squads, three officer's rooms, and a mess staffed by the local cadre of five. The walls are the same white granite as every building associated with the ward-wall, and the roof is of hard green ceramic tile.

There had been another reason for delaying Lorn's departure, he has discovered. Had he left Geliendra a day earlier, both his de facto company and the Fifth Forest Patrol Company would have been at the same waystation at the same night—a cramped situation. As it was, the two patroling groups had merely passed each other the day before.

Lorn rides the gelding out into the center of the courtyard and waits. He is in command, for the trip to Westend, of the equivalent of two squads, each headed by a very fresh junior squad leader.

Before long the two squad leaders ride up.

"Ser?" asks Kusyl, the older of the two junior squad leaders. "You want us to start on the wall?"

There are two perimeter roads that follow the ward-wall. One is set fifty cubits back from the wall—the other more than a kay back from the wall, roughly a hundred cubits back from the area of deadened soil. Patrols ride in a line abreast, one squad strung out from the wall road, one in a line inward from the outside perimeter road.

"You had the perimeter yesterday afternoon, right?" replies Lorn.

"Yes, ser."

"Then you start on the wall road. I'll be riding with you." Lorn turns in the saddle. "Fynyx . . . you and your squad patrol in from the perimeter road."

"Yes, ser."

Kusyl has already ridden back toward the lancers clustered around the stable doors. "Form up! First squad starts on the wall road!"

Fynyx follows. "Second squad here! Column by twos! Now!"

Once the squads are formed up, Kusyl reports, "First squad ready, Captain."

"Second squad, ser," Fynyx reports next.

Lorn nods and uses his heels to nudge the gelding forward and out through the open courtyard gates. A low ground mist, no more than a cubit high, covers the grass to the south and west of the waystation, fading away over the salted ground that borders the ward-wall.

"Line abreast!" go out the orders from the squad leaders.

Riding side-by-side, Lorn and Kusyl ride toward the Accursed Forest, turning their mounts onto the wall road. The column follows, each lancer turning until all are in the line abreast. Then, the first squad heads northwest in the shadow cast by the forest crown that towers over them, even though the massive trunks do not rise until they are almost seventy cubits back from the wall.

Muted sounds that Lorn cannot make out exactly drift across the comparatively low ward-wall, barely audible above the *clopping* of his mount's hoofs on the white granite stone of the road. A scent that is partly floral, partly something else, swirls past Lorn intermittently. His nostrils twitch as he tries to identify the sources . . . and fails.

"Quiet morning, ser," offers Kusyl. "Is it this quiet in the Grass Hills?"

"Sometimes, it's much quieter, except for the wind. The wind blows most of the time there." Lorn stands in the stirrups, trying to readjust to the riding he has not done for nearly half a season.

"Times . . . you can hear the big cats scream . . . eerie . . . comes across the wall like an arrow."

"I've never heard one," Lorn confesses.

"You'll know," promises the squad leader. "You'll know. No mistaking that."

The squad rides parallel to the wall road at a steady walk, passing ward after ward as the sun rises until Lorn and the lancers are riding in sunlight instead of shade.

As mid-morning nears, he wants to yawn. After two days of riding the wall, and time spent in the evening studying the ward-wall patrol manual that Maran had provided, his eyes tend to blur whenever he looks toward the chaos and whitened granite that prisons the Accursed Forest. Yet . . . he will be doing this for years to come.

Lorn glances at the wall once more, sensing the cascading webs of chaos that hold the dark order back.

"Ser!"

Lorn follows the yell and the gesture from one of the junior lancers. In the midst of the dead soil, perhaps a hundred cubits west of the wall road, rising from the salt-dead soil is a sprout of green, a shoot that is nearly three cubits high and beginning to branch out.

Lorn can sense the pulse of dark order within the green, and it almost seems as though the shoot is growing as he studies it. "Lances ready," he orders Kusyl.

"First squad! Form up! Lances ready!"

"Have them attack and discharge."

"First duad! Advance and discharge!"

Lorn watches as the first two lancers ride toward the green sprout, then rein up ten cubits short of the growth, train their lances, and discharge them. Golden-white chaos floods over the greenery, but little occurs except a shivering of the growth that is nearly shoulder high on the lancers' mounts.

"Second duad!"

As the first pair turns and rides to the rear of the column, the next two lancers ride forward and repeat the effort.

Lorn watches. It takes six lancers before the growth blackens and begins to crumble, and four more before nothing remains.

"Ser! There's no sign of anything remaining," calls Kusyl.

"Good. Have them reform while I ready the message to the Engineers."

"Yes, ser."

Lorn turns the gelding toward the wall, reining up perhaps five cubits from the shimmering granite beside one of the chaos-pulsing crystal wards. There, he takes out the grease pencil and jots down the ward number on the blank message scroll. "Ward West 163 South, 150 cubits due west of the wall road. One sprout three cubits high. Destroyed with firelances." Then he signs the missive and rolls it, riding back toward the column that has reformed. He also makes a note of the location on a blank scroll for himself.

"Ser?" asks the squad leader.

"Kusyl, here's the message to the Mirror Engineers at Westend. Pick someone to ride ahead and deliver it."

"Yes, ser." The squad leader scans the ranks. "Prytr! Forward!"

A small and wiry lancer ranker moves his mount to the side and rides along the side of the column, where he reins up. "Yes, sers?"

Kusyl extends the scroll. "You're acting as messenger. Take the captain's scroll directly to the duty desk of the Mirror Engineers at Westend."

"Yes, ser."

As Prytr rides off ahead of the column, and as the first squad resumes its measured pace and study of the wall and the deadland, Lorn glances back at the residual chaos, slowly leaching away from where solid black order and focused white-gold chaos had met. The firelances have destroyed the sprout, and infused the trunk with enough chaos to destroy the root structure, from what Lorn can sense. That he will tell no one. And it has taken full charges from a half-score of lances to destroy one thin green growth.

Under what seems an unseasonably warm winter sun, his

eyes fix on that distant spot where the white shimmering line of ward-wall merges with the darker bulk of the Accursed Forest and the horizon. Ahead of them, twenty kays or so, there is another chaos tower, just as the midpoint chaos tower lies thirty kays behind them.

Yet the chaos towers all over Cyador are weakening. How much longer will these hold, and what will hold the Accursed Forest back when they fail? Lorn snorts to himself. Unless he can determine a way to deal with both the Forest and Maran before Maran deals with him—and without alerting anyone else—Lorn will find himself failing long before the towers do.

He keeps riding, his eyes scanning the wall and the dead land stretching out from the white granite chaos bulwark.

LXV

THE COMPOUND AT Westend is a smaller version of that at Geliendra—whitened granite buildings within a square granite wall, polished oak timbered gates that stand open, and a spacious courtyard with smooth granite paving stones set edge to edge with scarcely space for the thinnest of knife-blades between them.

The sun hangs just above the western wall of the compound as Lorn leads his squads of replacement lancers in through the gates. Even before Lorn can dismount and lead his gelding into the smaller stables reserved for the officers passing through or posted at Westend, a figure hurries across the spotless white paving stones of the courtyard.

"Captain!"

Lorn turns in the saddle to see a man wearing a uniform cut like that of a lancer, but in the shimmering white of a magus, and with a tunic piped with red trim. He wears the triple-linked and lightning-crossed bars of a majer on his collar.

"Yes, ser?"

"Gebynet, Majer, Mirror Engineers. I assume you're Captain Lorn—the one who sent the message earlier today?" asks the Engineer majer.

"Yes, ser." Lorn dismounts and waits for the other to continue.

Gebynet smiles. "There's no problem. I wanted to thank you for your diligence and your accurate report. I also wanted to catch you. After you get your lancers settled, if you'd join me in the officers' dining hall . . . there are some things we should go over."

"I hope I didn't do something wrong." Lorn lets a worried frown creep across his face.

"No. The report was by the manual. But . . . if you encountered that, you may see worse on the trip to Jakaafra. . . . These things come in spurts, and I'd like to fill you in . . . just in case."

Lorn returns the smile. "I can use all the knowledge you'd like to share."

"I'll see you in a bit, then." Gebynet, a half head shorter than Lorn, turns and bustles across the courtyard.

As the sun drops below the compound walls, and shadows cover the white granite paving stones, Lorn walks the gelding into the stables, glancing around, looking for a hint of where to stable the gelding.

"Captain . . . I'll take your mount, if you would." A youth emerges from a stall, setting a pitchfork against the stall wall.

"Thank you." Lorn hands the reins to the stableboy, then unfastens the two green bags from behind his saddle.

"He'll be in the second stall here."

Lorn fumbles for a copper.

"Oh, no, ser. We're paid by the Mirror Engineers."

"Well . . . thank you."

"You're welcome, ser." The dark-haired youth smiles as he leads the gelding toward the stall.

Lorn purses his lips, then lifts his gear and heads out of the stable.

There are two officers' rooms empty, each with little more than a bunk, a table with a lamp, and wall pegs on which to hang uniforms and gear. Lorn chooses the second, seemingly slightly larger, and slides the bags under the narrow bunk. Then he closes the door, hoping that his gear—and the sabre wrapped within it—will be safe for a time. It should be, but he wonders. He'd once studied wards, years back, and read about the use of chaos-formed order to create a light-shield.

Maybe he should try that—but not at the moment, he decides, as he heads toward the officers' dining room.

Gebynet stands by a table for four with another Mirror Engineer, apparently waiting for the Mirror Lancer captain.

Lorn crosses the room that holds four tables, all vacant except for the one, and bows to the two engineers.

"Glad you could join us, Captain . . . Lorn, is it?" ventures the majer.

"Lorn. I appreciate your taking the time to fill me in."

Gebynet inclines his head to the other engineer. "This is Captain Sherpyt. He's in charge of the Second Heavy Engineers here at Westend." The senior engineer gestures around the small dining area. "Both Lancer patrol companies are out at the waystations tonight." Then he snorts. "Of course, each one's out seven out of eight nights. Much rather be an Engineer, thank you."

The three seat themselves, Lorn with Gebynet on his left, Sherpyt on his right.

On the bare wood of the table are four bowls, four large spoons, four heavy glass goblets, and a single bottle of wine—Byrdyn, Lorn suspects from the color and the aroma he can smell as Gebynet fills the three heavy glass goblets.

"The food isn't much," declares the majer. "We all eat the same, but the men's dining area is much noisier, and the service is better here."

"Not much," suggests Sherpyt. "That's why you always bring the wine."

"Of course." Gebynet smiles. "While we're waiting, I'll start." The majer takes a sip of his Byrdyn. "How tall was the shoot you fired?"

"Three cubits, maybe a shade more."

"Now . . . the Fifth Forest Company passed that area no

more than two days before, and they saw nothing," Gebynet points out, looking at Lorn.

"I don't know anything that will grow a cubit and a half a day," Lorn concedes.

"It could be a root, or a seedling that was launched from the Forest."

"If it's a root, you'll hear lots of heavy equipment moving in the morning," adds Sherpyt morosely. "We'll be working there for a good eightday."

Lorn does not speculate or reveal his sense that no root from the Accursed Forest had been involved. "I hope it wasn't a root."

"It could have been worse. If you hadn't been there, that shoot would have turned into a tree eight to ten cubits tall by the next patrol."

Lorn fingers his chin. "I don't think all my firelances could have burned something that large down."

"That's where Sherpyt and his heavy equipment come in," suggests Gebynet. "But most don't grow quite that fast." He pauses. "You're sure it was that tall?"

"At least. It was shoulder high on the mounts."

The Engineer majer shakes his head, then takes another swallow of the Byrdyn. "It could be that we'll have another breakout period. That's when you get shoots, roots, and trunks falling across the wall everywhere. Stun lizards crawling into the nearby villages. Cattle killed by the big cats . . . all sorts of amusing things."

"How do you even find the cats?"

"We don't find them all. That's why stun lizards and crocodators show up in the Great Canal or in the rivers. That's why there are giant cats throughout this part of Cyador . . . but the offspring of those that survive are smaller than those that first escape." Gebynet's lips twist into a crooked smile. "The animals aren't the problem; the trees and the vines and bushes are."

"Speak for yourself, majer," suggests Sherpyt.

"Ah . . . well, it shouldn't affect you, Captain Lorn, but the cats and stun lizards seem to seek out people who handle chaos—mages especially, and then engineers like Sherpyt who handle chaos-powered equipment."

"Have any attacked you?"

Sherpyt pulls back his sleeve. A long red gash runs up his forearm, disappearing under the white shimmercloth. "There's another on my leg. Two different attacks."

"That's another reason why all the Engineers on duty beyond the compound carry the short firelances in sheaths," Gebynet explains.

A server in solid green appears with a casserole dish, and a basket of bread, then vanishes without speaking.

"Best we eat while it's hot." Gebynet serves himself two ladlefuls of the mutton stew, consisting mostly of mutton chunks, carrots, and some other root vegetable that Lorn does not recognize by sight. Gebynet passes the casserole to Lorn, and breaks off a chunk of the rye bread. "Eat hearty."

The primary taste of the stew is salt. The carrots are orange mush, while the roots have been cooked until they are soft masses held together with stringy fibers. Lorn alternates stew, bread, and very small sips of the Byrdyn.

"Exactly what do engineers do here?" asks Lorn after several mouthfuls. "Besides destroying growth that escapes from the Forest. Or is that all?"

"We're the ones who repair the wall if it gets breached. That doesn't happen often," the majer explains. "We also repair anything else that needs it."

"How often?" Lorn persists.

Gebynet frowns, then wrinkles his forehead. "Only about once or twice a year, and those aren't big breaches—usually only a course or two of stone—and replacing the cables. That's the harder part because you have to break the connections on two of the wards, and that usually means replacing those as well."

Lorn lifts his eyebrows, hoping that the Engineer majer will add more.

"Repeated chaos flows make anything brittle. The wards have chaos flowing through them all the time. They're solid when they're in place, but if anything breaks through the chaos net—or moves them—most of them shatter."

Lorn takes more of the stew, and more bread, and enough of a sip of the wine to provide a hint of seasoning, pondering what the two engineers have conveyed. "You're more like Magi'i than Lancers. . . ."

"Almost all of the officers are about the same as third or fourth level mage adepts," concurs Gebynet. "At some point, it was suggested to each of us that our talents might be better used in the Engineers."

"We're Magi'i with tools, Lorn," adds Sherpyt. "With tools and with far less status and power."

Lorn frowns.

"Have you ever seen a Mirror Engineer in Cyad?"

The Lancer officer shakes his head.

"You never will." Sherpyt delivers his words in a matter-of-fact tone that offers more caution than would any amount of bitterness or emotion. "When they need us to work on a fireship, it goes to the yard at Fyrad. The Magi'i handle chaos repairs in Cyad."

Lorn nods.

"Our talents are necessary, and best kept where they can be employed most fully," Sherpyt adds.

"Just like those lancer officers who are unwise enough to reveal that they can handle chaos," Gebynet adds smoothly. "But enough of details. I trust you understand why we wanted to let you know why we appreciated your timely report on that shoot, and why such reports save us in the Engineers from even greater . . . difficulties."

"I had not realized the speed with which the Accursed Forest grew." Lorn takes a last mouthful of the stew, knowing he can stomach no more.

"Until they have seen it with their own eyes, most do not," answers Gebynet.

"It can be frightening," agrees Sherpyt, pushing his bowl away, and taking a slow sip of the Byrdyn.

Lorn finds himself yawning.

"You have had a long patrol already, with another three

days to go." The Engineer majer lifts an empty glass. "Do not let us keep you."

Lorn rises. "I must thank you both for the wine, the hospitality, and for enlightening me about my duties and the dangers that accompany them."

"Our pleasure. Our pleasure." Gebynet's voice is warm, and his eyes and mouth both smile. "Anything we can do . . . please let us know."

"I will." Lorn bows slightly, before he steps back toward his temporary room. "I certainly will."

LXVI

THE ALMOST-SETTING SUN falls on Lorn's left shoulder as he rides northeast along the outer perimeter road toward the white walls a kay ahead—walls that mark the Mirror Lancer compound at Jakaafra. The sky above the compound is already darkening with clouds sweeping in from the east. A chill wind blows into the Lancer captain's face, a wind bringing a raw dampness that foreshadows rain—or sleet. Behind Lorn rides a half-squad of lancers, just gathered in from their line abreast formation, the senior ranker riding beside him.

Despite the warnings from the two engineers three days earlier in Westend, neither Lorn nor any lancers in the squad have seen any other sign of the Accursed Forest attempting to escape the confines of the ward-wall.

Lorn's eyes flick to his right, toward the ward-wall itself where Kusyl rides with the other half of the replacement squad, then back to the compound ahead, and the white granite bulk of the chaos tower adjoining the compound and looming over it.

"Not too far to go," Lorn offers, his words barely louder than the sound of hoofs on the granite stones of the perimeter road.

"No, ser. Should get there before the rain," replies Ubylt, the ranking lancer in the squad.

A hundred cubits ahead, to Lorn's left, splitting off at an angle from the outer perimeter road runs another road, to the northwest.

"That goes where? Do you know, Ubylt?"

"To the town of Jakaafra, ser. Folks use the outer road to get to the towns around Westend. Be faster that way."

Lorn nods to himself.

Hoofs *clop* on the hard granite of the road as Lorn and the half score of lancers with him ride toward the compound, an oblong of light compared to the towering darkness of the Accursed Forest just to the south.

Kusyl brings his half of the replacement squad toward the compound on the western kay-long connecting road that parallels the wall running from the ward-wall proper to the white-granite bulk of the structure housing the chaos-tower. The stone glows faintly with the suffused energy of chaos in the growing darkness of late twilight, a glow invisible to those without Magi'i-like talents.

"Didn't see anything, ser, not on this last leg," the squad leader reports to Lorn.

"We didn't either, and I'm grateful for that."

Lorn and Kusyl lead the recombined squad through the open gates. The compound at Jakaafra could almost be a duplicate of the one at Westend, except that the gates are in the middle of the southern wall, rather than in the middle of the eastern wall.

Two lancers are lighting the lamps on the wall behind the gates, and lamps have already been lit on several of the low stone structures deeper within the outpost.

"Stables that way, ser," suggests Kusyl, gesturing ahead and to his left.

"Thank you." Lorn urges the gelding leftward.

A heavy-set and jowled lancer waits by the stables, his round face impassive in the light of the lamp in the holder to the left of the door, his eyes cold as he surveys the approaching column. He steps forward as he catches sight of Lorn. "You're the new captain, ser? For Second Company."

"I am. Captain Lorn, squad leader."

"Olisenn, ser." Olisenn's mouth smiles; his eyes do not. "Senior squad leader."

"Pleased to see you, Olisenn." Lorn swings out of his saddle and gestures to Kusyl. "Squad leader Kusyl. I believe he'll be leading the second squad."

Kusyl dismounts quickly.

"Good to meet you, Kusyl." Olisenn nods to the junior squad leader before turning back to Lorn. "You have the second room in the officers' section, ser. I'll be taking Kusyl to show him the quarters, if that be to your agreement."

"Once the mounts are set, that would be fine." Lorn nods to both squad leaders.

Both bow before they turn away.

As in Westend, a stableboy scurries up to take Lorn's gelding, and he has to remind himself to recover his gear.

Lorn walks from the stables, carrying his gear, and starts toward the end of the barracks building that should hold the officers' quarters. As he nears the lamp-flanked door on the south end, another lancer captain emerges and struts toward Lorn.

The oncoming officer is dark-haired, slightly taller than Lorn, but slender, with a thin mustache, and black eyes. His uniform is tailored to show a narrow waist, and the custom white boots shimmer, reflecting the courtyard lamps. He stops a good five cubits from Lorn. "You must be the new Second Company officer, I take it."

"That's right. I'm Lorn."

"Meisyl. I'm the one you're relieving. You picked a good time to arrive. We just finished patrol."

"So we'll have tomorrow standing down."

"Exactly."

Belatedly, Lorn lifts the hand with the seal ring, and starts to reach for his orders.

"We can handle that in the morning." Meisyl laughs, a languorous sound, as if he finds the exchange both amusing and boring simultaneously. "I'll take you through the records and all the reports that Commander Meylyd so enjoys."

"When you think it best," Lorn demurs.

"Tomorrow is early enough. I won't be leaving until tomorrow afternoon anyway."

"How will you get back to Geliendra?" Lorn asks. "You aren't riding back by yourself? Or taking a detachment of lancers for rotation?"

"Oh, no. The rotated lancers won't leave for an eightday. I'll catch a ride on the Engineer's small firewagon on its next run for replacement wards or whatever." Meisyl shrugs almost delicately. "It only takes two days to get to Geliendra from here that way.

"You have the second room. It's the same as the first, and when I leave you can take your choice. The third is smaller, and that belongs to Undercaptain Juist. He heads the First Company; they do the domestic patrol. He's been an undercaptain for a long while, but he was promoted from senior squad leader when they did such." Meisyl dismisses Juist's promotion with a graceful wave of his long-fingered left hand.

Lorn nods.

"I'll see you in the officers' dining room—just the two of us tonight—after you're settled. Olisenn will take care of the incoming men."

"We've discussed that," Lorn says. "He was waiting for Kusyl and me."

"Very conscientious, Olisenn is," Meisyl replies. "Most knowledgeable about many matters as well." With another smile he turns.

Lorn picks up the green bags and begins to cross the courtyard, following Meisyl's steps. The wind has continued to rise, and the faint *splatt* of rain on stone begins to fill the courtyard.

The second room in the officers' section is more spacious than that in Westend, and it even has a wardrobe and a narrow desk with a separate lamp in a bracket over the table desk.

After closing the white oak door behind him, Lorn unpacks his uniforms, hanging the tunics in the space in the wardrobe and the waterproof and winter jacket on the wall pegs. The screeing glass goes under his smallclothes in the wardrobe, but he leaves the Brystan sabre in one of the two green bags that he folds and slips into the shelf under the single bunk. Then he goes to find the wash chamber where he shaves and cleans up before repairing to the officers' small dining room.

Meisyl is waiting, but does not stand as Lorn approaches, merely gesturing for him to seat himself. Meisyl has a bottle of wine before him, and there are two of the heavy goblets on the time-darkened but bare and smoothly polished white oak of the table.

"That's one thing, Lorn. You have to make arrangements for your own ale or wine. I'd suggest the chandler in Ja-kaafra. His name is Duluk. Very fastidious about his wines. Sometimes he can even get Alafraan."

"All the way from Escadr?" Lorn lifts his eyebrows.

Meisyl laughs. "I'll win a gold from Juist on that."

"The Alafraan's better than Fhynyco. At least, I think so."

"Depends on whether you like body or bouquet better." Again, Meisyl's tone is almost bored. "The Alafraan goes better with meat. I like the Fhynyco better with fowl. Only desperate men drink Byrdyn." He fills the two goblets three-quarters full and nods to Lorn.

"Thank you." Taking the nearest goblet, Lorn reflects that, while he enjoyed Zandrey's Alafraan while he was stationed at Isahl, he has never been desperate for any kind of wine. "Desperate men do have strange tastes."

A server in green appears with platters and cutlery which he sets on the side of the table, quickly leaving and then reappearing with a larger serving platter and two baskets. "Sers?"

"Just put it down," Meisyl orders off-handedly.

"Thank you." Lorn nods to the server, who bows and re-treats.

Dinner is a platter with sliced mutton covered with a brown sauce and boiled potatoes in one of the baskets. The second basket holds bread—cool.

"The other company here? Juist's?" asks Lorn. "They patrol the northeast perimeter?"

"Not except for the eightdays when Second Company's on furlough." Meisyl shakes his head. "They're the peacemaking company for the villages on the north side of the Accursed Forest. Juist acts as a justicer about half the time. They also chase bandits . . . when there are any."

"Peacemaking?" Lorn raises his eyebrows.

"Once you get north of the Forest, there aren't that many towns between here and the Westhorns or the Hills of Endless Grass. It's almost like a province. So someone has to act as the Emperor's Presence. Juist is good at it; he understands those people." Meisyl offers a condescending sniff before he takes a small swallow of the purplish Alafraan.

"So there's no Engineer detachment here? Just the two Lancer companies?"

"This is the only perimeter base that has no Engineers. They send a detachment here every third day to check the tower. I'll ride back on their firewagon."

Lorn wonders. Is he stationed at Jakaafra for just that reason? That it is the only base without the engineers who are effectively low-level adept mages? Who else like him has been stationed at Jakaafra? How would he find out?

"How many engineers do they send up here?"

"Three or four, usually. Mostly officers." Meisyl breaks off a chunk of bread and dips it in the brown sauce. "You'll get to know them all . . . such as they are."

"Has there been much trouble with the Accursed Forest lately?" Lorn takes a bite of the dry mutton, glad for the sauce.

"Not for a season. Oh, you always have shoots and seedlings popping up somewhere, but that's to be expected. We haven't seen a limb bridge in . . ." Meisyl frowns. ". . . since late summer. There are always a few trunks falling over a season, but it's been a while lately. So you won't have many lancers left who are prepared for more than the occasional order-assault."

"I suppose the records tell how long. . . . Where are the

records on the Second Company?" asks Lorn guilelessly.

"You have a study. Or you will tomorrow. It's the building across from the north end of the barracks. Olisenn keeps the records on the men, and they're in a chest in the outer study when he's not working on them." Meisyl looks at the already half-empty bottle of Alafraan. "It will be pleasant to return somewhere that one can get a decent wine besides Alafraan."

"Where will you be going?"

"The port detachment at Summerdock. My consort-to-be will be joining me there, as my consort, then, of course."

"You must be nearing sub-majer."

"A mere formality." Meisyl refills his goblet and glances at Lorn.

"No, thank you." Lorn smiles, knowing he must be scrupulously polite all the while Meisyl remains. "Tell me about how you came to Jakaafra, if you would."

"There's little enough to say. I grew up in Fyrad, and went to the Lancer Academy, as had my sire, and his sire. . . ."

Lorn smiles and nods, taking another sip of Alafraan, one so small that the wine never really passes his lips.

LXVII

MEISYL AND LORN stand in the rear study by the desk table. Outside the single window the morning is gray, and fat drops of rain splat against the ancient glass panes. Meisyl reads the single sheet of paper drafted by Olisenn, then smiles, and affixes his signature before handing it to Lorn, who reads it himself.

> . . . certifies that Meisyl, Lancer captain commanding the Second Forest Patrol Company, hereby relinquishes that command to Lorn, Lancer captain, and that upon signature this fourday of the ninth eightday of winter, in the year one hundred ninety-seven of the founding of Cyad, Captain Lorn assumes command of the Second

Company, with all duties and privileges associated thereto. . . .

Lorn signs the bottom of the document, below Meisyl, with scripted characters far less flamboyant than those of the dark-haired captain who is departing.

"You have it all, Lorn, and I wish you well." Meisyl's smile is clearly one of relief. He fumbles two bronze keys from his belt wallet and extends them to Lorn. "The first key here is the key to the records' chests. The second one is to the door locks for the officers' rooms. If you have any questions, I won't be leaving until late this afternoon or tomorrow, depending on the engineers."

"Thank you. I'll find you, if I do."

After Meisyl departs, Lorn looks over his study closely, for it is the first individual study he has had in his duties with the Mirror Lancers. The room is small, seven cubits by seven, with only a narrow table-desk set against the wall, and a single chair pulled up to the desk, and a window with a chest-high sill behind the chair. The sole lamp is fixed in a bronze bracket on the wall over the desk. Set on the granite floor tiles, just in front of the desk, there is a foot chest, two cubits broad, one cubit high and one deep. A single armless chair completes the study's furnishings. With the exception of the lamp, every item in the room is formed of white oak, and all hold the gold of age.

Lorn nods and then steps out through the open door into the outer study where Olisenn is seated at a larger table, an open foot chest on the floor to his right.

"Yes, ser?"

"Captain Meisyl mentioned that you maintain two sets of records, Olisenn. . . ."

Olisenn smiles. "Just one, ser. There are two sets of records." He points to the foot trunk beside his work table. "The ones I keep are the individual personnel records. There is one sheet on each lancer . . . the lancer's name and rank, a simple physical description, place and date of birth, his closest family, when the lancer joined, his term of service, and past duty stations, and expected date of rotation. The reverse side is used for remarks, either for commendations or disciplinary actions." Olisenn lifts his ample shoulders. "Now . . . I have to make a sheet on each new lancer."

"The ones who arrived yesterday?"

"Yes, ser. I'll start each sheet, and Kusyl will be here shortly to finish them. They all go here in this chest." His hand drops to indicate the foot chest to his right.

"And the other set?"

"Those are the patrol records in the chest in your study, ser. Those are the only records we keep. The bronze key Captain Meisyl gave you . . . it opens the lock on either chest."

"He mentioned that." Lorn nods. "Later today, or perhaps after the first patrol, I'd like to read through your records."

"Whenever you wish, ser. It would be better after we update the records."

"I'll try not to impede your work." Lorn turns and re-enters the smaller rear study. He closes the door, and then lifts the records' chest onto his desk. The key slides smoothly into the lock and turns easily.

As Olisenn has said, the trunk holds the patrol records, a report on each patrol, written and signed by the company's captain. Leafing through the most recent of these, Lorn notes that most of the time a number of patrols have been reported on a single sheet, with little more than the notation "Patrol on schedule. No Forest activity," followed by "Meisyl, Captain, Second Forest Patrol Company."

Others have more description:

. . . ward cube crushed by limb, north 45˚ east. Killed small stun lizard, seared seedlings, found giant cat tracks, but no cat. Sent messenger to First Engineer Company at Eastend. Held station on fallen limb until Engineers arrived. No casualties . . .

. . . two ward cubes destroyed by double limb, north 323 and 324 east. One giant cat attacked second squad.

Cat killed. Two other cats fled as Second Company arrived. Stun lizard tracks noted. Sent messenger to First
Engineer Company Eastend. Held station until Engineers arrived. Casualties: 2. Kyscyt killed by cat at
ward-wall. Onymt slashed, will probably lose right
arm . . .

Lorn leafs through the reports more quickly, more trying
to get a feel for the pattern of what has happened with the
Accursed Forest than deeply analyzing the reports. Roughly
three years earlier, patrol reports for nearly three eightdays
have been signed by Olisenn, as senior squad leader. Lorn
picks up the report just before the first one signed by Olisenn,
but, like so many of the others, it merely states, "Patrol on
schedule." It is signed, "Dymytri, Captain, Second Forest
Patrol Company."

After studying Dymytri's last report, Lorn flips through
the papers more rapidly until he reaches Dymytri's first report—only three seasons before his last. Then he looks at
the reports before that—four eightdays' worth, all signed by
a senior squad leader named Fyondr. The previous head of
Second company had been Undercaptain Zylynt, who had
been in command only a few eightdays more than a year.
Zylynt's demise, unlike Dymytri's, is listed in the first report
signed by Fyondr: ". . . Casualties: 2. Undercaptain Zylynt,
killed by giant stun lizard when firelance failed. Lancer
Hyun, killed by lizard while supporting Undercaptain . . ."

Abruptly, Lorn comes to the end of the Patrol reports.
After a moment, he nods and replaces the files in the small
foot trunk and closes it. "Olisenn?"

After a moment, the heavy squad leader opens the door
and lumbers into the rear study. "Yes, ser?" He bows slightly
following his words.

"The Patrol reports only go back about five years," Lorn
observes.

"Yes, ser. We just keep five years here, sometimes almost
six, but since you were scheduled in, Captain Meisyl sent
off the older ones last eightday. They're all in Majer Maran's

files in Geliendra." Olisenn nods. "It keeps matters easier here."

"I can see that." Lorn smiles. "Thank you,"

"That's not a problem, ser. It's what I'm here for." Olisenn nods and waits for a moment before asking, "Is there anything else, ser?"

"No, thank you." Lorn stands. "I'm going to inspect the compound, Olisenn. I'll be gone for a while."

Olisenn's eyes lift to take in Lorn. "Would you prefer me to accompany you?"

"I don't think that's necessary. If I have questions, I'll ask you when I get back. You and Kusyl have more than a few records to update with all the replacement lancers that arrived."

"That is true, ser." The senior squad leader turns and walks back out through the door, closing it behind him.

Lorn replaces the Patrol reports in the foot chest and locks it, replacing it on the floor where it had been, then opens his door and steps out into the outer study.

"Ser!" says Kusyl, who has apparently just arrived.

"Just keep on with getting the personnel records in order, Kusyl, Olisenn. I'm going to get more familiar with everything in the compound." Lorn nods and steps past the junior squad leader out into the short corridor that leads out to the courtyard.

The rain that had been falling earlier in the morning has given way to a fine and cold drizzle. Lorn readjusts the summer garrison cap and steps out into the courtyard, heading toward the stables.

The mist-shrouded courtyard remains empty as Lorn crosses the damp stones to the stables, where he eases through the barely open sliding door into the warmer and drier air of the stable. He blots his forehead and glances around, then begins to walk farther back into the stable. The main corridors are swept clean, and each stall contains fresh straw. He glances upward, but he sees no cobwebs, or any piles of dirt in the corners.

"Ser? Is something wrong?" The thin-faced blond-haired

stableboy appears, a worn broom in his right hand.

"Not a thing." Lorn glances toward the stall where the gelding is. "Since I'm new here, I'm just trying to learn about things. What's your name?"

"Suforis, ser."

"I'm Captain Lorn, Suforis. How long have you been here?"

"I only started here when Captain Dymytri was in charge . . . winter turn when I was twelve. Say the captain afore him was nice, too, but I didn't know him."

"Do you like it here?"

"Yes, ser. So long as I keep the stable clean and the officers' mounts and the spares groomed, and all of them fed, Clebyl doesn't look my way, and that's fine by me. Lesyna— she's agreed to be my consort next winter turn, and Clebyl says I can be the assistant compound keeper if I keep working good. Haven't had an assistant here in two years. Assistants get the second quarters with the kitchen." Suforis smiles brightly.

"How many stalls do you have?"

"Stable has two score and twelve—enough for two companies and a half score spares. Not that many, though, 'cause Undercaptain Juist only has a score and a half for the domestic patrol. Says he doesn't need that many, really, but I'm not supposed to know such."

"He must not have much trouble."

"Almost never. Towns north of here real peaceable, ser. Good reason to live here. They say some of the rankers settle down here when they get through."

"How are the mounts?" Lorn gestures toward the gelding.

"Yours be a good'un, ser. Most are. Have to rotate the mount the big squad leader rides, even if he gets the biggest. . . ." Suforis shakes his head. "Other 'n that, n' gettin' the farrier up here from Jakaafra regular like . . . well . . . take care of the mounts, and they take care of you. Get to ride the spares . . . make sure that they get exercise . . . it be a good life. . . ."

"Good." Lorn smiles. "Anything I should know?"

"Well . . . ser . . . not that I'd be knowing, but I heard tell that if'n you run into a stun lizard best you stay leastwise fifteen cubits back. Cats don't matter much . . . have to get claws into you, and if'n they do . . ." Suforis shrugs.

"I appreciate the advice, Suforis. If there's any way I can help out . . . let me know."

"Thank you, ser." The young man bobs his head.

"Thank you." Lorn turns and slips back out into the courtyard and the drizzle. Looking up into the clouds, he nods abruptly and heads back to his quarters.

Once he crosses the courtyard and enters his quarters, Lorn locks the door, then opens the wardrobe and extracts the screeing glass Jerial had stolen from their father's study and given to him. Carefully, he sets it on the desk and studies it. Can he do what he knows can be done? What his father and the Senior Lectors can?

Finally, he pulls up the chair, seats himself, and concentrates on the circular mirror. His thoughts go to the enigmatic Olisenn. Lorn doesn't want to try Maran unless he becomes proficient.

The glass fills with a grayish mist, which silvers into a blank and bright surface reflecting nothing. Finally, a small image swims into view—two squad leaders at a table.

Lorn swallows, surprised, and loses his concentration. A blank glass reflects his own perspiring face back at him. A single drop of sweat falls on the glass.

He can do it!

He leans back in the chair and takes a deep breath. How can he develop and use the skill . . . without revealing that he possesses it, for revealing it will certainly create greater incentives for the senior Magi'i and Mirror Lancer officers to ensure his death—and the Second Company records illustrate a high mortality for company officers—a mortality higher than for the average lancer, and far higher than it would be reasonable to expect.

LXVIII

IN THE GRAYNESS of dawn in late winter, Lorn leads his white gelding from the stable in the first waystation on the northeast side of the Accursed Forest—exactly thirty-three kays southeast of the compound at Jakaafra.

Olisenn is waiting, standing by the oversized mount that will bear him.

"It looks like another cool morning, Olisenn," Lorn offers.

"Yes, ser. It won't be long before the Forest truly stirs."

"I wouldn't be surprised." Lorn waits for whatever the senior squad leader has in mind.

"You intend to keep riding with the second squad and Kusyl, ser?" asks Olisenn.

"It seems like a good idea for now," Lorn temporizes. "You have the experience to command the first squad, indeed all of Second Company, should anything happen to me. Kusyl does not."

"But I cannot offer easily any insights."

"That is true, but perhaps you can continue to share them in the evenings at the waystations. In that fashion, all can benefit." Lorn smiles easily.

"I will as I can, Captain."

"I'm sure you will, Olisenn, and we all appreciate your knowledge and experience." With another smile, Lorn mounts and then guides the gelding to his right, to where Kusyl has begun to form up the second squad.

"Ser?"

"I'll be riding with second squad today, possibly for the entire patrol." Lorn shrugs. "We'll have to see how things go."

Kusyl nods.

Once both squads are formed up and mounted, waiting in waystation courtyard under the heavy but formless gray clouds, Lorn gestures for Kusyl and Olisenn to bring their mounts nearer. He waits until they have reined up before he speaks. "This morning, second squad will ride the wall position; first squad will do the perimeter."

"Yes, ser."

"Yes, ser."

"Let's go."

The sound of hoofs on stone echoes for a brief time as Second Company rides through the gates and toward the ward-wall, each squad deploying into the spread line-abreast formation used for surveillance of the border of the Accursed Forest.

Lorn rides about twenty cubits to the right of Kusyl, closer than the normal spread of fifty. Despite the lingering dampness, the ward-wall is dry and sparkles in the indirect light filtering through the low-lying clouds.

The sun continues to struggle to burn through the mist left from the rain of the night before, but without complete success, so that the second squad rides along the ward-wall under a sky that shifts from dark to bright gray, then almost brilliant white, before it turns darker once more.

One stretch of wall looks precisely like another, white-gray blocks evenly matched, topped with crystal wards that flicker chaos. The wall stretches southeast, seemingly an endless line to the horizon.

ZZZZzzzzzpt! Lorn frowns as he turns toward the sound above the wall. At a second loud *zapping* sound, he glances toward Kusyl. "Kusyl?"

Noting Lorn's expression, Kusyl calls back an answer. "One of the big flowerflies, ser, the bloodsucking ones. Some reason, they can't cross the wall. Heard an engineer explain it once, something about the bloodsuckers coming with the firstborn, and that there aren't any in the Forest."

"I'm not sure how that makes sense," Lorn says slowly, his eyes still on the wall along which the gelding carries him. "The chaos barrier is there to keep the Forest in. So why would it choose an insect that's not part of the Forest?" Why would and how could the chaos barrier choose anything? He frowns. Does the Forest choose to destroy foreign insects?

Why? Or would it destroy any foreign body that crosses the ward-wall?

Kusyl shrugs with both hands. "That, I'd not be knowing, ser."

The two continue to patrol, silently, since the distance between them makes conversation uncomfortable.

The second squad patrols another kay of wall and deadland, then another.

"Ser! . . . Ser . . . Ser!" The yell comes from near the end of the line, a good six hundred cubits to the northeast, relayed by nearer lancers.

"Line halt!" Kusyl orders.

As the lancers rein up to a halt, Lorn guides his mount away from the wall to the lancer with the raised firelance. "Yes, lancer?"

The lancer points to the ground. On the deadland soil is a single bone, and a line of giant cat tracks. The bone—looking like it might have come from a sheep or goat—has been there for a time. There are no other signs of the giant cat's prey, and the tracks are indistinct, blurred by the light rain of the night before.

"Just keep an eye out. It looks like that happened yesterday."

"Yes, ser."

Lorn turns his mount back toward the ward-wall, gesturing for Kusyl to give the order for the patrol to resume.

The morning warms until the air is almost uncomfortably damp, and sweat collects under the edge of Lorn's white garrison cap.

The *clop-clop-clop* of hoofs offers a regular, almost soothing rhythm as the second squad continues in a spread formation that stretches from the road wall in a double line abreast, each rider a good fifty cubits from the next.

Lorn suppresses a yawn. He can understand why officers can get killed on Forest patrol duty, lulled into boredom by the endless sameness and suddenly confronted with the danger of a great cat or a giant stun lizard.

He has individual bits of information that should allow

him to form a better image of the situation he faces. He just needs to look at them differently, but it is difficult to think after a day of painstaking and mind-numbing patrol, looking for any trace of the Forest's breakout.

Suddenly, he straightens, fully erect in the saddle. That, too, is another bit of information. He thinks about what the Engineer Gebynet had said, something about patterns . . . of immense breakouts following a shoot as vigorous as the one he and his squad had destroyed on the southwest side of the Accursed Forest.

Patterns? What are the patterns? He shakes his head. The other question is who knows what the patterns are? Who has all the Patrol records?

Lorn nods grimly.

LXIX

To LORN'S RIGHT, a good dozen kays northeast, high and white puffy clouds scud along, swiftly, in the direction of the Westhorns. Between the clouds, sunlight falls in shafts that angle toward that distant ground. Directly overhead, the early afternoon's green-blue sky is mostly clear. At times, the slightest hint of a breeze wafts by Lorn, but the air has been largely still, despite the fast-moving clouds above.

Beyond the deadland and the outer perimeter road, the grass, and even farther away, the fields and woodlots are slowly greening, with the winter-gray leaves returning to their spring colors and the new leaves and shoots showing a lighter and brighter shade of green.

Lorn looks to his left, along the line of the second squad lancers riding the deadland inside the perimeter road. Beyond them are the riders of the first squad. Lorn can even make out the rounded bulk of Olisenn near the ward-wall.

After nearly seven days on patrol, with a day's respite at Eastend—a virtual duplicate of Westend—Lorn will be happy when they reach the compound at Northend, although it is always called the compound or Jakaafra, just as the compound at Geliendra is always called by the name of the nearby town as well, rather than the official name of South-end.

"Ser! Shoots ahead!"

"Shoots ahead! . . . ahead!" The report is echoed by the other lancers in the patrol line and relayed toward Lorn and Kusyl.

Lorn shakes his head as he uses his heels to nudge the gelding into a trot toward the lancer with the upheld fire-lance.

"Line halt! Line halt!" After barking the order, Kusyl turns his mount to follow the company commander.

Both the squad leader and Lorn rein up a good thirty cubits short of the shoots sighted by the lancer. At less than two cubits high, the twin green fronds are far shorter than the one Lorn had seen and has destroyed on his ride/patrol to Jakaafra, and they seem far more slender. He can sense only a hint of the black order that looms behind the ward-wall, but he studies the greenery for a long moment.

"Ser?"

"Have them flame by duads," Lorn orders Kusyl.

"Yes, ser. Form up!" Kusyl orders. "Prepare to flame by duads!"

After the lancers of the second squad reform from their line into the standard column of twos, Kusyl looks to Lorn. The company captain nods.

"Advance, and discharge lances!"

Under the warm afternoon sun, Lorn watches, but the shoots wither under the chaos flames of the firelances, leaving nothing but a black ash that disintegrates into a power, and then disperses under a light breeze that fades into still-ness.

Lorn watches the ashes disperse, letting his chaos-order sense probe the ground, but there is no sense of any under-lying well of dark order. Then he pulls out a message blank and turns his mount toward the ward-wall to note the ward location before dispatching a messenger to the Engineers at

Eastend. He knows that the Engineers will find nothing, but he will not suggest that, not at all. He also adds the location in his own small notebook.

He erases the momentary frown from his face as he rides toward the ward-wall—and Olisenn. The frailty of the shoots bothers him, especially after he has sensed the incredible dark order that lurks behind the whitened granite stones of the ward-wall.

LXX

LORN SETS ASIDE the bronze-tipped pen as he finishes the second of the two patrol entries, then lays the paper at the side of his study desk to dry. He turns in the chair and glances out the window at the clouds flowing from the south and building and darkening to the north. With the warm dampness of the morning and the clouds, he has little doubt that it will rain, perhaps for several days. But the Second Company will have to set out on patrol the next morning, rain or no rain.

He turns back to the desk, fingering his clean-shaven chin before he lifts the thin manual that Maran had given him, already showing smudges and scuffs. Inadvertently, he compares that to the ancient and spotless silver-sheened volume that Ryalth had presented to him, and he shakes his head, forcing his thoughts back to the patrol manual as he slowly searches for something he had seen—or thought he had—when he had first read it.

> . . . a Lancer company captain cannot halt breaches in the ward-wall, nor can he prevent the inimical creatures of the Accursed Forest from escaping such breaches, but he must do all within his power to ensure such creatures are destroyed before leaving the deadland barrier and before they can inflict damage upon the people of Cyad or upon their livestock and lands.

A wise captain will manage his deployments in such fashion so as to assure that his lancers are exposed to no unnecessary danger and so that casualties are minimized while making sure that as many creatures as practicably possible are destroyed before they can create harm. . . .

Lorn snorts as he sets down the manual. Destroy the creatures, but don't lose many men, and a wise captain will best know how to do that. Except that the manual offers no real tactics for such situations—just cautions.

After more time of silent contemplation, he stands and lifts the foot chest containing the Patrol reports. Those of the past five years, he reminds himself as he sets the chest on the clear side of the desk and unlocks it.

He re-seats himself, then begins to leaf through the older reports again, trying to check a nagging thought. He reads the last season of reports from Captain Dymytri, checking the events reported by the captain more closely, trying to focus on details that might just tell him something more.

. . . limb fallen short of guard wall from northwest mid-point Chaos tower . . . Casualties: 2. . . .

. . . trunk [twenty cubit diameter] smashed through chaos cables and a single course of wall stones . . . attack by three giant cats and one stun lizard . . . one cat escaped . . . casualties: 4. . . .

. . . long limb bridged ward-wall seventy cubits into deadland . . . night leopards attacked Engineers. . . .

Lorn frowns. Night leopards? He has not seen references to such before. Or had he overlooked them? He continues studying the patrol reports, apparently showing more than a score of problems.

. . . double trunk breach . . . rendered five hundred cubits
of ward-wall inoperable . . . Casualties: 15. . . .

. . . limb fall in heavy rainstorm . . . casualties: 4. . . .

Just as suddenly, the reports revert to the standard, "Patrol
on schedule. No Forest activity."

Lorn sits back in his chair, thinking. From late spring to
early summer, three and a half years earlier, Dymytri's reports
chronicle an outbreak of limb and trunk fallings which claim
scores of wards, nearly three score injuries to lancers and engineers, and at least a score of deaths. In that time period, several dozen wild creatures from the Accursed Forest escape.
Then, the outbreaks cease. And shortly thereafter, with nothing
on the record, one Captain Dymytri disappears or is killed.

Lorn replaces the records, then adds his own latest report,
and closes the foot chest. He stands and replaces the chest
on the floor before the desk, then walks to the window, looking at the thickening clouds, and at the Second Company
banner that flies above the barracks. The green-trimmed pen-
nant with the numeral two in the center is held out almost
stiffly by the steady wind, whipping but little.

Thrap! At the knock on the study door, Lorn turns. "Yes?
Come in."

Olisenn enters, leaving the door open. He bows. "A scroll
for you, Captain Lorn. It arrived by private local messenger."

Lorn steps forward to take the missive that the senior squad
leader extends to his captain. Although Lorn can sense that the
seal has been removed and then reheated somehow, he accepts
the scroll effortlessly and without hesitation, stepping back
and sideways so that he stands over the desk. "Thank you." He
breaks the blue wax without looking at it, even before Olisenn can move or retreat to the front study office, and lets
the wax fall on the golden-aged oak surface of his desk.

Lorn begins to read.

Honorable Lancer Captain Lorn . . .
I am pleased to inform you that the goods you

ordered from Ryalor House have arrived and that,
once you have inspected them, we will be more
than pleased to deliver them to whatever destination is your desire. . . .

Lorn manages neither to smile nor frown.

"Ser? Do you require me further?"

"Oh . . . no. I'm sorry, Olisenn. It's a private matter . . . not
about the Lancers. It's about some things I ordered." Lorn
smiles at the heavy senior squad leader. "You can go."

"Yes, ser." Olisenn bows deferentially, then leaves the inner study, gently closing the door behind him.

Lorn continues with the scroll.

We would suggest a slight haste in dealing with
the case of Fhynyco and the two cases of Alafraan,
but remain at your bidding, honored ser.

The missive is signed and sealed by one Dustyn, factor in
spirits and liquids, with the phrase beneath the seal, "Off the
main square, Jakaafra."

Lorn nods slowly to himself. Although he does not doubt
that the wines are from Ryalth to make his duty easier, he
wonders what else will come with the shipment . . . perhaps
a scroll that has not been already read.

LXXI

THE WARM MISTING rain of spring enfolds the Palace of
Light, and within the private study of the Emperor and his
consort, Toziel stands by the wide window overlooking the
harbor he can barely see through that mist.

He turns, but does not step onto the Analerian wool carpet
of subdued green and gold geometric designs that has graced
the study from the time of the Emperor Alyiakal. "I am troubled. I should not be troubled by this trifle, and yet I am.

You have noted that my sleep has not been as it should be."

"That I do know." The Empress Ryenyel smiles knowingly, and affectionately. "What trifle?" she asks after a moment, looking up from the black oak desk at which she is seated, the sole item of furniture within the entire Palace of Light made of that dark oak.

"The murder of a trader." A thin and humorless smile crosses the Emperor's mouth.

"That is a trifle. Yet . . . if it bothers you, it may be the first shoot of a noxious vine. Tell me of it." She smiles warmly. "That is what you wish, is it not?"

"I have no secrets from you, my dear."

"Nor should you, not if I am to assist you."

"You . . . you have always been of great assistance, and without it, as both we know. . . ." He shrugs and half-turns to study the mist.

"Enough of your flattery, my dear, welcome as it always is."

Toziel clears his throat. "Bluoyal'mer brought the matter to my attention several eightdays previous, and he mentioned it but once. Yet I have not dismissed it. The first heir of the Yuryan Clan of merchanters was murdered nearly a season ago. He was killed by a sabre tinged with chaos, a lancer's sabre, say the Magi'i. The day after the murder someone reclaimed an iron Brystan sabre that had been plated with cupridium. This merchanter used a stolen Dyljani trade plaque as authority and paid ten golds for the work. The cupridium master and his journeyman have been truthread by several Magi'i, and the truthreading confirms their tale. Both master and journeyman swear that the blade was in their care and not ready when the murder was committed. The journeyman also swears that the enumerator who picked up the blade was unfamiliar with weapons." Toziel turns back from the window and watches his consort.

"Who is the new heir?" asks Ryenyel.

"Veljan—a man far more suitable, according to all. Yet . . ."

"Yet, what?"

"His consort is the daughter of Liataphi, the Third Magus of the Magi'i. Liataphi has no sons and heirs. And this Veljan is honest and straightforward. Too honest and straightforward, from all I discover."

"That is far too obvious, dear one," observes Ryenyel. "Liataphi is too intelligent and too devious to have done such. He would see that such a ploy would illuminate him as if with a score of lamps."

"Then . . . who wishes to plant such an appearance? And why?"

"Who else would benefit, if far less obviously?" Ryenyel slips the cupridium-tipped pen into the holder on the left side of the desk.

"Rynst'alt, clearly."

Ryenyel shakes her head.

"Oh . . . Luss'alt, you think?"

"Luss'alt would benefit, but he could not have created such a scheme. I would guess that the one with the most to gain would be Kharl'elth."

Toziel nods. "When you put it that way . . ."

"What thinks your Hand?"

"He says but little, saving that it would appear to be a matter of trade and personal affairs, and trade rivalries best be solved by traders, and that using the Hand to meddle in trade or the personal lives of traders can lead but to disaster."

"Has he been right in what he advises?"

"More often than not."

"So it is unlikely to be a plot hatched here, though many here may seek to benefit by such." Ryenyel smiles but faintly. "Now, my dearest . . . that is the fashion in which it makes the most of logic, but not all plotters are of such logic. You must . . ."

"I know . . . set small traps to see who understands, and would use such, or who refuses to understand." Toziel's laugh is mirthless.

"Then, too," Ryenyel continues, "there is the matter of the sabre. Does anyone know who could wield such? None of the Magi'i would dare, for the deadly danger it would pose to them. None of the lancers would benefit from the attributes of such a weapon. And the merchanters could neither wield it nor comprehend its power."

"So there are two plots?" Toziel frowns. "And the second plotter a descendent of Alyiakal?"

"Only in spirit," Ryenyel says quietly. "You must tread carefully, for I would wager that neither knows of the other, nor should they."

After a moment of silence, they both nod.

Outside the mist lightens as the sun begins to struggle through the spring rain, and the greenery of the City of Light begins to reclaim the first city of Cyador from the gray-green of winter.

LXXII

THE RAINS OF the previous day have passed, but the air is warm, humid, and heavy, even in the early morning, as Second Company leaves the first waystation southeast of Jakaafra. The deadland is still muddy, with pools of shallow standing water, and with early mosquitoes humming everywhere. Mist hangs over and around the Accursed Forest to Lorn's right, and above the ward-wall. The sun is barely above the fields to the east, a fuzzy orange-white ball in a sky more a mist-shrouded green than blue.

"Be a hot day, specially afternoon, ser," says Kusyl from where he rides to Lorn's left.

"Very hot." Lorn glances toward the ward-wall nearly a kay away and at the mist that shrouds the massive trunks beyond the wall. Something does not feel right. He glances toward Kusyl. On the morning of the second day of the patrol, the second squad is deploying inward from the outer perimeter road, while Olisenn's first squad will deploy in a line outward from the ward-wall road. "Kusyl—this morning, I'll be riding with the first squad. I'll ride with second squad this afternoon."

"Yes, ser." The squad leader's cheerful voice indicates nothing.

Spreading the lancers into a line abreast and slogging through the mud will make for a long day, but keeping them on the roads will mean that too much of the Forest's activity could go undetected, particularly roots or new shoots carried above or beyond the ward-wall during the storm of the night before. Lorn turns the gelding southward and urges him to catch up with Olisenn and his overlarge beast. Absently, he brushes away an inquiring mosquito.

Zzzzzzpp!

Lorn does not wince at the sound of a flowerfly being destroyed by the chaos-net cast upwards by the wards, but the sound does remind him that the peaceful scene is not what it seems.

At the sound of another mount nearing, Olisenn turns in the saddle and offers a puzzled glance as Lorn rides toward him. "Ser?"

"I'll be riding with first squad this morning."

"As you command, ser."

The two ride silently and slowly as the line abreast forms and begins to ride parallel to and out from the ward-wall.

"Even it up, there!" Olisenn calls—more than once.

Lorn does not offer suggestions, or orders, but watches. Once the line is formed, and he and Olisenn ride on the opposite sides of the wall road, Lorn turns his attention to the ward-wall itself.

Although the wall *looks* the same as it always does, it is not. The relatively even pulses of chaos—if one can call any chaos energy regular—that are carried within the cupridium conduits and cast upwards in the net that restrains the Accursed Forest are different. While the chaos pulses are always different, always changing, usually each pulse does not differ greatly in power or duration. Lorn is not certain those are the right terms, but are closest to what he feels. This morning, there are larger pulses, much larger ones that feel *shallower* and some that feel like they are scarcely there at all.

After a time, he studies the road and the deadland past

Olisenn to his left, but there are no signs of shoots or seedling—or roots. Nor fallen trunks.

As the lancers ride, more slowly than ever, through the mud of the deadland, and as the morning passes, Lorn continues to watch, trying not to overstrain his eyes and senses, but knowing that all is not well somewhere along the wall. He also knows that to reveal that will leave him all too vulnerable in the seasons ahead. So he rides and watches. And the spring heat and hot dampness builds. While the discomfort rises, at least the deadland's mud has become less viscous, and progress somewhat less laborious.

Sometime after midmorning, Lorn nods, finally seeing a line of darkness on the horizon, a line that should not be there.

"Have them watch more closely," he finally tells Olisenn.

"Eyes sharp now, the captain says!" orders the senior squad leader. "Eyes sharp!"

"Ser! Trunk down! Trunk down!"

The line of blackness has become clear to all the lancers—a huge trunk jutting more than a hundred cubits out from the ward-wall—a trunk thicker at its uprooted base than the portion of the wall itself that is visible above ground.

Lorn glances at the nearest ward marker, then shakes his head. The closest engineer company is beyond the breach in the ward-wall, and to send a messenger past that without an escort would be foolhardy, considering the possible wildlife that the forest has had time to send forth. "Olisenn. Form up by duads on the road!"

"Ser?"

"On the road! A lancer won't have much chance against a cat in this muck."

The senior squad leader nods, then turns. "First squad! Duads on the road! Duads on the road!" Olisenn's voice carries, and lancers guide their mounts toward the Lancer captain and the first squad leader.

"Send a messenger out to Kusyl," Lorn adds. "Have him form up by duads on the perimeter road—and have the messenger stay clear of the trunk." Lorn blots away the sweat that has been gathering under the brow of his garrison cap.

"Yes, ser."

Lorn lets the gelding carry him ahead of the reforming squad, his fingers brushing the firelance in its holder, reassuring himself that the weapon is fully charged. His eyes go to the ward-wall, and then his senses. While the chaos-net is still intact, its web is fragile, and, closer to the fallen trunk, that chaos will do little to halt whatever the Accursed Forest intends to cast across the wall that will become little more than mere granite in a kay or so.

"Vyon! Message to squad leader Kusyl. From the captain. They're to form up by duads on the outer perimeter road and advance. They should be ready to repel creature attacks!"

"Yes, ser."

As a second thought, Lorn also checks his sabre, then glances at the huge trunk once more. The closer the two squads draw to the massive trunk—a grayish brown wall so dark it is almost black—the more Lorn begins to understand deep within himself the concerns expressed by both Maran and Commander Meylyd about the Accursed Forest. The trunk dwarfs any fireship Lorn had seen and, were it upright, could shade the Palace of Light with fifty cubits to spare.

Small catlike animals are racing down the trunk, jumping clear even before they reach the twisted and crushed branches of the brilliant green crown. Some are already clear of the toppled foliage.

The fallen trunk towers above the ward-wall a good fifteen cubits, a dark wall stretching perpendicular to the ward-wall. Only the lowest course of the ward-wall's granite is visible. Yet the granite of the wall appears to have held, except that it has cut into the trunk like an axe, and the trunk is firmly wedged in place. Then, Lorn reminds himself, under the five-cubit visible section of the wall is fifty cubits of granite foundation laid on solid rock, and reinforced with chaos bound in order.

"Prepare lances," Lorn says quietly to Olisenn.

"First squad, lances at the ready. Lances at the ready!"

Two blackish gray shapes seem to elongate from the trunk,

then separate. Lorn blinks, to realize that two huge cats sprint toward Lorn, their long bounding strides narrowing the distance, far faster than a galloping horse or a racing firewagon.

"Lances ready. Prepare to discharge!" Olisenn's orders are flat. "Discharge at will."

Forcing himself to be calm, Lorn lifts his firelance, and focuses it on the leading giant cat.

Hssstt! A single narrow beam of chaos flies, seemingly curving to strike the cat. The half-charred body tumbles into a heap.

Hhsstt! The second cat begins a spring before Lorn's followup bolt takes it in the chest.

Lorn pulls the gelding toward the wall, and turns in the saddle, checking to scc where Olisenn's lance might be pointed, but the squad leader's eyes remain on the trunk that lies less than two hundred cubits away.

"Company halt!" Lorn orders.

"Company halt!" Olisenn echoes.

"We can do five abreast for now," Lorn suggests.

"Five abreast! Stay on the road."

Lorn glances to the northeast, but can see little except the formation of the second squad—and a series of flares that are firelances discharging. He turns to study the trunk wall ahead.

A pack of smaller cats—the night leopards?—each perhaps ten stone, charges toward the first squad.

"Discharge at will!" Lorn orders, wheeling his gelding so that he can bring his lance to bear while continuing to watch Olisenn.

"Discharge at will. Short bursts! Short bursts!" Olisenn orders.

Hssst! Hssst!

Three of the cats fall. A fourth comes up under one of the men's lances, and the lance falls, and before the lancers—or Lorn—can react, the man is down.

Three quick firelance bursts sear across the smaller cat's back and upper shoulders. The cat spasms, then falls still. The fallen lancer does not move.

"Stop discharges. Save your lances!" snaps Olisenn.

Two of the cats flash back toward the gray-brown trunk, scramble lithely up it, and then sprint northward along the tops of the trunk away from the ward-wall and toward the crushed vegetation that is the crown.

"Gythet's dead, ser," one of the lancers announces to Olisenn.

"Strap him over his mount, quickly," responds the squad leader.

Lorn turns his mount to the northwest, paralleling the massive trunk, but at a good hundred and fifty cubits. He glances back at Olisenn. "We need to ride around the crown. That's to make sure we can send a messenger safely to Eastend."

"Ah . . . yes, ser. There are many creatures in the tops of the fallen trees. They wait until it falls, and then they hurry down and hide there, lying in wait."

"I'm sure they do. We'll try to give it a wide berth."

"Reform! Lances at the ready. Follow the captain."

At Olisenn's orders, Lorn lets the gelding slow, until he is riding to the left and slightly behind Olisenn. The hint of a frown appears on the squad leader's face, then vanishes, replaced with an expression of professional competence.

Neither Lorn nor Olisenn speak as the column rides out along the trunk to where the smashed limbs of the tree's crown form a small hill.

The captain wants to shake his head, but refrains. In the scurry and the attacks by the cats, he had forgotten that Olisenn presents as great a danger as do the creatures of the Accursed Forest. Lorn has his own firelance ready, if but with a fraction of its original chaos charge, and from where he rides he can cover both the squad leader and survey the fallen forest monarch.

Kusyl rides to meet them. His left sleeve bears a rent, but shows no blood. "Ser."

"How many casualties?" Lorn looks from the squad with at least one empty-saddled mount to Kusyl.

"Two dead, ser. Two wounded."

"One dead, ser. One wounded," Olisenn adds. "Thus far."

At the sound of crackling and rustling branches, all three men turn in their saddles toward the middle of the mound of branches and leaves. A single branch, more than two cubits thick, falls outside the crown, snapped by whatever stirs within the vegetation.

The light wind out of the south carries a musky bitter scent to Lorn, that and an acrid odor of crushed leaves.

"Prepare to discharge lances!" Lorn snaps. Anything that moves branches a cubit thick and whose power and mass move the entire fallen crown is something that will require more than a single firelance.

"Prepare to discharge—"

The last words of Olisenn's orders are lost under the crashing of displaced limbs and vegetation.

MMMMMmmmmmmmmmmmmmmnnnnnn. . . . A soundless, yet paralyzing mental scream slams into Lorn, and his mount. The gelding seems to stagger and steps sideways. Lorn wants to hold his temples, so intense is the pain, and for a moment he cannot see, for what feel like knives ripping at his eyes.

He blinks through the involuntary tears at the monster that emerges from the crushed crown, strewing aside vegetation like wet paper.

A huge gray lizard slithers from the crown, except that it is so large that it appears at first as if the gray trunk were turning and growing—or extending itself toward Kusyl and the second squad. Fully five cubits at the shoulders, and more than twenty cubits in length, the lizard pounds toward the second squad. A black tongue whips out, looking like a lash.

Before the mental order attack, three of the second squad's mounts have actually gone down, one to its knees. A lancer scrambles for his lance, not realizing the lizard's speed. The webbed and clawed left foot flashes, and the lancer vanishes under it.

Lorn winces. "Discharge lances! Now! Discharge lances!"

Hssst! A single line of fire flare from one of the second company lancers, but the chaos flame rolls off the gray hide of the monster stun lizard.

Hsssst! Hsst!

In response to the lines of chaos fire, the lizard swings its head from side to side, then pauses, as if calculating which lancer will be its next victim.

Almost without thinking, Lorn sheaths the firelance, and pulls out the lancer sabre, willing the chaos that surrounds him and the lizard into the blade. He nudges the gelding. The mount shivers. His heels dig into the gelding's flanks, and the white starts forward, slowly, then moving into a quick trot.

Lorn rides toward the lizard, angling from behind its head on the left side. He hopes the lizard will hold for just an instant.

Abruptly, the giant snout turns, impossibly quickly, toward the lancer captain.

Lorn hurls the sabre with all the force he can muster. The chaos-infused cupridium sabre spins lazily end-over-end as Lorn *wills* the point to strike the lizard's head or eye point first. Even as he wills the impact, he is leaning in the saddle, turning the gelding away from the stun lizard's gaping mouth and hot breath, and angling toward the second squad, pulling his own nearly depleted firelance from its holder.

MMnnnnnnnnnnnnn. . . . The stunning soundless metal scream is followed by an enormous grunt. Then the lizard convulses, thrashing, and a webbed forefoot claws at the sabre that protrudes from the platter-sized eye.

Lorn can sense the raging flames within the lizard's skull—as order and chaos war.

He reins up the shivering gelding.

Kusyl looks blankly at his captain.

"Discharge firelances! Now!" Lorn snaps at Kusyl.

"All firelances! Now!" echoes the junior squad leader.

"Aim at the head!" Lorn commands.

"The head!" Olisenn's and Kusyl's orders merge.

Firelance beams play across the thrashing lizard, winking out of existence as lance after lance is depleted.

The long tail lashes sideways and high.

Lorn cannot even yell before it smashes through a lancer from the first squad who has ridden too close. Then that tail, like a serpent, or an independent being, thumps up and down in slow beats, pounding itself into the ground, and pulping both dead lancer and mount.

Mmmnnnn. . . . The last mental scream rocks Lorn, both with its dying force, and the sense of despair.

Lorn takes a deep breath.

The lizard twitches . . . and keeps twitching. . . .

"Hold your discharges! Hold discharges!" Lorn orders.

The lancers watch the dying lizard.

The squad leaders watch the lizard, the crushed mound of the tree's crown, and the trunk that leads back to the Accursed Forest.

Lorn watches the lizard, the crown, trunk, and the senior squad leader.

There is a sigh, like a dying wind, and a last twitch, and the monster lies inert.

Lorn and the two squad leaders still study both the crushed vegetation of the crown and the lizard's corpse for a time before any speak.

Finally, Lorn clears his throat. He has to do it twice before he can speak. "We need to check the far side as well."

Both squad leaders nod slowly, reluctantly.

"Form up!"

While Second Company forms up, Lorn rides toward the dead lizard, looking for his sabre, but there is no sign of the weapon. The lancer captain nods and eases the gelding away from the dead beast.

Second Company rides slowly around the crown of the fallen tree. While there are rustles from the crown, and the acrid odor of crushed leaves comes and goes, nothing emerges from the twisted and splintered vegetation.

The company reins up on the southeastern side of the gray-brown trunk.

Lorn beckons to Olisenn, who edges his mount closer to the captain.

"We still need to send a messenger to the Engineers."

"Ah . . . yes . . . ser." Olisenn blots a face drenched in sweat.

Kusyl does not speak, but nods.

"We'll have to keep watch here until the Engineers arrive."

"Yes, ser." Both squad leaders reply, neither with great enthusiasm.

Lorn takes out the grease stick and begins to jot down the particulars of where the trunk fell, and the ward locations, on the blank message scroll. Finally he hands it to Olisenn. "Warn the messenger to ride well clear of anything else that may have fallen." Lorn pauses, then adds, "Have a half-score escort him around the trunk."

"Yes, ser." Olisenn eases his mount away from Lorn and toward the first squad.

Kusyl's eyes stray to the enormous bulk of the dead stun lizard. "Never . . . never seen anything that big. . . ."

Neither has Lorn, and he nods, slowly. "You wonder how many more there might be waiting on the other side of the wall."

"Rather not think on that, ser." Kusyl glances from Lorn to where Olisenn briefs the lancer acting as messenger.

It will be a long afternoon and a longer night, Lorn suspects.

LXXIII

LORN DOES NOT sleep well, or long, and is up even before dawn, as worried by the comparative silence as by the bulk of the trunk and the section of ward-wall that does not function. He ignores the griminess he feels because the little water they have has to be carried from three kays to the north and does not even try to shave or wash, but merely takes a long swallow from his water bottle.

In the gray that will precede a clear dawn, with only a hint of mist rising from the Accursed Forest, he walks past the duty sentry toward the granite of the ward-wall. While he carries both a sabre that had belonged to one of the dead lancers, and his firelance, he knows he will need neither, and doubts that knowledge as well.

As he faces the wall, dry and smooth in the dawn despite the dew that coats the wall road and the ground, he can sense where the chaos flows end, perhaps a hundred and fifty cubits to his left, at the last functioning ward. Without the flaring webs of the chaos net, Lorn can sense the order-chaos depth of the Accursed Forest, and the solid granite wall by itself seems a frail barrier to the height and power of that intertwined order and chaos.

Lorn cocks his head, trying to recall words from his days as a student magus. "Always called the Forest order-death . . . never mentioned twined order and chaos," he murmurs to himself. He looks up again, both with chaos-order senses and eyes, but he is not mistaken. The Forest has a depth of order wrapped in chaos, or chaos wrapped in order.

Despite the breach in the chaos net, as he continues to study the Accursed Forest, Lorn senses no probes of either order or chaos, and no creatures massing beyond the granite. He studies the Forest for a time longer, until the sun begins to rise above the deadland and fields to his left, but the silent presence and lack of overt threat does not change. When the sun falls on his shoulder and side, he turns and walks silently back toward the bivouac area.

By the time he reaches the tielines where the mounts are tethered, Olisenn is waiting, looking as bedraggled as Lorn feels. "You were at the wall, and it is not warded there. Was that wise, captain?"

"Probably not." Lorn laughs. "I'll learn, I'm sure." He pauses as Kusyl walks toward them. "Good morning, Kusyl."

"Good morning, ser."

"I checked with all the sentries before I left." Lorn's eyes fall on Kusyl. "I was inspecting the ward-wall this morning. It's been quiet all night."

"Might be more creatures this morning," hazards the junior squad leader.

"There might be," Lorn agrees, looking at Olisenn. "How long before the Engineers arrive?"

"They have firewagons that can make good speed on the perimeter roads, and I would judge that they might arrive by midday—if they left last evening or early this morning."

Lorn nods. "Both of you set some pickets, say, four from each squad. Just use the firelances to keep anything away. We're not going to try to destroy anything else right now." His smile is wry. "We don't have the charges for that."

"No, ser, we don't," Kusyl says strongly.

Olisenn frowns, but nods.

"I'm going to take a few men and ride back around the crown." Lorn unties the gelding from the tieline. "Does it matter who I ask?"

"No, ser."

After picking four men, nearly at random, Lorn checks the girths and the bridle and mounts the gelding. He and the four lancers slowly ride around the mass of tangled branches and crushed and uncrushed leaves that had formed the crown of the enormous tree. They circle the tangled mound at a distance of well over two hundred cubits from the nearest greenery. While there are occasional rustlings, and more than a few birds, including two enormous vulcrows that burst from the branches, they see no other creatures.

On the northwest side, a dozen vulcrows are tearing at the carcass of the stun lizard, but the birds scarcely raise their sharp hooked beaks. Two night leopards slink back to the branches as the riders near the dead creature.

After studying the area of the struggle with the lizard, and determining, again, that there is no sign of his lancer sabre, and no other creatures visible, at least, Lorn turns the gelding. "We'll ride back now."

As the five riders return to the main body of Second Company, Lorn watches the deadland and the battered crown, but while the rustlings continue, nothing emerges except occasional birds that he does not recognize, not that he has ever spent much effort in studying avians.

Olisenn and Kusyl are waiting, eyes expectant, as Lorn and his lancers reins up.

"Nothing. Vulcrows, two leopards that scurried back to the

tree, some birds." Lorn shrugs and dismounts. He pulls out a water bottle that will need to be refilled before long and takes a swallow, then blots his forehead. "We watch and wait for the Mirror Engineers."

He is blotting his forehead again, in the midday heat, when a voice rides through the silence.

"Ser!" calls the duty sentry, pointing to the north.

Lorn unties the gelding and mounts, as do the four lancers he had selected earlier. From the saddle he can see three firewagons approach, crossing the deadland from the outer perimeter road, and angling toward the point where the trunk and the ward-wall intersect.

"Mount up! Engineers are here."

"Mount up!" Kusyl and Oliscnn echo Lorn's orders.

Lorn fingers his grimy and stubbly chin, then eases the gelding toward where the three firewagons are slowing along the inner road that flanks the ward-wall. The third firewagon is armored in cupridium plate and tows an armored two-wheeled device with a tubular projection that can only be one of the special firecannons that Commander Meylyd had mentioned.

A thin-lipped engineer majer steps out of the first firewagon. He glances around, then spots Lorn, and marches toward the mounted lancer captain.

"Majer Weylt, Captain. I'm in charge of the engineer detachment at Eastend." The thin lips twitch into a smile. "When we received your message, I had some questions about the size of the trunk. But your lancer messenger was insistent, and I decided to come with the large firecannon. I'm glad we brought it."

"Captain Lorn, Majer. We're glad to see you." Lorn smiles. "The tree seemed large, but I'm new to this. I just followed the procedures." He calls up what he has read. "You'll cut away the trunk from the ward-wall. . . ."

"Exactly." Weylt bobs his narrow face up and down. "We make sure that the road is clear first, and then destroy the crown to make sure it harbors no creatures, and that there's no residual order poison."

"What do you need from us?"

"Just a loose guard while we set up. That's so we're not surprised. Then you pull back and let us get on with it."

"Yes, ser."

"Good." The majer almost spins on one boot and heads back to his firewagon.

Lorn remains mounted, with Kusyl to his left, as the half-score of Mirror Engineers unhitch the armored firecannon on the wall road, and wrestle it into a position roughly three hundred cubits from where the trunk rests on the ward-wall. One turns a crank-like handle, and a hatch opens on one side of the cannon. The engineer vanishes into the hatch.

Another rolls a long cable from the firewagon that has towed the cannon to an assembly on the rear of the cannon and inserts it into a square bracket. Lorn senses that the cable is cupridium sheathed in something, almost a shimmercloth substance of many layers, clearly designed to keep the chaos flows within the cable.

Seemingly from nowhere, Majer Weylt appears, again marching briskly toward Lorn. "Pull your lancers back behind the cannon, Captain—and out from the ward-wall," orders the thin-lipped Mirror Engineer. "At least a third of a kay back. Have them ready for more creatures."

Lorn wonders about how many more cats and stun lizards will rush from the crown and the upper trunk, but only nods. "Yes, ser." He turns and stands in the saddle. "Second Company! Pull back to seven hundred cubits!"

Half-wondering just how accurate any of them will be judging seven hundred cubits, Lorn guides Second Company to a position perpendicular to the trunk, closer to a half kay, he suspects, back from the crown itself. He turns his mount and reins up, watching Olisenn from the corner of his eye, and observing the engineers as well.

Two of the three firewagons roll back down the ward-wall road, almost a kay, leaving only the firecannon and the firewagon to which it is connected. All the Mirror Engineers have vanished, except for one, who then climbs inside the hatch door on the right side of the cannon and closes it behind him.

Of the score of Engineers, none remain in the open, Lorn notes.

HHHSSSTTT! With a whining, whooshing hiss, a single jet of flame slices through the dark order of the trunk. The heat radiates even to where the lancers are reined up.

Clunnnnnk! The ground shakes, a half kay away, as the trunk outside the ward-wall drops onto the road and the deadland.

A second jet of flame—somehow both blue and black—flares skyward from where the trunk has contacted the ward-wall. Smaller explosions follow, and sections of wood, shredded and twisted, begin to fall.

A dull *clunking* announces the impact of a ten-cubit length of branch on the armored shell of the firecannon.

Lorn turns in his saddle and studies Olisenn. Is the heavyset squad leader pale? Lorn's eyes go to Kusyl, who is definitely pallid and tense. Then his eyes go to the tree's fallen crest, where the branches keep twisting.

In an instant, a half-score of the night leopards appear at the edge of the crown. Abruptly, all charge the Second Company, clearly without any hesitation, as if they had known all along where the lancers were.

"Discharge lances at will! Short bursts! Short bursts!"

"Short bursts!" Olisenn adds in an even louder bellow.

Nine of the leopards fall before reaching the Second company. The last slams into a lancer's mount, but the man keeps his head and drives his sabre down and through the beast's neck, awkward as the blow is.

The mount screams, a long slash across the point of her left shoulder, but the lancer manages to remain mounted, and slowly gentles the mare.

The rest of the lancers reform into their squads, watching the vegetation, but no other creatures emerge.

Discreetly readjusting his garrison cap, and blotting his forehead, Lorn glances back toward the cannon, where the engineers are working to reposition the weapon. "Steady! They're going at it again!"

Another whining whistling blast follows, and a gap ten cubits wide appears between the ward-wall and the remainder of the trunk.

The second blast dislodges no more creatures, although a number of birds circle the trunk.

There is no sign of the vulcrows—none at all. Once more the engineers reposition the firecannon, and after each searing blast do so again until they have opened a gap between the wall and the remainder of the trunk that is more than fifty cubits wide.

Once the gap has reached that width and the inner road is clear, the Engineers turn the firecannon. The armored firewagon slowly tows it outward until it is roughly a hundred cubits from the crushed crown, between the crown vegetation and Lorn's company.

The Engineer Majer strides from the cannon toward Lorn, and Lorn rides forward to shorten the senior officer's walk.

"Thank you, Captain." Weylt smiles.

Lorn waits.

"Captain Lorn . . . now we're going to fire the crown. It's going to burn hot. I'd leave your men where they are until the worst dies down. You might get another giant cat or two. You might not."

"We'll be ready, ser."

"Fine." Weylt turns and walks back to the firewagon.

Shortly the cannon screams again, except the fire flares into a broad fan, and immediately flames begin to shoot up from the center of the mangled limbs and leaves. As the fires spread, one section of the branches shudders, and a long gray-black giant cat leaps from the twisted branches and greenery, padding right past the armored firecannon.

The cat pauses two hundred and fifty cubits out from the spreading flames. Its dark eyes study the Second Company, lined five abreast at least a good five hundred cubits away. Then, as suddenly as the others had attacked, the giant cat lopes almost due north, well away from the lancers and the engineers and their equipment.

Lorn has no intention of chasing it, not with the state of his company's firelances.

The flames continue to rise, crackling a fierce orange, and thick and acrid black smoke, twined with plumes of lighter gray smoke, rises into the now-clear green-blue sky, forming a haze that begins to spread.

At the ward-wall, several engineers are working, replacing the smashed crystal wards with others, ignoring the flame that flares three hundred cubits northward.

The flames are subsiding, leaving the trunk seemingly untouched, when the engineer majer returns, striding briskly toward Lorn, who urges the gelding forward again.

The majer begins without greeting, without preamble. "The wards are working, and there's little enough more we can do."

"Do you just leave the trunk now?" asks Lorn.

The majer laughs. "We're through with it. So are you. There's a timber factor who has a contract on anything like this. There will be a team out here in a couple of days, and within two eightdays, you won't know that there ever was a fallen trunk here. Good timber, they say. I wouldn't touch it, not with the residual dark order in it, but they ship it down the Great Canal and then sell it to the coastal traders. Get a good price, I understand. The fees they pay help pay our stipends, Captain, yours and mine."

Lorn nods. He understands the logic, but he wonders about the merchanters profiting on the deaths of lancers. "This seems like a large trunk," he observes, watching the Majer. "Is it, ser?"

"Thirty-five cubits at the ward-wall. That's the biggest I can recall. Be a few loads of solid timbers for the merchanters." The majer smiles ironically. "More than a few, I'd wager. They can handle it. I wouldn't. Once this dies down, we'll be returning to Eastend, and you'll be free to continue your patrol."

"We'll need to recharge or replace our lances at Eastend,"

Lorn says quietly. "There probably aren't a dozen lances left with charges."

"That we can handle, Captain. I'll see that a full set of lances is waiting for you."

"Thank you."

"Least we can do." The majer nods, then turns and leaves Lorn.

Lorn rides back to the Second Company. They will have a long ride to the next waystation, a very long ride, that will last well into the evening. Even when the return patrol is over, he will have no rest, not with the need to request replacements and draft letters to the families of the fallen lancers, and to handle all the other details that must wait until Second Company returns to Jakaafra.

LXXIV

IN THE LATE afternoon, Lorn leans forward in the saddle. He rubs his forehead, ignoring the burning in his eyes, and the itching of salty sweat on the two-day old stubble on his neck. Then he straightens, forcing himself erect as Second Company nears the locked and sealed granite structure that is the northeast midpoint chaos tower.

". . . too bad didn't put a waystation here . . ." murmurs a lancer riding behind Lorn.

". . . make too much sense . . ."

Lorn motions, and the second squad turns out from the ward-wall and follows the road that loops around the midpoint chaos tower and the low wall that connects it to the ward-wall.

In the fading afternoon light, as he rides within fifty cubits of the solid granite walls, Lorn studies the bulk of the midpoint chaos tower. Is it his imagination, or does the granite of the tower somehow seem less solid than the tower at Jakaafra? He frowns, concentrating on the tower with both sight and fatigued chaos-senses.

He shakes his head.

"Ser? You all right?" asks Kusyl.

"I'm fine." He offers a laugh. "As fine as any of us are, anyway."

As Kusyl nods and looks away, Lorn's lips tighten. From what he can tell, the midpoint chaos tower has failed. There are no pulses of chaos energy flowing in the cupridium conduits from the building to the ward-wall, although the wards along the wall proper still hold and flare their chaos net.

The flow of chaos must be traveling all the way from Eastend and Jakaafra. Is that why the Accursed Forest is now attacking along the northeast ward-wall? Or had the tower failed years earlier and the failure been kept silent?

Again . . . what he does not know would fill endless scrolls. He rubs his forehead once more, knowing that they still have another sixteen kays to cover before they reach the waystation.

LXXV

As the Second Company forms up in the courtyard of Eastend, its compound a mirror image of Westend, Lorn walks toward the long building that holds the Mirror Lancer detachment, wondering if anyone will even be there. The corridors and studies are empty, and Lorn heads back to the officers' dining area. With each step, his boots click faintly on the polished stone floor of the corridor.

There, at the sole occupied table in the dining area, he finds Majer Weylt and two engineer captains. All three rise as he approaches the table.

"Captain," offers Weylt, "can you join us?"

"I fear not," Lorn says. "My company is forming up now." He bows to the majer. "I just wanted to let you know that I appreciated your having the firelances ready, Majer. Your efforts were most welcome."

"Thank you for your courtesy." Weylt's eyes twinkle

above his thin lips. "I see you found another . . . appropriate
. . . sabre."

"There were some spares in the armory here." Lorn's lips
quirk momentarily. "I'm not the first, I gather."

"You broke yours?" asks the squat captain to Weylt's
right.

"Ah . . . not exactly. I put it in a stun lizard's eye, and it
dissolved, I think. At least, I couldn't find it after the lizard
died."

"You . . . killed a stun lizard with a sabre?"

". . . and most of the charges in my company's firelances,"
Lorn adds smoothly. "We still lost more than a few lancers."

"The lizard was over twenty cubits in length. I saw the
carcass before we burned it," Weylt adds. "Most impressive."
He nods his head. "We won't keep you, Captain, but it has
been a pleasure meeting you and working with you."

"And you, also." Lorn returns the nod with a bow and
smiles. "You will pardon me if I hope we do not work together too often?"

Weylt laughs. "Indeed! Indeed. Have an uneventful return
patrol."

"We hope to. Thank you again."

With a smile and a last bow, Lorn turns and walks back
to the courtyard where he reclaims the gelding from the stableboy. He checks his gear, leads the gelding into the courtyard, and then mounts quickly.

While the courtyard remains in shadow, the sun has risen,
and the deadland beyond the gates is flooded with light as
Lorn lets the gelding carry him toward the waiting lancers.
He frowns as he considers he should have looked for Weylt
earlier. There are so many little aspects to his job that are
not in the manual and on which he has not been briefed.
Then, he supposes, that is true of many positions within Cyador and the Mirror Lancers.

"Wondered where you were, ser," offers Kusyl as Lorn
rides up to the head of the column where both squad leaders
wait.

"I was offering our thanks to the head of the Mirror Engineer detachment for the replacement firelances and sabres. He was out on his own patrol yesterday, but he was the one who ensured they were waiting for us."

Kusyl nods. "He seems solid enough, if a bit brisk."

"He has to cover twice as much ward-wall as we do," Lorn points out. "Is everyone ready?"

"Yes, ser," reply both squad leaders.

"Let us go. First squad will start on the wall."

"First squad, advance!"

"Second squad . . ."

As Second Company rides through the gates and toward the ward-wall, Lorn wonders what awaits them on the patrol. Was the other Engineer majer—Gebynet—correct in predicting a rash of excursions by the Forest? Or will the ward-wall offer another quiet and uneventful patrol?

Thinking about the non-functioning midpoint chaos tower, Lorn doubts that many patrols will be uneventful, but ensures that a pleasant smile remains on his face as he rides beside Kusyl.

LXXVI

In THE LATE early morning, the sun hangs just over the Accursed Forest, its towering trees revealed and then obscured by the scattered and white puffy clouds that scud westward. A cooler breeze blows out of the northeast, reminding Lorn that the season is spring, where summer heat is followed by chill and then by rain or mist . . . and then by wind or more heat, before the irregular cycle begins once more.

To Lorn's right, the two squads of lancers are spread in a long line abreast, searching the deadland for signs of Forest activity beyond the ward-wall. To his left is the ward-wall, that seemingly unchanging low rampart of chaotic permanence that stretches northwest to the horizon, reflecting as it has for generations the vision and the skills of the Firstborn. And the power of the Accursed Forest.

The low clopping of hoofs and the breathing of lancer mounts are the only sound beside the sighing of the breeze that is slowly changing into a cold wind. Lorn hopes the chill will be dry, and not one that leads to cold rain or sleet.

He looks to the wall and notes the chiseled marker: N 480 E. They have another ten kays to ride before they reach the midpoint of the northeast ward-wall—and the granite structure housing a chaos tower that does not work.

His shifts his weight in the saddle and glances once more to his right, out at Olisenn and the first squad, riding methodically across the deadland, looking for signs of growth Lorn doubts they will find.

As the sun rises, so does the wind, and the cold air, sweeping off the winter heights of the distant Westhorns, chills more than the spring sun warms, but the Second Company's lancers ride steadily northwest.

After covering another two kays, Lorn glances toward the wall, and both his eyes and chaos-order senses study it. The chaos pulses through the cupridium cables are less regular. Does that mean another fallen trunk? A breach in the wall itself? Trouble with a chaos tower? Or his own imagination?

He shivers as another cold chill washes across him—that of someone using a chaos glass to scree him. Maran? Or a higher-level magus from the Quarter of the Magi'i? He maintains a faint smile until the chill fades.

Is the screeing because of what he senses? Or is what he senses independent of the user of the chaos-glass?

Whatever it may be, he must wait. Still, Lorn gestures for Kusyl to ride closer.

With a puzzled expression, Kusyl follows Lorn's gesture and guides his mount almost beside Lorn's gelding. "Ser?"

"Do you think we should space the men farther apart when we go five abreast?" Lorn asks. "Say another cubit or so apart?"

Kusyl frowns. "Too far, and there is a greater risk that their lance fires will strike each other if leopards or cats get too near."

Lorn nods, his eyes on the wall ahead, waiting until he can make out the faintest hint of darkness where the ward-wall touches the horizon. Finally, he turns once more to Kusyl. "There's another tree trunk down, across the ward-wall up ahead. I can just barely see it."

Kusyl stands in his stirrups and squints. "I see nothing."

"In a kay or so you will," Lorn assures the junior squad leader.

They ride nearly another kay and a half before, abruptly, Kusyl peers forward. "There is a trunk. You have good eyes, Captain."

"It's in knowing what to look for," Lorn replies. "I didn't know what that was when I started. Let's form up on the road, and send a messenger out to Olisenn. He might have seen it, but he might not yet." After a moment, he adds. "We can ride five abreast on the road for a while, until we get nearer the tree."

"Form up on the road!" Kusyl orders. "On the road, five abreast!"

". . . not another fallen tree . . ."

". . . would draw unlucky bastard of an officer . . ."

". . . more angel-fired cats . . . stun lizards . . ."

". . . don't know that . . ."

". . . by Steps of Paradise, I do . . . better believe I do. . . ."

Lorn ignores the mutterings, keeping a pleasant smile on his face as he lets the gelding carry him forward.

"Formed up, ser," Kusyl reports. "A messenger is riding out to first squad."

"Good. We'll move out from the wall once we get within a half-kay of the trunk." Or sooner if the chaos-net of the ward-wall is gone.

Lorn scans the area ahead as the second squad rides forward, checking the ward-wall, the area around where the trunk spans the wall, and the crushed green crown of the forest giant farther to his right. While he sees small creatures scurrying from the Accursed Forest down the trunk to the crown area, Lorn cannot be sure what they might be, other than they do not seem to be large enough to be stun lizards or the giant cats.

Some three hundred cubits from the trunk, Lorn raises his hand and reins in the white gelding. "Squad halt!"

In the silence, he studies the ward-wall, noting to himself that the chaos-net has vanished. While the fallen trunk is not so large as the one they had encountered on the first half of the patrol, even from where he is reined up, he estimates that the diameter is still greater than fifteen cubits.

Beyond the trunk, he can see the bulk of the non-functioning midpoint chaos tower.

"Don't usually see 'em this close to a chaos tower," offers Kusyl.

"That's our luck," Lorn offers. "Send another messenger out to Olisenn. Have them form up five abreast and ride toward the crown. We'll wait here a moment while I write out the message to send back to the Engineers. Then we'll ride toward the crown, say, a hundred cubits off the trunk."

"Yes, ser."

Lorn finishes the message as quickly as he can and hands it to the squad leader. "Here."

In turn, Kusyl rides to the rear of the column and turns the scroll over to a thin lancer, who immediately turns his mount and heads back toward Eastend. The squad leader rides back to Lorn and reports, "On its way, ser."

Lorn nods. Both men know that the Engineers will not arrive until late the following day, if then. "Let's see what this trunk holds."

"Yes, ser. Lances ready! Forward at a walk!"

The horses' hoofs powder the dead soil, not quite crunching the lifeless ground, turning up white streaks of the stones and stones of salt once poured onto fertile soil.

They have covered no more than fifty cubits, and are still close to two hundred cubits from the trunk, when two of the giant cats bound from the trunk, one to the left of the line of lancers, and one to the right. Both animals angle toward the lancers, running at speeds that seem to halve the distance with each breath.

"Discharge at will!" Both Lorn and Kusyl shout the orders near-simultaneously.

Hhssst! Hssst! Firelance bolts flare toward the cats, and all appear to miss.

"Short bursts!" Lorn adds.

Hssstt!

One cat falls, growling, before the firelances converge on it. The other cat dashes sideways at an incredible speed and sprints northward through the gap between the two squads, heading away from the lancers.

"Hold your discharges!" Kusyl orders. "This one's dead, and you'll need 'em!"

The fallen cat seems slightly smaller than the one that had escaped the firelances, although it is hard to tell with most of the forward part of its body charred.

"Lances ready," Lorn orders, urging the gelding northwest, edging along the trunk toward the crushed mound of vegetation that had been the crown—a circular matted mass clearly smaller than that of the tree they had encountered on the outward patrol.

Perhaps fifty cubits short of where the tree's crushed upper branches begin lies a separate branch, nearly two cubits across, Lorn judges, and more olive colored and without smaller branches, almost like a huge vine torn from the Forest.

The branch undulates along its entire length, creating salt smears on the dead soil, and the lizard-like triangular head of a serpent rises beside the darker gray-brown of the tree trunk. The jaws open, extending wide enough to swallow a man.

". . . mother of the Steps!"

". . . barbarian's she-boar . . ."

"Advance and discharge at will! No closer than thirty cubits," Lorn adds. "Aim for the head. Short bursts!"

"Short bursts!" adds Kusyl.

The serpent curls, as if coiling for a strike.

Hsstt! Hssst! Hsst! The firelances probe, searing the unprotected serpent's head, which twists and turns as if trying to avoid the chaos-fire.

Then the head lifts and turns toward the lancers, slowly moving outward, trying to strike at the source of its pain.

More lines of fire converge on the slow-moving giant snake, and a series of shudders ripple up and down its length. The huge triangular head, blackened beyond any recognition, drops onto the deadland with a dull *thump!*

"Hold your discharges! Hold discharges!" Lorn orders.

He and Kusyl watch carefully from a good thirty cubits, but the shudders that shake the serpent slowly die away. Measuring the dead snake with his eyes, Lorn gauges the serpent to have been at least forty cubits in length.

He looks up as Olisenn leads the first squad toward them, at a slow and deliberate pace, far too slow, Lorn decides, although he says nothing.

The heavy-set senior squad leader reins up and looks at the dead serpent, then at Lorn. His mouth opens, then closes, then opens again. Finally he speaks. "One of those . . . I have not seen before. Nor have I heard of such."

"If you and the experienced lancers haven't heard of these, I hope we don't run into more of them," Lorn says quietly. "It wasn't near as bad as a giant cat or a stun lizard. It was much slower. You need to stay a good thirty cubits back."

"That I will remember." Olisenn nods, his eyes still on the snake.

Lorn tenses, turning the gelding toward the bottom of the tree's crown, where the branches have begun to rustle. "Lances ready!"

Even as the words leave his mouth, with another rustling of branches, a half-score or more of night leopards bound toward the two squads. One mount in the first squad shies sideways, and several lancers struggle momentarily to bring their horses back into formation.

"Discharge at will! Short bursts! Short bursts!"

Hsst! Hssst! Hssst! . . .

Short firelance bursts crisscross, forming almost a wall

against the smaller leopards—smaller only in comparison to the giant cats.

Before Lorn can issue another order, the firelances are silent. Eight of the leopards are down, dead.

Lorn turns the gelding, watching as the two surviving night leopards sprint northward, their paws barely touching the soil, leaving the faintest puffs of dust as they make their way toward a distant woodlot.

"That be not good," observes Olisenn, "the Forest creatures amid the woodlots and fields of the people of Cyad."

"No," Lorn agrees, "but we have no way to track them or catch them." And forty lancers and firelances are not enough to deal with all that accompanies one of the tree trunks that topple, or are toppled, from the Accursed Forest across the ward-wall. "I'd be surprised if we have charges in half the firelances."

"More like a third," suggests Olisenn.

"If that," adds Kusyl. "And half a patrol to go yet."

"We still have to wait for the Engineers and make sure nothing else shows up," Lorn points out, probably unnecessarily, but he wants the lances spared, if possible.

"They will not soon arrive," predicts Olisenn.

Lorn fears that as well. "We need to circle the crown and go down the other side. We'll keep the squads together."

"Yes, ser." The quick response from both squad leaders conveys definite approval of that tactic.

Although Lorn thinks he hears some rustling in the branches, he sees nothing on the slow ride around the fallen tree. Nor do his squad leaders or any of the lancers see any more aggressive creatures.

The only animals they see are when they circle back to the southeast side of the tree in completing their circuit. The vulcrows and other carrion birds have already begun to feast on the dead serpent and the fallen night leopards.

Lorn looks south toward the Accursed Forest, wondering how many more trunks will fall across the ward-wall in his three years at Jakaafra, and how many more surprises like the giant serpent await him.

LXXVII

LORN WAKES THE next morning, just after dawn, stiff from lying on the hard soil of the deadland with only a thin blanket for padding and for warmth against a night that had almost been close to freezing. His skull aches, both from fatigue and from a vague memory of dreams—dreams of white walls being poured into the very earth itself, trees being scythed from the forests, and acid being dripped on his skin, except his skin had been the ground itself. His eyes turn south to the bulk of the Accursed Forest, but the Forest offers no answers.

He shakes his head slowly and stretches, gingerly. He drinks nearly an entire water bottle before he has any of the hard biscuits and cheese that comprise the emergency rations. The combination of liquid and food seems to clear his thoughts somewhat, and he studies the day, seemingly as cool as the previous one, although the wind out of the northeast has died down into an intermittent, if cool breeze.

As Lorn is smoothing his uniform in place, wishing again that he had been able to shave, Kusyl appears.

"The sentries say that nothing happened with the tree, ser," Kusyl reports. "No cats, no leopards, no serpents."

"Good. I'm going to have another look at the serpent. I won't be long. Besides, there's little enough we can do except try to keep any more leopards from breaking free."

"Yes, ser." Kusyl's tone is not quite dubious.

"The sentries are still on duty?"

"Yes, ser."

"When I get back, we'll discuss the day—both for first and second squads."

Kusyl nods.

Lorn walks the five hundred cubits or so from the bivouac area beyond the crown of the tree down the east side of the tangled branches. Four vulcrows flap off as the lancer captain nears the trunk and the dead snake. The astringent smell of crushed leaves mixes with the odors of musk and death as Lorn steps closer to the charred remnants of the serpent's head.

For a time, he studies the mass of charred scales and the blackened white bone showing through. Then he studies the trunk, and then the branches. Finally, he walks back to where the two squad leaders wait. His boots are covered with the powdered dust of salt- and chaos-killed soil even after his short walk.

Olisenn raises his eyebrows as if to ask why Lorn had been studying the dead serpent. Kusyl merely waits.

"We need to maintain the guard to keep any more creatures from leaving the Forest or the tree. We'll need to continue the sentry with four lancers with firelances behind him, until the engineers arrive and fire the crown."

Both squad leaders nods reluctantly.

"We won't mount anyone else until the engineers arrive, but we can rotate groups of lancers to that stream to the north to get water for themselves and their mounts—and to wash up if they want."

"Yes, ser."

"Why don't you take the first group, Olisenn," Lorn suggests. "You and Kusyl alternate groups of four from each squad."

"As you wish, ser."

Lorn nods. His thoughts are still on his dreams and the puzzle of the giant serpent.

"I'd like to report that to the second squad, ser," Kusyl says.

"Of course."

Lorn does not join the rotation for washing until well after mid-day, with the last group from the second squad. The cool water clears his head more, and he feels less itchy and more presentable after shaving.

It is late afternoon before two firewagons appear with the armored cannon. The officer who emerges from the lead firewagon to seek Lorn is one of the captains Lorn had met when thanking Majer Weylt the morning Second Company had left Eastend.

Lorn rides the gelding closer and reins up, waiting.

"Captain Lorn, Captain Strynst. Majer Weylt sends his apologies, but the spring rains were too heavy, and there was a break in the retaining walls for the Great Canal, and he was summoned to assist there."

"From Eastend?" Lorn asks.

"It's a distance, even by firewagon, but there aren't that many good engineers, and the Majer is one of the best." Strynst smiles apologetically.

"We're glad to see you," Lorn replies. "I was just surprised that he'd be called from so far."

"There aren't that many Mirror Engineers any more. Most of us are here, except for the few that are in Fyrad working on the fireships." Strynst turns and studies the trunk. "Not too bad, this one." He gives a wry smile. "Of course, it fell right on a ward. Happens nine times out of ten. Biggest reason to believe the Accursed Forest thinks in some way. That couldn't happen by accident—not year after year."

"I never thought anything with the Forest was an accident." Lorn laughs once.

"Some lancer officers do. Most of them end up dead." The engineer captain gestures toward the upper branches three hundred cubits northward. "Have many creatures running loose?"

Lorn's eyes follow the gesture momentarily, then fix back on the engineer. "Two giant cats, one serpent, and a pack of night leopards. Vulcrows, of course."

"A serpent? Never heard of one of those."

"It's a big one," Lorn says, gesturing in the general direction of the crown. "Forty cubits, maybe longer. Two cubits thick."

"We'll take a look when we fire the crowns." The captain pauses. "You get all the creatures?"

"One giant cat and two of the leopards escaped. There wasn't any real way to catch them."

"There never is once they leave the trees and get past the

lancers. Until some holder gets killed trying to protect his stock or kills them because they get cornered in a pen or something." Strynst shakes his head. "Might as well get started. Pull your men back, and we'll set up the firecannon."

"They're all back at the crown area now, Captain. I thought it would be better to set up there to keep any more creatures from breaking loose. If you want, I can move some up here."

"A half-score—behind the firewagons," Strynst suggests.

"I'll have them there shortly." Lorn turns the gelding and rides back north, knowing, again, from the order-chaos patterns that he feels and cannot yet fully explain, that nothing more will occur. Not with this fallen trunk.

"Thank you." Strynst turns and walks back to the firewagon.

Lorn turns the gelding, letting the horse walk slowly toward the waiting lancers. He takes a deep breath. Spring has just barely begun.

LXXVIII

THE BRIGHT MID-MORNING light of spring is pouring through the window of the inner Mirror Lancer study as Lorn struggles with the last lines of his latest patrol report. He looks it over once more, then signs it and looks up at the closed door, beyond which is the empty outer study.

Theoretically, he has the day off, as a stand-down period, but if he does not use part of the day to catch up on the reports and the letters to the families of the fallen lancers, it will be another eightday before he can, and then he will have twice as much to write, with a memory far less fresh.

After he sets aside the patrol report to let the ink dry, he picks up the next sheet of paper to begin the summary reports that will go to Majer Maran in Geliendra—carried by the next firewagon of the Mirror Engineers. In one patrol, Second Company has dealt with two breaches of the ward-wall by the fallen trees—a giant stun lizard, something like four giant cats, three packs of night leopards, and a giant serpent—and lost five lancers.

Lorn dislikes mentioning the number of creatures that escaped, but does, since all the reports in the file do so, even if the format does not necessarily require such. But, as Lorn knows, what is required and what is expected are not always the same. After finishing that scroll, he lays it by the first, and then begins writing the scroll he dislikes.

> ... with great sadness I must inform you that ... was killed while performing his duties as a Mirror Lancer. He died in protecting the land that he served and loved from the continual dangers of the Accursed Forest. ...

After five such letters, Lorn finally picks up the other scroll, the sealed one that has been waiting for him.

Rather, it is addressed to: Lancer Captain, Northend, Jakaafra. The seal is blank maroon wax, without even an initial on the glob that holds the scroll closed. Lorn breaks it, unrolls the missive, and begins to read.

> Honored Captain:
> I am writing this scroll on behalf of my family, and my brother in particular. They have suffered great depredations as a result of the failure of the Mirror Lancers at Jakaafra to destroy wild creatures from the Accursed Forest. ...
> Last eightday, a black leopard entered the sheep pen and dragged off a prize ewe, two nights in a row. The day following, my brother found dead a bullock he had been fattening for market. Little was left, save the head and bones. The prints in the ground were of a cat whose size could scarce be imagined. ...
> I am fortunate in that I do not require livestock for my livelihood, but all too many in and around Jakaafra will not survive in winter, save in despair

and poverty, unless these awful creatures are destroyed. . . .

Whatever needs be done, we beseech you do
so. . . .

The signature reads: Kylynzar.

Lorn takes a deep breath. So . . . now he must worry about
sacrificing even more lancers to save cows and sheep—or
possibly save those farm animals. Or can he task Juist with
rooting them out? How? He takes a second breath, considering that the victims could have been children as easily as
livestock.

Yet . . . he has not had enough charged firelances or
enough lancers to kill and contain all the night leopards and
giant cats they had faced, let alone the giant serpent.

He frowns, catching himself. Knowing what he knows, he
has not been able to do such. Will he have to? He worries
his lips. He certainly has no intention of attacking every stun
lizard with but a sabre or trying to chase down giant cats.

The serpent still preys on him. Setting aside the scroll for
a moment, he searches for the patrol manual that Majer
Maran had provided. When he finally pulls it from the single
desk drawer, he flips the pages slowly, going all the way
through the volume. Not finding what he seeks, he starts on
the first page and begins to scan each page, if quickly.

When he has completed a second search, he sets the manual down slowly. There are no references to serpents. The
manual lists the dangers from the night leopards, from giant
cats, from the stun lizards, even from a kind of tortoise Lorn
has never seen, and from vulcrows and the circular nests of
giant paper wasps—wasps as long as a man's index finger.
The captain winces at that thought, and resolves to keep that
possibility in mind with the next fallen trunk.

Lorn had not seen teeth in the serpent's jaws, nor had the
serpent actually attacked the lancers. Yet it could have swal-
lowed a lancer.

Lorn fingers his chin and glances down at the scroll he

must answer—or send back to Majer Maran. He likes neither alternative.

Finally, he begins to write. . . .

> Honored ser,
>   I appreciate the magnitude of the calamities which have befallen you and your family and your brother. . . .
>   . . . do the best that we can, but Second Company patrols a wall ninety-nine kays in length with but two score lancers. . . . At the time of your difficulties, we were opposing the Accursed Forest and killed near-on a score of creatures, including four giant cats, two packs of the black night leopards and a giant stun lizard . . . in these endeavors in which five lancers lost their lives it may have been possible that some creatures did escape, but not through the lack of effort or the unwillingness of lancers to die to protect the folk of Cyador . . . and we will continue to do our best in this struggle. . . .
>
>   With all best wishes and heart-felt condolences. . . .

After the third scroll dries, Lorn locks all eight responses into his chest, since there is no way to send them at the moment, and since he may reconsider his wording of the last response.

He closes the door and walks down the empty corridor, turning at the cross-corridor and going through the double doors to the courtyard of the compound. The courtyard is also empty, since Juist is patrolling the roads somewhere thirty kays to the north, as Lorn recalls.

On the other side of the courtyard, the stable doors are open, and Lorn steps inside.

"You're about early, ser," offers Suforis, the thin-faced blond stableboy, scurrying up to the lancer captain, "that be, for a stand-down day." He glances toward the stall that holds

Lorn's gelding. "You're not going to ride him far, ser?"

"Only to Jakaafra."

"He'll do for that. The farrier'll be here after your next patrol, ser."

"How many of the mounts need new shoes?"

"Could be a half-score, ser. Not as bad as undercaptain Juist's mounts; they ride the roads, mostly, and it's hard on 'em. He needs most of the spare mounts."

Lorn nods, then asks, "You said that you were allowed to ride the spares for exercise?"

"Have to, ser. And Undercaptain Juist, he uses me as a messenger, at times."

"You're good at it, I'd bet," Lorn answers. "I might ask you to do that, as well, except it's for me to send scrolls to order things. Could you do that, say for a copper a scroll— carry them to a factor in Jakaafra?"

"Did that for Captain Meisyl, half copper each." Suforis grins.

"So a copper would be fine." Lorn grins back. "Now . . . If you'd saddle the gelding."

"Yes, ser."

Lorn does not wait long before the stableboy returns.

"You best be riding easy, ser," cautions Suforis, after leading the saddled gelding out to Lorn.

"I will." Lorn smiles at the earnest young man.

The lancer captain lets the gelding set his own pace. It is not as though Lorn is in that much of a hurry, although it is far later than he had intended to get back in touch with Dustyn the factor. Then, when has he had any stand-down days to do so before this?

The air has warmed from the previous two days, but a light breeze from the east remains, making riding comfortable. Green has suffused the shoots in the fields, and the winter-gray leaves retained by the trees in the woodlots and orchards have turned deep green, while the fresh leaves are a lighter and more intense shade. The apple trees in one orchard already show white blossoms, although the pearapples' limbs are near-bare yet, with winter-gray leaves still furled.

The gelding's hoofs tap-click on the granite stones of the road, a smooth way, but narrow, only ten cubits wide. Twice Lorn goes onto the grassy shoulder to pass wagons headed for the town. He nods politely to both drivers, and both nod back, somberly, without speaking.

Although the town is supposedly only five kays from the compound, it is nearly mid-morning when the gelding brings Lorn to where the houses begin to gather together, past the kaystone announcing the town lies yet one kay farther. Lorn rides past the yellow-brick houses, each with the green ceramic exterior privacy screens, and the trimmed privacy hedges that circle rear porticos. Most of the green shutters are open. With all the dwellings of one story, to Lorn, Jakaafra seems something less than a town, if more than a hamlet.

The single square in the midst of Jakaafra is small, merely an open, stone-paved expanse no more than a hundred cubits on a side. Lorn rides slowly around the square, making a full circuit before his eyes light on a building on a short lane just off the square. There is a narrow storefront, above which is a green barrel. Lorn hopes that the green barrel is the symbol for a factor in spirits and liquids. It should be, since Dustyn's scroll had indicated he was "off the square."

With a smile, Lorn guides the gelding to the granite hitching post below the narrow porch, and ties his mount to the bronze ring, slightly tarnished. He steps onto the porch and through the single doors and finds himself in a small room, bare except for a counter, behind which no one stands, but on which is a handbell. Lorn rings it.

"Coming . . ."

Lorn waits, but no one appears.

Finally, he rings it again.

". . . said I was a'coming." The curtain behind the counter is drawn back and a man appears a span or two taller than Lorn. His straight brown hair is pulled back and held by an ornate silver clip. "I said . . . oh, Captain, didn't know as it was you. Captain Lorn, I take it, since you'd be the only Mirror Lancer captain around, and today being your stand-down day, I'd wager, seeing as you wouldn't be here on any other day. . . ."

Lorn laughs. "I'm Captain Lorn." He lifts his hand and shows the seal ring.

"And I'm Dustyn, factor in spirits and liquids, only one north of the Accursed Forest, only one 'tween here and the barbarians, 'tween here and the Westhorns. . . ." Dustyn bows. "If you would accompany me, honored captain."

As he follows Dustyn through the narrow curtained archway, Lorn wonders why he is an "honored" captain, but he follows the older man along a corridor and down the narrow brick steps to a cool cellar. Against one wall is a long platform, on which rest kegs and barrels of differing sizes, made of staves of various woods. On the adjoining wall are racks containing hundreds of bottles.

Before the racks are three wooden crates and two baskets.

"You see . . . we have two cases of the Alafraan and one of the Fhynyco. . . ." Dustyn lifts both hands theatrically. "And of course, the two baskets of dry goods we accepted on your behalf, as they were so small."

Lorn nods. The baskets are small, no more than two cubits long and slightly less than a cubit in diameter—small enough to be fastened behind his saddle. He extends silver to the factor. "I appreciate your care." He smiles. "You did well to treat with Ryalor House. It is small . . . but not without influence."

Dustyn offers a lopsided smile in return. "Indeed, ser. I know some who trade with both the Yuryan Clan and the Dyljani, and my inquiries, always discreet, you understand, they have returned the words to me that the Ryalor House is honest and returns value." Dustyn shifts his weight from foot to foot nervously.

"All kinds of value?" suggests Lorn.

"Ah . . . yes, ser."

"I will put in a good word for you, Dustyn." The lancer captain smiles. "Perhaps we could work out something." He pauses. "I would rather not accept all these bottles at one time, and you do have some storage here."

"Yes, ser." Dustyn's smile loses its nervous edge. "If you would wish a few bottles every eightday . . . for a small fee. . . ."

"How small?" asks Lorn warily.

"Very small—a half copper an eightday?"

"We have an agreement." Lorn extends another silver. "This should accommodate you until fall, should it not?"

"Yes, ser."

"Do you know a holder named Kylynzar?" asks Lorn. "From somewhere around here?"

"Kylynzar? Yes, ser. A most respected man. He holds much land to the north, in the red hills, and he grows melons, and some of them he turns into the gold melon brandy. It is good brandy, though most in Jakaafra prefer the rice beer or the ale."

"Hmmm . . . do you have a bottle of the brandy?"

"I have several . . . more than several."

Lorn nods. "I have a suggestion. I will be sending a scroll to someone I know at Ryalor House. You can make those arrangements, can you not?"

"It would have to accompany some goods . . . or for a fee. . . ."

"The golden melon brandy. I would suggest sending a small case to Ryalor House. A gold in shipping?"

"Ah . . . yes, ser, and a gold for a half-score of the smaller bottles."

Lorn nods, and extends two golds, hoping he will not need to spend much more for at least several eightdays, when his next stipend as a lancer captain arrives. "Consider it done. You send my scroll—you will receive it tomorrow or the next day—with the shipment back to Ryalor House."

"Yes, ser."

"And for that, Dustyn, you could spare me one small bottle of the golden brandy to go with the Alafraan and Fhynyco I will take with me, could you not?" Lorn smiles winningly.

"If I like it, and Ryalor House likes it, you might find more trade with them."

"A bottle I could spare." Dustyn's smile is half-relieved, half-speculative.

"And you know that Ryalor House respects confidences, and expects its confidences to be kept?"

"Ah . . . yes, ser . . . many have said such."

"Just so we understand each other."

"Yes, ser."

Lorn gives up a last silver. "For your assistance and continuing efforts, Dustyn." He *thinks* the combination of implied lash and honey will keep the factor dealing honestly, and his own rudimentary truthreading skills indicate that Dustyn has not lied to him or tried to deceive him.

Lorn does need to borrow some cord to fasten the straw-padded sack with the brandy and wine and the two baskets to the gelding, and he ties them securely behind his saddle.

With a nod and a wave, he turns the gelding back toward the compound. Concentrating on all that must be done, his thoughts flicking from one problem to another, the return ride seems far shorter.

Once he is back in his quarters, with the three bottles of wine—one of Fhynyco and two of Alafraan—and the brandy sitting on his small desk, he opens the brandy and pours a finger width of it into his mug.

Then he sniffs it, slowly. The aroma barely holds the scent of melon, and there is a deeper and warmer flavor there. He takes a sip, and cannot help but smile. If Ryalor House can arrange matters quietly, there will be more golds from the brandy. If. . . .

Then . . . all of life holds its ifs.

Lorn bends down and opens the first basket. On top is a set of smallclothes, and then a lightweight summer shimmercloth Lancer tunic. Under that is a second set of smallclothes. Within the second set is a folded and sealed paper. He smiles and sets aside the clothing for the words written in Ryalth's bold script.

My dearest captain,

As promised, here are some goods that may be
of value in the seasons ahead.

Much gossip came of the death of Shevelt. I believe that occurred after you departed. The Dyljani
Clan offered its respects to the new heir, in golds.
They also presented an exquisite Hamorian tapes-
try. At the moment, all is calm.

Ryalor House suffered some loss when the *Redwind Courser* foundered in a storm in the Gulf, but
not so much as many, and recouped some of that
in other trades. . . .

Lorn nods. While he had hoped the ship would last for a
few voyages, he had warned Ryalth, and she had acted ac-
cordingly. He would like to wait to respond to Ryalth, to
take time to answer properly, but time he does not have, not
when he will ride out on the morrow for another patrol out
and back, another eightday before he can send a scroll in a
manner he knows will reach its destination with far less
chance of being read than sending it through the lancer courier system.

Still . . . he had the forethought to make arrangements with
Dustyn—the forethought, and the luck, he reminds himself.

Below the garments, and wrapped in heavy oiled leather
are several other packages—some cheeses, dried fruits, and
nuts. The second basket holds a package of fine linen paper,
three bottles of ink, and a cupridium-tipped pen that has
clearly come from a craftsman. Concealed in the middle of
the paper are ten golds. Also at the bottom of the second
basket are more dried fruits and nuts.

Lorn smiles at the clear reminder that he is expected to
write, and at the suggestion that the golds are to be used to
ensure such missives arrive.

Once he has emptied the baskets and stored their goods,
Lorn lights the lamp in the bracket above the desk, seats
himself, and begins to write, using the new pen and ink.

> My dearest lady trader,
>
> Thank you for the Alafraan and the Fhynyco . . .
> and for all the manner of fine goods you have sent.
> You are truly amazing. . . . I have made arrange-
> ments, through Dustyn the factor, to send you a
> small case of a gold melon brandy. Dustyn rec-
> ommended it, and I have tried one bottle. It has a
> good and mellow taste, strong as it is, and I've
> never seen it before. Perhaps it might prove useful
> and profitable as an item to sell to the Austrans or
> Hamorians. . . .
>
> I also suggest you look into the timber gleaned
> from the Accursed Forest. It's carried down the
> Great Canal and sold to coastal traders and Ha-
> morians . . . wouldn't be surprised if it made good
> shipbuilding timber, but couldn't tell you why. The
> Brystans might be interested. . . .

Lorn pauses, holding the pen, wishing he could offer her
more insight, for it seems that is all he can offer in these
days. Finally, he adds a few more lines and closes it.

> From your faithful partner, one most apprecia-
> tive of the clothing, the sustenance, and the wines
> and the spirit in which they were all conveyed.

He lays that scroll aside for the ink to dry while he begins
the second, also overdue, to his family, but that will go
through the lancer courier system, where it will doubtless be
read, and will say little that is not expected.

> It was a long trip to Jakaafra, and it has taken
> some time to become familiar with all that is nec-
> essary here. My immediate senior officer, Majer
> Maran, is most friendly, and reminds me of my old
> school-mate Dettaur. . . .

Only Jerial will understand the full meaning of that. . . .
and his mother. . . .

. . . patrols here different from those in Isahl . . .
we ride three days, have a day of stand-down, then
ride three more—unless there is a problem. . . . Jakaafra is the smallest of the compounds around the
Forest. . . . I have met some Mirror Engineers and
am developing great respect for their work. . . .

After he adds more pleasantries, and allows the second
scroll to dry, Lorn seals both scrolls and sets them on the
corner of the desk, for dispatch, in their differing ways, in
the morning.

Then, he stands and stretches, before moving to the wardrobe, and slipping the chaos glass out and setting it upon his
desk. He frowns. He has only felt one magus screeing him
since he came to Jakaafra. Does the Forest inhibit such? Or
does no one care about his actions in distant eastern Cyador?

Laying the glass on the golden-aged white oak, Lorn concentrates on the silvered glass, trying to call up the image of
Ryalth. The mists appear, and swirl for what seems an in-
ordinately long time, but they do clear and present an image.

A red-haired woman walks along Second Harbor Way in
the fading light of early evening. Abruptly, her step hesitates
and she turns. For a moment, Lorn looks full into the face
in the glass, then lets the image go. He does not wish to
disturb her—not too much.

His forehead is beaded with sweat from that short effort,
and he can tell he will need practice, much more practice.

What of Maran? He shakes his head.

Then he smiles and concentrates on recalling Dustyn the
factor.

When the mists clear, Lorn finds himself blushing, for
Dustyn is within a bedchamber, and not alone. He quickly
allows that image to fade.

Does the Forest inhibit a chaos glass?

He concentrates on the last tree trunk that had fallen across
the ward-wall, trying to recall the location near the midpoint
chaos tower and even the shape of the trunk that remained
after the engine captain had fired the crown.

The mists take far, far longer to clear, and Lorn can feel the heat pouring from his brow, but he continues to seek the image.

Finally, he is rewarded with an image. Four wagons flank a trunk that appears half what it had been. A score of men labor with shimmering long saws. Lorn tries to shift the image to see beyond the wall, but nothing appears except a black-silver curtain. He tries again.

His head feels light, and tiny stars flash before his eyes. He sits on the edge of his narrow bed until the flashing and dizziness subside. Then he stands and replaces the glass in the wardrobe.

He needs to find something to eat. He reclaims the opened brandy bottle and steps out into the corridor, turning and locking his door. Then he starts for the dining area, where he knows he can find bread and cheese, at least. Perhaps Juist has returned and will like some of the brandy.

Lorn shrugs, smiling. The day has not gone that badly, and he does not have to think of the morrow's patrol. Not yet.

LXXIX

THE SPRING-LIKE breeze gusts past Lorn as the lancer captain rides along the perimeter road just north of the white granite structure that holds the northeast midpoint chaos tower—the tower that Lorn is convinced has not operated perhaps in several years. The gelding's hoofs barely tap on the smooth granite of the road, and the faint chirping of insects in the fields to his left occasionally lifts above the sighing of the wind in the meadow grass that is already knee-high there.

With the breeze, Lorn feels cooler, and the perspiration he has blotted from his forehead does not return, not until the breeze dies down. To his right, the second squad continues riding forward in their line abreast formation, looking for signs of any Forest incursions, but in the three patrols since the last fallen tree, there have been no shoots or any additional fallen trees.

Behind Lorn's saddle is fastened a second sabre in a battered sheath. All the men know it is there, and none remark upon it, not after seeing that their captain had lost his first sabre battling a stun lizard. Yet that is not why Lorn carries it. He can sense the dark order within the cupridium forged-exterior of the blade, and he knows that, in some instances, it will have greater effect against the order-backed attacks and creatures of the Accursed Forest, for it has become all too clear that the Forest employs linked order and chaos, and that such is far more effective than either order or chaos alone. Where and how—of the exact circumstances—he is less certain.

He readjusts his garrison cap.

"Going to be a hot summer, ser," Kusyl says, raising his voice to cross the stretch of road that separates the two men. "All the signs point to it, every one. Vytly says the grapes are coming in early, and not a late frost to nip 'em, either. Melons, too, and even the redberries are fruiting early."

"I hope it's not as hot as the Grass Hills," Lorn answers with a laugh. "I could do without that."

"No, ser. Nothing that hot. Maybe feels hotter here, though, 'cause the air's damper, you know." Kusyl gestures to his left, toward the silent bulk of the Accursed Forest. "Always rains more around the Forest. Be why folk live here, even worrying 'bout the creatures." The junior squad leader pauses, then asks, "Heard any more about the big cats?"

"Every so often, I get a scroll complaining that a bullock or a sheep's been killed. I try to explain."

"They should be out here, looking at one of them trunks after it falls. Give 'em a real different look at things. Wager none of them be pensioned lancers."

A murmur rises from the lancer fifty cubits to Kusyl's left, one that Lorn barely hears, and Kusyl does not. ". . . such a man as a pensioned lancer . . . not Paradise likely!"

"I'm sure they're not," Lorn answers across the ten cubits

between them. "I doubt a pensioned lancer would stay too close to the ward-wall."

Kusyl laughs. "Not me. Be going back to Kynstaar, I am, when that day comes. Open a tavern there, and take golds from lancer officers."

Lorn smiles.

Ahead is the place where the last tree had fallen, but, as Majer Weylt had told him eightdays before, there is no sign that a Forest tree had ever toppled across the ward-wall. The wind has filled in the depressions in the deadland with loose salty soil and carried away the sawdust. Poorer peasants have crept out into the deadland at dawn and at twilight and carried off the remaining branches for firewood. And the wind and the insects have removed the leaves. To the south, Lorn can discern no noticeable gap in the huge trunks that comprise a second wall behind the ward-wall itself.

It is almost as though no tree had ever fallen across the ward-wall.

Except . . . Lorn recalls that there are dead lancers, strange animals roaming the northern lands of Cyad, and farm animals killed and dragged off into the dark. And he knows that other trees will fall, as falls the rain, as blows the wind.

LXXX

IN THE BRIGHT light supplied by the wall lamps and their polished cupridium reflectors that are unnecessary for those within the chamber, First Magus Chyenfel moves deliberately, almost cautiously, to the armchair beside the desk in the austere study on the uppermost level of the tower that crowns the Quarter of the Magi'i. It is a tower in name only, for it rises but five levels, far less imposing than the Palace of Light—except to the Senior Lectors of the Magi'i and those who know what transpires within the Quarter. Silently, Chyenfel'elth seats himself, then waits for the Second Magus to take the chair before the desk.

"Ser?" asks Kharl'elth. "You do not summon often in the evening."

"When I am tired, and less on guard? You are right. I do not." A smile appears and vanishes. "I wish to know why you discourage Captain-Commander Luss from voicing his support of the sleep-ward project to the Majer-Commander, and why you have likewise discouraged the Emperor's Merchanter Advisor."

Kharl smiles warmly, his green eyes dancing. "I have said not one word against this effort. Not one word against it to anyone, ser."

Chyenfel offers a dramatic sigh. "That is the same as discouraging it, and we both know it. I have held my counsel, believing that we had time, and that in the fullness of that time, the need would become obvious without having to raise one's voice or the power of the Magi'i."

"That was wise, ser, for the replenishment towers here in the Quarter may fail soon, if one by one, and the barbarian attacks are increasing, requiring more firelances, and more charges for those lances." Kharl's words are bland. "As you know, I fear the barbarians more than the Accursed Forest."

"Failing to deal with the Accursed Forest may be wise for a season or so, perchance, even a year, but not longer." The sungold eyes of the First Magus lock upon the green eyes of the Second Magus, which carry but a shade of the sungold sheen. "Yet you know as do I that the ward-wall on the northeast side of the Accursed Forest is barely holding, and that we have lost yet another chaos-tower there."

"I have read the reports from the Mirror Engineers that have suggested such." Kharl shrugs offhandedly. "We both understand the dangers. Yet we do not wish to incur the Emperor's displeasure—or that of the Majer-Commander of Lancers—by limiting further the chaos charges we supply to the Mirror Lancers. Or by reducing the number of firewagons that travel the Highways of Cyador. We have already limited the use of tow-wagons on the Great Canal."

The First Magus waits.

"That is why we ... intimated that Captain Lorn—or

should I say, Lorn'elth?—be assigned such patrols on the northeast ward-wall border." Kharl brushes back a stray reddish hair, almost absently, yet affectedly. "He is likely to be . . . more effective."

Chyenfel'elth's mouth smiles, but his sungold eyes are politely intent, never leaving the Second Magus. "That was indeed wise, Kharl, if not precisely for the reasons you discussed with Captain-Commander Luss."

"We also need the time to ensure your project works," Kharl continues, "and that is another reason why I have not yet pressed for its implementation. All the while, the ward-wall must seem as strong as ever until we are most certain we can complete your project."

"I almost believe you, honored Second Magus." Chyenfel steeples his long delicate fingers before him.

"Are you convinced it will work, ser?" asks Kharl abruptly. "This great project of which you speak to the Emperor so intently?"

"Completely? No. But it matters not. If it does not work, then Cyad is better served by knowing such while other chaos towers yet remain. There will be no towers in a generation, and only a handful of firelances charged by the laborious concentration of the scattering of first-level adepts. Each year will find but a few score cupridium blades produced to hold back the barbarians of the north." The sungold eyes flare. "You know this. The risk is worth it." An ironic smile follows. "Except to those who wish to seize power now—or in the poor handful of years to come."

"I have never opposed you, ser." The warm smile plays once more across Kharl's face.

"But . . . knowing how I can truthread you, most honored Second Magus, you are most careful of what you say, and how you say it."

"As are you, ser," replies Kharl. "As are we all."

"Again, you are most accurate, Kharl, most accurate. I would that you consider turning your considerable charm and judgment to support what we must do to confine the Accursed Forest for more than the handful of years left to the chaos towers and their crystal wards."

"I hear, honored First Magus, and I will begin."

A faint smile once more appears on Chyenfel's lips, and he rises to signify the meeting is at an end.

Kharl also rises, and his smile could be a mirror of that on the lips of the First Magus.

Neither the sungold eyes nor those of dancing green with the intermittent gold cast bear any semblance of a smile.

LXXXI

THE WAYSTATION IS silent, under an early summer sky so cloudless, dark, and still that not even the stars overhead twinkle. Lorn does not look skyward as he slips silently across the granite stones of the courtyard to the small side postern that is neither locked nor guarded. Wearing the Brystan sabre on his right hip, in addition to his lancer sabre on his left, Lorn slides into the shadows, melding with them as he opens the gate and departs, walking silently southward on the stone walkway that flanks the walls.

Once clear of the walls, he places his boots as quietly as possible on the dry deadland soil, for he would rather not take the narrow road that leads from the front gates of the waystation past the perimeter road and inward to the ward-wall. Even so, his steps carry him steadily through the darkness toward the ward-wall and the presence that looms behind the whitened granite and the chaos-net that flares above it—a net unseen except by the Magi'i—and a lancer who remains magus.

He stops on the inner wall road, where he studies the subtly glowing granite, the chaos net, and the deep twining of black order and golden-red chaos. He wonders again how something that incorporates such chaos can be as evil as the Magi'i have depicted. Yet there is no denying the *animosity* that the forest creatures have toward the engineers and the lancers. Or is it exactly animosity?

"Do you want to try this?" he murmurs to himself, knowing as he does that merely continuing as a skillful lancer is not enough. After winter and spring, with summer continuing the same pattern of scattered Forest shoots and too many fallen trees, and escaping creatures too swift and numerous and dangerous for the numbers of lancers and firelances in Second Company, he knows that sooner or later, he will make a mistake that will be fatal—or that could be, and he has no wish to trust his future to fate alone.

He unsheathes the Brystan sabre, holding it before him. Then . . . Lorn concentrates, much as he once did in transferring chaos from the tower in the Quarter of the Magi'i to the chaos cells that power the firewagons of Cyad. Except this time, he merely shifts that energy away from a single ward, in order to create an unshuttered window—or a door temporarily open—to the Accursed Forest.

With the fading of the small section of chaos-net, Lorn can fully sense the power—the white chaos and dark order of the Forest that is greater in its own way than the combined energy of all the chaos towers that weave the chaos web that holds the Forest within its bounds. And he understands, and he shudders.

A dark lance flares through the window in the ward-wall, straight at Lorn, attacking the lancer-magus as if he were the Forest's gaoler.

Lorn lifts the Brystan sabre, lifting untested chaos-order shields, shields he has practiced only in private since leaving the Quarter of the Magi'i, and letting the ordered iron within the cupridium catch the Forest's bolt of order-chaos . . . catch and turn it upward into a flare that flashes upwards.

Nonetheless, he staggers, and with his staggering releases his hold on the chaos diversions, and the chaos-net surges back, confining the Forest.

Lorn's face burns, and sweat drips from his forehead. He has been foolhardy . . . and survived by luck, and his own lack of chaos control. He smothers a bitter laugh, knowing

390 ◇ L. E. Modesitt, Jr.

he has barely begun to understand what he must learn.

As he walks back through the darkness he glances at the sabre once more. Within the shimmering cupridium is a core of ordered iron—and iron that feels darker, almost black, and far stronger than either the original wrought material iron of the blade or of the comparable cupridium lancer sabre that remains in his scabbard.

A faint glow surrounds the Brystan sabre. Lorn sheathes it carefully and walks even more silently and circuitously back toward the side gate from whence he had departed. Overhead, the stars have begun to twinkle once more with the slight breeze that helps to cool his fevered countenance.

Lorn slides through the shadows, and is walking across the courtyard, almost to the courtyard door that will lead to his quarters.

"Ser! That you, Captain?"

Footsteps cross the stones, and Lorn hears the *hiss* of a drawn sabre.

"Yes. I just wanted some air. It's all right." Lorn lets the lantern show his face.

"Ah . . . yes, ser." The sabre is sheathed. "You see that, ser?"

"See what?" Lorn temporizes.

"Been so quiet . . . then there was this flash out by the wall. I thought maybe another of those big trees falling. But nothing happened. Thought I heard footsteps, you know, but there was just a glow moving by the wall, and it vanished."

"You can't ever tell with the Accursed Forest," Lorn points out, truthfully.

"No, ser. Sorry to bother you, ser." The lantern is lowered.

"It's not a problem. I'm glad you're watching for us." Lorn inclines his head, though he doubts the lancer can see the gesture fully. "I'm going to turn in. We still have a long ride tomorrow." And again the day after, and the day after that—and for who knows how many more days and seasons of trees falling and creatures escaping.

LXXXII

UNDER HIGH BUT thick gray clouds, Lorn watches as Olisenn orders his squad into the line abreast formation that runs inward from the perimeter road toward the line already formed by Kusyl's second squad. The heavy squad leader's voice is firm and carries, yet Lorn finds himself watching the senior squad leader more and more, trying never to turn his back on the man at any time when firelances are in readiness. Even so, there have been a few times when Lorn has forgotten, and sooner or later, that will create problems.

Lorn reaches forward and pats the gelding, grateful that his mount has proven more trustworthy than all too many people in Cyador. Lorn frowns at his thought. It is not that so many have proven untrustworthy; it is that his observations, and those of his father, have shown that so many will prove untrustworthy. The gelding is what the gelding is, unlike people who change in response to their perceptions of events that may benefit or threaten their power.

He glances toward the clouds that do not seem to promise rain. Second Company has but one more day's patrol before reaching the compound at Jakaafra—and the two full days off they receive after every fourth complete patrol to Eastend and back.

As he turns the gelding northwest on the wall road, Lorn studies the white-granite wall to his left. The chaos-flows are once more irregular—the response to his efforts of two nights before? Or another fallen tree? Or both?

A faint smile crosses his lips.

There will be another tree trunk down. That he knows. And there will be more wild creatures—and another day on station before the Mirror Engineers arrive.

"Was it worth it?" he murmurs.

"Ser, you speaking to me?" asks Kusyl from the other side of the wall road to his right.

"No, Kusyl. I was thinking out loud. How I'll be glad when we finally get back to Jakaafra."

"You and me, too, ser. Been a long summer, and it's hardly been two eightdays since it even started."

Lorn nods. Will he ever see the ripening—of pears and praise—or of anything for which he has silently worked?

LXXXIII

THE FOUR OFFICERS sit around the small table in the dining area at the Jakaafra compound. Only a single lamp on the wall is lit, illuminating the table but dimly, to Lorn's advantage. Lorn takes a sip of the Fhynyco, then glances across the table at Gebynet, the Mirror Engineer majer, on his way through on one of the periodic inspections of the chaos tower that lies just beyond the compound. To Lorn's left is Captain Ilryk, a tall and blond officer, with a high forehead and an angular face and pointed chin. After a moment, Lorn's eyes travel to Undercaptain Juist, sitting to Ilryk's left. "How do you like it?"

"Good!" The stocky Juist takes a solid swallow.

An enigmatic smile curls onto Ilryk's lips, but he does not offer an opinion.

"It's better than Byrdyn," admits Gebynet, after a more refined sip, and another sniff of the bouquet. "How did you get it here?"

"I have some contacts with merchanter houses," Lorn admits. "They have been kind enough to ship some items to a factor in Jakaafra."

"You don't look or act like you come from a merchanter clan," Juist states bluntly.

"I don't," Lorn says easily, taking what appears to be a deep swallow, but is not, more like a bare sip. "I just know a few people, and Captain Meisyl suggested that it would be wise to order in a few bottles of a decent wine for times like these." He laughs. "Few enough that they are with each of us gone off some place or another most days and nights."

"True," admits Gebynet.

"As I am when I am here," says Ilryk, who commands the Fifth Forest Patrol Company based in Westend. As Lorn patrols the northeast ward-wall, so does Ilryk patrol the northwest wall.

"We're all riding somewhere most of the time," Juist says after another swallow from his goblet of Fhynyco. "Leastwise, none of you have to chase bandits."

"I think, Juist," offers Ilryk sardonically, "Captain Lorn and I would prefer the handful of bandits to facing stun lizards, giant cats, and night leopards. The bandits fear firelances and lancers, and fight seldom."

"Most days . . . we ride longer," counters Juist.

"Through more pleasant surroundings," suggests Ilryk.

Gebynet laughs. "I've heard this before, and you two won't change. I'd rather enjoy the Fhynyco, if you don't mind."

Ilryk smiles, still sardonically, while Juist looks at his empty goblet mournfully.

Lorn half-fills the undercaptain's goblet, then addresses the Engineer majer. "Do you have to do more inspections when they send Majer Weylt off to work on the Great Canal? Or do they send him sometimes and you other times?"

"We do different things beside maintaining the chaos towers. Last year, after the storms, I spent almost a season in Fyrad, repairing the trading piers there." Gebynet sips more of the wine. "Rather good vintage, captain."

Lorn swallows obviously, then lifts the second bottle. "You should have some more. No sense in letting the bottles stand unused." He refills both goblets and appears to refill his own as well. "Not these days."

"You been having a lot of fallen trees, I hear," offers Juist.

"Have the local people been complaining to you about the escaped creatures?" Lorn's smile is crooked.

"We did get a night leopard last eightday, out east of

here," Juist answers. "That made a big melon grower happy."

"Kylynzar, I'd wager," Lorn suggests.

Ilryk shakes his head. "It would be that one."

"How did you know?" asks Juist, glancing from Ilryk to Lorn.

"He's been writing scrolls to me." Lorn rolls his eyes, letting his words slur ever so slightly. "He wishes us to make sure that no creatures escape from the Accursed Forest. None at all. So I must risk lancers and myself—or risk myself even more." Lorn turns to Gebynet.

"You have been here the longest of us. Are more trees falling this year?"

"Quite a few more than normal," says Gebynet, adding quickly, "but not an unheard-of number."

"Not unheard of," Lorn says, looking blankly at the Mirror Engineer, "but how many companies have handled so many fallen trees in three seasons? Not quite three seasons," he corrects.

"We have seen more this year than last on our wall," interjects Ilryk, "but there are always more on the northeast. In the past two years, anyway."

"I would not know. . . ." the majer answers slowly.

"Perhaps one?" asks Lorn idly, letting his truth-reading senses scan the Engineer.

"Three or four, I would say."

Lorn nods. Gebynet is lying, and unhappy about it as well. He lifts the bottle again. "Some more. No sense in letting the bottle stand unused."

Gebynet and Juist exchange glances, but allow Lorn to top off their goblets. Ilryk refuses, his amused smile still in place.

LXXXIV

IN THE MID-AFTERNOON sun, Lorn stands in the stirrups to let damp trousers dry as much as to stretch his legs. As on every afternoon in the recent days nearing harvest, the few scattered clouds provide little relief from the damp heat, and the late-day rainstorms only add more moisture to the steamy heat. Each patrol day ends with uniforms soaked in sweat, and the soil of the deadland is powder under the hoofs of the patrol mounts, rising and infiltrating boots and uniforms, and leaving every lancer's skin dry and itchy from salt and sweat and dust.

Lorn glances to his left, along the line-abreast of lancers, riding almost a hundred cubits apart now that first squad has but thirteen lancers out of the twenty when he had arrived three seasons earlier. The second squad has but twelve. No replacements are scheduled until the end of fall or the beginning of winter, and Lorn wonders how small Second Company will have gotten by then.

As he looks back to his left, as he takes in and ignores another *zzzzzppp* for a dead bloodsucking flowerfly, he can sense the intermittent pulses of chaos in the cupridium cables that link the crystal wards. Another tree is down across the wall, but how far from Second Company he cannot tell.

"Hot . . . never gets any cooler . . . be glad when it starts to frost," grunts Kusyl from the outer edge of the wall road.

"Then we'll have to slop through mud," Lorn reminds the squad leader.

"I think I'll take that."

"That's what you say now." Lorn grins.

As they ride through the afternoon, Lorn keeps looking to the southeast, until his eyes confirm what his chaos senses have told him far earlier. Yet another trunk has fallen across the ward-wall.

"Another tree is down."

"Five abreast!" Kusyl turns in the saddle and calls to Lorn. "Olisenn's already seen it. His squad is going to five front now."

"Set up the containment pattern for the crown," Lorn tells Kusyl. He no longer bothers with checking the trunk first. If there are giant cats, they will attack no matter where the lancers are. Stun lizards are slow enough to be chased down if necessary, and the night leopard packs are always in the crown. As for the giant serpents, Second Company has seen but the one in three seasons.

"Five abreast! Move out to the tree crown!" Kusyl orders. "Ubylt! Ride out and inform squad leader Olisenn that we're riding out to join them to block the tree crown!"

"Yes, sers!" Ubylt turns his chestnut northward.

As Lorn and the second squad angle their way toward the tree crown yet several kays away, Lorn tries to estimate the size of the fallen giant, judging that its base diameter is about twenty cubits, larger than many, but not so large as the mammoth trunks they have sometimes encountered.

"Think the forest'd run out of big trees," mutters Kusyl.

"With ninety-nine kays on a side to work with?" Lorn laughs.

"Didn't used to be so many."

"Maybe it was waiting for the big trees to get bigger."

Kusyl snorts.

The two squads join at the perimeter road to the northwest of the crown. Lorn estimates that the nearest part of the twisted greenery lies almost three-quarters of a kay from them.

"First squad . . . you take the left side, second squad the right."

"You heard the captain."

"First squad to the left!" booms Olisenn.

With roughly a hundred fifty cubits between them, the two lancer squads ride toward the forest crown, lances at the ready.

Lorn blots the sweat from his forehead, ignoring the heat from the continual sunburn on the back of his neck and the way his sweat-soaked uniform clings to him. He shifts his weight in the saddle, but his eyes remain on the crumpled green canopy.

The first creature that lumbers outward, angling more to the east and the first squad, is a smallish stun lizard—if a lizard a mere three cubits at the shoulder and fifteen cubits in length can be termed small.

MMMnnnnn . . . The silent mental scream halts several mounts, and one lancer sways in his saddle.

"First squad," Lorn orders. "Discharge at will! Now! Short bursts!"

"Short bursts at will!" repeats Olisenn.

MMMnnnnn . . . The stricken lancer slumps in his saddle, and one mount rears.

"Second squad, lances ready! Stand by," Kusyl orders.

Hhssst! Hssst! . . . The orange-golden-red of firelance discharges flares across the lizard, which, uncharacteristically, turns as if to retreat into the tangle crown foliage. The firelances lash again and again, and the lizard is still.

"First squad, let the second squad lead a little," Lorn orders, nodding to Kusyl.

The lancers of the second squad move forward faster, closer to the tip of the crown. Lorn looks back, and it appears as though the stunned lancer is beginning to recover, being supported in his saddle by another lancer.

Lorn glances toward the vegetation ahead, now well less than two hundred cubits away. "Company halt!" He reins in the gelding, watching the mass of green and brown, sniffing for the musky odor that goes with the cats, but for the moment, he smells but the astringency of crushed leaves.

First company reins up to Lorn's left, their lances at the ready as well.

The forest canopy is silent, almost too silent, Lorn thinks.

Then, both Lorn and Kusyl see the telltale shifting of branches and the rustling of leaves that always precedes an attack by the black night leopards.

"Stand by to discharge! Short bursts!" Even as those orders are in the air, Lorn has to add, "Discharge at will!"

Nearly a score of the night leopards bound from the greenery, straight at the second squad.

Hsst! Hssst! . . .

Firebolts from lances flare, and golden-red chaos collides with streaking blackness.

Three leopards converge on Lorn, and while his lance

strikes two, the third flattens itself and springs toward the gelding.

Lorn slashes down with his sabre, reinforcing it with his own personally guided chaos force, and the night leopard drops, leaving but a thin scratch along the gelding's shoulder.

Dark bodies strew the deadland soil.

"Ser! There it goes!"

Lorn's eyes follow the sole surviving leopard. It has sprinted back toward the ward-wall, then to the east, and then outward toward the perimeter road well clear of any area where lancers are positioned to intercept the lithe dark cat.

"Ser! We can't catch it!"

"Hold where you are!" Lorn orders, ignoring the grim, almost pleased smile on Olisenn's broad face. He takes a deep breath, thinking about another leopard's escape about which he will doubtless hear, one way or another. No one will care that of nearly a score of the night leopards, they have killed all but one.

"Hold fast!" Both Kusyl and Olisenn echo his orders.

Lorn blots the sweat from his eyes with the forearm of his sleeve. He studies the canopy again wondering if they will see a giant cat again—or a serpent—or anything.

He has been commanding Second Company for nearly three seasons of patrols . . . and encountered a fallen trunk practically every second or third patrol. Is the Forest going to continue probing the northeast ward-wall? Even if it does, what could he do about it? Except position his lancers and watch every move Olisenn makes?

"Stand by," Lorn orders tiredly. "We need to send a messenger to Eastend."

Again.

LXXXV

LORN GLANCES AT the scroll on the desk in the inner study, and then at the window. Outside, a warm drizzle is falling, and a hot fog rises from the granite stones of the courtyard. It is afternoon of his stand-down day, and he has not finished all the reports that have piled up. He cannot remember when he last had a clear-eyed moment in which to write Ryalth or his family, and he still must write a request to Commander Meylyd to pay the farrier for reshoeing ten mounts.

Finally, the lancer captain picks up the scroll from Majer Maran a second time and re-reads it slowly.

> . . . while it is true that Second Company has been forced to deal with a singular amount of activity from the Accursed Forest, that does not relieve you of the responsibility for the safety of the people of Cyad.

Lorn snorts. It is not as if he has not already been made well aware of that requirement by many souls—beginning with the Patrol Manual itself. His eyes go back to the scroll.

> Commander Meylyd has received more than a dozen message scrolls begging greater efforts in containing the creatures from the Accursed Forest, and I am hereby conveying his concerns to you. All in the Mirror Lancers know the difficulties of carrying out the duties laid upon us, often without the ideal support and supplies. This necessitates long eightdays, and fortitude not required of others. Such is the life of, and the glory of, an officer of the Mirror Lancers. As are all officers in the Mirror Lancers, you are required to accomplish your duties to the fullest of your abilities. Rationales and

excuses may serve for merchanters and outlanders, but the duty of a Mirror Lancer in the service of the Emperor and of chaos is to comply, and the accomplishment of the unbelievable and the impossible must be the commonplace for us. To allow a single creature to escape from the order-death realms of the Accursed Forest is not acceptable, not when the lives and livelihoods of the people are at stake. . . .

Lorn sets down the scroll and looks out the window once more at the steaming mist rising from the courtyard.

What can he do? Does he have any choice? If he does not bring greater use of his personal control of chaos to the fore, he will end up discredited. If he does, he may end up dead. After a time of blankly staring at the window, he bends and reclaims the scroll, then seats himself at the desk and begins to write his reply—his short reply.

I have received your scroll reminding me most persuasively of the responsibilities and the glories of serving as an officer of the Mirror Lancers. You have made most clear what is required of me, and I hear and obey.

He lets the ink dry before he seals the scroll and summons his senior squad leader. "Olisenn?"

The heavy-set lancer opens the door and steps into the inner study. "Yes, ser?"

Lorn gestures to the scroll on the desk he is sure that Olisenn has already read. "Majer Maran has more clearly outlined our responsibilities, and I have acceded fully to the scope of duties required of us. If you would make sure this reply is sent with the next Engineer firewagon . . . ?" Lorn extends the sealed scroll.

"Yes, ser." The senior squad leader nods.

"And Olisenn?"

"Yes, ser?" The oily politeness of the squad leader covers a deeper contempt.

Lorn continues to smile, almost blandly, waiting several moments before he speaks. "If I recall, is not the Accursed Forest the largest concentration of order and death in all of Cyador?"

"As you say, Captain, that it is."

"And does order not have the property of converting the power of chaos into sterile death if chaos is not used in perfection?"

"That be what the Magi'i say. Me, being but a simple lancer, I'd not be knowing."

Lorn nods. "Majer Maran has suggested that we must make greater efforts to keep the Forest creatures from reaching the holders and their herds and flocks." He frowns. "We may have to make some changes to ensure that forms of sterile death are restricted to the Forest, and that, somehow, we can do such without casualties. It will be a challenge, but, as Majer Maran has pointed out, that is indeed our duty."

"We've not been losing many lancers, ser. That is, not so many recently."

"True . . . but we'll have to stop more of the creatures."

"Order it as you see fit, ser, and we'll carry it out."

"I'm sure you will. Still . . . one never knows when matters change, and I wanted you to know that we have been ordered to make changes." The captain nods politely, waiting before adding. "It's been said that in the past, some senior squad leaders developed their own communications with the command in Geliendra. You wouldn't know of that, would you?"

"Me, ser? That would be against the line of command, ser."

"So you never thought of anything like that?"

"Me, ser? No, ser."

"I'm glad to hear you say that, Olisenn." Lorn smiles. "That's all for now, and please make sure that scroll gets to Majer Maran."

"That I will, ser."

Olisenn is lying about communicating with Geliendra, not

that Lorn has expected otherwise, but now it is clear that matters will change . . . must change.

After checking the Patrol reports he has written once more, Lorn puts them in the foot chest and locks it, useless as that clearly is against Olisenn's surveillance, but somewhat effective, he hopes, against Olisenn's understanding of what Lorn knows.

Then he steps into the outer office, but Olisenn has already departed.

Lorn ponders his next steps as he walks slowly toward his personal quarters. Maran's scroll is clearly an attempt to put Lorn in an impossible situation. Use of chaos by lancers is effectively forbidden, and now Maran has insisted that Lorn not let a single Forest creature escape. Under the current circumstances, that will run lancers and mounts into the ground, and increase casualties. Increased casualties mean fewer lancers and more likely more animals escaping.

He takes a deep breath as he enters his deep quarters. He paces in a narrow circle for a time, then takes the silver volume from its concealed resting place and begins to page through it, half-wondering if the ancient Firstborn who had written the lines contained in the imperishable pages had ever faced a Majer Maran. What sort of steps would he—or she— have taken. What provisions made?

He continues to page through the volume. Suddenly, he stops, and reads.

> I have no soul,
> but a nibbled kernel . . .
> feelings dried and stored
> on the shelves of self
> in the deep cellar where
> provisions must be made
>
> Provisions must be made.
> I made them
> gleaning
> those wild leftovers of

        unharvest days,
        hoarding hard-to-come-bys
        of cold reason
        against colder seasons.

        Provisions must be made,
        and I have made them.

Slowly, he nods. While not exactly analogous, the basic truth is there. Provisions must be made, provisions of cold reason against colder seasons. Perhaps . . . just perhaps . . . the Firstborn were not all that different, after all.

That does not comfort him, and he shivers ever so slightly as he closes the volume.

LXXXVI

PROVISIONS MUST BE made . . ." The antiquated words run through Lorn's thoughts as he rides the white gelding slowly to the southeast, this time patrolling the perimeter road with Kusyl and the second squad. He feels as though his neck and back get twice as stiff when he rides with the first squad, and it is a tremendous effort not to watch Olisenn all the time.

Yet he has nothing that he would actually call proof against the heavy-set squad leader, only the knowledge that the man is communicating with Majer Maran and lying about it, only the growing contempt the senior squad leader has for Lorn. And Olisenn's contempt does not seem based in fact, for all the other officers, and even Kusyl, have acknowledged in some fashion that Second Company has handled far more ward-wall breaches than has been common, and with far fewer casualties for all the dangers involved.

No . . . Lorn had not done as well as he should have at the beginning. This he acknowledges, at least to himself, but no one offered assistance, and he had had to learn on his own.

He also had to learn, that, as part of its efforts to strike against Cyador, the Accursed Forest always seemed to have its wild creatures attack the lancers before making their escapes. Or was that because they do not attack until they somehow *know* the Lancers and the Engineers are going to destroy each particular fallen tree? Which of those may be true, Lorn still does not know, only that the pattern has held for the time he has directed Second Company.

He puts his weight on the stirrups for a moment, lifting himself off the saddle, then looks to his right at the too-spread, line-abreast formation. Are he and the lancers being asked to hold back the Accursed Forest with no real hope of success in the years ahead? Just to purchase years or seasons for Cyador?

He laughs to himself. Nothing lasts forever. That he already knows. Some time, the ward-wall will fail. Even if the project Ciesrt had mentioned works and another way—whatever it may be—is found to restrain the Accursed Forest from reclaiming all of eastern Cyador, in time that, too, will fail. Is that why duty becomes important?

With a headshake, he smiles. Some men seek power, like Maran, because life ends. Others, like his father and Myryan, seek meaning. But the world is the same for both, and makes no effort to accommodate either.

His eyes survey the whitened granite of the ward-wall—stretching endlessly to the horizon, or so it seems, without a break, without a stream, without a river. Lorn straightens. He wants to shake himself—not that the observation would change anything—but he should have noticed. In all of Cyador, even in the Grass Hills, is there a diamond-shaped area ninety-nine kays on a side without a watercourse leaving or entering it? One with trees and high vegetation? One with flat lands immediately around it, which turn into rolling hills and plains within two kays?

Because the Accursed Forest *is,* he and everyone else have just accepted it. But what sort of power had it taken for the Firstborn to create such a containment—one that moved rivers and watercourses? And what sort of power did the forest possess to survive without such watercourses? Can it reach upward and tap the clouds? Is that why there is always more rain around it?

"Ser!"

Lost in his thoughts, for once Lorn is not the first one to spot the fallen tree—another of the mid-sized forest monarchs.

His eyes confirm the alert, and he turns his head toward Kusyl. "Form up five abreast here on the perimeter road. Send a messenger to Olisenn. Have him join us a kay this side of the crown."

"Yes, ser."

To the south, over the Forest, clouds are forming, and darkening. Lorn wonders if the rain will reach the deadland where they ride and if they will have to wait through a storm for the Engineers and then ride through mud to reach Eastend. With all that seems to be happening, he will not be surprised if Second Company will face rain and mud.

The second squad gathers itself back into a loose formation on the road, and Lorn and Kusyl ride just ahead of the first rank of the five lancers abreast, and on the inward side of the perimeter road.

"Still say more trees fall on the northeast side. Reyt—he's an engineer lancer—he says it's 'cause the winds come out of the northeast." Kusyl snorts. "So why do the trees fall *into* the wind?"

Lorn laughs softly. "Engineers have to explain, whether they can or not."

"Like we got to fight, whether we like it or not?"

"Something like that."

The two lapse into silence as they near the point on the perimeter road closest to the fallen tree.

"Squad halt!" Kusyl orders. "Easy in the saddle."

He and Lorn turn to watch the approach of the other squad.

"Ser." Olisenn nods as the first squad draws up parallel to the second.

"Staggered lines! We'll advance now," Lorn calls out. "Lances at the ready."

"Staggered lines. Lances ready. Stand by to discharge."

With a hundred fifty cubits between the two wide-spaced, five-abreast formations, the two squads move southward, each almost flanking a side of the tree's crown. The staggered lines allow the second line to fire past the first, as necessary, or to move forward when a lancer ahead exhausts his firelance.

The squads are still two hundred cubits from the crown when a pair of giant cats, their shimmering gray coats almost the color of the clouds gathering over the Accursed Forest, bound toward the lancers—toward the second squad, seemingly almost directly at Lorn himself.

"Discharge at will! Short bursts!"

Hssst! Hhhssssssst!

"Short bursts! Angel-fire! Short bursts!" Kusyl bellows.

Hsst! Hsst!

Five beams crisscross and find the leading giant cat, and it stumbles and rolls forward in a heap, dust rising around its body. The second creature sprints to the left side of the second squad. Lorn can see that, unless he does something, it will escape. He lifts his own firelance, and sights, boosting the chaos with what he has learned and practiced both in the Grass Hills and in secret—and confining it with the order binding he has seen from the Accursed Forest.

Hssst!

The narrow beam curves and burns through the huge cat's skull, and it skids along the powdering soil of the deadland.

". . . see *that!* . . . captain's getting good with that lance. . . ."

". . . always been good . . ."

Lorn's eyes do not remain on the fallen creature, but fix on Olisenn, and the self-satisfied and sardonic smile that fades as the senior squad leader glances up to meet Lorn's eyes. Lorn returns Olisenn's expressionless scrutiny with an insouciant smile that he maintains almost as an insult.

Olisenn cannot conceal a frown.

Lorn wipes the smile from his face. He should not have given any warnings to the contemptuous senior squad leader, but he has had to pretend and ignore so much from the man that it is difficult to remain impassive all the time.

He hears a rustle in the branches, and his eyes and senses refocus on the greenery that appears dull in the afternoon sun that is dimmed by the high thin clouds to the west. He can almost sense the night leopards gathering.

"There's something coming from the crown. Leopards, I'd guess." Lorn raises his voice and gestures toward the vegetation. "Olisenn, move your line in closer! We don't want any to escape between us. Not after Majer Maran's last orders."

"To the right!" Olisenn repeats, frowning.

"Move it up. Lances ready!" Lorn orders the first squad, urging his own mount to the left so that he is almost beside Kusyl. "Second squad, lances ready. Prepare to discharge!"

The leaves twitch and rustle one more time, and then the leopards burst forth, not toward first squad, but toward the second squad.

Absently, Lorn wonders if that is because he bears some concentrated chaos, even as he orders, "Second squad. Discharge at will. First squad! Hold your lances!"

The leopards almost reach second squad before firebursts stud the air.

Hsst! Hsssttt!

"Short bursts!" Kusyl insists.

Hssst! Hssst! Hssst!

The short bursts that Kusyl has demanded rain across the fifteen or so night leopards that are almost among the lancers.

Lorn lifts his own lance as if toward the leopards, raising it slightly and turning it just beyond the leopards.

Two leopards scream . . . and one claws at a lancer's mount to Lorn's left before it falls.

Hssst! Hssst!

Lorn's eyes cross Olisenn's, and the senior squad leader's mouth opens, as if to protest, before the single chaos bolt blasts through his throat.

Seemingly without looking near Olisenn, Lorn sweeps his lance across two other leopards, letting his own chaos senses bend the flame to take them down. Other dark cat figures, some charred, some with but small-looking wounds, lie across the salt-streaked and powdery deadland soil.

"Close, ser!" Kusyl says, glancing around nervously. "Too close."

Lorn scans the area, but surprisingly, not a single leopard has escaped. This time. Nor are there movements or any rustling from the snapped and twisted limbs and crushed leaves of the tree's crown.

"Ser! Ser!"

Lorn looks up, surprised.

"It's Olisenn, ser!"

Lorn urges the gelding the seventy cubits or so toward the first squad.

When he reins up, two lancers, white-faced, are on the ground with the prone figure of the senior squad leader.

"What happened?" Lorn asks.

"Don't know, scr. When the leopards attacked you and second squad, ser . . . maybe a firelance . . . See . . . he's burned."

Lorn swallows hard. That he can do. "It could have been anyone's. It could have been mine. They were closer than I thought. It was probably my fault." He shakes his head. "I didn't act quickly enough." And that is certainly true, Lorn knows.

After a moment of silence, he adds. "He was a good squad leader. We'll miss him." He looks down. "If you . . . Frygel . . . would . . ."

"Yes, ser."

"And Askad, too."

"Yes, ser."

Lorn glances at the tree crown, as if to check to see that nothing else lurks there, then back at the two lancers. "I'll be acting as squad leader . . . for the rest of the patrol. . . ." He lets his words trail off, before straightening in the saddle. ". . . wish . . . otherwise." He closes his mouth and slowly turns the gelding.

"Captain's upset. . . ."

". . . wouldn't you be. . . ."

". . . he charged that lizard . . . saved three-four last spring . . . and those cats . . . doesn't get upset . . . just killed three . . . right here. . . ."

". . . doesn't like to lose lancers . . ."

Lorn rides slowly back to Kusyl, shaking his head. "It shouldn't have happened this way."

"That sort of thing happens, Captain," Kusyl replies with a long face. "Happened before, try to avoid it, but you spread out too much, and they get away. Won't be the last time 'less we get more lancers."

"We won't get enough." Lorn laughs, a harsh bark. "We're not getting any until winter turn." He takes a deep breath. "If you'd set up the sentries, Kusyl. I need a moment. Then . . . then we'll have to send another messenger to the Engineers."

"Yes, ser."

Lorn needs more than a moment, but a moment is all he will get, since he will have to take over the first squad, and watch them as well.

The slow roll of thunder from the south, from over the Accursed Forest, passes across the Second Company, and the south wind rises, with the hint of dampness that foretells the rain and the mud Lorn is expecting.

Then too, before long, he expects Majer Maran will be arriving. Of that, Lorn has no doubts.

LXXXVII

Lorn glances out the inner study window into the courtyard, where the early fall sunshine bathes the white granite in a clear light. Then his eyes drop to the stacks of papers on his table desk.

In the outer study, a dazed-looking Kusyl is reading through all the personnel files in the foot chest. Lorn worries about Kusyl's administrative abilities, but Kusyl can read and write, if slightly laboriously, since lancers are not promoted to squad leaders, even junior ones, unless they can. More important to Lorn is that Kusyl, rough-edged as he is, is loyal to Lorn and to the Mirror Lancers, not to blind ambition.

Should Lorn have acted against Olisenn? How could he not? Maran would not have transferred the man, and even a request for transfer would have created the incentive for Olisenn, or Maran, to act against Lorn, and Lorn does not wish to have to deal with both Olisenn and Maran at once. Lorn has no doubts, even if he has no proof, that Olisenn was an accomplice in the removal of Captain Dymytri. And Lorn has seldom regretted acting; he has regretted more the times when he has not acted, as in the case of Myryan's consorting, which he fears will harm her more than he knows. Still . . . that he has been forced so to act troubles him.

He glances over the scrolls.

Although he has finished the patrol report summary to Majer Maran and the request for a replacement squad leader and the authority to promote Kusyl permanently to senior squad leader, Lorn has more than a few tasks of his own remaining.

One of them is to request, again, replacement lancers for his understrength company. Another is to write to his family, carefully, since Maran will certainly intercept such a scroll and read it. He must also consider how to change the tactics of approach to the fallen trees, in such a way that seems, if not natural, at least understandable to his men.

Lorn picks up the pen. A scroll to Commander Meylyd for more lancers will be the easiest. He does not expect much, but knows that if he does not request such, he will be considered lacking in concern for accomplishing his duties and protecting both the people of Cyad and his lancers.

After he completes it, his eyes scan the page.

> . . . the first squad of the Second Company stands at twelve lancers, with no squad leader, only an acting leader from those twelve. The second squad consists of thirteen lancers and the new senior squad leader. Second Company is less than two thirds its normal complement . . . but has been

tasked with handling double the number of ward-wall breaches seen in past three-season periods running from winter through summer. Therefore ... requesting replacement lancers to bring the Company to full complement, and your action, insofar as dispatching or promoting a permanent junior squad leader. . . .

Lorn sets aside the scroll to dry and starts on the second one, the one to his family that will doubtless be read by Maran or Meylyd.

... the past seasons have exacted a toll on my company, for the Accursed Forest has continued to press against the ward-walls with continued presence. More than that, it would not be proper to say, save that we have persevered against all manner of obstacles foreseen and unforeseen ... most difficult charge is to ensure that the wild creatures do not escape to plague the people of Cyad and yet not to expose the lancers to untoward harm or attack from such creatures ... few understand the true need for the tasks which I now undertake, nor would I before I had come to Jakaafra. . . .

... trust that all is well with you in Cyad, and that Myryan's gardens have indeed borne the fruits she has hoped for and that Jerial continues to find satisfaction in her duties as healer. . . .

Lorn smiles as he adds the next line.

... I have not had the time to discover new vintages here in Jakaafra, and so doubtless will return to Cyad in years to come with my palate at a great disadvantage. . . .

A few more lines about the apples in Jakaafra, and the joy of cooler weather, and he signs it and sets it aside to dry.

Then he leans back, thinking about tactics. Exactly how can he change formations and approaches to let him use chaos more freely without close scrutiny—and make such a change seem acceptable to the lancers, without their noticing what he must do?

He closes his eyes, mentally trying to visualize what Second Company has done so often, and dares do no longer.

The scroll to Ryalth will wait until he is in his own quarters and probably until evening.

LXXXVIII

OUTSIDE LORN'S INNER study, the first cold rain of fall splats on the ancient blued-glass panes, and chill radiates from the glass far, far older than Lorn—or than Majer Maran, who lounges in the single chair across the table desk from Lorn.

"You have had some time to consider the message in which I conveyed the sentiments of Commander Meylyd." Maran's blue eyes express concern. "Those are also the sentiments of the Majer-Commander in Cyad."

Despite the headache engendered by the storm outside, Lorn returns the smile with one equally warm. "I appreciated that you made the effort to make matters clear. When one is spending most of his days patrolling the ward-wall and attempting to contain the Accursed Forest's creatures and efforts with far too few lancers, one has a tendency to forget that there are other concerns."

"You have indeed grasped the difficulties facing the Mirror Lancers and Commander Meylyd," Maran says warmly. "He and the Majer-Commander must ensure that all lancer officers, especially captains who command patrol companies, carry out their duties in a way that is harmonious with the distinguished reputation of the Mirror Lancers, and that their enthusiasm for the accomplishment of their individual duties and the well-being of their lancers does not create a situation at variance with the higher goals of the Mirror Lancers. You understand that, and it is indeed rewarding to work with such a perceptive officer."

"I doubt that I am that perceptive," Lorn demurs, "and for that I have welcomed your instructions and advice."

"You have obviously considered in great depth my earlier suggestions, Captain," Maran observes, "and I look forward to telling Commander Meylyd that there will be no more reports of creatures that have escaped from the Accursed Forest to plague and disturb the people of Cyad. In fact, I will be assuring him that you have gone to great lengths in using the traditional methods of patrolling to make sure of such."

"Second Company will be employing all the truly traditional means at its disposal to carry out the instructions you have conveyed," Lorn replies.

"The Commander will be most pleased." Maran's seemingly endless smile is replaced with an expression of mild concern. "There is one other matter."

"Yes, ser?" Lorn responds in a tone of respect.

"We were all so disturbed to hear of the death of senior squad leader Olisenn. He was experienced and well-respected." Maran touches the end of his short and trim mustache. "I suppose that an accidental death from a misaimed firelance was one of the few ways such an experienced lancer could have died."

Lorn nods. "It's always the things you don't prepare for, I've discovered, Majer, that are the ones that are the most dangerous. That accident was something that none of us anticipated, and that could not have been foreseen. I have been reviewing approach plans to ensure that nothing of that sort will occur again in Second Company."

"You make it sound as though one must be prepared for everything." Maran laughs warmly and gently. "No lancer officer can prepare for everything. No matter how hard he works, there will always be surprises. That's what makes life interesting." The laugh is followed by the warm smile that Maran always bears. "Still, your efforts under slightly strenuous circumstances have revealed that your emphasis on preparedness may indeed bear welcome fruit, and we look forward to your future reports."

"Have you and Commander Meylyd had a chance to consider the replacement lancer request which accompanied my last reports?" Lorn smiles off-handedly. "I understand that you and the Commander have much to consider, but since you are here in Jakaafra . . ."

"Ah . . . yes." Maran nods knowingly. "You will receive replacements at the turn of season, some three eightdays from now, as will all the ward-wall patrol companies. The Commander would wish that we could have fully reinforced Second Company, rather than only return you to three-quarter strength, but trained lancers are becoming more scarce. And you have been dealing with the Forest without . . . permanent . . . casualties for the last half season, excepting the unfortunate accident with senior squad leader Olisenn. But that was not a result of the actions of the Forest creatures."

"We have been fortunate," Lorn admits. "It would be best to be at full strength, but we understand all the many requirements that the Mirror Lancers and Commander Meylyd and you must address." He raises his eyebrows. "The barbarians? Are their depredations . . . ?"

"We are not informed of such, but I would surmise so." Maran's smile widens, and he stands. "I fear I have little else to add."

"You have been most kind and helpful," Lorn responds as he also stands.

"Oh . . . and Captain Lorn, I must tell you again that Commander Meylyd will be most pleased to learn of your success in containing the Accursed Forest with the traditional methods. He looks forward to your continuing success with such." Maran's smile and blue eyes remain warm.

"As do we," Lorn replies, adding after a slight pause, "Will you be staying at Jakaafra tonight?"

"Alas, those higher duties call, and I will be returning to Westend with the Engineers' firewagon, so that I may attend Commander Meylyd tomorrow." Maran offers a last smile. "I do appreciate your concern for my comfort and welfare, and I would that you know I feel the same for yours."

Lorn bows. "A fruitful journey, Majer."

"It has been, Captain Lorn, most fruitful." The majer returns the bow before he departs.

LXXXIX

SER?"

Lorn glances up from the papers on his table desk, papers covered with lines and angles and distances—and the rough-scrawled shape of a fallen tree . . . and a set of double lines that represent the northeast ward-wall.

"Yes, Kusyl?"

"The replacement lancers just rode in, ser. There's someone to see you, ser."

"Have him come in."

"Yes, ser."

The tall and broad-shouldered lancer with the single stripe of a junior squad leader on his sleeve steps into the inner study. "Squad Leader Shynt, ser. Reporting, ser, as junior squad leader to the Second Company." The swarthy and black-haired Shynt utters the words as though they were a sentence to death or exile, his baritone voice bleak and without emotion.

"Close the door and sit down, Shynt." Lorn gestures to the chair across from him and carefully stacks the papers, then replaces the pen in its holder.

"Yes, ser."

Shynt sits lance-straight on the edge of the armless chair across from Lorn.

"Black angels only know what you've been told about Second Company, Shynt." Lorn's voice is conversational. "Would you care to share any of that, or would you prefer I guess?"

"Ser . . . I've been told nothing." Shynt's voice remains bleak.

Lorn ignores the lie, then tilts his head to the side slightly. "You are a very good squad leader, and you also dislike incompetent captains. You aren't good at concealing that fact, and as soon as the opening for a squad leader here appeared, you were selected."

"Ser?" For the first time, Shynt's voice loses its almost brittle edge.

"You were doubtless allowed to learn—and someone will ensure you hear it if you haven't already—that I'd managed to lose the most experienced squad leader in all of the Forest patrol companies through a totally avoidable mistake. Then, I'm sure through overhearing and 'accident,' you were allowed to discover that more Forest outbreaks occur along the northeast wall than along any ward-wall, and that Commander Meylyd and others are most concerned about that and about Second Company. Finally, someone suggested, most indirectly, that only you could put it right, leaving matters to your own initiative."

Shynt remains rigid in the chair, as if he dares not speak.

"You also probably escorted the most inept group of replacement lancers you have ever seen, and have just discovered that they won't bring either squad up to more than three-quarter strength."

When Lorn stops talking, silence is the only response.

"And now you don't know what to say," Lorn laughs softly, ironically, but Shynt remains immobile. "That's because most or all of what I've said appears true to you, and because you know you can't lie convincingly, which is why you were picked for this impossible duty assignment." He pauses. "Except it's not impossible. Only Majer Maran believes it's impossible, because he believes concealment and evasion are stronger than truth." Lorn's amber eyes lock on Shynt's black ones. "Tell me, squad leader Shynt, are you strong enough to deal with truth?"

"Yes, ser." Shynt's tone is close to defiant.

"Good. Before you leave the outer office, before you do anything, you will read all the patrol reports for the last five years, and you will tally up all the fallen tree trunks encountered by Second Company under each of its captains. You will also tally the casualties by year under each captain. You may ask senior squad leader Kusyl any questions you wish, and I suggest you do. Then, you will come back into my office and report what you have discovered. Is that clear?"

"Yes, ser." An edge of bewilderment colors the squad leader's voice.

"Good." Lorn stands. "I will be here as long as it takes you. But, since we'd both like to eat, I suggest you set to it." He bends and lifts the unlocked foot chest, setting it on the side of the table desk. "You may read anything else in here as well, if you think it will help your understanding."

"Yes, ser."

Shynt takes the chest carefully, and Lorn opens the door to the outer study for him, then closes it and returns to the diagrams and calculations on the papers that he unstacks and spreads once more before him.

It is late afternoon before there is a *thrap* on the door, although at times Lorn has heard voices, often intense, if whispered, as though Lorn might have been listening.

"Come in," Lorn says, restacking the tactics sheets, with which he *thinks* he has reached a solution.

"Ser?" Shynt stands in the doorway with the foot chest in his arms. "Might I return this?"

"Come on in and close the door. Set it on the floor against the wall there."

Shynt deposits the foot chest carefully, then straightens. "Ser . . . I apologize."

"Accepted, without reservation. Now . . . sit down and tell me what you discovered." Lorn gestures to the armless chair.

"Ser . . ." After he seats himself, Shynt raises a single sheet of paper. "I could tell you the numbers, but you know them. Else you would not have asked. You had a few more casualties in your first season than the other captains. Your— Second Company had close to four-fold the number of fallen trunks. You have continued to encounter more fallen trunks, but your casualties for the past two seasons are less than any other captain's in a season."

Lorn nods. "Do you see why I wanted you to read those reports?"

"Yes, ser."

"Did you talk to Kusyl?"

"Yes, ser."

Lorn nods.

Shynt looks down, then the black eyes meet Lorn's. "Ser . . . it be not my province to ask. . . ."

"But you'd feel more comfortable knowing what you stepped into and how it happened?"

"Yes, ser."

"That's understandable." Lorn fingers his chin, leaning back slightly in his chair. "I am not certain that there is a simple answer. I'll try. When the large trees fall, they create a breach in the ward-wall. With each breach, Accursed Forest creatures wait for lancers to arrive. We don't know why this is so, and it is not written down anywhere, but it happens. The more trees that fall, the more attacks on lancers, and if the lancers are not very careful and very good, the more creatures that escape to attack the people and herds and flocks beyond the deadland." Lorn smiles. "There is nothing new about that. But . . . you know there are only so many chaos towers that charge our firelances and that not every person makes a good lancer?"

"Yes, ser."

"And you have heard that the barbarians to the north are mounting more attacks every year."

Shynt nods.

"If the Mirror Lancers do not provide more lancers in the north, then the Emperor will not be able to protect his people from the barbarians. If there are more lancers in the north, but not that many more lancers in all the Mirror Lancers . . ." Lorn waits.

"There must be fewer lancers here."

"And you have seen that this is true," Lorn concludes. "But if we have fewer lancers, and more trees falling, what will happen here in Jakaafra?"

"Second Company must face more wild creatures with

fewer lancers . . . and there is the possibility that more will escape?"

Lorn nods. "Let us say that one giant cat escapes—just one—for every tenth tree-fall. If three tree-falls occur in a season, how many cats will escape over the year?"

"One . . . three over two years."

"Now . . . what happens when a company faces twenty-four tree falls in not quite three seasons?" Lorn answers the question before Shynt can. "You would have six giant cats loose." He smiles crookedly. "I suggested such to Commander Meylyd in requesting a full replacement complement. It was not well-received." Lorn shrugs. "We have done better than that—with only three giant cats loose, as I recall, but there have also been more than a few night leopards that escaped.

"I have changed the Patrol procedures slightly. We do not send a messenger for the Mirror Engineers until *after* we have been attacked by Forest creatures. We move toward the crown of the tree from the perimeter road, with two squads flanking it at a half-square angle, and we use but short bursts on the firelances."

"Such procedures have worked. Your casualties have been reduced."

Lorn nods. "I have been strongly requested to return to 'traditional' lancer patrol techniques, but I have been also ordered not to allow any wild creatures to escape." A crooked smile follows. "Squad leader Olisenn was most committed to traditional procedures, and I fear that his inability to adapt to the new procedures may have contributed to his ending up in the line of a firelance. I do not know that, but that is all I can surmise."

Shynt nods slowly. "If I might ask, ser . . . what patrol tactics will you adopt?"

Lorn grins. "I am informing Majer Maran that I am abandoning those procedures about which he and Commander Meylyd had expressed concern and that Second Company intends to do its utmost to stop any wild creatures from escaping the deadland."

Shynt almost smiles. "Ah . . . I see."

"Then we will see." Lorn looks at the black-eyed squad leader. "So long as no creatures escape and I do not disobey any direct orders, we will doubtless hear little."

Shynt nods. "Thank you, ser."

Lorn stands. "I'm glad you're here. Kusyl will introduce you to First Squad, and I'll ride mostly with you on patrols to begin with, until we're comfortable."

As Kusyl leaves with the junior squad leader, Lorn closes the door, then turns. He looks out the study window at the gray clouds that will become more prevalent as winter nears, recalling the lines from the poem in the silver-covered book.

Provisions must be made.

Lorn has made them.

XC

THE EVENING IS cold and overcast as Lorn walks across the damp stones of the courtyard to the stable, and the mist rising from the stones swallows much of the light from the lamps set in their bronze brackets along the walls. The captain wears two sabres—a lancer officer's sabre on his right and the Brystan sabre on his left. He also carries a firelance. His steps are sure, silent, as he slips into the warmth of the stable and the welcoming scent of dry straw.

"Suforis?"

"Coming, ser." Suforis scurries out from the tack room. "You going out tonight, ser?" asks the blond ostler. "It be mighty chill and damp, and with you starting out on another patrol tomorrow. . . ."

"I know. I won't be riding far or hard, and I won't over-heat him." Lorn smiles. "I promise. It's just a short ride."

"Be but a moment, ser." The young ostler hurries off.

Lorn glances around the stable as Suforis saddles the geld-ing. As always, the structure is swept and clean, without a trace of cobwebs or dust, and the wood of the stall boxes gleams in the dim lamplight.

Suforis returns, leading the gelding and looking anxiously at the lancer captain as he hands over the mount's reins. "I'd be going, ser, but if you'd not be long . . ."

"You like being consorted?"

Suforis flushes. "Ah . . . yes, ser. Much, ser."

"Good for you." Lorn's laugh is warm and friendly. "I will not be long, but I can groom and stall him, and I would not wish that you keep your consort waiting." Lorn slips the single firelance into its holder.

"I could wait, ser."

"Go." Lorn smiles before leading the gelding out through the stable doors and into the mist of the courtyard. "You've been here late enough."

Outside, in the thickening mist, Lorn mounts and rides slowly to the open gates. The clicking of the gelding's hoofs is preternaturally loud, amplified by the mist and dampness.

"Ser?" asks the gate guard on the right as Lorn reins up in the light of the lamp. "You going out?"

"I won't be too long. I just need a quiet ride to think."

"Ah . . . yes, ser."

Lorn nods and guides the gelding out into the misty darkness beyond the walls. He hopes that the combination of the mist, the darkness, and the closeness to the ward-wall will preclude anyone using a chaos glass to determine exactly what he does. The sentries' low voices are carried through the dampness to Lorn as he guides the gelding toward the ward-wall.

". . . got much to think of . . ."

". . . all do . . . not be an officer for a guarantee to the Steps of Paradise. . . ."

". . . not like as we'd be getting either such, Myttr . . ."

". . . none of them, neither . . ."

A faint smile appears and disappears, unseen, as Lorn continues to ride along the cross-road that leads to the ward-wall. To his left, he is aware of, but cannot see, the granite structure holding the northpoint chaos towers. Once he reaches the ward-wall, he rides to the southwest for perhaps another kay before he turns the gelding to face the ward-wall and then reins up, roughly midway between two of the wall-ward crystals.

For several long moments, he studies the whiteness of the granite wall and the darkness that looms behind the wall and the chaos-net broadcast by the crystal wards. Among the scents that drift out of the darkness is that of erhenflower. Did it originally come from the Accursed Forest?

Lorn draws the Brystan sabre, then concentrates on the flickering chaos-net, grasping that flow with his chaos senses and turning it aside, to open once more that narrow window or door to the massive intertwining of order and chaos beyond the white granite of the ward-wall.

This time . . . although a narrow aperture is open—there is no immediate thrust of power toward the lancer captain, not of chaos or of black order.

Lorn waits, the black-iron-cored Brystan sabre in his right hand, his eyes and senses on the Accursed Forest.

As he waits, an image builds, one of bubbling red-white fountains of chaos, of dark pillars of order, and deep ponds of a different kind—or color—of order, more shaded in deep gray, and then vines of golden-white chaos twining around the dark order pillars. That mental image vanishes and is followed by a second image—one of which he has dreamed more than once.

Knives of white fire gouge the very earth, laying down deep trenches that stretch across the land, and from those trenches rise white walls, walls that burn into Lorn's flesh if he is to so much as move toward them. Beyond the trenches is fire, an endless fire that turns the very land and trees into ashes. Rivers are wrenched from their courses, and hills are flattened by other knives of focused chaos.

Lorn finds he is sweating profusely as the images break off, despite the misty chill.

A single beam of chaos-order lances through the aperture that he has created. The sabre flashes up, almost without Lorn's volition, and catches that narrow line of power.

Lorn struggles, both instantly and endlessly, it seems, to re-cast the fire back at the base of the ward-wall where it splays across the granite and fountains upward in a flare of light. Even as he directs that energy, so much vaster than any mage firebolt he has seen, even as he lets the chaos-net flow back into place, cutting off the flow of linked order and chaos, Lorn understands that what the Accursed Forest has cast out is but a fraction of the power it possesses.

Lorn also understands not just within his thoughts, but with every sense and feeling he has, that the Forest's power lies in the melding of all that is within the Forest—and that Cyador and the Forest cannot occupy the same lands. With that feeling comes a sadness, a melancholy, as if it should not be so, and yet cannot be otherwise.

After sheathing the sabre, he turns the gelding, without looking back at the ward-wall or the Forest beyond, wondering, not for the first time, why the Forest has not tried in greater fashion to overwhelm him. Because it cannot, or because it understands that his death would avail it little? He laughs softly. The latter is true enough, for if he died, the chaos net would flow back in place. But does a forest, however filled with order and chaos, have that kind of understanding? Or does it just play the very patterns of order and chaos, without understanding, in the way that a river must follow the lines of the land?

It comes to him, as he nears the gate to the compound, that he will never know that answer, and that, too, casts another kind of melancholy over him.

"Ser?"

"It's me. Captain Lorn."

"Getting worried about you, ser."

Lorn avoids looking surprised. Has he been gone that long? "I appreciate your concern."

"Saw some torches out there. . . ."

"I was trying something with a firelance," Lorn explains. "It must have taken longer than I realized."

"That be no problem, ser."

"Good night." Lorn offers a smile and guides the white

gelding through the gate. He can tell now that he has not been gone that long, but he wonders how bright his manipulation of order and chaos was to have been seen through nearly two kays of the misting rain.

Suforis has indeed gone, but left a single lamp lighted, and the stable door slightly ajar.

Opening the door, Lorn smiles and leads the gelding back to the stall to unsaddle and groom him.

When he finally returns to his quarters, the first thing he does is set the unused firelance in the corner. Then he goes to the wardrobe and studies his face in the mirror on its door. His skin is flushed, red, as if sunburned, as it has been when he has manipulated the ward-wall chaos-net before.

He shakes his head, then removes his belt and sabres, followed by the damp tunic that he hangs on one of the wall pegs. His sits on the chair and pulls off both boots before he returns to the second drawer on the side of the wardrobe. From there he removes the chaos glass and carries it to the narrow desk.

With a half-cynical smile, Lorn looks at the glass, then concentrates on Maran.

The silver swirls part slowly, and the image of the dark-haired and mustached Majer Maran appears in the center of those swirls. Maran sits before his own desk, pausing as if thinking, with a scroll below, and a half-empty goblet of an amber wine to his left. The majer's face stiffens, as if he too can sense a chaos glass scrutinizing him.

Lorn smiles coldly and releases the image, quickly replacing the chaos glass between the smallclothes in the wardrobe.

He has barely found Ryalth's volume of ancient poems and stretched out in his trousers and undertunic on his bed, looking at the silver-covered book, before he can feel the chill of someone using a chaos glass to see him. He smiles faintly, but does not reveal that he senses the screeing. Nor does he nod, but merely continues to study the shimmering cover of the volume of poems, knowing that Maran will puzzle over that cover.

As the mental coldness created by the distant user of the glass lifts, Lorn finally opens the book, selecting a page he has read before, the one Ryalth selected for him so many years before, yet one whose feelings seem familiar despite the antique slanting characters and the references and the style used by the ancient writer.

SHOULD I RECALL THE RATIONAL STARS?

There I had a tower for the skies,
where the rooms were clear . . .

Should I recall the Rational Stars?
Or hold my ruin on this hill
where new-raised walls are still,
Perfect granite set jagged on the dawn,
with striped awnings spread across the lawn . . .

Lorn thinks about the concluding words, then reads them softly, aloud, in the stillness of his chamber.

Oh . . . take these new lake isles and green green seas;
take these sylvan ponds and soaring trees;
take these desert dunes and sunswept sands,
and pour them through your empty hands.

Almost . . . almost . . . those words bring up feelings like those evoked by the Accursed Forest with its images. Or were the images his—created within his mind by something different from the Forest?

Lorn closes the silver cover of the thin volume, shaking his head slowly. Then he stands and replaces the volume in his wardrobe and begins to complete his disrobing. The words of the ancient writer and the melancholy they hold flows over and through him.

Should I recall the Rational Stars . . . ?

XCI

ALTHOUGH LORN HAS expected more treefalls as a reaction to his "practice" sessions along the ward-wall, there have been none for two full round-trip patrols to Eastend and back since Shynt's arrival. The only remnant of Lorn's efforts in the nights along the ward-wall is the occasional sense of melancholy he feels when he looks beyond the white granite of the ward-wall at the towering trunks and high canopied greenery of the Accursed Forest. He has also had one more dream about walls that burn and rivers being wrenched from their beds.

The lancer captain pushes that thought away as he rides with junior squad leader Shynt on the wall road, his eyes scanning the ward-wall, the Accursed Forest, and the granite stones of the road. As always, the Forest retains its greenery, even as winter is arriving beyond the ward-wall, with chill winds and graying winter leaves, even as Lorn and Second Company ride through a gray early morning on the second day of another outbound patrol from Jakaafra. He is reminded once more of the differences outside and within the wall by the *zzzzpp* of an expiring flowerfly against the chaos-net.

Lorn wonders how long before they will confront another fallen tree, and how long before Majer Maran again appears at Jakaafra and under what pretense. Lorn also ponders how he also must carry out his commitment to Ryalth in a manner that meets the full requirements of consortship, yet in a way which protects her more than it threatens her. And he must continue to improve his control of chaos and order while not letting his lancers know that is what he does. That is one reason why he bears two firelances in a specially adapted holder. He smiles at that thought, for no one, not even Kusyl, has asked about the twin lances.

"Cool and damp, maybe get wetter, ser," offers Shynt.

"Colder, I'd say, but not wetter." Lorn is beginning to sense irregularities in the chaos net and the flow of chaos force along the wall, but says nothing, just keeps watching the wall ahead as the lancers ride southeast.

It is not quite mid-morning when Lorn senses what he has known must be coming, and not much after that when a lancer reports, "Fallen tree ahead, ser!"

"Shynt, have them form up five abreast and ride out to the perimeter road," Lorn orders.

"Yes, ser."

Lorn turns the gelding across the dampened but not yet muddy earth of the deadland, and he and the first squad cross soil that smells vaguely of a harbor, and more so with each hoof that strikes it.

Kusyl and the second squad are waiting at the perimeter road for Lorn and the first squad, reined up a good kay to the south of the point on the road directly north of the fallen tree.

"First squad stands ready, ser," Kusyl reports as Lorn and Shynt ride up.

"Good. We'll stay on the road until we're opposite the crown, and then reform into two squads. The men know we'll be trying something different this time?" He looks at Shynt, then Kusyl.

"Yes, ser."

Lorn nods and urges the white gelding along the perimeter road, his eyes checking the tree canopy as they ride closer, but he sees no creatures on the trunk or beyond the canopy, not that he would expect such.

Finally, he turns, "Halt here."

"First squad, halt!"

"Second squad, halt!"

Lorn turns the gelding off the road and rides forward perhaps a hundred cubits before reining up and waiting for the two squads to form up flanking him.

"Second squad forward!"

"First squad, right turn."

As the squads draw into their staggered five-abreast formations, Lorn continues to watch the fallen tree, but sees nothing. To his left, he knows, perhaps as few as five kays southeast, lies the non-functional midpoint chaos tower, but it is just beyond his vision.

"Second squad stands ready, ser!" Kusyl calls.

"First squad ready."

Lorn raises his hand, then begins to ride forward, alone between the squads as they close the distance to the crushed canopy of the fallen tree. Approximately seventy-five cubits separate Lorn from the first squad on his right, and seventy-five cubits from the second squad on his left. He now wears the Brystan sabre on his waist, although he has never called attention to his switch in weapons. And he carries the two firelances in their specially adapted lance-holder.

When Lorn is about five hundred cubits from the tangled and crushed crown vegetation, he removes one of the two firelances, and calls, "Lances ready! Prepare to discharge."

Both squad leaders echo his command.

In near silence that follows, as Second Company rides closer, Lorn's hearing seems to sharpen and he can pick up a few phrases across the distance.

"Why is he doing it like that?"

". . . maybe since the old squad leader got killed . . ."

". . . like he's mad . . ."

". . . more like bait, 'cept he's got teeth . . ."

"Cats get him sometime . . ."

"You haven't seen him . . ."

At two hundred cubits from the tree's canopy Lorn can sense the tension ahead, and calls out again, "Prepare to discharge lances!"

The gelding has carried Lorn to within a hundred and fifty cubits from the canopy when the pair of giant cats break from the screen afforded by the twisted limbs. They bound, predictably, toward Lorn, drawn by the sense of chaos and order he embodies.

Lorn raises his firelance, aiming at the rear cat, the one that will always turn and angle away, given the opportunity, waiting until the beast is almost within the range of a traditional firelance.

Hhsstt! The animal drops as the single bolt drills through it, a firebolt that does not curve that noticeably under Lorn's chaos control.

The first giant cat seems almost to stumble, then launches itself toward the lancer captain.

Hhhsssttt! The line of fire burns away its eyes and upper skull. Lorn does not lower the firelance until he is certain the beast is dead.

". . . see what I mean . . ."

". . . no one that good with a lance . . ."

". . . captain is . . ."

"First squad! Close in about fifteen cubits!" Lorn orders, mentally checking the angles as he overtly switches firelances. Next, once they are within a hundred cubits, will come an attack by the night leopards.

Lorn slows the gelding until the first squad has eased toward him, closing the gap that had widened back to about seventy-five cubits, before he lets his mount resume a slightly faster walk southward and toward the creatures that await them.

The strange sense of melancholy passes over him, but he pushes it aside, his eyes and senses centered on the danger ahead.

The canopy branches rustle, then tremble, but no leopards appear. Lorn slows the gelding, knowing that the attack will and must come, that it will follow patterns that the Accursed Forest has set.

"Stand by to discharge lances! Short bursts!"

That command is barely repeated before the two packs of leopards emerge and accelerate toward the lancers.

"Discharge at will!"

Hhsst! Hssst! Hssst!

Firelance bursts flare across the packs. Lorn wheels the gelding to the right, charging just behind the first squad, moving to anticipate the pair of lagging leopards who will sprint northwest to escape the lancers.

Focusing his firelance on the leading black cat of the two that trail, he discharges the entire lance before the cat staggers and tumbles. The trailing cat, cut off by Lorn's charge, abruptly shifts and springs straight toward the captain.

Lorn takes down the last leopard with the Brystan blade—or actually—the chaos-fire he extends beyond the cupridium tip of the curved blade. At the angle he has used, he doubts that his lancers have seen what he has done, and even if they have, few if any will understand or remember that the sabre seemed impossibly long for one short moment, but Lorn has no intention of allowing the cat close enough to harm him or his mount.

Breathing heavily, Lorn reins up the gelding. He still holds the depleted firelance and the Brystan sabre. Once he is certain both fleeing leopards are dead, he switches firelances, and turns the gelding back toward the point where, as he has ordered earlier, the two squads have drawn up facing and flanking the crushed canopy of the fallen tree.

The two squad leaders ride from their squads and toward Lorn, reining up perhaps fifteen cubits away from their captain.

"First squad reports, no creatures escaped, ser," reports Shynt.

"Second squad reports, no creatures escaped, ser," states Kusyl.

"Good." Lorn nods. "I'll have the message for the Mirror Engineers in a moment." His eyes burn, and his head throbs from his use of order and chaos. As he continues to look at the two squad leaders, his vision blurs, and for a time, there are two images of the two men.

He blinks, and the images merge, but the headache remains. Also, he is aware that his uniform is far damper than those of his squad leaders and lancers, and even the muscles in his thighs are close to cramping. Still, he turns in the saddle and says easily, "Kusyl, Shynt, have the squads stand by with lances ready, but if there's no movement for a while, then you can set up the sentries for the afternoon and evening."

"Yes, ser," reply both squad leaders in near-unison.

Lorn slowly replaces the sabre and the firelance, and then pulls out the message blank for the Engineers. Even at one tree-fall every three patrols, it will be a long winter.

XCII

LORN REINS UP under the green barrel and just beyond the narrow porch that leads into Dustyn's establishment. As he dismounts, the lancer captain glances upward at the heavy gray clouds, hoping that his business with the factor will not take too long and that he can ride back to the compound before the downpour that threatens actually begins. He ties the gelding to the bronze ring of the hitching post outside Dustyn's narrow porch, then climbs the steps and enters the narrow foyer.

He reaches to pick up the bell when the thin face of the factor appears.

"Morning, Captain," offers Dustyn. "Must be a stand-down day for Second Company, seeing as you'd be here so early in the day."

"It is one of those few days," Lorn admits.

"You'd be wanting some of the Alafraan, I'd wager, not waiting for your messenger fellow to bring it."

"I could do with a bottle or two," Lorn admits, "but that's not the reason I came."

Dustyn opens the door and gestures for Lorn to follow him along the corridor and into a side study even smaller than the one assigned to Lorn at the northpoint compound. Besides the small high desk there are but two stools. The inner wall is stacked with foot chests, three abreast and two high. The gray curtains on the single window are dusty. Lorn ignores the cobwebs as he takes the proffered stool.

"And what can this poor factor in spirits and other liquids be doing for a mighty captain of lancers, might I ask?" Dustyn grins at his own words.

"Well might you ask," Lorn returns, grinning as well, "for you are a well-respected factor, and one who can accomplish tasks that none would know or suspect, saving that they be accomplished, and none beside you could have done the same."

Dustyn guffaws, shaking his head. "Aye, and you should a' been a factor with such words, or stayed in the family trade, if'n that were their lineage."

Lorn looks at Dustyn, continuing to grin. "Well . . . you are a factor, one who can arrange many things."

"So it is said, but what is said is often more than I can do." Dustyn chortles loudly. "And I tell folk that I can do anything!"

"Do your talents go so far as to arranging for a consorting, one to be recorded here in Jakaafra?"

Dustyn frowns. "One of the parties, the man to be sure, would have to live, say . . . in some proximity and be known by someone . . . if one of your lancers . . . you and I could . . . you know, such is frowned upon. . . ."

"But not forbidden," Lorn points out. "All who have left their families' households or established their own have the right to a consort of their choice."

"Aye, and like as it is not always easy for such . . . should the households from which they come differ more than a fingertip in . . . shall we say, the style of their lace and their privacy screens?"

Lorn nods. "But I would have this arranged. You—or those respected in Jakaafra—know the man, and some even know of the woman."

"Why would . . . I should not ask."

"Let us just say that both the man and the woman wish this consorting, and both are old enough and established in their doings that consent is not required."

"Consent is always required of woman of altage or el-thage," Dustyn suggests carefully, "and even of women who are merchanters, unless they hold the house."

"Consent is not required," Lorn emphasizes, with a grin, "although discretion may be advisable."

Dustyn frowns.

"No ill will come to you," Lorn says. "Has not your trading prospered from my suggestions?"

"Mightily, Captain, else I'd not be listening." Dustyn's face is expressionless, except for his eyes, which contain a hint of amusement. "Now . . . you want this to be a real consorting?"

"A very real one."

"And am I to know the names of the parties?"

"Not until that day, or as close to it as possible." Lorn smiles. "You understand merchanting, for you are an excellent factor, and you could call this consorting a matter of trade. It is, in a way, as you will see when the season is right."

At the terms "a matter of trade," the factor's brow furrows slightly. "Now, Captain, I'd been thinking this might be a lancer officer consorting with a lovely lady from, some might take it, understand, a senior commander's household or even a Magi'i hold or a high family . . . a love match, you might say."

Lorn smiles. "It is a love match, Dustyn . . . and I promise that you will not be disappointed in either the match or the trade that benefits you which will come from it."

The factor finally grins. "Captain . . . all say you keep your word in a place that it be most hard to do, and I must confess that I am mightily curious, but there be times to wait for the cat to move, rather'n chase it, and this, I'd be thinking, is one of those times."

"It is indeed one of those times."

"Still . . . for it to be recorded here, as a real consorting, I needs must know the names two days afore. Should be an eightday, but . . . two days I can arrange, if that be suitable."

"Two days before you shall know, and you will understand then." Lorn grins. "If you do not do so before." He inclines his head. "Now . . . the second matter . . . the one less difficult."

Dustyn inclines his head.

"You have seen that goods are coming to reach me . . . ?"

"Ah, yes, ser. In point of being, that I was going to tell you, it dropped clean from my thoughts at your . . . request . . . you have received three more cases, and two others, of which I cannot fathom."

Lorn nods. "It appears as though I will be stationed here for a time, perhaps for many years, and my family is attempting to make my life more comfortable, yet . . ."

"You'd be looking for a small place a yer own? Thinking on . . . consorting, say?"

"I'm too young for that, yet," Lorn says with a straight face, "as this business has shown me for sure. But . . . I'd not want to go through what this fellow will face when the time might come. And, I cannot keep leaving cases in your cellar, not dry goods, nor . . ." Lorn shrugs. "You know that officers often do such, because we cannot keep much more than uniforms and weapons. I think I have a local woman, a consort of one of those who maintain the compound who will keep such a dwelling for when I need it. If you can find such a dwelling."

Dustyn laughs. "That be easier, far easier than the first, for I know of four such, and that be without lifting my eyes past the road east."

Lorn frowns.

"Ah . . . captain, the young folk now flock to Cyad or Fyrad or even Geliendra. Even my own Asbyl—she be consorted to a factor's son in Geliendra, and never shed a tear on her way south." Dustyn shrugs. "Fact be . . . my ma's place. I fixed it for her, Asbyl, I mean, even new tiles on the roof. I'd been wondering . . . you could have it for a silver a season, if you'd be keeping it neat. If it's as you say, I'd be selling it to you for ten golds, any day you wish."

"I would not wish to. . . ."

"There's but three of us, and Hyul took Da's place last year. Wryul'n I . . . our place got rooms we don't use from one season to the next. Now . . . I couldn't give ma's place away. You'd be doing me a favor, a' sorts, and, well, without the trade you and your friends at Ryalor House brought me . . . be a harder life for us. . . ." Dustyn smiles almost sheepishly.

Lorn lifts his hands helplessly. "Done." He extends two silvers. "I'll take two bottles, and if this would pay for the use of the dwelling for a pair of seasons."

"Your trust speaks well for you, Captain, but best you see it, first." Dustyn glances outside, not taking the coins. "Not yet. You have a mount. I'd be meeting you in front."

Not long after Lorn has mounted, Dustyn appears on an almost sway-backed brown mare, and the two men ride along the narrow lane until it joins the road leaving Jakaafra to the east.

Lorn hopes that what Dustyn has said about the dwelling is accurate, but the factor has been reasonably fair in all his dealings. So the lancer captain rides and watches to see what awaits him on the east road.

The dwelling sits on a low rise on the eastern road from Jakaafra, less than a kay from the square, and just beyond the kaystone that notes the town center is one kay away. The new roof tiles glisten pale green, even in the dim light of the cloudy day.

Dustyn dismounts heavily, and limps slightly, past the privacy screen and to the door, which he opens with an ancient bronze key. Lorn follows, and silently walks through the house.

The dwelling is small, as Dustyn has said, with but a bed-chamber, a larger room containing a tiled stove and space for eating and meeting, a bath-chamber, and a rear room for storage, no more than five cubits on a side. There is a serviceable bed, even a doorless armoire, in the sleeping chamber, and a table with three old oak chairs in the main room.

"Even got a handful of pots there." The factor gestures to the golden oak cabinet beside the stove. "And a few pieces of crockery."

The floor tiles are a pale blue, faded by time, but not cracked, and the joins have been recently grouted. There are both interior and exterior ceramic privacy screens, and the hedge providing privacy for the small rear portico needs but little trimming. There is a stable that will hold two horses, but without space for a carriage.

As the two stand looking at the privacy screen before the front entrance, Lorn nods. "This will do well for me."

"I was thinking it might."

Lorn extends the silvers again, adding a third. "If I could trouble you to bring the goods in your cellar sometime in the next eightday or so . . . ?"

"A pleasure, Captain, a pleasure." Dustyn glances upward. "Best we be getting back. I'd not be thinking I'd like to be getting too damp, and you've a much longer ride than do I."

Lorn nods at that and remounts the gelding.

The first drops of rain begin to dribble out of the gray sky when Lorn is little more than a kay out of the town of Jakaafra on his return to the compound. By the time he rides through the gates the rain is falling so fast that he can scarcely see a hundred cubits ahead, and he is most grateful for the stone-surfaced roads of Cyador.

Water pours from his uniform and has plastered his garrison cap and hair flat against his skull as he leads the gelding from the downpour into the stable.

"Ser . . ." Suforis looks at Lorn wide-eyed.

"I know," Lorn says tiredly. "I know. But there are few days I even have free to get to Jakaafra."

"Yes, ser. I'll make sure he gets dry and rubbed down."

"Thank you." Lorn takes the wine and marches back through the rain-filled courtyard. His feet squush in his boots as he walks down the corridor to his quarters. After wringing out his uniforms, and hanging them out to dry—slowly, he suspects, Lorn changes into dry trousers and a dry undertunic. Then, he dries and oils the sabre and leaves it out of the scabbard, hoping both will dry before he has to leave on patrol again.

Only then does he seat himself at his desk and read through the last scroll from Ryalth once more.

> . . . we are a quiet house and becoming regarded as
> an example for the Clanless Traders. I have tried

to keep our image that way. This has been helped by the occasional appearance of a senior enumerator from elsewhere. It has also been aided by the growth of our shipments of a golden brandy that is of high quality. Since it and many of our more profitable items are shipped through Fyrad, we are known to have distant contacts. Some of those contacts date from the other ship disaster that we discussed. They are now pleased to see that house reborn through its heir. That is well these days.

While we remain on the topmost level, we are now paying for three times the space we had previously, and I have purchased a warehouse from the Jekseng Clan that has never been regarded as well-fated since it was once rented by a Hamorian trader. It helps to know the past of some matters.

I see I have forgotten to tell you that, because of certain information about timbers, Ryalor House has become involved in other ventures which we should discuss before too long. The serving lady you never met also says all is well.

. . . and I look forward to hearing from you.

Lorn smiles and begins to pen his reply.

My dearest trader,

My two-eightday furlough begins the ninth eightday of winter, and I have made the arrangements discussed a year ago, and am well-pleased with the thought of keeping my word on this matter. I am hoping that it will be convenient for you to come to the town of Jakaafra at that time, and I have arranged a modest dwelling for you, so that all can be handled with decorum and grace. Should I not be immediately present on account of my duties, inquire of the factor who has arranged much. . . .

Should you wish to demur, I will make other

> arrangements to keep this word whenever you de-
> sire it to be such. . . .

Lorn frowns at his words. He does not wish to seem too
formal, but he does not wish Ryalth to be compromised in
the event the scroll falls into the wrong hands.

Finally, he concludes.

> As you know, I am less than most perfectly able
> to express myself under these circumstances, and
> must trust to words more formal than what I feel,
> but I trust that my actions will express me far better
> than my poor words, and that you will understand
> as you have done so well and so often over the
> years.

He looks blankly toward the window and the rain beyond
as he finally seals the missive, his eyes fixed far beyond the
grayness of the compound.

XCIII

AS THE WHITE gelding carries him southeast along the road
beside the white granite of the ward-wall, Lorn wipes the
cold drizzle off his forehead. Sweat continues to ooze from
under the garrison cap to mix with the fine rain. Without the
oiled white leather winter jacket, he would be soaked, but
cold as it had been when they had left Jakaafra, he had chosen the warmer jacket over a waterproof. The weather has
warmed somewhat, and under the jacket, even unfastened as
it is, he is too warm.

No lancer can carry enough for all types of weather, not
and be able to fight giant cats—not and carry two firelances
and two sabres.

"Far too wet and cold not to wear a jacket," Shynt observes from where he rides on the outer side of the ward-

wall road, echoing Lorn's feelings, "and too warm to wear such."

Lorn shakes his head. "And it's not really wet enough for this to help crops much, and too damp for healthy riding. No one really benefits. Some patrols are like that."

"Most . . . in the winter."

The lancer captain nods in agreement, then glances ahead. Through the mid-day drizzle, the white granite oblong bulk of the structure housing the non-functioning midpoint chaos tower looms ahead and slightly to the left of the ward-wall road. Before long, the first squad will have to ride around the mid-point tower, and then, somewhere beyond that, farther southeast, they will find another fallen tree.

It has been almost two eightdays and two complete patrol circuits since he sent off his fateful scroll to Ryalth, and he has heard nothing, but still he must deal with patrols and trees and escaped creatures. Then, he reminds himself, it is still early for her response. He turns back to study the wall. His eyes and senses check the chaos-net and the increasingly irregular pulses of the chaos flows confirm to him that another tree has fallen across the white granite barrier—several kays to the southeast of the midpoint tower. The irregularity of the chaos—greater irregularity, he corrects himself, for chaos flows are never regular—remind him again that he pursues a dangerous path . . . as his father had suggested more than once.

Yet, being who he is, what other can he do? Other than smile and make provisions.

Smile? The ancient words, in their slanted characters, run through his mind.

Smiles . . . *images on the pond of being, reflections only made possible by the black depths beneath.*

Black depths—he has black depths. That he knows as he pushes the words away. He knows, too, that what he must do in dealing with the fallen tree ahead—riding alone as a target—will work, and that no wild creatures are likely to escape. He also knows that if too many more patrol reports show neither casualties nor escaped animals, it will not be that long before Majer Maran returns to Jakaafra with another chore in mind—one for which Lorn is not certain he is fully prepared.

Provisions must be made . . . and I have made them.

But are they enough? That . . . he will never know, unless he fails, and then it will be too late. With a faint smile, Lorn leans forward slightly in the saddle and runs the fingertips of his right hand over the two firelances, one after the other. Both are fully charged. Then he straightens up and studies the ward-wall to his right once more, trying to guess how many kays they will ride before a lancer will spot the fallen Forest tree, how many kays before he will have to use concealed chaos once more, because a magus-born lancer cannot be suffered to be successful.

XCIV

LORN LOOKS UP from the patrol report he is writing as Kusyl stands by the door to the inner study.

"This came with the Engineers, ser." The senior squad leader extends the white and green sealed scroll.

Lorn stands to take it. "Thank you. It will be a bit before I have the reports ready to go."

"Myserk will stop back before they leave," Kusyl replies. "He understands." With a nod, he steps back and closes the door.

Lorn looks at the scroll, then forces himself to set it on the side of the desk. He picks up the pen and continues until he reaches the last lines of the summary that will be dispatched to Majer Maran.

> . . . no casualties, and no creatures escaped. Patrol remained on station at the fallen trunk for two days until Mirror Engineers could respond. Return patrol without Accursed Forest events.

With a smile of relief, he lays the summary beside the completed full report for both to dry and finally picks up the scroll Kusyl had brought him. Lorn is not that surprised to see that the seal has been carefully slit from the paper and then re-heated—as shown by the blurring of his father's "K" on the wax.

He breaks the seal and begins to read.

> . . . is always good to hear how well you are doing. I have received favorable reports on your progress from many, including the officer who recommended you for lancer training so many years ago. He continues in that post today as well as then. Apparently, younger lancers are the ones who move more from duty assignment to duty assignment. . . .
>
> Jerial has spent more time with me lately, and perhaps I was too hasty in my suggestions about future consorts. This is indeed something that we should discuss when you return, but I would like to assure you that I now believe your earlier inclinations may have true merit, and would be in your best interests if you still remain so inclined. . . .

Lorn frowns. Has Jerial talked about Ryalth to their father? Or has Ryalth's success become more noted? Or is something else afoot about which Lorn knows nothing?

> Vernt continues to pursue his efforts with both diligence and recognition. He has been raised to a lower second level, as has Ciesrt, although both are in very different aspects of magial endeavors. Myryan's garden is a wonder, and she is most pleased with that aspect of her life and dwelling. . . .

Lorn winces. He suspects he knows exactly what his father's words convey, and he can only hope his younger sister is not too terribly unhappy.

Sylirya has been taken as a consort by a cabinet-maker, so that Kysia has become the head of the household staff. She is good enough to run the household of a trading magnate and will in time perhaps have the skills needed to assist some high functionary in the Palace of Light, though we would certainly miss her here. In time, she will doubtless leave us for a younger family, but her loyalty cannot be faulted . . .

Lorn shakes his head with a wry smile.

In the end, little has changed within the house since last you were here, excepting that we all miss you, and wish you well in your struggles along the ward-wall of the Accursed Forest.

The lancer captain lowers the scroll, then lifts it and studies the writing itself, rather than the words. While his father's writing retains its ability to offer detailed observations between the lines and the characteristic angular flow of the letters, there is something . . . Lorn studies the scroll more closely, noting the slight wavering of some pen strokes. Age? The toll of being a senior magus?

Lorn sets aside the scroll and fingers his clean-shaven chin, thinking about his father's apparent change of heart—or thought—concerning Ryalth.

Does Ryalth's scroll give any indication of any reason for that?

He takes out the other scroll—the one Suforis had delivered with two bottles of Alafraan from Dustyn the night previous, after Second Company had finally returned to Jakaafra, once again running almost three days late, this time because of tree-falls earlier along the southeast ward-wall. With only two of large moveable firecannons, and the need to recharge them after use, tree-falls close together meant one lancer company or another had to guard a fallen trunk for several days, at times. This time, it had been Second Company's fate.

He unrolls the scroll.

> My dearest lancer,
>
> I told myself I would not be disappointed had you forgotten our discussion of a year ago. I would have been disappointed. That I can tell from my reaction to your scroll. I will be in Jakaafra for this venture as you have requested. The trip will allow me to visit some factors in Fyrad and in Geliendra and other towns along the route.
>
> All is well with Ryalor House. We have been able to broker some additional timber shipments when the amount of timber increased past the anticipated contract levels, as I had suspected might well occur. . . .

Why had she suspected? Because the timber came from fallen trunks and because Lorn's presence meant more falling trunks?

> . . . our interests in coastal shipping have also offered solid results, for equally predictable reasons. . . .

Lorn sets down the scroll of his consort-to-be and laughs. His father and Jerial must have just looked. Jerial's wagering ventures have let her overhear much of the gossip, and many of the facts could not have been hidden. Not when Ryalor House has trading spaces three times as large as before, its own warehouse, interests in coastal ships, and who knows what else that Ryalth has not told him.

And all because a student mage saved a pretty face from being attacked years before? A pretty face that hid so much more?

Lorn glances to the cold and sunlit green-blue sky beyond the study window. He hopes that Majer Maran will wait a season or two before returning, but doubts he will have that much time. If . . . if Lorn is fortunate, he and Ryalth will be consorted, and she will have returned to Cyad before the majer reappears. If . . .

XCV

LORN PUTS HIS saddle bags on the top of the barrel of grain set beside the gelding's stall and carefully props the pair of firelances between the barrel and the stall wall, waiting for Suforis to finish saddling his mount.

"Be just a moment, ser," the ostler calls.

Lorn smiles to himself, and studies the stable, still as neat and clean as ever, then runs his fingertips over one firelance and then the other, making sure that both are fully charged. Although the patrol before the last one had found a fallen tree—the one they'd had to wait two days for the Engineers to clear, the fact that there had been no fallen trees on the last patrol made it more likely that he and Second Company would encounter one on this patrol—or the next.

"We'd be wishing you a good patrol, ser," offers Suforis as he extends the gelding's reins to Lorn.

"We?" asks Lorn with a grin.

"Me and Lesyna. She is most pleased to be cleaning and watching over your new dwelling, now. Her da even said it was worth the old mare he gave her, 'cepting the mare's not for much but carrying her. Leastwise she can go to town now and visit her folks." Suforis grins. "Or carry a scroll or two when it be not wise for me."

"You don't mind her riding alone."

"Lesyna? Always liked the horses, she has. 'Sides, captain, what sense it be to say she'll not ride? Be different when Clebyl gets pensioned off and we get proper quarters, screen and all, instead a' just a big room . . . and have children . . . but now?"

"I'm glad it worked out and that you're pleased."

"That be two of us, ser." Suforis bows his head and gestures toward the next stall.

"Go ahead," Lorn says. "You've work to do."

After Lorn fastens his saddle bags in place and slips the two firelances into the holder, the captain leads the gelding out of the stable into the courtyard where the lancers of Second Company are mounting up. The high thin clouds that had been visible at dawn are thickening into a more solid gray—or perhaps the dawn clouds just foreshadowed the heavier clouds moving in from the northeast. The brief gusts of wind seem colder as well.

Outside the stable, Lorn mounts the gelding and rides to the north end of the stable building where Shynt is mustering the first squad. "Good morning, Shynt."

"Good morning, Captain." Shynt glances past Lorn toward the double column of riders. "We be ready, ser."

"How is Hykylt?"

"He will ride, ser." The junior squad leader looks at Lorn and lowers his voice. "Were you trained by a healer, ser?"

"One of my sisters was fortunate enough to become a healer, and I watched closely," Lorn replies. "I would rather that word not be spread." Lorn laughs softly. "A fierce lancer officer must not be seen as a gentle healer."

"Don't know many as would call you soft, ser."

"That's best." Lorn nods and guides the gelding back southward toward Kusyl and the second squad.

"Ready, ser," Kusyl reports, even before Lorn reins up.

"We might as well get started."

"Yes, ser. Second squad, forward, in column by twos!"

"First squad, forward, in column by twos!" echoes from behind them.

Lorn's heels urge the white gelding forward, and his eyes go to the clouds. A light snow would be better than rain, but only a light snow. So they will have rain or heavy snow, he suspects from the twinges in his skull that foreshadow a storm-headache, as he rides out through the compound gate toward the chaos tower building to his right. His face offers but a pleasant smile when he turns the gelding to the southeast and the patrol ahead.

XCVI

LORN STEPS OUT of the stable at Eastend and into the twilight of a winter day. Carrying his saddlebags, he stretches his legs, and readjusts his grip on them. The firelances have already been collected and delivered to the Engineer detachment for replacement or recharging.

The Lancer captain keeps trying to stretch his legs as he crosses the courtyard toward the quarters he will occupy as a transient officer, much as Captain Ilryk does when Third Company finishes a patrol at the Jakaafra compound. Although Second Company's latest patrol offered no tree-falls, the ride had been cold and seemed longer than usual. Lorn's breath leaves white clouds as he walks briskly across the white granite stones, glad this time for the white winter jacket that he wears.

"Captain!" A figure in the uniform of a Mirror Engineer waves from fifty cubits away.

"Majer." Lorn raises his hand in reply as he recognizes Majer Weylt.

Weylt waits for Lorn to reach him before speaking. "I'd hoped you'd get here this evening. Otherwise, it would have been a lonely evening meal."

"Are all the other officers gone?" asks Lorn.

"Yes. Be just us here tonight. Captain Strynst is off checking a tree-fall on the southeast ward-wall. And the patrol captain here . . . have you met Gowl?"

"Just in passing. We've shared a few meals."

"He's the one who found the tree. So that leaves us." Weylt shrugs, then smiles briefly. "I'll see you in the officers' dining area shortly."

"I need to clean up a bit."

"That's fine." With a nod, Weylt turns and walks toward the building adjoining the quarters.

Lorn shaves and washes quickly, and pulls on his one

clean tunic before leaving the transient officer's room and walking out across the now-empty courtyard. When he enters the next building, Lorn can hear the hubbub from the larger hall where the lancers are already eating. In the officers' area, the engineer majer is waiting at one of the two tables, alone.

"I did hurry," Lorn says as he nears.

"I can tell. The food may not be worth the haste." Weylt gestures toward the bottle on the table. "All I have is Byrdyn, Captain. Scarcely repayment for that Fhynyco you had for me at Jakaafra."

"After a cold and long patrol, the Byrdyn is most welcome," Lorn replies, seating himself across from Weylt.

A server in gray appears and deposits a small casserole dish on the square table, a poor rendition of emburhka, from what Lorn can smell. A small loaf of a rye-like bread in a basket accompanies the dish.

"How long were you working on the Great Canal?" Lorn asks while Weylt fills both goblets.

"Near-on a season. That's the way it seemed." Weylt lifts his goblet. "To better days." After a quick small swallow, the majer heaps some of the emburhka onto his crockery platter.

"To better days," Lorn reiterates as he lifts his own goblet and takes a sip. Then he serves himself, then breaks off a chunk of the bread in the basket and sets it on one side of his platter. "What happened? I heard the retaining walls of the Great Canal collapsed. . . ."

"In a way." Weylt tilts his head, as if thinking of a way to explain. "You know that the Accursed Forest lies in the middle of Eastern Cyador. It's raised just a little, and the land is flat around it, and then slopes down . . . well, if it rains too much over or around the Forest the water has to go somewhere. And if the land to the south and west is already soaked, then the Fryadyr River overflows. It overflowed, and broke through the levees near Geliendra and then carved a way to the Great Canal. . . ."

"So . . . when the rains stopped, the river was flowing into the canal?"

Weylt nods. "Almost like there had been a river there once. Maybe there was, before the Firstborn changed things. That made it hard. We had to build a dam and then replace the levees before we could even start on repairing the Canal." He frowns. "I didn't realize that they've started using oxen to pull the freight boats along the canal."

Lorn shrugs helplessly. "I wouldn't know. I didn't come that way."

"No one could tell me why. Oh . . . they said things like the chaos-cells for the tow wagons were needed elsewhere. But that doesn't make sense. There are plenty of cells."

"Is there plenty of chaos-force away from the Accursed Forest?" asks Lorn, almost idly. "Or maybe they need it to charge firelances used against the barbarians."

"That could be." After taking a swallow of the Byrdyn, Weylt glances at Lorn. "You've been carrying two firelances for the past few patrols."

"Seems like I've had to. Even with reinforcements, we're only at three-quarters strength." Lorn but sips from his goblet, looking guilelessly at the major. "We've had a lot of fallen trees on the northeast ward-wall."

"I can see where the extra lance might help." Weylt's tone is even, unforced. "Of course, we don't have enough lances to issue two to every lancer."

"I wouldn't be using a second one if we had a full complement," Lorn points out.

"There don't seem to be enough lancers anywhere, these days. That's true." Weylt pauses to take several mouthfuls of the casserole before speaking again. "Be glad to get home leave, and some good emburhka."

"How long for you?" Lorn asks between bites of the too-heavily peppered and overcooked emburhka.

"Another three seasons, at the end of summer." Weylt's lips twist. "Afterwards, I'll be back here, just like you will be."

Lorn nods, waiting, knowing from the edge in the engineer's voice that more is coming.

"You make reports on every patrol, don't you?" Weylt asks.

"We all do."

"Reports . . ." Weylt snorts. "We even have to report on every lance we recharge or replace. By squad and company, of course. And a separate place for the officers. They all go to Majer Maran. Don't know what good they do."

"I think every report must go there," Lorn suggests. "I suppose he could figure out how much chaos energy it takes each squad to handle each tree-fall. Except each one's different."

"They might be trying to find out how much chaos energy it really takes. If they have trouble powering the Canal tow wagons . . ." Weylt refills his goblet, and glances at Lorn.

The lancer captain looks down at a goblet still half full. "I think not. With more Byrdyn, I might not wake up that easily in the morning."

"Then, Commander Meylyd or your Majer Maran might have something else in mind," suggests Weylt.

"They might," Lorn agrees. "Who would know, though?" He takes another small sip of the Byrdyn. "I thank you for the wine. It's been most welcome . . . and the conversation."

"Not at all. I hate eating alone, and you're one of the very few who understands the position of a Mirror Engineer." Weylt raises his eyebrows but slightly. "Now . . . or even perhaps in the future."

"I think I do," Lorn replies. "And it's clear you're one of the few here who understands what a lancer captain such as I might face." He lifts the goblet.

Weylt lifts his in return.

They both smile.

XCVII

THE EMPEROR TOZIEL'ELTH'ALT'MER, who carries the elthage lineage although he has no magely talents, remains at ease in the malachite and silver chair as he listens to those who speak before him. In her smaller chair, back behind his right shoulder, also listens the Empress Ryenyel.

"Why can we not continue to use the chaos towers that surround the Accursed Forest to recharge the firelances and replenish the chaos-cells for the firewagons? I have heard many and elegant words and more words about this," declares Majer-Commander Rynst, "but I cannot say that I have heard an explanation that fully satisfies me."

"We are using those chaos towers exactly for that," replies the First Magus smoothly. "As well you and His Mightiness know. We are sending firelances from Geliendra all the way to the Cerlyni and even the Jeranyi border in some cases. Now is not the problem. It is the future that presents the difficulty." After a long pause, Chyenfel adds, "I have not been exactly silent on the difficulties posed by the Accursed Forest."

"You have been most eloquent in stating that the Accursed Forest presents a difficulty," Rynst agrees, his words warm. "Yet . . . my lancers, even my Captain-Commander, as I am most certain you know from your Second Magus, would know what is so deadly about the Forest that it is to be feared more greatly than the barbarians of the north. Their blades claim far more lancers than do the creatures of the Forest."

"There are none so deaf as cover their ears and will not hear." Chyenfel's smooth voice drips honey. "Not that you have ever covered your ears, wisest and most powerful of lancers and Warrior of Light, but it may be that other lancers, more concerned about what may happen in the handful of years immediately before us, have done so."

Only the slightest tightening of the muscles around his

eyes betrays the interest of the Emperor. There is no visible change in the Empress, who continues to look vaguely amused, as her eyes rest not on either the First Magus or the Mirror Lancer Majer-Commander, but upon Merchanter Adviser Bluoyal.

"My dear friend, never have you been so effusive in your compliments." Rynst smiles indulgently. "But I beg you explain in terms simple enough for me to convey to those lancers who may die without the chaos-cells charged by the Forest towers."

Beside Rynst, Bluoyal looks at the white and glistening stones of the floor of the audience chamber.

Chyenfel turns toward Rynst once more. "Perhaps I have tailored my previous presentations to your great perception. I will attempt greater simplicity. The chaos towers are beginning to fail. Yet we cannot move the chaos towers without causing them to fail immediately. We now have barely more than the minimum number of chaos towers required to maintain the wards. At times already, the chaos-net on the northeast ward-wall is breached. If . . . if our effort is not undertaken soon, it cannot be undertaken at all. Then the Forest will breach the wall and surround the remaining towers so that they cannot be used. So . . . we can contain the Forest, and lose the excess power from the chaos towers, or we can refuse to contain the Forest and lose the excess power from the towers—and turn much or all of eastern Cyador back to the Forest." Chyenfel bows to Rynst.

"You are most clear, O master magus." Rynst pauses. "Yet you and your predecessors have assured us of the power of your magely towers. We have relied on such. Now . . . you say such powers will vanish within years—or sooner."

"The Firstborn said that the chaos towers would not last forever, only that their power would be uncontested while they endured. Now . . . one by one, they are failing. We have but one tower more than the minimum we need to create the sleep-ward barrier, and thus restrain the Accursed Forest for generations to come. *If* we do not act now, we cannot act in the seasons and years ahead."

"I could say, although I will not," Rynst declares, "that if we do not have more firelances, the barbarians will take northern Cyador. Nor will I suggest that a barbarian can lop a poor lancer's head from his body more effectively and more swiftly than can the fastest growing of trees."

"You are most eloquent, my dear Majer-Commander." Chyenfel laughs. "Most eloquent. Not that I would call you verbose. Nor vain. Nor simplistic. No, for you see far beyond what passes in this chamber. You are most wise, and you know that the barbarians remain raiders and bandits. You even know that, even were our northern borders undefended, the barbarians would move but a few dozen kays southward in your lifetime or that of your children or grandchildren. And you know, too, that the Accursed Forest can grow a large tree in two seasons. And that you lose half as many lancers to the Forest as to the barbarians—and that is with the ward-walls." Chyenfel shrugs. "So I do not have to tell you that if the ward-walls fail because we maintain them to charge a few score firelances, you will be fighting both the barbarians and the Forest, and you will indeed lose. You are wise enough to see that and more. Would that others saw as much." Chyenfel bows deeply to the Mirror Lancer Majer-Commander.

"I thank you for your most cogent explanation." Rynst's tone grows more indulgent. "I truly understand that all Magi'i have limitations that we can but dimly grasp. We of the Mirror Lancers also have limitations, for it is difficult to contest with blades alone and far fewer numbers, an endless flow of barbarians, whether they be raiders or not."

Toziel laughs—long and loudly. "I applaud you both. For both of you have outlined the dilemma most eloquently. So eloquently that I must ponder the wisdom you have so masterfully conveyed." He stands. "Until tomorrow."

Ryenyel rises silently, then follows the Emperor from the chamber.

When Toziel and Ryenyel have returned to her salon, he seats himself on one side of the white divan, she the other. Toziel studies her face. "You are tired."

"Much occurred."

"Rynst has never been so intemperate. Nor Chyenfel," muses Toziel. "Yet I could sense no anger. Both were acting."

"That is because they were trying to get you to act, my dear. They know that what you decide and how you decide will determine the power to be in Cyador for generations."

"Because we have no heirs."

"Because I would not bear heirs and have them twisted by what must happen in the Palace of Light. You understood that from the first, my love."

"It makes matters more difficult."

"You have time yet," Ryenyel points out.

"Not so much as others think, and those others would replace both Rynst and Chyenfel. That is clear, but beyond that . . . who might know? A dozen rationales, or more. . . . Yet Chyenfel cannot live too much longer. He is already almost consumed by chaos."

Ryenyel nods for the Emperor to continue.

"Liataphi? Do you think he wants Kharl'elth to be First Magus to expose his venality and weaknesses?"

"That could be," responds the mahogany-haired Empress-consort, "but what of the plot to place his daughter in control of the Yuryan Clan through her consort Veljan? She advises him on everything."

"As you do me," Toziel reminds her.

"Veljan is forthright and honest and devoted to his consort-mistress. So is an ox."

Toziel laughs gently. "I trust I am not an ox."

"Far from that, my dear." Ryenyel frowns slightly, showing the tiredness on her lightly freckled face. "There is still the missing ordered-death sabre. I fear we have not seen the last of that plotter."

Toziel raises his eyebrows.

"Ten golds . . . a stolen trade plaque . . . a dead heir . . . and a cupridium-plated sabre filled with iron order-death . . . and silence." Ryenyel smiles. "Each is by itself a trifle. Less than a trifle. Yet your Merchanter Advisor Bluoyal was worried enough about that to ask of Luss and Kharl. Did Shevelt know something? And why is Bluoyal so concerned about a Brystan sabre?"

"It makes one wonder." Toziel's voice is near-expressionless.

"It makes *me* wonder," she replies. "Shevelt's death is tied to that weapon, and Liataphi would not have dared such. Nor could he have used such a weapon. Someone wants the calmer Veljan to succeed his father, and Bluoyal is most concerned about that." She smiles. "Then there is the silence. Silence is the surest of assurances that an able plotter still lives. All crow when such dies, and they crow sooner and louder when an inept one dies."

"What else troubles you?"

"Bluoyal was telling me—"

"You meet with my advisors without me?" Toziel's eyes twinkle.

"As necessary." She arches her eyebrows. "He was telling me about a clanless trading house that is wealthier and more influential than many of the smaller clan houses."

Toziel waits.

"It is called Ryalor House. He but mentioned it in passing, and Bluoyal never mentions anything without a reason."

"That tie is stretching, my dear," says Toziel, grinning. "It is run by the mistress of a lancer captain who could have been a magus, and the captain is the son of a magus who is a senior lector—" He breaks off and looks at her.

They both laugh, almost joyously.

After a time, Toziel shakes his head. "So why does Bluoyal wish this known? He knows we talk."

"Kien'elth's daughter is consort to Kharl's son . . . and Bluoyal does not trust Kharl."

Toziel raises his hands helplessly. "So we have an unknown plotter advancing both Liataphi and Kharl. The pair so dislike each other that none will have them in the same chamber save on the most formal of occasions."

"Who lies below them?"

"Any number of senior lectors—Kien, Abram, Hyrist—

they're the most senior. Hyrist and Abram are thought arrogant and self-centered. Kien'elth is well-regarded, but he is almost as consumed by chaos as Chyenfel, and so cannot succeed him, for that, as well as for the reason we both know. Kien's younger son is solid, but not brilliant enough for what we have seen. Kharl will not support Liataphi, nor Liataphi Kharl. Luss is Kharl's tool, and for that reason alone, we dare not replace Rynst, arrogant as he has become, for Rynst knows that, and that is why he suffers Luss to remain as his second."

"There is something else," offers Ryenyel.

"Oh?"

"The Lady Trader of Ryalor House—her fortune cannot be reckoned . . . but she has gained on ventures that only one with knowledge from the Quarter of the Magi'i would have. And she has left on a coaster for Fyrad."

"Most convenient for Bluoyal, I would say."

"What of Bluoyal?" asks the Empress.

"That is the question, is it not? Who does he scheme to put in Chyenfel's place?"

"Someone we do not know—or could not pick." Her lips turn up. "Or we would know already."

"So . . . my dearest . . . what should I decide?"

"Agree to Chyenfel's plan. Immediately. That will ensure that Rynst must concentrate on defeating the barbarians without the extra firelances from the Accursed Forest. Also, if Chyenfel is accurate, if Cyador is to survive, then it must be done, and about purely magely things, he is usually accurate."

"And then we wait to see who betrays who and why? And we watch Bluoyal? And Kharl and the heirs of Kien."

The Empress nods.

XCVIII

THE DAY IS cold but clear as Lorn reins up the gelding before Dustyn's narrow front porch, and it feels warmer than it is because the winds of the previous day have died away. Winter has raced by, or so it seems to Lorn, for it is sixday of the seventh eightday of winter, ten days until Ryalth is supposed to arrive. Already, Juist is muttering about having to take patrols for Second Company's two eightdays of furlough.

Because Lorn will leave on the morrow for another patrol and because he may not be back until just before Ryalth arrives, he needs to talk to Dustyn. He dismounts and ties the gelding to the bronze ring, then mounts the steps and opens the door. For the first time since he has come to Dustyn's establishment, the proprietor is actually standing at the half-door counter.

"Captain, I been wondering when you might be arriving to let me know about this mysterious consorting."

"I'm here," Lorn grins. "I do have a question about it. The lady is traveling here, and while she is expected by firstday of the ninth eightday of winter." Lorn shrugs, "Traveling does not always lend itself to exact days."

"That be no problem. The Emperor's rules say that the recorder must know at least an eightday before. Wasyk'll bend that to two, knowing how hard it be for some folk to come up with the silver, but there's folk tell him a season in advance."

Lorn nods. "That is good."

"And who be these folk, Captain?" Dustyn asks.

"I am one of them," Lorn says quietly, "although it would be better if it were not widely known until afterwards."

"I thought maybe it might be you, Captain," Dustyn says slowly. "But when I asked some merchanters I know about you . . . no offense, you understand . . . they said best they say little." The factor frowns. "Seems like you have powerful friends and as many of power that may not be such, especially . . ."

"For a mere lancer captain, you mean?" Lorn offers a sardonic smile.

"Captain . . . none'd be calling you mere. Even old Kylynzar been mumbling about how he didn't like much what you wrote him, but he couldn't complain none about how you'd stopped the wild creatures. For him . . . well . . . he complains about aught any time."

"I told him we did our best, and that I couldn't guarantee killing every wild creature that escaped."

"You been killing most of 'em, isn't it so?"

"So far," Lorn admits, quickly changing the subject. "I haven't been consorted before, and I was in Isahl when my sister was. So what do I do?"

"Consorting be simple enough. It be after the consorting that it be no longer simple." Dustyn laughs hoarsely, then clears his throat. "Wasyk be the recorder of consorts and the tax farmer for the Emperor here in Jakaafra. Be easier 'n I'd thought, 'cause your havin' a place of dwelling means no winking at whether you be proper in consorting here. Doesn't say which dwelling, but a man's supposed to be consorted where he has one. Anyway . . . you and your lady . . ." Dustyn frowns. "Don't recall your saying her name, and I'll be needing that to give to Wasyk." He waits.

"Ryalth . . . she's an independent trader, and the head of Ryalor House."

Dustyn shakes his head, even as he smiles. "Now . . . some matters be making more sense. A lancer captain from a Magi'i family—I did find that out, not much more—consorting to one of the powerful rising trading houses . . . more 'n a few not be pleased to see that kind of alliance. . . ."

"Why . . . because they worry about mage blood in merchanter offspring? The children can only claim either merage or altage heritage. So what do we have to do?"

"Plain forgot to finish . . . you sign the register in front of

Wasyk and seal it there with a silver. That be it, so far as the Emperor's concerned."

Lorn somehow doubts that.

"And then your troubles are your own."

"They're always our own." Lorn pauses, then adds, "I have to be on patrol starting tomorrow. If the lady should arrive . . . well, she has the welcome of the dwelling . . . if you understand and would assist in that?"

"That I can do with great pleasure." Dustyn frowns. "She be truly the house leader of Ryalor House?"

"Absolutely."

"Ryalth . . . Captain Lorn . . . Ryalor . . ." Dustyn shakes his head. "Should a' figured . . . I should."

Lorn forces a laugh. "Leave the figuring to others, Dustyn, and Ryalor House will continue to help you prosper."

"Oh, that I will, ser. That I will. Owe you two far too much to be flapping my chin, outside a' my own place, you see, that is. . . ."

"And to make sure you prosper . . ." Lorn slips a silver into Dustyn's hand.

"Ser . . . you needn't . . ."

"I need not, but times have not been easy for you."

"Thank you, ser, and I will be taking the best care when the lady trader should arrive."

"I know you will." Lorn glances toward the door. "And I have to ready a company for another patrol."

"You do that, ser, and I'll be watching out for you."

Lorn nods as he steps toward the door, and the cold ride back to the compound.

XCIX

FAT AND WET snowflakes swirl past Lorn, so heavily that he cannot see the ward-wall from the perimeter road from where he rides with Kusyl and the second squad, so thickly that he is continually brushing slush and water from his forehead.

He ignores the headache that accompanies the snow.

After briefly considering stopping the patrol, he decides against it, at least for a time. The biggest danger is fallen tree trunks, and even the heaviest snow won't hide anything that large.

"You think this will last, ser?"

"I hope not. Usually, the big flakes don't. Then, we're going on furlough after this patrol." Lorn says with a rueful laugh that carries the fifteen cubits between their mounts. "With our luck, a cubit of it will fall on the deadland."

They both know that while the green crowns of the giant trees of the Accursed Forest may accept some snow, it will neither remain nor filter into the warmer green below.

"Or it'll turn to rain and freeze," counters Kusyl.

"Let's hope not." Lorn has had enough of patrols in cold and wet rain.

"May not get any tree-falls."

"Let's hope not."

Snow clings to the gelding's mane, and creates wet splotches where it melts on the thighs of Lorn's trousers. The two ride silently, through the hushed whiteness created by the fast-falling snow, and Lorn continues to brush away snow and water.

Then, as abruptly as it has started, within the space of riding less than a kay, the snow stops falling, leaving the deadland covered with white less than a fraction of a span deep. Only puddles of slush remain on the granite of the perimeter road itself.

Lorn looks to his right. White steam-like vapor rises from the heights of the Accursed Forest, creating a misty effect above the high crowns and around the ward-wall.

Above them, the heavy gray clouds move swiftly north-ward.

"We'll get rain before we're done," predicts Kusyl.

Lorn has no doubts about that. He just hopes it does not create another fallen tree or delay the patrol too much.

C

LORN CHECKS THE locks on the armory door, then nods to the duty guard—from Juist's company. "Everything's secure. The Mirror Lancer firewagon should be here to replace these tomorrow. Pass that along to your relief. Squad leader Shynt knows already." Shynt also knows how to send a message to Lorn through Dustyn, although Lorn does not wish any interruptions on his furlough.

"Yes, ser."

The lancer captain offers a nod before turning and leaving the small white granite building. In the chill of late afternoon, Lorn walks quickly across the courtyard to pack his bag. As he nears the quarters building, he sees Kusyl standing by the door, waiting for Lorn.

"You be moving quickly, ser," observes the senior squad leader, a hint of a smile running across his face.

"I am. What about you?"

"I be leaving early in the morning."

"You're riding to Geliendra and leaving the mount there?"

"Yes, ser. That be allowed."

"I know. I wasn't questioning." Lorn offers a smile. "You're glad Shynt's the one staying, and not you?"

"Bein' senior squad leader has some privileges, ser." Kusyl grins. "What you be doing on furlough, Captain? If you don't mind my asking?"

"I've got a place outside Jakaafra. I'm from Cyad, and it's too far to try to get home without spending nearly half the time traveling. I'll just try to enjoy myself here. It'll be good not to be patrolling. What about you?"

"I'm from Fyrad. Only four or five days down. Want to see my family. So I'll travel . . . and travel."

"Have a safe journey."

"Thank you, Captain."

Lorn slips into the quarters building and back to his own

room. There, he begins to gather what he will need. He forces himself to pack the formal uniform carefully, although shimmercloth does not wrinkle easily, and he slips both the chaos glass and Ryalth's book in with his other clothes. He certainly doesn't want to leave them behind.

As the familiar mental chill of a chaos glass being used to scree him falls across his quarters, he concentrates on not allowing himself to stiffen, but instead fastens the bag and checks the wardrobe, as if to see what he may have forgotten. He already wears the Brystan sabre. The chill fades, but Lorn wonders how often he will feel it over the next two eight-days.

The sun is touching the horizon when he finally rides out through the compound gates and turns the white gelding toward Jakaafra. He looks ahead, wondering if Ryalth has come . . . or if she is still on the way. He does not dwell on other possibilities.

The sun is below the horizon when he passes the keystone that indicates he is one kay from the square, and his breath leaves white clouds in the fading light.

Lorn rides slowly through Jakaafra in the dimness of late twilight, toward the dwelling he has scarcely used. The glow of a few lamps glimmers past shutters mostly closed against the chill of a winter evening. Will there be a lamp glimmering at his small dwelling, or will he be the one to light it and wait?

The scent of burning wood fills the air as he nears the small dwelling on the east road. Lorn smiles as he sees lights past the front shutters, and he forces himself to ride to the stable. A chestnut is stalled in the small stable. As he unsaddles the gelding, his eyes pick up the blue-and-green-bordered saddle blanket.

With a smile, he closes the stable doors and carries the bag with his formal uniform and other clothing to the front door. He pauses, then knocks, listening for footsteps he does not hear in the dimness of evening, with the scents of burning wood and cooking spices sifting around him.

After a moment, the door opens, and Ryalth smiles. "You could come in. It is your dwelling."

Lorn just stands there, at the door, looking at Ryalth, her red hair, faint freckles, and creamy skin. He finally speaks. "I'm so glad you're here."

He steps forward. So does she.

How long the embrace lasts, Lorn does not know. Nor does he care.

When they step apart, he studies her again, unable to stop smiling.

"The way you look at me . . ." She looks down.

"I missed you. Each time I see you after we're apart, I realize that more."

"Sometimes . . . you're still that student I met that night. After all these years, it's hard to believe you still want to see me that much."

"More than when I was that student," Lorn admits. "Much more."

"For that, I am glad . . . more than glad." Her eyes twinkle and her lips curl into a smile as as she steps around him and closes the door, clicking the bronze latch in place. "We might be better off with this closed."

Lorn looks back. He had forgotten the door. "I suppose I do need to clean up," he finally admits as she turns from the door. "I didn't want to take the time after we finished the patrol. I was just thinking about how you might be here. . . ."

"You were more than thinking, my lancer captain. *That* I can feel."

Lorn can feel his face redden.

"So was I." Her voice is gentle.

After a moment of silence, Ryalth continues. "There is a stew and some bread. I have tried my cooking skills. I find I'm not preparing meals as often these days. This stove is like the one at my Aunt Elyset's. . . ."

"Old, I know." Lorn grins. "Of course, cooking is possibly beneath your wealth as a rising trading house?"

"Wealth . . . ?"

"Wealth, I suspect. I've heard from many sources . . ."

"Go . . . and wash up." Although her voice is stern, her eyes sparkle.

"As you command, Lady Trader." Lorn can't help grinning. "As you command."

"Your supper will be ready before you are," she cautions.

"I'll hurry." Lorn finds himself flushing again.

Ryalth smiles as she shakes her head, before turning and walking back to the ancient ceramic stove that is built out from the far wall.

Lorn carries his bag to the bedchamber. He unfolds the formal uniform and hangs it in the armoire. He smiles as he sees the two sets of blues—one very formal on one side of the hanging part of the armoire. After unclipping his scabbard and leaning the weapon in the corner of the bedchamber, he makes his way to the small bathing room where he washes quickly with the two buckets of water and the pitcher of hot water Ryalth has clearly heated for him.

Then, before he comes to the table, he retrieves a bottle of the Alafraan from the small rear storage room. "Such cooking deserves a good wine." He looks for glasses in the small cupboard but can find none and settles on two mugs that are but slightly chipped. After uncorking the bottle, he fills the mugs two-thirds full, and stands by the table.

"We deserve it, one way or another. I hope as reward. You may need it as recompense. You can sit, dear lancer." The redhead sets the stew kettle on the cracked green ceramic trivet in the middle of the table. She sniffs. "Oh . . . something's burning." She scurries back to the stove and uses a heavy woolen mitt to open the oven door. A curl of gray smoke drifts upward as she struggles to get a short baking paddle under the roughly circular loaf of dark bread. After a moment, she turns and eases the loaf into a dry woven grass basket that she carries to the table. "Good. It didn't burn. It was just the dough that I slopped on the bottom of the baking grate."

"You don't slop things." Lorn pulls out the ancient armless wooden chair and seats himself.

"When I cook, I do." Ryalth seats herself.

Lorn takes the battered wooden-handled cupridium ladle and dishes the stew into Ryalth's crockery bowl, then into his own. He nods toward the basket and the steaming loaf.

"You don't trust my cooking?" Her tone is mock-plaintive. "Even before we're to be consorted?"

"My most honored lady trader, I have always trusted your cuisine . . . long before I proposed this coming consortship. Or have you forgotten that so soon?" Lorn does his best to mimic her plaintive tone.

Her laugh is a warm caress, and he smiles inanely.

"The sole worry I have had about you," he says, "is your traveling all this way from Cyad into the near wilds of the east of Cyador."

"I did not travel alone, but your factor friend Dustyn was kind enough to provide lodging . . . for Eileyt—I thought it wise to bring an enumerator—and a hired guard."

"You were probably most wise, and even wiser not to have them here."

"Wiser for you . . . or for me?" Ryalth arches her fine eyebrows.

Lorn finds himself flushing, and takes refuge in a mouthful of the crusty hot bread. He swallows abruptly, reaching for the crockery mug that holds his Alafraan, as he senses the chill of a chaos-glass casting for him.

"Still?" Ryalth murmurs, her lips barely moving.

"It is the second time since I came off patrol," he murmurs back, lifting the mug in a toasting gesture he does not feel, forcing a smile.

"To us, despite those who watch." Ryalth responds with a smile that appears less forced than Lorn's feels to him.

"To us." His smile feels more natural as the chill of the glass fades.

"Has this happened often?" she asks quietly.

"At times since I've been here, but more often recently. A majer in Geliendra suspects that I am more than I appear. What of you?"

"But a time or two, and the chill was not near so . . . unfriendly . . . not so cold."

"Perhaps it was my father. He has recently hinted that I was right about you, and that he was mistaken."

Her fine eyebrows arch. "Your father of the Magi'i—the renowned Fourth Magus?"

"There is no Fourth Magus," Lorn points out.

"Not in name, but that is what many call him, in respect," Ryalth says. "All throughout Cyad."

Lorn laughs. He cannot help it. "He tries to discover more of you, and you of him, and neither tells me."

Ryalth shrugs so helplessly that Lorn finds himself shaking his head, half in admiration, half still in amusement.

After a moment, Ryalth takes a sip of the Alafraan, and then some of the stew. "It does have a good taste."

His mouth full, Lorn nods.

They both eat for a time, until Ryalth looks up. "I've never been consorted," she says slowly.

"Nor I, dear lady."

"I know it must be recorded for the Emperor."

"Recorded for, but not sent to him," Lorn points out. "Unless requested. It may be that no one will request the records of the town of Jakaafra for a long time." He shrugs. "If they do, what will they find? That a lancer consorted with a merchanter lady?"

"That is but what they would find in Cyad."

"But where they find it conveys a far different message. Were we to consort in Cyad, all manner of schemes would be placed at our doorsteps. Here . . . the message is that we wish to escape notice."

Ryalth frowns slightly. "You think that to be true?"

"I hope many will take it so. If indeed they discover such."

"With Magi'i screeing us both?"

Lorn shrugs. "They may not scree farther, now that they have seen us together in a quiet dwelling. If none see the signing of the book tomorrow . . ."

"I care not who may know."

"I would prefer none know till you return to Cyad. I will give you scrolls to my parents, and Myryan."

"You would make me a messenger, now?"

Lorn flushes. "I meant just for you to carry them to Cyad and send them by messenger from there. That way, they would learn earlier."

"So long as that is what you intended . . ." The serious phrasing that begins her admonition gives way to lilting, almost laughing, words that are followed by a grin.

"Woman . . . trader . . . you are most dangerous."

"*You* are the dangerous one."

"Not me. Not now."

Ryalth brushes off his disclaimer. "You worry about this majer?"

"I would not have him strike at you."

"No. He will not strike at me. His lancer honor is too precious for that. Were he a merchanter, now . . ."

They laugh again, together.

CI

LORN PACES BACK and forth in the dwelling's main chamber, trying not to let the Brystan sabre bang into anything. He supposes he should have worn the lancer weapon, but he feels more comfortable with the older weapon, and it feels somehow right.

He glances toward the bedchamber where Ryalth is fastening a scarf over hair that she has laboriously curled, pinned, and braided. She wears a formal blue tunic with loose flowing blue shimmercloth trousers. Then comes a blue woolen cloak, with a narrow cream and green border, before she studies herself in a hand-mirror.

"Are you ready for me to get the mounts?" he asks.

"Are you worried?" Ryalth glances at Lorn, wearing his formal Lancer cream uniform with the green and white piping. "You keep walking back and forth."

"No. I just feel useless at the moment."

The redhead turns and studies him. "You're going to make

sure that everyone knows you're a lancer." She grins. "So much for a quiet consorting."

"Everyone in Jakaafra would know no matter what I wore," he points out. "Besides, they'll all be looking at you, not at me."

"Go get the mounts."

He bows with a smile. "As you command, my lady."

"Go." Both her mouth and eyes return the smile.

The clear mid-morning remains chill, but the breeze out of the northeast is light, sometimes even dying away, as Lorn leads both mounts from the small stable to the door. He had saddled them before he had washed and dressed. A carriage might have been more appropriate, but he knows of none for hire in Jakaafra.

He waits for a time longer before the door, holding the reins of the two mounts, shifting his weight from one foot to the other, and wondering what other preparations Ryalth makes behind the privacy screen. He is almost ready to tie the horses to the hedge and go back inside when Ryalth steps out and latches the door behind her.

"You see? I wasn't long." She glances at his face. "Not too long, anyway."

"You're even more lovely than usual." Lorn offers a hand as she mounts.

"I should get consorted more often."

"I'm sorry it wasn't earlier." Lorn mounts easily.

They ride slowly toward the square and the center of town. As they pass one of the larger dwellings—on the north side of the road, two women standing outside the green ceramic privacy screen watch closely without speaking. Once Lorn and Ryalth have passed, the women's voices drift toward them on the barely perceptible breeze.

". . . there! Looks like a consorting . . . ever I saw one. . . ."

". . . captain, all right, handsome as he is, but who be the lady?"

"That's shimmercloth, and the cloak—that says there's lancer and Magi'i blood in the union. Don't see that often, not here."

"Love match . . . I tell you . . . no other reason it'd be here."

Lorn smiles and leans toward Ryalth. "It is a love match, you know?"

"I know. I've known that for years. It took you a while."

He shrugs expansively, but the wide smile remains on his face.

The recording building lies on the west side of the small town square, around the corner and a good two hundred cubits from the side lane that holds Dustyn's establishment.

More people watch from the porches around the square, a good half-score from the wide porch of the cooper's, and half that from the weaver's adjoining building.

"I've never seen so many people here," Lorn says quietly.

"Dear . . ." Ryalth laughs. "They don't get to see this often."

"A consorting? It happens all the time."

"There are many lancers, and few lancer officers," she points out.

"You're the one," he counters. "There are but a handful of trading houses, and none so large headed by a woman." Still, Ryalth's words nag at him. Despite his mother's words, he has never considered, not fully, how few lancer officers and Magi'i there truly are in Cyador. He pushes that thought away as he looks at the far side of the square.

Dustyn stands on the stone walkway to the right of the steps up to the yellow brick recording building. He wears a rich brown cloak, trimmed in blue, over brown trousers and a good blue tunic. Beside him is a silver-haired woman who smiles broadly as Lorn and Ryalth ride toward her. Alongside the factor and his consort stand an enumerator in blue—Eileyt, Lorn assumes—and a guard wearing merchanter blue.

Eileyt's gray eyes take in Lorn. Lorn smiles politely. The slender enumerator bows, a bow of respect.

Ryalth dismounts gracefully, barely placing any weight on the hand that Lorn offers. The guard steps forward to take the reins of both mounts.

"Greetings, Captain, and my best wishes to you, Lady

Merchanter." Dustyn inclines his head first to Lorn and then to Ryalth. "This be my consort Wryul." The spirit factor gestures to the silver-haired woman.

"Thank you." Lorn nods, as does Ryalth.

"You look lovely," Wryul addresses Ryalth. "And to come so far . . ."

"We would have had to wait years for Lorn to return to Cyad," Ryalth explains. "I'm very happy to be here."

As the couple turns toward the steps of the small building, a closed carriage of polished golden oak and drawn by a pair of matched grays approaches from the eastern end of the avenue and enters the square.

"That be Kylynzar, I do believe," exclaims Dustyn as the coach draws to a halt and as a wiry white-haired man in a maroon cloak steps out. The white-haired man turns and offers his hand to a gray-haired woman in a matching maroon cloak.

"A quiet consorting?" Ryalth murmurs under her breath.

"I told no one except the ones I had to," Lorn murmurs back.

"Then why is half the town here?"

"It's not half. . . ." Lorn protests.

"It is if you look behind us around the square." Ryalth touches his hand to call his attention to the two who have arrived in the coach.

"Captain, Lady," offers the man in the maroon cloak, "with your decision to honor Jakaafra in your place of consorting, we could do no less than to honor you." A wry smile follows the words. "We have not met. We have corresponded. I am Kylynzar, and this is my consort Mylora."

Lorn and Ryalth incline their heads.

"We are pleased to meet you," Lorn says.

"Not so pleased as are we."

Dustyn clears his throat. "Ah . . . ser . . . lady. Wasyk be waiting for you."

Ryalth lifts her eyebrows. Lorn finds an embarrassed grin on his face. They walk up the two stone steps to the open double doors of white oak, then step inside.

The recording hall is but fifteen cubits deep and half that in width. The floor is over-polished white marble. Four tall windows—two on each side—provide the illumination. The panes are glazed with ancient, blue-tinged glass. The hall is empty of all furnishings except for a single white sunstone pedestal.

A heavy-set figure stands behind the open book that rests on the stand of white sunstone. Each page of the book is a cubit in height and two thirds that in width. The man wears a sash-like white shimmercloth scarf wide enough almost to conceal his brown tunic, despite his bulk.

"I am Wasyk, the recorder of consortings. Approach . . . you who wish to record your consortship here in the town of Jakaafra." The recorder inclines his head to the couple.

Lorn and Ryalth walk slowly toward the book and sash-wearer.

Only Dustyn and Wryul and Kylynzar and Mylora have followed the couple into the building, and the four of them stand at the back, just inside the doors.

Lorn and Ryalth stand two cubits back from the sunstone pedestal and the book upon it. Both look to the recorder.

"Do you two—Captain Lorn of the Mirror Lancers and Lady Ryalth of Ryalor House—declare your intention to take each other as consorts?"

"I do," Lorn replies.

"I do." Ryalth's words are as firm as Lorn's, if more melodic.

"Would you each inscribe your name in the book before you, signifying that such is your choice of your own free will, in the prosperity of chaos and light and under the oversight of the Emperor of Light?" Wasyk extends a shimmering white pen.

Ryalth takes the cupridium-tipped pen and writes her name. She passes it to Lorn, who in turn, writes his name.

Wasyk takes the pen and replaces it in the ceremonial cupridium holder, then clears his throat before declaiming, "As entered in the book of Jakaafra, you are hereafter consorts." Wasyk beams at the couple. "May you always be fulfilled in the light and in the fullness of time."

Lorn slips the shiny silver onto the pages of the book, as Dustyn had told him. He stands there for a long moment.

"You could kiss me," Ryalth murmurs.

Lorn does.

He can hear a gentle sigh from the back of the small building.

"Such a lovely couple . . ."

Arm in arm, the newly consorted pair walks toward the door.

Kylynzar steps up, coughs gently, and speaks. "It be forward, we know, but Dustyn and Wryul and Mylora and me, we'd like you to come to the Brick Hearth. Our treat, if you would. It not be that often that a consorting such as yours happens in Jakaafra."

How can they refuse?

"We would be more than happy to join you," Ryalth says brightly. "Our families are far from here, and your hospitality is most welcome."

"Most welcome," Lorn adds.

"It has been three generations since a lancer officer has lived in Jakaafra, leastwise with his consort, if only part of the time," says the gray-haired Mylora.

"We'll be here when we can," Lorn says, recalling his mother's words just before he had left Cyad—her observation that lancer officers were almost as exalted and rare as the Magi'i outside of Cyad.

When they step inside the Brick Hearth Inn, propelled forward by Dustyn and Kylynzar, Lorn's mouth drops open. The public room has been cleared, and a table set against the side wall. On the green linen of the table are platters heaped with slices of melons, wedges of cheeses, and baskets of bread. At the left end of the table are a score of bottles of amber wine.

Kylynzar and Dustyn both laugh.

"Little enough we can do," Kylynzar says. "If you'd not mind, we did ask a few other folk to join us."

"Of course." Lorn hopes his voice does not betray too much surprise.

Kylynzar gestures, and within moments near-on a score of others have flocked into the public room, all dressed in their best. Lorn recognizes only one couple—the ostler from the compound—Suforis—and his consort Lesyna. Both wear cloaks of brownish red. Suforis smiles broadly as his eyes meet Lorn's.

To the right of Suforis is Eileyt, and he smiles as well.

"Quiet consorting?" Ryalth murmurs.

"I had no idea. . . ." He whispers back.

"I can tell. You look like a stunned bullock."

"One moment!" bellows Dustyn. "Kylynzar's better with words 'n me, and he's got a few."

The hubbub dies away.

"Just a few," announces the grower. "Most of you know I never was too fond of lancer officers, and outside of Dustyn, not passing fond of factors, either. These two are different, and I wanted to let them know that the real folk of Cyador are most glad of it. Now, let 'em have a first bite, and then join in."

Still flushing, Lorn edges toward the table.

Dustyn extends two mugs in which he has poured the ruddy yet amber vintage. "You haven't tried the like of this."

Lorn grins and accepts the mug, as does Ryalth.

Lorn tries a wedge of the white cheese, and sips some of the amber wine as he steps back from the table and turns to his redhead. "This is different, sweet and dry at the same time."

She takes one sip, then a second. "It's strong."

Kylynzar approaches. "That's my amber melon ice wine." He glances at Ryalth. "Perhaps you might . . . Later, of course." The wiry grower flushes. "I did not mean to talk of trade."

Ryalth laughs gently. "It is good, and we will talk later."

"You are gracious, and you have dealt fairly, yet firmly." Kylynzar shakes his head. "I *will* talk no more of trade." He bows slightly to Lorn. "We have not seen exactly eye-to-eye, Captain, yet you have lived up to your duty. And my cousin, he has told me that you always face the wild creatures first, and not last like so many officers." He laughs, "And your consort has done far better by us than all the other factors of Cyador combined. In fact, much of our decision to be here and offer hospitality arises from her, and it is a pleasure to see that she is as beautiful and charming as she is an effective merchanter." The grower inclines his head to Ryalth again.

"She is beautiful and charming, and very effective," Lorn agrees.

Eileyt slips through the crowd and bows. "Captain, my best wishes to you."

"Thank you. My gratitude to you for all the assistance you have provided to Ryalth and Ryalor House."

Before either can say another word, a heavy-set man in a brown tunic so dark it is almost black steps up. Lorn recognizes Wasyk without his shimmercloth scarf.

"Never seen such a handsome couple," says the recorder. "Really created a dither here. Hasn't been a lancer consorting or a merage consorting here in more than a score of years."

"We didn't know," Lorn admits, keeping his eyes on the big man, even as he wonders how long the not-quite-impromptu festivities will continue.

"You both from Cyad?"

"I grew up in Fyrad mostly," Ryalth explains, "until I was older."

"I was raised in Cyad," Lorn acknowledges.

"Won't talk long, but wanted to tell you both that folk'll remember this day." Wasyk raises his mug.

Lorn takes but a tiny sip, knowing he will have many sips yet to come.

After taking a sip of her wine, Ryalth reaches out and squeezes Lorn's hand, warmly. "We'll remember it a long time, a very long time."

Lorn has no doubts about that. And he'd thought it would be a quiet consorting. . . .

CII

LORN STRETCHES GINGERLY, yawning, his arm still around the redhead sleeping beside him. The mid-morning light seeps through the closed shutters of the dwelling's bedchamber, thin slivers of light angling toward the floor. The air is chill, because they had gone to bed early the night before and not stoked up the ceramic stove in the main room.

Smiling reflectively, and looking at the peaceful and lightly freckled face of his consort, Lorn still finds it hard to believe that the festivities of their consorting two days earlier had lasted most of the day and into the evening. He and Ryalth had finally slipped away near sunset, to more than a few knowing looks. The day after the ceremony they had spent quietly—the first day Lorn can remember in years where he or Ryalth had not had to rise early for some reason or another.

"Mmmmm." Ryalth nuzzles up to his cheek and kisses him gently.

"Mmmm to you, too, sleepy-head."

She yawns quietly, then snuggles against him. "You don't know how good it feels to sleep in the morning."

"I was just thinking that."

"But you woke up. . . ."

"It *is* mid-morning," Lorn points out.

"It's still cold." She shivers and pulls the worn quilt up to her ears—one-handed.

"I'll start the fire in the stove."

"Mmmmm . . . if you don't mind . . . too much?"

He grins at the mock-plaintive note in her voice. "I'll start it and then come back until it's warmer."

The stone floor—the part not covered by the few braided rugs—is indeed cold to Lorn's bare feet. He pads into the main chamber where he sorts out some of the thin strips of wood in the starter basket, and then piles some of the larger pieces above it in the firebox. Then he concentrates.

Hst! The tiny chaos bolt is sufficient to create a small blaze within the stove.

Lorn smiles and walks back to the bedchamber, where he slips under the covers again.

"Your feet are *cold.*"

"I did get the fire started in the stove."

"Good." Ryalth kisses his cheek, then pauses, before asking, "Have you ridden around Jakaafra much?"

"Except for the ward-wall? No. When you're on duty most of the time . . . well . . . the only riding I really did was to Jakaafra to deal with Dustyn and to arrange for the consorting and dwelling."

"You should. Now that you're consorted, you can wear that uniform when you ride with me."

"I hadn't thought of wearing anything else."

"You hadn't thought of wearing anything at all today, you lecherous consort," Ryalth teases.

Lorn flushes. "We've never had days like this together before, and they won't last that long."

"I know." She sighs softly and hugs him, then kisses his cheek again. "I hoped for this for a long time. I didn't think it was possible."

"Lancers consort with merchanters."

"But Magi'i don't, and you were a student magus."

"I still would have."

"The way you are now, you would," she admits.

"I don't think I could have been otherwise." His arms encircle her, and they kiss, a long and lingering kiss.

They both stiffen as they sense the chill of a chaos glass screeing them, and they hold to each other, barely breathing, until the scrutiny ends, and the chill fades away.

"Whoever . . . has no decency." Ryalth snorts, leaning back just slightly.

Lorn wonders if his small use of chaos drew Maran, for it could be no other, or if the majer is merely curious about Lorn's furlough.

"I didn't feel that yesterday or at the consort signing . . . did you?" she asks.

"No."

"Then he must think you've enticed your mistress to Ja-kaafra. I hope he gets very jealous. Very jealous."

"He might be."

"It's getting warmer," she says. "What did you do? Stoves don't heat up that quickly."

"A trick I learned as a student," Lorn admits.

"Be careful who sees that." She frowns.

"I am. You're the only one who knows."

A trace of another frown crosses her brow before she speaks. "Best it remain that way, my very dear lancer." She half sits up, pulling the coverlet around her. "You didn't read me a poem. One from the book. You brought it, didn't you? You know it was really my first present to you?"

He smiles, thankful he can. "It's in my bag. You want me to read one now?"

"One . . . we're waiting for the stove to warm things up."

Lorn eases out of the bed a second time, extracts the silver-covered volume from the bag, and then extends it to her. "You read one. Your favorite." He slips back under the covers.

"Tonight, you have to read me one."

"I will."

She leafs through the book, then stops, nodding. After a moment she reads.

> Like a dusk without a cloud,
> a leaf without a tree,
> a shell without a sea . . .
> the greening of the pear
> slips by . . .

Lorn smiles gently to himself as she finishes the verses.

> . . . and wait for pears and praise
> . . . and wait for pears and praise.

"I like that one, too," he says, leaning next to her and kissing her cheek. After a moment, he takes the book and gently closes the cover.

Her fingertips hold him at bay. "You promised we could take a ride."

"Do you really want to ride around Jakaafra?"

Ryalth nods. "People should see us, and the air will feel good."

"And?"

"I might get some more ideas. I think I know where I can sell that amber melon ice wine, if it will travel."

"Always the trader?"

"Not always." She kisses his cheek again. "Not always."

CIII

LORN COCKS HIS head to the side, then looks down at the draft of the scroll he writes on the table that serves for eating and writing and anything else in the small dwelling. He glances toward the glassed panes of the window whose inner shutters he has opened to get more light. Outside the warmth of the dwelling, a light but cold wind blows through a gray mid-morning.

When he had saddled both mounts earlier, Lorn had been glad for his winter jacket. From the table, warmed by the ceramic stove, he studies the sky once more. The clouds are high, and still do not look to bring rain or snow, or not soon.

He dips the pen again and adds a sentence to the draft of the scroll before him, then pauses before crossing out several words and penning in changes to the side.

"You are busy this morning," Ryalth observes as she emerges from the bedchamber, wearing working merchanter blues. She walks over to Lorn, and bends down and kisses the back of his neck.

"Are you ready?" he asks, replacing the pen in its holder and looking up at her.

"As ready as you, my dear lancer." She smiles warmly. "You do not mind accompanying me on merchanter business?"

"Not at all."

"Even after yesterday?"

Lorn laughs. They had ridden nearly ten kays to a hamlet where a smith supposedly forged unique iron implements, only to find that their uniqueness was only in their size and crudeness. Then they had talked to a pearapple grower whose fruit was renowned in the region, but Ryalth had decided even from the dried and winter stored samples that the fruit would remain a local delicacy because it bruised too easily. Most of the day had been like that.

"It is just that I seldom get this far east and north. . . ." She shakes her head. "I would never get this far were it not for you." She sets a blue leather wallet on the edge of the table, and there is the dull clink of coins. While Lorn has seen it before, he had never looked that closely, thinking it a trader's wallet, and little more. This time, he sees, embossed on the leather, a green emblem—the intertwined letters "R" and "L" set within an inverted triangle.

Lorn studies the emblem, his lips curling into a smile.

"That's the symbol I've been using from the beginning," she explains.

"You never showed me."

"You never asked."

Lorn shakes his head. "I can't ask what I don't know about."

"Neither can I." She laughs. "Someone I love taught me that a long time ago."

They both laugh.

"What do you think of this?" Lorn hands her the scroll he has written. He stands and looks over Ryalth's shoulder as she reads through his revised and crossed out words.

> . . . Father had written some time back that, after discussing possible consorts with Jerial, he had decided that the lady I have spent so much time with

over the years is most suitable. Because that was
also my inclination, and because she is my love,
and because it appears likely that I will not be returned to Cyad at any time in the years immediately before me, she traveled to Jakaafra, where we
were consorted.

I know this was not exactly as we all had hoped
for the placement and timing of such an event, but
you all know how unwise making such a union
public in Cyad would be at this time. Mother has
also told me that she views the lady as most lovely.

Ryalth looks up. "You didn't tell me that."

"I didn't? I thought I did."

She shakes her head ruefully. "Lorn . . . my dearest lancer,
there are times when I can almost see that there are thoughts
running through your mind, and you look as though you
ought to be talking, and I think you are hearing all the words
you would speak. Then, I think you sometimes feel you have
spoken them."

"I will try to be better with you," he says slowly.

"Do not fret about it. That is the way you are."

"Sometimes I dwell in my thoughts and words too much."
He glances from the redhead to the scroll. "What do you
think?"

"Do you think they'll be too terribly upset?"

"I don't think so. Did you know that mother told me not
to spend too much time with them when I was in Cyad? She
said to spend it with 'my friend.' "

"I hope they won't be too upset."

"They won't be. They want us to be happy."

"People say that," she points out, "until someone else's
happiness upsets them. I still worry about upsetting your parents."

"If you'd rather I not tell them. . . ."

"You have to . . . I understand that. All may be as you say.
But I worry. So do you, or you would not take such care in

drafting your scroll." The redhead looks toward the door. "It's colder out, isn't it?"

Lorn nods.

"It won't get warmer while we wait."

He smiles as he takes the draft scroll from her and sets it on the table. Then he takes the sabre from where he has set it in the corner and attaches the scabbard to his uniform belt. Then he dons the white leather winter jacket and his winter riding gloves.

Ryalth wears a wool-lined blue leather vest over her tunic, and then a heavy dark blue woolen cloak. Her gloves are also dark blue.

"I've already saddled them."

They walk the fifty cubits to the stable together. Lorn leads out the chestnut first, then the white gelding, closing the stable door and then mounting.

The raw and damp wind blows in their face out of the northwest as they ride toward the square, and the smells that had hinted at coming spring in the days immediately after their consorting have vanished with the return of winter. Neither speaks as their mounts carry them the kay into the center of Jakaafra.

Eileyt and Usylt, the trade guard, are standing under the narrow porch of Dustyn's establishment as Lorn and Ryalth ride down the lane from the square. As Lorn and Ryalth rein up, the two men hurry down from the porch to untie their horses and mount.

"We're only going across the square," Ryalth says, "to the cuprite master's shop."

The shop is on the south side of the square, close to two hundred cubits from the recording hall, and distinguished by a small square sign fastened to the eaves of the overhanging front porch. The sign shows a yellow lamp, and the porch is empty. Lorn dismounts and ties the gelding to the short hitching rail at the very end, then offers a hand to Ryalth.

She smiles as she takes it. "I'll have to get used to doing without all this courtesy before long."

"Enjoy it while we can."

After she dismounts, Ryalth unfastens the blue leather Ryalor House wallet and extends it to Eileyt. She nods to Lorn. "It's custom in the smaller towns. If you have an enumerator, then he should disburse and collect the coins."

"I'll watch the mounts," Usylt says, more to affirm that he wishes to remain outside, Lorn suspects.

"Thank you," Ryalth replies.

Lorn hurries up the three wooden steps and crosses the wide porch from which many had watched their consorting nearly an eightday earlier. He wonders at how quickly the time has passed for them and how soon he must return to duty and Ryalth must return to Cyad. He cannot help but worry that her absence will not help her trading. With those thoughts on his mind, he opens the door for Ryalth, then motions for Eileyt to enter as well.

The enumerator shakes his head and stands back to let Lorn follow Ryalth.

Inside, Ryalth steps forward to study the items on a small table which include several ornate lamps, a kettle, and a lamp that looks more like a storm lantern of some sort. Ryalth studies the storm lantern.

The odor of hot metal permeates the shop. In the rear are a small forge, two workbenches, and a rack containing tools Lorn does not recognize. A man appears to be heating something in or over the forge, but his back is to Lorn, and a youth pumps a bellows, sweat streaming down his forehead. The young man's eyes widen as he sees Ryalth, and he says something to the crafter.

The crafter turns. He is a squarish man, short, not even to Lorn's chin, but muscular, with stubby fingers that set aside what appears to be an ornate bronze vessel. He steps toward the three figures at the front of his shop. "Lady Trader . . . Captain . . . I be Ghylset." The crafter's eyes flick from Ryalth to Lorn and back to Ryalth. "What might I do for you?"

"You show good work, master crafter," Ryalth offers. "Better than many I have seen, even in Cyad and Fyrad."

"Thank you." The hint of a frown accompanies his words. "Do you seek something?"

"I seek good work." Ryalth half-turns and gestures at the table and the objects upon it. "Which of these might show such?"

"The one you be looking at, Lady."

Ryalth studies the bronze lamp carefully.

"Begging yer pardon, Lady Trader . . . but if you'll be looking at the way the mantel's set . . . that's the secret . . . that lamp . . . really more a lantern but small enough to carry by mount or ship or set on a carriage, and it will burn through a gale and the heaviest of rains."

Lorn can sense the truth of the crafter's words, and he knows Ryalth can as well.

"Could not another cuprite master copy this?" questions the redhead.

"Well . . . supposing they could, but it'd take someone good as me, and I've figured some ways to make the seals with the glass tighter 'n most, and quicker to form." Ghylset shrugs. "At five silvers a lamp for a lamp that'll burn in the worst of storms. . . . I don't think there's none can match me for quality nor price."

"Four silvers apiece if I order in lots of a half-score," Ryalth suggests flatly.

"Half-score?"

"Can you make a score of them by the turn of spring?" Ryalth asks.

"A score . . . mayhap more." The crafter frowns. "But four . . . that is low."

"Nine golds for a score," Ryalth says firmly. "If they sell, I will order more."

"Nine golds . . . aye . . . that be not too burdensome. Yet . . . I cannot begin so many . . . not without some estimation of faith . . . beggin' yer pardon, Lady Trader."

While Ryalth and the cuprite crafter talk, Lorn studies another series of lamps set on the shelf against the outer wall, taking in those of various sizes. He smiles as he sees one that is smaller than his clenched fist, wondering as he does what use such a lamp might have.

"... three golds now ... so you may begin ... and two more—Dustyn will deliver them—when you bring the lamps to him to be shipped to me. I will send four more golds when I receive the lamps."

"They say you have been most fair. . . ." Ghylset nods slowly.

Ryalth looks to Eileyt, who produces three golds from the Ryalor House wallet he carries for her.

"I look forward to your lamps, master crafter." Ryalth's smile is professional, yet with the suggestion of warmth.

"They be the best."

Lorn nods to himself as he follows her from the shop. Because she can assess both worth and character, Ryalth has a definite advantage, and she offers enough warmth so that she does not have to haggle endlessly.

"Which crafter do you wish to see next?" Lorn asks as they step out onto the windswept porch.

"No crafter—an oilseed grower." Ryalth adjusts her cloak.

"The one with the perfumed oils?"

"There's always a market for good oils, and if they're different . . ." She shrugs, then mounts her chestnut.

"Dustyn says his place is a solid four kays out the west road," Lorn says as he quickly mounts. "I hope this works out better than the pearapple grower."

"Most don't," Ryalth cautions him, turning her mount toward the recording hall. "You should know that by now. That's why I visit so many."

"I know." Lorn guides the gelding alongside her chestnut.

Behind them, Eileyt nods as he and Usylt ride after them toward the west road from the square.

CIV

IN THE CLEAR gray light preceding dawn, Lorn and Ryalth ride side by side on the perimeter road to the southwest, toward Fyrad and Cyad, and away from Jakaafra. Behind them ride Eileyt and Usylt, the guard.

The air is still, and frost has settled on the deadland, and on the winter-gray trees to their right, well out beyond the deadland. Lorn wears his winter jacket over his duty uniform, as well as the winter garrison cap. Ryalth wears her vest under the heavy blue woolen cloak. Faint puffs of steam indicate their breathing.

Lorn glances to his left, at the glow of the sun about to rise from behind the ward-wall and the Accursed Forest. Somehow, the days of Lorn's furlough have raced by until none are left, and he and Ryalth must return to their duties.

"You have the scrolls?" he looks at Ryalth, taking in the red hair, the light freckles and the deep blue eyes he will miss more than he had ever thought. "And you will send them by private messenger?"

"We agreed on that." Her lips curl into a smile that is both ironic and resigned, yet warm and accepting.

He laughs once, gently. "You will take care on the ride to the Great Canal?"

"We will, and I will send you a scroll when I reach Cyad." She smiles softly. "You need to get back. I would not have you fail to be where you must be."

Lorn reaches out and takes her gloved hand in his as they ride side by side. "I dislike parting, especially now."

"I will visit as I can," she promises. "But you need to go."

Lorn nods. "Take care." He gives her hand a last squeeze, then releases it.

"I will." Her smile is sad.

Lorn eases the gelding to the edge of the road, where he watches as the three ride southwest. Ryalth looks back several times. Finally, he turns the gelding and starts back toward the compound. He has not ridden two hundred cubits when he looks back over his shoulder. Ryalth is looking at him, as well, and he raises his arm. After a time, they both look away.

Lorn continues slowly back along the perimeter road, and the orangish light of dawn floods up from behind the ward-wall and the green canopy of the Accursed Forest. He studies the unseen darkness that is all too real, and wonders how the coming Patrol will fare.

Shortly, he eases the white gelding past the duty guards and through the compound gates, his eyes checking the courtyard, noting that both Kusyl and Shynt have begun to muster their squads outside the quarters building.

He dismounts outside the stable and leads the gelding inside.

Suforis hurries up. "Ser, you'd not be going on Patrol today?"

"Tomorrow. That's soon enough." Lorn extends his mount's reins to the blond ostler, then unfastens his gear from behind the saddle.

"She be a lovely lady, ser," Suforis observes, as he takes the gelding's reins from Lorn. "Though I was surprised that Dustyn asked me 'n Lesyna to the festivities."

"We were glad you were there." Lorn laughs, almost ruefully. "You two and Dustyn were the only people I really knew." He shifts his grip on his gear, then nods to Suforis. "I'd best be getting where I should be."

"Yes, ser."

Lorn walks briskly to the quarters building, stopping but long enough to drop his gear bag in his duty quarters, and then returns to the courtyard to see Kusyl, waiting before the formed up second squad.

"Ser." Kusyl bows as Lorn approaches.

"Squad leader."

"Halfscore and four, ser. One missing, ser."

"Very good, Kusyl. You may dismiss them to their duties. We will inspect all blades and gear before the noon meal.

Once they are working on their gear, I'd like to meet in the outer study."

"Yes, ser."

Lorn nods and heads to the first squad.

"Ser, halfscore and five, ser. All present," Shynt announces.

"Very good, squad leader. You may dismiss them to their duties. We will inspect all blades and gear before the noon meal. Kusyl and you and I will meet in the outer study once they're working on their blades and gear."

"Yes, ser."

Lorn turns and heads for the study, hoping that there are no scrolls or messages bearing ill news. There, the door has been unlocked, doubtless by Kusyl, but the outer desk is bare. He opens the door to the inner study, but his desk is equally bare.

For some reason, that disturbs him more, he feels, than would have scathing scrolls from either Majer Maran or Commander Meylyd. Slowly, he takes off his garrison cap and hangs it on one of the wall pegs, then doffs the winter jacket.

Tomorrow, Second Company will resume its patrols, and Lorn has few doubts that the struggles with the Accursed Forest will continue.

CV

THE EMPEROR LEANS forward in the malachite and silver chair that dominates the smaller audience hall. His eyes are hard as he fixes them upon the First Magus. "If you would, most honored of Magi'i, explain just how you plan to make this barrier work, and how long the process will take."

Chyenfel bows. "But, of course, Your Mightiness. All know that there are chaos towers that confine the Accursed Forest. As you have been informed, of the dozen towers that once enfolded the Forest, three have failed. Two of those were at the cardinal points of the wall. Where once every tower station at the cardinal points had two functioning towers, now only the south and west stations have two towers. The other failed chaos tower is the northeast midpoint tower, and that has meant forcing more chaos energy through the cupridium cables on the northeast ward-wall. That requires more chaos energies precisely from the cardinal point tower stations most burdened. Thus . . ." the First Magus shrugs, ". . . the barrier on that wall is not so strong as on the other walls, and there have been more attempts by the Accursed Forest to break through the wards there."

In the far more modest malachite chair behind the Emperor's shoulder, Ryenyel sits, her eyes not upon the First Magus nor upon the Majer-Commander of Mirror Lancers, but, once again, upon Bluoyal, the Merchanter Advisor to the Emperor of Light.

"We will use the remaining power in the towers to create a barrier," Chyenfel continues, "a barrier like that which separates the inner part of a tower from the outer, and that barrier will also place a slumber-ward, if you will, over all of the Accursed Forest. We think re-setting the chaos fields to do this will take a good two-score mages. It will take a season to assemble all that is necessary, and but an afternoon to accomplish it."

"*If* it can be done," suggests the Emperor.

"So you should be able to move the towers by the fall if His Mightiness agrees to this now?" asks Bluoyal quietly.

All faces turn to the merchanter advisor at his interruption. To Bluoyal's right, Rynst nods slightly, almost as if urging the merchanter to go on.

"We are seeing more pirate attacks upon our trading vessels," the heavy trader continues. "Yet we understand that we can expect less support from the fireships and fewer Mirror Foot on our ships with firelances. For generations, those chaos towers have sat around a forest that hasn't caused a shade of the trouble that the barbarians or the pirates have, all because the ancients thought there was something there. So a few wild creatures escape, and a few cattle and sheep are killed. It would be far cheaper to pay for the lost live-stock, and move the lancers and the towers to where they can do real good."

"If you may recall," offers Chyenfel, "no chaos tower can be moved, unless it was placed in something that contains it and can be moved, such as a fireship. The records and history are quite clear on that. They are also quite clear on the dangers of the Forest."

"Has anyone tried to move them in, say, the past five generations?" counters Bluoyal.

"Which one would you like to lose, honored merchanter? If we try to move one surrounding the Forest, we cannot contain the wild order, even under the new barrier. Why would we wish to move any of the others?"

"I was not thinking of the others, most honored First Magus."

"As we have told the Emperor before, although you may have missed such, honored advisor on trade and commerce, the towers will still be there, although none will be able to see or sense them."

"Not sense them?" Bluoyal raises his bushy eyebrows.

"They and the wards will be twisted so that they will not quite be as they are . . . or that they do not appear as such, more precisely."

The Emperor of Light frowns. "If the towers . . . vanish . . . will this not alarm the people? You had not mentioned this aspect of your barrier. What of the lancers?"

"We would see no need of the present numbers of lancers," answers Chyenfel cautiously.

"So that they could be moved northward, or placed on the new sail-powered warships?" interjects Bluoyal.

"That would be the decision of His Mightiness, in consultation with the honored Majer-Commander," replies the First Magus.

"A moment." Toziel lifts his hand. "Let me make this most clear. You are telling me that unless I agree to your plan, I will have no choice?"

"Sire . . ." Chyenfel offers patiently. "You have no choice.

If you try to move the towers, they will fail, and the Accursed Forest will reclaim much of eastern Cyador. If you do nothing, the towers will fail within years, if not sooner, and the Forest will do the same."

Toziel looks at the perspiring magus. "I cannot say that I am pleased with the performance of the Magi'i."

"Sire . . . this day has been foretold from the very first. You have read the original writings of the Firstborn. . . ."

"And I would be the man to be Emperor when it may occur?" Toziel's words are like cold cupridium. "So . . . for how many more years will your plan confine the Accursed Forest, so that Cyador may continue to prosper?"

"Sire . . . as you know, we would use all the power in the Towers to create a barrier, the slenderest barrier of time passing, and by doing so, we would layer order and chaos about the Forest, and place the Forest in a type of sleep, so that it would come to resemble a normal forest. . . ."

"You have told me that. How long?"

"Twenty-five to thirty score years, we would judge—if . . . *if*, no one brings a focused order or chaos of that same magnitude to the ward-walls."

"How could that occur, if there is no other source of focused chaos or order besides the chaos towers—which are failing—and the Forest which you will lull into an enchanted sleep?"

"We know of no such way, sire." Chyenfel bows.

"As you say . . . I have no choice. Let it be done." Toziel stands. "We will not visit this issue again." He turns and moves toward the exit from the chamber.

A smile flits across Bluoyal's face, a smile noted by Ryenyel alone before she turns to follow her consort.

Rynst's cold eyes scan first Bluoyal and then the First Magus. The three advisors remain standing in place until the chamber is vacant of imperial presence.

As is their custom after the audience with the advisors, the Emperor and his consort return to the Empress's salon, where she seats herself on the white divan.

Toziel studies his consort. "I do believe we have finally

had enough meetings on the barrier for the Accursed Forest so that Chyenfel can create it without interference."

"You could have ordered him to proceed a year ago," Ryenyel points out, "were it not for other considerations."

"Folk—even high advisors—must talk and talk and repeat themselves until they are confortable with an idea, for if they are not . . ."

"The delay is greater," Ryenyel finishes drily.

"And I must appear almost dense, as if forced into acceding to the plan." Toziel shakes his head.

Faint smiles appear on both their faces.

"And all the Magi'i had to understand that the towers there *will* fail."

"You mean Kharl and Liataphi . . . perhaps Kien," she suggests.

"Kien understands. He always has. He prefers to advise, and stand in the shadows. That is why he will never seek to be First Magus. Or even Third."

"Many would not agree."

Toziel grins at her. "But you do, and I trust your judgment." The grin fades, and he paces to the window. There he looks out at the heavy spring rain for a time before he turns and speaks again. "Each eightday we delay, we risk failure of another tower, and the chance that the Accursed Forest will leap the wards beyond our ability to contain it."

After a silence, the Empress-consort speaks. "Rynst now understands that Bluoyal only wishes the towers and the lancers in order to support the merchanters' trading ships. He also understands that while he cannot brook Chyenfel, the First Magus can be trusted far more than the Second. Or the Third."

"Only now?" Toziel snorts. "Or is it that he fears Bluoyal more than the Magi'i?"

"Bluoyal walks a narrow and dangerous path, trying to ensure that the lancers and the Magi'i do not see that their interests are closer to each other's than to his." She reaches for the goblet of spring water on the table, nearly draining it in a single swallow.

"They see that. They have always seen that." The Emperor's smile is cold. "But neither can afford to trust the other allied to Bluoyal. Yet they know that both Magi'i and Lancers are few outside of the three cities. They cooperate like a pair of giant cats against a pack of night leopards. Most carefully."

"And when the towers fail?" she questions.

"There will be towers after we are gone," Toziel answers.

"Not many, and not for long. You hesitate to answer?"

"You know, as do I, my dear. There will need to be more lancers against the barbarians, but the Magi'i who can draw chaos from around them will be far fewer." He shrugs. "That will make each more powerful individually, but the families far less so, and there will be fewer. Bluoyal's successors will find they still need lancers, but not until many perish, and more than a few vessels are lost."

"Little will change," she prophesies.

"The appearances will not, but the emperors to come must either be powerful Magi'i or inspire loyalty within the Mirror Lancers, for either lancers or Magi'i can destroy an Emperor. Yet they must have the support of the Merchanters, for without that there will not be the golds to support the Mirror Lancers."

"Bluoyal is coming to believe that he can decide who will succeed you, even now. I wonder if he holds the Brystan sabre in reserve . . . or the man who does."

"That part of the riddle has not surfaced." Toziel sinks onto the divan beside her, breathing slightly heavily.

"No," she replies, "but it will. Bluoyal already believes that the merchanters will purchase the Palace of Light in years to come."

"For a season, perhaps, in two generations. Sooner, if we fail, and blood will stain the sunstone so deeply it will not be removed, should that occur." He studies her drawn face. "You give too much to me."

"What else would I do, dearest? We know there is no one else."

"Not yet." Her fingers rest lightly on his cheek.

CVI

IN THE MID-AFTERNOON gloom, Lorn sits at the narrow desk in his study, reading over the last lines of his patrol report, before he begins the summary report that will go to Majer Maran. Outside, the heavy rain that began the day before on the final day of patrol continues to beat down on the tile roofs of the compound and to run in sheets across the slightly slanted stone pavement of the courtyard, pouring into the drainage canal leading westward.

The lancer captain massages his forehead with his left hand, closing his eyes for a moment, listening to the drumbeat of the rain, rain that usually seems to provide headaches.

Ryalth has returned to Cyad, and Lorn has completed one complete patrol, surprisingly without a tree-fall or another excursion from the Accursed Forest. Those will come. That he knows, but he hopes that he will have some time, for he has yet to decide how he will handle what must come from Maran, if not by spring, then later.

Thrap. The knock on the study door is gentle.

"Yes?"

Kusyl opens the door and peers inside. "Ah . . . ser . . . the engineers brought the replacement firelances."

Lorn beckons for the squad leader to come in.

Kusyl does and closes the door behind him.

"They're not fully charged, or there aren't enough?" Lorn suggests.

"Just a score and a half, ser. If Frynyl hadn't run for the north, well, ser . . ."

"I know. There wouldn't even be one for me. I could have borrowed one from Juist, but only one. He generally has a few extras, and they don't discharge theirs as rapidly as we do." Lorn smiles. "I appreciate your telling me. It won't change anything." He glances toward the window. "I just hope the rain lets up soon."

"Not quite so heavy as earlier, ser." Kusyl bobs his head. "There be anything you want, ser?"

"No, thank you."

Once Kusyl leaves, Lorn looks out at the still-falling rain. He shakes his head sadly. Maran has made Lorn's decision for him, although Lorn doubts Maran will understand the reasons for that decision. The captain fingers his chin. In a way, Ciesrt has also helped to make Lorn's decision, and his sister's consort would not understand either.

Lorn takes out another sheet of report paper and begins drafting the summary report to Majer Maran. Since nothing occurred, it is short, and before long, Lorn has handed it to Kusyl for dispatch.

Then he crosses the courtyard to his quarters quickly, but Kusyl is right, for the rain has diminished to a fraction of its former intensity.

He bolts the door behind himself, pacing around the small room, thinking. After a time, he recovers and opens the silver-covered book, searching for a poem that may reflect his conflicting emotions, either his sense of loss at Ryalth's absence . . . perhaps his growing understanding of how fortunate he has been to have found and held her or his anger at Maran's smallness. He passes by page after page of verse, feeling the weight of melancholy, until he pauses, caught by an image, though it is not what he has sought.

He reads the words slowly, and aloud, for the combination of the subtle strangeness and the angular characters always suggests restraint.

> An ornamented garden, filled with flowers,
> statues surrounding lovers' bowers,
> these we will not find in granite walls,
> nor in the heights of Palace halls,
> vain images of a world long lost in space
> that none can bear to view or to replace.
>
> Love you I will these last days we hold,
> loving till we are ash and order cold,

> for ancient images are not for keeping,
> nor Palace walls and second falls for weeping.

He frowns, wondering again who the writer might have been. Then he shakes his head, looking for something slightly less melancholy, but the best he can find is the first stanza of another verse.

> Virtues of old hold fast.
> Morning's blaze cannot last;
> and rose petals soon part.
> Not so a steadfast heart.

"Not so a steadfast heart . . ." he murmurs to himself. Is his heart that steadfast? He shakes his head and turns to the lines about pears, recalling Ryalth's voice as she had read the words on a chill morning that had been warmer than most he has known.

Then, only then, he slowly closes the book. Ryalth had asked him so long ago what he knew of the ancients. He still does not know, only that they had somehow seen an age end, a life end, and it had colored everything written in the small, seemingly eternal, silver-covered volume he holds.

CVII

TO LORN'S RIGHT the ward-wall glimmers white in the steam of the morning of Second Company's second day of patrol—outbound from Jakaafra compound on the second full patrol since Lorn has returned from his furlough and seen Ryalth off on her way back to Cyad. While it is too early to have heard from her, he worries.

He also worries about the weather and the Accursed Forest. The cold rain has been followed with still air and a sun that seems as hot as early summer. The air is damp and warm, and steam rises from the road and even from the deadland, so much so that Lorn can barely make out the second squad's lancers in the line abreast stretching in from the perimeter road.

Lorn blots his forehead with the back of his hand, even though his jacket is fastened behind the saddle. His eyes and chaos senses focus on the ward-wall ahead, for the chaos field set up by the wards is truly chaotic and seems almost to fade away at times. He turns his head left and calls to Shynt, "Tell them to watch things closely."

"Aye, ser." In turn, the junior squad leader calls out. "Watch close now! Could be aught all in this mist! Watch close."

As the gelding carries him along the wall road, headed almost directly into the sun, Lorn struggles against the glare of sun and reflected light to make out the midpoint chaos tower that the company must be approaching—that and the fallen trunk he knows must lie ahead. Still, Second Company rides another three kays before Lorn sees the line of darkness crossing the ward-wall ahead—and behind it, the white granite of the midpoint chaos-tower building rising above the ground mist, less than half a kay behind the fallen tree. For a long moment, he studies the point nearly a kay away where the tree has struck the granite of the ward-wall, noting that white oblongs are strewn across the wall road—the first time he has seen such.

He turns in the saddle and calls to Shynt, "Form up into five abreast. We'll head out to join the second squad." His fingers touch the single chaos lance in his holder—fully charged and then some.

"There's a fallen tree ahead. Form up five abreast, staggered! Pass it out!" orders the junior squad leader. "Five abreast!"

After guiding the gelding away from the ward-wall, Lorn urges his mount up alongside Shynt's. The lancers fall into their five-abreast ranks as Lorn and Shynt pass, until they have gathered the understrength squad together. Shynt barely has the first squad formed up a quarter kay from the wall and riding outward toward Kusyl and his second squad—

already formed up on the perimeter road—when a messenger rides toward Lorn, reining up and then turning his mount to ride beside the lancer captain.

"Ser," the messenger blurts. "Squad leader Kusyl, ser, he wants you to know that there's another trunk down on the far side of the chaos tower."

"Another?" murmurs Shynt to himself.

"Thank you," Lorn replies. "Tell him we'll join him on the perimeter road off the crown of this trunk. And tell him to stay well back until we get there."

"Yes, ser."

The lancer rides back toward Kusyl, and Lorn and the first squad continue riding in formation, outward through the ground mist that has begun to dissipate, out toward the perimeter road and the second squad.

Lorn keeps studying the dark trunk whose length they parallel, but he sees nothing overt, no giant cats on the trunk, no night leopards—just a huge trunk-wall that seems blacker than most of the fallen forest giants he has encountered on previous patrols.

As Lorn nears the second squad, formed up on the perimeter road, Kusyl rides forward to meet his captain. "Two of 'em down, ser," reports the senior squad leader. "You can see the second, on the other side of the tower building." He points. "Looks big as this one. Could be bigger. Hard to tell from here."

Following the gesture, Lorn nods. "Two or not, we'll have to check this one first. We'll follow the road and then head straight at the crown."

"Yes, ser."

Lorn continues to watch the two fallen forest giants, separated by almost a kay, with the bulk of the midpoint chaos tower and its connecting wall between them, yet he can see nothing moving except dark birds that are clearly vulcrows.

When they are opposite the first tree, Lorn reins up, then turns. "Form up on me for the approach to the crown." The captain looks from Kusyl to Shynt.

"Yes, ser."

"Yes, ser."

Lorn eases the gelding forward, then slips the white fire-lance from the holder. He also checks the sabre. Once the squads flank him, with seventy-five cubits separating him from the forward lancer on each side, and he rides alone once more, he urges the gelding toward the mass of twisted and splintered branches and greenery that lie six hundred cubits before him.

A vulcrow flutters to land on a branch protruding higher than the others, its black feathers glistening under the hot spring-like sun, something dangling from its mouth before the morsel disappears when the scavenger swallows. Lorn rides closer to the forest canopy. He can see long strands of moss-like vegetation.

The air smells of splintered and resined wood, of acrid crushed leaves, and slightly of the acrid and musky scent that tells of stun lizards. The branches rustle, then crack ominously, and the crackling is followed by a greater odor of musk and an intensified acridity.

"Prepare to discharge firelances!" Lorn orders without turning his head, his eyes sweeping the twisted greenery.

"Firelances to the ready."

The two stun lizards that crash from the fallen tree are five cubits high at their front shoulders, and stretch more than twenty-five cubits. The heavy tails do not lash. The nearer and fractionally larger lizard halts, then watches Lorn through black eyes that do not blink. Soundlessly, a black tongue flicks out like a lash, pulling a gray sparrow Lorn had not even seen from the air.

After taking the bird, the first lizard remains perfectly still. So does the second.

A gap of a hundred cubits separates Lorn and the two squads of Second Company from the pair of lizards.

The first lizard lumbers forward a good twenty cubits, then halts. The tongue flicks the air once more.

Lorn waits.

The trailing lizard angles to Lorn's right and continues

forward slowly until it comes to a halt ten cubits forward of the first.

The first lizard takes another dozen ground-covering strides, then lifts its head.

MMMMnnnnnnnn . . .

At the mental scream of the lizard, several lancers sway in their saddles. One drops a firelance and clasps his hands to his forehead, as if to try to keep his skull from exploding.

"Discharge at will!" snaps Lorn.

"Fire at will!" echoes Kusyl.

MMMMnnn . . . The second lizard charges for Shynt.

Hssst! Hsstt! Hssst! Firelances flare everywhere, but most concentrate on the second lizard, the one that has almost reached the five-abreast formation before slowing under the flash of lances.

MMMnnnnnn! Lorn feels rocked in his saddle by the mental blast, even though he knows the sensation is but within his mind.

The giant lizard half-turns and the tail swings. A lancer tries to duck, but is swept from the saddle, and the return swing, lower, sweeps his mount from its hoofs.

Lorn digs his heels into the gelding's flanks and urges him forward. Recalling his previous encounters with the lizards, he directs his lance blasts at the first lizard's left eye.

Hssstt!

MMMMMMmmmm . . . The stun blast contains a sense of pain and rage. *MMMnnnnn . . .* The big tail thumps the dead-land, then lashes toward the second squad.

Mmmmnnnn . . . Lorn fires again, glancing toward the first squad momentarily. Two mounts are down, but the second lizard's head is a charred mass. He concentrates on the lizard that continues to lumber away from him and toward Kusyl and the second squad.

The first lizard flees Lorn, its tail sweeping through the legs of another lancer mount, and sending mount and lancer down. Lorn urges the gelding more to his left, trying to circle past the flailing tail to get another blast at the lizard's eye.

Abruptly, the big creature slows and its tongue flashes toward a lancer, but the lancer has the presence of mind to slash with his sabre.

MMMMnnnn!

The lancer shakes his head, managing to hold his blade against the lash-like tongue.

HHHssssTTT! Lorn focuses a long bolt, one that curves under his control, into the lizard's left eye.

A deep roaring groan fills the air, and the tail slams the ground, once, twice. Lorn senses that the beast is dying, and lets loose another fireblast before he turns the gelding. His eyes travel toward the ward-wall, where, even as the two lizards are still twitching, another set of four large dark forms come streaking, not from the foliage, but down the massive tree trunk from the forest.

"Giant cats! Reform!"

"Lances ready!"

Before the second squad can turn toward the south and the ward-wall, one of the giant cats has struck a lancer.

Hhhsttt! Hssst!

The bursts from the lances are shorter, weaker, and many lancers have dropped exhausted lances and are using their sabres.

Lorn finds the Brystan sabre in one hand, and the firelance in the other. His eyes are watering, and his head is splitting, but he lets loose with another chaos blast, this time at a giant cat that has started to spring toward Kusyl from the side, while the senior squad leader is using his sabre on a third cat that has slashed the shoulder of a lancer in the first rank.

The cat squalls, then crumples, and Lorn tries to scan the area between the lancers and the crushed canopy.

A round tannish object rolls out of the canopy, surrounded almost by a dark fog, that starts to swirl away from a rough sphere.

Paper wasps! Lorn turns his lance in the general direction of the nest and lets loose a chaos bolt. *Hssst!*

Knives slash his vision, and he understands he is drawing chaos from around him, that the charge in his weapon is long since depleted. He drops the lance. This is one time that he isn't worrying about the weapons, not with all the wild creatures swirling around and attacking Second Company.

He glances back at the tan sphere, but the wasp nest flares yellowish, as do some of the finger-long wasps. A handful escapes the chaos flash, and the insects whine toward the nearest lancers—those on the left end of Shynt's company.

Lorn jerks his attention back to the crushed green leaves of the canopy, and the rustling that foretells night leopards. "Night leopards!"

"Frig!"

"Dark angels . . ."

Lorn manages to drag out the other sabre and wonders just how effective he will be guiding the gelding with his knees. He swallows and blinks as the smaller cats continue to bound from the greenery—far more than a score.

Hssst! Hssst! Hssst! The handful of firelances left from those lancers who had been in the third rank flare, and lines of chaos crisscross the dark feline forms, those that have not already reached lancers and their mounts.

"Short bursts! Short bursts!" Shynt bellows.

A mount screams.

Lorn finds himself swinging the Brystan sabre left-handed to drop a night leopard that has streaked toward him, while holding the second sabre ready in his right.

Hsst! Hsst!

Lorn does not recall well the next moments, only that he employs both blades, and that no leopards turn and flee, but all continue to attack.

Abruptly, impossibly, it seems, there are no creatures attacking.

Lorn glances down. One trouser leg is slashed, and there is blood splattered across his boots and legs. His eyes feel like knives are being driven through and behind them, and his skull feels as if it had been split with a dull wedge. He blinks and tries to assess what remains around him.

Close by, he can see five mounts lying on the deadland. One shudders and tries to rise, shudders and tries again, but the mare's right foreleg is crushed and twisted, possibly from the lashing tail of one of the stun lizards.

One lancer lies on his back, his body swollen, and his face covered with red blotches from the attack of those paper wasps that had escaped Lorn's firelance.

Other unmoving forms—five—lie beside the charred forms of the lizards, the giant cats, and the night leopards.

Kusyl rides slowly toward Lorn. Dark splotches cover his gray's coat, blood is smeared across the forearms of both sleeves.

Not sure that the attack is over, or that the comparative stillness is a lull, Lorn keeps scanning the area, with both chaos senses and sight. The only sounds come from the lancers and their mounts, and the pitiful whimpering of the mount that will have to be destroyed.

A vulcrow flaps overhead, then glides above Lorn and down toward one of the lizard carcasses. Lorn blots his forehead to keep the sweat from eyes that already burn and slash into his skull, but he does not close his eyes, but keeps watching.

"Form up on me!" Kusyl orders.

"Reform!" yells Shynt, his voice cracking slightly.

Lorn watches the greenery as the lancers reform, those that remain and can, then rides to where Kusyl sits on his mount before the remaining eleven members of the second squad.

"Never . . . ever seen aught like that, ser," observes the squad leader.

Lorn shakes his head, but only minutely, for each movement sears his vision. "I haven't either." He swallows, but that helps little with the dryness in his mouth and throat. "Best we remain formed up and see what happens for a bit. Except . . . have a couple of men look to the wounded . . . do we have any?"

"Yes, ser." Kusyl frowns. "Seven down, I think, both squads. Those that stayed mounted be all right, save slashes . . . excepting Thylt . . . lizard tail snapped his arm."

Shynt eases his mount to join them, as all three continue

to survey the twisted branches of the fallen tree. "We have no charged lances remaining."

"I doubt if anyone does," Lorn says hoarsely.

The silence continues for some time, yet the only movement is that of the handful of vulcrows that are gathering, flapping down to feed on the dead lizards.

"There is a second tree," Lorn says. "Have second squad remain here with the wounded. First squad and I will circle the other tree, but we'll stay well back. Well back," he adds.

Shynt nods.

"We won't send a message to the Engineers until we look at the second tree—carefully." The captain looks at Kusyl. "If you'd have someone collect the lances that were discarded or dropped, and see how many are left with charges. . . ." He laughs once, harshly. "If there are any at all."

"Yes, ser."

Lorn turns in the saddle to Shynt. "First squad ready?"

"Yes, ser."

Lorn and the first squad slowly ride past the midpoint chaos tower, then continue almost another half kay before turning southward and beginning a circuit around the second fallen trunk, at a distance of a good five hundred cubits. Lorn watches the trunk . . . and listens. All he hears are the murmurs of lancers.

". . . two stun lizards . . . never saw so many of those angel-dead leopards . . ."

". . . captain killed one lizard himself . . . big cat . . . lots a' small ones . . ."

". . . better . . . got the worst luck of any officer . . ."

". . . not worst luck . . . worst wall . . . northeast always been bad . . . say it be the winds . . ."

". . . heard he got consorted on furlough . . ."

". . . might as well . . . lots don't live to get back to Cyad. . . ."

Lorn concentrates on the fallen tree, but no branches rustle, and there are no signs of any other wild creatures—besides the vulcrows that perch on the trunk, and then fly back to pick at the carcasses.

"Not a thing on this trunk. Strange it be," Shynt observes. "They were waiting for us at the first."

Lorn nods, his eyes going to the ward-wall that lies still ahead, continuing to ride parallel to the second trunk, the firelance held out, even though the chaos charge is gone. He compares the bark to what he has seen earlier, a bark that is darker, smoother—harder perhaps.

As they near the wall that hardness is clear. Once again, the trunk has also destroyed or knocked out of the wall a good three courses of the granite stonework.

"Tough tree, this one," Shynt says. "Hope we don't see more like this."

More like what they have just endured, and there will be no Second Company Yet not a single wild creature has escaped—unless they had left well before the lancers arrived. Lorn shrugs. If that is the case, he can do nothing, but accept that Maran will blame him for that as well.

No matter how carefully Lorn writes his patrol report, Maran will find a way to blame Lorn.

CVIII

AFTER TURNING THE gelding over to Suforis and ensuring that the firelances are locked in the armory, Lorn hurries back to his study, stopping only to drop his gear, and reaching the Second Company studies even before Kusyl—if Kusyl even intends to do so. Lorn carries the scroll passed to him by Suforis, who has informed Lorn that Lesyna has actually brought it from Dustyn. A second scroll waits in the outer study, one from Cyad through the lancer courier system. The one from Cyad has been opened and resealed, if most carefully.

Once he is in his study, and has lit the lamp to lift the twilight gloom, Lorn opens Ryalth's scroll first, smoothing it out gently.

My dearest,

I have returned safely. It is most late tonight, but I will write now, else I will have little time for eightdays to come. No . . . Ryalor House did not suffer in my absence. Having three enumerators and a junior trader sufficed. There are many opportunities, and some I see clearly for the first time. . . . I already have a buyer for the lamps, and an offer on the melon ice wine. . . .

He skips over the rest of the general references to trade opportunities, looking for her reaction or his family's reaction to their consortship.

You had asked I send the scrolls. I did, but I sent them with a scroll of my own, requesting their leave to call. Your sister Jerial appeared at the Plaza herself and escorted me to the evening meal. Your father apologized for not coming personally, but he asked that I understand his presence in the Plaza would have negated all we had done in our arrangements. They were not only kind, but far warmer than I would have believed. We will continue to be circumspect, and I have officially engaged your sister as my personal healer. That is rare, but not unheard of. . . .

Rare for a merchant, but not for a Magi'i family without healers, Lorn reflects. Trust his consort and his sister to immediately find a way to work matters out.

. . . Eileyt is now a senior enumerator, and pleased with that. So am I.

Lorn nods.

If matters progress as well as may be possible, I may be able to return to eastern Cyador to arrange future goods and shipments as early as next fall. That would please me no end, and I trust you, as well.

The words, "my love," are written above her signature.

Lorn smiles, looking at the last words. Finally, he reaches for the second scroll. While he knows Ryalth reads people well, he still frets as he breaks the seal and smooths out the heavy paper.

Your scroll arrived, accompanied by another, and I must say that you surprised us, not so much for your choice or the location, but for the timing. Yet I must admit that this was not totally unexpected, considering the situation in which you find yourself. The lady asked our permission to call, and Jerial escorted her to us, the best arrangement possible. I told her that while her courtesy was charming and her discretion remarkable, that she was welcome at any time. She is indeed remarkable, and I must praise your ability to see far more than either your mother or I would have ...

Lorn laughs to himself. Those circumspect words were as close to a compliment of Ryalth and an admission that his father had been wrong as he was ever likely to get.

... Jerial is also pleased, although she has been hard-pressed lately as a result of recent unfortunate incidents, such as occurred the last time you visited.

Recent unfortunate incidents?

Myryan has also been pressed into service, and has had far less time with her new dwelling and her garden than she would have wished, but her skill is undeniable. Vernt may well be considered for elevation to a full second level adept in the year or so ahead, so devoted he is to his work. Your mother and I have introduced him to several young ladies, and, in light of recent events, he might even consider seeing one of them.

Your mother and I are well, if not possessed of quite the vigor of our offspring, and I am most pleased to be where I am at this time in my life . . .

Lorn frowns. From what he can tell, there has been another chaos-explosion, perhaps on a fireship, and a great deal of stress and pressure has been placed on the highest level of the Magi'i. The very highest level, Lorn knows, for his father is just below the three who lead the Magi'i.

The lancer captain looks at the locked foot locker on the far side of his desk. Tomorrow . . . tomorrow he will deal with the patrol report and the other administrative duties.

Tonight, he is relieved.

Half-relieved, he corrects himself as he leaves the inner study.

CIX

LORN IS IN his study early the next morning, working on the patrol report. Short as it is, he writes three versions, and it is well after mid-morning before he is satisfied. Then . . . he must plead for replacement lancers in a scroll to commander Meylyd. Drafting that request is almost as laborious, but finally he finishes a draft.

He glances out the study window at the green-blue sky and the puffy white clouds that drift out of the north, then looks back down at his request, his eyes taking in what he has written.

. . . as I had noted in a previous meeting with Majer Maran, Second Company was well under strength

even before the extraordinary demands placed on
it by the excursions of the Accursed Forest . . .
have managed to restrict the wild creatures using
the most conventional of Mirror Lancer tactics, and
without use of additional firelances . . . toll has
been high, and both squads now number less than
half their normal strength . . . should the most recent level of activity by the Accursed Forest continue, it would appear unlikely that even the most
esteemed and loyal Mirror Lancer officer could
continue to restrict the escape of wild creatures
without reinforcements. . . .Therefore . . . requesting replacements necessary to bring Second Company up to full strength, . . .

Lorn reads through the draft. He purses his lips. The wording is still not right, and it nears mid-day.

Thrap.

He looks up at the knock. "Yes?"

Kusyl opens the door. "There be a Majer Wcylt here, ser."

"Have him come in." Lorn stands.

Weylt enters the inner study, and Kusyl shuts the door.

"Majer, what can I do for you?" asks Lorn.

"I wondered if we could have something to eat before I
leave. We were checking the tower," Weylt explains.

"There's not much at mid-day," Lorn says. "Usually just
bread and cheese, maybe some dried fruit." He smiles. "I can
offer some wine."

"I'd appreciate that."

"I can go now." Lorn gestures toward the papers on the
desk. "Reports, but they can wait until after we eat."

"Thank you."

"If you would like, I'll meet you there. I keep the wine in
my quarters," Lorn points out.

"That would be fine."

Lorn crosses the courtyard. He notes that the Engineer
firewagon is being loaded with several firelances—those ex-
pended by Juist?

There is but one bottle of Alafraan left in his room, but Lorn suspects that it will be worth serving for the majer, who has often provided good, if indirect, advice before.

Weylt sits alone at the table, a platter with a large wedge of cheese and a basket with two cold loaves of bread in the middle of the battered but polished golden oak surface of the table.

Lorn uncorks the bottle, then seats himself and uses his belt knife to cut several slices of the hard white cheese. He pours a half goblet of the Alafraan for himself and closer to a full one for the Mirror Engineer majer.

Weylt takes a slow sip. "Thank you, Captain. You have the best wine of all the compounds around the Forest."

"I was lucky. My trader provided it."

"You were lucky in more than that." Weylt breaks off a chunk of bread, eating it with some cheese before speaking again. "You were fortunate we were free when your messenger arrived. When we returned to Eastpoint, there was a messenger from Captain Tysyr."

"He's at Eastpoint now?"

"That's right. He replaced Ivinyt . . . about half a season ago. He had a trunk down on our side of the southeast mid-point chaos tower. So . . . a bit later, and you'd have been out there another day, perhaps two."

"I'm glad we weren't." Lorn takes the bread and a large wedge of cheese. "We were there long enough."

Weylt nods deliberately, slowly. "I did notice the charred remnants of a large paper wasp nest, purely by accident." Weylt smiles. "I trust you did not bother to put such an insignificant addition into your patrol report."

"With the giant cats and the stun lizards?" Lorn laughs. "It didn't seem that important, I must admit, and I never did get an accurate count of the night leopards. So I just mentioned that there seemed to be two packs, and none escaped."

"Most sagacious, Captain." Weylt lifts the goblet, but does not drink. "I would say that you are not in the most enviable position. Those two trees were the largest I have seen. They were among the most substantial to have fallen, according to the Engineer records. We keep very accurate records, you understand?"

The lancer captain nods.

"Normally, those falls would release large numbers of creatures. Yet you have indicated that you reported success with keeping a modest number from escaping. A . . . skeptical superior might question the numbers. He would request our report, which would verify the size of the fallen trees. Then he would wait for reports of escaped creatures. If such reports occur, of course, there might be disciplinary action for falsification." Weylt shrugs. "You do not falsify, and . . . well . . . sometimes the truth is even less palatable." He takes a sip of the Alafraan. "Did I tell you that this is excellent wine?"

"No, but I believe it is, and I am fortunate to be able to share it with you."

"There are times when I wonder whether I should have attempted to remain an insignificant magus, and times when I wonder if I should have tried for the Mirror Lancers." The Mirror Engineer looks down at the wine left in his goblet. A wry and sardonic expression appears. "Then we have an event such as this, and I am most happy to be an Engineer. I'm glad I'm not a lancer. We are but expected to do what may be necessary, and no one lets us near anything, especially in Cyad."

"We also do but what is expected." Lorn takes another sip of wine. "It can be difficult to attempt more."

"Ah, yes," replies Weylt, "and yet the time may come when more is necessary. It is difficult to recall that at times." The majer swallows the last of the wine. "Best I go, for we need to return to Eastpoint before too late tonight." He stands. "I thank you for the wine, and the company, and wish you the best with your patrols and reports."

Lorn follows the majer to his feet. "Thank you. I appreciate your observations."

"Sometimes, that's all a good Engineer can do." He looks

at the table. "Don't let me keep you from finishing your meal." With that, Weylt nods and departs.

Lorn re-seats himself and cuts another slice of cheese, his brow furrowing as he considers Weylt's words and what they signify.

CX

LORN TAKES A deep breath, and blots his forehead. Despite the breeze from the open window, the study is warm, a heat of a spring that foreshadows an even warmer summer, he fears, and one that may bring even more fallen trees and wild creatures. The lancer captain has just completed his patrol report for the second uneventful patrol since the one that had involved the two fallen trees. He has heard nothing from either Maran or Commander Meylyd, nor have any replacement lancers yet arrived at Jakaafra. Lorn doubts that they will, but if he hears nothing after another patrol, he will again request replacements. He has also noted his requests for replacements in the patrol reports kept at Jakaafra.

He has just begun the summary report for Majer Maran when there is a *thrap* on the door of the inner study. He looks up to see Kusyl standing there, a slight frown on his face.

"Majer Maran, ser."

Maran walks past Kusyl even before the senior squad leader has finished announcing him. "Greetings, Captain."

"My greetings to you, Majer," Lorn replies, standing, if somewhat indolently. "I had not expected you so soon."

Kusyl quickly retreats and closes the door.

"I am gratified to see that you are so industrious on your stand-down day," Maran offers. "Not that one would expect any less from such a creative and hard-working captain."

Lorn smiles politely.

"I have received your patrol report—the one where Second Company encountered two fallen trunks." Maran again offers his warm and concerned smile, and the brown eyes beam gently. "It was a rather amazing report."

Lorn shrugs gently, his eyes and senses fully upon the more senior officer. "It was accurate."

"Oh, I am most certain it was accurate. Every report you have submitted has been most truthful in every detail you have provided."

"And I have provided every important detail, Majer," Lorn continues, "so that you and Commander Meylyd will be kept well informed."

"We both appreciate that. Yes, we do." Maran's smile turns vaguely apologetic. "Captain . . . there are a few items we should discuss. Better alone, I would think. I suggest that we should take a ride."

"Perhaps that would be best," Lorn concurs. "Is your mount . . . ?"

"He is tied outside. I will meet you by the gates," Maran suggests. "Shortly." He flashes his warm smile once more before he turns and leaves.

For several moments, Lorn looks to the open window, knowing that he must face the results of his decisions, and that, after today, there is no turning from his course, that he—he and Ryalth, for his decisions no longer impact but himself—are committed to long and dangerous years. He shakes his head. Being who he is, there never was another course, and all he can do is work to ensure she is not too adversely affected. That will be more than difficult, for his failure will lead to death.

He laughs, once, harshly. Turning from one's dreams is a greater death than failing to reach them. A far worse death— that he has already seen in others—for one experiences it each day anew.

Lorn stacks the reports and places the thin Lancer manual on them to hold them against the breeze from the window before reclaiming the Brystan sabre and clipping the scabbard to his belt. Then he steps out into the outer study.

"Ser?" Kusyl looks up.

"I'll be taking a ride with Majer Maran," Lorn tells the

senior squad leader. "He has requested I accompany him. I would doubt it will be long." He grins ruefully at Kusyl. "With senior officers, one never knows, though."

"No, ser." Kusyl's brow furrows, but he does not speak further.

"I hope to be back soon." Lorn adds as he leaves.

When he crosses the courtyard, he looks for the majer, but Maran has already left or is on the other side of one of the courtyard structures.

Suforis is not in the stable, and Lorn has finished saddling the gelding and is leading him out before the blond ostler appears.

"You won't be riding him hard today, will you, ser? I could get another mount . . . ? It would not take but a moment."

"No. I doubt I'll travel more than a few kays. Majer Maran has something he wants to talk about or show me."

"Yes, ser." Suforis's assent contains some doubt.

"There's no rain or chill, Suforis, and I won't be riding hard. Or far." With a smile, Lorn mounts the gelding. He rides at a walk across the stone-paved courtyard and past the duty guards.

Maran is waiting, reined up a half-kay from the gates on the road that leads past the chaos-tower building and toward the ward-wall. The majer's mount is the same white stallion he had ridden earlier when he had given Lorn a tour of the ward-wall near Geliendra.

"You took your time, Captain."

"The ostler was out, and I had to saddle up my mount. I wasn't expecting to take a ride." Lorn's voice is even, casual.

"No, I suppose you were not. At least, not today." A hint of amusement colors Maran's deep and warm voice. The majer's heels touch the stallion's flanks, and the big mount carries the majer along the access road.

Lorn follows Maran's lead, suppressing a knowing nod as the majer follows the road that flanks the wall connecting the chaos tower building to the ward-wall. They turn southwest on the wall road, riding toward Westend.

Lorn does not speak, just rides on the side of the road closest to the wall, as the two officers cover first a kay, then nearly a second, before Maran looks at Lorn again. "It is too bad you were not born five generations earlier, Captain."

"I appreciate the compliment." Lorn laughs. "But I like this time, thank you." He glances back over his shoulder, but he cannot make out any figures near the compound, just the walls.

"This time does not behoove you." Maran continues in his deep and thoughtful tones, almost as if Lorn were not riding a handful of cubits away. "You are capable, Captain, far too capable for a mere lancer."

"All lancers should strive to be capable," Lorn says conversationally, breaking into the older officer's monologue, "as a mere beginning."

Maran glances at Lorn, the brown eyes momentarily flat, instead of warm.

"Tell me, Maran," Lorn adds, deliberately omitting the senior officer's title. "When does a senior officer have the right to threaten the lives of a junior's company and men for the sake of secretive plotting? Or for the interests of a few senior officers in Cyad?"

Maran raises his eyebrows, and the warm smile returns to his deep brown eyes. "I do not believe that has ever occurred. Threatening the lives of lancers, that is."

"By the way," Lorn says, "I thought you might wish to know that you have made my decisions far easier . . . oh, and that I have taken the liberty of taking a consort."

"You did not consult with the Commander, or me, and that is usual. Then, you seldom do the usual."

"But not required," Lorn says, "not under the Lancer Rules of Procedure." He continues to smile.

"There are many things which are not required, but wise, nonetheless," Maran adds, "as you will doubtless discover in your short career."

"No," Lorn replies quietly. "As you will discover in a shorter career." He draws the Brystan sabre that looks little different from a lancer sabre now that it shimmers with a cupridium finish.

"You do anticipate, Captain, but . . ."

Hssst! The firebolt of a full magus flies at Lorn.

Lorn raises the sabre and twists it, also twisting the shields he holds, and flings the firebolt, energy he has now encased in black order—ordered chaos-fire—back at the majer. He turns the gelding so that he faces Maran's right side.

"Trifling." Maran languidly raises a hand as if to dispel the firebolt.

Lorn follows the returned firebolt with the sabre, letting it fly, guided by chaos-order, and filled with the twined order and chaos he has learned from the Accursed Forest.

"Uhhh!" As the firebolt shatters, the Brystan sabre's sharpened point drives through the majer's shoulder.

The warm smile vanishes from the majer's face, and Lorn uses his chaos senses to drive another order-chaos beam at Maran.

"Black . . . angel . . ." Those are Maran's last words. There are no hisses, no screams—Maran's body just *flares* as the glowing golden white of chaos, enfolded by the deep black of order, flows around it. Then, there are no traces that he had ever been there, except for a handful of buckles, some coins—and the two sabres, Lorn's and Maran's, all of which slide off the white leather of Maran's saddle.

Lorn sits stock-still for a moment, somehow both surprised that his attack has been so successful and gratified that his understanding of Maran has been so accurate. He also silently thanks Majer Brevyl.

After that short moment, Lorn rides forward and grasps the reins of Maran's stallion, then dismounts.

First, he reclaims the Brystan sabre, gleaming as if it had never drawn blood. Then, he gathers Maran's sabre and the metal in his gloved hands. He walks toward the ward-wall.

There he lifts the sabre . . . and tosses it over the ward-wall, followed by the other metal remnants. As the weapon crosses the chaos-net, it flares, and the heat-shimmering blade tumbles into the greenery on the inside of the granite.

After remounting the white gelding, Lorn leads the majer's mount along the road for a time, although the stallion tosses his head more than once. After another kay, Lorn loops the reins over the saddle and then, with a yell, he slaps the fractious stallion's rump. The bigger mount trots a distance, then slows, but continues to the southwest.

Lorn watches until he is certain the stallion will travel for at least a time before he turns the gelding and begins the ride back to the compound.

As he nears the gates, Lorn reins up and addresses the pair of guards. "Majer Maran should be back later. Tell him I'll be in my study."

"Yes, ser."

Suforis hurries from the tack room even before Lorn has fully led the gelding into the stable.

"You see? It wasn't all that long, and I never had him at more than a fast walk."

"That be good, ser." Suforis studies the gelding, then nods.

Lorn leaves his mount with the ostler and crosses the courtyard to re-enter the company study.

"Ser?" asks Kusyl.

"Majer Maran had a few words for me." Lorn does not smile. "He said he would be back later when I had a chance to consider them."

"Ah . . . yes, ser. I'm sorry, ser."

"We often have to do what our seniors wish, Kusyl." Lorn's laugh is harsh. "As I'm sure you know."

"Ah . . . yes, ser."

With a nod, Lorn closes the door to the inner study.

He looks out the window once more. From now on, even more than in the past, he must watch and weigh every action, every word. And he must anticipate.

He wishes he could talk to Ryalth, but perhaps it is better that he not, for a time.

Lorn shakes his head and seats himself at the desk, where he continues work on the patrol summary report that Maran had interrupted. He will send that off, as required, with the next Engineer firewagon. Then he begins drafting yet another request to Commander Meylyd for replacement lancers. He has completed the second draft and is reading it when there is a knock on the door.

"Ser? There be some lancers here, asking of Majer Maran."

Lorn frowns. "He hasn't come back? Have them come in." He remains seated as two lancers step into the inner study.

"Ser. . . . squad leader Jugyt, ser, and Shalar, ser," offers the broad-shouldered junior squad leader. "We had been expecting the majer . . . but none be seeing him."

Lorn offers a puzzled look. "We took a short ride. He said what he had come to say, and then said he would be back later. I came back, and I haven't seen him since. I thought he had come back and left with you, since I hadn't heard anything."

"No, ser."

Lorn fingers his chin. "The last time I saw him, he was riding the wall road, toward Westend, but we were only a few kays from here." He stands and calls, "Kusyl!"

"Yes, ser?" Kusyl re-appears.

"Do you know if anyone has seen Majer Maran?"

"No, ser."

"He said he was coming back, but his men here haven't seen him," Lorn explains.

"I don't know as anyone has seen him since he left the compound, ser."

Lorn purses his lips. "If you'd check with the guards and any of the men—or see if Juist's company saw him. They rode back in a while ago."

"Yes, ser."

After Kusyl leaves, Lorn looks at the two lancers. "All we can do is look and see if anyone saw him. I'll have my company check the area. It seems strange that he'd leave without you, but maybe he did."

"He rides alone at times, it be true, ser, but always he returns," says Jugyt.

Lorn shrugs helplessly. "I scarcely know what to say. We can check to see if there has been a tree-fall nearby, or if there are any tracks on the deadland." He glances toward the window, and gestures toward the sun that hangs just above the compound walls. "Best we hasten."

"Yes, ser."

Lorn reclaims his sabre, then heads for the stable. This time he will use a spare mount, for despite the search for Majer Maran, Second Company will still begin a patrol tomorrow. After all, Maran would certainly not to have wanted Lorn to deviate from accepted Mirror Lancer procedures.

The captain who would be more offers a brief smile as he nears the stable.

CXI

AS SECOND COMPANY rides slowly toward the gates of the compound at Jakaafra, Lorn looks down at his bloodsplattered trousers, and then at the depleted firelance in the holder. The sun is almost touching the western horizon, outlining the silhouettes of distant orchards to the west, and casting long shadows from the walls of the compound.

Lorn does not look back at a company that is now really but the size of a single full-strength squad, nor at the three mounts that bear dead lancers. They have not permitted any wild creatures to escape despite another fallen trunk, but that is due to luck, and to the renewed tendency of the creatures to attack the lancers, rather than to attempt to escape beyond the deadland.

"We getting any replacements, ser?" Kusyl asks quietly, from where he rides alongside Lorn.

"I've requested more lancers three times, Kusyl. Majer Maran never offered much encouragement, but he didn't say no, either. That's if he got back to Geliendra, but I haven't heard about that, either."

"Funny about that, ser. His men found his mount, but not him. Think the Forest got him? They say that happens, sometimes."

"It could have happened, but we didn't see any traces of wild creatures." Lorn shrugs tiredly as they near the gates. "I just wish he had sent us some more lancers. The men are accomplishing the impossible, but it can't go on."

"What if we just waited until the Engineers arrived? Before getting near the trunk, ser?" asks Kusyl.

"We'd have as many dead lancers and some dead Engineers, probably, and Second Company would have a new captain and new squad leaders," Lorn replies.

"Thought it be like that, ser." Kusyl shakes his head. "Can't be saying as I understand. Do you, ser?"

"Not totally, Kusyl. I've heard that the Magi'i are going to try something, but that was seasons ago, and nothing has happened. Maybe they just want us to hang on until they can. Or maybe it's something else."

"Whatever it be, ser, best they do something or they'll have creatures running free throughout northeast Cyador."

"The other companies are short of lancers, too," Lorn points out.

"Not near so short as Second Company."

"They don't face so many tree-falls."

Kusyl shakes his head sadly.

"Evening, ser," calls the gate guard as Lorn nears the gates. "Hard patrol?"

"Hard patrol," Lorn confirms.

He will send another request for replacements, little good as such requests seem to do, but how can he not make such requests?

His fingers clench momentarily as he considers that senior officers—Maran, and now Meylyd—are forcing him to choose between his own life and risking his lancers. Yet, were he to step aside, or let himself be killed, nothing would change.

It may not, anyway, for all that he has chosen to follow dreams.

He pushes that thought aside. He also pushes aside the desire to use the chaos glass to view Meylyd. If Meylyd is at all sensitive to its use, that will create more problems, and Lorn knows of nothing to be gained by using the glass for such a purpose.

For the moment.

CXII

SPRING HAS COME to Cyad, and the green and white awnings fill the streets to the south of the Palace of Light under a clear green-blue sky. The Second Magus and the Captain-Commander of the Mirror Lancers stand on one of the smaller western balconies of the Palace.

Kharl looks out at the harbor, where scaffolds enfold two white-hulled fireships moored at a guarded white stone pier.

Luss glances at the two ships, then at Kharl. "Matters do not look so bright for the Quarter, these days."

"Nor for the Lancers. Your casualties in the north are climbing, as are they in the companies along the ward-wall of the Accursed Forest." Kharl's green eyes shimmer with the hint of overlying chaos-gold. "And . . . Maran is dead."

"Mirror Lancers do die in the course of duty," Luss says. "We do believe in duty, you may recall."

"You were the one who had expressed interest in Majer Maran, as I do recall."

"It should bother me that a renegade mage who posed as a lancer has died?" asks Luss.

"It might, if you consider the implications," suggests Kharl.

Luss raises his eyebrows. "Perhaps you should educate me, devious one?"

Kharl merely shrugs. After a time, he says, "The glass shows but the ward-wall . . . and nothing beyond—as usual." The Second Magus smiles brightly. "As I recall, he was supposed to deal with a certain captain. It would appear that the captain is clearly more experienced than some had anticipated."

"In direct combat, he has much experience," concedes Luss. "You had assured me that he has little capability and experience as a magus."

"Perhaps he used a sabre," suggests Kharl. "I merely suggest some caution."

"And how would you suggest such caution be applied, O devious Second Magus?"

"It would be best the Majer-Commander not discover this effort. Nor the Emperor, for who knows what he might ask of the Hand? Yet . . . that is up to you. Were I, say, a captain-commander, I might send word to Commander Meylyd that the Majer-Commander feels that unless there is some evidence of what befell the majer, evidence that the Emperor would regard as convincing, that the matter should be dropped with a quiet warning to the captain."

"You think that wise?"

"Very wise . . . the captain will fight to survive. If he is attacked by another officer, such as your Overcaptain Hybyl, Hybyl will also die, and then this Lorn will flee . . . or cover it up. Either way, the Majer-Commander will discover what has occurred. He will need to blame someone, perhaps someone rather high in the Mirror Lancer Court in Cyad . . . someone he does not like. It is better that this not come to light yet . . . until later, and then it will appear that *he* ordered it to be suppressed."

"Meylyd will try to find something," suggests Luss.

"I am certain he will attempt such. If he does, the problem is resolved. If he does not, there will be another field commander skeptical of the Majer-Commander, and one willing to tell the Emperor that the Majer-Commander attempted to cover a murder. Since the murder cannot be proven, the rumor will be more effective."

Luss nods slowly. "Devious as you are, that makes much sense. But what of the captain's future?"

"He appears to have developed certain skills . . . in anticipating or avoiding certain uses of chaos. To deal with him at Jakaafra would make the effort, shall we say, rather obvious. Then, if the First Magus is successful in the effort to put the Forest to sleep, any effort against the captain would become even more obvious." Kharl smiles. "Were I a senior lancer officer, I would promote him to overcaptain and then transfer him to where there is much . . . conflict."

Luss shakes his head. "A third such tour? For the son of the Fourth Magus? That would come to Rynst's eyes before the captain reaches Assyadt, and then the Majer-Commander would look far deeper. I think something like a port detachment, say in Biehl. For a short time, until he is forgotten. He also may encounter . . . certain difficulties there. . . ." Luss smiles. "Then, if necessary, a tour in Assyadt, after another promotion, so that he will be most inexperienced and also less . . . conditioned to combat. Also, if he is transferred now, before a full turn of duty . . . his time in Cyad will be limited."

"Best he be in Cyad for but a short period now, rather than a longer time later," Kharl agrees. "And best he be away from the Accursed Forest while the sleep barrier of the First Magus is created."

Both men nod.

"If he should survive yet more conflict, then he should come to Cyad as an aide to the Majer-Commander . . . say, when it is most appropriate," suggests Kharl.

"After certain other events?"

"Exactly."

Without another word, the two turn away from the view of the harbor and from the striped awnings whose unfurling heralds spring in Cyad.

CXIII

SITTING BEHIND HIS study desk, Lorn looks at the pen holder, and then at the open window, and the low clouds that promise rain that has not yet arrived. Second Company has completed another full patrol, encountering only shoots from seeds, and Lorn must write another patrol report, and a summary, and decide whether to again request replacement lancers—and sit and wait to see how Commander Meylyd will react to Maran's disappearance.

Finally, Lorn picks up the pen and begins to detail the last report. He has barely written three lines when Kusyl steps into the study.

"Yes?"

"Ser! There's a firewagon here, and Commander Meylyd. He's coming this way."

Lorn finds a sardonic smile on his lips. "Perhaps he will tell us about our replacement lancers, then."

"Ser?"

Lorn shakes his head, standing quickly.

At the sound of voices, Kusyl steps back and holds the door to the inner study as the Commander enters, followed by a smaller officer, an overcaptain. The squad leader closes it gently but firmly as he leaves.

Meylyd does not take a chair, but addresses Lorn directly. "Captain . . . I am sure you know why I am here. This is Overcaptain Hybyl. He was Majer Maran's deputy."

Behind two officers, Kusyl opens the door and slides in a chair and then silently closes the door once more.

"I am afraid I do not." Lorn offers a polite but confused expression. "I must admit I cannot honestly say I know why you are here, saving for my continual requests for replacement lancers."

"You cannot say?" Meylyd now offers a quizzical expression. "Majer Maran indicated he was not pleased with you before he left. And you pretend you don't know that? When he disappeared immediately after meeting with you? At a meeting outside the compound where no one but you two happened to be present?"

"No, ser. I knew that the majer was displeased. He took me for a quiet ride, where none would hear, he said. And he told me that while you were pleased with my results in containing the wild creatures, he was not happy with the strategies I had adopted. He said they were against patrol doctrine."

Hybyl nods. "He reported such before he departed Geliendra."

"For the record, Captain, with exactly what tactic was Majer Maran displeased?" asks Meylyd.

"My using myself as a target and carrying two firelances." Lorn shrugs. "There isn't anything against it in the manual, and since we're understrength, I didn't think one extra firelance would be a problem—at the time, that was still something like fifteen less than full complement, and it left the extra in the hands of an officer."

Another puzzled look passes between the two officers.

"Now, we have but half the requisite complement, and I had thought you might be here to discuss my requests for replacements." Lorn gestures to the single chair. "Ah, ser . . . if you'd like a seat?"

The Commander takes the chair Kusyl had shoved into the room, and Hybyl takes the armless one before the desk.

Lorn seats himself slowly, after the other two, waiting.

"Now, if you would continue, Captain . . . With an account of your meeting with Majer Maran," commands Meylyd.

"I don't know that there's that much more to say, ser. Majer Maran told me to use standard patrol tactics, and he said that I needed to contain the wild creatures without wasting chaos charges. He said that you expected I follow standard procedures. I told him what I just told you, and he said that sometimes junior officers needed to understand that not all accepted procedures were written out. He made that very clear. I told him I'd give up the extra firelance . . . if that would help."

"And?"

"He got very polite, ser. He said that I was not quite hopeless and that I had better act like every other captain, and that he would be watching me closely. Except that he said all of that much more politely and indirectly, and very pleasantly." Lorn shrugs. "I could not begin to repeat the way he said things."

A faint smile crosses Hybyl's lips.

"And what did you do after your ride?" asks Meylyd.

"I came back here. He said he needed a moment, and that he'd be back in a bit. I kept looking for him, but he didn't come back. I'd thought at first he'd decided to ride to Westend, but when his lancers came back and said he hadn't, we all went looking. We found his mount some three kays from where I left him, but we didn't find him. We didn't find any boot tracks either. You know that, I think, from the report I sent."

"I think we'll talk to your men, if you don't mind, Captain. I'd appreciate your remaining here in your study." Meylyd rises. "Then, I'll be back to talk to you."

Lorn stands. "Yes, ser. They'll tell you everything they know."

"I'm most certain that they will." Meylyd smiles coldly.

Hybyl does not smile at all as the two leave.

After a long moment, Lorn shrugs and sits down. While it may make no difference, he returns to drafting the last patrol report.

He has long since finished it, and trusting that his analysis of the commander's position is correct, grateful that, if his decision of how to deal with Maran was wrong, at least, the results will not directly affect Ryalth. As he is looking out his open window at the clouds that have gotten ever darker as the morning has turned into afternoon, he turns at the sound of voices and is standing behind his desk when Meylyd and Hybyl step back into the study.

Hybyl closes the door.

Meylyd motions for Lorn to sit down, then takes the larger chair and seats himself.

Both officers from Geliendra glance at the closed door.

"Everything *appears* as you have said, captain," Meylyd begins. "And all the men are telling the truth. That presents a puzzle. Majer Maran was most capable. So, clearly, are you. Yet the majer had no reason to disappear, and you were the last to see him."

Lorn waits.

"Do you have anything to say about this?"

"Nothing I haven't said, ser. I know the majer intended to

do something as far as I was concerned, but he didn't tell me. And he never returned to the compound."

"His lancers found his mount."

"Yes, ser. I was with them. So was squad leader Shynt."

Meylyd glances at the overcaptain. "If you would go, Hybyl, and make sure the outer study is empty, and stays that way."

"Yes, ser."

Meylyd studies Lorn as he waits for the two doors to close. His mouth smiles before he speaks, but his eyes are cold. "We have a difficult situation. On the one hand, there is a lancer captain who is holding the most difficult stretch of the ward-wall. He tends to, shall we say, use lancer techniques in a somewhat different manner. But his results are good, and all the local . . . eminences . . . are pleased. On the other hand, we have a distinguished lancer majer who is most concerned about the ward-wall and the captain. The two meet; the captain returns; the majer rides off and is never seen again. There is no evidence of anything. Even the horse tracks show that. Yes, I checked with the lancers on that. The two men rode together; they sat mounted and talked. One of them dismounted and walked and then remounted, and they rode southwest for a time and then they parted. And the majer vanished from his mount. Was he plucked from it by something from the Accursed Forest?" Meylyd shrugs.

Lorn remains silent, waiting.

"I asked for guidance from the Majer-Commander. I was told that it was best that I not act unless there were facts to support me. So . . . I guess there's nothing more to be said, Captain." Meylyd pauses. "It's clear that the majer had something in mind. A pity that he didn't tell me . . . or you. Whatever happened, it's also clear that no one will ever know. Perhaps it's better that way." Meylyd looks out the study window for a long moment, as if considering whether he should say more, before turning back to Lorn. "I do expect you to follow the guidelines he laid out, to the very letter. Overcaptain Hybyl will be taking the majer's place. He'll be promoted to sub-majer shortly, and you'll send your reports to him. I cannot stress how accurate I expect those reports to be."

"Yes, ser."

"And, Captain, Majer Maran was very capable. I hope you understand that."

"Yes, ser."

"I intend to hold you to those standards." Meylyd rises. "And, to ensure that there are no more deviations from lancer tactics, your replacements will arrive within the next few days. They are on their way from Westend."

"Yes, ser. I understand, ser."

Meylyd nods coldly. "Good day, Captain." After a last cold stare, he turns and walks out, leaving both doors open.

Lorn wonders if the Majer-Commander of lancers really had been consulted, and if so, why?

Still, for the moment, there will be replacement lancers, even if every one has been ordered to report anything strange that Lorn does.

Lorn takes a deep breath.

Outside, a warm drizzle has begun to fall.

CXIV

OUTSIDE THE JAKAAFRA compound's stable, Lorn slowly dismounts from the gelding, noting again the long scratch along his mount's shoulder, a scratch he has helped heal with minute amounts of the black order, as he had been taught so many years before by Myryan and Jerial. While in the lancers, of necessity, he has held his healing efforts to those which take little effort and which are little remarked.

His own uniform has rips in the trousers at boot level and more than a few splatters of blood from the latest attacks by giant cats and night leopards. He now has but one uniform left that is not soiled beyond repair and cleaning with blood or other gore—and that is only because it is the one that arrived from Ryalth with the latest shipment of wine. In his next scroll, he will have to ask if she can have another tailored and sent, although he dislikes asking for such, when she has given and risked so much for him already.

Lorn glances back across the courtyard, then shakes his head. He has already seen to the collection of the firelances and their storage in the armory, not that they pose much danger in their discharged state.

"Ser?" asks Suforis as Lorn leads the gelding into the stable. "You have another hard patrol?"

"Yes." Lorn does not elaborate on the two latest lancers Second Company has lost, or upon the cold scrutiny that falls over his every move from many of the replacement lancers.

"Sorry to hear that, Captain."

"Some patrols are like that." Lorn unfastens his gear, and the spare sabre, easing the saddle bags onto his shoulder.

"Yes, ser."

"That's my problem, not yours. How is Lesyna?"

"She be fine, ser." Suforis smiles.

"Good." Lorn nods and, in the early twilight, walks from the stable toward the quarter's building. The courtyard is almost empty, the lancers already in the meal hall, he suspects.

Juist walks from the small administrative building, glancing around, then calls, "Lorn!" The undercaptain motions, and Lorn forces himself into a walk demonstrating energy he does not feel, not after another patrol extended by a fallen tree.

As Lorn nears, Juist holds a scroll that he lifts. "Hybyl's squad leader came with the Engineers. Dropped this off for you. Insisted I give it to you personally." He grins and holds up a small leather pouch. "And this. If I be not mistaken, in here are the arched bars of an overcaptain."

"After all the admonitions I've received?" Lorn asks.

"Could be, just might be, that the Majer-Commander likes results," Juist suggests. "Meylyd likes to do things the way the Lancers always did 'em. Doesn't work so well, from what I'm hearing."

Lorn offers a wry smile. "What are you hearing?"

"Other captains losing almost as many men, except they're seeing half the tree-falls. Those reports go to Cyad, you know?"

"I know they go. I wasn't sure anyone read them."

Juist hands over the pouch. "Going to open it?"

Lorn shifts the saddle bags and takes the pouch, opening it gingerly. Juist is right. Inside are two sets of linked double bars, with the arch above them, signifying an overcaptain. He eases the insignia back into the pouch, and slips it inside his tunic.

"Told you," says Juist. "You're going to be someone, and I'll be happy to tell everyone I knew you—'cept I'll be doing it from in front of a hearthstove for years afore you're out of the saddle." The undercaptain grins.

"You're not upset?"

"Me?" The shorter and older officer shakes his head. "Lucky to be an undercaptain. Don't come from the right places, and don't talk fancy, and except for covering furloughs a few times a year, I don't have to mess with the Forest. Another three years, and I can take my pension. Few enough lancers get 'em." He glances at the scroll.

Lorn breaks the seal and reads quickly, squinting to make out the words in the dim light of the courtyard.

"Well . . . Overcaptain?" Juist asks after a moment.

"They're sending me to Biehl, to head the port detachment there."

Juist laughs. "Hard to believe. It makes sense. Give a good officer a tour where someone's not out to kill him every day . . . maybe learn something besides tactics."

Lorn shakes his head.

"Take the good, Lorn," Juist advises. "You taken enough of the bad."

The new overcaptain forces a smile. "Thank you. I'll try." Even as he speaks, he wonders just how good the promotion and transfer are. With a last nod to Juist, Lorn walks to his own quarters.

After lighting the lamp, he reads the order scroll again . . . and a third time. Then he washes up quickly, but does not change out of his uniform, and he heads to the officers' dining area, carrying a bottle of the Fhynyco. Juist and Ilryk have already begun to eat the mutton stew, overpeppered enough that Lorn can smell the seasonings even before he sits down.

"Didn't know as you were coming, lucky fellow," offers Juist, with a laugh.

"Is it true?" asks Ilryk.

"It looks to be," Lorn says.

"The bottle he brings says so. 'Sides, it was that sub-majer Hybyl's squad leader that brought it. Sour face he had too." Juist laughs.

Lorn uncorks the bottle and half-fills the three heavy goblets.

"At least with a sour face, you can read something. Maran always smiled, always looked like he cared." Ilryk pauses, then turns to Lorn. "You saw him last. He was headed to Westend, wasn't he?"

Lorn takes a sip of the Fhynyco before answering. "He was riding in that direction. He didn't tell me what he had in mind. Except complaining about the way I handled Second Company."

"He didn't like the way I handle my company," Ilryk replies. "He said I should always be well in the fore, so that my men could see me." The blond captain shrugs. "I am always in the front rank, but too far forward, and I cannot see where they are, and that makes it difficult to give orders."

Lorn shakes his head. "He told me not to be well in the fore. He said I was too far forward."

Ilryk laughs. "Senior officers." He raises his goblet. "May you not be as they, Overcaptain! May you remember what it was like to be a mere captain."

"You'll be an overcaptain before long," Lorn suggests after accepting the impromptu toast. He breaks off a chunk of stale bread and dips it in the overseasoned stew.

"One never counts on a promotion until the emblem is on your collar. Not in the lancers." Ilryk raises his glass. "One can but count on the wine one drinks today."

"That be too true," Juist agrees.

Lorn has to nod to that, and then he takes another mouthful of the mutton stew.

"Good wine," Ilryk adds. "Thank you."

"I'm glad you like it."

Although the day has been long, Lorn finds he can barely eat one helping of the thick and heavily spiced stew, and excuses himself early, leaving the remainder of the Fhynyco for the other two officers.

Back in his quarters, he reads the scroll again. From what it says, his promotion is already effective, and he can wear the new insignia immediately. While the next day is a stand-down day, he needs to get a message to Ryalth immediately.

He sits down at the narrow desk in his quarters, under the pool of light cast by the small lamp, and lays out one of the few remaining sheets of paper, then dips the pen in the ink-well. The scroll will definitely go by Suforis through Dus-tyn—early on the next day.

> My dearest,
>
> I have been notified rather suddenly that I am being promoted and transferred, almost two years before I expected such. Within three eightdays, I will be in Cyad, on my way to take over the Mirror Lancer port compound in Biehl . . .

He pauses, then continues.

> I will only be in Cyad for an eightday and a few days, because I am not due for home leave for another two years, and I dearly hope that this does not find you traveling elsewhere. Still, we must take the opportunities we have in an uncertain world.

He can think of no news that may help her trading, nor of anything else of import as great as his coming to Cyad. Re-luctantly, he adds another line.

If you would arrange for another three sets of uniforms for me, I will repay you when I arrive in
Cyad. I will be there so short a time, I fear that
they would not be ready were I to wait until I arrive.

He looks out his window, but the clouds block the stars.
Finally, he picks up the pen and dips it again and closes.

I look to those moments we will have together, and
to seeing you again far sooner than I had thought
possible. . . . With all my affection and love . . .

Yawning, he sets aside the pen. He must still write his
family, and, on the morrow, finish another set of patrol reports. The day after will be another patrol. There will be one
more after that before he can leave Jakaafra, more than
enough time to find himself in trouble if he does not maintain
his guard and his skills in dealing with the Accursed Forest.

Then . . . will he ever not find himself facing trouble in
such times, he being who he is and not what others would
wish?

He looks into the darkness. Is that not what all men believe? How is he any different from them?

For that, he has no answer, not one that does not flatter
his self-esteem.

CXV

LORN RECOGNIZES THE face of the officer who rides into
Jakaafra compound late in the afternoon, but for a moment
cannot recall the name. The black-bearded captain is swarthy,
and his height is well above average.

Akytol—the name comes to Lorn—was the older lancer
officer candidate with whom he had ridden in the firewagon
to Kynstaar when he had first left Cyad for lancer training.

Lorn nods to himself and starts across the courtyard. He reaches the stable just behind the big lancer officer.

"Stable!" Akytol calls.

Suforis steps out into the courtyard and looks up at the tall captain. "Yes, ser?"

"Is this where I can stable my mount?"

"Yes, ser."

Lorn walks toward the older, but now junior officer, as Akytol dismounts outside the compound stable.

The black-bearded officer frowns as Lorn approaches, but then looks back at Suforis to hand over his mount's reins.

"You're here to take command of Second Company?" Lorn asks pleasantly.

"Yes." Akytol turns, and adds, quickly, "Ah, yes, ser," as the late afternoon light of spring glints off the linked bars with the overcaptain's arch that are fastened to Lorn's collar.

The ostler glances from Akytol to Lorn.

"This is Captain Akytol, Suforis," Lorn explains. "He is a well-respected and very solid Lancer officer."

Akytol continues to wear a vaguely puzzled expression, as if he still cannot place Lorn.

"I'm Lorn. We left Cyad together for Kynstaar a number of years ago."

Akytol swallows. "Oh . . . I am sorry, ser. I did not recognize you."

"That's all right. We all change over the years. You always wore a beard, and that made it easier for me. If you will get your gear, I can show you the quarters. You can either have the first room, or mine after I leave tomorrow. It's your choice. Then I'll show you the studies, and we can talk over the evening meal, such as it is."

"I would appreciate that." Akytol nods awkwardly. He turns to unfasten the two large kit bags from behind his saddle, then follows Lorn across the courtyard.

"This is the only compound without an Engineer detachment, and the other company here is really a domestic peace-keeping company. It's commanded by Undercaptain Juist," Lorn explains. "They'll take over patrols during company furloughs, but otherwise, you have full responsibility for the northeast ward-wall."

"Sub-Majer Hybyl did say something about that."

Lorn opens the door to the quarters. "You can put your gear in the first room. I've always used the second." While Akytol deposits his bags, Lorn takes the last bottle of Alafraan from his wardrobe, and rejoins the captain. Then Lorn leads the taller officer back into the courtyard and to the small administrative building.

"Our spaces are the first ones. The outer study is for the lancer records, and the senior squad leader." Lorn opens the door, but Kusyl has already left for the day. Lorn opens the inner door. "This will be your study. The small foot chest there holds the patrol reports and other papers. I'll give you the key in the morning."

Akytol nods.

"Now . . . let's get something to eat."

The officers' dining area is empty, as Lorn had guessed, since Juist had left early in the morning to handle a problem some forty kays to the west at a town Lorn had not heard of before that morning and since Ilryk is not due for several days, assuming Fifth Company has not found another downed tree.

Lorn uncorks the wine and fills one of the goblets, but only half-fills his own. Then he sits. As if waiting for them, a server appears and drops a casserole dish on the table with the usual basket of bread.

"Fowl, I think," Lorn guesses. "It's more often mutton." He gestures to the dish. "Go ahead."

As Akytol serves himself, Lorn continues, "You have to keep patrol reports, just as with the barbarians, but you also have to send a summary report to Sub-Majer Hybyl after each complete patrol—out to Eastend and back. . . ." Lorn goes on to explain the location of reports and lancer records, serving himself as he does.

As Lorn speaks, Akytol's eyes take in the overcaptain's bars again, for at least the third time since they have been seated in the officers' dining area.

". . . handled by the senior squad leader—that's Kusyl." Lorn stops, and refills Akytol's goblet.

"Thank you."

"Where have you been?" asks Lorn.

"At Inividra—that's one of the outposts under Assyadt. I had Third Company there."

"The last year or so, you've had more barbarian attacks, they say."

"Almost twice as many as before. We're seeing more Brystan weapons, too. Better iron, sometimes nearly as hard as cupridium." Akytol refills his platter. "The size of the raiding parties is larger, too."

"Archers?" Lorn asks almost idly, taking a small sip of the Alafraan.

"Some. They say there weren't any years ago. They're not very good. Take a good firelance any day." Akytol swallows the last of the Alafraan in his goblet. "Good wine."

"It's Alafraan. A friend sent me some. It would be hard to take it with me." Lorn refills Akytol's heavy and crude glass goblet.

"It is good."

"The barbarians just charged us when I was at Isahl," Lorn observes. "Was it that way at Inividra?"

Akytol nods, his mouth full.

Lorn waits, encouraging the bigger officer to go on.

". . . just take those big blades and charge at you. They didn't seem to care who they charged . . . officer or ranker. Lately, a couple of groups showed up with local lances— long poles with billhooks on 'em. Nasty if they got too close." Akytol takes another large swallow of the Alafraan. "Except they're better suited to a footman."

"Or if your firelances charges are low."

Akytol nods again. "A couple of times, we didn't get full charges before we had to go out. Lost a quarter score just on that count. Sub-majer said he couldn't do anything, that the Magi'i were having some sort of trouble, he guessed." The bigger officer snorts.

"I understand an old acquaintance of mine is at Assyadt.

A Sub-Majer Dettaur. We grew up together. Have you run across him?" Lorn refills Akytol's goblet a second time.

"Sub-Majer Dettaur . . . he's number two at the headquarters in Assyadt. Sometimes, takes a patrol. Good man."

"He was always good with blades, any kind," Lorn suggests.

"He still spars a lot, I hear, but I wasn't there much. It's a good sixty kays from Assyadt to Inividra." Akytol frowns. "You have a sister . . . ah, ser?"

"I have two. Sub-Majer Dettaur once courted one of them."

"You have a . . . certain reputation. . . ." Akytol says slowly. "I had not realized . . ."

Lorn nods. "I'm aware of that. That's why you're getting Second Company, I'm sure. Commander Meylyd and Sub-Majer Hybyl wish that my replacement be a lancer who is very traditional. They're quite pleased that you were available, I am certain."

"Sub-majer didn't say much beyond outlining procedures, and providing a patrol manual."

"It is a good idea to read it carefully," Lorn says, almost dryly. "I might add that it is acceptable to use a staggered line of five abreast in facing the wild creatures. The giant cats and stun lizards are more durable than the barbarians, and you will need as many firelances as you can focus on them. And the giant serpents—we only came across one of those—I don't think they're terribly dangerous so long as you stay back from them. So I'd suggest dealing with a serpent after all the other dangers and creatures. . . ." He smiles. "The manual doesn't mention serpents, but squad leader Kusyl can tell you more, if you wish to know."

"Giant serpents?"

Lorn nods, looking down at his empty platter, not that he has eaten all that much. "I will sign over Second Company in the morning." Lorn pauses. "Do you have any other questions I might answer?"

"Any place where I can get wine like that?" Akytol grins.

"You might try the spirit factor in the town of Jakaafra.

His name is Dustyn. He can get any number of types of spirits. So can the chandler, I've been told, but I used the spirit factor."

"Good to know." Akytol nods. "Where are you going, ser?"

"A port detachment in Biehl. A partial tour, I think, although no one has said."

"You're lucky, ser. Like to get one of those myself, one day."

"Perhaps you will." Lorn stands. "I need to take care of a few things. You can have the rest of the bottle. I'll see you in the morning."

"Are you sure . . . I would not wish to impose." Akytol stands.

"Enjoy it." Lorn laughs gently, gesturing for the taller officer to sit down.

"Thank you, ser." Akytol remains standing until Lorn departs.

As he returns to his room, Lorn is glad that he has already made arrangements for shipping all the remaining goods in the small dwelling on the east road from Jakaafra back to Cyad and to Ryalor House—as well as paying Dustyn an extra pair of silvers for two seasons' use of the house.

He also hopes that the lancers of Second Company will not suffer too much before either the Magi'i complete their mysterious project to contain the Accursed Forest or before the Forest kills Akytol. He fears the latter is more likely. Although he does not dislike the big officer whose traditional approach may prove all too convenient for Sub-Majer Hybyl, there is little he can say or do that will change Akytol.

As he lifts the silver volume once more, Lorn smiles, recalling pears and praise. He hopes his brief season in Cyad will be one he can recall and praise. His smile broadens as he thinks of Ryalth and begins to pack the last of the few items he will carry with him when he leaves with the engineer's firewagon on the morrow.

Will he see the Accursed Forest again? Or will whatever project the Magi'i have in mind render it a memory, its reality changed before he returns—if he returns.

His lips curl into a smile. He will see Ryalth, again, and for a time he had even feared that might not occur.

As Ilryk has said, "One can but count on the wine one drinks today." And it looks as though he and Ryalth will have at least one other day. Beyond that, neither knows.

CXVI

IN THE FRONT compartment of the firewagon, only Lorn is awake. The Mirror Lancer Majer to his right sleeps, as does the corpulent factor seated across from them. Lorn looks out into the darkness, a clouded darkness deep and lit—only to him—by the hints of chaos escaping from the cells of the six-wheeled vehicle as it rumbles westward across the smooth stones of the Great Eastern Highway toward Cyad—and Ryalth.

Lorn has killed a senior officer. Maran is dead, and Maran should be dead, for Maran would have let lancers die, unwisely and unnecessarily, rather than see Lorn survive. Lorn frowns. Scores of barbarians are dead because of Lorn, and some lancers in Isahl live because Lorn has been effective at killing. Is Cyad worth all the deaths it causes to come to pass—one way or another? Or are Lorn's dreams worth those deaths?

Life without dreams is death, but are Lorn's hopes to lead a better Cyad worth more than Maran's dreams of holding together an old Cyad, or worth more than the barbarians' dreams of bringing it down? Does the best dream win? Or the most powerful dreamer? Or are all dreams merely illusions that crumple in the end upon the Steps to Paradise with the deaths of their dreamers?

And what of Ryalth? Although she knows his dreams, and has helped him in surviving, and in feeling that what he dreams is worthy . . . with each action he takes, the possible repercussions are greater, and so are the threats to her.

The merchanter across the compartment snores, shifts his weight, and lapses back into heavy breathing.

As the firewagon carries him ever closer to Cyad, Lorn continues to look into the future and the darkness, a darkness lightened by the chaos only he can see—and lightened but dimly for all that.

CXVII

LORN WALKS ACROSS the Plaza to the wide steps leading up to the topmost level. For the first time, he wears his lancer uniform in the Plaza, and more than a handful of merchanters in blue glance in his direction. He cannot help smiling, half in apprehension, half in anticipation as he nears the steps.

". . . overcaptain . . . don't know him . . ."

". . . don't see many here . . ."

"Someone's heir . . . guess . . ."

With his smile still broad, he climbs the wide steps in the middle of the two wings of the structure, wondering whether to turn right or left at the top, since he only knows that Ryalor House now holds the entire upper level. He turns left, and discovers that all the doors are closed. Retracing his steps to the stairs and past them, he comes to a set of open double doors.

After noting the painted emblem above the open double doors—the intertwined R and L within the inverted triangle— Lorn nods and steps through the doors. Amid the tables and the handful of merchanters in blue, he does not see Ryalth immediately, although there is a closed door that looks to lead to a private study.

"Ser?" asks a thin-faced junior enumerator, standing from a table on which are piled stacks of wrinkled papers. He steps forward as if to question Lorn's very presence. "Might I help you in some way?"

A thin-faced, slender and gray-eyed senior enumerator rises from a table desk in the corner and slips forward quickly. "Sygul . . . this is Overcaptain Lorn—*the* Overcaptain Lorn," Eileyt says quickly.

"Oh, ser . . . I'm so sorry." Sygul bows deeply. "I'm so sorry. It's . . . well . . . no one ever described you. . . ."

Lorn laughs gently. "I'm not five cubits tall with shoulders that touch both sides of the door? I'm afraid not." He looks at Eileyt. "Is she here?"

"She is, and I think that all of us will feel better if we escort you there before she sees you being detained here." Eileyt turns toward the closed door at the left side of the trading tables.

". . . didn't know . . ."

". . . don't let *her* know that. . . . You think she be tough on an improper invoice . . ."

Lorn smiles sympathetically as he follows the senior enumerator.

Eileyt knocks on the closed door. "Lady . . . there is a most important personage here to see you. Most important." He grins.

"Show him in, Eileyt."

Lorn opens the door and steps inside.

Ryalth and an older balding trader in the orange of Hamor are seated on opposite sides of a desk table. The study is almost stark, with but the desk table and a handful of chairs, several chests lined up against the side wall. There are two high rear windows, both barred.

The gray and balding trader turns, and Lorn can see the annoyance in his eyes. Ryalth's eyes widen and she stands.

Lorn smiles. "I can wait, but Eileyt suggested I should make my presence known."

Ryalth gestures to the sitting trader. "This is Duhabrah. He is the representative of his house in Cyad."

Lorn bows. "I apologize for the interruption, and I am most pleased to meet you."

"The overcaptain and his house were the first backers of Ryalor." Ryalth smiles. "He is the one who made the trade of the amber gold spirits possible . . . and a number of other unusual goods. Some of the goods we were talking about."

The trader surveys Lorn more closely. "You are not a trader born, I would say."

"No. My family is elthage." At the trader's blank look, Lorn adds, "Of the Magi'i."

"A Lancer officer of Magi'i blood who is involved in trade!" Duhabrah laughs, a full rumbling laugh. "Lady trader . . . I see more from this than from all else, and I am pleased I am here."

Lorn bows. "I will leave you two to your trading. Eileyt will show me around," he adds. "I have not seen all that is here."

Ryalth returns his bow with a smile.

Lorn steps back, closing the door gently, and turns to Eileyt. "She told you to bring me in, even if she were with someone?"

"Yes, ser."

Lorn nods. He gestures around the large room. "Tell me a bit about each person and what he does."

Eileyt clears his throat. "Sygul—the one near the door— is a junior enumerator. He checks the commodities boards in the Plaza below, and lets me know if anything changes by more than a twentieth—or if he thinks something is happening to the prices of grains, fruits, the more widely traded metals. We don't trade them, except for dried fruits and at times iron and cuprite, but the Lady Ryalth can tell from knowing that prices are changing what else may be affected. He also checks the bills of lading against the invoices to make sure the quantities are the same, and . . ."

Lorn follows the enumerator's restrained gestures, listening.

"Kutyr—the one in the blond beard in the corner—he is a trader, mostly in fruits and spirits. . . . He will travel to Hydlen in several eightdays to purchase the advance contracts on dried fruit. . . ."

Lorn nods as Eileyt goes around the large room, although the overcaptain doubts he totally understands about half of what the enumerator says—or rather the meaning beyond the words themselves.

"And you," Lorn says, when Eileyt has finished his summary, "you're the one that makes sure everyone does what they must, and the one who keeps the ledgers?"

"The Lady keeps the ledgers, but she requires that I check them to ensure aught is well, and accurate."

"You find mistakes . . . but not many, I'd guess."

"Few," Eileyt says, "but it is best that way, for the Emperor's tariff enumerators require double any discrepancies as penalties. And Bluoyal—the Emperor's Merchanter Advisor—is hardly loath to suggest that those houses that are caught cheating steal from the others because the rest of us must pay more in tariffs while they pay less."

Lorn has never heard of the tariff enumerators, but he nods, wondering what else there is that his education and experience have overlooked. He also notes the vaguely distasteful manner in which Eileyt refers to Bluoyal, and reminds himself to ask Ryalth about the man.

The study door opens, and Ryalth escorts Duhabrah to the main doors of Ryalor House, where the foreign trader bows twice and departs, smiling effusively.

Eileyt slides away as Ryalth returns to where Lorn stands. Without speaking, he follows her into her study where she is the one to close the door.

They embrace.

After a long time, they separate, and Ryalth looks at Lorn, eye to eye. "You came here first, didn't you?"

"Almost . . . I dropped my gear inside the door at my parents, said hello and left. I did kiss my mother. I wasn't sure about trying to enter your quarters, if you even have the same ones, my wealthy merchanter lady . . ."

"I'm not that wealthy."

"Everyone thinks you are." Lorn grins. "And most beautiful."

Ryalth shakes her head. "You are impossible. Still."

"Very impossible . . . and wondering if we can depart before too long."

She smiles. "I am almost through for the day, and we can leave shortly."

"Ah . . . mother did ask if we could join them for dinner."
Lorn shrugs apologetically. "I would not . . . with so little
time . . . yet . . ."

"I know. Jerial has already conveyed an invitation for
whatever night you arrived, and I agreed." She grins back.
"I told her we would not stay late, and she said that she
would make sure of that, as well."

"You have everything arranged." Lorn shakes his head.
"You two."

"Not everything, but your family has been far warmer than
ever I would have imagined." Her smile fades. "They are
most cautious, though." The redhead shivers. "I would not
live like that, knowing every word be measured, every action
watched."

"It may come to that," Lorn says. "You have seen that . . .
or felt it . . . with me."

"For you, that I will accept, but not merely because of
birth and station."

Lorn kisses her again.

"We will not soon leave here, and we will be late for
dinner . . . if you do not permit me to finish."

"Finish what?"

"The report that goes with the seasonal import tariffs for
the Emperor."

"I would ask," Lorn says, letting go of her hands.

"I will hasten. Then we will take a carriage and pick up
your things. From now on, you are staying with your consort
in Cyad." She smiles.

"I would hope so."

"You have lecherous thoughts, my dearest of lancers.
Were this not for the Emperor's enumerators, we would already have departed."

Lorn reaches out and squeezes her hand once more. "Then,
do what you must." He pulls out the seat on the side of the
desk table and seats himself, wondering how to tell her what
else he must, yet knowing that he must, for all that he does

affects her, and she is in Cyad, where all are watched, both for power and weakness.

Ryalth continues to page through the sheets before her, occasionally lifting her pen. Finally, she signs the last page and looks at Lorn once more. "I am done, but you are not."

He nods, then stands and moves toward her, embracing her gently, and murmuring in her ear as he does, "I am here . . . and I am most glad to be so. Yet . . . it is because Maran vanished . . . the Lancer officer of whom I told you, the one who was a magus. Commander Meylyd and perhaps the Majer-Commander of Lancers suspect I managed to remove him—but he was never found. He . . . Maran . . . kept putting more and more restrictions on my patrols. . . ."

"He wanted the Forest to kill you. . . ."

Lorn nods, his head against Ryalth's warm cheek. "Yet . . . all I do . . . it may come to bear upon you. . . ."

"Long have I known that." She returns his embrace—gently, but more tightly. "You stood by me . . . when none did . . . you have risked your ties with your family for me . . . and always have you kept your word to me. That you could not do, were you to die."

"You know . . . for what I hope . . . and strive . . . and the dangers . . ." he murmurs, his arms still around her.

"Had you not risked yourself one night, long ago . . . I might be dead—or a fearful woman at any trader's beck. Had you not stood for me to your family . . ." Her lips brush his cheek, and she lays her cheek against his. "Now . . . for what you have done, they see me as I am, not as they thought I was."

"I worried . . . about Maran . . . yet I could see no other course."

"Many worry . . . few act. You act, and I will be with you." Her fingers tighten around his. "I will, and never doubt it. Never." Her last word is whispered fiercely.

Whatever will come, whatever will be . . . they will face it together.

"... even if we are thousands of kays apart," Ryalth murmurs.

He holds her tightly, without barriers, without reservations ... and her arms are as firmly around him as his are around her.

THE SOPRANO SORCERESS

Book One of The Spellsong Cycle

L. E. Modesitt, Jr.

Anna Marshall is a singer and music instructor at Iowa State University who wishes she could be somewhere else. The world in which she finds herself, however, is not what she had in mind. For on Erde, Anna Marshall is not just a professional singer: on Erde, her ability makes her a powerful sorceress. And this means that she immediately becomes a target, not only of the political factions, who fear the unknown, but also of the men of Erde, who fear a woman with the power she possesses. Anna must learn enough magic – and enough about Erde – to protect herself before it's too late.

The Soprano Sorceress begins an epic new tale of sorcery, song and political intrigue by one of the most exciting storytellers in fantasy.

THE SPELLSONG WAR

Book Two of The Spellsong Cycle

L. E. Modesitt, Jr.

When Anna Marshall wished she could be anywhere
but Iowa, and anything but a music intructor, she did
so at exactly the wrong time – and found herself
pulled into the very different world of Erde. On Erde,
music is magic, and Anna's ability as a singer has
made her an enormously powerful sorceress.
But the fight has only just begun.

With her unique power, Anna saved the kingdom of
Defalk from invasion and became its regent. After six
years of war, however, Defalk is weak and the
kingdom's southern neighbour is already encroaching
on the border. Rising to power may have been the easy
part – now Anna will need all her skill just to hold on
to what she's managed to accomplish so far.

Orbit titles available by post:

☐	The Magic of Recluce	L. E. Modesitt, Jr.	£6.99
☐	The Towers of the Sunset	L. E. Modesitt, Jr.	£7.99
☐	The Magic Engineer	L. E. Modesitt, Jr.	£7.99
☐	The Order War	L. E. Modesitt, Jr.	£7.99
☐	The Death of Chaos	L. E. Modesitt, Jr.	£7.99
☐	Fall of Angels	L. E. Modesitt, Jr.	£7.99
☐	The Chaos Balance	L. E. Modesitt, Jr.	£7.99
☐	The White Order	L. E. Modesitt, Jr.	£7.99
☐	Colours of Chaos	L. E. Modesitt, Jr.	£7.99
☐	Magi'i of Cyador	L. E. Modesitt, Jr.	£7.99
☐	Scion of Cyador	L. E. Modesitt, Jr.	£7.99
☐	The Soprano Sorceress	L. E. Modesitt, Jr.	£6.99
☐	The Spellsong War	L. E. Modesitt, Jr.	£7.99
☐	The Parafaith War	L. E. Modesitt, Jr.	£6.99

The prices shown above are correct at time of going to press. However, the publishers reserve the right to increase prices on covers from those previously advertised without prior notice.

ORBIT BOOKS
Cash Sales Department, P.O. Box 11, Falmouth, Cornwall, TR10 9EN
Tel: +44 (0) 1326 569777, Fax: +44 (0) 1326 569555
Email: books@barni.avel.co.uk.

POST AND PACKING:
Payments can be made as follows: cheque, postal order (payable to Orbit Books)
or by credit cards. Do not send cash or currency.
U.K. Orders under £10   £1.50
U.K. Orders over £10   **FREE OF CHARGE**
E.E.C. & Overseas   25% of order value

Name (Block Letters) _____

Address_____

_____

Post/zip code:_____

☐ Please keep me in touch with future Orbit publications

☐ I enclose my remittance £_____

☐ I wish to pay by Visa/Access/Mastercard/Eurocard

Card Expiry Date

_____